To Tame A Texan

To Tame A Texan

FOUR NOVELLAS BY

EVELYN CROWE
LORRAINE HEATH
VIVIAN VAUGHAN
EILEEN WILKS

St. Martin's Paperbacks

TO TAME A TEXAN

ISBN: 0-312-96886-8

Printed in the United States of America

St. Martin's Paperbacks edition / March 1999

10 9 8 7 6 5 4 3 2 1

Contents

To Tame a Texan

Long Stretch of Lonesome

A Novella
By Lorraine Heath

For Pete Denby
Who casts a tall shadow

One

LONESOME, TEXAS
1884

Chance Wilder was a man with his back against the wall.

Finding comfort in the rough wood of the saloon pressing against his slender shoulders, he tilted his chair farther back. As was his habit, he studied the comin's and goin's, always alert to the potential for trouble. He didn't fear the bullet that might hit him dead-on. It was the one that might come up from behind that weighed heavy on his mind.

Barely shifting his gaze, he scrutinized the young man standing at the bar. The man hadn't taken his eyes off Chance since Chance had sauntered through the saloon doors. He'd watched the man down half a bottle of whiskey, his fingers caressing the butt of his gun in between swallows as though unable to find courage in either the liquor or the sidearm. Chance figured the fidgeting man would meet his Maker before Chance rode out of town.

With a slight shift in his hips, Chance eased forward and the front legs of the chair hit the wooden floor with a resounding thud. The saloon suddenly became quieter than a prayer meeting. His gaze cautiously roaming the room, he slowly tipped the bottle of whiskey until he'd refilled his glass without so much as a splash, his hand steady as a rock. A man in his line of work relied on a steadfast hand. He set down the bottle, picked up the glass, and dropped back against the wall, balancing the chair with the ease that he used when cradling his gun in the palm of his left hand.

He sipped the amber liquid like a man in no hurry—which he was. He had no one waiting on him, hadn't had anyone waiting on him since he'd killed his first man at fourteen.

He heard one man clear his throat and the harsh whisper of another. He didn't have to hear the words to know what they were discussing.

Every person in the saloon—every person in the town—wanted to know who Chance Wilder had come to Lonesome, Texas, to kill.

Toby Madison hurtled through the swinging doors of the saloon. The thick smoke burned his eyes, and he thought the stench of sour whiskey might make him puke. Or maybe it was the blood trickling down the back of his throat that made his stomach heave. He thought the bully might have busted his nose.

"Hey, boy, get out," someone ordered, clamping a large hand onto Toby's shoulder.

Toby jerked free, his frenzied gaze darting over the glaring faces. He hadn't expected half the men in town to be lollygagging in the saloon this time of day. He'd never find the man he was anxiously seeking.

Then he realized that everyone was crowded on one side of the saloon, leaving the other side practically empty. He swung around. His stomach knotted up tighter than a hangman's noose when he saw the stranger sitting in the far corner, alone, his chair tipped back, and his silvery eyes narrowed as thinly as the sharp edge of a knife.

Toby swallowed hard and limped hurriedly across the room. "You the gun-for-hire everybody's talkin' about? Are you Chance Wilder?"

The man's eyes narrowed further, and Toby figured he could slice a man open with that gaze.

"If'n you are, I wanna hire you," Toby said.

"Already been hired," Wilder replied in a quiet, raspy voice that still managed to echo around the saloon.

Toby heard somebody gasp and another whisper fiercely. Even with the blood trailing down his throat, his mouth went dry. "But them bullies is beating up my sister. I want you to make 'em stop."

"You look old enough to stop them."

"I tried to stop 'em from hurtin' Lil, but them bullies is—"

The bartender grabbed him, his beefy fingers biting into Toby's skinny arm. Toby bucked, unable to wrestle free of the relentless grip.

"This is no place for you, boy," the bartender announced as he hauled Toby across the room. Toby felt like the sack of flour he'd dropped when the bullies had grabbed his sister and dragged her behind the general store. Desperation edged his words as he fought frantically to keep his eyes on Wilder. "I'll pay you everything, everything I got!"

Wilder slammed the front legs of his chair against the floor. The bartender froze. Toby wrenched free. Wilder unfolded his tall, lean body and tugged on the brim of his black Stetson.

"What the hell," he murmured. "I ain't never been paid everything before."

"You want to steer clear of this mess," the bartender said.

Toby thought he didn't sound too sure of what he was saying.

Wilder pulled one side of his black duster back to reveal a pearl-handled gun housed in a holster slung low on his hip. "*Everything* is a hell of a lot. You gonna better the kid's offer?"

"No . . . no, sir," the bartender stammered.

"Then don't tell me my business because you ain't paid for the privilege."

"We gotta hurry," Toby said as he scurried out of the saloon. He heard Wilder's spurs jangling as he followed. He figured Lil was gonna have a cow when she found out he had hired a gun to save her.

Chance sauntered after the towheaded kid, increasing his pace as they distanced themselves from the saloon. Skinny as a willow branch, the boy couldn't be any older than seven or eight. But he had spunk. Chance had to give him that. And if he wasn't mistaken, the boy had a broken nose. He hadn't noticed it until the bartender grabbed the kid. It had to hurt like hell, but the boy's only worry seemed to be his sister. Chance chuckled low. He was looking forward to receiving everything—and how much trouble could it be to chase a couple of bullies away from a little girl?

The boy raced past the general store, flew around a corner, and disappeared between the two buildings. Chance stepped over the split sack of flour that littered the boardwalk and gave the wagon in front of the general store a passing glance. He heard the boy's indignant yell and quickened his pace. He rounded the corner and staggered to a halt.

One of the bullies had grabbed the boy and was holding a pistol to his temple. The boy stood as still as a stone statue, his eyes holding his sister's gaze. Her skirt and petticoats were hiked up to her thighs . . . up to her slender womanly thighs. Her burnished hair tumbled past her shoulders. Her torn bodice revealed the creamy curve of a small breast with each labored breath she took. Blood trailed down from a split lower lip and a bruise was forming on her cheek.

The man who had pinned her against the wall began to unfasten his britches. "Figured you'd stop fighting now," he drawled.

Defiance shot into her startling blue eyes and quickly faded into acceptance of her fate. She must have fought like a wildcat to hold the five men at bay as long as she had.

"Don't think the lady is interested," Chance said with feigned calmness, wondering why no one had come to the lady's defense until now.

The apparent leader snapped his head around and glared. "This ain't none of your business."

Chance slipped a matchstick out of his shirt pocket and wedged it between his teeth. In his youth, he'd discovered that he had the embarrassing habit of rolling out his tongue when he slid the gun from his holster. As if looking like a panting dog in the middle of a gunfight wasn't bad enough, he'd damn near bit off his tongue a time or two. Gnawing on the matchstick kept his tongue behind his teeth where it belonged. And it had the added advantage of making him look a little more dangerous. He rolled the matchstick to the other side of his mouth with practiced ease. "The boy paid me to make it my business."

"Toby," the woman gasped, snapping her worried gaze to her brother. Chance's gut clenched. Her voice sounded like she'd just crawled out of bed after a long night's sleep or a long night of making love.

The boy proudly puffed out his chest even though he still had the barrel of a six-shooter pressed against his temple. Chance tried to remember what the boy had called his sister—Lydia? Lilly? Lil? That was it. Lil.

The leader released a sharp bark of laughter. "Head out, mister."

"Where I come from, men don't paw ladies like that," Chance told him.

"Well, she ain't no lady. She's a whore. Jack Ward's whore."

She let loose a stream of spittle that hit the leader in the eye. He swung his arm back—

"Don't even think it," Chance commanded in a voice rife with authority. "Can't tolerate a man who hits a woman."

The leader lifted a corner of his mouth in a sneer. "That so?"

"Yep, that's so." He wrapped his fingers around the edge of his duster and drew it aside, hooking it behind his gun.

One of the other men started to twitch, his eyes growing round. "Hey, Wade, I'm thinking this is the fella—"

"Shut up," Wade growled, knocking the woman to the ground before planting his feet apart, facing Chance squarely, and issuing his challenge. "Stop me from hitting her."

Chance met and held each man's gaze briefly before letting his icy glare settle on the leader. "I want your boys to know that I'll kill every man who draws a gun."

"Holy hell," the nervous man said, throwing up his arms. "He's the gunslinger, Wade. I ain't gettin' myself killed over no woman."

Wade's smile faltered. "That so? You the gunslinger?"

"He sure is!" Toby yelled. "And he's fast, too. Faster than anybody!"

"They say you're reckless and wilder than most,"

Wade said, doubt lacing his voice. "They say you've killed twenty-four men."

Chance gave a short nod. "That's what they say." He slid his gaze over to the man who still held the boy. "The first bullet goes right between your eyes if your gun ain't holstered by the time mine clears leather."

With a shaking hand, the man slid his gun into his holster and released the boy. "This ain't my fight."

Chance jerked his head to the side. "Get outta here, boy."

The boy rushed to where his sister was crouched in the corner. He curled up in her lap, and she wrapped her arms closely around him. That wasn't exactly what Chance had in mind for the boy. He didn't like for children to see death. At its best, it was an ugly sight. At its worst, it guaranteed nightmares.

He locked his gaze onto Wade. "If you and your friends want to just stroll on outta here—"

Wade went for his gun. Everything else seemed to happen within the same moment. Chance slid his gun from his holster, aimed, heard an explosion, and felt a bullet bite into his shoulder as he hit the dirt, rolled, and fired. He saw surprise flitter across Wade's face—just before he crumpled into a lifeless heap.

Chance struggled to his feet. The woman stared at him in horror as though she'd forgotten the man he just killed had planned to rape her. Chance had accepted long ago that the reality of death usually made people forget that only moments before they'd desperately prayed that the deceased would die. "That your wagon in front of the general store?"

She gave a brusque nod. Chance pinned three of the men with a steely-eyed glare. "Reckon she'd appreciate it if you'd finish loading the wagon for her." They bobbed their heads like apples tossed into a barrel of water. "See that you get her a new sack of flour while you're at it."

They scurried off to do his bidding. He looked at the man who had held the boy earlier. "Go get the sheriff."

The man balked. "Wade drew first."

Chance nodded slowly. "Yep. Be sure you tell that to the sheriff 'cuz I can't tolerate liars and you just saw what happens to people who do things I can't tolerate."

The man was still nodding when he disappeared around the corner.

The boy scrambled out of his sister's lap and came to stand before Chance, his head bent back as he looked up at him with something akin to hero worship reflected in his eyes. "You saved Lil." The boy dug a hand into the pocket of his britches. "I'm gonna pay you everything just like I promised."

Chance held out his hand, and the boy dumped *everything* into his cupped palm: a length of frayed string, a rusty harmonica, and a bent penny.

Two

Lillian Madison stared straight ahead as she guided the wagon home. She found it impossible to believe that her brother had hired a man to protect her—or that the man seemed intent on honoring his end of the bargain.

She cast a sideways glance at Chance Wilder. Sitting on a dun-colored horse, he rode beside the wagon, his face set in rigid lines, his body held stiff. She'd heard of him. He had a reputation for drifting into a town and not leaving until he'd killed someone. She supposed now that Wade was being buried, Wilder would move on. She'd be glad to be rid of him. How could a man kill with no remorse? His eyes had been icy, calculating. He had moved with the grace of a striking snake when he'd jerked his gun from his holster. He held the weapon as though it were a part of him. She shuddered with the memories.

"Have you really killed twenty-four men?" Toby asked as he bounced on the wagon seat, turning toward Wilder. She had taken Toby to see the doctor before they left town. The physician had stuffed cotton up Toby's nostrils to halt the bleeding from his broken nose. He had to breathe through his mouth, and when he talked, his voice honked like a goose. She imagined it was a sound that could easily grate on the nerves of a man like Wilder.

"That's what they say," Wilder said in a flat voice.

"Reckon it's twenty-five now on account of Wade dying."

"Reckon so."

"How do you keep count?" Toby asked. "Do you notch your gunbelt?"

Wilder remained silent.

"I heard gunslingers notch their gunbelt. Want me to do it for you—notch your gunbelt, I mean? I could borrow your knife—"

"Nope."

"Then how will you remember?"

"Boy, I do my damnedest to forget."

"Then how do you keep count?"

Silence followed. Lillian wanted to explain to the man that she couldn't tolerate anyone ignoring a child, no matter how bothersome he became.

"You ever been to Houston?" Toby asked. "Me and Lil used to live in Houston."

Silence.

"What about Austin? You ever been there? Me and Lil got to spend the night in Austin when we was moving here. It's only a day's ride away. I bet you come through there on your way here."

Silence stretched between the man and the boy. Toby rolled his tiny shoulders forward, and Lillian knew Wilder's disinterest had hurt her brother's feelings. She wanted to slap the man. She'd spare Toby from all the hurt in the world if she could. It was the reason she had accepted the land and the house that Jack Ward had offered her.

If only she'd realized all the trouble that bit of foolishness would cause.

Toby lifted his blue gaze and gave her a lopsided

grin that revealed his latest missing tooth. "I gave him everything, Lil."

She slipped her arm around him and drew him up against her side, hugging him fiercely. He'd given the man his dearest possessions, and Wilder had dropped the treasured gifts into his duster pocket as though they were less valuable than dirt.

She drew the horses to a halt in front of the white clapboard house. She climbed down from the wagon and trudged over to Wilder. She peered up at his cold, immobile face. "We're home now—safe. I'd appreciate it if you'd head back to town."

Only his silvery eyes moved as he slid his gaze to her. "The boy paid me . . . *everything*. Never had *everything* before . . ."

He closed his eyes, slumped forward, and tumbled off his horse. With a small startled screech, Lillian jumped back as he landed with a thud near her feet.

"Gawd Almighty!" Toby cried as he scrambled down from the wagon. He skidded to his knees beside Wilder.

The man's duster parted to reveal a shirt soaked in bright crimson blood. Lillian thought she might be ill.

Toby snapped his head around, fear reflected in his youthful eyes. "He got shot. Why didn't he say something when we was at the doctor's?"

Shaking her head, she knelt beside Wilder and gingerly unbuttoned his shirt. Carefully lifting the material to peer inside, she saw the ragged, gaping hole still oozing blood from his shoulder.

"He's bleedin' something awful," Toby said. "You gotta help him, Lil."

Lillian hesitated. If she helped a man who made a living killing others, would she, in effect, become an accomplice to future killings? If she left him as he was, perhaps he would not survive, and no one else would die.

He had come to Lonesome for a reason—to kill someone. As much as she hoped Wade had been his intended prey, she thought it very unlikely.

Toby slipped his small hands beneath the man's shoulders and struggled to lift him. "Come on, Lil. We gotta get him into the house." He raised his troubled gaze to hers. "He saved you, even though I paid him to do it."

She considered what Wade might have done to her if the man hadn't shown up. No one would have stopped him. Everyone in town would have thought she'd deserved it.

Toby strained to heft the man. Wilder's hat tumbled off his head to reveal a riot of ash-blond curls. His hair looked incredibly soft, like Toby's had as a baby. She hadn't expected that of a man who killed others to make money. Unconscious, his face completely relaxed, he looked young, much younger than she'd originally thought he was.

"Help me, Lil," Toby pleaded, his breathing labored.

She gave a sharp nod and bent to help her brother carry the hired gun into the house.

The raging fire burned through his shoulder. Chance wanted to stay huddled behind the wall of agony, but the softness beckoned him, touched him, spoke to him.

He struggled to open his eyes. His shoulder was swathed in bandages. The woman sat on the edge of the bed, patting a warm damp cloth over his bare chest, humming a tune—"Red River Valley." Ruby shadows shimmered over her hair. He decided the muted shades were caused by the flame from the lamp sitting on the table beside the bed. She appeared young and innocent, too innocent to be an old man's whore. He knew all about Jack Ward because the man's family had paid him to come to Lonesome.

"What's Lil short for?" he croaked.

Her hand stilled, right above his pounding heart. "Lillian. Lillian Madison."

"Pretty name." A tinge of scarlet crept into her cheeks, and he thought he could easily drown within the fiery blue depths of her eyes.

"You should have told someone you'd been shot," she scolded as though he were a child.

"Would have brought out the vultures," he said in a tired whisper.

Her delicate brows knit together. "The vultures?"

"Men looking to gain a quick reputation. It wouldn't have mattered that I was bleeding like a stuck pig. Killing me is killing me."

She drew back her shoulders. "Yes, I suppose it would be quite an accomplishment to shoot the fastest gun west of the Mississippi."

With difficulty, he rolled his head from side to side. "I'm not fast at all."

"Then how in heaven's name did you gain your reputation?"

"I'm deadly accurate."

She bolted from the bed, the movement jarring his shoulder. Groaning, he slammed his eyes closed. He heard the steady staccato beat of her heels as she paced the floor. Then the pacing came to a sudden stop. He opened his eyes, knowing what she would say before she spoke the words.

"As soon as you're strong enough, I want you off my property."

She left the room in a flurry of whispering skirts. He sank into the softness of the bed. The pain had shifted from his shoulder to his heart, the incredible pain almost unbearable.

But he would bear it as he had since he was fourteen. He'd live with the pain, the guilt, and the loneliness . . . until the day that he came upon a man who was more accurate than he was.

He drifted into the welcome oblivion where the past was merely a shrouded mist.

"Is he gonna die, Lil?" Toby asked.

Lillian studied the man lying in her bed. When he had awoken earlier, she'd thought he was well on his way to recovery. Now she wasn't so sure. Although his fever was raging, he was shivering as though he'd just emerged from a river in winter. "I don't know," she whispered as she dipped a cloth into a bowl of warm salt water. She wrung it out and began to wipe the sweat from his throat. She felt his body stiffen beneath her fingers.

"Don't go for the gun," he rasped. "Goddamn it! Don't go for the gun!"

He jerked, kicking at the blankets. She pressed her hands to his shoulders. "Mr. Wilder?" His breath came in short little gasps. "Mr. Wilder?"

"He's gonna draw, dammit!" Groaning low, he convulsed, waving his hand frantically. She wrapped her hand around his, and he settled into stillness. His breathing slowly evened out, and he opened his eyes. She saw pain reflected in his eyes, pain that traveled clear to his soul. "He's dead," he whispered. It wasn't a question, but she nodded anyway.

"I didn't want to kill him," he said, his voice low.

Then why did you? hung on the tip of her tongue, but she couldn't bring herself to voice her true thoughts when he seemed so weak.

"I know," she said softly, not fully understanding

why she needed to comfort this man who was clinging to her hand. She felt him relax as though her words gave him absolution. She leaned forward. "Mr. Wilder, do you have family? Is there someone I should notify if you should . . . should die?"

He rolled his head from side to side. "No family. No one who cares." He smiled, reminding her of a small boy about to play a prank. "I won't die in your bed, lady."

Her stomach lurched. Her troubles had begun the night Jack Ward died in her bed. "See that you don't."

His eyes drifted closed, but his hand remained firmly wrapped around hers. He had stopped shivering, and his cheeks felt a little cooler to her touch. She sat on the bed and stared at their clasped hands. He was a killer, but for a few moments, he had simply been a man haunted by demons. She wished she hadn't witnessed his vulnerability—wished she hadn't wanted to hold him close and make the pain go away.

Chance awoke exhausted, his shoulder aching. Shafts of sunlight pierced the room. A woman's room. It carried the fading fragrance of roses in bloom. Turning his head slightly, he saw the boy standing beside the bed, reverently touching the harmonica that lay on the bedside table.

"Do you—" He'd planned to ask the boy if he knew how to play, but he couldn't push the words past his parched throat.

The boy jerked his head around. "Bet you're needing some water," the boy announced with authority.

Chance struggled to sit up as the boy poured water from an earthen pitcher into a glass. He felt weaker than a newborn babe. He took the glass the boy offered, hating the way his hand shook as he gingerly sipped on the cool water. He studied the boy. He no longer had cotton stuffed up his nose, but he had an ugly black bruise framing one eye. "Your nose hurting?"

The boy shook his head vigorously. "Lil said it'll probably be somewhat crooked, but that it'll give me character."

Chance couldn't prevent a corner of his mouth from lifting. "Character, huh?"

The boy nodded. "I reckon that's a good thing to have—whatever it is."

Chance's smile grew. "Not too many people have character these days."

"Do you have character?"

His smile withered away. "None at all."

"I'm supposed to get Lil if you wake up." The boy hightailed it out of the room. Breathing heavily, Chance sank against the pillow and rested the glass on his chest.

Wiping her hands on a crisp white apron, the woman strolled into the room. "You're awake."

"You say that like you had doubts."

"You ran a fever for two days."

Shock rippled through him. "Two days? What day is it?"

"Thursday."

"I need my clothes," he barked.

"You need to rest," she insisted.

He narrowed his eyes. "I need to get some fresh air, start gathering my strength—"

He started to sit up, and she pushed him down with one hand pressed against his shoulder. "Let me feed you some broth first—"

"Where's my gun?"

"I put it away—"

"Get it."

"You're not in any danger—"

"Lady, the only time I don't wear a gun is when

I'm making love to a woman, so unless you're aiming to climb into this bed with me, bring me the damn gun."

Fire flashed within the blue depths of her eyes. She stomped to the bureau, jerked open the top drawer, and snatched out his gunbelt. She stalked to the bed and flung it at him. Groaning when it thudded against his chest, he grabbed the holster and closed his hand around the smooth handle of the Colt. He captured her gaze, certain she wanted to tell him exactly what he could do with his gun. "Does anyone know I'm hurt?"

She shook her head. "No, I considered going for a doctor yesterday evening when you were delirious, but you threatened to put a bullet between my eyes if I did."

He nodded. "The boy?"

"Hasn't left your side."

He heard the anger building in her voice. And he didn't blame her. "I'll eat now," he said quietly.

She stormed from the room, her fists swinging at her sides. Lord, she was a ball of fire. He slid his gaze over to the boy.

The boy furrowed his brow. "You wouldn't really a killed her, would you?"

Chance slowly shook his head. "Nope. But in my line of work, you live longer if people believe the lies."

Three

Lillian heard the low, haunting melody of a harmonica fill the late afternoon air. She stepped out of the barn. Chance Wilder sat on the porch, his back against the wall, the front legs of the wooden straight-backed chair in the air, the harmonica pressed to his lips.

Toby sat beside him, his chair in the same reclining position, his eyes fastened on Wilder.

She didn't like to admit that it had impressed her to see Wilder summon up the strength to make his way to the front porch. He'd sat there all afternoon, Toby pestering him more often than not. He was more patient with her brother this afternoon than he'd been the first day. She realized now that all his efforts had been geared toward staying on his horse that day.

She didn't like seeing his patience. It was much easier to dislike him when he'd been short-tempered with Toby. Much easier to dislike him before she'd seen his vulnerability and held his hand through the night.

She strolled to the house and rested her arms on the railing of the front porch. The slight breeze toyed with the curls circling Wilder's head. His mouth moved slowly over the instrument, and she imagined his lips trailing a path along her throat. A heat surged through her that had little to do with the late summer afternoon.

As though reading her thoughts, Wilder paused in his playing and lifted a corner of his mouth. " 'Evenin'."

Her heart thundered as though she'd never had a man speak to her with a sparkle in his eyes. "Toby, you need to finish up your chores before supper," she announced, trying to ignore the blatant attraction she felt for this man, this hired killer. She couldn't explain it, much less understand it.

"Ah, Lil—"

"Do what your sister says," Wilder said.

With a scowl, Toby dropped the chair onto all fours and tromped toward the barn.

"Don't take offense, Mr. Wilder, but I'd rather you didn't encourage him—"

"Encourage him to do what? His chores?" he asked.

"Encourage him to spend time in your company. He's at an age where he's easily swayed. I'd rather he not be influenced by a man . . . a man who kills."

"You'd rather he be influenced by an old man's whore?"

Lillian stepped back as though he'd slapped her. "What Jack Ward was to me is none of your damn business!"

Chance watched her storm past him and disappear into the house. He cursed long and hard under his breath. He had no right to say what he had, but every time he thought of an old man's gnarled hands touching her, touching her the way he wanted to, the way she'd never let him . . .

The boy loped to the house, his smile bright. Chance was surprised the kid's jaws didn't ache as a result of his constant grins. The boy leaped onto the porch. "You comin' in for supper?"

"Think I'll stay outside a little longer. Smells like

your sister cooked up some stew. Why don't you bring me a bowl?"

"I'll sit out here with you," the boy offered.

Chance shook his head. "Your sister needs the company."

Toby nodded reluctantly before going inside. Chance slipped the harmonica into his pocket and gazed toward the horizon. Evening would arrive soon. Over the passing years, he had most missed sitting on a porch in the quiet of the evening after a day filled with exhausting work. Now when his body ached, it was more often from a bullet wound than from laboring in the fields. In the evening, his back was usually against a wall in a saloon. He didn't want that final bullet to come from behind.

He heard the footsteps and shifted his gaze. Lillian stood in the doorway, a wooden bowl in her hands. "Toby said you wanted to eat out here."

"Thought it best."

She gave him a brusque nod, handed him the bowl, and turned to go back inside.

"Miss Madison?"

She stopped, but didn't look at him.

"I owe you an apology. I had no right to say what I did."

She met and held his gaze, a corner of her mouth lifting. "Well, we finally agree on something."

"We agree on something else. I won't be influencing the boy. I'll leave come morning."

Her smile fell, and she furrowed her brow. "You can't be fully recovered."

"Thanks to your tender ministrations, I'm strong enough. I'll bed down in the barn tonight and be gone by first light."

"When you're finished eating, come inside and I'll change your bandage."

He waited until she went into the house. Then he lifted the bowl, inhaled the spicy aromas, and knew a longing so intense that he nearly doubled over with it.

He missed all the things he'd never have: meals prepared by a woman with loving care, a home where he could sit in the middle of the room, children who looked up to him . . . and a woman who loved him.

Lillian cursed her shaking hands as she unwound the bandages from around Chance Wilder's shoulder. Her gaze slipped lower. A fine sprinkling of hair covered his chest. Tenderly, she touched her fingers to the wound and felt him stiffen. "I'm sorry. I just want to make certain there's no infection brewing. You're really fortunate that the bullet went clean through."

"Yep."

Her fingers strayed to a scar on his shoulder, the remnants of another wound. Other scars marked his arm. "You have several scars. Do you always get shot in a gunfight?"

"I usually come away with a nick or two." He captured her gaze. "Like I said, I'm not fast."

"Then why do you do it?"

"Why do you stay here when you're not wanted?"

Her fingers stilled as she studied his eyes. Silver like the gun he wore. She reached for clean bandages and began to wrap the wound. "I have my reasons," she stated softly.

"And I have mine."

He grunted when she jerked the bandage into a knot. "But you kill!" she spat, loathing laced through her voice.

"You wanted him to rape you?"

Horrified, she stepped back. "No! But you could have wounded him."

He gave a long thoughtful nod. "Could have."

"You should have. Wounding him would have stopped him as effectively as killing him."

"Would have stopped him this week. But what about next week? Or the week after that? You act like I killed an innocent man. One of his boys held a gun to your brother's temple. You think he wouldn't have given the order to shoot?"

Pressing a hand to her mouth, she spun around. Yes, he would have killed her brother to gain what he wanted from her. She pivoted back around. "Who are you to be judge, jury, and executioner?"

"He knew my reputation. He drew first. If I'd wounded him, he would have come after me, and he would have seen to it the odds weren't so even because then it would have been a matter of revenge. I learned the hard way that if I don't kill a man when he draws on me, he'll have another opportunity to shoot me—usually when my back is turned."

"How can you live like that?"

Averting his gaze, he reached for his shirt, but not before she caught a glimpse of loneliness reflected in his eyes. Grunting, he pulled his shirt over his head. Without thought, she tugged his shirt down and began to slip the buttons into place. She felt the touch of his gaze roaming over her face like a gentle caress. She didn't move when she saw him slowly lift his hand. Tenderly, he cradled her cheek with a hand that killed. She raised her gaze to his.

"I remember you holding my hand, caressing my brow—"

"I'd caress a snake to keep it from dying in my bed."

His unexpected smile sent unwanted shafts of pleasure swirling through her.

"You know the legend, lady, but you don't know

the man. And damned if I'm not tempted to introduce you to the man."

She saw his nostrils flare, his lips part as he lowered his mouth. She knew she should step away, but her feet were rooted to the spot like an ancient oak tree. He was wild and dangerous, everything she feared, all that she longed for. She welcomed the strength in his hand as he tilted her face. She heard thundering footsteps.

Toby burst into the room. "Riders are comin'!"

She felt the tension ripple through Wilder as he pierced her with his narrowed gaze. She shook her head, knowing by his guarded expression what he was thinking. "I didn't tell anyone you were hurt."

He snapped his gaze to Toby. "How many?"

"They're workin' up a cloud of dust. I couldn't count 'em."

Chance released her, withdrew his gun with the hand that had just caressed her cheek, checked the bullets, and slipped it back into his holster. He grabbed his duster, grimacing as he pulled it on. He settled his hat low over his brow. "You and the boy stay inside. If bullets start to fly, you take cover."

"Not every person is a threat—"

"If I'm wrong, then you can invite them in for tea," he growled as he stalked from the room. She heard the front door slam in his wake.

"I don't think he's wrong, Lil," Toby said.

She slipped her arm around him. "You stay here. I'm going into the front room so I can see what's happening." She crept to the window, eased the blue gingham curtains aside, and peered out. Wilder stood on the front porch, one hip cocked, his duster pulled back to reveal his gun. The riders drew their horses to a halt. One man urged his horse forward.

"Are you Chance Wilder?"

"Yep." Wilder pulled a matchstick from his pocket and wedged it between his teeth.

"They say you always work for the man with the best offer."

"That's what they say," Wilder replied.

"Mr. Ward wants to see you up at his house."

Wilder withdrew the match from his mouth and pointed toward the corral. "I'd be obliged if one of your men would saddle my horse. It's the dun-colored beauty."

Lillian sank to the floor, her heart thundering. She could think of only one reason why Jack Ward's son would seek an audience with Chance Wilder. John Ward wanted to hire the man, and she knew he'd offer Wilder more than a harmonica, a bent coin, and a length of string.

Chance's spurs jangled as he followed John Ward's foreman through the sprawling ranch house to a room decorated with cow skulls and horns. A man in his mid-thirties glanced up from his chair behind a large oak desk. "Come in, Mr. Wilder, and have a seat."

Chance ignored the chair set in front of the desk and ambled to a leather chair that rested against the wall. He sat and casually crossed his foot over his knee. He studied the man who was studying him. The man looked as though he'd earned his place in the world.

"You're dismissed," John Ward said without taking his gaze off Chance. The foreman backed out of the room and closed the door behind him.

"You were supposed to meet with me this afternoon," Ward said.

"Had something else to do."

A muscle twitched in Ward's jaw. "Wade Armstrong worked for me." He leaned forward. "I thought you did, too."

"I got a better offer."

"What's my father's whore paying you? I'll better the offer."

Chance chuckled. "Can't be done since I'm being paid everything."

Ward narrowed his blue eyes and set his mouth into a grim line. "I don't take kindly to being betrayed. You and I had an understanding—"

"I never commit myself to an offer until I get a lay of the land and a feel for the stakes involved. I spent two days riding your land. I can't see that it's hurting you not to have that little patch the woman's living on."

"How in the hell do you think my mother feels knowing that her husband died in his whore's bed?"

Chance's stomach knotted. Jack Ward had died in Lillian's bed, in her arms? Something akin to jealousy shot through him at the thought. "Make her an offer—"

"My father gave her all she'll ever get from the Wards. I want her and the boy run off that land, and if you won't do it, I'll find someone who will."

"Be sure that he's as good as his reputation because he'll have to get past me first." Chance unfolded his body and strode from the room.

Four

With trembling hands, Lillian dunked the plate into the bucket of hot water. Wilder had returned earlier, dismounted, and sunk to the porch. He'd ordered Toby to see after his horse. She wanted to tell him to get back on his horse and ride out, but he'd gripped the railing post so tightly that his knuckles had turned white, and she'd realized that he wasn't nearly as recovered as he'd led her to believe. His face had dripped sweat, and she'd seen the small tremors racking his body. She would have offered to help him if he hadn't given her a steely glare. It was several long moments before he was able to pull himself to his feet and deposit his body in the chair on the porch.

Frustrated, she'd returned to the kitchen to wash the dishes she'd let soak while he was gone. She heard Toby's excited voice. He'd no doubt finished tending to the horse.

She set the last dish aside. Wiping her hands on her apron, she walked quietly to the front door and gazed out. Toby had curled three fingers against his palm, was pointing one finger, and had raised his thumb in the air.

"Pow! Pow!" he cried, flinging himself to the ground and rolling like he'd seen Chance do that first day in Lonesome. He jumped to his feet, a wide grin splitting his freckled face in two. "They didn't shoot today 'cuz they was scared of you," he said.

"They weren't scared of me, boy. They were scared of death," Wilder drawled.

"When I grow up, I'm gonna be just like you," Toby said, his face beaming.

Lillian's throat tightened. She wanted Toby to have the influence of a man in his life, but not when that man was a killer.

"You don't want that, boy," Wilder said, and Lillian suddenly realized that he never called Toby by name.

"Sure I do," Toby said, easing nearer to the porch, his head bobbing. "I'll be famous—"

"What you'll be . . . is staring down the road at a long stretch of lonesome," Wilder said, his voice a deep rumble, but in the midst of it, she thought she heard a sigh of regret.

Lillian stepped onto the porch. Wilder slid his gaze over to her. He'd removed his hat and the slight breeze toyed with the soft curls that looked so out of place on a killer. She dropped onto the top step and gazed toward the horizon where the sun painted its farewell tapestry.

"Where do you live?" Toby asked, inching forward on the balls of his feet.

"Under the stars."

"Ain't you got a house somewheres?"

"Nope."

Toby darted a quick glance Lillian's way before looking back at Wilder. She knew Toby had always longed for a house instead of a room over a saloon. His dream brought her here.

"How 'bout kids? You got kids?" Toby asked.

"None that I know of."

Lillian felt the heat warm her cheeks as the image of this man in bed with a woman fluttered through her mind and took root. He wouldn't be wearing his gun . . . or anything else for that matter. "Toby, you need to stop pestering Mr. Wilder."

"I ain't pesterin' him," Toby protested. He angled his head and studied Wilder. "Am I pesterin' you?"

Wilder shot his gaze to Lillian, and she realized she'd dug herself into a hole. She'd asked him not to encourage Toby. To fulfill her request, he'd have to hurt Toby's feelings and tell him that he was a nuisance. Wilder glanced off into the distance. "I'm just feeling a little tuckered out."

"On account of you bein' shot?" Toby asked.

"Yeah."

Toby twisted around, scooted to the end of the porch, dug his bony elbows into his skinny thighs, and, with a deep sigh, leaned forward to watch the sunset. Lillian lifted her gaze to thank Wilder for sparing Toby's feelings. A knot formed in her chest at the raw tenderness she saw reflected in his gaze just before he turned his attention away from her brother and stared at the sunset. The loneliness he'd mentioned to Toby earlier was wrapped around him like a shroud. What would it be like to have no home, no family? As hard as things had been growing up, she'd always had the love of her mother, and now Toby's unfettered devotion.

"Is your shoulder hurting?" she asked.

He shook his head slightly, but didn't look at her. "Aches a little."

"Maybe we should put your arm in a sling, to ease the pressure on your wound."

He slid his narrow, silvered gaze over to her. "It's best not to care, lady."

She turned away, allowing the silence between them

to thicken, the chasm to widen. The man sitting on her front porch seemed so different from the man who wore his reputation. She had not expected tenderness from a killer or a show of respect for her wishes. He had never harmed her or Toby, but she couldn't overlook the fact that he had hurt others.

"Beautiful sunset," he said quietly, with reverence.

Lillian snapped her head around, unable to keep the surprise from reflecting in her voice. "I didn't expect you to be a man who would notice—"

"I notice everything, lady. It's what's kept me alive." He leaned the chair back, resting his head against the wall. "Boy, if you decide to follow the path I've tread, you'll need to learn that."

Toby swiveled his head around. "Learn what?"

"To appreciate every minute you're given. You never know which one will be your last."

Toby furrowed his young brow. "I figure the last one will come during a gunfight."

"The last one will come when you don't expect it, when your back isn't against a wall."

Lillian eased forward. "You think someone would shoot you in the back?"

He shrugged.

"How can you live always expecting to die?"

"If I expect it, maybe it'll be longer in coming."

"And what do you gain?"

"Another sunset."

She turned away, not certain what to make of this man. The low strains of the harmonica floated around her, a seductive melody echoing loneliness. She felt a strong urge to reach out to him, but he'd chosen his path. The music faded into the silence as the darkness blanketed the land.

"Where did you get the mouth organ, boy?" he asked.

Toby twisted around. "It belonged to my pa. He carried it with him during the war."

"Where is he now?"

"Dead."

Lillian wished that the night hadn't turned Wilder into little more than a silhouette. She wanted to see his face, to know what he was thinking as he held her brother's precious gift.

"What about the string?"

"Nothing special about it. Just figured you never know when you'll need a length of string so figured it was a good thing to carry about. But the penny is a lucky penny. I put it on a railroad track and a train ran over it."

"You're lucky the train didn't run over you," he said.

"That's what Lil said. That's why it's a lucky penny."

Lillian heard Wilder's low chuckle. She stared through the darkness. She *had* said those exact words to Toby. The memory unsettled her. She rubbed Toby's shoulder. "Need to get yourself ready for bed."

"But it ain't late—"

"It's late enough for you."

She heard Toby's disgusted sigh as he scrambled to his feet and tromped onto the porch.

"Here, boy."

In the shadows, she was able to make out Wilder extending the harmonica to Toby.

"That's yours now," Toby told him.

"I figure I'm alive because you talked your sister into tending my shoulder. This is payment."

Toby snatched it out of his hand and held the harmonica to his mouth. His quick burst of air sent a squeaky noise into the night. As he walked into the house, more followed.

"He's a good kid," Wilder said quietly.

"He has a name," she snapped. "It's Toby."

"You call a person by name, it makes it harder to forget him."

"What about the people you killed? Did you know their names?"

"Some of them."

She moved her feet up to the next step and wrapped her arms around her drawn-up knees. She thought she might actually like the man if he didn't kill people. "How much was Ward going to pay you?" she asked softly. When his answer was silence, she glanced over her shoulder, pinning him with her gaze. "He is the one who brought you to Lonesome, isn't he?"

"No, lady. You're the one who brought me to Lonesome."

Her heart pounded frantically against her ribs with the realization that she was the person he'd come to kill. "How much did he offer?"

"Ten thousand," he said quietly.

"That's a lot of money."

"Sure is, and he's gonna offer it to someone else. Whether you want to admit it or not, lady, you need me."

"I don't need you. We have a sheriff who is paid to protect the citizens of Lonesome."

"And where was he the other day?"

She wrapped her arms around her middle. "Maybe he was busy with other business, but I plan to speak with him tomorrow about John Ward."

"I'll go with you."

"You said you were leaving in the morning."

"I'll leave as soon as you've talked with the sheriff."

She heard the hushed click of the chair hitting the porch as though it were as weary as the man who sat in it. His boots reverberated over the porch and thudded on the step. She jerked her head up.

" 'Night," he said as he hit the ground.

She shot to her feet. "No."

He stopped, turned, and took a step back toward her. "No?"

She licked her suddenly parched lips. "I . . . I just don't think it's a good idea for you to sleep in the barn. You increase the chances of your wound getting infected."

"Figured you'd prefer for me to be out of the house."

She nodded, trying to understand why she didn't just let him go. Maybe it was the manners her mother had bred into her, or more likely, it was the fact that this man had honored the word he'd given Toby when *everything* was now only a piece of string and a bent coin. "If John Ward should come back tonight—"

"He won't."

"How do you know?"

"He hasn't had time to hire my replacement, and he's not about to risk his life until he feels like he's got someone to cover his back." He took a step closer, and she watched the moonlight play over his golden hair. "Why do you want me in the house?"

"As payment," she blurted, the heat flaming her face. "Payment for your kindness to Toby . . . and for saving me. I hate that you killed the man—" Tears burned the back of her eyes. She despised the weakness that made her sink to the porch. She wrapped her arms around herself and rocked back and forth, memories assailing her of the glittering lust and hatred burning in Wade's eyes. "He was going . . . going to . . . no one would stop him."

Strong arms embraced her, and she pressed her head

against the warm sturdy chest. She heard the constant thudding of his heart.

"No one wants you here. Why don't you leave?" he asked in a low rumble.

She shook her head. "This place was the only gift Jack Ward ever gave me. It means everything to me."

"You loved him?" he asked quietly.

She nodded her head jerkily. "I shouldn't have. God knows I should have hated him, but I never could bring myself to hate him. Even now when his gift brings me such pain, I can't overlook the fact that he gave it to me out of love."

"Have you ever talked with John Ward, tried to settle the differences?"

"No. John threatened to kill me as a trespasser if I ever set foot on his land. Makes it hard to reason with a man when you can't get near him."

"It's even harder to reason with him if he's dead."

Lillian's heart hammered against her ribs. Trembling, she clutched Wilder's shirt and lifted her gaze to his, trying to see into the depths of his silver eyes, but his eyes were only shadows hidden by the night. His embrace was steady, secure, his hands slowly trailing up and down her back. "Promise me you won't kill him," she demanded.

A silence stretched between them, as though he were weighing the promise against the offer that he'd cloaked as a simple statement. "If he's dead, you and the boy will be safe."

She tightened her fingers around his shirt and gave him a small shake. "I don't want the blood of Jack Ward's son on my hands. Give me your word that you won't kill him."

His hands stilled. "What are you willing to pay me to keep me from killing him?"

Her heart thundered, for even though she couldn't

see it clearly, she felt the intensity of his gaze. She had no money, nothing to offer him—nothing to offer a killer except herself. And she knew that he was aware of that fact.

Had she actually begun to feel sympathy for this man whose solitary life gave him no roots, allowed him no love? He was worse than Wade, for Wade had at least barreled into her, announcing loudly and clearly what he wanted of her. The killer wanted the same thing, but he'd lured her into caring for him and trusting him, catching her heart unawares.

Tiny shudders coursed through her body and tears stung her eyes as she answered hoarsely, "Anything."

He cradled her face between his powerful hands. "Anything?" he whispered. "And if I want everything?"

She nodded jerkily. "I don't want John Ward killed." And how could she warn John Ward when approaching him meant her certain death?

Wilder leaned more closely toward her. His warm breath fanned her face. He shifted his thumbs and gently stroked the corners of her mouth. "Give you my word that I'll let the bastard live."

He slashed his mouth over hers, demanding, claiming all that she offered to willingly pay. Everything. Her body, her heart, her soul. She could not give one without giving the others.

His tongue delved deeply, hungrily, as though he were a man coming off a fast. Then, like a man who had felt the easing of his hunger, he gentled his touch. He threaded his fingers through her hair while the callused pads of his thumbs caressed her cheek. She had never been kissed with such tenderness, had never experienced so great a yearning to give back in kind what she was receiving. She twined her arms around his neck and heard his guttural groan. He tore his mouth from hers and blazed a trail of hot, moist kisses along the column of her throat. A tiny gasp escaped her lips.

Without warning, he surged to his feet. She stared at his rigid back and listened to his harsh breathing echoing through the night. She rose, clinging to the porch post for support, afraid her trembling legs would give out beneath her. "Chance?"

"Go to bed, Li—lady," he growled.

She licked her swollen lips, tasting where he had been. "Are you—"

"I'm sleeping in the barn."

"I don't understand. I thought you wanted—"

He spun around. "Christ, lady, I do want you . . . more than I've ever wanted anything. And that's the very reason why I won't take what you're offering."

She watched him storm toward the barn, the disappointment slamming into her. Disappointment with him because he'd left her with a woman's yearnings. Disappointment with herself because she wished he'd satisfied those longings.

FIVE

''Not a damn thing I can do. They haven't broken any laws.''

Lillian glared at Sheriff Bergen. The graying mustache that drooped down on either side of his mouth gave him the appearance of frowning whether he was or not. She placed her hands on her hips and leaned slightly over his cluttered desk. ''But he threatened to run us off our land.''

''No law against threatening people.'' His brown eyes held an acceptance she wasn't willing to tolerate.

She leaned over farther. ''He is going to hire someone—''

''Ain't against the law to hire someone.''

She jerked back. ''It's not against the law to hire someone to kill me?''

The sheriff snorted. ''John Ward isn't going to hire someone to kill you.''

Anger surging through her, she spun around and locked her gaze onto Chance's. He stood with his back against the wall, his arms crossed over his chest, his face void of expression as though he had expected the sheriff's words. ''Didn't he offer to hire you?''

He gave a long, slow nod.

''To kill me?''

He twisted his lips into a sardonic smile. ''He's too smart to put it that bluntly. All he told me to do was run you off the land. A man can take that any number of ways.''

''I imagine a hired killer would only take it one way,'' she snapped, turning her attention back to the sheriff. ''You have to do something.''

He moved his mouth as though he were chewing an idea. ''I know it's hard to understand, but until he's actually broken the law, I can't arrest him just in case he might break the law.''

''This is ridiculous. Can't you at least talk to him?''

''And tell him what?'' Sheriff Bergen countered. ''If he kills you, I'll arrest him? He knows that.''

''I can't believe there is absolutely nothing you can do.''

He shook his craggy head. ''My job is to enforce the law—''

''And to protect the citizens,'' Chance said. Lillian jerked her head around. He shifted his hard-edged gaze from her to the sheriff. ''Why don't you arrange a meeting between Miss Madison and Ward? Maybe they could come to a peaceful agreement.''

''I don't imagine there will be any peace unless Miss Madison leaves or John's mother dies. Mrs. Ward can't stand the thought of her husband's . . .'' The deep red circles burning brightly on Sheriff Bergen's cheeks seemed out of place on the older man. He cleared his throat. ''Jack's mistress living near Lonesome. And you can understand if you look at it from her point of view—she was married to Jack for forty years, helped him build something out of nothing. A woman don't take kindly to evidence of the man's unfaithfulness and him dying in your bed was damning evidence—for him and you.''

Lillian tasted the bitterness of defeat. They had lived

here for only three months, and the happiness she and Toby longed for hovered just beyond reach. She straightened her shoulders. "Thank you for your time, Sheriff."

Trembling with fury, she marched out of the sheriff's office and stumbled to a stop on the wooden boardwalk. Toby turned away from the horses, his grin wobbly. "How'd it go?"

She forced herself to smile. "The sheriff doesn't think we have anything to worry about."

She turned her head slightly as Chance came to stand beside her. "You knew the sheriff wouldn't do anything to help me, didn't you?" she asked, her anger smoldering.

He tugged the brim of his hat lower. "Figured there wouldn't be a lot he could do. What you need is to hire someone to protect you. Fortunately for you, your brother already did that."

"You said you were going to leave."

"Changed my mind."

Relief coursed through her, then warred with doubt. "I don't want a hired gun—"

"Don't argue with me, lady. I know you don't like what I am, but I'm the only chance you've got right now if you want to stay alive. If you won't keep me around for yourself, keep me around for the boy—until we can arrange a meeting with Ward and work out a better solution."

"I don't understand you. Toby gave you—"

"Everything."

Everything. A length of string, a bent coin, and a harmonica. He'd returned the precious harmonica to Toby. She could almost believe Chance Wilder was a man of honor, a man of compassion.

"Wilder!"

She jerked her gaze to a man standing in the middle

of the street, his hands flexing over a pair of guns strapped on either side of his hips. She turned her attention back to Chance as he slowly turned to face the man, who began to fidget.

"They say you're the best gun this side of the Rio Grande," the man announced.

Chance gave a long, slow nod. "That's what they say."

"I'm calling you out."

She heard Chance release a low sigh as he reached into his pocket, pulled out a matchstick, and wedged it between his teeth. "Lady, you and the boy go into the sheriff's office."

Her heart leapt into her throat. "You can't possibly—"

"Do it now," he snarled between clenched teeth.

She grabbed Toby by the arm and pulled him into the sheriff's office. With the door slamming in her wake, she scurried to the window. She watched Chance amble confidently into the middle of the street. The sheriff came up behind her and gazed over her shoulder. "You've got to stop them," she told him.

"Can't. They ain't broke no laws yet."

She snapped her head around. "Damn you! Wilder will kill him."

Sheriff Bergen shrugged. "Probably, but Wilder always works within the law or he'd be wanted for murder."

"As long as the person who wants the killing done makes the best offer."

He raised a thick brow, but didn't take his gaze off the street. "Like that widow in Dripping Springs? Heard all he got from her was a pig. Besides, from what I hear, he's never killed anyone who didn't deserve to die. Take that fella who just called him out. He killed a sixteen-year-old boy in Sherman. Said he was cheating at cards.''

Gunshots cracked the air and unexpected terror ricocheted through Lillian. She jerked her gaze to the street. Chance was walking stiffly back toward the sheriff's office. Grabbing Toby's hand, she hurried outside. She saw the other man sprawled in the street, his blood pooling over the ground and soaking into the earth. She rushed to Chance's side, her gaze flicking over him. ''Where did you get shot?''

''Get on your horse,'' he said.

''How bad are you hurt?''

He gripped her arm and gave her a small shake, his cold eyes holding hers. ''Get on the goddamn horse now.'' He shifted his gaze to Sheriff Bergen. ''I've got witnesses—''

''And I'm one of them,'' the sheriff said. ''I saw that he drew first. His name—''

''I don't want to know his name,'' Chance cut in as he dropped some coins in the sheriff's palm. ''See that he gets a decent burial.''

Toby was already sitting astride his horse when Lillian mounted hers. She heard Chance groan low as he pulled himself into his saddle. She hoped they'd get home before he tumbled from his horse.

Chance winced as Lillian dabbed alcohol on his wound. The bullet had creased his right arm. The advantage to being left-handed was that his opponents had a tendency to aim for his right out of habit.

''You have got to learn to draw faster,'' Lillian scolded.

A corner of his mouth curved up. He couldn't remember the last time anyone had shown an ounce of concern over his well-being. ''Careful, lady,'' he warned. ''I might begin to think you care.''

His stomach knotted when he saw the tears well within the depths of her blue eyes. He felt as though someone had emptied a six-gun into his chest.

"Why couldn't you have ignored him?" she rasped.

"Because he wouldn't have let up. He was in the saloon the day I got here, trying to gather the courage to challenge me. He was looking to gain a reputation. At least by facing him, I was able to control from which direction the bullet came." Cradling her cheek, stroking her soft skin, he knew he was inviting danger. Walking away last night had been the hardest thing he'd ever done—and he couldn't explain why he'd done it. She wasn't innocent. She'd been an old man's . . . lover. But never his whore. No matter how many men Lillian Madison took into her bed, she'd never be any man's whore. She was too fine, too gentle for that. So he admitted to her what he'd never told another soul. "I don't want the bullet with my name on it to come from behind."

The tears brimmed over and trailed down her cheek, rolling along the curve of his thumb. "Is that why you always keep your back against the wall, even here?"

He nodded. "I think about how nice it would be if I didn't worry about that last bullet, but the thought gnaws at me like a squirrel eating a pecan."

She blinked back the tears and sniffed. "Why do you stick a match into your mouth? You only seem to do it when you sense danger."

"If I tell you, you gotta promise not to tell a soul."

She gave a curt nod. "I promise."

"In the heat of a gunfight, my tongue lolls out of my mouth. I damn near bit it off once. Biting down on a match keeps it where it belongs."

She laughed and touched her fingers to the hair curling around his ears. "You are nothing like I expected."

"You're everything." Her laughter dwindled along

with her smile. He brought her hand to his lips, holding her gaze. "You're everything I want, and everything I can never have."

Lillian watched Wilder walk through the fallow fields beyond the house. He'd taken his supper on the porch even though she'd invited him to sit at the table inside the house. It wasn't reasonable to want to know everything about him. It wasn't wise to be glad that he was staying a little while longer. It wasn't logical to realize she might be falling in love with him.

She strolled through the tall grass and weeds. He crouched down as she neared. When she reached him, she saw him scoop up the dirt and sift it through his fingers.

"It's good soil," he said. "What are you going to grow?"

She knelt beside him and shrugged. "I haven't a clue. I don't know anything about farming."

"Corn would be good."

She watched his gaze roam over the fields and was left with the distinct impression that he could actually envision the corn growing. "Were you a farmer?"

He dumped the remaining dirt out of his palm, stood, and slapped his hand against his thigh. "Once. A long time back."

She rose to her feet. "What turns a farmer into a hired gun?"

She watched his Adam's apple slowly rise and fall as he swallowed. "A desire to die."

In long strides, he strode across the fields. She hurried to catch up to him. "Why would you want to die?"

"Because I didn't want to live."

"Why?"

He staggered to a stop, and she nearly slammed into him.

"Why the sudden interest?"

"I've always been interested, but I think I was afraid to know the truth. What sort of man are you, Chance Wilder? A man offers you a fortune and you turn your back on it for a piece of string and a bent coin. You've killed twenty-four men, twenty-five counting Wade—"

"That's what they say."

She stared at him, comprehension slowly dawning. "*They say* you've killed twenty-five men. *They say* you're fast. *They say* you always work for the best offer." A knowing smile crept over her face. "But you don't say." She angled her head. "How many have you killed?"

"Before I came to Lonesome?"

She nodded.

"Eight."

Relief swamped her. He had killed, but not to the degree she'd expected. "Tell me about the woman in Dripping Springs. The one who paid you a pig."

"Two pigs. She paid me two pigs to make her neighbor think twice before trampling his herd through her garden."

She laughed. "You're not as tough as you pretend to be."

His eyes narrowed into silver slits. "I'm tough, lady. Never make the mistake of thinking I'm not. I've been on my own since I was fourteen."

"What happened when you were fourteen?"

He hesitated.

"Are you afraid to tell me?" she goaded. "Afraid I might realize you aren't so tough?"

She saw a muscle in his jaw clench.

"I went hunting . . . with my brother. James was four years older than I was. It's been ten years, but I can see him clearly—like he was standing in front of me. We lived in Palo Pinto. Lot of Indian raids going on back then.'' A far-off look came into his eyes. ''We separated, thinking we'd have better luck finding game. Then I heard him scream.'' Anguish reshaped the lines of his face. ''By my count close to two dozen renegades had taken him by surprise. They were torturing him, and his screams for mercy were echoing around me. I couldn't save him.''

Her heart went out to the child who had seen his brother in pain. It had nearly torn her heart in two to see Toby hurt when they'd been attacked in town. She couldn't fathom how he must have felt hearing his brother's screams. ''What did you do?''

As though catapulted from the past, his gaze snapped to her. ''I killed him. One bullet between the eyes. I've always been a damn good shot.''

Tears welling in her eyes, she touched his arm. ''How awful, but I'm sure he was grateful.''

He laughed mirthlessly. ''My parents didn't see it that way. They kicked me out with nothing but the clothes on my back. I should have tried to save him.''

''You would have been killed as well.''

He shrugged. ''Maybe. We'll never know. I only know that he's dead, and for a long time, I wished I was, too. I went wild, got into fights, goaded men into drawing on me. But at the last second, the need to live always won out over the need to die.''

Watching him walk back to the house, a lone figure silhouetted by the retreating sun, she fought the overwhelming urge to comfort him.

Six

Lillian lay in bed, unable to sleep. Shafts of moonlight pierced the room. When she closed her eyes, she saw Chance standing in the fields, reciting his tale in an emotionless voice. But his eyes, his silver eyes had revealed his anguish.

She slipped out of bed. He wouldn't stay, and when he left, she feared he'd take a portion of her heart with him. She padded down the hallway and peeked into Toby's room. His face relaxed in innocent sleep, he was sprawled across his bed. His fingers were curled around the bent coin Chance had returned to him earlier in exchange for tending his horse. She closed his door quietly before walking out of the house.

The night was warm, the sky a blanket of stars. The full moon guided her journey to the barn. She climbed the ladder and peered into the loft. Chance stood beside the loft opening, limned by moonlight, gazing out at the night. The ladder creaked as she climbed higher. He snapped his head around.

"Go back to bed, lady," he said harshly and dismissed her with a simple turning of his head.

Taking an unsteady breath, she crawled into the loft, ignoring the straw pricking her through her nightgown.

She strolled toward him. "Your parents were wrong to send you away."

"I'm a killer—"

"No, I don't think you are." She touched his arm, the place where she'd bandaged his wound earlier.

"I shouldn't have told you that story."

"Why? Because I might come to understand you, to care about you?"

"I hurt people, lady. That's what I do. And I hurt worst those I care about the most."

Her heart soared with the unguarded admission that he cared for her. "Hold me."

"Lady, I'm hanging on by a thin rope." Despair and something akin to fear delved into the depths of his silvery eyes. "If you don't get out of this loft, my gun's coming off and so are your clothes."

"I'm staying."

He cradled her cheek. "In a few days, I'm leaving."

She nodded, her voice catching in her throat. "I know."

"No matter what happens tonight, I'll ride out of here and never look back."

Every doubt she had melted away with his words, with his attempt to send her away. Whatever else Chance Wilder might be, he was a man of honor. "I want to be here, tonight, with you."

She heard his breath hitch, and in the moonlight, she watched his Adam's apple slide up and down as he swallowed. Slowly, as though to give her time to change her mind, he reached down and untied the strip of leather that kept his gun anchored to his thigh. Even more slowly, he unbuckled his gunbelt and set the gun and holster in the corner behind him. When once again he stood before her, she thought she saw a flicker of doubt flash within his eyes.

"What's gonna pass between us will make it harder

for me to leave, but I will leave, Lillian,'' he whispered, cupping her face between his hands.

She smiled softly. ''I like it when you say my name. You'll have a harder time forgetting me.''

''I'll never forget you,'' he rasped. ''Whenever I see a stormy sky, I'll remember the color of your eyes.'' He pressed a kiss to each of her closed eyelids. ''When the leaves turn in autumn, I'll remember the way your hair looked when the sun glistened over it.'' He rained kisses over her face and throat. ''And when the night comes, I'll remember what it was like to hold you in my arms.''

His words brought tears to her eyes. She knew she would forever remember him. His arms closed around her, pressing the soft curves of her body against the hardened planes of his. She had tended his wounds, but she longed to tend his heart. When his mouth covered hers, she denied him nothing. He groaned and she felt him shudder.

With nimble fingers, he unbuttoned her gown and slid it past her shoulders. The soft cotton traveled the length of her body and pooled quietly at her feet. She fought the urge to hide her body from his appreciative gaze. He never took his eyes from her as he stripped out of his own clothes. She stepped into his embrace, and he carried her down to the quilts spread out over the straw. Warm and protective, his body blanketed hers. She pressed a kiss to a scar on his chest. How she longed to ask him to seek another means of living, a living that would keep him out of harm's way. How would she bear it when the news came that the notorious gunslinger had been slain?

She fought back the depressing thoughts and wrapped her arms more tightly around him as though by doing so, she could keep him with her forever. She slipped her hand behind his head, threading her fingers through his curling locks, and brought his mouth down to hers. Eagerly, she kissed him, desperate to send the reminders of death into the shadowed corners. "Say my name," she rasped.

"Lillian." Chance lifted his mouth from hers and held her gaze in the moonlight. If death weren't nipping at his heels, he'd offer her more than a roll in the hay. He'd give her everything he had, little as it was.

But he'd been reminded today how easily something that touched him could touch her. He gave his hands the freedom to roam over every inch of her body, memorizing the texture, the curves, the hollows. And where his hands traveled, his mouth followed, bringing her pleasure. Her soft moans were the sweetest sounds he'd ever heard. Her gentle touch ignited a fire that he feared might never burn out.

"Chance," she whispered with a ragged breath. He wanted to die hearing his name on her lips, feeling her hands on his flesh.

Rising above her, he joined his body to hers, felt her tightness close around him. He rocked against her, hearing her tiny cries grow with intensity as she met his thrusts. She held his gaze, and when her body arched beneath his, he thought he'd never seen anything more beautiful—and that beauty carried him to new heights.

Breathing heavily, he collapsed against her. He pressed a kiss to the hollow at the base of her throat where the moisture gathered like the dew on a petal. Then he rolled to his side, tucked her within the curve of his body, and drifted off to sleep.

Lethargically, Lillian awakened. The warmth was gone, and in its place, she felt an unaccountable cold. She glanced toward the loft opening. Chance stood there, the moonlight playing a shadow dance over his nudity. She thought he looked magnificent.

As though sensing her gaze, he turned slightly. She was unprepared for the anger flashing in his silvery eyes.

"They say you were Jack Ward's whore," he said through gritted teeth.

She eased up onto her elbows. "That's what they say."

"They say he died in your bed."

She nodded. "He did."

"But you weren't his whore." He glanced down at his thigh, and she saw the thin trail of her blood that spotted his flesh. "Until tonight no man had ever bedded you." He turned to face her squarely. "I want to know exactly what Jack Ward was to you."

She swallowed hard. "He was my father."

Chance stared at Lillian as though she'd spoken words he'd never before heard. "Your father?"

She nodded jerkily and the moonlight shimmered off the tears welling within her huge eyes. He dropped to the quilt beside her and cradled her soft cheek within his roughened palm. Guilt gnawed at him. If he'd known she was untouched, he never would have laid a hand on her. "Why didn't you tell me?" he asked, his hoarse voice clogged with emotion.

She lifted her bare shoulder slightly and snuggled her cheek more closely against his cupped palm. "Two reasons. I was afraid if I told you that you wouldn't believe me, and I wasn't certain I could stand the pain." She turned her face and pressed a kiss against his hardened flesh. "But more, I was afraid if I told you the truth—if you knew I'd never lain with a man—you wouldn't touch me."

He brushed a kiss across her temple, inhaling her

sweet fragrance, mingling with the scent of the straw and their earlier lovemaking. "Ah, lady, you shouldn't have come to me. You deserve so much better—"

"You would have sent me away if you'd known, wouldn't you?" she asked.

"Yes. Hell, I should have sent you away anyway." He leaned back slightly and held her gaze. He wanted to tell her that she filled a hole inside of him that he hadn't even known existed. But telling her anything about his feelings might prompt her to reciprocate—and forgetting her was going to be damn near impossible as it was without any declaration of love. "Does John Ward know?"

She shook her head. "No. He was out of town when Toby and I moved here. I don't know why Jack didn't tell his family before he moved us here. He had plans to tell them about me as soon as John returned, but he never got the chance."

He leaned back on an elbow and trailed his fingers along the inside of her thigh. "Tell me everything."

She sighed heavily. "My mother met Jack Ward during the war. He served in Galveston. She fell in love with him, and I think . . ."

Within her eyes, Chance saw the stark truth warring with what she wanted to accept as the truth.

"I think he loved her. When she died, I found a letter he'd written her shortly after the war ended. He was returning to his family, and he'd never forget her. Along with the letter, I found newspaper clippings she'd collected, all heralding his success as a rancher near Austin. The night he died, he had brought me the letter that she'd written to him, wishing him a lifetime of happiness." She clutched his arm. "She never told him about me."

"Then how did he find out?"

"I wrote him after Mother died. I thought he might want to know that she was gone."

"What about Toby's father?"

She smiled softly. "Shortly after I was born, Mother moved to Houston. She worked in a saloon. I think the bartender, Ben, must have loved Mother for years, but he felt he had nothing to offer her." She shrugged. "I'm not sure of the details, but I remember that she stopped looking tired all the time. He doted on her. They'd planned to marry, but he was killed in a barroom brawl. Shortly afterward, Mother discovered she was carrying his child. We lived in a room over the saloon. Wasn't fancy, but we had love. Mother died of influenza last year. After I wrote Jack Ward, he came to Houston and told me he wanted to make things up to me. He had a little house and some land he wanted to give me. I had always wanted a house, and so had Toby. And I'd always wanted my own father's love. The night he brought my mother's letter, he clutched his chest and collapsed. I got him to the bed, and he died in my arms. Everyone assumed I was his whore."

"And you didn't correct them?"

"Everyone was in a panic. Mrs. Ward was hysterical. John arrived the next day and wanted to protect her. I've thought of leaving, but this property is the only thing Jack Ward ever gave me other than my life. It's everything to me."

"Then I'll do all in my power to see that you keep it." He shifted his body and laid her back down on the quilt. Covering her body with his, he kissed her tenderly. He understood her desire to hold on to the land because, in the short time he'd known her, she'd become everything to him.

SEVEN

The late afternoon air hung heavy around Chance as he walked among the trees lining the banks of the river, Lillian's small hand nestled within his larger one as though it belonged there. They'd brought the boy swimming, and Chance could hear the muted sound of the flowing stream nearby. They'd left the boy to give him some privacy for putting his clothes back on, but he figured Toby recognized a lame excuse when he heard one. The truth was: Chance was dying for an opportunity to kiss Lillian.

He stopped walking and faced her. The sun had kissed her face, leaving her cheeks glowing a rosy red. If he lived to be a hundred, he'd never forget the shape of her face. "I want to have a meeting with John Ward. I'm thinking the troubles would go away if he knew the truth."

She hesitated a moment before she nodded thoughtfully. "And when the troubles go away, you'll go away."

He saw the sorrow sweep into her eyes. He was both humbled and terrified with the knowledge that she cared for him. He lowered his head, touched his mouth to hers, and kissed her, gathering the memories close so he could unfurl them at night beside the campfire.

She welcomed him as no one else ever had. She made him want to stay—when he knew he had to go.

He drew back and brushed his thumb over her swollen lower lip. "I'm not what you need, lady."

"But you're what I want."

Explosions rent the still air. Chance felt the pain tear through his back as he pulled Lillian close, withdrew his gun, and plunged over the embankment, giving them some protection. "Can you get to the boy and horses?" he asked.

"Who do you think is out there?"

"My guess is that Ward hired his gun. Ride out of here and get the sheriff. I'll hold them off while you get away."

He heard more gunfire, stretched up slightly, and shot off two bullets before quickly ducking back down. Several guns fired, chunking bits of bark off the nearby trees.

"You can't stay here," she told him.

"I've got no choice. Someone needs to distract them. Now go!"

She leaned forward as though to kiss him briefly, then reeled back, horror etched across her face as she stared at the bright red blood coating her hand. Her gaze darted from her hand to his face. She wrenched his duster aside and gasped at the freely flowing blood that drenched his shirt and trousers. His side felt as though someone had built a blazing fire within him.

"We've gotta get you to a doctor," she said.

He cradled her cheek, despising the way his hand trembled. He held her gaze, hating the truth he had to impart. "I'm hurt bad, Lillian. Take the boy and get to safety. Tell the sheriff that Ward finally did something he can arrest him for."

"I won't leave you to die. I'll send Toby—"

He grabbed her arm and jerked her close. "And who

the hell is gonna take care of your brother if you're killed? You were a sweet roll in the hay, lady, but that's all you are to me. Now get the hell out of here."

She pulled back, tears brimming in her eyes. "That's a damn lie. You're just trying to make me leave."

He drew her against him, unable to stand the anguish in her eyes. He brushed his lips against her soft hair. "My life has meant nothing. For God's sake, let my death mean something. Take the time I can buy you and get out of here."

He heard her muffled sob before she withdrew from his hold and gave him a jerky nod. He slipped his shaking fingers into his pocket, but couldn't latch onto a matchstick. She brushed his hand aside, reached into his pocket, withdrew a matchstick, and slipped it into his mouth. His voice nearly strangled him. "Thanks."

"I love you," she whispered hoarsely before scrambling down the embankment toward the horses and Toby. He peered over the edge and fired twice, taking satisfaction in one man's yell. Then he dropped back down. He looked over his shoulder and saw Lillian and Toby riding out. Relief swamped him along with the blackness; his last thought was that he'd finally acquired something worth living for.

The rain fell softly on his face, and the fragrance of roses in their first bloom wafted around him. He heard the voice of an angel whispering his name and felt her gentle fingers caress his brow. He'd expected to drop straight into Hell and here he was: on the other side of Heaven.

Struggling through the agony, desperate to gaze upon the angel's face, he forced his eyes open. Darkness surrounded him and a halo of light surrounded the angel. Tears glistened over her lovely face as she smiled tenderly. His heart tightened with a bittersweet pain that made the throbbing in his side pale in comparison.

"Hello," she whispered, her voice low as though she feared any sound would bring him pain.

He licked his parched lips. She brought a glass of water to his mouth. He drank slowly, having been shot too many times not to know better than to take his time adjusting to the land of the living. "I'm not dead," he croaked inanely.

Her smile widened. "No. You were lucky."

Nodding, he drifted back into oblivion.

Lillian pressed a kiss to Chance's brow before gently wiping her tears from his face.

"Think he'll live?" Toby asked.

She glanced over her shoulder at her brother. "He'll be weak for a while, but I think he's going to be all right."

"He ain't gonna like what you did, Lil."

She touched his shoulder. "We're not going to tell him. It'll stay our secret."

Toby nodded.

She squeezed his shoulder. "And as hard as it'll be, we have to let him go."

Chance slung his saddlebags over his horse's rump. A week of being laid up in bed had nearly driven him insane. He hadn't regained all his strength, but he'd gained enough to know Lillian Madison was anxious to see his back headed down the road.

"Where do you think you'll go?" Toby asked.

"Whichever way the wind blows," he said. He darted a glance at the woman standing calmly on the porch, watching his actions as though they meant nothing to her. "So how long do you think this 'understanding' with John Ward will last?" he asked.

"Forever. You were right. Once I explained everything, he was extremely understanding. He won't bother me and Toby anymore.''

He didn't believe her, not for one minute. Something had happened between the time he'd blacked out and the moment he'd awakened in her bed, but he wasn't exactly sure what. The woman had been incredibly vague with the details, refusing to meet his gaze whenever the topic came up. Even when she'd despised what he did for a living, she'd met his gaze head-on. He was willing to bet his life that she was hiding something. He pulled himself into the saddle.

''You got the string?'' the boy asked.

Chance smiled. ''Yep.'' He shifted his gaze to Lillian. His throat constricted, and he knew he wouldn't be able to push any words out so he simply touched his finger to the brim of his hat and gave a brusque nod.

He guided his horse around and began galloping toward the sunset. And he never once looked back.

''It's my understanding that you won't be bothering Miss Madison anymore,'' Chance said, standing in John Ward's office.

''That's right.''

''And how do I know you won't change your mind?''

''No reason for me to. She traded the deed to her land for your life.''

Chance's gut knotted up so tightly he nearly keeled over. ''What?''

John Ward shook his head, smiling. ''It was something to see. She came galloping up from the river, waving her petticoat like a white flag. Said you'd been shot. She swore she'd sign over the deed to her land if I sent one of my boys for the doctor. Couldn't pass up an offer like that. Brought the land agent along with the doctor, and she signed the deed over to me right on the spot. Now that you're well enough, she ought to be packing up and moving on."

"Where's she gonna go?"

"I've got no idea and I don't care. She'll be off the land and that's all that matters to me. Her presence here was breaking my mother's heart."

"I imagine your father is rolling over in his grave," Chance said.

Ward stiffened. "He had no right to bring his whore here."

"She wasn't his whore. She was his daughter."

Chance heard a soft gasp. He spun around. A silver-haired woman stood in the doorway. She pounded her cane on the floor. "John, make this man take his lies out of this house!"

John Ward narrowed his eyes and studied his mother. "Are they lies, Mother?"

Tears filled her eyes. "I told him not to bring her here, but he said he owed her. He loved her mother during the war, but it was just to punish me because I wouldn't live in Galveston with him. I didn't want to be where the Yankees might be." She hit her cane on the floor. "I don't want her here."

"Why did you tell me she was Father's whore?"

The woman sank into a chair. "Because I knew you wouldn't send her away if you knew the truth. If you knew she was . . . your sister."

Ward crossed the room and knelt before his mother. "You're punishing an innocent woman for the sins of my father."

"He had no right—"

Chance strode across the room. Ward snapped his head around. "Where are you going?"

"I'm leaving. I found out what I came here to learn."

* * *

Lillian saw the rider silhouetted against the late afternoon sun. Her heart sped up, and she took a deep breath to calm it. She set the box into the back of the wagon and lifted her hand to shield her eyes from the glaring sun. Clothed in black, the man sat tall in the saddle. Her heart leapt into her throat. He wasn't supposed to return.

Toby rounded the corner. "Heh, Lil, can I—" He came to an abrupt halt. Then his eyes widened as the rider drew his horse to a halt. "Chance!" He bounded across the short expanse separating him from Chance. Smiling broadly, he tipped his head back. "You came back!"

"Sure did," Chance said in a low voice as he slowly dismounted. Reaching into his pocket, he withdrew a length of frayed string. "Here, Toby, you can have this back."

Toby snatched it out of his hand. "Great! I was needing some string."

Lillian stared at Chance. "You said his name."

"Sure did," he said as he stalked toward her, his eyes narrowed. "You gave Ward the deed to the land. You told me it meant everything to you."

"You meant more."

He jerked her into his embrace, and she felt the rapid pounding of his heart beneath her cheek. "Damn you, lady, why didn't you tell me?"

"Because I knew you'd get angry, or worse, you'd feel that you owed me."

"Why, Lillian, why did you give him the land?" he asked in a hoarse voice.

She tilted her head back and met his gaze. "Because I love you."

He cradled her face between his hands. "I've got

some land west of here. There's nothing on it but a couple of pigs—''

She shook her head. "Once before I took land in place of a man's love. It's a poor substitute. I won't do it again.''

"And what if my love comes with the land?'' His thumbs caressed her cheeks. "I don't know if it'll work, but I'm thinking if I hang up my gun and we live a quiet life for a while . . . that maybe my reputation will fade. Right now all I have is a long stretch of lonesome waiting for me down the road, and I want more. I want everything, Lillian. A home, a wife, a family. I want you.''

She smiled warmly, her heart humming with happiness. But the sound of thundering hooves made her turn her head. Chance released her and stepped back, slipping a match between his teeth. She didn't know if she could live like this, constantly wondering when the last bullet would come.

The rider drew his horse to a halt. Her heart slammed against her ribs as John Ward stared down at her.

"You have his eyes,'' he said quietly. "I didn't notice that before, and I should have. I owe you an apology, Miss . . . Ward. Your name should be Ward, and I'm ashamed my father didn't do right by you. Even more ashamed that I treated you unfairly. If you'll come into town with me, I'll deed the land back over to you.''

Chance slammed his eyes closed. Ward was giving her back the land. All his hopes and dreams died with the offer. The land meant everything to her, and he couldn't stay. He was too well known here.

"No, thank you, Mr. Ward. I no longer want the land.''

Chance opened his eyes. She was watching him.

"I've been offered some land west of here, and I always take the best offer."

Chance felt his heart swell with love, and he knew he'd do all in his power to make certain she had accepted the best offer.

"At least let me pay you what the land is worth," Ward offered.

Lillian shook her head and smiled warmly at Chance. "I don't need the money, Mr. Ward. I already have everything."

Chance drew her into his arms, holding her close, knowing he'd never let her go. "Ah, lady, you've just given me more than everything."

Epilogue

FIVE YEARS LATER

Pushing herself up from the rocking chair on the porch, Lillian Wilder pressed her hand against her swollen stomach where her unborn child kicked. She was hoping for a girl this time.

She walked to the edge of the porch and saw her husband strolling in from the cornfields, his three-year-old son perched on his shoulders, Toby loping along beside them. She watched as Chance threw his head back and laughed, and she knew Toby had told him something outrageous. She loved Chance's laughter, loved his smiles, loved him.

She heard a rumble and glanced toward the road. Her breath caught at the sight of the unfamiliar wagon. Slowly, she released her breath. Men looking to gain a reputation usually rode in on a horse. In the passing years, only two men had come to the farm seeking out the notorious Chance Wilder. They'd left disappointed, discovering that Chance Wilder could not be goaded into strapping on his gun.

She didn't think the elderly couple pulling their wagon to a halt in front of her house had come to challenge Chance's fading reputation. She stepped off the porch. " 'Evening."

The man pierced her with a silvery gaze. "We were told this is Chance Wilder's place."

She wiped her suddenly damp hands on her apron. "Yes, that's right. Chance is coming in from the fields now."

The man climbed down from the wagon, and then helped the woman to the ground. The woman riveted her light blue gaze on the man striding from the fields. The older man slipped his arm around her shoulders and drew her close as though what needed to be faced was better faced together.

Lillian saw Chance's stride falter and slow as he neared the house. Wariness guarding his features, he came to stand beside her, his eyes drawn to the couple. He wrapped his hands around his son and lifted him off his shoulders, setting him on the ground between him and Lillian. A heavy silence stretched between him and the couple. Lillian slipped her hand into Chance's, surprised to find his trembling.

Tears welled in the old woman's eyes and spilled onto her cheeks. She pressed a shaking hand against her mouth. "Chance," she whispered brokenly.

"Mama," he croaked.

She held out her arms. "We're so sorry. Forgive us, son. Please forgive us."

Chance shook his head. "There's nothing to forgive, Mama."

Chance released Lillian's hand and crossed the short expanse, taking his mother into his arms. Lillian heard the woman's heart-wrenching sobs.

"We were wrong, wrong to send you away," his mother lamented.

"It's all right," Chance murmured.

Lillian watched as Chance's father hesitated, then

stepped forward to wrap his arms around his wife and son. They held each other for long moments as the years and regrets melted away. Finally Chance drew back. "I want you to meet my family."

He held his hand out to Lillian. She stepped within the circle of his arm. "This is Lillian, my wife."

Lillian smiled warmly. "I'm very happy to meet you. Chance has often spoken of you." She introduced them to Toby.

Chance lifted his son into his arms. "And this is our son," he told them.

More tears welled in his mother's eyes. "Oh, Stephen, we have a grandchild. How wonderful! What's his name?"

Chance hesitated, shifting his gaze to Lillian. Nodding, she slipped her arm through his.

"James," Chance said quietly. "We named him James."

They had selected the name in memory of his brother. Lillian watched as understanding dawned in the older couple's eyes.

"We were about to sit down to supper," Lillian said. "Will you join us?"

"We'd love to," Chance's mother said. "We have so many years to catch up on."

Chance stayed back, watching his parents stroll to the house, James between them, holding their hands. Toby opened the door and led them inside.

Lillian slipped her arm around Chance, and he drew her more closely against his side.

"They hurt you, and yet you forgave them so easily," she said softly.

"If they hadn't sent me away, I wouldn't have you."

"I'm not worth the years of loneliness and pain—"

He touched his finger to her lips. "Lillian, you're worth everything."

Lowering his mouth to hers, he kissed her deeply, tenderly. He remembered Toby's offer to pay him everything. He'd thought everything was a length of string, a harmonica, and a bent penny.

Everything was love.

Best Laid Plans

By
Evelyn Crowe

One

In forty-eight hours all hell was going to break loose.

Kathleen Calhoun felt a flash of panic as she gazed at her raised fist. It shook. The emotional reaction was so foreign to her nature that she stared at her hand as if it belonged to someone else. No one had ever accused her of being a coward, and she wasn't prone to bouts of paralyzing fear—until now. Taking a shaky breath, she allowed herself to be distracted by the scenery.

The Texas Hill Country was alive with an early spring. Birds tittered from the big cottonwood trees, and bees were busy above a profusion of flowerpots shoved in corners of the front porch of the ranch house. In the distance cattle and horses grazed lazily under an early morning sun.

In forty-eight hours she would deliberately destroy three lives.

She'd delayed long enough, and wiped a sweaty palm down over her hip. From years of habit, she straightened her skirt, tugged at the jacket of the no-nonsense business suit, then touched her neat cap of short blond hair.

Time was her nemesis, and as if to put it off just a second longer, she bolstered her flagging courage by shining the dusty toe of each high heel on the back of a shapely calf. Kathleen raised her fist again. She faltered.

In forty-eight hours, one way or another, her life would be forever changed.

Before she could turn tail and run, she squared her shoulders and rapped her knuckles, hard, against the weathered door. All her bridges had been efficiently torched. Forty-eight hours seemed a pitifully short time to gamble her future on. But there was no going back, not now that she'd come this far. Suddenly, she heard sounds from behind the door and her heart kicked up a fuss. She clutched the manila envelope she'd brought against her chest like a shield.

Kathleen found her voice first. "Hello, Cole." He looked wonderful—a tall, muscular man who moved with strength and grace. Her tongue suddenly seemed to be glued to the roof of her mouth and she could only stare at him, matching memories and dreams with reality.

Cole's shock at finding her on his doorstep quickly disappeared. His beautiful eyes cooled to green ice and his mouth tightened as a muscle along his square jaw jumped. At a loss for what to do, he raked his fingers through his hair, leaving it boyishly tousled.

"Well, counselor," Cole responded first. "What tears you away from the courtroom and brings you here?"

The eighteen months since they'd parted hadn't altered him. He was still her handsome cowboy. But by the way he was glaring at her he wasn't going to give an inch. Kathleen braced herself and tried to smile even though her lips felt frozen and strangely numb.

"I have something for you, Cole."

"What's that? Another knife in the back?" His laugh was rough and barbed, leaving little doubt how he felt. "No, thanks. The last time you gave me something, it was the shaft. You sold me out." He started to close the door in her face, but she boldly crossed the threshold. Cole Jackson, a man who backed down from no one, retreated a couple of steps. "You cost me, lady, too much. I thought I made myself clear when I walked away from you in Dallas. Nothing's changed."

Oh, but it had.

Something in his eyes made him seem vulnerable, a look of hurt, maybe pain. In the split second before he recovered, she saw hunger. If it had been night and a full moon, she would have howled at it with joy. Cole was controlled. Sarcastic. Polite. He was furiously angry—but he still wanted her.

Kathleen held out the manila envelope. "Would you look at this?"

"Nope."

"It'll explain so much, Cole."

Turning sharply on his heels, he headed for the door and said over his shoulder, "What's to explain?" No way in hell was she going to get the upper hand. He'd been down that road and it only led to heartache.

Her task wasn't going to be easy, but Cole's careless, unemotional recovery scared her. She was left standing in the living room with only the smell of freshly brewed coffee and the sound of two voices, low and muted, to remind her she was alone.

Following Cole, she experienced a moment of panic. A horrible thought, one she'd never considered, went through her head. What if Cole had another woman—or worse, what if he was married? She pushed the idea away, refusing to think of the possibilities, and glossed over her anxieties by clinging to the unforgettable memories they shared.

Kathleen walked through the house, sensing more than seeing everything as she passed through rooms.

She had never visited the Rocking J Ranch but she knew every inch of it by heart. What astonished her was the homey ambience with a feminine touch to it. Which was surprising considering the household had been all male for years.

She knew the hundred-and-fifty-year-old, sprawling stone house had been added to with every generation until it was in jeopardy of becoming a monstrosity. The last major project on the ranch had been the half-acre retention pond Cole and his brother had installed before William had been killed.

Aware of her fears, she lagged behind, dreading the moment she would enter the kitchen. Then, as she stepped through the doorway, and the two occupants fell silent, she knew without a doubt they had been talking about her. She took a second to muster her courage by glancing around. This room was the family gathering spot with all its modern conveniences and comfortable, overstuffed furniture. The room was spacious and airy, surrounded by windows that captured the warmth of the morning sun. A lifetime ago, she and Cole had had a good laugh over the fact that her culinary skills were limited to a few of the simplest dishes.

Cole's back was to her, blocking her view of the other person. When he moved aside and reached the stove, Kathleen slowly exhaled, unaware she'd been holding her breath until that moment.

Kathleen's smile flashed bright and friendly, but quickly evaporated as she met a fierce scowl and a pair of keen, and judgmental, black eyes. The pigeon-chested, diminutive woman was in her late sixties. Her skin was the color of rich bittersweet chocolate. Her face was deeply marked with character, pride, and fierce loyalty. In direct contradiction to her rather forbidding look were telltale lines lacing the corners of her eyes and her mouth that spoke of great humor. Her features were made even more striking by the startling contrast of dark skin against snow-white hair and eyebrows. She was surprisingly beautiful in her own individual way.

Kathleen refused to be the first to look away from that all-knowing gaze. A silly woman thing—but she needed an ally in the household. Besides, she had too much to lose to back down, and was too stubborn to reveal she was scared to death.

The absence of sound in the kitchen as the women eyed each other made a startling tableau. Cole picked up his Stetson, adjusted it lower on his forehead so his eyes were shadowed, and successfully hid his amusement. He coughed and broke the awkwardness. "This is Kathleen Calhoun. She won't be staying." With a satisfied twist of his lips, he left the women still sizing each other up.

The door slammed behind him, and Kathleen spoke first. "I didn't betray him, Lovey."

"Only my family and friends calls me Lovey, missy."

Kathleen was uneasy under the hard-eyed inspection and worked to keep from fidgeting. "Gemma then. A precious stone," she said. "Your father named your sisters Pearl, Ruby, Opal, Sapphire, Emerald, and Garnet. When you came along, he called you his last jewel, his Gem because you were the most precious of all."

"More like I was the sickly runt of the litter." Lovey busied herself by taking a couple of angry swipes at the big oak table with her dishtowel. "How'd you know that?"

"Cole. I know everything about this place and the people he loves."

"Don't mean diddly-squat to me nohow." A wry smile twitched at her mouth before her lips immediately thinned in an angry line. "Not the way that boy's been hurtin'."

Cole was thirty-eight and calling him a boy made Kathleen want to laugh, but a stabbing glance from those all-knowing black eyes was more sobering than a dash of cold water.

"I—" Whatever Kathleen wanted to say petered out on a gasp. Movement beyond the bay window diverted her attention. She watched as a horse and rider stopped beside a metal-rail gate. Cole leaned sideways in the saddle, unlatched the gate and let the horse nudge it open.

"What does he think he's doing?" she whispered, all too aware of time slipping away. "He can't leave." But he was. Cole expertly backed the horse up and secured the gate, then rode away.

"He's heading for the pond, isn't he?" She knew it was one of the places he liked to go when he needed to be alone and think. She didn't wait for an answer but headed toward the front of the house, vaguely aware Lovey was right behind her.

Kathleen hauled in her suitcase from the porch, a case large enough to make Lovey's beetle-white eyebrows shoot up like accent marks.

"What do you think you're doing?"

Kathleen kicked off her high heels and dropped to her knees. She threw out jeans, a cotton shirt, and socks. She didn't own a pair of cowboy boots and held up her hiking boots. "I'm going after him."

"What for?"

Kathleen jumped up and stripped down to her underwear. "Because I didn't betray him and I brought the proof with me." Stepping into the jeans, she paused and gave Lovey her best straightforward look. "And because I love him and I think he still loves me."

"Them's mighty powerful words for what you done to that boy."

"But that's just it. I didn't do anything." Slipping on the shirt, she hastily tucked it in, then sat on the floor to put on her socks and boots.

"He's riding Lucky Lady."

Kathleen glanced at Lovey, knowing the cryptic remark was loaded with meaning. But Lovey's lips were tightly clamped together, her expression grim. There would be no help from that quarter. Kathleen desperately searched for the clue in the grudgingly given information.

Her shoulders slumped and she asked, "Lucky Lady's the quarter horse he rides when he's searching for strays?" That meant Cole was trying to put as much distance between them as he could, leaving her no way to follow. "He can't shake me that easily, you know."

Lovey grinned, a rather wicked look that was tinged more with mischief than malice. "Can you ride?" she asked, her eyes shining like dark polished stones on a clear river bottom.

Kathleen hesitated for a heartbeat. "Some," she admitted, trying to conceal her inexperience. "Is there someone who could saddle a horse for me? I don't know how."

"This is Saturday, gal, all the hands are off till Monday."

Time was ticking and Kathleen was all too aware that she didn't have any to spare. She was an intelligent, resourceful, thirty-one-year-old woman and wasn't about to let a little thing like a saddle defeat her. Heading toward the kitchen with Lovey at her heels, she said, "I'll figure it out somehow."

"I've saddled a few horses in my day."

Kathleen stopped, holding the door open. "Will you help me?" Pretending a calm she was far from feeling, she anxiously waited through the intense inspection.

"These Jackson men," Lovey grumbled. "They're more trouble than they're worth." She yanked off her apron and tossed it on the table along with the dish-towel. "I don't know why I get involved. Cole's a grown man. Come on, missy."

"Kathleen or Kate, please."

"Well, come on, Katie-girl, that damn horse ain't going to wiggle into her gear all by herself. No sirree, she surely ain't."

Lovey moved with surprising speed and Kathleen found herself jogging to keep up. She decided to stretch her good luck. "Is Cole seeing anyone special, Lovey?"

"Oh, that boy's been a regular gadfly." Lovey didn't break her stride as she cut the young woman a sideways glance. "Nothing serious, I 'spect."

As they approached the barn, Kathleen, bedeviled by her doubts, began to lag behind. For the past year, all she could think about was facing Cole with the truth. It never crossed her mind that he might refuse to see her. It was inconceivable that he wouldn't listen to her explanation. Sure, she knew there would be the hurdle of his initial reluctance to resolve. But she had carefully worked it out in her mind, and everything had gone so smoothly then. Now, it looked as if she were going to have to chase him down and devise a way to make him stay put long enough to listen.

There wouldn't have been a problem if she was in a courtroom. She'd know exactly what to do and say. But here—she looked around—she was out of her element. The weight of her inexperience suddenly seemed daunting.

Then Kathleen remembered what was at stake.

* * *

Cole heard Kate long before he caught sight of her. He always admired her strong will and a stubborn streak that prevented her from surrendering when she believed she was in the right. At least, that was what he'd once admired until she'd proved him wrong. Cole smiled when he heard the colorful curses that tinged the air. He rose up in the stirrups to get a better view, then bit down hard on his lip. She was posing, for God's sake.

"I know you're out here, Cole Jackson." Each word was spit out in fits and starts, as if she were afflicted with a bad stuttering problem. Her teeth were clenched to keep from biting her tongue. Worse still, her butt was being mutilated.

She should have guessed that Lovey was far too cooperative, and would pick the oldest and most unpleasant horse for her to ride. No matter what her command was, the animal knew only one gait—teeth-rattling rough. His pace was a bone-jolting, stiff-legged trot that jarred every nerve in her body. She was beginning to feel dizzy and afraid she might have shaken-brain syndrome. If and when she finally found Cole, she'd be a blithering idiot unable to put two coherent words together.

Giving up wasn't a part of Kathleen's nature. She followed a combination of Lovey's directions and memories of conversations with Cole about the ranch's layout. When laughter rang out, Kathleen yanked the horse to a butt-slapping, boob-bouncing stop. He was somewhere close and laughing his fool head off.

She searched a thicket of trees, scanning them with the same intensity she would have studied a Bev Doolittle painting. The thought of her favorite artist forced her to remember that nothing was ever as it first seemed.

Cole's horse was a peculiarly marked animal, a murky brown splashed with tan and black that blended in perfectly with its surroundings. All she could do was wait and watch. Then, just as she was about to give up, Lucky Lady's tail swished and Kathleen could distinguish between shapes. She folded her arms across her chest and waited, watching as horse and rider wound their way out of the thicket.

Cole figured the ride had done him good—cleared the cobwebs out of his head. He'd had time for the initial shock of Kate's arrival to wear off and the rush of pain and anger to subside. He shouldn't have been surprised that she'd followed him. Kate was a little like a pit bull with a bone. He had two choices; he could hear her out, or bodily kick her off the ranch. He asked himself what harm it could do to hear her out as long as he kept her at arm's length emotionally.

"Who," Kathleen snarled as Cole drew closer, "named this nag Pegasus?"

"I did."

Kathleen nodded. "I see. You're certainly no Bellerophon. That was probably your father or William." The Stetson hid Cole's eyes, but she could have sworn a smile hovered around his mouth. "You must have been Chimera."

Cole laughed as a deep well of memories bubbled to the surface; memories of endless family nights with books and stories. It had astounded him that he had found a woman who shared his love for reading. "You think I make a fitting Chimera?"

She tilted her head to one side and gazed at Cole, her heart beating faster the closer he came. "A fire-breathing monster. Oh, yes. I've seen that monster, remember?"

"Then it might be wise for you to leave, Katie, before you get more than your fingers burned. You and I have nothing left to say to each other."

Kathleen let out a deep sigh of frustration that rustled her bangs. Her gaze narrowed on Cole as he rode off. How was she ever going to make him understand if he wouldn't stay still long enough for her to carry on anything but a one-sided conversation with herself? Kathleen gazed at Pegasus's twitching ears and wondered if the damn animal was laughing at her, too. Then she shrugged, gritted her teeth, and tapped her heels in the horse's side. As they set off at a bone-rattling trot, she cheered herself with the thought that she could always use a few less inches off her thighs.

Two

She couldn't have asked for a more perfect day for a ride. The morning was crystal-clear and the air full of incredible fragrances, strange scents she'd yet to identify. An urbanite, she was more accustomed to car fumes, smog, and humanity. Actually, she was amazed that she had any sense of smell left at all. Kathleen wanted to stop and take in everything at once. Instead, she trailed after Cole, grumbling to herself, forced to face the fact that her careful plans could be chalked up to the casualties of overconfidence. A new plan was in order, one to permanently nail Cole's hide to one place long enough that he'd have to hear her out. Time, after all, was slipping away too fast for her liking. She had less then forty-eight hours to clear up their misunderstandings.

Two years ago she and Cole had met and fallen in love in the mists of the most tragic of circumstances. Cole's brother, William, a boy of twenty-two, sixteen years Cole's junior, was killed in a car accident in Houston. William had been one of those menopause babies, born into the world as his mother passed out of it. He'd been raised by Cole and his father, Matthew. William's death had dealt them a terrible blow, made worse by the fact that he was killed by a drunk driver.

The shock had taken its toll on Matthew, already in poor health, who died soon after William from a heart attack.

Cole had lost too much, too quickly—no one blamed him for his voracious desire for vengeance. She was an assistant district attorney assigned to prosecute the driver. Of her own volition, she'd become Cole's willing instrument to sate his hunger for justice. Only she'd failed him—and herself. That tragedy was something she still had trouble reliving.

She would much rather cling to the happier times. The surprise and delight that despite the tragedy and heartache of the situation that threw them together, the endless court delays, heated arguments, and the clash of their strong-willed personalities, she and Cole had fallen in love. Theirs wasn't just a passing physical attraction, either, but one with an intensity, a depth of feeling that they'd found so much joy in. As much as she wanted only to remember the perfection of what had been, she wasn't one to bury her head in the sand for long. Eighteen months ago her life had changed dramatically. She had changed drastically. And it all started the first day of the trial. Everything had fallen apart.

Kathleen sighed long and soulfully as a ploy for attention. Her only response was a twitching of Pegasus's ears. Cole had come into her life like a whirlwind. He'd departed the same way, leaving her devastated. The nature of his exit left no route for her to follow until she could go to him with the truth of what had actually happened.

Kathleen wiped a bead of sweat from her forehead. The sun was getting high and the heat of the morning rising. She attempted to drill a hole in the center of his back with an angry glare. How, she wondered, was it humanly possible to sit in a saddle, atop a horse, and look as if he were part of the animal? She tried to mimic his more relaxed movements, and was rewarded by being bounced even higher in the saddle. Pegasus had four pogo sticks for legs and she grabbed the saddle horn before she slid sideways.

"You can ignore me if you want, Cole, but I don't intend to give up. I'll follow you all day if necessary." Under her breath she snapped, "Even if it kills me." Which, she thought, was becoming more and more likely.

Cole's attempt to ignore Kathleen's antics was failing. He struggled to keep a clear head and his heart whole, but both were betraying him. Time had taken the edge off his hurt and anger. He hated the way he longed to touch her, to feel her in his arms. Hell, it didn't take much of an effort to recall the taste and smell of her. But those were memories that usually visited him in the middle of the night. Kathleen's sudden appearance convinced him that passion and love weren't so easily dismissed or forgotten.

"You're making it hard on yourself, Katie." He refused to look around, afraid that his iron-willed resolve would crack. "Put your heels down in the stirrups and grip the horse's sides with your thighs. Keep your back straight and relaxed." He sensed her adjusting her position, and settled the Stetson lower on his head to hide his grin. Pegasus was old and arthritic. Nothing short of a miracle would change the old boy's gait, but he didn't have to explain that to Katie. Cole smiled beneath the shadow of his hat. He gave her an hour before she called it quits.

Kathleen trailed behind Cole at a much slower pace, struggling to follow his advice. It didn't take much effort to realize her efforts were useless. The only way she could keep her mind off her discomfort was to get back to the reason she'd come. "Cole, that last day in court—"

He wouldn't let her finish. "How's your family?"

"Okay. About that day, Cole—"

"Your mom and dad are good?"

She ground her teeth together. "Yes."

"And your sister and her family?"

"Sandra, Gary, and the kids are great. So are my brother and his family." She decided that a little tug at what was left of his heart wouldn't hurt. Her nieces and nephews had been fascinated with Cole. He was a real-life cowboy who wore boots and a Stetson and talked of rodeos, cattle drives, longhorns, open ranges, and wild horses. Her sister's youngest, Becky Ann, had fallen head over heels in love with him. The children had bonded with Cole and roared with laughter over his clever renditions of a few Shel Silverstein stories. Her entire family had been enchanted when Cole would recite the funniest Western poems they'd ever heard. Everyone had their favorites. Kathleen's were Robert Service's "The Shooting of Dan McGrew" and "The Cremation of Sam McGee."

Kathleen's throat closed up and her voice roughened as she said, "Becky misses you."

"What did you tell them, Katie? That you threw the trial because it served your purposes to further your career in the DA's office?"

The silence was made more intense by the creak of leather and the movement of the horses. Though his accusation hurt, at least it was out in the open. "I know you believe that to be the truth, but you're wrong. By the way, I quit the DA's office."

They were moving single-file up a narrow path that cut through the limestone canyon. Cole reacted to her remark by stiffening his back and increasing Lucky Lady's pace. Kathleen did the same, determined to keep up. "Cole, you know I was as committed to prosecuting William's killer as you were to seeking justice."

Cole's silence, as unnerving as it was, also gave her hope. At least he wasn't riding off. She bounced in the saddle and just managed to duck under a low tree limb. She was numb from the waist down but figured it was a blessing. "What happened at the trial wasn't my fault. That's one of the reasons I'm here, Cole, to explain the truth of what happened. Darby Middleton can't hide behind Senator Middleton any longer, and the Senator won't be using his money or his political influence this time." She wasn't ready to tell him what her actions had cost her personally and professionally.

"You can be as uncooperative as you want, but I'm staying until you know all the facts. You see, Cole, I'm not a coward. Not like you." She was tired of being treated as if she were invisible. His anger was preferable to indifference. "I don't make snap judgments, and I don't walk out on people I love."

She decided to go for the jugular. "You always told me William was the fairest-minded person you'd ever known. You said your father taught you to face your demons. What would they have done in this situation, Cole?"

Her words had the sting of a sharp-edged razor. At first there was surprise, then the pain took his breath away. Cole twisted around in the saddle. With his emotions firmly hidden behind an unreadable expression, he said, "Don't go there, Kathleen. You'll get hurt."

She laughed, and it wasn't a pretty sound. "You couldn't hurt me any more than you already have. Dammit, Cole, can we stop and talk? My brains are getting scrambled."

"Sorry. I have some strays with new calves missing."

At least he hadn't told her to get lost. "I'm not giving up."

"Suit yourself."

There was nothing more maddening, she thought, than a stubborn man with righteous indignation on his side.

By the time they'd traveled the edge of the canyon, Kathleen was reduced to tight-lipped restraint. For most of the trip she'd simply closed her eyes and held on, trusting Pegasus to safely find his way. When they reached the rocky floor of the canyon, she groaned as she saw Cole and Lucky Lady jump the banks of a narrow stream. Kathleen didn't think she or the horse could survive any attempt to follow Lucky Lady's graceful leap. She hauled back on the reins, making noises that were supposed to reinforce her order to stop. Her efforts were about as effective as an ant trying to stop an elephant. When Pegasus did halt, they were in the middle of the streambed and he was taking a long drink.

Enough was enough. She was hot, sore, scratched, dirty, and angry. Kathleen pried her hands from the saddle horn, wrapped it with the reins, then carefully dismounted. Her feet no sooner touched the bottom of the shallow streambed than her legs buckled and she suddenly bounced on her bruised backside. If the cold water hadn't felt so good, she would have cried with frustration. Instead, she closed her eyes and let out a long sigh.

Cole wheeled Lucky Lady around and waded into the water. He gazed down at Kathleen. "It's not quite deep enough for a swim, Katie." He leaned down and held out his hand.

Kathleen accepted his offer of help and was being pulled to her feet when she said, "You remember Officer Louis Ramsey, don't you? Our star police witness who developed a case of memory loss, among other things, on the stand?'' She was almost standing when Cole suddenly let go and she fell back into the stream.

''Oops,'' Cole said, and tapped Lucky Lady's sides.

Kathleen wasn't going to let him get away with it. He wasn't going to shut her up. ''Senator Middleton bought him off.'' Cole glanced over his shoulder with just enough interest in his expression. As she struggled to stand up, she continued. ''I've got Ramsey's signed confession.''

Cole had that tight-jawed, cheek-muscle twitch that told her more clearly than words that he was dying to know more, but too obstinate to admit he might have been wrong. Kathleen deliberately ignored him, enjoying a brief sense of satisfaction. The delay also gave her time to glance around for Pegasus, who was at that moment heading back up the canyon path with more speed and grace than had been afforded her. ''My horse.''

Following the direction of her gaze, Cole said, ''If you'd dropped the reins to the ground, he'd have stayed put till hell froze over.'' He gently nudged Lucky Lady's sides and started off, leaving Kathleen standing in the middle of the stream. ''It's a hard lesson to learn, but one not likely forgotten after the first time.''

''You're not going after him?''

''No.''

''I have to walk?''

''It won't take you very long to reach the house. Just follow the trail.''

''Oh, no, you can't get rid of me that easy. I'm going with you.''

"Now that's a much longer walk."

"It can't possibly be worse," she said, "than riding that beast."

Famous last words.

Three

As an avid shopper, she'd walked miles in malls wearing high heels. She had danced and stood for hours at parties, precariously perched on stilettos. But she'd only worn hiking boots for casual wear, never on long hikes. Someone should have warned her that boots required a breaking-in period and perhaps a thicker pair of socks.

The blessed coolness, the welcome relief of being soaking wet, had worn off. She was uncomfortably damp, but determined to hide any sign of weakness. She walked beside Cole, holding tightly to the leather stirrup as a safeguard just in case he got a wild thought and decided to ride off and leave her stranded. If he tried, he'd have to bodily drag her along. A small amount of caution was called for, and she refrained from any further discussion of why she'd come, deciding to wait until he wouldn't walk away.

Cole felt as low as a snake. He glanced at the top of Kathleen's head, noting the way the sunlight played on her hair, making it shine and change color. Her hair had been the second thing about her that had attracted him. It was thick, straight, and the color of polished gold. He used to love watching the way it bounced and swayed with the slightest movement, as if it had a life and will all of its own.

He didn't miss the dampness that plastered her bangs against her forehead. He never thought she'd actually try to stay with him, much less keep up. She was full of surprises.

But his ingrained good manners gnawed at his conscience. He'd been too rough on her and should have given her a ride. At that moment she gazed at him. Kate had a cat's calm blue eyes, and he knew from experience that she had patience, as well. She intended to make him miserable—make him suffer. He didn't care. Maybe he deserved it.

Lucky Lady threw up her head and the bridle jangled with her impatience at the prolonged plodding pace. Cole absently reined her in. If he offered Kate a ride now, she'd probably give him a wounded look to make him feel worse than he already did. He'd wait and let her make the next move. After all, he thought, this was her game. Cole was struck by his choice of words. Was she playing a game with him? And if so, why? Why now after all this time? More disturbing, what did she hope to gain?

Kathleen stumbled into Lucky Lady's shoulder, sending the startled horse dancing sideways. Cole quickly regained control of Lucky Lady. Then he held out his hand to Kathleen. "You better ride with us before you cause Lady to throw me." Katie didn't argue and Cole shook his boot loose from the stirrup. "Put your left foot in there. Get a firm grip on my arm. Good. Now when I pull, give a push and swing your right leg over the horse."

She settled behind Cole and wound her arms around his waist. In that moment, even though he stiffened at her light touch, it seemed the eighteen months of separation had never happened. She was where she was supposed to be. Where she was meant to be.

Surprised by the horse's sudden move, Kathleen grasped Cole tighter. He smelled like sunshine, soap, and leather. Just holding him, feeling his heart beat under her hands, made her dizzy with longing. More than anything in the world, she wanted to rub her cheek against his back—to close her eyes and let go of the iron grip she'd maintained from the second he had opened the front door. She wished she could turn back the clock.

Before leaving Dallas, Kathleen had promised herself she would never use her body as a bargaining tool. It didn't matter how much she wanted him, Cole wasn't a man to be manipulated, used, or fooled. He would hate her if she tried. Besides, she didn't think she had the nerve for seduction. Cole was nursing a grudge at the moment and any attempt to use their physical attraction would end in disaster.

Kathleen settled into the fluid motion of Lucky Lady's surefooted trot. They traveled along another rocky ridge on the opposite side of the canyon. Kathleen felt an abrupt change in Lady; she was suddenly full of nervous energy. Cole sensed it and settled deeper into the saddle just as Lady's gait shifted to a smooth, barely contained canter.

With a suddenness that made Kathleen catch her breath, they burst beyond the confining cliffs and out into the open. Then they were racing down into a lush green valley with a scattering of large trees, scrub oaks, and cedars, and ringed by a bald limestone butte. A sense of peace like a rush of warmth settled over her.

Kathleen lifted her face to the sun, savoring the dry wind that tugged at her hair. At that moment she knew everything Cole had told her about living so close to the land was true. She felt its magic, the way it seemed to pull at her soul. She belonged here.

"Dammit, Cole." She knuckled his ribs, making him yelp and jump. "Don't you have anything to say about Officer Ramsey?"

He slowed Lady's enthusiastic romp. "I knew the minute he lied in court that he'd been bought. It was obvious the Senator got to him. The judge knew it. You did, too, Katie."

"But only at the moment it happened, Cole." She couldn't believe he was actually talking. "I was in shock."

"Really? I don't think so. You looked just as self-controlled as usual." Before she could say anything, he continued. "Don't forget, Katie, I'd seen your courtroom talents. Remember before Dad died, we were in town for a lot of the preliminary meetings? I caught a couple of your trials. And don't forget that you told me all about the drama class you took in college because a law professor made the course a requirement for trial lawyers. Oh, I'm well aware of your acting talents."

"You're wrong. What you saw that day in court had nothing to do with deception. It goes beyond shock, Cole. I was stunned senseless. Dammit, I had talked to Ramsey right before we went into court. He gave no clue that he would come down with memory loss, or that he would lie outright. Then when I started to present the evidence, the Breathalyzer and blood tests . . ." It had been eighteen months and she still got a sinking sensation in the pit of her stomach just thinking about that awful morning. "I can't believe you'd think I would or could make vital physical evidence disappear from the police property room."

Cole stopped Lady and twisted in the saddle so he could face Kathleen. "You're right. I never thought you removed the evidence, but I think you knew it would happen. I think you let it happen because it would have been advantageous to your career. And let's not forget your boss. The district attorney's office is about as political as you can get."

"And I went into court and made a fool of myself to further my career?"

He silently admitted he didn't understand that part. But he couldn't block out the memory of her face that morning as she realized there was no evidence. She didn't flinch, or gasp, or scream her outrage at what had occurred. Instead, she had simply tried to continue the case until the judge called a halt.

"You're ambitious, Katie, and a deal with the Senator would have put you in a plum position. And there was your boss the DA to consider. I'm sure the Senator's money and political influence extended to your office."

"Tell me how, Cole. How could my losing the case and looking incompetent in court and to the media be beneficial to my career?" When he shrugged and started to turn around, she grasped his arm. "Why is it so hard for you to believe I was set up?

"That morning in court, when Ramsey changed his story, I went into shock. I'm a good lawyer, Cole. I've had witnesses, for whatever reasons, lie on the stand before. But Ramsey yanked the rug out from under me. I had interviewed and coached him right up to the time he took the stand. You knew that, Cole. We discussed the importance of his testimony to the case at length.

"His sudden switch—I was dumfounded by it. For a second I thought I'd done something wrong or that I didn't hear him right. Then, to make matters worse, I saw in his eyes he wasn't going to tell the truth. No matter what I did or said, I wasn't going to break him. He had too much at stake. That's when I tried to submit the evidence. I don't know—I just shut down. I was speechless.

"But do you know what haunts me? I blamed myself for not picking up the evidence from the police property room. I let someone from my office go get it. Well, you know what a disaster that was. Everything was gone. Even Ramsey's written reports never made it to court. The judge had no choice but to stop the trial. But I didn't make a deal or throw the case. I never would have done that to you or William."

Until now he'd refused to think about that awful day in court. Now, with Kathleen so close and touching him, he couldn't shut the memories off as easily. Time and distance had allowed him to revisit the scene and see it differently. He sensed his resolve weakening and forced himself to remember that she talked a good game. It was all part of her profession. Was he wrong?

Cole looked at Kathleen. Spellbound, he saw the vulnerable mouth and the hurt in her eyes. A burst of desire as startling as it was sudden shook him to the core. It was the insatiable hunger of a lonely man. The gnawing pain of it forced him to admit that no matter what she'd done, or how he'd tried to lie to himself, he'd never stopped wanting her. He'd fooled himself into thinking he could forget her. Kathleen was always with him, locked away in that safe place in his mind just waiting to be freed.

Lucky Lady broke the magic of the moment by forcing Cole to turn his attention to controlling the nervous, prancing horse.

"What's wrong?" Kathleen grabbed at Cole to keep from sliding off.

"Listen," he said.

"I don't hear anything."

The horse pawed the ground, then reared up a few feet. Kathleen clutched Cole's waist tighter as Lady danced sideways and struggled to charge forward, but Cole held the reins tightly. "Do you think she smells a wolf? You said you had wolves here, didn't you? Could it be one of those piggy things—the javelinas you told me about? Maybe a rattlesnake? What's happening?"

"If you'll stop chattering a second, Lady'll tell me." Cole got a jab to his ribs and laughed under his breath. Katie wasn't fond of being told to shut up.

"How can a horse tell you any—" Whatever she'd planned to say next was cut off as the horse leaped from a standstill to a full gallop. Kathleen fought to keep from falling by digging her fingernails deep into Cole's shirt until she felt firm flesh. She experienced a moment of pure terror as she floundered, slipping one way and then the other. Then she righted herself, settled into the motion of the horse, and began to enjoy the thrill of speed and power underneath her.

Lucky Lady slowed to a trot and Kathleen had a second to catch her breath before she started talking to Cole again. It was at that moment she heard what must have spooked the horse. A sound so heart-wrenching that what she was about to say froze on her lips. Human or animal, she recognized the cry of an infant in fear and pain. She was drawn, pulled instinctively, toward the source of the pitiful crying. A small calf had his front leg wedged between the spiny trunks of some scrub cedars.

Kathleen didn't wait for Lady to completely stop. She slid clumsily to the ground, fell to her knees, then was up and running toward the trapped calf. Rushing headlong toward the animal, she was unaware of Cole shouting her name. She was dimly aware that he and Lucky Lady were headed in a diagonal line away from her.

The closer she got, the louder and more distressed the cries became. "Poor baby," Kathleen crooned softly a couple of times. The wailing grew weaker and a pair of big brown eyes, round with fright, stared back at her. Kathleen lost her heart. The baby calf was ginger-colored, all soft orange with a wet velvet-black nose and soulful dark eyes. "Did you get yourself stuck, Pumpkin?" she whispered in baby talk, grinning at the apt name.

Kathleen crouched beside the calf and surveyed the problem. "You look like you're okay. I don't think this is going to hurt much. Poor little thing. You want your mama, don't you?" She grasped hold of the cedar branch in one hand and the quivering little leg in the other.

Everything seemed to happen at once. Pumpkin set up an earsplitting racket as Kathleen pulled the branch away and grabbed the freed calf with the other. She suddenly had an armload of wiggling, kicking, and bawling bovine. Crouched with the struggling calf clasped to her chest, Kathleen was thrown off balance and pitched backward onto the ground and into the scrub brush. Poked, scratched, and kicked, she managed to regain her footing. When she was finally standing, she turned to where Cole and Lady were, triumphant with her trophy held tightly against her chest. It was at that moment that Kathleen realized what Cole had tried to say.

She turned to stone—unable to move. No more than fifty yards away an enraged mother, a longhorn with a lethal set of horns that spanned six feet, was pawing up clods of grass and making the most frightening snorting noises Kathleen had ever heard.

"If the calf is okay," Cole said calmly, "please put

him down and back up toward me. Now, Katie.''

She couldn't move. It was as if her feet had sprouted roots. All she could do was watch the huge longhorn rush toward her, as frightening as an oncoming freight train.

Four

To say that her life flashed before her eyes was an exaggeration. She had time to feel the pain of leaving loved ones behind and to regret unfinished business. Then everything changed. Suddenly there was time for wonder and surprise and the opportunity to see the mastery of horse training in action.

Cole dismounted in one fluid motion and hit the ground running. Before his feet actually touched the earth, he whistled two sharp sounds that sent Lady in the direction of the charging longhorn.

"Let go, Katie." Cole attempted to take the wiggling, bawling calf from her arms.

Kathleen's attention was fixed on Lucky Lady. She clutched the calf tight. "I always thought you were pulling my leg when you told me they could do that." The riderless quarter horse was working the cow, anticipating her every move, cutting every access route off as expertly as if Cole were atop her and giving commands.

"Come on, Katie, let go." He wasn't interested in her observations. "You should know better than to come between a mother and her baby. Dammit, you'll squeeze him to death if you don't stop."

She tore her gaze away from the ongoing battle between horse and longhorn, kissed the top of the silken head, and carefully set him down. "Get along, little Pumpkin." With only a brief backward glance that tugged at Kathleen's heart, the calf scampered away.

Cole bit his lip. "Pumpkin? You named him Pumpkin?"

They watched as horse and cow ceased their battle, each eyeing the other until the calf rejoined his mother. "It fits, don't you think?"

Cole didn't answer. Katie closely resembled something his old tomcat might drag through the back door. As he tallied the damage, he struggled to keep a straight face. Both knees were wet and soiled by manure. Her shirt was streaked with mud and torn at the elbow. Her hair had lost that neat, sleek look. What wasn't stuck to her face and neck from sweat was a wind-tossed mess. There was a dark, slimy streak on one cheek and a splash of mud on her chin. Katie either was oblivious to her current state or didn't care. She was a paradox and full of surprises.

He admitted he was more than a little disarmed. During all the time they had spent together with her family and around her young nieces and nephews, Katie hadn't once used that silly tone of voice with them. Now his smart, streetwise, tough-talking Katie was baby-talking to a calf. This was a whole new side he'd never seen. For some stupid reason he couldn't explain, he felt a warm rush of pride. Katie hadn't had an easy morning and she hadn't whined or complained all that much. But the day wasn't over yet.

"Just look at him, Cole. He's as orange as a pumpkin. Are they going to be all right out here alone?"

"Alone?" The question was asked in all seriousness. Cole glanced away for a moment to hide his amusement. "They'll be fine. They're not alone, Katie. There's plenty of company."

Cole's eyes were overbright and sparkling with suppressed laughter. She hadn't missed the fact that he was struggling to keep from making her feel a fool and loved him even more for the effort. "Of course, they're just cattle to you, but I saved Pumpkin's life." She couldn't look at him without giving away more than she was ready to, and turned her attention to dusting off her clothes. "I got sort of attached, and I'll worry. So sue me."

"He'll be fine now." Cole made a show of clearing his throat. He was having a hard time stopping himself from hugging her. "Are you okay?"

"Shaken, not stirred," she said carelessly then could have bitten her tongue off. It was a joke, shared between them because they both loved the older, campy James Bond movies. A quick glance and Kathleen saw that the remark hadn't slipped past Cole. "I wish you'd talk to me. At least let me finish what I've come to say. It's important, Cole."

"To whom?" Instead of staying to find out, he walked away. "I know what I know, Katie. You can't change that."

"What if I could?"

"Maybe it's too late, Katie. Maybe it's just not important anymore." He refused to dredge up all that pain again. God knows he'd worked too hard burying it.

"It's important to me, and it should be to you, too. What if I could show you undeniable proof that you're wrong, Cole? You think I betrayed you and William. That I sold out." He whistled for Lucky Lady as Kathleen hurried to keep up. "Are you afraid you made a mistake and threw away everything we had together?"

He swung up on the horse before he answered. "How could I be wrong? I was there and saw the whole ugly business."

The weight of his continued rejection stung, and she

blinked back the blur of tears. For the first time she thought she understood. Cole had gambled everything on her, on her abilities as an attorney, and their love. With a mumbled thanks, she accepted his hand, stepped into the empty stirrup, and was pulled up onto the horse.

In his eyes she'd failed him, but Cole had also failed himself. He just wasn't aware of it. Whether deliberately or as a subconscious defense mechanism, he had never taken the time to mourn William's or his father's death. At first he'd been too eaten up with getting revenge. Then she and Cole had fallen passionately and giddily in love. When she had attempted to talk about William and Matthew, Cole had shut down. He'd made it clear he didn't want to think about facing the pain waiting like a dark curtain ready to be pulled aside.

When the case was lost and the trial over before it really started, Cole must have felt betrayed in the worst way. That dark curtain he'd so dreaded had come down and all his bottled-up pain must have bubbled to the surface like acid. He'd lashed out, and she had been his whipping post.

Knowing Katie so intimately, Cole was uncomfortable with her long silence. It usually meant trouble for someone. Since he was the only one around, he stepped into the void in self-defense. "I'll take you back to the house."

"I don't think so. You're stuck with me."

"Suit yourself. But the day's not over and I still have work to do."

His indifferent tone and careless attitude put her teeth on edge. "Oh, I just love being with you, Cole Jackson. You're so talkative and entertaining." Kathleen wiggled into a more comfortable position on Lady's rump and wrapped her arms tightly around his waist.

"Have I told you how I traced the money the Senator paid Ramsey?" She didn't bother waiting for his response. "It's all in the papers I brought but since you won't look at them I'll have to fill you in." Cole didn't show any sign of renewed interest. Lucky Lady jumped forward and Kathleen lost her next words to the wind as they galloped across the valley. All she could do was hold on and wait for an opportune moment to force the issue once more.

The ride gave Kathleen time to witness the mystery and beauty of the ranch. Up until that moment, she'd thought Cole had been overly eloquent with his descriptions. But words were poor substitutes for what the eyes beheld. The Rocking J Ranch landscape continually changed. There were limestone canyons tumbling with boulders and bristling with brush and cactus. Rolling hills cut through with ribbons of rushing water and the wide lush pastures. Everywhere she looked there was something new to marvel at. And probably the only way to take advantage of the sights was on horseback.

The sun rose higher and the day lengthened. As taken as she was with the passing scenery, Kathleen didn't intend to give up easily, even though at times she was forced to shout.

"After you left me, I had a talk with Ramsey." She didn't mention it had taken days to recover after Cole left. There had been those miserable days and nights remembering the way he'd walked out, and the awful things he'd said.

"I'll give Ramsey credit for guts, or maybe fear, but he pretty much stuck to his story. I did some digging and uncovered a few facts about Ramsey and his wife. They were in the midst of a messy divorce. Louis was involved with another woman and spending a lot of money on her. I didn't think his wife, Karen, would appreciate hearing that bit of information, and I was right. I also discovered that Louis had bought a new truck and put it in the girlfriend's name. There were other so-called gifts. Expensive repairs to his lake property, and a new boat. He was stupid and greedy and I went after him through Karen."

Kathleen refused to be silenced even as they half waded, half swam across a river so crystal-clear she could see fish darting out of the way. When they plunged up and over the riverbank, the land opened into wide green pastures full of cattle. They were all the same deep bloodred color, and though bigger than the longhorns they were not as impressive without a set of horns.

"I told Karen Ramsey I was sure Louis had gotten a large sum of money from Senator Middleton. She certainly wasn't getting any for herself or their two girls. Texas law is very clear about community property laws. Judges tend to get really testy when one or the other attempts to hide assets. Things can get nasty." Cole had let Lucky Lady slow to an amble and she was sure he was listening. His silence was beginning to wear on her nerves, though.

Cole stopped to observe a small herd of about fifteen horses. Kathleen watched, speechless at the sight of the majestic stance of the American paint stallion standing guard over his mares. Suddenly, as if sensing danger, he threw his head up and stamped the ground. Then in a flash the entire herd was racing across the pasture, finally disappearing over the rim of a hill.

"I gave Karen's attorney a few tips on where he might locate Ramsey's hidden money."

His own noisy sigh of frustration amused him. He'd tried to shut Kathleen out, but the more she talked the more intrigued he became. He twisted in the saddle so he could watch her, to study her face. She was a good actress, but a poor liar. A difference he could spot in a minute.

"Ramsey was trapped," Kathleen said. "He couldn't lie about having money, and he couldn't hide the fact that he had deliberately concealed it from his wife, the judge, and the court. He knew he had to make a full financial disclosure."

Cole saw the hole she'd dug for the cop, and smiled. "There was no way his paycheck could have paid for everything. He had cash he needed to account for, but couldn't reveal where it came from. You put him between a rock and a hard place."

"Damn right, just where I wanted him. Ramsey had to tell the judge where all that extra money came from. If he refused, he'd go to jail—if he confessed, well, he knew I was just waiting to put him behind bars. That was my cue and I stepped in with a deal."

Kathleen didn't mention the threats Ramsey and a few of his cohorts had made. Nor did she tell him that by Monday morning, when all hell broke loose, she might very well lose what she'd worked so hard to reclaim over the last eighteen months.

"The deal with Ramsey, in return for his signed confession, would have given him a light jail sentence and probation. But I had to have it all in writing. Who gave him the money? How much? What did he do with the evidence he stole from the police property room? And lastly, who in the DA's office helped him pull it off?"

The mention of her job and the DA was like throwing cold water in Cole's face. His expression settled back into grim lines as he turned his back to her and kicked Lucky Lady into action. Kathleen grabbed at the back of the saddle, silently cursing her big mouth.

Cole had never hidden his distaste for her boss, District Attorney Albert Hazelwood. On that last disastrous day in court Cole had accused her of being Hazelwood's puppet. He thought she'd sold her soul because of ambition and greed.

"Jesus, Cole," she bit out between clenched teeth. "Can we please stop for a while? My bottom's killing me. I'm getting cramps in my legs and I think I've lost all feeling in my feet. And—I have to go to the bathroom." For a moment she thought he was deliberately ignoring her, but then he turned the horse toward a small wood-shingle shack.

Cole swung his leg over Lady's neck and slid to the ground. Without a word he grabbed Kathleen by the waist and helped her down. He didn't let go.

As soon as she was upright, her knees buckled. Her legs felt like rubber, and if Cole hadn't been holding her, she'd have fallen flat on her face. "If you say one word, so help me, I'll kick both your kneecaps off. That is, when I can move." Grabbing hold of the stirrup and part of the saddle, she asked, "Are my feet on the ground?"

"Yes." Cole laughed, startling some of the cattle that were gathering to watch. He elbowed Katie aside, flipped open the saddlebag, and handed her a plastic bottle of water. Kathleen moaned, leaned her shoulder against the horse, and upended it until the bottle was dry. "I would have loved a drink myself," Cole said with no trace of his earlier sarcasm. He was having trouble staying detached. He dug once more in the saddlebag, held out a roll of paper and pointed to the trees behind the shack.

"You, you can't possibly mean . . . ?" She concentrated on keeping any trace of a whine out of her voice and searched the trees as if hoping to spot a restroom or maybe an outhouse.

" 'Fraid so," Cole said with a careless shrug.

Kathleen gave him a narrow-eyed, assessing look,

hoping he was joking but knowing better. He didn't think she'd do it.

"What else have you got in there?" She attempted to peek into the saddlebag but he moved so she couldn't see.

"A cellular phone, first-aid kit, and a knife."

She snatched the roll of paper and stomped off toward the tree line.

After a lengthy time passed Cole began to get worried. Then, just as he was about to go in search of Katie, she burst through the trees, looking panic-stricken. Close at her heels were a couple of his cattle.

Kathleen glanced over her shoulder, saw the animals were gaining and started to run. "Cole, make them leave me alone."

He'd held back as long as he could and burst out laughing as she skidded to his side and slipped behind him, shoving the roll of paper at him.

"Why are they following me? What'd I do?"

"They're curious animals." Cole headed for the shack with Kathleen glued to his side. He unlocked the door and half disappeared inside. "Here, take this salt lick over by the water tank." Her attention was on the gathering cattle. "Katie."

She looked at the large whitish block, and the others that were stacked high inside the shack. Cole placed it in her outstretched hands and she almost fell forward under the weight. "By the water tank, Katie."

"What's a salt lick for?" She juggled the heavy block a moment until she got a better grip.

"To lick. Now take it over by the water tank."

Kathleen spotted the enormous metal tank a distance behind the building. It reminded her of one of those aboveground backyard swimming pools. With each step she realized the cattle were moving in on her, and more were coming from all directions. "Cole! Cole, help!"

They were gaining, some so close that she could see just how big they were. She panicked, dropped the salt lick, and ran a few steps before she realized the cattle weren't threatening her. They only wanted to get to the block of salt. She looked at Cole and knew by the gleeful amusement he tried desperately to hide that she'd been set up.

It was a mean trick, and he'd stood by and watched as the herd started to converge on her. Then he saw that Katie realized they were tame, and he smiled as she got the courage to pet a few by running her hands over their sides as she headed back to where he was standing. Cole tucked a block of salt lick under each arm. "Shut the door and lock it, then bring that last block there on the ground."

She did as asked, silent, her eyes drilling a hole in his back. "They're as tame as puppy dogs, aren't they?"

"Most of the time."

Cole pointed out where to drop the salt lick she was carrying and she followed him to the far side of the water tank. When he'd set the last one down, and had turned, he was between her and the edge of the tank. He'd taken his last shot at her. He'd used up all his jokes at her expense. She was tired, dirty, and sore to the bone, frustrated and just plain mad. As if her hand had a mind of its own, she reached out and shoved. Cole tumbled into the tank.

Frightened by Cole's startled shout and the wave that swelled over the edges and soaked the ground, the cattle spooked and scurried away to a safer distance. Half soaked herself, Kathleen stood with her arms crossed and for the first time in days she smiled with real humor.

Five

Cole climbed out of the shallow water, sputtering and laughing. One glance at Kathleen and he quickly sobered. "I wondered how long you'd last before you blew your cool. Silent suffering has never been your strong suit."

The water came up to his knees and filled his boots. The algae-slick bottom made each step risky. Cole grabbed his hat as it floated by, gave it a couple of hard slaps against his thigh and set it on his head. He grabbed the metal rim of the tank with the intention of getting out, only to find himself on his back and sinking into the water once more.

When he was on his feet again, he thought it prudent to stay where he was. "Why don't you join me? Water's warm and it looks to me like you could use a bath right now."

"Very funny, Cole, since I'm this way because of you." She didn't trust the glint in his eyes and slid a couple of feet away from the tank as she watched him step over the rim. "You think you can drag me all over God's creation, wear me down, and get me to give up. That would make you happy; then you wouldn't have to face the fact that you're wrong. There are things that

I have to tell you, things you have to know, before it's too late.''

Cole leaned against the outside rim of the tank, stamping the water out of his boots. His head jerked up and his gaze narrowed. ''Too late for what, Katie? What are you pulling now?''

Kathleen flapped her arms like an angry bird. ''I'm trying to make you see the truth, and not the truth according to Cole Jackson.''

''Okay. I'll listen.''

She shook her head, wondering if she'd heard right. It wasn't like Cole to give in so easily. Still, her uneasiness couldn't stop her heart from beating crazily against her chest. She searched his face, trying to find a chink in his armor or a sign of a trap. ''Just like that,'' she said, ''you'll listen?''

''Well, hell, Katie. It's as plain as your grimy face that if I don't, you're going to dog my every step till either you drop dead or I strangle you.''

Taken at face value Cole's surrender seemed genuine, but it didn't make her any less suspicious. He was up to something. She gave an uncertain nod, but was still reluctant to get too close, afraid she'd find herself in the water, too. ''Fine.'' She looked pointedly at him. ''Okay. Good. Where was I? I had Ramsey on the hot seat.'' Cole walked toward her and she jumped back a couple steps. ''I was his only way out. What are you doing?''

Cole waved his hand as if embracing the world. His smile was watchful, really no smile at all. ''This is not the place to have this conversation.'' He whistled sharply and Lucky Lady trotted toward them. Cole swung up in the saddle and held out his hand for Kathleen.

She couldn't decide what diabolical scheme he had up his sleeve. Keeping her mouth shut, she fixed her attention on the stirrup and positioned her foot. When she looked at Cole, his face was tight and closed, making her hesitate for a second.

Kathleen slapped her hand into Cole's, gripped it tightly, and was pulled up behind him. After she'd settled comfortably, she asked, "Where're we going?"

"A place of truth, Katie. A place where there can't be any more lies."

Kathleen would have challenged his cryptic answer but Lucky Lady leaped forward and galloped across the pasture.

The fact that Cole still thought she was lying was a bitter pill to swallow. Breathing deeply, she gulped the sweet afternoon air and fought to mask the pain and hold back tears. She fixed her gaze between his shoulder blades, longing to recapture the feeling of pleasure and humor she'd experienced at seeing his ungainly backward flop in the water tank. But the brief moment gave her little solace.

Thank heaven, he couldn't see her face. Crying wasn't an option, not for her and not with Cole. She used to be strong and able to hide her emotions. Acting came so easily to her. Certainly, no one had ever accused her of being a crybaby. But her life had changed so drastically in the past eighteen months that her emotions were much closer to the surface now. She found herself crying for the dumbest reasons and at the most inopportune times.

The sun was uncomfortably hot on her back, and Kathleen realized suddenly they were heading in a different direction. She glanced around, saw that they were skirting the edge of a small lake, and asked, "Is that William's pond?" Cole's nod seemed to be the only answer she was going to get. She had the distinct impression that William's name on her lips was blasphemy to his ears. Or maybe it was her own feelings of guilt and failure. There hadn't been a day or night that passed since Cole left her that she hadn't questioned her every action. As much as she'd reminded herself the fiasco at the trial wasn't her fault, she knew better. Her relationship with Cole had been a distraction.

Lucky Lady's slower pace jarred her back from that dark road where her thoughts seemed to dwell. She realized what Cole had meant when he said they were going to a place where there would be no more lies. On an emerald-green hill, lovingly manicured, stood a single ancient live oak tree. It spread its massive limbs over the Jackson family cemetery. Gray headstones, some blackened with age, stood proudly erect, memorials to the men, women, and children who were once a part of the land. A black wrought-iron fence surrounded the boundaries like a band, a ring, Kathleen thought fancifully, to keep them united as one.

Cole stopped at the gate, dismounted, and without a word helped Kathleen down. He let the reins fall to the ground and gave Lady a light slap on the rump. For a moment he watched as she wandered a few feet away and began grazing on the lush grass. Then, as if gathering his strength, he took Kathleen's elbow and escorted her through the gate.

She knew where they were headed and was relieved. Cole was finally willing to listen to everything she had to say. They followed a worn and winding path between the headstones until something caught her eye. Kathleen stopped. She pointed to the narrow stone slab set between an arch made of weathered timbers that had turned as gray as the stone. On top of the arch sat a magnificent and imposing set of longhorns.

Cole once laughingly told her the horns always reminded him of a crown. Maybe it was a fitting tribute to both man and animal. Both had been instrumental in starting a cattle empire. The longhorns were as much a part of the Jackson history as the men themselves.

"Is that Joshua Jackson's grave?"

"Yes."

"Tell me about them again, Cole."

"You've heard it all before, Katie."

"But not like this. Not here at the family cemetery, knowing each and every one may have stood where I'm standing now. On this very spot." Once they'd shared so much. Cole had teased and laughed at her insatiable appetite for hearing about his colorful history. She knew she was bewitched by his stories, but also felt a deep connection with the ranch and his family, too.

Cole was touched more than he wanted to admit that Kathleen was still enchanted with his past. His heritage was as important to him as the land. He had buried a young wife and stillborn twins here. After that he had pinned his hopes on William to carry on the Jackson name. That wasn't meant to be, either. Since leaving Dallas, he'd been haunted by the realization that he had failed. He'd failed as a man, and failed in his responsibility to his family. He was the last Jackson. His throat tightened painfully as the guilt and loneliness rolled over him. There would be no Jacksons to carry on. Who would care for what he left behind?

Kathleen waited through Cole's silence, sensing his shifting moods. She wished she could tell him everything, but complete truth was out of the question, at least until she knew in her heart that he still loved her. She touched his arm and snapped him out of his gloomy thoughts.

Cole picked up his story. "Joshua Jackson, his widowed mother, five brothers with their families, and Joshua's wife and the first five of his fifteen children came from Missouri with Steven F. Austin's group.

They were among the first three hundred families to arrive in Texas.

"There have been Jacksons on the land under our feet and as far as the eye can see since 1829 when Texas was still under Mexican rule. Jacksons died at the Alamo, at Goliad. They fought at the Battle of San Jacinto and helped defeat Santa Anna and his whole Mexican army. Jacksons fought the Cheyenne, marauding Apache, and the Comanche. See the monument over there, the angel with her wings spread wide and half covered by the climbing pink roses? That's Hannah Jones Jackson's grave. My great-great-great-grandmother."

Kathleen jumped in and finished for him. "She was taken by Comanches in a raid and held captive. Her husband and two uncles rode after her and brought her back. She had been badly treated and partially scalped but lived to an old age. Old enough to scare her great-grandchildren with her gruesome tales."

Cole grinned and his eyes came alive. He was amazed. She'd remembered so much. "That's right. Hannah had grit." At one time, he'd thought Katie reminded him of Hannah. "Come on. There's a marble bench under the tree and there's always a breeze."

As they drew nearer Kathleen realized that the bench was angled in such a way that they would be facing William's and Matthew's graves. To tell a lie in a hallowed place was blasphemous. Mottled sunlight cascaded through the massive limbs of the live oak tree, adding shafts of color to the ghostly light. Spanish moss, strung on branches like tattered rags on a clothesline, undulated on the delicate breeze. Kathleen shivered and wondered if Cole felt the slight chill in his wet clothes. But he didn't mention it.

"Now. Tell me what's going on, Katie. I can tell you're holding something back."

Shadows darkened and shifted shapes. The scent of roses mingled with honeysuckle grew stronger. ''There's more, of course there is,'' she snapped, overcome by her own frustration. The strain of the past months was beginning to crack her calm facade. She'd worked hard for this moment, rehearsed and planned so carefully that now she had her chance, she balked. Kathleen's smile was quick and apologetic as she struggled to hide a wave of panic. So much hung on what she was about to say. Not just her own life, her own peace of mind or happiness would be affected; others would be, too.

Kathleen swallowed. She turned her attention to William's headstone, then dropped her gaze and stared at the ground between her feet. ''I made a nasty deal with a liar and a thief in an attempt to catch the devil.''

Her voice was soft, apologetic, and Cole had to lean closer to hear. ''What deal?''

Kathleen wasn't ready to answer questions and kept talking. ''Ramsey knew he was headed for jail. Either his wife was going to get him or I was. He just needed to be reminded of a few truths to make up his mind who he wanted to deal with. I made it clear if he didn't cooperate with me, I'd see to it personally that his jail time would be spent locked up with the general population. Career criminals. Drug dealers. Rapists. Child molesters. They don't much like cops, and they have some crazy code—they especially hate dirty cops. I promised Ramsey that with his full cooperation and a signed confession he'd spend his time in a secure facility.''

''You could do that?''

With a careless shrug, she said, ''Of course.'' She didn't reveal that she had been willing to call in every favor owed, do whatever it took to make it true. He'd never know about the heated screaming matches and outrageous threats that flew back and forth between her and Ramsey and later her boss. Cole would never know how scared she'd been when the threats started. They were insidious at first—phone calls and hangups in the middle of the night that switched to long periods of silence or heavy breathing. The calls quickly turned vulgar and graphic and were followed by vile letters.

Cole had picked up a dry twig and was breaking it by slow inches. It sounded like bones snapping, and given their location and the fact that she imagined they were her bones, she was decidedly uncomfortable.

"Ramsey broke and I got my signed confession. He admitted that Senator Middleton paid him off, and promised him a job after the media attention cooled down on the trial. Ramsey was also the one who stole the evidence from the police property room and lied on the stand about the night he interviewed Darby Middleton at the accident site."

"You're not telling me anything we all didn't know, Katie."

She refused to look at Cole. "I had to make another deal with Ramsey. He won't be going to jail, after all."

"What?" Cole tossed what was left of the twig away and glared at her. "What did you say?"

"Ramsey's greedy and corrupt, but he's not totally stupid. He told the Senator he destroyed the evidence against Darby. He didn't, though. He figured he might need it as leverage, blackmail, whatever you want to call it. When he realized I wasn't going to back down on the jail sentence, he pulled out his ace in the hole. I made the deal and got his signed confession plus the evidence he stole."

"But he walks?"

"It's how the system works sometimes, Cole."

"It stinks, Katie. That creep was willing to let my brother's killer go free for a few pieces of gold."

"More like thirty thousand dollars cash and the promise of a future job." From Cole's thunderous look, she wished she'd kept her mouth shut.

Cole didn't like the way Kathleen's eyes avoided his. Something bad was missing from her rendition. "Okay, what happened?"

There was no easy way to tell him; she had to blurt it out. "Ramsey's dead. Supposedly, he committed suicide." She rushed on. "Though it weakens my case somewhat not to have Ramsey personally testify, remember I have his signed confession and all the evidence."

Six

"When did Ramsey die, Katie?"

"Two days ago."

Cole cursed under his breath. Then, as if he couldn't sit still any longer, he started back down the path, his long legs eating up the distance between them.

Shocked by his abrupt departure, Kathleen watched in disbelief as he walked away. Like a shot out of a cannon, she sprinted after him. "I'm not through, Cole. Dammit, you said you'd listen this time." She grabbed his arm. "Stop, Cole."

He shook her off and kept going. "Sweet Jesus, Katie, I've heard enough."

Time was passing too fast. Seized by a growing sense of dread, she picked up her pace. Whatever it took, she had to tell everything to Cole. "Cole, stop. You have to know the rest."

"Why? Dammit, Katie. I'm sick to death of having my guts wrung out. I've suffered enough. I lost my brother, my father, and you. God knows not a day or a night has gone by that I haven't rehashed everything. Every detail, Katie, every second. All I can see is that you're trying to salve your own conscience."

Kathleen made up her mind when she realized Cole was headed for Lucky Lady. She'd talk until she was blue in the face or until Cole physically tried to gag her.

"Ramsey's death ties up everything nice and neat for too many people: the Senator, his son, the DA, and you, too, Katie."

"What a rotten thing to say."

"I know, but it's the truth."

"See! There you go again. The truth? Cole Jackson, you wouldn't know the truth if it jumped up and bit you on the butt."

This wasn't the time to be amused, but Katie always had a way of turning the tables on him. That was one thing he had to watch out for. Katie could make him laugh when he wanted to be serious.

A chuckle slipped past his lips. He tried to stop it but with little effect. Suddenly, he found himself laughing and wondered how close he was to losing his sanity. He avoided looking at Katie, knowing it would be a mistake as she seldom lost her cool. He stood aside and waited while she exited the cemetery. As Cole secured the gate, he spotted Lucky Lady grazing a few yards away and whistled.

Kathleen wasn't about to let it go and trailed him as the horse approached. "Ramsey's death, untimely as it was, doesn't make a difference."

Cole grabbed the saddle horn with both hands and swung himself up in the saddle. He held out his hand for Katie and studied her face, waiting for her to fit her foot in the stirrup. As hard as he tried to stay aloof, unmoved, he could feel his self-control ebbing. Once he'd had a clear line of blame, but lately that line had begun to fade. It was becoming harder to stay angry. Katie fitted her foot into the stirrup, grabbed Cole's arm, and was lifted up behind him.

"What do you mean his death doesn't make a difference? Dead men don't make good witnesses, Katie. They can't talk."

"This one can and did," she said and smiled at his back, pleased he was still willing to listen. He hadn't totally hardened his heart against her.

"What happened to his evidence after his death?"

"I have it."

"In a safe place, I hope?"

"You could say that. They're sitting on your kitchen table."

Something she'd said suddenly struck him as odd. "You said Ramsey's death was *supposedly* suicide. Is there some question about it?"

"Not as far as I know, not with the police anyway, but I thought it was awfully coincidental. Besides Ramsey, the DA was the only one who knew I was still digging around in the case. I told him about Ramsey's confession."

"Yeah, there's something you've conveniently managed to skip over. If what you say is true and you didn't know the evidence was missing on the morning of the trial, and if you had nothing to do with making a deal with Middleton, then who at the DA's office helped the evidence disappear? That's something I'd like to know, Katie. I read the spin control Hazelwood put on the disaster of the trial for the news media. He blamed you. So how did he react to your reopening it?"

"The case was left open, Cole. The judge dismissed it with prejudice—for lack of sufficient physical evidence. I had the right to keep investigating."

He read a wealth of emotions in her voice. "That may be, but DA Hazelwood wanted you to back off, didn't he? How deep is the DA's office in bed with Middleton? How about you? What did the good Senator promise you?" Before she could answer, he asked another question. "Just when did you quit the DA's office, Katie?"

"Two weeks ago," she said, and perversely refused to add any more to her statement.

"Two weeks, huh? Around the same time you took Ramsey's confession to Hazelwood?"

It was impossible to carry on a conversation with Cole's back. They were heading down the slope of the hill, drawing closer to the ranch house. Kathleen could make out the lines of neat white fences and the roof of the house.

The hush of the afternoon was shattered by a racket loud enough and sudden enough that she floundered behind Cole as she twisted around to find the source. The noise seemed to be coming from everywhere at once, then three large dogs burst from the trees and charged Lucky Lady from different directions, as if they'd been stalking her. Lucky Lady never so much as flicked her ears at the noise, only shook her head with arrogant dismissal.

Kathleen punched Cole in the ribs. He had told her about them—these three demons of comedy. They were William's two Labrador retrievers, one black, one chocolate—dogs that he'd tirelessly trained—and the third dog, a mutt that belonged to Cole. She knew them by name and said out loud, "Caesar, Brutus, and Et Tu." Knowing so much of the Jackson history, and the entire family's love of reading everything from poetry to the classics, Kathleen didn't find the dogs' names that odd. She grinned and glanced around. Lurking about somewhere, never too far from the dogs he loved to bedevil, was a thirty-pound tiger-striped, mysterious mixed-breed tomcat named Iago.

Cole hollered for quiet and the commotion stopped as abruptly as it started. The dogs, their tongues hanging from the sides of their mouths, romped next to Lucky Lady as Et Tu took the lead.

Lovey met them at the door. Her sharp gaze missed nothing. "Lord Almighty, just look at you." Her eyes roamed over Cole. "Did you go swimming in them clothes and with your boots on? And just look at that new hat." She didn't wait for an answer and turned her interest to Kathleen. Pearly white teeth gnawed at her lower lip. "You needn't give old Lovey that evil eye, missy. I called Cole on that silly phone he carries and told him you was headed his way."

She gave Kathleen another, closer and slower inspection. "And what happened to you? Appears you been"—she sniffed the air and her nose crinkled—"rolling in somethin' awful. And how'd your clothes get torn?" She shot Cole a hard look. "Well, it ain't no concern of mine nohows what ya'll been up to. But I say it don't look like you two had much fun. No." She laughed. "No sirree, it don't look that way a'tall."

"If you're through, Lovey," Cole said, and hung his misshapen hat on the rack by the back door, "I'd like to know why you put Katie on Pegasus."

"Why? Cole Jackson, you ain't gonna put the blame on me! 'Cause you put every greenhorn comes through here on that horse and make 'em spend all day with it so's they'll 'preciate what a good ride's supposed to feel like. That's why."

Cole knew there was no use arguing, but he'd never stop trying to get the better of Lovey. He sniffed the air. "Something smells good."

"You're too late with the flattery. It ain't gonna get you nothing but the back of my hand, boy."

Kathleen let their banter flow over her. All she could do was close her eyes and inhale and savor the aromas as her stomach made loud protesting noises. When she opened her eyes, she spotted the large envelope she'd left on the kitchen table. It had been opened. She reached out to pick it up and paused. Her purse was on one of the chairs. She distinctly remembered leaving it beside her suitcase.

Lovey watched the young woman. She pursed her lips to hold back a smile. "That satchel you call a purse was ringing. It near drove me crazy, so I answered the darn thing."

Kathleen sensed Cole's eyes on her and at the same time felt her heart plummet to her toes. She was torn between fear and worry.

Lovey said, "It was your sister." She saw the flicker of fright in Kathleen's gaze before it was swiftly masked, and hastened to add, "She just wanted to know if you was okay. Said not to worry about her, everything's just fine."

Kathleen couldn't hide her relief. She pulled out a chair and collapsed.

"Why would Sandra be worried about you?"

"You know Sandy, the worrier in the family."

"Funny, I never thought of her like that, just the opposite, really. But why would she be worried about you being here?" Cole scowled when Katie's answer was only a speaking glance. "Where is she?"

Kathleen looked away. "Austin. Shopping."

"Austin? Why Austin? I thought Sandra hated shopping. At least that's what she told me."

"What is this sudden interest in my sister's likes and dislikes? Who cares where she is? You're just trying to keep me from finishing what I've come to say."

"I was not. Dammit, Katie—"

"Children, children." Lovey stepped in. When she had their full attention, she made a show of untying her apron. She folded it neatly and put it away, then picked up her purse and car keys from the counter.

"There's roast with all the fixin's in the oven. Salad and a pitcher of iced tea in the refrigerator." Cole glanced at the clock, and frowned. Before he could give her the third degree, Lovey hurried on. "My niece called. Two of her youngest is down with the itchy-spots."

"The what?" Cole tried to hide his dismay at being left alone with Kathleen.

"Chickenpox. I'll be going over to help out."

"When will you be back?" Cole unsuccessfully tried to hide his unease.

"Oh, maybe Monday. Maybe Tuesday. You got a problem with that?"

Cole's frown turned darker. His gaze ricocheted between Lovey and Katie. Lovey's innocent expression made him nervous. Lovey didn't know the meaning of innocence. She was a born mischief maker and a snoop. He hadn't missed the fact that she'd read the papers Katie brought. Lovey was loyal. She was a part of the Jackson family. Hell, she'd wiped his bottom. She gave him hell about half the time, bitching and griping, but when push came to shove Lovey would never take sides against him. He had told her much of what had happened in Dallas. The parts he'd glossed over she had filled in for herself. It was clear she'd skin Kathleen Calhoun alive if she ever got the chance. So why did he suddenly feel as if Lovey had crossed the line and he was left standing alone?

And there was Katie's neutral expression to consider, too. There was something going on here. He was sure some woman thing had passed between them. Cole was left standing and staring after Lovey as Kathleen excused herself to go wash up. He had a sudden sense of having walked into a trap.

* * *

The hot bath and clean dry clothes revived them. It didn't go unnoticed that they each seemed fortified enough to take on the other. Cole's suspicions continued throughout the meal. They were both ravenous and ate pretty much in silence. He did notice that Kathleen kept glancing at the door as if she expected someone to walk in. When he finished eating, he pushed the plate aside and said, "You know, everything you've told me so far could have been put in a letter. So why the trip out here, Katie?"

Did he think her stupid? She was sick of being put off, dismissed, and accused of lying. Most of all, she was tired of repeating herself every time Cole decided he didn't want to hear any more and walked away. She was exhausted from chasing him down.

"Would you like more iced tea?" Pushing the chair back, she picked up their glasses. For a second she froze. She'd been sitting too long and every muscle in her body suddenly screamed with pain. Refusing to look at Cole, knowing he was grinning like an ape, she concentrated on putting one foot in front of the other. Kathleen circled around behind Cole, set the glasses on the counter, then eased toward the door.

He knew her too well and wasn't fooled. The sweet smile tinged with malice was a dead giveaway. He'd seen her in action in court just as she was about to rip apart a witness on the stand. Knowing she was up to something didn't make him any less curious about her intentions. It wouldn't surprise him if he got the remaining pitcher of iced tea poured over his head.

Kathleen had it all figured out. She'd seen what she needed hanging on the hat rack. Cautiously, she took the lasso off the peg. She walked back toward Cole, letting the rope trail out behind her until she was left holding the noose. Before she changed her mind, she flipped the noose over Cole's head and shoulders and pulled hard, forcing the rope to tighten and pin his arms to his sides.

"What the hell? Katie!"

"Sorry," she said. "But it's the only way." She wound the extra rope around, securing his arms and effectively tying him to the chair. Cole wasn't going anywhere—not until she'd had her say. She'd vowed she would never use sex or their attraction for each other, but with Cole a captive the temptation was too great to pass up. With only a slight hesitation, she leaned over and kissed him. It was meant to be quick, but once her lips touched his the kiss unexpectedly became passionate. Breathless and struggling to hide her emotions, Kathleen was the first to pull away. The kiss was more telling than a declaration.

Cole wasn't as unaffected as he would have liked. His hesitant tone of voice gave him away. "This is crazy, Katie."

"I know." Kathleen put the table between them in case he got loose. At least she'd have a head start. She eyed her handiwork proudly, grinned and grew braver.

"Untie me."

"Don't think so. And you needn't give me that nasty snarl. It's just you and me, Cole. You and me and a long, long night."

"You're crazy."

"Yep, that's possible, but whose fault is that? You deliberately antagonized me today, so you can blame yourself for whatever happens."

"This won't accomplish anything, Katie."

"We'll see."

"You won't change my mind."

"We'll see."

She cleared the table while ignoring his threats and struggles. When she realized he could stand, even though he was bent double in an impossible position, it startled her into action again. She improvised and tied his legs to the chair with dishtowels.

"I don't want to go over old ground again."

"We'll see."

"Dammit, Katie. I've heard it all."

"Have you?"

She flicked a few missed crumbs from the tabletop, then opened the envelope she'd brought and spread out the papers. "You haven't heard nearly enough, certainly not the whole story." She returned his glare, her bright sapphire-blue eyes filled with anger. "We never seem to have time for an intelligent conversation. Now we can. Clever of me, don't you think?"

Seven

''Let's start, shall we?'' Kathleen separated four sheets of paper and arranged them side by side on the table in front of Cole. ''This is Ramsey's confession. Read it.''

''We've gone over this, Katie. Why don't I just take your word on what it says and you can untie me?''

''Read it, all of it. Or I swear, Cole, I'll tape your eyelids open and stick pins under your nails until you do. Read!''

At first Cole skimmed a few paragraphs, then, despite his reluctance, he slowed down and studied the document carefully. When he finished, he was quiet. ''Okay,'' he said, ''In a nutshell, Middleton paid him to lie about Darby being drunk that night. He gives all the details, the cash amount and the promise of a future job. Ramsey also says that he bribed his buddy in the police property room to turn his head while he stole the evidence out of the marked bags. What he doesn't say, Katie, is who at the DA's office was in on the deal.''

Kathleen scooted to the edge of the chair and leaned forward eagerly. ''He didn't know it but I knew there had to be someone in my office working for Middleton. You blamed me for what happened and you were right.

I screwed up, but not deliberately—I didn't sell out.

"You see, Cole, the night before the trial I was supposed to check out the evidence, review it, then lock it up in our office vault. Then the morning of the trial it was my job to see that the evidence was checked in at court. But I didn't do that." She waited, watching his face, her heart pounding so loud she wondered if he could hear it. Cole's expression and the quick flush of color in his cheeks told her he hadn't forgotten even though he would have her believe otherwise. "We had plans for that night. Remember?"

"Yes," Cole mumbled and shifted his gaze to the tabletop.

"You were there with me when I called the office. You heard me tell my secretary to have one of the ADAs pick up the evidence and deliver it to me the next morning." Kathleen watched him closely.

Cole remembered. He could never forget that night, no matter how hard he tried. They had been uptight and excited over the start of the trial. The long months of strain had taken their toll. Suddenly, it was going to come to an end and all the pain would magically be swept away. They were giddy with success, high on love, and for the first time enjoyed the luxury of making future plans. The night was going to be special, and it was.

"Do you remember, Cole?"

God, yes. Every minute detail of that evening at Katie's apartment was branded on his memory. There had been nights over the past eighteen months when he'd wished and prayed that he could forget. "This has gone far enough. Untie me, Katie."

"No." There was no need for Kathleen to ask if he remembered that night again, and no use for him to deny it. She could see her answer in the way his jaw clenched and his lips tightened, but the softening of his gaze spoke volumes. She remembered, too.

They'd dined at a posh Dallas restaurant, but they had no appetite for food after all. She smiled, thinking about the drive to her apartment. It was pure luck they'd made it at all. Later, they had snuggled together and laughed, blaming their abandon and lack of caution on the champagne and absence of food.

Kathleen gathered Ramsey's confession then placed a single sheet of paper on the table. "I didn't take care of business, Cole, and we were late to court the next morning and I didn't have time to go through the evidence box. But why should I have? I knew what was in it—what was supposed to be there."

"The evidence had to be signed out of the police property room. Whose signature was it?"

"It was mine, but a poor forgery."

"What did the DA have to say about that?"

Kathleen almost smiled but caught herself in time. Cole had curbed his dislike for her boss, Albert Hazelwood. It was Matthew Jackson, Cole's father, who had taken one look at the district attorney of Dallas and pronounced him as slick as a snake-oil salesman and about as low. Cole never disagreed.

"Once he realized the signature wasn't mine and that someone in the office had been paid off, he was furious. Or at least I thought that was the case."

"You're not sure now?"

"That's right. He knew I would never give up the case. He actually encouraged me to stay with it, but it had to be on my own time. If and when I found something solid, I was to go to him first."

"You didn't buy that line, did you?" Cole snapped, angry over the way they had all been duped not only by the judicial system, but by two men who had taken oaths to uphold the law.

"At that moment, yes." She couldn't stand Cole's

look of disgust. "Dammit, it was all I had to hold on to. He promised me an internal investigation."

Cole shrugged, rankled by being kept stationary so long when he wanted to walk the floor, or put a fist through a wall. "I bet nothing ever came of the investigation."

"You're right. But by then I'd told him about my ace in the hole. He couldn't do anything but agree that Ramsey had been bought by the Senator. Yet, even with all I had, he put up the convincing argument that I would never be able to make a case that would stand up in court. He gave me all the legal reasons it wouldn't work and they were believable. When I didn't cave in, something I can't explain changed. Something I felt rather than observed."

It would be years before she shook off that awful feeling. It was always with her—the flash of fear like a searing flame and the nausea that followed so swiftly on its heels. The man she'd worked for was corruptible. "Hazelwood told me I had stepped into the big league and didn't have the resources or manpower to fight, and neither did the DA's office. He insisted I turn over all Ramsey's evidence. That was two weeks ago."

"The day you quit?"

"Yes."

"And Ramsey's death was two days ago?"

She nodded but gazed elsewhere, knowing he had another question he was waiting to ask. Her ploy didn't work.

"When did you leave Dallas?"

"Two days ago."

Cole stared at her, silent, deep in thought. He felt a band of unease tighten around his chest. "Did something happen, Katie? Did Hazelwood or someone threaten you?"

"I didn't wait around to find out. Cole, I'd already

planned to come here, nothing or no one could change my mind.''

That she was evading his question was obvious, but Cole decided not to push it—not yet. ''Untie me, Katie.''

''Not yet.'' Pointing to the single sheet of paper on the table, Kathleen said, ''That's a list of what should have been in the evidence box. Ramsey's accident-scene reports, the results of the Breathalyzer test, the hospital blood test, and a videotape. That tape was important because it was taken at the accident scene, clearly showing Darby failed the sobriety test. Ramsey gave me everything he stole, Cole, except the original videotape. He had to turn that over to Senator Middleton as part of his deal to get the money.''

Kathleen placed a file on top of the growing stack of papers. ''This is Darby Middleton's juvenile record. He had four arrests for drunken driving before he reached sixteen.''

''You told me the DA's office couldn't use those in court, that they were sealed because Darby was underage at the time.''

''That's right, but this isn't a courtroom.'' Kathleen hoped time and separation hadn't made the emotional wounds fester to a point where he wouldn't admit he'd been wrong, even when he was confronted with the evidence that she'd never betrayed him.

''No, it isn't,'' he said softly under his breath while he kept his gaze on the table, refusing to look at her. ''Untie me, Katie.''

Kathleen's hands froze, suspended above the papers. This time something was different, something about his request she couldn't put her finger on, an emotion in his tone she couldn't identify. She'd done all she could and would have to trust him sometime. Without argument she did as he asked.

Cole didn't feel the loosened rope or the binding on his ankles fall away. He was mired too deeply in his miserable thoughts to hear anything Katie might say. A troubled man, with the weight of his mistakes resting heavily on his shoulders, he rose from the chair and walked over to the wide expanse of bay windows. He stared blindly at the panoramic view beyond.

He'd been wrong. Any fool could see that, but like a fool he'd embraced his pain and nursed his grudge against Katie far too long to let it go without one last nasty shot.

Eighteen months ago he had returned home from Dallas with an iron resolve to stay clear of any entanglements. The old cliché "love hurts," was right on the mark. Love had cost him too much. He'd lost too many loved ones. The first was his mother, then sweet, young Sally and the twins. William's death had seemed the cruelest blow of all. God, he had loved that wild, brilliant boy. When his father died he'd almost given up.

All that heartache should have hardened him, and it probably would have if not for Katie. Now she was here, and even though he'd been wrong to accuse her, he couldn't allow himself to weaken. He wanted her to stay forever, but knew from sad experience there were no guarantees for tomorrow.

"As I've said before," Cole said, "you could have explained everything you've told me in a letter. So why did you come?"

Kathleen knew in her heart she wasn't prepared for Cole to know everything. She had to be careful because she was still hoarding secrets she couldn't share. Of all the people in her life, including her family, Cole knew her best. The rest of her life depended on what was to come.

"Monday morning all hell's going to break loose."

He waited as she gathered together the papers, straightened their edges neatly, then slipped them back in the envelope. "Copies of everything here, including my statement detailing what happened, will arrive at the offices of the governor in Austin and the state attorney general. The same copies were sent to five newspapers spread out around Texas and to the major network TV stations in Dallas, Houston, and Austin." She tried for a little levity. "While I was on a roll, I sent the same package to all the Washington, D.C., media—newspapers and television."

Cole glanced over his shoulder at Kathleen. For the first time since they'd sat down, real amusement touched his face and smoothed out the worry lines. "Sounds like overkill. You covered yourself pretty good, though." He smiled when the bloom of color tinted her pale cheeks pink. "Did you send a copy to the President?"

"No, to someone equally as powerful who can handle this sort of thing. The attorney general of the United States. I threw in the head of the Senate Ethics Committee as well."

He had an overwhelming urge to take her in his arms. From the moment she'd arrived he'd kept his distance. When her arms were wrapped around his waist, with the heat of her body pressed against him, and her breath and voice in his ear, he still kept his distance. Strange, he felt closer to her now than he had all day, even with the width of the kitchen between them. "So you came to warn me. Or are you here to escape the fallout? There is going to be fallout, isn't there?"

"Yes." She shivered when Cole turned his back on her and continued staring out the window. "The truth, and it will prevail, Cole, will ruin three lives and taint a dozen or so more. The Senator, depending on how slick his lawyers are, might not spend time in jail, but he will be publicly and politically ruined. Darby will be tried again, a fair trial this time, for intoxicated manslaughter. He'll be convicted because the evidence is there.

"I don't kid myself about Senator Middleton. He won't take what I've done lightly. His son's freedom is at stake. He'll play rough." She had an idea just how dirty it was going to get. That was the compelling force that drove her to Cole.

"He'll go after you?" Cole asked.

"With both barrels."

She wished he'd look at her. "Then there's Albert Hazelwood."

"The third person?"

"Yes. I could never prove conclusively that the DA or anyone in my office was in Middleton's pocket. Just the fact that he interfered, then advised me to drop the case, looks bad. Albert knows the system and how to wiggle around it. Hazelwood has as many enemies in Dallas as advocates. Those who are against Albert will go after him with a kind of fanatical enthusiasm. I think he'll resign his office and go into private practice."

Something wasn't right. Kathleen felt a chill whisper across her skin and hugged herself. The distance that separated them suddenly seemed like a chasm growing wider with each passing minute. Desperate to stop it, she said, "I came here, Cole, because I wanted you to know everything. You had to hear the truth from me."

Cole still remained silent and her fears grew. Even as she warned herself not to push her luck, she attempted to break the increasing silence. "I understand why you reacted the way you did in court. If the circumstances had been reversed, I might have done the same. At first I was devastated that you could ever imagine I'd betray you, or William's and your father's memory.

"After you left, I told myself you'd come to your senses and realize you were wrong. So I waited for you to come back, then I waited for you to call. When I didn't hear from you, I got really angry. For a while, I hated you. I . . ." Kathleen's voice trailed away as she summoned up all her courage.

"I love you. I've never stopped loving you." Suddenly, the room seemed be sucked dry of air. "There wasn't a day or night that passed that I didn't think of you." Kathleen couldn't breathe. "Please don't tell me it's too late. You still love me, too. I know you do." Cole was so still she didn't know if he'd heard anything she said. She grabbed the edge of the table to steady her trembling legs.

"Dammit, I can't stand here with my heart in my hand and have you ignore me. Please look at me." He turned, and she wished she'd never asked.

Eight

"Maybe you shouldn't have come at all."

Kathleen could hardly breathe. When she started to speak, her throat closed up and the words came out in a whisper. "You don't . . . you can't mean it?"

Cole swung around and stared out the kitchen window again. "Can't I? Why not? You show up after eighteen months. Eighteen months, I might add, during which I never heard one word from you. Not a denial, not even *I'm sorry, Cole*. I heard nothing but silence, Katie. Now you come to me with all this proof." He waved his arms as if to take in the world. "You swear it's the truth and you've always been honest with me. But dammit, Katie, I know you, and you're lying. Why? What is it you don't want me to know?"

He glanced over his shoulder and asked, "Are you in danger?"

"No," she lied. The degree of danger was debatable. How could she tell Cole that Senator Middleton's and probably Albert Hazelwood's revenge would be to put every detail of her life under the microscope of the media. The headlines, tongue-wagging, and gossip would be horrendous. Her enemies would turn her own tactics against her. Just imagining the field day the media would have tearing her apart made her queasy.

There would be things revealed that she didn't want Cole to know. She had to be the one to tell him and she couldn't bring herself to do it until she knew if he still loved her.

"Then what aren't you telling me, Katie?"

For a moment he lost himself in his thoughts as he watched the sun setting on the horizon. Dusk threw shadows across the land. They expanded and stretched and sucked up the brilliance of the day. He could barely make out the location of the cemetery because of the deepening shadows on the hill. Then suddenly, as it had done every evening, the sun backlit the massive live oak tree. A rainbow of color like flashes of lightning shot between limbs and leaves. For a second the old tree glowed like a stained-glass window.

The truth. Kathleen watched and waited, tortured by that word. Once again she asked herself—could she afford to tell him everything without knowing if he still loved her?

Cole steeled himself as he faced her for the last time. "I know you had nothing to do with what happened at the trial." He gazed at her, taking in every detail, every nuance, his eyes the lens of a camera, and his mind the pages of an album. The way one eyebrow quirked higher than the other had always amused him. "I'm sorrier than you'll ever know that I was so quick to judge you and jump to the wrong conclusions." Her lips, soft and full, curled upward at the corners as if she had a secret only she knew.

"But there's been too much unhappiness between us." She was shaking her head, unwilling to listen and accept what she knew was coming. He'd lost too much of himself in his pain. The fact was he was too frightened to take that step, to free his heart, again, especially with Katie.

Kathleen's resolve almost weakened until she

thought of what was at stake. She screwed up her nerve and asked, "Do you love me, Cole?" She held herself stiffly erect to keep from collapsing.

Cole sensed the urgency behind her question, the desperate need to hear those three words from him once more. He could see the sadness and the longing in her gaze. How could he tell her he was a coward? The kindest thing he could do for Katie and for himself was to send her away.

Silence separated them far more than a few feet. Cole could no longer look at Kathleen. He couldn't bring himself to watch the pain he was about to inflict. Cole sighed and delivered the last blow. "Face it, we just weren't meant to be together, Katie. It's time to call it quits. Life has a way of fooling us and refusing to turn out the way we think it ought to." He brushed past her and left the room.

She stood stock-still, listening to his retreating footsteps fade away. It shouldn't be this difficult, she thought. She'd planned so carefully. Kathleen felt wetness on her cheeks and wiped it away with the back of her hand. Cole was wrong. "What a crock," she whispered. "You're just plain butt-headed, that's all." She looked around the kitchen, spotted her purse on the counter, and grabbed it.

Cole listened to the front door slam shut, the sound echoing a final good-bye through the empty house. He heard a car start. He waited, waited until there was only silence again. What he'd done was for the best.

The next morning was too sunny and pristine for Kathleen to stomach. She felt as jumpy as droplets of water on a hot skillet. After she'd stomped out of the house and left Cole, she'd driven to the hotel in Austin where by prearrangement her sister was waiting. Kathleen spent a miserable night pacing the boundaries of their room, talking until she was hoarse. Sandra, as only an older sister could, was her sounding board, interjecting advice when the opportunity presented itself. But Sandra's good intentions had been stretched to their limits at about three in the morning. She had seriously threatened to shoot Kathleen and put her sister out of her misery—then go after Cole with the same intent.

The one and only point the two sisters had agreed on wholeheartedly was that Calhouns, especially Kathleen, weren't quitters. Once that was established, they knew what had to be done.

Kathleen pulled the front door of the ranch house shut. Birds tittered in the big cottonwood trees. Bees were busy above a profusion of flowerpots shoved in corners of the front porch of the ranch house. In the distance cattle and horses grazed lazily under the early morning sun. She viewed it all with an eerie sense of déjà vu.

Cole was nowhere to be found. His truck was parked in the same spot as it had been the day before. The coffeepot on the stove was still warm and there was a single cup in the sink. She concluded he was out riding and she'd just have to wait. But she had a sudden feeling he was close by. Lost in the turmoil of her thoughts, she started to step off the porch and glanced down to make sure of her footing when she froze. As silent as a whisper, three dogs had crept up on her. Caesar, Brutus, and Et Tu stood stock-still, watching, sniffing the air. Four sets of eyes assessed each other, hers the only one that showed fear. Cole's stories about the three were always laced with humor, but he'd made it clear that for all their buffoonery they were excellent watchdogs.

Kathleen cleared her throat, praying her voice carried more authority than she was feeling at the moment. "Good doggies," she said. "Where's Cole?" Ears perked up and in unison they wheeled around and trotted a few feet away. Then as if puzzled that she wasn't following, they stopped and waited for her to catch up. Using the dogs as her guides, she trailed behind them, suddenly aware where they were heading.

It was a long, winding trail and a hot trek up the hill. The gate to the cemetery was open and she strolled through, spotting Cole immediately. He was sitting on the bench, his back to her as she approached. Kathleen stopped before she reached him, deliberately keeping some distance between them.

She realized he was so lost in his own world that he hadn't even heard her approach. The dogs, sensing the severity of the situation, slinked away to a safer distance to watch. There was an unbearable pressure in her chest, and she felt as if the ground were shifting under her feet. She was almost overwhelmed by the urge to cry. There was too much at stake for her to make a mistake. She was not a gambler by nature and for the first time in her life she was trusting her heart over her head.

"You said you know me so well." He straightened but didn't turn. "That works both ways, Cole Jackson. Was I lying to you? No, I didn't lie. I just wasn't telling you everything. I had my reasons. Good ones." She needed to say what she'd come to say before he faced her. "But you, Cole, you looked me in the eye and lied. You see, I know you, too.

"Even when you thought I'd betrayed you, you still loved me. That must have rankled. When you realized you were wrong and you tallied up the loss of everyone you'd loved, then tried to balance it against your pain, the scales tipped in favor of never loving again. You decided you couldn't afford to take another chance and that you could live without me and my love. It won't work. You can't hide from the past or the future, no matter what it brings.''

His silence gave her hope. Kathleen rushed on, her heart in her throat. Her pulse was going wild, pounding in her head so noisily she couldn't tell if she was speaking loud enough. She sent up a silent prayer of thanks that he still hadn't looked at her. It was important that she finish first. ''Do you think I don't know what's in your heart?''

Cole swung around. How could he push her away again? How could he . . . ? His gaze took in everything at once. The tenderness in her eyes and the soft curve of her cheek as one dimple winked in and out uncertainly. She shrugged, obviously at a loss for words, which was unusual for his Katie. Then whatever he was about to say died on his lips.

He stared, unable to speak, at the little boy standing unsteadily beside Kathleen. The child had one arm wrapped tightly around her leg, the other arm lifted so he could suck his thumb. Silky brown hair stirred in the morning breeze. Cole's breath was shaky as he looked into green eyes—his green eyes.

Kathleen touched her son's head, the movement more protective than she realized. ''Do you remember the night before the trial? We were reckless and careless.''

''How could I forget?'' Cole forced himself to answer. He couldn't take his eyes off the boy. ''I asked you once before if the reason you came here was because you're in danger. If you are, for both your sakes, you have to tell me, Katie. I can make the ranch a fortress. No one could touch either of you. There's nothing I wouldn't do to protect—''

''The fact that I had your child is going to become public knowledge very soon. Middleton and Hazelwood are too savvy to bypass that juicy tidbit of news.

They'll try and find a way to use it against me. I didn't want you to find out that way.''

If there were a thousand questions he wanted to ask, Cole couldn't think clearly enough to voice them. He moved closer and squatted down before the little boy. All of a sudden he dropped his head and tears ran unabashed down his cheeks.

Kathleen saw Cole's shoulders shake with emotion. She bent down so they were both on the child's level and took his hand in hers. Funny, she thought she would need words of love and promises of forever, but his tears said all she ever needed to hear. ''Cole, I named him after you and William. Cole William. We call him C.W.''

The child heard his name and laughed as Cole looked up. Father and son gazed at each other and smiled identical smiles. Kathleen watched for a second, then glanced away as if she were intruding on a private moment. She sighed deeply, feeling relieved and elated, and sad all at once. Looking around, she smiled. There could not have been a more fitting place for them to meet, here under the old tree with generations of Jacksons looking on, especially William and Matthew.

A smile touched Kathleen's eyes, making them sparkle. She remembered her family, who were gathered in Austin, waiting to join them and show Cole he had more family and people who loved him than he was probably ready for. It was a fitting beginning.

Sweetheart of the Rodeo

By
Vivian Vaughan

For my son Bobby,
Who loves horses almost as much
as he loves his mother.

Thanks for the 350 bright,
shiny red ones!

1

BALLOU HILLS RANCH
TEXAS, WEST OF THE PECOS
JUNE, 1883

"Wish me luck, Cat."

Catarina Ramériz stood outside the corral, oblivious to the husky voice that reached her through a haze of expectancy. With one hand she held her black skirt against a billowing gust of wind. Black curls struggled from her bun and wisped untended about her intent black eyes.

Around her, Ballou Hills cowboys perched on top of the corral fence, boot heels hooked over the rail below; others stood to either side, arms folded over rails, chins resting on crossed wrists. The hot, dusty air shimmered with impending disaster.

In the center of the corral stood the cause of all the commotion, a wild black stallion named Texan who had already sent one Ballou Hills cowboy to the hospital over in Pecos. Now Monte Ballou had decided to show the outlaw who was boss of this ranch.

And Catarina was scared.

Monte might be the son of Ballou Hills' owner, but Catarina had a feeling, a deep, horrible, fearful feeling, that Texan had no intention of relinquishing his position as king of the Ballou Hills outlaws.

"That hoss cain't never be rode," Baldy, a cowboy to Catarina's right, commented under his breath.

"Monte can do it," spoke up another, this one called Tipper. "If anybody can," he added skeptically.

"What'll you give me?" The challenge came from down the line.

"Let me in on that bet." Skeeter Owens leaned across Catarina, hand outstretched to shake on the deal even before it was struck. Even before Monte climbed aboard the outlaw horse. "I'll take Monte an' . . ."

Catarina's head throbbed with fear, but before she could berate the cowboys, Monte spoke again.

"What'd you say, Cat?" As if carried into the corral on a whirlwind of dust, he stood before her, six feet of lanky, sun-bronzed arrogance. Only the five-rail fence separated them, and it wasn't nearly enough to head off the potent effect his presence had on her.

"These boys believe in me," he was saying, "how 'bout you?"

Catarina drew so sharp a breath she almost choked on the intake of dust and grit. She rarely saw Monte, except at mealtimes when she helped her mother serve the cowboys. Her mother, Tina, had been Ballou Hills' cook since before Catarina was born; her father, Raul, had been ranch foreman longer than that.

With Monte's blue eyes peering at her from that lean, tanned face, Catarina felt herself the center of attention, even though she could tell from the cowboys' voices to either side that everyone else was intent on the upcoming ride and paid them no mind. They continued to banter, brag, and argue the merits of Monte over Texan—and vice versa.

While she swallowed, tried to answer, Monte hitched

the saddle he carried by its horn. Pee Wee Johnston called from the center of the corral.

"Hurry it up, Ballou." Pee Wee's plea was laced with exasperation. Since he bested the other cowboys by a good ten years, he naturally fell heir to the more vexing tasks. Snubbing an outlaw horse could be called vexing and worse. "I cain't hold on to this bucker all day long."

Monte gave no indication he heard. Monte was like that. Always had been. When he gave his concentration to something, he concentrated all the way. Now Catarina was the object of his attention. His expression was a mixture of gravity and amusement.

"Cat's got her tongue," he sang gently, just loud enough to be heard by those nearest them, "locked inside her throat; if she don't laugh, she's a-bound to choke."

It was a silly, mindless ditty, guaranteed to produce giggles from a morose little girl. But today it had the uncomfortable effect of a shower of falling stars pummeling her scalp. Gooseflesh rose along her arms, even as she felt her skin quiver with a sudden increase of inner heat.

She hadn't heard the ditty in a good six years. Chuckles from either side reminded her that she and Monte were not alone. The audience didn't appear to bother him.

Before she could recover, he lifted a free hand to his lips, kissed the rough pad of his forefinger, and swiped it gently down her nose. "For luck, Cat." With a wink he turned and headed for center stage. His swagger further jarred her sensibilities with every jangle of his spurs.

He had touched her.

For the first time since he had returned to Ballou

Hills after a six-year absence, Monte acted like she actually existed, like he remembered . . .

He *had* remembered the ditty. Fortunately, at this moment her fear for him was too great for anything akin to hope to take root.

Encouraging calls followed him to the center of the corral. Beyond, Pee Wee struggled with the frightened black horse. While he pulled the halter rope so taut the stallion's muzzle almost rested in his lap, Carlos Santero raced out and reached across Pee Wee to blindfold the outlaw.

Approaching quietly, his attention fixed firmly on Texan, Monte lifted a hand, silencing his audience. A hush followed. The only sound Catarina could hear was the thrashing of her heart.

Through a world that had slowed to half-speed, she watched Monte stop beside the outlaw. She watched him lift the saddle and throw it on the already sweating black back.

But the animal would have none of it. Even before contact, Texan's back legs shot out. Monte jumped aside, but recovered quickly. He reached under the heaving belly, caught the trailing end of the cinch, and fastened it tight.

Mesmerized, Catarina tried not to look but was unable to tear her eyes away from the lanky cowboy she had loved since she was thirteen years old. She reasoned that if she were to close her eyes, something horrible might happen to Monte. Her heart seemed squeezed as tightly as the cinch around Texan's belly.

She felt it burst when Monte reached for the saddle horn. With one smooth, quick movement, no motion wasted, he stepped into the saddle.

"Turn 'em loose, Pee Wee."

Pee Wee obliged, then backed his mount away, bringing Monte and the outlaw into full view. Everything turned hazy. Dust flew like a tornado had set down inside the corral.

Then Monte released the blindfold, and Texan sprouted wings. Back arched to form the shape resembling a horseshoe, the outlaw stallion bunched his feet as neatly as a toe dancer and from that position, he bounded straight into the air.

"Now we'll find out if ol' Monte can stick!"

"Hell, cain't nobody stick on a frog-walker like . . ."

But Monte did.

Skeeter's words drifted off when Texan landed on all fours with a force that lifted Monte from the saddle.

Quickly, though, he regained his seat, while Catarina gripped her hands together, fingers entwined, as if by sheer will she could help him hold on.

"Please, dear God . . ."

Before she could finish her prayer, Texan had squatted back on his haunches. Monte gathered slack, drawing the halter rope closer to the glistening black mane, then as quickly he eased the rope back through his hand when Texan reversed himself with a mighty backward leap that looked for all the world like he couldn't keep from falling over backward.

"That dang sunfisher. He's a-gonna—"

"Fan 'em, Monte! Fan the bucker!"

But the best Monte could do for balance was to fling his left arm back and forth—rather spasmodically, Catarina thought. His Stetson, the object generally used to fan for balance, had flown off at some undetermined time.

As things turned out, fanning this outlaw wouldn't have helped. Swapping ends, Texan brought his front hooves down with a bone-jarring thud that served as a springboard for another skyward jump that left the cowboys around her spellbound.

"Dang, if that ol' hoss don't think he can chin the moon!"

"Yeah . . ."

When a stiff-legged landing failed to unseat his unwanted cargo, Texan gave a couple of smaller sheepjumps, then flung himself into a spin.

"He's a-windmilling, boys."

"We can see that, Skeeter. What about Monte?"

"Hold on to him, Monte!" Carlos called.

By now the dust was so thick and Catarina's mouth was so dry, she could roll grit between her teeth. *Hold on to him,* she prayed. *Wear him out.*

But that was not to be. Two spins and a jackknife later, Texan left his rider tumbling head over booted heels into the air. As if the outlaw horse knew exactly what he had done, he stepped aside and watched Monte fall to the ground.

Except for Texan's heaving sides and Catarina's thrashing heart, all movement ceased. Then Catarina was scrambling over the rails.

Only later did she realize what she had done.

"Come on back here, Cat." Skeeter Owens grabbed her around the waist.

"No. Monte's going to be trampled."

"We ain't about to let that outlaw stomp another Ballou Hills cowboy into the dust, Cat. You stay right here."

When her vision cleared, Catarina saw that Pee Wee had already caught Texan's halter rope. Carlos had reached Monte, who sat up and gingerly ran fingers through his hair. Skeeter turned her loose.

"Ain't that your mama callin'?"

Catarina shook her head to focus her attention. From behind she heard the dying echoes of her mother's voice. But the scene inside the corral held her enthralled. She watched Monte stand, test his legs, and grin sheepishly. Carlos fetched his Stetson.

" 'Bout time we turn that outlaw back to the wild," Pee Wee was saying to no one in particular.

"Yeah," Skeeter agreed.

Monte slapped his hat against his chaps a couple of times. Catarina watched, feeling each slap as she would have a blast of cold air. *Yes, turn the outlaw loose.*

"No way," came Monte's voice. "Not till after the rodeo in Pecos." It was an order, undisguised as anything else. Turning, he scanned the assembled cowboys, daring each by turn to dispute the boss's son. "No human hand's to touch this outlaw till that rodeo. I want him mean as the stallion that sired him."

The Ballou Hills mess hall was a long adobe building with plank tables and bench seats for a hundred or more cowboys at roundup time. Regular times, like now, a couple of tables in one corner were all that were used. The kitchen was attached to the rear.

Catarina had no more than rushed through the door when her mother thrust a white canvas apron in one of Catarina's hands and a long-handled spoon in the other. "Pin your hair back, then stir the frijoles, *hija.* Señor Ballou does not pay me to feed his cowboys burned beans."

Tina Ramériz's brusque tone, or perhaps the fact that she called Catarina "daughter," instead of "my daughter," alerted Catarina to her mother's mood—aggravation headed straight for peevishness.

"Sí, Mamá." Catarina fitted the huge apron over her simple white blouse and black skirt, then reattached the combs that held her long black hair in a bun at her nape. At the wood-burning range pinto beans burbled in a ten-gallon cast-iron pot.

She knew exactly what she had done to cause her mother's displeasure; if she hadn't, when Tina continued, the topic would have become clear as branch water.

"I think it's time you took up Tía Juana's offer to spend some time in Cuero."

"Mamá." Protesting, Catarina stirred the beans vigorously, scraping the bottom of the pot to prevent scorching. "You need me here."

"Not if you can't stop mooning over . . ." Exasperated, Tina flung her hands in the air. "You know how the señor and señora feel about you and their . . ." Again words failed her. Catarina didn't need to hear them spoken to grasp the situation.

Despair rose like steam inside her. *Cat's got her tongue, locked inside her throat; if she don't laugh . . .* But this was no laughing matter.

"Monte has been back two months, Mamá," she argued, "and I have done nothing to cause Señora Ballou alarm."

"Until today."

"Today? What did I do today?" Her nose actually twitched where he had touched it.

He touched me. I did nothing.

"You don't belong out there with the cowboys," Tina replied. Her tone had gentled, which made it harder to ignore than her previous belligerence. "Go call them to supper, *mi hija.*"

Outside Catarina banged the iron triangle harder than necessary. Perhaps she should move to Cuero to live with Tía Juana. Perhaps she should leave Ballou Hills. She had stayed this long because her mother's health was poor. Tina needed her help to keep up with the demands of cooking for two dozen ranch hands day in and day out.

Indeed, Catarina had positioned herself to take over when her mother could no longer carry on. Even Señora Ballou had said as much.

But that was before Monte returned. Monte, her childhood playmate. Her first, and only, love. As the only children at Ballou Hills, they had been inseparable. Monte taught her to ride, to shoot . . .

Cat's got her tongue. . . Monte taught her to laugh . . . and to cry . . .

"Whatcha tryin' to do, Cat, call cows from the back forty?"

At Skeeter's question, Catarina stopped banging the triangle. Her mind returned fuzzily to the present.

Hungry cowboys filed into the dining hall and took their places at the long plank tables where Catarina had already set out large bowls of beans and potatoes and platters piled high with three-inch steaks. The next half hour was so full she had little time to think. Then things settled down. Fetching the coffeepot from the kitchen, she began to refill the cowboys' cups.

Table talk centered around the major event of the day: Texan, or more precisely, whether Monte could ride the outlaw stallion in the upcoming Pecos rodeo. Odds seemed pretty evenly divided.

The rodeo, scheduled as the main event for the annual week-long Fourth of July festivities, would be the first time cowboys from area ranches performed their skills in front of an audience. No one remembered exactly whose idea it was to begin with, but everyone west of the Pecos was excited about it. Plans for the rodeo had taken precedence over just about everything else for the last three months.

With Monte's father, Matthew Ballou, and Stewart Krandall, of the neighboring Jagged Skyline Ranch, serving as co-chairmen, the event had been organized as well as any political organization. Various ranches were placed in charge of the chosen events: steer wrestling, calf roping, cutting horse competition, and of course, the highlight event—bronc riding.

Tina Ramériz was in charge of the food, and she and Catarina had spent long hours coordinating menus with other ranch cooks. A separate committee, made up of ranch wives and daughters, headed the Rodeo Ball, which would follow the rodeo the night of July Fourth.

Tina had even found time to make Catarina a special gown for the occasion, although most of Catarina's time would be spent cooking and serving.

Now, she didn't even want to go to Pecos. She didn't want to hear about the rodeo again. She didn't want to think about Monte riding—or trying to ride—an outlaw horse they called Texan. But on this night she would have had to be standing on the other side of El Capitán, fifty miles west, not to hear the cowboys' banter.

"Tell you what I'd do, Monte, were it me . . ."

"I know your ol' man has rules against spurring in front of the cinch," Baldy was saying, "but you rake a couple of rowels across that ol' hoss's shoulders and he'll likely settle down some."

Comments up and down the table ranged from scoffs to downright ridicule.

"What kinda man talks like that?" Pee Wee wanted to know. Skeeter quieted down the table with a general fear.

"Frankly, boys, I'm bettin' ol' Texan'll turn out to be one of those hosses that cain't be rode."

"Could be you're right, Skeet." This from Tipper. "We all gotta remember what ol' Texan did to Curly Red."

Catarina felt her insides go limp. She watched Monte take a bite of his rolled tortilla, set it aside, and favor the speaker.

"We're not gonna think about Curly Red, Tip."

Silence fell over the naturally gregarious crowd. Each cowboy studied his plate, as if eating were the most important thing on his mind. Only Monte remained relaxed. He cut a bite of steak, stuck it in his mouth, and reached for his cup.

Without a moment's thought, Catarina jerked it away from him. Only then did she realize that her hands were shaking so badly she couldn't pour coffee into it. Disconcerted, she slammed first the cup, then the coffee pot, back on the table.

"Oh, no," she rebuked. "Don't think about Curly Red. Texan just bunged him up a bit, broke a leg, a collarbone, and an arm. Maybe he'll finish you off."

"Finish me off?" Monte held her attention, his brows knit over those deep-set crystal-blue eyes. His lips rested softly closed, and the sight did squiggly things to her stomach. She felt like he had poured the pot full of scalding coffee down her throat. When it hit the writhing mass in the pit of her stomach, fire flashed through her.

Monte finished his question with a hee-haw. "Listen to that, boys. Cat's found her tongue."

Too angry to retort, she clamped her lips closed again.

"Catarina," came Tina's call from the kitchen. "We're out of tortillas, *hija*. Quickly, now. *Andale*."

Embarrassment fueled her anger and fear. Just as she picked up the coffee pot and turned to leave, Monte slapped her playfully on the behind.

"Don't worry 'bout me, darlin'. I'm not fixin' to get myself throwed in any man's corral."

The masa mixture was cold and wet. Catarina slapped it angrily between her palms, shaping circle after circle of raw tortillas. When enough were made, she slammed them one by one onto the hot griddle where they sizzled a few minutes on each side before she transferred them to a heated platter and covered them with a clean, damp towel.

Stirring up a new batch, Catarina had just pinched off a ball of it when Monte came into the kitchen.

"Cat?"

Ignoring him, she strove to concentrate on the ball of wet dough, which she slapped from one palm to the other. He came to stand before her.

"Hey, Cat. Look here."

To avoid looking into those blue eyes, she turned away. But he caught her by the shoulder.

"If I embarrassed you, I'm sorry."

Tense, she held her ground. Inside she burned.

"Come on, Cat. Let me apologize."

Her jaws ached with a wholly different sensation. Her spine sizzled. She felt tears well.

"I'm not gonna get myself killed, Cat."

She slapped the dough. From sheer habit, she formed a round, flat raw tortilla. She struggled to concentrate on the dough, on her job. Tossing the tortilla to the griddle, she pinched off another ball of dough and began the process all over again. Cowboys could eat their weight in fresh tortillas. And with two dozen to feed . . .

Monte persisted. "Darnit, Cat. Stop that a minute and talk to me. I didn't mean to embarrass you. I'm not gonna get myself killed. What else can I say? I'm glad you . . . I mean, I appreciate your concern."

Red-hot anger seemed to leap from the griddle when she started to toss the tortilla on it. Then something else seized her. Neither anger nor fear, she recognized it as humiliation. The feeling weighted heavily on her arms. Why had Monte returned? Why hadn't she been forewarned? Why hadn't she left Ballou Hills long ago?

Of a sudden, she turned. Seeing his apologetic expression, her humiliation grew. "I don't want your appreciation, Monte Ballou. Or your apology. And I don't care whether you get killed ten times over."

Later she thought it must have been the astonished look on his face, or perhaps the way his strong chin dimpled, or the way his blue eyes penetrated hers, taking in her true meaning, that drove her. At the time, however, her only thought was to escape. But could she, ever?

Staring at that face, a face she had tried desperately to avoid during the two months since he'd returned, a face that had haunted her dreams for the past six years, she suddenly despised it. And its owner. Yes, she hated . . .

Hated . . . With trembling arms and a mighty thrust she flung the perfect wet tortilla into his earnest face. Then she fled through the rear kitchen door.

It wasn't the first time Monte had embarrassed Catarina; although she had no way of knowing whether he was aware of the first. By the time his mother demanded the return of her garnet ring, Monte had been on his way to school in St. Louis. Why hadn't he stayed away forever?

The answer was simple. Because Ballou Hills Ranch was his home. At over three thousand feet above sea level, the ranch enjoyed a well-balanced climate. While summer days were hot to the point of frying eggs on the front steps, with sunset, coolness crept down from the mountains, rejuvenating all living things.

Tonight Catarina didn't feel the coolness. She ran until she reached the horse-trough well, a good thirty yards from the kitchen. Oblivious to the star-studded velvety sky, she buried her face in her hands and drew shallow breaths. Why was she such a fool? Why hadn't she kept her big mouth shut?

Why hadn't she left Ballou Hills before Monte returned?

Why had he returned? The rumor was much too probable to ignore—that he'd returned to court and wed Suzanna Krandall, daughter of Stewart Krandall, whose ranch bordered Ballou Hills to the east.

Suzanna, another childhood friend. Blond and beautiful even then, Zanna had not let her china-doll looks interfere with the rough-and-tumble life of ranch children. The times she visited Ballou Hills, she, Cat, and Monte had gotten into enough mischief for a dozen city children. Or so Señora Ballou had been known to say with a lilt to her voice.

The lilt in the señora's voice had died soon enough when she learned that instead of setting his cap for the respectable neighboring rancher's daughter, her son had chosen the daughter of their foreman and cook.

"We should have kept Catarina away from that boy," Catarina's mother had worried later, after they learned the truth and Monte had been sent away. "Now she's hurt, and our life here is sure to be ruined."

"She'll get over being hurt," her father insisted. "She's only thirteen, a child, a *niña.*"

At the time Catarina had not been able to interpret her mother's intense embrace, or the way Tina crooned, *"Mi hija. Ooooh, pobrecita. Mi hija."*

Now Tina's insistence that Catarina take up her aunt's offer to move to Cuero explained what Tina had known all along. Regardless of what her husband thought, childhood infatuation could grow into a woman's love.

Now nineteen, Catarina knew her mother had been right to worry—she would never get over Monte. He could marry Zanna Krandall, probably would marry Zanna, should marry Zanna.

Suzanna had been sent away to school, too, a few years later, to somewhere in the East. She was due to arrive back in time for the rodeo. It was the talk of the country.

Catarina's imagination created vivid mental images of her childhood friend now grown to womanhood. Once a tomboy like herself, Zanna was certain to be a lady through and through. She would be more blond and beautiful than ever. The curious side of Catarina wanted to see Zanna; but her serious side, where the primeval need for self-preservation resided, didn't want to come within a country mile of Monte's rumored intended. She never wanted to see them together, hear them . . .

Monte's hands on her shoulders caught Catarina unawares. Deep in thought, she hadn't even heard his spurs. Before she could get a grip on herself, he had turned her to face him.

"Cat? Are you crying?"

For a second too long Catarina stared into those blue eyes, now deep, almost black with the night. Mesmerized, she could not draw her eyes away.

When he questioned her again, she remained mute. She dared not speak. She tried not to shudder as the pads of his thumbs wiped tears from her cheeks. She felt the sticky masa on his fingers.

He grinned, then flung his hand into the night. Droplets of dough scattered. As though oblivious to his actions, he licked the remaining dough from his finger, then cleaned Catarina's cheek with it. *Is this a dream?* she wondered. *More likely a nightmare.*

"What's this all about, Cat?"

Dough still clung to his cheeks and eyebrows. She was tempted to wipe it away but dared not touch him. She pressed her lips together.

"Cat's got her tongue," he sang softly, "locked inside her throat. If she don't laugh, she's a-bound to choke."

His gentle teasing seared away her anger and a good deal of her embarrassment. "I hadn't thought about that song in forever."

"Me, neither," he admitted. Then he chuckled dangerously low in his throat. "But you gotta admit, it fits. I never realized how well."

"Maybe I just don't have anything to say."

"I think you have a lot to say," he responded. "You proved that at supper."

She drew a much too shallow breath. Already the night sky spun around her.

"Hold still," he said, taking her chin in two fingers. "Let me get this dough off. Dang if you didn't make a mess."

She smiled in spite of herself, but when he took out a handkerchief and tried to wipe her face, she took the cloth and did it herself. Although she was sorely tempted to clean up the mess she had made on his face, she slapped the handkerchief in his hand. Again, she had startled him.

"Whoa, Cat. What's gotten into you? You never used to be so touchy."

"You never used to try to kill yourself, either."

"I'm not going to kill myself." Using his handkerchief, he cleaned dough off his eyebrows while he spoke. She watched, unable not to. Expectancy grew insidiously inside her . . . along with anger.

"You won't have to. Texan will do it for you."

"No he won't." By now his handkerchief was covered with wet dough. Holding it by one corner, he shook it a time or two, then grimaced as he wadded it up and stuffed it in his pocket. She almost smiled, but the topic was too serious.

"No one's ridden that horse yet," she reminded him.

He cocked his head, arrogant even after being showered with masa. "I haven't tried."

"Did you leave your memory back East? What about today? Being thrown once doesn't count?"

He shrugged. "Not if you don't get hurt."

"How can you joke about it?"

"I'm not joking. Riding broncs is what I do. What we all do."

"Not your father."

"Not anymore," he corrected. "Papa broke his share of buckers in his early years. Now he has cowboys to do it."

"I take back my earlier question," she retorted. "It isn't your memory that's missing, it's your ability to reason. This isn't about breaking horses, and you know it."

Moonlight played off the band of white skin on his forehead where his Stetson had shielded it from the elements. His eyes gleamed with mischief.

"No? What is it about, Cat?"

"Pride."

"Pride?" He held up his hands in surrender. "Guilty as charged." When she didn't comment, he added, "Sure it's about pride. This is my job. I'm good at it."

Pride goeth before a fall, she wanted to say, but instead chose to remind him, "Curly Red was good, too."

He grinned. "Not good as me, darlin'."

She ignored the endearment, outwardly at least. Except for her skin, which seemed afire. She longed for him to touch her again, longed for him in a way that consumed her. And all he wanted to do was show his prowess by riding wild horses. Or getting himself killed by wild horses. "How many broncs have you ridden that're as mean as Texan?"

"Question is, how many bronc busters have tried to ride Texan who're as good as me?"

"You're arrogant, Monte Ballou. You know that? Arrogant. And it'll get you killed, or maimed for life."

He remained silent a moment too long for it to have not been the entertaining of a serious thought. Finally, he grinned that wicked grin. "Who's the best bronc rider you know, Cat?"

"You won't listen to reason, will you?"

"Come on, Cat, tell me. Who's the best?"

Failure settled over her like a black cloud. She could talk until she was blue in the face, and he wouldn't hear. Or heed.

"I know who *thinks* he's best."

This time it was Monte who didn't respond. Not in words. Silently, he lifted a hand and ran his fingers through loose strands of her curly black hair. The contact sent stars tingling across her scalp and down her spine. She wondered whether he sensed her reaction. How could he not?

Still without speaking, he licked his finger. "Yuk! Raw tortillas." He ran the wet tip of his finger down her nose. "I like mine cooked, darlin'."

It was a moment rife with possibilities. She stood paralyzed by her own insidious desire and sensed that he was held back by some war of his own. Every second that passed ticked with intensified pressure inside her head. But still she resisted making the first move.

Finally he dropped his finger, turned and walked away. She stared after him until he disappeared into the black shadows of the corral.

He was going to see Texan.

She knew that as surely as she knew he could never be persuaded to free the wild horse without trying to ride him in the big rodeo in Pecos.

And she knew what she had to do. Somehow, she had to save Monte from himself. Then and only then would she be free to leave Ballou Hills. Forever.

11

The following week Suzanna Krandall arrived at Ballou Hills, accompanied by her parents and a contingent of Ragged Sky cowboys.

"I got tired of hearing those boys claim to be able to whip up on your team, Matt," Stewart Krandall told Monte's father. "Thought we'd give 'em a little practice before the big rodeo."

Catarina wasn't sure whether to be glad or sorry. Six new witnesses increased the odds that Monte wouldn't be able to back down from riding Texan without losing face.

She, on the other hand, wasn't concerned about his face, but his life. More so every day. In the week since Monte announced his intention to ride the wild stallion in the rodeo, Texan had proved himself the outlaw he had been labeled. His nickering could be heard late at night, but still Monte insisted that no one go near him.

"I want him mean," he commented more than once.

Mean, the horse probably was, but Catarina sensed that determination and even fear had more to do with the violence the wild stallion wreaked on Ballou Hills. After he had almost thrashed his way out of his stall on two separate occasions, Monte designed a pen himself. Fashioned of ropes, it was meant to keep Texan safe from himself. So intricate was the design that it took every cowboy at the ranch to construct it.

"Figure we might all join the Navy after this," Skeeter Owens groused. "I'll pit knots against any ol' seadog."

Catarina wasn't interested in knots. She needed cohorts. One, at least. During the week she had approached one cowboy after the other, hoping to find one person who shared her fear and would be willing to buck the crowd.

Zanna Krandall represented Catarina's best chance to persuade Monte to forgo his foolish plan to ride Texan.

Zanna was a surprise. If she had learned sophisticated ways back East, she must have shed them in the month she'd been home. Instead of dainty slippers and multiple petticoats, she rode up to the Ballou Hills ranch house astride a powerful palomino stallion, which was as blond as she. Even Catarina caught her breath.

Always slender, Zanna had now filled out in all the right places. Her hair, if possible, was even blonder, even longer, even silkier. It was tied back with a length of bright red-dyed rawhide that matched her belt and was the only color on her otherwise no-nonsense riding garb—buckskin-colored pants, boots, Stetson, and vest, the latter worn over a starched white shirt.

Catarina felt a surge of pride and joy, combined with a sickness that flooded into every part of her system. A hoity-toity, sophisticated lady would have been much less of a threat for Monte's affections than this beautiful cowgirl.

"Papa wasn't telling the whole truth about why we rode over," Zanna replied now to her father's claim. Although definitely matured and more cultured than Catarina remembered, Zanna's voice reflected her heritage as a ranch woman, West Texas born and bred. "I'm the one who needs practice."

The hot summer breeze blew hotter, fanned by a captivating smile and Zanna's unaffected honesty. Not a male present gave the slightest indication that she wouldn't be welcome in the roping arena. No one voiced or otherwise gave a hint that she wouldn't be accepted as one of the boys.

Even though Zanna Krandall was definitely not one of the boys. When Monte stepped forward to give her a hand in dismounting, Catarina felt the sour sickness in her stomach turn to clabber. But Zanna brushed him away with a radiant smile and familiar giggle.

"When have I needed help to get off a horse, Monte Ballou?"

"Not since I've known you," he admitted good-naturedly.

Something incandescent and bright as the Milky Way on a clear summer night shimmered between them.

Then Zanna found Catarina.

"Cat!" Brushing past Monte, she flung herself into Catarina's arms. "My dear, dear friend. I've missed you!"

And Catarina could truthfully reply that she had missed Zanna. "It's been a long time."

"Too long. We have a lot of catching up to do." Zanna tilted her very pretty oval-shaped head. "Why didn't you answer my letters?"

Before Cat could reply, Monte took charge.

"Come on, everybody, let's go show Zanna and the Jagged Sky boys our secret weapon."

Enthusiastic whoops greeted this proposal, followed by muffled boasts and general bantering. Zanna looked quizzically to Catarina, and Catarina knew suddenly that she had an ally.

If the rumors were true, Zanna wouldn't be any more anxious than Catarina for Monte to get himself stomped to death by an outlaw horse.

"You too, Cat," Monte was saying. "Just because you're a doubter, we won't cull you." He grinned and Catarina's senses windmilled.

So she fell in step. How could she not? They strode across the clearing to the barn and beyond, to the rope corral where Texan was held captive. As they neared, the stallion peaked his little pointed ears, bowed his neck, and watched them approach with wild-eyed rage . . . or fear.

"Your secret weapon, huh?" Zanna's challenge held awe, or admiration, rather than ridicule.

"You bet," Monte replied. "Zanna, meet Texan, the meanest outlaw horse west of the Pecos."

Zanna studied the animal, who had begun to paw at the earth with his front hooves. After a few strokes, which filled the air with clouds of dust, he backed off with a hobbled sort of gait.

"Can he turn on a dime?" Zanna wanted to know.

"On a pinhead."

Zanna's concentrated expression gave way to a lovely, brilliant smile, and without warning, she snickered.

"I suppose that next, Monte Ballou, you're going to tell me that you intend to try to ride this magnificent animal in the rodeo?"

"Not try, Zanna. Ride. *R-I-D-E.* And *W-I-N.*"

And die, Catarina thought, more angry now than worried. The arrogance of this man amazed her. That her feelings for him had grown so strong amazed her even further. Why couldn't she forget him? Let him rot on the arena floor after Texan stomped the life out of him? Thank heavens Zanna was here. Zanna, her best hope—

Zanna winked at her, then turned her attention back to Monte. "You remember that secret game of two-card draw I won just before you disappeared?" Zanna asked him. As children they used to slip off behind the barn with a deck of Señor Ballou's playing cards. By the time Monte went away all three of them were fairly accomplished, but Zanna and Catarina knew enough to let Monte win more often than lose.

"Uh, yeah," Monte said, attempting to hide his lapsed memory with a grin. "If you say so."

"I never had a chance to collect my prize."

"So?" Monte challenged softly.

Too softly, Catarina thought, feeling again the magic simmer between them. Or did she, knowing the rumor that they were going to marry, imagine the attraction?

"So, I'll claim it now," Zanna was saying.

Monte raised a brow. Catarina held her breath. She knew what was coming. They'd been children together. If anyone was a bigger daredevil than Monte, it was Zanna. She might have been slender to the point of frailty, fair-skinned to the point of blistering without a bonnet, but Zanna as a child had been a risk-taker of the first order.

"I want to ride Texan, Monte." Zanna's request, voiced in a fervent tone that left no doubt of her sincerity, caused an intake of breath from those of the gathered cowboys who hadn't grown up with her.

"Why am I surprised?" Monte laughed.

"I'm serious, Monte."

"You're crazy."

No, you're both crazy, Catarina wanted to shout. But the voice of caution would not be heard here. With this turn of events, she doubted it ever would be.

"You really think you could ride him?" Monte challenged.

"I know I could, cowboy."

"You admitted you're rusty."

"I've got three weeks to practice."

"Roping, not riding killer broncs. Bustin' broncs is man's work."

"Man's work?"

"You bet, Zanna. And this bronc has my name on him. He's mine, darlin', ain't he, Cat?"

Catarina had listened to their bantering with a weakening heart. Not only had she lost the one person she thought she could count on as an ally—she chastised herself now for having forgotten so much about Zanna—but the evidence before her was as good as proof that the rumors were true.

The phrase "meant for each other" took on a whole new meaning. If ever two people were meant for each other, they were standing before her. Her two oldest friends, one of them, the man she loved. The man they both loved, judging from Zanna's beguiling expression.

Meant for each other. Zanna was not only Monte's social equal, which Catarina would never be, but Zanna was a cowgirl, fearless and cocky. And at this moment, no one standing within a mile radius of them could deny they were meant for each other.

"Come on, Cat," Monte urged. "Tell Zanna who's the best bronc rider in this whole dang country."

While Catarina struggled to find her voice, Zanna winked at her again. Then she gave Monte exactly the kind of high-and-mighty expression he deserved.

"We both know who claims to be best, don't we, Cat?"

"Cat! Dang, it's good to see a friendly face."

Catarina stood in the doorway to the austere hospital room where Curly Red recuperated from the trompling Texan had given him. She tried not to stare, but Curly looked even worse than she had imagined he would.

His left leg, encased from thigh to foot in a thick white cast, was suspended by a rope and pulley anchored on the ceiling. His right arm was also in a cast that went from shoulder to wrist. It was crooked at the elbow in an awkward angle and propped on pillows. His face was so pale his freckles seemed to have faded. His shock of curly red-gold hair was all that remained of the once-gregarious cowboy, and it was more matted than curly.

"You don't look so good," she said without thinking.

That morning Catarina had jumped at the chance to ride into Pecos with her parents. Señor Ballou had sent her father to check on the progress of the new arena, and since Tina needed supplies to feed the extra Jagged Sky crew for a few days, Raul decided to take the buckboard. Catarina saw this as her last opportunity to garner an ally in her quest to save Monte from himself.

Looking at Curly Red now, her spirits rose a measure. If anyone could persuade Monte of the foolishness of trying to ride Texan, it would be the mangled cowboy in the bed before her.

"Come on in, Cat." With his free hand, he swatted a fly toward the open window. "Catch me up on ranch gossip."

She blurted out the only thing on her mind. "Monte intends to ride Texan in the rodeo."

Curly didn't take a minute to reply. "Figured he would."

"Stop him, Curly. You know how dangerous that horse is."

"Me stop him? I couldn't stop him, Cat. Wouldn't try if I could. Somebody's gotta ride that outlaw."

"Somebody's going to get killed," she objected.

"Naw, don't think like that. Monte's 'bout the best buster there is out there."

"*About* isn't good enough."

Curly took his time answering. "You talk to him 'bout this?"

"He won't listen. Nobody will listen. Not even Zanna."

"Zanna's back? Hey, that's good news. What's she like? I've heard so much about that woman I almost dream about her."

You and others, Catarina thought bitterly. "She and the Jagged Sky riders are spending a few days at Ballou Hills, practicing for the rodeo. I'd forgotten how fearless she's always been. She tried to get Monte to let her ride Texan."

"Zanna Krandall? A woman? She's just pullin' ol' Monte's leg."

"You didn't know her growing up."

"What I've heard, she might could do it," Curly allowed. "Be a shame to mess up a pretty face, though."

"But not Monte's?"

Curly Red chuckled, then grinned. "Dang this ol' leg. Don't think it'll ever stop hurtin'."

"Yet you're willing to see one of your best friends ride the horse that did all this to you?"

"Willing? Wouldn't exactly put it that way. It's just what we do, Cat. You've been around the ranch long enough to know that."

She turned to the window to keep Curly from seeing the distress that flooded her eyes. Yes, she knew cowboys rode broncs. Taming broncs was the way they got enough saddle stock to run a ranch. Yes, she knew she was being silly, probably making a fool of herself.

But she didn't want Monte to get killed or maimed. She didn't want to come into a room like this and see him bound and swaddled, strung from the ceiling like a hunk of curing beef.

She didn't want him to die. It no longer mattered whether she could have him or not. That had never been an option. But why was she the only person to see the danger? To accept the danger? And to reject it?

"Look at it this way, Cat," Curly explained. "That ol' hoss's gotta be rode sometime. Monte's got a burr under his saddle blanket to ride him. Well, he ain't a-gonna be satisfied till he's tried it."

"He tried once. Last week."

"Texan throwed him?"

She nodded.

"Don't reckon it counts, less'n he was hurt some."

"He was hurt," she muttered to the dust-smudged windowpane. "He just doesn't realize it. Texan poisoned him with the deadliest of all diseases—the challenge to do something no one else can do."

She stood a moment, watching a roadrunner skitter across the road outside, gathering her wits. Curly wouldn't help. Why had she thought . . . ? Two horses rode into view.

Catarina felt herself grow warm. "Here he comes now," she told Curly. "Zanna's with him."

As though to punish herself, she watched the two horsemen approach the hitching rail, step down and hitch their mounts. Both were lithe and blond; the major differences were Zanna's curves and Monte's height. He rose half a head above her as they strode side by side up the walk.

Curly Red had followed her line of vision. He let out a weak whistle. "That Zanna Krandall? She's as comely as they say. Reckon she knows she's lassoed herself the wildest critter west of the Pecos?"

Catarina felt like she had tumbled out the window, or off the back of an outlaw stallion. A deep sorrow pierced her every time she heard Zanna and Monte spoken of as a couple, even though the rumors were undoubtedly true.

"Some fellers have all the luck," Curly was saying behind her. "If my folks had fixed me up at birth like that, it'd be my luck the child would grow up to be a crone. But look at ol' Monte—not only does he get a big ranch and a beautiful wife, but the best dang cowgirl around. She's gonna make him one hell of a ranch wife."

"Not if he kills himself on Texan," Catarina blurted out. "If Zanna intends to marry him, she ought to start by saving his life."

Overwrought, she mouthed a quick good-bye to Curly Red and rushed out, only to run smack-dab into Monte as he came up the stairs.

"Cat?" He caught her by the shoulders.

She struggled free, wriggled past him, and hurried away without speaking.

That night at supper, Monte changed the topic of conversation. Texan was no longer the center of attention; Catarina was. Before the cowboys had settled down good, Monte began teasing her.

"How was your visit to ol' Curly, Cat?" He had to call down the entire length of the table, to where Catarina set out heaping bowls of mashed potatoes. Tina followed with cream gravy.

Catarina ignored him. "I'll get the steaks, Mamá."

"Everything looks wonderful, Cat." Zanna inhaled a deep draft, a pleasurable expression on her face. "And smells heavenly."

"Thank you." Catarina was glad for the distraction. "Mamá deserves the credit."

"I'll bet you—"

"Hey, Cat"—this from Skeeter—"got your tongue?"

Others took up the chant.

"Locked inside your throat?"

"Hurry, let it out!"

"Or you're a-bound to choke!"

Ignoring the good-natured cowboys, she glared down the length of the table at Monte, jaws clenched, furious.

"Tell us about your visit to Curly," Monte prompted.

"He looked like he'd been run through Mamá's meat grinder," she retorted. Turning away, she headed for the kitchen, but before she could get there Tina met her with platters of steaks, which she thrust into Catarina's hands, leaving her no choice but to return to the table.

Monte continued relentlessly. "Since Cat's not inclined to tell you 'bout it, boys, reckon I'll have to. Ol' Cat here went to see Curly today. Three guesses what they talked about."

"Naw," Skeeter mocked, scratching his chin as though in thought. "Let me think now, couldn't a'been 'bout you ridin' ol' Texan?"

"You got it, Skeet."

"Dang, Cat," Carlos chimed in. "Can't you tell a feller's got his pride?"

"What good is pride without his life?" she challenged.

"I'm gonna show you, Cat, darlin'," Monte vowed. "Wait an' see. I'm gonna dedicate that ride to you."

The thought, spoken in jest she was sure, struck Catarina a wicked blow. Suddenly she had taken enough. Growing up on a ranch, she was as aware as anyone that ridicule and joking were a way of life. Everyone was fair game; and she had made herself a target by her relentless campaign. But suddenly she could take no more.

She wasn't sure why. The idea that she would forever be linked with this fatal ride was bad enough, but at the moment, Monte's calling her "darling" in such an offhand way, and in front of Zanna, seemed demeaning . . . and more . . . unbearable.

Darlin', darlin', darlin'. The word spun in her head. The table spun in her vision. As steadily as she could manage, she set the platter of steaks in front of Zanna, and fled. She walked, or thought she did, straight to the kitchen, then she ran. Through the kitchen and out the back door, like before.

And like before she soon heard the back door slam a second time. She cursed her stupidity. Had Monte come after her again? She wanted to disappear into the night, but there was no place to hide. She made it as far as the well, before a voice called after her.

"Wait up, Cat." It was Zanna.

Relief came instantly, but was brief. She didn't want to talk to Zanna. She didn't want to talk to anyone. She was sick and tired of talking and arguing and pleading . . . and pretending. She leaned against the well and felt the mortar cool her heated hands.

"Monte was a beast to tease you like that." Zanna came to a stop beside Catarina. "Someday he'll realize how fortunate he is to have a friend as concerned about his welfare as you are."

"If he lives that long."

When Zanna put a comforting arm around Catarina's shoulders, Catarina had to force herself not to pull away.

"He'll live through it, Cat."

"You're not worried?"

"Of course, I'm worried. Seeing Curly Red brought home the truth. You and I've both seen cowboys badly hurt riding broncs, but—"

"Then stop him, Zanna."

"I can't. You can't, either. We shouldn't even try, Cat. Carlos was right. This is much bigger than just riding a bronc. Texan is a symbol of strength and power. It's like, well, like knights slaying dragons."

"They didn't, Zanna. Dragons are fantasy; Texan is real."

"I know, but it's the same thing. A man has to have his pride, Cat."

"I know that," Catarina admitted reluctantly. "I don't understand it, but I realize it's a fact. Why can't they see that pride is no substitute for two good limbs, for an uninjured brain?"

"A man won't understand that. To a man . . . well, a man has to find that out for himself. You and I face a different challenge, Cat. We're going to be taking care of Monte Ballou for the rest of his life. Believe me, we'll make things a lot easier on ourselves if we allow him this period of . . . of freedom."

Catarina had stopped listening halfway back. "What do you mean, *we* are going to be taking care of him?"

"Haven't you heard?"

"The rumors of a pending marriage?" Forcing a smile, she turned to her friend of many years. "So they're true? He proposed?"

"Not proposed. In our situation, a proposal isn't required, although I'll admit I'd like to hear one."

Catarina was confused now. Had their parents proposed for them? What a dreadful way to have your life determined for you. "What does that have to do with me?" she questioned, hoping her true concerns were not obvious.

"That's the best part. Just today Mrs. Ballou reminded me that your family has traditionally worked here. Your father took his father's place as foreman. And you, dear Cat, will take your mother's place. We'll have to find you a husband to be foreman, just like your—''

Catarina heard only Zanna's claim of the best part, and it struck a sour chord. If it had been her, the best part would have been marrying Monte. But, of course, Zanna had always known it would happen. Then Zanna got her attention.

''I'm thinking maybe Carlos. How do you feel about Carlos? Is he a good enough cowboy to make a good foreman? Of course, Monte would ultimately decide—''

''Zanna.'' Catarina was surprised by her own gentleness. ''I will choose my own husband.''

Zanna laughed, lighthearted, unaware that she had just signed and sealed Catarina's lonely life. ''We are good friends, and a good thing. Ranch life is miserably lonely for a woman. Since my mother died so early, I didn't realize how lonely it is for women, but Mrs. Ballou confided that she would never have remained sane out here without the friendship of your mother.''

The friendship and the work, Catarina wanted to reply. But she would not spoil her friend's sunny outlook. Life could well do that in a very short time.

The following afternoon Catarina, cursing herself for being a glutton for punishment, ventured to the roping pens to watch the Ballou Hills cowboys compete with their Jagged Sky rivals.

Zanna was in the pen when Catarina arrived. She sat proud and beautiful, strong and courageous, atop her palomino stallion, Rhubarb. Pee Wee manned the gate between the two pens, which separated the roping arena from the calves waiting to be roped. All told, a couple of dozen cowboys ringed the arena, shouting encouragement.

Catarina thought she had slipped in unnoticed, until Monte appeared at her side.

''Who would've thought growing up that Zanna

Krandall would make such a fine cowboy?"

Words jumbled in Catarina's head and caught in her throat, so she just nodded and managed a feeble smile.

"Feels good, the three of us together again."

His camaraderie was confusing. Didn't he know what "everyone" knew? The thought that he might not know the rumor, combined with his low, confidential tone, was more dangerous to her than all his taunting and ridicule rolled into one. Lately, he was like that. In public he found any excuse to taunt her, but in private, which essentially they were now with the cowboys' attention focused on Zanna, he was open, gentle, as though he spoke with someone who really mattered.

She did matter to him, or she had. Catarina had never doubted that. That was what had gotten them in trouble in the first place. Six years ago, when he first realized she was a girl.

"Dang, Cat." He'd looked at her with that confused, baffled expression that always gave her heart a twitch. "I get all tongue-tied around you now."

They'd ridden out to a stock tank a couple of miles from the house. He had insisted on helping her remount the pinto pony he had taught her to ride. She could still feel his hands span the waist of her simple cotton skirt.

Instead of lifting her to the saddle, his hands had slipped a notch to settle on her hips. She had just realized she had hips, and was still a bit self-conscious. But when Monte touched her, a sizzling sensation rippled through her.

He had felt it, too. For he turned her around and they stood like statues. He'd looked her up and down. His expression had been a mixture of confusion and something that warmed her, but one for which she had no words.

Then without speaking, he had moved his face in a

self-conscious sort of way, touched her lips, and kissed her. Lips to lips. Quickly. No lingering.

Their eyes had spoken for them that day. Both were surprised. Neither had been prepared. Then he kissed her again.

This time his lids had narrowed over his blue eyes, as though he still couldn't figure out what was happening. To be truthful, she couldn't either. But from that day on, kissing became an obsession, for her and for him. It had gone on all summer. They fished in the pond, went swimming, rode horses. Every second they could steal away from duties, they spent together.

It went little beyond kissing, except for a bit of experimental touching. They were both young and willing, but still not fully conscious of the demands their bodies would soon make.

It was beside the pond one day in late July that Monte proposed to her. Catarina would never forget the day or the words . . . or the aftermath.

"When we get older, Cat, we're gonna get married," he had said.

"Only if you propose in the right way," she'd countered. Her aunt had gotten married the previous spring, and Catarina was completely smitten with romance and all its trappings.

"I'll do it right now," Monte responded, going down on one knee, taking her hands in his. "Will you marry me, Cat?"

"My name's not Cat."

"Same as."

"A proposal doesn't count unless you use the whole name."

"All right. Catarina Ramériz, will you marry—"

"That isn't my whole name."

"It isn't? How was I to know?"

"Repeat after me. Catarina Rosa María Josefina—"

"You're pulling my leg."

"No I'm not. If you want me to marry you, you'll have to ask all of me."

"When we get married, you'll have to change your name anyway, so I'll just change it now," he decided. Holding her hands again, he gazed intently into her eyes. "Catarina Ramériz, will you marry me and change your name to Catarina Ballou?"

"Sí, Monte. Now, kiss me."

Kissing was the best part for Catarina. That summer all she wanted to do was kiss Monte. But he had other concerns.

"I don't have a ring."

"You have plenty of time. We can't get married for ten years."

"Ten years? It'll be before then. But you need a ring now. An engagement ring, so everyone will know that you're my girl."

As it turned out, everyone did know.

The next day, Monte put a garnet and gold ring on her finger. It was too big, of course, but he also brought a roll of gauze and together they wrapped it to fit.

It was the best day of her life, for the future belonged to them.

Then, like a blizzard was wont to blow in unexpectedly from the north, freezing everything in sight, her world changed overnight.

The next day Monte vanished, although she didn't realize the truth of it at first. For twelve miserable hours it was as if he had never existed. He wasn't at breakfast; his horse remained untouched in the barn; his saddle in its place. He didn't appear at dinner, or even at supper. Later that night her parents explained.

"Monte has gone away to school," her mother responded to her incessant questioning.

"Without saying good-bye?"

"I'm certain he said good-bye to his parents."

"He didn't tell me good-bye." Even as tears welled in her throat, Catarina knew something inexorable had happened to her dreams. She cried herself to sleep that night and for many nights to come.

Later that first week, Señora Ballou came to the clothesline where Catarina was hanging out the wash.

"My dear Catarina, I believe Monte gave you something before he left that should be returned to his family."

Catarina didn't understand at first.

"The ring," the señora explained. "It's a garnet, my dear. It has been in my family many years. I shall pass it along to a granddaughter someday, or perhaps to a daughter-in-law, when Monte chooses a wife."

Monte has chosen a wife, Catarina cried inside. Looking back, she marveled that she had exercised such control. She did not question Señora Ballou, she did not object, she did not relate the truth to Monte's mother. The truth, that Monte had already chosen a wife; that Monte would return to her. That the grandchildren the señora awaited would be her children.

Neatly pinning the corner of sheet she held in her hand to the clothesline, she had lifted her left hand to study the ring on her finger. When she tore it off, it was as though a falling star had streaked through her. Bright and sparkling, it faded into complete and utter darkness as she placed the gold and garnet ring into the señora's outstretched palm.

During the six years that followed, Catarina received only scraps of news about Monte. After completing school, he was sent to run the Ballous' ranch in New Mexico.

Not that he never returned to Ballou Hills. He had not missed a holiday that Catarina could recall in all the six years. But Catarina hadn't been there to see him.

It took only one year for her to face the truth. Every time Monte was due to arrive home, Catarina was sent to visit her aunt in Cuero.

They were being kept apart. Now, suddenly, six years after he vanished from her life, Monte had returned to Ballou Hills without fanfare. Six years.

Was that the length of time it took an improper childhood romance to die?

For Monte, obviously, the answer was yes. For her, it would never die. And so she must leave. She knew that, now more than ever with the plans being made for her future—cooking and cleaning for the new Mr. and Mrs. Ballou. She wouldn't do that. She couldn't.

She couldn't cook for them and clean for them and wash the bedclothes where their children were conceived. The thought left her covered with cold perspiration, here in the midst of a West Texas summer day.

"Are you all right, Cat?" It was Monte. As though drugged, she pulled herself back to the present, to the corral.

A shout from Skeeter drew their attention. "Look at that Zanna ride!"

Shaking out her rope, Zanna formed a wide loop, which she twirled expertly above her head, while expertly guiding Rhubarb toward a mottled young calf with her knees.

"Ain't she the best dang cowboy west of the Pecos?"

Zanna let go of the loop. It sailed through the heat waves and dust, before dropping over the calf's head. Within a split second, Zanna had dismounted and raced toward the calf. Without a second thought, she fell to her knees in the boiling dust, pulled a length of rawhide from her hip pocket, and bound three of the calf's legs.

When she scrambled to her feet, triumphant, a cheer arose from the onlookers.

"Hell, Monte," Pee Wee called from his place beside the gate, "bet she could ride ol' Texan if she had half a chanc't."

"Fat chance," Monte replied beside Catarina.

She wondered whether he meant that he didn't want anyone but himself to ride Texan, or whether he would be afraid for Zanna to ride the outlaw.

Either way Catarina was the one left out. Out, where she had always really been. During the night she had allowed herself to recall the details of Monte's childhood proposal for the first time in years. Now she wondered whether he had known even then the future that had been planned for him.

When he got down on his knees that day on the rocky ground and proposed to Catarina, had he known that his wife was already chosen for him? That he was destined to marry Zanna, their friend?

He hadn't proposed to Zanna. But that was of no consequence. Zanna had said so herself. No consequence at all.

Then Catarina knew what she would do. And how she would do it. Before she left Ballou Hills forever.

"I don't mean I'll try to tame Texan," Catarina explained to her grandfather, Este Raméríz, when he immediately objected to her plan.

The idea had been simmering in the back of Catarina's brain ever since Zanna mentioned the Raméríz family's heritage at Ballou Hills. With no place else to turn, it had formed into the last possible if improbable solution. After supper that evening, Catarina sought out her grandfather. One look at her beloved Papacito, old before his time, an invalid from the numerous bone breaks suffered during his long cowboying career, strengthened her resolve to save Monte from the outlaw stallion.

"I just want to take the killer edge off him," she insisted.

In his day Esteban Raméríz, shortened in ranch-country fashion to Este, had been the leading horse-gentler west of the Pecos. Ranchers from near and far regularly depended on his skills to gentle a horse when spurs and whips failed to work. Generally, spurs and whips made a horse meaner, Este believed.

Although he resisted adamantly when Catarina approached him for help with the outlaw stallion, she finally persuaded him with the promise, "I won't get in the pen with Texan, Papacito."

"I don't reckon it'll hurt you to walk around the outside of the corral," he finally allowed.

"It won't do much good, either," she objected.

"More than you think. You must remember, *hijita,* a wild horse, any wild animal, for that matter, uses all his senses for protection."

"Then I know it won't work," Catarina lamented. "Texan will never look at me and see Monte."

"Sight may be the least important," Este advised. "Wild horses are generally so frightened of humans their eyes don't focus. You've heard of wild-eyed fear?"

"*Sí.*"

"Smell, touch, sound—those are the senses you can control."

"The scent, I can do," she said, confidence returning. "Today I removed Monte's shirt, duckins, and socks from the laundry before Mamá and I do the wash tomorrow."

"Excellent," the old man said with a formal nod.

Her grandfather's approval added another measure of confidence. Then she considered the other senses. "Touch? How can I touch him from outside?"

"Through the ropes," her grandfather replied.

"Once that wild stallion gets used to your scent, he will allow you to reach through the ropes and touch him."

"My hands are half the size of Monte's."

"*Sí,* but next you will introduce the hackamore. That will feel the same regardless of who puts it on him. You must use Señor Monte's hackamore."

"But how? I mean, without getting into the pen?"

"You can reach through. By the time you introduce reins, Texan will be standing patiently beside you."

Catarina doubted that. "How long should it take, Papacito?"

"You must have patience, *hijita.* And you must remember your goal. You are not trying to tame the stallion, but only to take the edge off him."

The killer edge.

During the hour that followed, Old Este instructed Catarina in a technique she had heard some call magic.

"That ol' Este," they would say, "he's got magic in those hands."

The more she heard from him now, the more absurd she felt to even think she could succeed in such an undertaking.

"I am sorry to be of no use to you, *hijita,*" he bemoaned once, patting his infirm legs with bony fingers, which he then brushed across the lids of his failing eyes.

"You have been of great help, Grandfather." But one thing still bothered her. "Even if I croon low, as you have instructed, my voice will never sound like Monte's."

"Then we must find another way." And Este again instructed Catarina how to leap another obstacle on this uncertain path she had set for herself. If it weren't a life they were talking about, Monte's life, she would not attempt such an impossible task.

"You must promise me something else, *hijita.*"

"Que es, Papacito?"

"Do not risk your life with that horse. He can hurt you even through the ropes. Pay close attention. Learn to read his thoughts before he acts upon them. It will be especially difficult in the dark of night." Then he called on the most powerful argument of all. "I can see you truly care for this young gringo. You would not want him to go through a long life with your blood on his conscience. Promise me you will abandon the project the moment you sense danger."

"I promise, Grandfather."

"Then go." He kissed her forehead when she leaned over his chair. *"Vaya con Dios, mi hijita."*

"Gracias, Papacito."

By the time Catarina left her grandfather's little adobe house a silvery half-moon had risen in the huge dome of black sky. Glancing at it, she was struck by the foolishness of her plan. She had as much chance of sprouting wings and flying to the moon as she did taming Texan.

Papacito's method was good, he had worked it countless times, but the method and even her inexperience were not the only obstacles. Her very nature held her back.

For Catarina and Monte were opposites in more than their cultural heritage and their social positions. Monte was naturally gregarious, whereas Catarina was quiet and retiring. It went against her nature to step forward and make the first move in any situation. Especially this thing she was about to do.

But there was no other way. She had exhausted all other paths to saving Monte from his own pride. This plan must work; but for it to work, she must step forward and make it happen.

She headed straight for the corral, although her steps

were admittedly shaky. Her great determination fought her innate reticence, and she wasn't certain which would win. Then she arrived and found Monte exactly where she had expected.

The jolt of seeing him combined with the clandestine nature of her plan, and stars seemed to explode inside her.

He stood exactly where he had stood this time every night since he decided to ride Texan—back in the shadow of the stable watching the outlaw horse. Upwind, of course, so Texan wouldn't become accustomed to his scent. It was up to Catarina to use this habit for her own purposes.

Uncertainty washed over her. She fought the urge to turn and run. How could she ever be so bold? Why had she ever imagined she could do this?

Approaching him, she felt again the strong natural tug of expectancy that had sprung poignantly to life the moment she heard he was returning to Ballou Hills; the same insidious yearning she felt every time she came within a country mile of him. By now this feeling had intensified to the point that she felt continually consumed by it; her arms turned to jelly and her brain spun in a dizzying kaleidoscope of fascination and anticipation and despair.

The color of darkness, this despair threatened to overtake her more vibrant emotions. Since she had learned of his family's plans for him, the darkness had spread inside Catarina. High noon more resembled midnight for her.

Then he glanced up and she felt like the moon had suddenly become full and shone directly on them. She stopped in her tracks. The world seemed to stop, too, and her heart. In the tense stillness, neither she nor Monte moved.

His face was in shadow, but the upward tilt of his

strong jaw was all she needed to visualize the rest. His blue eyes would be staring at her; his thoughts, even if she could see his expression, would be unreadable. Serious.

It struck her then that Monte had changed in that regard. Since returning, his demeanor had been unusually somber. A strange seriousness pervaded even his joking and unmerciful teasing.

She wondered what had happened to him in the six years they were apart to bring on such somberness. She knew from whence her own had sprung. She entertained no fleeting hope that Monte's had been brought about by the same thing.

"You come to badger me 'bout Texan?" His query was spoken softly and carried no trace of displeasure.

"No."

"Given up, have you?"

"Yes," she lied quietly.

"You've seen the error of your ways?"

"No. I don't see any advantage to making an idiot of myself for no gain."

He chuckled softly. "You always were able to cut to the meat of the matter."

Stifling every tendency to fidget, shuffle her feet, clasp her hands, or just plain turn and run, Catarina held her ground. Moments passed while she summoned her nerve and tried to think of a way to proceed. Finally, she came right out and asked.

"Will you walk over to the pen with me?"

His silence told her she had taken him off guard. Caution advised stepping gently.

"I, uh, Zanna said I shouldn't be afraid. I thought if I could stand close to him, maybe I could conquer my fear."

Unaccustomed to lying, she wondered whether he could tell. At length he pushed away from the post and came toward her. It took all her willpower to stand her ground.

She wanted to run from him.

At that moment she was more afraid of Monte than she was of Texan—more precisely, of her reaction to Monte. She had never felt anything as strong as this pull toward him; it fairly incapacitated her. It was a pull fashioned from that dark skein of despair.

If she couldn't be with him forever and ever, she never wanted to stand close to him again. He stopped within inches of her. She could see his features clearly now—his brush-stroke straight brows, his perfect nose, his flat cheeks, strong jaw. The only things she couldn't see were his eyes, which were in shadow, and his remarkable lips, which were pursed inward.

"You always did have the guts of ten men, Cat."

"Hardly," she whispered. "I just, well, don't you think I've made a big enough fool of myself?"

"Yeah, I suppose you have."

"Help me conquer my fear of Texan, and I'll keep my mouth shut from now on."

"It's a deal. Come on. I'll walk you over there. But just for a minute. Don't want ol' Texan to get used to me."

Guilt tied her tongue. Then Monte touched her and the spread of liquid heat through her body made things infinitely worse. She was glad to have guilty feelings to contend with.

When she failed to move forward, Monte nudged her again. "What's the matter, Cat? Getting cold feet?"

Determinedly, she stepped ahead of him, away from him.

"Oh, I see. You're anxious."

"No." Breathless, she knew her only hope was to talk. "I'm not anxious. It's just . . . necessary."

"Necessary?" By the time they reached the rope

corral, Texan, who had watched their approach warily, had bolted for the other side.

"If you want to get close to this critter, we'll have to climb the fence."

"No!"

He chuckled.

"Isn't there another way?" When he failed to respond, she tried again. "I know. Let's walk around."

"Won't do any good. He'll bolt ahead of us."

She wondered whether Texan could hear them talking as he ran around the pen. That was all she wanted tonight. For Texan to hear their voices, to become accustomed to their voices and not associate fear with them. If it took bolting . . .

"That's what you want, isn't it? For him to be afraid of you?"

Before she realized it, he had stopped and turned her by her shoulders.

"What's this all about?"

"I told you. I have a fear. I need to conquer it."

"Like the time you jumped in the Pecos? Before you could swim?"

"I could swim when I came out," she challenged softly.

"Yeah."

His husky reminder set her skin afire. This was not the topic she had planned to use to keep him talking.

"I remember it well," he said, a whisper now. "To this day I can't remember ever being more frightened."

"Frightened? You?"

"You knew that."

"Well, maybe at the time." Yes, she had known at the time how frightened he was. He'd jumped in, fully clothed, boots and all. But instead of hauling her out, he taught her to float.

The memory floated now, through her mind, and she

imagined through his, through her veins, through her heart. As badly as she wanted him to talk, she knew she couldn't bear to speak of so intimate a topic.

"We were kids, Monte. Just kids and . . ."

"And you nearly killed yourself."

"I didn't. You saved me, like always." The words slipped out. She regretted them the moment she spoke them. She could not allow herself to remember the past, certainly not standing this close to Monte.

"Like you're trying to save me now?" he quizzed.

Try as she might she couldn't deny it. She nodded, weak with the want of something she shouldn't even think about. Determinedly, she turned her gaze away from him, to the center of the pen, where the black horse stood eyeing them, motionless, ready to bolt at their slightest movement, frightened, skittish.

Like she was.

Monte took her chin in two fingers and turned her face toward him. "Look at me, Cat. I know how you feel."

When she tried to protest, he wouldn't allow it. "I know how you feel. I feel that way, too."

Catarina felt her knees turn to jelly and thought for sure they would give way. She envisioned herself hanging by her chin from his fingertips. It was an absurd, farcical image that almost dispelled the tension between them. Until he continued.

"We feel the same way."

Oh, no, Monte, she thought. *No we don't. If we felt the same way, you wouldn't be marrying Zanna. You wouldn't have stayed away six long years.*

"You can't grow up best friends," he persisted, "and not care about each other. We were best friends, Cat. You and me. Zanna was third. Day in and day out, it was us, you and me. Best friends. It'll always be that way. That's why it's important for you to know that I honestly, truly appreciate what you've been trying to do."

She doubted that, but instead of reacting in anger as she had a few days ago, she stood her ground. The truth was not only ominous, but terrible. It sealed her fate as nothing else could have. She would not, could not, remain at Ballou Hills and pretend to be Monte's best friend and Zanna's best friend, socially removed, of course.

She wouldn't attend their parties, she would serve them. She wouldn't eat at their table, she would cook their meals. She would be their maid, who came and went through the back door and listened to their woes and their joys while cooking and cleaning and ironing their clothes.

No, Monte didn't understand, not by a long shot. He had just admitted it.

"Come on, Cat. We'd best get on back."

"Go ahead," she told him. "I need a little more fresh air. That kitchen can get pretty hot this time of year."

"Yeah, I can imagine. Well, good night. Glad we've come to this understanding. Don't you worry anymore. I won't go getting myself killed on that ol' hoss. We've got a lot of living left to do. Both of us."

"All three of us."

"You bet."

"But not together," she whispered after he had walked away.

In the following weeks, Catarina carried out her plan with single intent: to protect Monte from the outlaw horse before leaving for Cuero to live with her aunt. She avoided Monte as though he carried the plague instead of her broken heart.

Night after night, she waited in the shadows until he left his vigil upwind from the pen where Texan awaited his role in the big contest. It was this role Catarina attempted to change.

The first night was the hardest. As soon as Monte was out of sight, she hurried to the tack room where she unwrapped the bundle she carried in a gunny sack. Monte's shirt and pants, snatched from the laundry earlier. Putting them on resulted in unexpected anguish. Even though she wore her own chemise and pantalets under them, the idea of being inside Monte's clothes, which still contained his scent, which had touched his body in the most intimate places, stirred such insidious yearnings in her that she considered calling the whole thing off.

But then she remembered her cause. To protect Monte from Texan—or rather to protect Monte from himself. So she took his work Stetson from its peg beside his saddle and tack, and headed for the pen.

It took three nights for Texan not to bolt to the other side of the rope corral when she approached. That the frightened horse finally stood still for her didn't mean she had her grandfather's gift, certainly not to the degree he had it, but that she followed his instructions diligently.

Each night she took several lumps of raw sugar and as she spoke softly, calling, "Texan boy, shush, Texan, Texan boy, Texan, come get some sugar," she crumbled the lumps of sugar on the ground just inside the pen.

When her grandfather suggested this action, she had objected. What if Texan wouldn't eat the sugar? What if Monte or some other cowboy found it the next morning?

"One thing a wild horse shares with his civilized brothers is curiosity. After you leave, ol' Texan will come over and investigate. He'll eat that sugar and want some more. In three nights, he'll be curious about you. He'll still be frightened, so be wary. But three nights and he'll come to you."

And he did. Catarina wasn't prepared for the thrill of seeing the powerful, sleek wild horse approach her, halting step by halting step. The fourth night, she petted his nose and he bolted. The fifth night she petted his nose and he stood still. Although he shook like a leaf in autumn, he stood and took her hand and she felt a power born of kinship. They had a long way to go before fear could be transformed to trust, but Texan had taken a chance on her. And she measured up.

Since she didn't intend to tame the stallion, just take the killer edge off him, as she'd told her grandfather, she wouldn't be required to get into the corral, but from the time Texan stood still and let her pat his nose, the temptation to do so grew.

At the same time another feeling began to develop within her—a sense of connectedness between herself and the horse . . . and Monte. She didn't actually think, *If I can't touch Monte, I'll touch Texan.* But in a sense this became the issue. *If I can't have Monte, I'll have Texan. If I can't be close to Monte, I can be close to Texan.*

And in those jumbled half-formed thoughts was born the awareness of how Monte felt about Texan, because she too became obsessed with this magnificent animal. Of course, Monte wanted to conquer the horse, while Catarina wanted to tame him, but wasn't that the same?

No, she insisted. She did not want to tame Texan. That wasn't her intent. She merely wanted to take the killer edge off him.

At the beginning of the second week after she began working with Texan, which would be the last week she had to accomplish her goal, she introduced Monte's bridle. It took a couple of nights, and again, it was Texan's innate curiosity that solved the problem. Instead of slipping the bit into his mouth, she rubbed it over his broad nose, gently, up and down, down and up, allowing him time to watch moonlight glance off the traces, allowing him to nose and smell, even to taste the leather.

The following night her defenses broke down, or was it her need that became too great to resist? Whatever the impetus, Catarina climbed into the pen. Texan's only reaction was to stiffen his legs.

"Be careful of those hind legs," her grandfather had warned. "That horse, any horse, can turn on a cent and kick out at you at the same time. A wild lead stallion owes his position in the herd to his agility as much as to anything else. He's cunning, clever, and mean."

She was careful. With flight foremost in her mind, she reached for his nose, stroked it, then tentatively patted his neck, then his withers. Only after he became fairly comfortable with that did she try to touch his back. It took another two nights.

She had lugged Monte's bridle and saddle blanket out with her. After letting Texan nose the blanket, she rubbed it lightly over his back, then laid it on top, holding it in place with a gentle touch.

By the time she finished that night, joy overwhelmed her. Next she would get the bit in his mouth. Once or twice, no more, just enough that when Monte did the same in the rodeo arena, Texan wouldn't lose his wits. Nothing more. Just take the edge off.

With that reminder, she crawled out of the pen, dropped the saddle blanket on the ground, and stood there a moment, admiring the magnificent stallion. "Good night, Texan," she whispered softly. "Until tomorrow."

She had just reached to touch him on the nose, when steps sounded behind her.

"So!" At Monte's call, Texan bolted. And Catarina wanted to, as well.

How long had Monte been standing there? Had he seen her in the pen? Had he seen her lay the saddle blanket on Texan's back?

He caught her by the shoulders and spun her around. "Change of heart, huh? Some change of heart—from trusted friend to liar."

Her heart leaped to her throat. He was mad, no doubt about that. She had never seen him so mad. *He's been gone six years,* she reminded herself. *She didn't know the man he had become.*

She might love him, but she didn't know him.

"Of all people," he was saying, "I would never have believed I couldn't trust you, Cat."

She heard something else in his voice now, and it sounded to her trained ears very much like despair. Still she had nothing to say. Regardless what he thought, lies didn't come easy to her, and the truth could not be spoken. When she tried to step away, he tightened his hold.

His hands bit into her arms, and for a moment she thought he might shake her, but at length, he sighed and shook his head instead. Tears welled in her eyes. She felt like the worst kind of ogre.

It shouldn't matter, she argued. If she could save his life, it didn't matter what he thought about her. But it did matter. She didn't want to disappoint him. She wanted to please him. How could she leave here with animosity between them?

How could she not?

Without warning, he drew her to his chest and held her there. His heart throbbed against her shoulder. She wasn't sure hers could beat anymore at any speed.

"You crazy woman," he whispered into her hair. His hold tightened, and she felt herself spinning, but not out of control, for he held her. Tightly. Securely.

She felt safe and right. She never wanted to move.

"You could have been killed," he muttered. "That horse is a dangerous animal. He could kill you even through the ropes, Cat."

Drawing her back, he looked in her eyes and she saw only concern. "You scared the life out of me."

Relief struggled for a hold on her senses. He hadn't seen her in the pen. Surely. Otherwise he would have known Texan hadn't threatened her. He would have known she was safe.

"Dangit, Cat." Expelling a heavy breath, he shook his head for a moment, as though silenced by the horror of his thoughts. "Promise me you won't come near this pen again."

She pursed her lips. It was then he noticed her clothing.

"What's this?" He picked a handful of his shirt, nipping her breast in the process. Acknowledgment passed over his face at the same time she realized what he touched. In that sizzling instant he moved his fingers.

"I don't mean that," he mumbled from somewhere deep in his throat. The silence became heavy and thick, and hot.

Catarina felt her jaws tighten and her cheeks burn. Deep down low an insidious expectancy began to strum, stunning her. Her arms quivered and her skin felt like he had torched them, the way cowboys set prickly pear afire to burn away thorns for cattle food in winter.

Taking in her attire, Monte tried to smile. She watched his lips quiver, then give up. "You crazy woman." He drew her close again. "You crazy, crazy woman. No one's ever cared this much about me before."

No one else ever will, she thought suddenly. She knew he could feel her trembling, the erratic beat of her heart, but for the longest time she didn't know what to do about it. Finally, she found the courage to break the embrace.

"You're just afraid I'll ruin your chance to kill yourself at the big rodeo," she charged.

His gaze penetrated the darkness to capture hers. At length, he laughed. It was a strained, throaty laugh, nothing like the easy, jovial laughter for which he was known far and wide. She tried not to read a single thing into it. For nothing she could think of, or nothing he could think of, for that matter, would change the life set out for them by his and Zanna's parents. When they were young.

Without breaking the spell, Monte lifted a forefinger to his lips, kissed it, and swiped it down her nose. She froze in place.

"Not a chance, darlin'. I'm gonna ride that hoss and dedicate it to you."

Curly Red returned to Ballou Hills the next day, one arm in a sling, one leg in a cast. He had a difficult time hobbling around on one good leg and one crutch. If Catarina's plans had been altered when Monte caught her with Texan, seeing Curly Red's condition restored her determination to tame Texan. No, not tame. To take the killer edge off.

She needed one or two more sessions with Texan to feel comfortable that her work had succeeded. Not that she would feel anything but fright when Monte stepped onto the animal, but she had to finish the project to ease the outlaw's fear, if not her own.

At supper that night she almost changed her mind. Besides the joyous homecoming for Curly Red, Zanna and the Jagged Sky cowboys were leaving for home the following morning. Supper was a celebration. Talk centered on Texan, with Curly Red giving Monte advice and the Jagged Sky crowd predicting he would get his head busted open all over the new arena floor.

Catarina served dessert, applesauce cake, without a word, and had just brought the coffeepot to refill cups, when Curly Red piped up.

"Hey, Cat, what'd you have to say 'bout all this? You still on your crusade to save ol' Monte's worthless hide?"

Catarina had already made up her mind to respond to any such comment with an evasive remark about how she was through making a fool of herself. But before she could do more than stammer, Monte jumped down Curly Red's throat.

"Shut your mouth, Curly."

A stunned silence followed Monte's demand. Every pair of eyes turned to Monte. His comment hung in the air like a question.

"Cat's got feelings, too," he charged. "So get off her back, all of you." His gaze held hers for a split second, before he turned to the cake.

She reached the kitchen before she took a single breath. He'd never, ever taken up for her. Since he'd been back, all he'd done in front of the others was to tease her. He had been the most unmerciful of all. But now . . .

His changed nature somehow made it even more imperative that she protect him from his own arrogance. More imperative, yet at the same time more difficult to go against his wishes. That night, she approached Texan expecting Monte to catch her at any moment.

The next morning she wondered why it mattered so much to her. After breakfast the Jagged Sky cowboys led their horses out of the stable, while the Ballou Hills bunch stood around taunting them.

"See you in Pecos."

"You bet. I'll see you on the corral floor."

"How much you givin' on Monte and that outlaw hoss?"

"Half a month's pay."

"Dang, I'll give a year's pay, an' throw in my cootie cage."

"Where is ol' Monte, anyhow?"

"And Zanna?"

Snickers followed the last questions, and Catarina experienced a sudden sickening in her stomach. Consumed by a morbid curiosity that rivaled Texan's, she headed for the stable, where she hadn't far to look to see them standing in each other's arms. Well, sort of.

Zanna's arms were thrown around Monte's neck, while his hands were anchored tentatively—Catarina thought—to either side of her waist. But there was nothing tentative about the kiss they exchanged.

Grateful for the foresight that had kept her from barging through the darkened corridor of the stable, Catarina quickly backed away and fled to the kitchen, where she busied herself collecting plates and cups and chastising herself for her very real and deep hurt.

You've known it all along, she admonished herself. But knowing and seeing were different things. As different as the domesticated pinto pony she rode as a child was from the outlaw called Texan.

That night she almost persuaded herself not to go to Texan's pen. Almost but not quite, for the chore she had set for herself was unfinished. She'd known when she began that her only objective was to protect Monte. And she had known she was protecting him for Zanna Krandall.

But that night, when she stepped into the tack room with her bundle of clothes wrapped in a gunny sack, Monte was waiting for her.

He leaned against the wall beside the carved wooden

tree his saddle rested on, fiddling idly with a leather tie string. Even before her eyes adjusted to the dark tack room, she knew he was there.

Call it intuition, call it premonition, call it what she would, nothing could settle the butterflies that fluttered insidiously in the pit of her stomach. Nothing. Not even her desperate attempt to call up every detail of the kiss she had witnessed between Monte and Zanna earlier in the day.

"You just won't give up, will you, Cat?"

She inhaled. Why couldn't she get mad at him? Angry? Anger would serve her well, but it wasn't in her. She shook her head, avoiding his gaze, wondering what sort of excuse she could give for being in the tack room at this time of night, holding a sack of his clothes, no less.

He took it from her.

"Gotta hand it to you," he said casually. "Putting on these smelly things night after night must have been torture."

Anything she said would be an admission, so she held her tongue.

"You ruined my horse yet?" he asked suddenly.

"Ruined?"

"With all that mumbo jumbo stuff ol' Este uses."

"I don't know what you're talking about." But she had to come to her grandfather's defense; anything less would be perfidious of her. "Papacito does not practice mumbo jumbo."

"No? Well, whatever you call it, you're one damned determined woman."

The accusation was voiced in a tone half irate, half gentle.

She nodded, unwilling to reveal anything.

Without moving an inch, he began to sing that ditty. "Cat's got her tongue . . ." He sang so softly, if she hadn't known the words by heart she wouldn't have recognized them. "Locked inside her throat; if she don't laugh, she's a-bound to choke."

Before he finished, he'd pushed away from the wall, and by the time the verse was over he was standing toe to toe with her. She stood stock-still by sheer force of will. She would not give in to the hopeless, debilitating emotions this man stirred in her.

While she struggled to control her thoughts, Monte kissed a finger, rubbed it down her nose, and she thought for sure she would faint. But she didn't.

At least she didn't think she did. The instant his finger left her nose, he took her in his arms, and his lips covered hers.

It was a kiss like nothing she had ever experienced. Nothing like the kisses they'd shared, reveled in, as children. There was nothing childlike about this kiss. It was full-blown, mature, and erotic.

And so long overdue that neither of them stirred for the longest time. It took her breath and left her weak, weak yet vibrant, powerful.

"Oh, Cat, Cat, I couldn't not do this. It's eaten at me from the instant I saw you when I returned. I . . ."

She stopped him with her lips. They couldn't talk. It would do absolutely no good. And in a few days she would be gone. She only hoped that now she would leave with his love, not his hatred.

Then time and thought disappeared. The kiss that followed could have lasted a second or a year. But who could count minutes when Monte's lips seemed to suction the very life out of her?

When his hands slipped through her hair, her brain, which for weeks now had swirled with despair, exploded in joyous sound and color, filling her head and her body with something akin to liquid quicksilver. She melted into him. And he into her.

She wasn't aware when he took her breasts in his palms, but when he drew back, he squeezed them gently. "You didn't have these when you were thirteen."

She wanted to tell him that he didn't have a probing body back then, either, but she dared not lead them any farther down the path they were headed. So, again she offered him her lips, and again he sent her spinning off the edge of the world.

Quickly it grew too hot. Monte realized it before Catarina, fortunately, she later thought. At the time he set them apart, however, she felt only abandonment.

They stood, chests heaving, eyes searching, arms reaching, hands touching. She placed her palm over his heart and felt it pound. She liked to think it pounded with his love for her. Love?

"I was wrong the other night," he said in a strangely hoarse voice that tugged at her until she returned to his arms and laid her face against his chest.

"We can never be just friends."

"I know." She almost cried the words, her mouth to his heart.

"I don't know what we're gonna do, Cat. I'm the man, and I'm supposed to have all the answers, but I don't." He threaded his fingers in her hair and pulled her face to his. "But I'll figure it out. I promise. Okay?"

Again she kissed him, full on the mouth, lips open, desperately, hopelessly, lovingly. He couldn't figure this out. No one could. Their fate had been sealed long ago. Monte would marry Zanna. His parents expected it. Zanna's parents expected it. Zanna expected it.

But Catarina couldn't stay and fit herself into their plans. And suddenly she knew she had to be the one to tell him. She couldn't leave him the way he'd left her.

Breaking the kiss, she blurted out, "I'm leaving."

"Leaving?" He sounded as though the thought had never occurred to him. "You can't leave."

"I can't stay." She started to add the part about him and Zanna—how she was supposed to cook and clean for them—but she couldn't speak the words. Here in his arms, in this one stolen moment, they were equals. She couldn't deny herself the fantasy of that feeling. "I'm moving to Cuero. Tía Juana has been trying to get me to . . . and . . . I—"

"You can't go, Cat."

"I can't stay, Monte. We both know that."

For the longest time he didn't speak. He just stared at her, chest heaving. "When?" he finally asked.

She shrugged.

"Not till after the rodeo."

That broke the spell for her. The rodeo. Texan. Zanna.

"Promise me, Cat. Please be there."

She nodded, for the truth could not be spoken. The truth, that she loved him too much not to be there in case he was hurt. The truth, that it would tear her heart out to watch him with Zanna.

So instead, she whispered, "I haven't ruined him for you. No one could ruin such spirit."

The strangest look came over his face then. It reflected all she felt and told her he felt the same things, with the same intensity, with the same hopelessness.

"Don't talk," he mumbled, closing his lips over hers again. "Just . . . don't . . . talk. I can't get enough . . ."

III

By the time the Ballou Hills crew arrived in Pecos on July first, the town was already bursting at the seams. The hotel was full, and every bed in every home was taken, either by friends in for the big event, or by paying boarders who had heard about the week-long celebration and come west to investigate.

"Looks like one of them gol'darn gold-rush towns," Skeeter commented.

All agreed.

"If we didn't have our saddles, we'd be out in the cold without so much as a piller," Baldy grumbled. No cowboy worth his salt liked a crowd.

"Nothing cold about it," Pee Wee observed. It was just after noon and the heat was hot and getting hotter. Had a vote been taken, "Hotter'n Hades" would have been the most often heard phrase in the dusty streets of Pecos, Texas.

Pee Wee and Skeeter pulled the wagon around back of the big red-rock Ballou house, located a mile or so from the center of town. Area ranchers kept their own town houses, most of them with quarters for staff.

Catarina had grown up staying in their little rock house, which was settled some thirty yards behind the big house. That this would be her last trip here added to the poignancy of the occasion.

"Reckon we'll get on over to the corral and see 'bout ol' Monte and his outlaw," Pee Wee told Mr. Ballou.

Left alone with supplies to sort and store and beds to freshen with sun-sweetened sheets brought from the ranch, Catarina found it even harder than she had anticipated to accept the truth that could no longer be denied since her experience with Monte two nights earlier.

"I'll never forget you, Cat," he'd said. "If we were free—"

"We're not," she had reminded him. But his plaintive words still rang in her head. *I'll never forget you.* She knew he meant it. She knew she would never forget him. But as usual, knowing and accepting were two different things.

The situation was made a bit easier, or harder, depending on which way her mood blew at any given moment, by Monte's daily absence. Once they arrived in Pecos, he spent almost every waking hour at the corrals, helping set up and prepare the new arena for the rodeo.

She saw less of Zanna than she had expected, also. Which was bittersweet, at best. Zanna had called her a dear friend, and Catarina had grown up considering her so. But grown up, Catarina knew her place, and Zanna should know hers.

Catarina's first sight of Zanna was a surprise. Zanna was coming out of her own family's town house two blocks over. Leather britches had been replaced by a split riding skirt—more appropriate town attire. Catarina knew the change would not slow down the beautiful, high-spirited girl.

Once the Ballou town house was aired and dusted,

beds made, supplies put away, Tina and Catarina spent their time with the other ranch cooks preparing food for the barbeque to follow the rodeo and precede the ball.

The ballroom, being decorated by ranch wives and their daughters, was a huge room on the top floor of the hotel with ceiling-to-floor windows all around and a balcony that overlooked the railroad.

Every Christmas ranch families joined forces to throw a big dance here at the hotel. The Cowboy Christmas Ball drew crowds from miles around. Catarina had always been sent to Cuero, but she had heard the stories—dancing till dawn, then feasting on scrambled eggs, antelope sausage, tortillas, and hot Mexican relishes. The ladies all wore special gowns.

This Fourth of July Catarina had a special gown, too. Tina had outdone herself making it. True to their Mexican heritage, it was designed with tiers of white lace, trimmed with row after row of red, blue, and green ribbons. It was breathtaking, off the shoulders, with a graceful, swirling skirt.

The gown required only one adornment—a happy smile. Already Catarina despaired of being able to carry out her part of the charade.

But the talk of the town, the topic on everyone's lips and minds, was Monte and Texan. Could he ride the outlaw? Or would the outlaw make straw of the would-be best cowboy west of the Pecos?

Catarina longed to see Texan, but she hadn't had a moment to escape to the corrals, which were located a good mile from the Ballou mansion. She could only hope and pray the reports were not true.

Texan had kicked out half the boards in his stall, one report said.

Texan tried to bite the cowpoke who fed him, another claimed.

Texan was so wild and dangerous, he had frightened the rest of the rodeo stock. No cowboy would go near the barn where he was stabled.

By the end of the week, everyone was breathless with anticipation, Catarina most of all. Disparate emotions flooded her. Underlying her worry for Monte and Texan was the certainty that regardless of how Monte came out, at the end of this celebration her own life would change forever. She could hardly stand to think about the future.

But neither could she keep it from her mind. She felt like she was approaching a precipice and would soon fall over the edge into some great black void. She found herself wanting to draw out every hour, every minute. Even the agonizing fear that Texan would harm Monte was better than finding out for certain.

To draw the suspense out as long as possible, bronc riding was saved for the final event of the day, following three rounds of steer roping, two of bulldogging, and a couple of events for the children. Pee Wee and Zanna went nose to nose in the roping contest. Pee Wee won the third round, but only by a few seconds.

Skeeter came in second to a Jagged Sky cowboy in bulldogging, while Curly Red stood on the sidelines with a scowl of disappointment on his face.

Curly Red considered himself the best bulldogger in the entire cowboy world.

"Wait'll next year," he groused to Catarina, who had stood beside him the whole afternoon, eating corral dust until she felt herself caked with a layer a good inch thick. Curly couldn't get around well enough to move from pillar to post, as he said. Catarina was frozen in place by fear.

She hadn't seen Texan since they arrived. Not only distance but her mother had kept her away, with tasks that didn't allow her time to slip off someplace that far away and get back to help with the next chore.

She hadn't seen much more of Monte, until today. Today he was everywhere. Racing here, racing there, encouraging the Ballou Hills cowboys.

"We have to win 'em all," he told his troops. "Take all the trophies home to the hills."

When Skeeter came in second, Monte was there to pat his shoulder, with a "Great goin', partner."

If Monte was nervous about his upcoming ride, it didn't show. His joviality seemed real, and Catarina could hardly hold her composure, seeing it.

Her palms were wet and her mouth dry, and only partially from the thick dust that bowled out of the arena with every contest. Before she was anywhere near ready, the announcer took his megaphone and climbed up on the fence.

Sandy Burgess had been appointed announcer primarily because he was the only man in the country who owned one of the newfangled contraptions Mr. Edison called a megaphone. Sandy had designed his himself. It was almost as big a curiosity as Texan.

"All right folks, it's time for the main event. Why don't ya'll take fifteen minutes, get yourselves something cold to drink, and come back ready to cheer ol' Monte Ballou on? Or," he added with good-natured ribbing, "you can cheer on ol' Texan, if you've a mind to."

Fifteen minutes. Catarina's heart thrashed beneath her already dusty white blouse. She tucked lengths of wispy black curls behind her ears and bit her lips, wondering whether she had done everything she could to prevent disaster.

Would Texan remember Monte's scent enough not to go completely berserk? *Fifteen minutes.* Her previous life passed before her eyes, especially the kiss. The last kiss.

The real kiss. The real good-bye.

"Why'd we have to wait?" came a call from the stands.

"Get on with the show!" shouted another.

"This bronc ride ain't gonna last that long."

Hee-haws followed the final call, and Catarina wanted to shout back at them. She wanted to run. Or at least close her eyes. Suddenly she felt so antsy, she knew she couldn't stand here beside Curly Red and watch. Before she could think of an excuse to leave Curly, Monte appeared.

"Come on, Cat. You gotta get up there with ol' Sandy."

"No!" The idea horrified her. His answer was to take her hand and pull her down a corridor he opened up between the gathered cowboys. When she protested again, he squeezed her hand. It felt like he'd squeezed her heart.

Around them the crowd buzzed. She'd never seen such excitement, never imagined such excitement. "I can't sit up there, Monte. Please."

"You're my lucky charm, Cat." They had reached the fence just below where the announcer balanced on the top rung. Monte grabbed her around the waist. Then stopped.

"You're trembling like a leaf."

No turning back now. There was nothing she could do to stop him or to control the situation. She had to find some way to support him. So she smiled, or tried to.

"I'm trembling for you, since you don't have sense enough to be afraid."

He laughed. Then like he'd done so many times before, he kissed his finger, ran it down her nose. This time it took her breath. Before she could regain her senses, his lips followed. The noise, the crowd, even the dust faded.

Brief was the kiss. Hot like the air around them. It sizzled on her lips even after he lifted his, incinerating every thought except of this man. Even her fear for him burned away.

"For luck, Cat." Catching her around the waist again, he heaved her upward. "Give her a hand, will you, Sandy? You know what to do from there."

"Sure do, Monte."

Catarina objected. "I have on a skirt, Monte. I can't sit on top of a fence."

"Keep your knees together, darlin'." His response was as quick and light as her heart was heavy. But heavy or not, he had no trouble hefting her up on the fence.

The next thing she knew, she was sitting on the top rung beside the announcer. Her heart stood still.

Behind them the thrashing had begun. When she looked over her shoulder, four Ballou Hills cowboys were dragging and prodding a terrified Texan toward the arena.

His eyes bugged out, glassy and terrified. His neck bowed. Every time he kicked out his back legs, the cowboys tugged, inching him toward the arena. The cheering, yelling crowd clearly heightened his terror. She had to do something.

When Catarina tried to scramble down the fence, Sandy stopped her. "Sit still, missy. You have the best seat in the house."

"Let me down. I have to—"

"Naw, Cat. Settle down. Show's 'bout to begin." With that he lifted his megaphone. She settled back, breath held, body tense.

"Listen up, you heathens," Sandy shouted. "Into

the ring comes one of the meanest outlaw hosses known to this country.''

For a second the cheering stopped, as though each of the several hundred people present paused to catch a breath at the same time. The silence was broken by a scream so piercing that it took Catarina a moment to realize it came from Texan.

The cowboys had managed to get him into the arena, where Pee Wee waited on his horse, ready to snub Texan's nose and blindfold him, to allow Monte to saddle and mount.

Frantically searching for Monte, Catarina first found Curly Red, standing in the spot where she'd left him earlier, his face white as the day he walked out of the hospital.

The traitor, she thought. Why hadn't he talked Monte out of this?

''Let's get the show on the road!'' It was Monte's voice. He stood directly below them, calling up to Sandy. When Catarina met his eyes, he winked.

''Wish me luck, Cat.''

She could but nod, while Sandy continued.

''This here outlaw's gonna be rode, folks, or let's say try to be rode, by a challenger for the title of Best Dang Cowboy West of the Pecos.'' Sandy paused, then added, ''An' we all know what that means. Hell, there ain't no cowboys nowhere else.''

The crowd loved it. Cheers, laughter, yah-hoos.

''Ol' Monte Ballou, the cowboy of whom I speak, asked me to announce that this here ride o' his is dedicated to one Miss Catarina Ramériz.''

More cheers and yah-hoos. They sounded the way Catarina imagined the roar of the sea would sound, for her head spun with fear and hope and love and despair. And not a little embarrassment.

But it was with fear alone that she watched Monte

step toward Texan, with that familiar, arrogant swagger, carrying his saddle by its horn, saddle blanket thrown over his shoulder.

The ride that followed would be related in chuck wagons and camp houses in the Pecos country for a hundred years to come. What the *Pecos Tribune* had termed the "Ride of Death" in that week's newspaper would the following week be reported as the "Ride of the Century."

At the time all Catarina could manage was to concentrate on each aspect of the ride as it happened. When Monte approached Texan and put his hand on his neck, the horse tried to toss his snubbed head and kicked his feet straight up in the air. But observing with a practiced eye, Catarina saw a degree less violence than she'd expected, considering the entrance Texan had made into the arena.

Monte set the saddle at his feet and picked up his saddle blanket. Gingerly, he laid it upon the outlaw's back. He must have been talking to the frightened horse, Catarina figured, trying to win cooperation. And it worked.

Before the very eyes of several hundred gathered witnesses, Texan's muscles began to relax. He still tried to jerk his head free, and his back legs twitched as if he wanted badly to kick, but Catarina sensed an easiness that hadn't been there a few weeks earlier.

The announcer obviously didn't detect the same thing. "He's a-bunchin', folks!" Sandy bellowed into his bullhorn. "Look out for him, Monte!"

Next came the saddle, and Texan resisted. He tossed his hindquarters, he kicked and pitched. Pee Wee gathered the snubbing rope tighter, and Monte reached beneath the heaving belly of the horse and pulled the cinch tight.

Catarina felt as though he had tightened it around

her own chest. She waited, as she knew every man, woman, and child in the crowd waited, for Texan to thrash his hind legs.

But he didn't. He twitched his back, as though trying to rid it of a pesky horsefly. But he didn't actually strike out.

He wasn't truly afraid.

But, of course, it was too early to tell, Catarina cautioned herself. When Monte climbed into the saddle, that horse could unwind. No human had ever sat on Texan's back, not for long.

She watched Monte give Pee Wee the nod. Pee Wee switched the taut halter rope to Monte's outstretched hand. Monte grabbed it, held it secure, then reached for the saddlehorn. Texan's flanks twitched; Catarina's insides fluttered.

It's too soon to tell, she cautioned herself.

A murmur rippled through the crowd. Catarina focused on Monte's hands. She watched him tug on the saddle horn, testing his weight against Texan's will.

Silence fell over the arena like the shadow of a rare cloud, broken only by the rustle of hooves when Texan sidestepped the man who tried to lift himself onto his back. At the second nod, Pee Wee freed the blindfold, then expertly backed his mount away from the outlaw.

Texan snorted, shook his head. His nostrils flared. He tossed his head, flung it back, his ears pointed skyward. Monte kept one boot toe hooked in the stirrup. Catarina watched him talk to the horse, trying to soothe and reassure him.

It took him three tries to get into the saddle, for Texan kept sidestepping in a circular pattern. By the time Monte sat gingerly in the saddle, he and Texan faced the announcer.

And Catarina. Their gazes locked. Monte lowered his full weight onto the wild animal. Texan's eyes flashed. He made an effort to buck. But it wasn't a wholehearted effort.

Monte cocked his head. Was his face turning red, or did Catarina imagine it? In the end he had to spur Texan to get a rise out of him, but it wasn't much of a rise.

The crowd had remained silent during this unexpected turn of events. After a few minutes Monte managed to guide Texan about the arena in an uneasy gait, which showed signs of promise even now.

Someone on the other side of Catarina snickered. Then someone else. Hisses could be heard from the crowd.

"Some outlaw!" came a call.

"Yeah, Ballou, what happened to that wild ride you promised us?"

"Hell, I can see a man ride a horse any day of the week. I'm getting me a cold beer."

The crowd quickly dispersed, peppering Monte with good-natured derision as they went. Only the Ballou Hills cowboys remained silent and still, obviously not believing what they had witnessed.

Monte continued around the arena until he returned to the spot beneath Catarina. He tipped his hat, then reached toward Sandy. "Hand me that newfangled contraption of yours." Sandy obliged by handing down the megaphone.

Catarina wanted to fall off the fence backward and run for her life. She didn't know what to expect. But she feared the worst. Was he mad? Surely. She had embarrassed him in front of the entire country. Family, friends, and strangers. As a practical joke it would rank with the best. But how would Monte take it? His pride had been at stake.

"Ladies and gentlemen," he called through the megaphone. "Wait up a minute. I want to introduce you to someone." He glanced up at Catarina. "Come on, Cat, take a bow. Ladies and gentlemen, Catarina Ramériz is one hell of a horse tamer. Ain't she, now? Cat's the one who tamed ol' Texan."

"You are going to wear that gown, Catarina, and you will attend the ball."

"No I won't." Then she added, "*Por favor, Mamá.* Please don't make me face . . . them. Not tonight."

So they compromised. Catarina wore the gown her mother had worked on so long and hard, but she did not go into the ballroom. Rather, she remained in the preparation room, arranging food trays and mixing punch, where she had time to recall every detail of the disaster she had made of this day.

With more luck than she had experienced in a month of Sundays, she had escaped the arena without having to confront or be confronted by Monte. No sooner had he handed the megaphone back to Sandy than he had been swamped by Zanna and his family. They gathered around, as near as he would let them come to Texan, giving Catarina a chance to scramble down the backside of the fence and escape.

She hadn't come face-to-face with Monte since then, and with a smidgen more luck, she wouldn't. As soon as she could leave the ball, she would return to their quarters behind the Ballou house. In the morning she would leave. She'd already talked her father into letting her take the stage from Pecos to Cuero. Her bag was packed. Money for her ticket was secured in the pocket of her traveling cape. In a few hours she would be gone.

A few hours . . .

Which made it impossible for her not to peep into the ballroom from time to time, or to stand a bit longer than prudent at the serving table when she slipped out with trays of cakes and cookies.

She hadn't intended to speak with anyone, much less dance. Carlos was the first to approach her.

"It's a polka, Cat. Come dance with me."

"Oh, no . . . uh, later, Carlos. Thanks."

Her next time out, it was Zanna who approached. Zanna was a vision of loveliness. Nothing less would describe her. Gone was the cowgirl attire, and in its place a delectable gown of filmy pink material, draped to perfectly reveal more than a hint of cleavage, a tiny waist, and the promise of perfect hips. Her blond hair was pinned up in a cascade of curls and pink silk flowers that nipped her bare shoulder on one side.

"You look stunning," Catarina told her honestly. "Nothing left of the cowgirl who ate dust all afternoon."

"You, too, Cat." Zanna plucked at a white lace ruffle that fairly dripped red, blue, and green satin ribbons. "Your gown is magnificent."

"Thanks to Mamá."

"Of course. She always makes you the most fabulous clothes. My mother has always said Tina should go into dressmaking. Of course Mrs. Ballou couldn't allow that."

It was said with a laugh, no intention of disparagement. But the words themselves left no room for speculation as to their separate places in life. Catarina wanted to hug Zanna for reminding her. She'd needed reminding too much lately. She didn't mention this to Zanna, for Zanna wouldn't know what she was talking about.

But as she lowered her gaze to keep her thoughts to herself, her breath caught. There on Zanna's hand was the ring.

Her garnet and gold ring. The one Monte had placed

on her finger six years before when he proposed to her.

The ring his mother took back after they sent him away. *You understand, my dear, it has been in my family for many years. I shall pass it along . . . a daughter-in-law . . . when Monte chooses a wife . . .*

"I see he proposed," she managed. That morbid curiosity again, clamoring to hear the worst.

Zanna followed her line of vision to the ring, which she lifted to the light. "Isn't it beautiful? Mrs. Ballou gave it to me this evening."

"The señora?" Catarina was stunned. She tried, oh how hard she tried, to smother the lightness that flashed through her.

"She said it has been in her family . . ."

The music closed in, swirling, taunting . . . When Catarina felt moisture sting her eyes, she knew she had to escape. "Excuse me, Zanna."

As she rushed, head down, the short distance to the preparation room, the noise stopped swirling in her head. The music faded, the cowboys' banter became intelligible. They were ribbing Monte, she realized. Of course he would take his new position as laughingstock in stride, as behooved a man in cattle country. Then she heard his voice.

"Hell, fellows, the joke's on you. Sure had you going, didn't we? But Cat gets the credit. Damn, she should be out here takin' it like a man. Hold on a minute . . ."

Panic spread through Catarina. Slipping past her mother, she gained the hallway before she heard Monte's voice again, this time in the preparation room.

"Tina, where's Cat? She needs to get out there and take her medicine."

His voice was light, his tone jocular, and Catarina knew she would remember it the rest of her life. As she would remember her mother's response.

"Catarina said something about going home to pack," Tina told Monte.

"To pack? Mama'll let her have time to pack in the morning. We're not leaving for the ranch till afternoon."

"Catarina isn't returning to Ballou Hills, Señor Monte."

"What?"

"She will take the morning stage to Cuero."

"Cuero?" He sounded like she had never told him. Had he not listened? Not believed?

"Her aunt Juana lives there. You remember. Catarina has decided to visit her, well, perhaps more than visit. With you and Miss Zanna fixing to marry, and with Raul and myself getting on in years . . ."

Catarina didn't wait for more. She hurried down the back stairs of the hotel and out the rear entrance—the service entrance, she reminded herself.

The night was cooler now and felt soft against the bare skin of her shoulders. The sky was black, and there must have been a million stars.

Stars to guide her, she thought. The same stars would shine in Cuero as here. The same stars would shine everywhere as here. She would never escape them. Not for the rest of her life. She would always . . .

About halfway between the hotel and the Ballou mansion lay the corral, arena, and stables. By the time Catarina reached them, she was breathless. She thought of Texan, and the stunt that cost Monte the title of Best Dang Cowboy West of the Pecos. Texan was an outlaw no longer, thanks to her shenanigans.

From the sound of his announcement after the rodeo, Monte would make Texan his own special riding horse. The idea left her aquiver with intimacy. She had tamed Monte's horse, a horse he would ride every day . . .

Without consciously considering her decision, she

turned into the stable. When she came to her senses, she stood outside Texan's stall. Moonlight streamed through the open stable behind her.

"Hello, Texan. You did good today."

The horse whinnied.

"I'm sorry I didn't bring sugar. But I'm sure you'll be getting your share."

Texan tossed his head as if he understood.

"I'm going, Texan, but I'll leave Monte with you." The tears she had fought so long stung her eyes. Reaching forward, she stroked Texan's long silky nose. "Take care of him, you hear me?"

"I hear you, Cat."

Her hand stilled on Texan's face, as if turned to stone. Monte had followed her. When she turned, he stood only a few feet distant, staring at her as if he had never really seen her.

"You heard . . . ?"

"You're not going to leave me, Cat."

"Yes, I . . ." Lowering her head to keep from revealing her deep distress, she fingered one of the multitude of colored ribbons that adorned the fiesta dress. While she wasn't looking, Monte stepped forward, reached out a gentle hand, and touched her bare shoulder.

She jumped back. "No, please."

"Come on, Cat. Come on, girl. I won't hurt you. Not ever again. I . . ."

The words were gentle, mesmerizing, like one would use to soothe a skittish horse. But there was no soothing her. "Stop, Monte. You shouldn't have followed—"

He didn't allow her to protest. Gathering her in his arms, he crushed her to his chest and held her so tightly she felt trapped. But for the life of her, she couldn't pull away.

"I've been such a fool, Cat." While he spoke, he

nuzzled his face in her hair, which had for the most part come loose as she ran through the night . . . away from him.

"I thought . . . I mean, I tried to do what was right, Cat. I mean, what my parents said was right, but it isn't right. It's wrong."

Without the slightest bit of enthusiasm, she pulled back and regarded him sadly. "No it isn't, Monte. They're right. Zanna is perfect for you."

He plucked at a curl that fell over her forehead, and she remembered how it had felt when he threaded his fingers through her hair, when he held her breasts in his hands, when he kissed . . .

"Please don't do this."

"They aren't right," he insisted. "You know it. I know it. You're the one who's perfect for me." His blue eyes were dark here in the barn, but his voice had lost none of its intensity. The way he looked, she thought he might kiss her, but he was intent on his argument. "And I'm perfect for you. We've always known that."

When she didn't respond, either to agree or object, he cocked his head and grinned. "Now that you've tamed me a little, we'll be even more perfect together."

She laughed, but quickly sobered.

He rested his forehead against hers, nuzzling, skin to skin, back and forth. "See? Who makes you laugh, Cat? No one but me."

"That doesn't mean anything."

"I think it does."

In truth, she did, too. But she couldn't allow herself to relent. "No one will ever tame you, Monte Ballou. You're arrogant and you always will be."

"Maybe, but I won't ever hurt you again." Threading his fingers through her hair, he pulled her head back and spoke directly into her face. "I promise you that, Cat. I'll be good to you."

She knew he would, given the chance. She had never doubted it. And that made it even harder. "You don't know what you're saying, Monte. There are other people involved. They would never allow me—"

"You mean my parents?"

"Maybe mine, too. We're different . . . I mean, we're from different—"

"Classes? Races? Social positions?"

She nodded, relieved that he understood and admitted it.

"That's a bunch of bull, Cat. We're more perfect together than any couple I've ever known. All these things you call differences, hell, they don't even matter. We grew up together, we *like* each other, we have fun, we made plans, Cat."

"I know. Do you think I forgot? I couldn't forget, not even when—"

"When what?" he prompted. But she couldn't talk about it. Certainly not to him. One of them had to remain sane.

He sighed. "I only came home for holidays so I could see you, but you were never there."

"They conspired against us," she agreed softly. "They think they're right, Monte. Maybe they are."

"You don't believe that," he challenged. And the sincerity, the intensity, in his tone brought a catch to her throat. She lifted a hand and stroked his cheek. Quickly, he covered her hand with his, holding it against his skin.

"I didn't know about the ring until tonight," he told her. "I thought maybe Zanna had one like it or . . . When she said Mother gave it to her, I knew. My mother took it away from you, didn't she?"

Catarina tried to shrug it off. But here was the perfect opportunity. "It was her ring, Monte. She had every right to keep it for her family."

"I told her why I gave it to you."

"Then they sent you away."

"Yeah. But they can't do that again."

"They can. I mean, maybe now that we're grown up they couldn't stop us, but think what we would be doing to them."

"To them? Look what they've done to us."

"It isn't just your parents, Monte, or mine. There are others . . . Zanna . . ."

"Zanna understands."

"Oh, no, you're wrong." Catarina stopped short of relating Zanna's view of their future—Zanna in Monte's bed, Catarina washing their bedclothes.

"Yep, Zanna understands. We had a talk tonight."

Catarina was totally speechless.

"She told me something that I'd rather hear from you."

"Zanna? What could she have told you?"

He took his time answering, tethering her to him with a gaze as intense as his voice when he finally said, "Zanna said you're in love with me, Cat. Why don't you tell me that yourself?"

Her heart stopped. Her first reaction was, how could Zanna do that? Then, how could Zanna know?

"Tell me," he prompted. "Please, Cat. Admit it. Right here. Right now."

Her despair had never been so black; her life had never seemed so bleak. "Never."

"Not even if I say it first? I love you, Cat. Don't run away from me. We've wasted too many years already. You belong at Ballou Hills. You belong with me. Will you marry me?"

"Marry you?" A chill seemed to pass over her skin, and it was only then that she realized Monte had slipped her gown off her shoulders, down to her waist. It didn't take much more to shed it completely.

"Yep, you've changed a mite since you were thirteen."

She stood before him in pantaloons and chemise, while he took her in. She recalled her grandfather saying a wild horse responded with all his senses.

Well, she did, too. And she had never felt as wild in her life. Not as wild, not as wonderful.

Monte's hands seemed to guide his gaze down her length, then back. While he cupped her breasts in large palms, his lips covered hers.

Before the kiss had ended—truthfully, she wasn't sure the kiss ended for several hours—he had lifted her in his arms and carried her to a pile of fresh hay in an unoccupied stall.

"This too sticky?" he mouthed, his lips laving her face with love.

She shook her head.

"Cat's got her tongue . . ."

"Don't talk, Monte. Don't waste a minute."

She realized he misunderstood her, for he stiffened in her arms.

"We have the rest of our lives, Cat. I won't take no."

"I won't say no. But I still don't want to waste another minute. We can talk later."

In years to come she would tease him about scrambling out of his clothes.

"You should have entered the calf scramble with the kids rather than trying to ride a tame horse."

"There wasn't but one tame horse in that barn, Mrs. Ballou," he would return, "and it was Texan."

She did surprise herself that night. On the other hand, she had felt reborn to a life of great possibilities, and she didn't intend to spend another moment of it as a timid, shy person.

But when Monte stretched his very nude body alongside her very nude body in the hay that night, she wasn't really aware of the future. Her mind was on him, this man she had loved for so long.

"You don't look much like you did six years ago, either," she teased, sifting her fingers through the fuzzy hair on his chest.

"You don't think so?" And with that he guided her hand lower until she held him in her hand, as she had held him in her heart for such a long time. And she reveled in her love for him.

And in his love for her, which he expressed in the most ardent terms, in the most intimate fashion, with the most loving touches.

With his lips to her lips, his hands to her throat and her breasts, he set her flesh aquiver and still she wanted more.

"It's all I ever wanted," she moaned. "Yet, there's something else, something . . ."

And so he lay over her and inside her and took her to places of fantasy and bright, bright lights, and she knew at last that the darkness was gone. Forever.

Clinging to her, he pulled her over onto his chest and held her, while the sweet scent of hay and lovemaking filled their nostrils and the cool night air dried their bodies.

"Now have I convinced you?" he wanted to know.

She nodded against his chest, so full of love and peace that she couldn't find words to express it all. Finally, her thoughts returned to the day just past.

"I didn't intend to tame Texan," she admitted. "I just wanted to take the killer edge off him."

"You surely did that, darlin'," he said with a

chuckle. Then he sobered. "Reckon when all's told, you tamed me a bit, too."

"I cost you your chance to be a hero, like you wanted."

"Until now I didn't know what I wanted, Cat. Now I know. I've always wanted to be your hero, yours and no one else's."

"You've always been my hero, Monte. Even with your rough edges."

"Rough edges?"

"I knew what was beneath them."

When he swept his hand down the length of her bare back, she shivered, and when he cupped her bottom seductively, she nestled snugly against him. But he tugged her gently upright.

"Time we got back to the ball."

"Oh, no."

"Oh, yes. We have to."

"But Monte, they'll know."

He stopped struggling into his breeches and watched her tie her chemise. "Maybeso," he admitted, before kissing her lips with utmost tenderness. "Will it embarrass you?"

She thought about it. "Yes. But that's all right. It's just . . ."

"Zanna left."

"Oh, no."

"She said to tell you she expects an invitation to the wedding."

"Zanna. She really is my friend."

"Mine, too," Monte said. Then he kissed her again. "But just a friend, nothing more."

"I know. You were right. It's always been us. You and me." After her dress was in place and she had plucked most of the hay from her hair, she reached across the space between them and hugged him. ''We're perfect for each other, Monte.''

He broke the ensuing kiss with a wide-eyed expression. ''Dang, Cat, I forgot.'' Dragging her by the hand, he headed for the hotel ballroom. ''We gotta get back up there. I forgot to tell you. The boys voted you Sweetheart of the Rodeo.''

A Tempting Offer

By
Eileen Wilks

One

On a crisp morning in early March, a rider flung herself and her horse at one of the hills that crumbled off the shoulders of the Davis Mountains in the westernmost corner of Texas. She had only one thought in her mind.

He's back.

The path up that hill looked as deficient as a drunkard's promise. The hill itself was rock. Loose rock, some of it. Hard rock still fixed to the earth's bones in places. Rock that had been broken and broken again by a thousand thousand freezing desert nights and hotter-than-hell days into sand, sand that slid treacherously beneath the horse's big hooves. Had anyone been nearby to see the rider on that big black horse taking that hill at such a speed, he could have been excused for cursing or closing his eyes—if he wasn't from around here.

Anyone who lived within a hundred miles of the Double Bar T Ranch, however, would have recognized the horse and its slim rider, and stood back to enjoy the wordless poetry of a local legend in action: Sammie and her Big Black Beast.

Just before Beast's feet started to skid, Sammie swayed, keeping her weight over the withers, balancing the animal through the tricky sand with an instinct as uncanny as it was automatic. It was just as well she rode instinctively, because most of her mind wasn't on her riding.

He's back.

She'd gone to check on Big Ben before breakfast. The big Brahman bull was her pride and joy, the start of what would someday be her own herd. A couple of years ago she'd bargained with her stepfather for the purebred calf as a bonus for overseeing his ranch. At six-thirty that morning she'd been kneeling to look at a healing sore on the bull's left hind leg. J.J. had come up and leaned on the top rail of the fence around the bull's paddock. He'd commented on the weather, which had been unusually chilly for early spring, and on the bull, who was healing nicely from having had a minor argument with a fence. He'd scratched the bristly gray stubble on his chin and he'd dropped his bombshell, ever so casually.

Tucker Evans was back.

The news had made Sammie break out in shivers of happiness.

Not that she'd let on, of course. She'd had plenty of practice keeping her feelings to herself. No one but J.J. would have guessed what the news meant to her. But the old cowboy was a noticing kind of man, and he'd known her ever since she and her mother came to the Double Bar T when Sammie was eight. There wasn't much that he missed.

Still, he was too tactful to comment on her reaction, except for adding that rumor claimed Tucker had hung up his rodeo spurs for good this time.

She'd gotten all shaky and made an excuse to go saddle Beast. The quickest route between the Double Bar T and the Evans ranch lay across the low, rocky hills that straddled the fence line between the two properties for several miles, and the only way across those hills was on horseback.

He's back.

Sammie and her Beast reached the crest of the hill and paused, letting the gelding catch his breath while his rider enjoyed the prospect of leaving her step-father's land behind.

The country she looked out on might have looked bleak to other eyes. Even the Apaches had considered this region good for little except passing through on their way to raid elsewhere—down in Mexico, maybe, where the huge *rancheros* with their thousands of cattle had provided such tempting targets, or well away to the north and east, where the grass grew green and lush instead of brown and sparse, and the missions offered little defense. But Sammie loved everything she saw, from the flat, dry land fit for only the stubbornest of God's creatures, to the worn-out mountains blocking the horizon to her left.

At the base of the hill lay the fence that divided the ranches. Set in that fence beside one of the scrub oaks that studded the mountains and straggled into the surrounding hills was the crude gate that her brother and Tucker had put in years ago. Back then, when Tucker and Dan were still home, folks used to complain about the way the three of them had run wild all over creation. At least, it had been "the three of them" whenever Sammie could catch up or keep up with the two boys. Time passed. The land didn't change much, but people did.

It had been a year since she'd seen Tucker, if she didn't count the Sandhills Rodeo a couple of months ago. She considered that. Waving at him from across the stadium didn't count as really *seeing* him, she decided. Maybe, she thought, half hopeful, half afraid, her feelings had changed.

Did she want them to?

Uncomfortable with anything resembling self-analysis, Sammie pointed Beast's head down the hill, and squeezed with her knees. He moved forward, as eager for speed and challenge as his rider.

Tucker was outside in what passed for a yard at his house, trying to bludgeon the faucet near the corral into working, when he saw Sammie coming at a dead gallop. He stopped to watch.

Sammie didn't just ride. She hunkered down and merged with the horse, the wind, and the moment. Seeing that dab of flame-haired female on the back of an ugly, black-as-hell horse bearing down on him like an out-of-control freight train made Tucker grin.

Damn, but it was good to be home.

She pulled up in a flurry of dust and hooves, kicking her feet out of the stirrups and leaping from Beast's back before the dust settled. "Tucker!" she cried happily.

That was all she had time for. He threw his arms around her and hugged her off her feet, knocking her hat to the ground and swinging her in a circle that made the big gelding dance back, flattening his ears.

"Hell, Sammie, I missed you." He set her back on her feet, beaming down at her. "Tell your monster not to eat me, okay?"

"Idiot." An untidy jumble of red curls hid her face when she bent over to pick up her hat. "If you missed me so much, how come you didn't ever write? Or call. You do know how to do that, I guess? Shoot, I didn't know until this morning that you were home!"

"I just got here yesterday. Anyway, you must have known I'd be here soon. Once I hired Felicia and her brother to get things back in order—"

"I heard about *that.*" She slapped her hat against

her jeans, raising a puff of dust. "But knowing you were getting the house ready to live in again, and knowing you planned to live in it yourself, are two different things."

"Well, what did you think, Sammie? That I was going to sell the place?"

She just looked at him, her features oddly expressionless. Sam had a funny little face, kind of skinny and pointed like the rest of her, blessed with a whole galaxy of freckles and dominated by eyes as green as an old 7Up bottle. Those eyes, her hair, and her temper had come to her from the Irish father who'd died when she was little.

He frowned. "Sammie? Is anything wrong?"

"No, what could be wrong?" She grinned suddenly, banishing his misgivings. "I guess I ought to know better than to think you'd be selling, huh? If you *had* put the place on the market, we would have had the paramedics out to revive Art. 'Cause I know you wouldn't be selling it to him, and he'd have a stroke if you sold to anyone else."

"Wouldn't he, though?" He took a minute to savor that notion.

Arturo Ochoa, Sammie's stepfather, had been trying to buy the Evans ranch for years, but Tucker didn't fault the man for that. Art wasn't the only one who had made him an offer. Tucker's father might have let the ranch buildings fall into disrepair before he died, but the land itself was good, with two deep wells for ranch use, and another one for the house. And it wasn't heavily mortgaged. Tucker had used his winnings on the rodeo circuit to make sure of that.

"Your stepdad know I'm home?" he asked. "I haven't heard from him since he cussed me out for turning down his last offer."

Sammie shrugged. "I haven't seen him today."

Tucker could have forgiven Arturo Ochoa for his rudeness. Being an easygoing man himself, he was willing to overlook what rose more from habit than malice. No, it was the way the man treated his stepdaughter that made Tucker's blood boil. "Can't have everything, I guess," he said regretfully. "Much as I'd like to send Art's blood pressure soaring, I'm not willing to give up the ranch to do it."

"That would be going a little far." She settled her hat back on her head, using both hands as if the operation took all her attention. "You *are* staying, then? You're home for good?"

"I'm a rancher now—or will be, soon." Lord, hadn't he planned this for years and years? Long before Pete Evans had finished drinking himself to death, his son had realized that he'd have to leave the ranch he loved in order to hang onto it. But he was back now, and it felt good. Real good. "Things will be tight at first, but I've got a line of credit set up, plus what I saved from my prize purses—"

"Including your win at the NFR last year," she said, grinning.

"Damn right." He grinned back, because that had been the best moment of his life. Until now. "Think there's any chance Art will sell me some of his breeding stock? I've got some cows coming in a couple weeks that I bought at auction, mostly Hereford with a few Limousins I got at a good price, but I could use some more. I hear good things about what you've done with the Triple Bar T range stock the past few years, Sammie, since you talked him into buying that high-dollar Brahman bull of his."

She flushed, looking pleased. "We're having pretty good success. You planning on running a pure herd, or mixing?"

"Probably keep the dams pure, but go for crosses

on the calves. Come on." He started for the barn. "I need to get a bigger wrench to hit that damned faucet with."

She fell into step with him. "Black ballys?" She named the most common cross, between Black Angus and Herefords, popular among cattlemen for their low birth weight and quick growth.

"Yeah, or, if I could buy a few good Brahman cows from Art, I might try some Brangus and Beefmasters." He sure was glad Sammie was here. She and Dan were his oldest friends, and he wanted her to see what he'd done to begin putting the place to rights. Even more, he wanted to tell her some of the things he planned to do.

They talked about bulls while they walked over to the hay barn. "I reckon you're using Dominion to sire the calves?" Art's prize bull had won trophies all over the West, and was worth in the neighborhood of forty thousand dollars.

"Mostly. I've just started using semen from my own bull on some of the cows, too."

He raised his eyebrows. "Big Ben? The Brahman out of Dominion you were telling me about last year?"

She nodded. "He's two now, and the vet's given him a clean bill of health. With his ancestry, all he needs is a year or two of good calves to be worth a pretty penny."

"Are you thinking about selling him, then, or just his seed? I wouldn't mind having a good breeding bull, and that Big Ben of yours sounds—"

"Tucker?" said a soft, feminine voice from behind them. "What's keeping you, hon?"

He turned and smiled at the other half of the plans he'd been working on for so long. A tall brunette stood in the open doorway to the barn. She looked just right standing there. Just like he'd pictured for so long while he was out on the circuit, breaking bones and records and saving up the money to get back to his real love—the ranch.

Tucker knew himself for a lucky man. From her pretty painted toenails to the long brown hair that tumbled down her back, Lynda was a real class act. "Come on over, sweetheart, and meet an old friend of mine," he said to her, holding out a hand.

When she reached him he hugged her up against his side and turned back to Sam, grinning proudly. When a man was truly ready to settle down, he needed someone at his side, building a home right along with him. And he'd found just the woman to do that. "This ought to prove to you I'm really home for good. Sam, meet Lynda. My fiancée."

Two

"You gonna get that wire tight, or do you plan for the cows to use it for jump rope?" J.J. asked. He stood at the other end of the barbed wire they were stringing.

Sam gave the wire-stringer several hard twists. Her blasted eyes were acting up again. They'd been doing that off and on all morning. She scowled and blinked. The dampness on her lashes made rainbow sparkles at the edges of her vision. She blinked again.

No stupid rainbows for her. She wanted to break things. Great big noisy things.

She was such a fool.

Not until she heard Tucker introduce his fiancée had she admitted the truth to herself. Deep inside, she'd nursed the hope that when Tucker finally came home for good, the scales would fall from his eyes. If he were home for more than a few days, surely he'd see that she wasn't his old roping partner anymore, or Dan's kid sister. She wasn't just "good ol' Sammie."

Surely, if he would only stay around long enough, he would see that she was a woman.

"Damnation, girl, if you're not going to pay attention, you might as well go do your nails or somethin'!"

She glared at her old friend. No doubt Lynda spent a lot of time on her fingernails, those long red weapons she kept filed and varnished to a hard shine. "The wire's tight. What more do you want?"

"Oh, it's tight, all right. Tight enough to snap, whip back, and blind one of us."

Startled, she checked the tension—and eased back. "Sorry."

He finished at his end in silence. J.J. was getting on in years, but he was sharp, even though he usually looked as if he'd gone on a three-day drunk several years back and never returned. He shaved once a week, for church, and believed in the old-fashioned values of hard work and "waste not, want not." In fact, he was downright tightfisted. His miserly ways were responsible for Sammie's one feminine accomplishment. When she was fifteen she'd learned how to sew in order to mend rips and replace buttons on clothes that the old man was too cheap to throw out or quit wearing.

He liked to say that he could still manage to hit a nail on the head with a hammer when he had to, and he was right enough about that. So she wasn't surprised when he said, elaborately casual, "So—what's she like, this fiancée Tucker brought home with him?"

"Dark-haired. And pretty." She gathered up her tools and started for the spot a hundred yards back where they'd left the horses. "I guess you'd say she's built. You know," she said, her empty hand shaping an hourglass in the air. "And she's got the kind of hair that looks like she didn't fix it, only it really takes forever to get it that way. She wears those fancy fingernails you have to pay someone to glue on, and she moves kind of slinky, like that gray barn cat that won't let anyone near her."

He snorted. "I thought she must be somethin' special, since he plans to marry this one, but she don't sound any different from any of his other women. A city girl."

"How can you tell?" she asked dryly. Tucker wasn't exactly known for his discriminating tastes in women. He liked them all—and they liked him right back, unfortunately.

J.J. shook his head sadly. "Playing the field is one thing, but Tucker seems to think he's supposed to pollinate the whole blamed thing single-handed, like he was a bumblebee or somethin'."

Sammie choked on a laugh. It was funny, but it hurt, too. For all Tucker's wholesale fondness for the female gender, he'd never made a pass at her. Didn't look like he ever would, now. Her spirits were ankle-high and sinking by the time they reached the horses.

"I don't see why he thinks she'll make a ranch wife," she said, gathering the reins in one gloved hand. She'd mounted Beast too often to find it awkward to get her foot in a stirrup that was higher off the ground than her waist. "She couldn't saddle a horse or throw a rope. Not with those nails." Probably couldn't cook a roast or bake up a pan of brownies, either, but Sammie wasn't going to mention that. She'd have trouble deciding which side of a pan to put the roast in, herself. Her cooking skills were pretty much limited to what could be fixed in a frying pan over a campfire.

J.J. sighed as he settled on the back of his buckskin mare. "Well, honey, men don't always use their thinking parts when it comes to picking a woman."

She knew that. Even good men weren't contemplating riding or roping skills when they got that look in their eyes . . . the look Sammie had always longed to see lighting Tucker's eyes.

Well, she'd seen it. But it hadn't been there for her. "She isn't really his fiancée. Not yet." She cued Beast, and he started walking.

"He called her that."

"But she didn't like it. 'Oh, honey,' " Sammie

mimicked in a sickly-sweet voice that made Beast twitch his ears in disdain, " 'Don't keep saying that, now, when you *know* nothing is really settled.' "

J.J. gave one of his all-purpose grunts as the two of them reached the nearest gate. When Sammie bent from the saddle to open it, the fluid movement was every bit as "slinky" as she'd accused her rival of being. On horseback, she was everything graceful. She didn't have trouble until she stood on the two feet she'd been born with, instead of the four she borrowed so often.

"This business of givin' a woman a test-drive like she was a car—well, they had another word for it in my day," J.J. muttered.

Being fair gave Sammie all the gloomy pleasure of poking at a sore to see how much it hurt. "Times have changed, J.J., and I think this trial period is her idea, not his." Tucker had told her in a goofy, pleased-as-punch voice that Lynda wanted to see how she fit in down on his ranch before she said yes.

Sammie knew darned good and well the woman was already saying yes to a different question—one posed privately—but she tried not to think about that.

"So, you going to that party he's givin' Friday night?"

Leather creaked as she shifted in the saddle. "I suppose." The first party given at the old Evans ranch in years would be to introduce Tucker's almost-fiancée to his friends and neighbors. She grimaced.

The old man scratched two days' growth of gray stubble on his chin. "Don't feel like you have to show up. Everyone knows you don't go in much for dress-up parties."

"I have to go," she said grimly. Good ol' Sammie had better show up at her friend's party, or people would wonder why. She couldn't stand that. The last thing she wanted was for everyone to know how she felt.

Especially him.

From somewhere on his person, J.J. unearthed a round tin of chewing tobacco. He opened it and pulled out a plug. "If he marries that Lynda, maybe you'll start dating from time to time." He stuck the plug in his cheek.

"As if anyone would ask me."

"They'd ask. 'Course, you might take a bit of trouble with your looks now and then. You might even quit scowling at anyone who notices you're female." He chewed meditatively for a minute. "I can't help thinkin' about what you told me that night you got into Art's brandy."

She scowled at him. "I never told you anything, and I don't want to hear about it." Brandy was strong stuff. The night she'd heard about her friend Janie getting pregnant was the first and last time she'd tried it. She'd ended up out by the corral, sobbing into Beast's withers. J.J. had found her there, and she'd told him something she'd never admitted out loud before.

"If your heart's dream is to have some babies of your own," he said now, "you'd better start dressing and acting more female-like."

"Oh, get real. I'm not any good at makeup and clothes and all that, and I'd look like a fool if I tried. As for *acting* female—well, I can just imagine how Charlie or Lonnie would stare at me if I were to start batting my eyelashes at them."

"Don't worry 'bout it," he said, and spat a stream of brown juice from his mouth. "I'll help you."

She glanced at him dubiously. J.J. knew everything there was to know about tending cattle, but he didn't strike her as being the best source for tips on feminine fashion and flirting.

"Don't look so doubtful, missy. I know how a woman gets a man's attention. That's usually enough. Once you get a man to lookin', you can let him take it from there. Long as you don't let him take things too far." He gave her a stern look.

Sammie thought it over, and decided it wasn't likely that J.J. knew any less than she did about attracting a man. At least he had the insider's view of the subject. She nodded, her spirits lifting slightly.

He smiled and tugged the brim of his hat down. "Red's a good color for catching a man's eye," he told her. "We'll get you somethin' red for the party."

Sammie lay awake in bed that night and brooded about names. Her name, to be specific. She wondered if anyone even remembered what it really was. Had anyone even once called her Sherry Ann since her mother died?

Her hand went to the little locket she wore around her neck. Tucker had given it to her when she turned sixteen. She'd replaced the chain twice, but she hadn't lost the little gold heart. Engraved on it in elegant scrollwork letters were her initials: S.A.M. From S.A.M. to Sammie had been a small, obvious step when she was little. It wasn't as if she disliked her nickname, either, and yet . . .

She wasn't just "good ol' Sammie," who was practically one of the guys. There was more to her than riding and roping. Only she didn't know how to get hold of the parts of herself that were buried and waiting. The scared parts.

All she really knew was ranching. At one time she'd thrown herself into learning everything she could about the one thing Arturo Ochoa seemed to love, hoping to earn his approval. She'd given up on that long ago, but in the meantime, her own love for the land and the life had grown. She had plans. She had a few cows now, breeding stock, and she'd twisted Art's arm into letting her lease a small strip of land to keep them on. And she had Big Ben. Eventually she wanted to have her own place.

She'd need money, of course. That would come from her bull. She could start selling his seed once he had a proven record. Eventually she'd save up enough money to get herself a little spread of her own, somewhere else.

Somewhere far away, she thought now. Someplace where she wouldn't have to see Tucker and his dark-haired bride once they started having children together.

Sammie hugged her middle. Her flat, empty middle.

A thought sprang, full-blown and absurd, into her mind. She shook her head as if she could physically dislodge it. No, that was crazy. She'd never . . . she couldn't ever . . .

But if she didn't, what then? The only man she'd ever loved was going to marry his red-nailed bimbo. Once that happened, Sammie could either leave the state or spend the rest of her life pretending to be his friend, and nothing more. Either way, she'd be alone.

Put that way, her idea didn't seem *entirely* crazy.

Sammie had always made decisions quickly. Some people accused her of not thinking at all before she jumped smack-dab into some crazy notion, but she knew better. She *did* think things through before making her mind up. She just thought real fast.

Especially when she already knew what she wanted to do.

Three

On Friday night Sammie sat out in the truck and stared at the Evans house, which was lit up like a Christmas tree. Inside, people were laughing and talking and drinking. Out here in the long, curving drive . . . out here, it was downright chilly.

Sammie gave her top another tug, but it hadn't grown one bit bigger since she put it on. She looked down at herself and wondered if J.J. had lost his mind. The old man had made the ultimate sacrifice and gone shopping with her, driving all the way to El Paso so she could find something special, and *this* is what she'd ended up with.

The salesclerk had called the top a ''bustier,'' which would be appropriate if you pronounced it the way it was spelled, since that top was definitely more busty than anything Sammie had ever owned. Since it was a French word, though, you had to say it funny—*boost-yay*. It looked like something a dance hall girl might have worn under her clothes a hundred years ago, being stiff with boning around the middle, and red. Really red. It had a wee tendency to slip down—at least, Sammie didn't think it could have been intended to ride as low as it kept trying to go.

J.J. had insisted she get some lipstick and stuff, too,

so she'd gotten a clerk at one of those fancy department stores to show her how to put it on. That had taken an entire hour, and then the woman rang it all up. Sammie had nearly fainted. Who would have dreamed you could pay that much for a few tubes and powders?

Now all she had to do was find the courage to get out of the truck and walk into Tucker's house with her bust all but falling out of her bustier. Sammie took a deep breath . . . and her top slipped a critical fraction of an inch. She pulled it back up, muttered under her breath, and opened the pickup door.

The house was so full of guests that at first she didn't see him. When she did, she almost wished she hadn't. Tucker had a bad effect on her breathing sometimes.

The wonder was that Tucker hadn't been ruined by his looks. Oh, he had his share of male ego, but his was an ordinary sort of vanity, not what you might expect from a man who looked like a walking invitation to sin. He was vain about his hair, for instance, and wore it long to show it off. It was nice hair, too—a light, shiny brown with lots of blond streaks. But it wasn't the man's hair that made females follow him like puppies. It was the whole package. He had a long, rangy body, and a way of moving that made a woman stop what she was doing to watch. His face was long and narrow, and when he smiled, the sun came out.

That, even more than his looks, was why women fell all over themselves for him. That sweet smile of his was genuine. Maybe he was a bit thick about some things, like how to tell the difference between flash and substance in a woman. But he was a good man, strong all the way through and gentle in the ways a man should be gentle. Tucker would walk a mile out of his way for a stranger in need. For a friend, he'd crawl a hundred miles through a blizzard.

Who wouldn't love a man like that?

The bimbo rejoined him just then. She took his arm in her hands and hugged it up against her, like he might not notice her breasts if she quit pushing them at him. She was smiling up at him like she'd just had her teeth cleaned and couldn't wait to show them off.

Sammie gritted her own teeth and looked away.

Yeah, he was sweet, but the good Lord knew he was thick as stone about some things.

"For heaven's sakes, Tucker. Would you look at her?"

"Who?" Tucker said, looking around obligingly and enjoying the way Lynda held his arm up against her.

"Your little friend," Lynda said, her full lips turning up in amusement. She was a real work of art tonight, Lynda was. Her fingernails were as red as her lips, and her silky black dress was thin enough to make every man in the room wonder what, if anything, she wore beneath it. "The one who came to see you a few days ago on that big, ugly horse. Didn't you tell her this was a dressy party?"

"Sammie's here?" he said, surprised. "I didn't know she was coming." She'd acted odd when he introduced her to Lynda on Tuesday—stiff and formal and not like herself. Maybe she'd felt shy. Lynda might have seemed pretty sophisticated to her, he supposed. Or maybe she had her nose out of joint. Sometimes a man's friends didn't like it when he decided to get married, but he hadn't thought Sammie would get bent out of shape about it.

After all, she was a girl, too. Sort of. Weren't females supposed to think a man was best off married? "I sure do hope you and she get to be friends," he said.

"So you keep telling me."

"So where is she, anyway? I can't see her in all this

crowd." They'd all come, he thought, satisfied. Ranching neighbors and townsfolk had all come to the Evans ranch, just like they used to do in the old days, before his father's drinking got bad. They eddied through the big, old-fashioned living room and dining room now like a school of lazy, tight-packed minnows.

"She's over by that chubby man with the toupee," Lynda said. "The banker you introduced me to. Really, Tucker, you should have told her to dress up. She looks like she belongs at a honky-tonk. The poor thing must feel so out of place."

"Sammie doesn't own any dresses," he said, but his reply was automatic. He was staring too hard to pay attention to what he said.

That wasn't Sammie he saw. Couldn't be. Oh, the red hair scooped into an untidy ponytail might look like hers, but it was on the head of the wrong woman. That cute little redhead could have been Sammie—the size and shape were about right, though he wasn't at all sure there was that much shape to Sammie, under those long-sleeved shirts she always wore—but Sammie would never, ever appear in public dressed that way.

"C'mon," he said, and grabbed Lynda's hand. "We'll go see."

"Oh, honey, you run along." She patted his cheek. "Your little friend isn't comfortable around me, I'm afraid. I'll just mingle."

He felt a twinge of disquiet. Lynda's mingling always seemed to involve men rather than their wives, sisters, or daughters. But that twinge got swallowed up in a whole ocean of other feelings as he crossed the room. The closer he got to his goal, the worse he felt.

The cute little redhead *was* Sammie. He stopped right in front of her and couldn't deny that. Only it wasn't the *right* Sammie, not the one he'd known for fifteen years. This Sammie had brown stuff on her eyelids that made her eyes look different. She had lipstick on, for God's sake. Red lipstick, the same color as the top she was almost wearing.

He was outraged. He wanted an answer, even if he wasn't sure what the question was. And he'd get one, too, by God. "Sammie," he demanded, "what the hell are you doing?"

She frowned. "I'm talking to Mr. Peterson. What the hell are you doing?"

It occurred to him that maybe he was being an idiot. Maybe Sammie got dressed up for parties these days. Just because he'd never seen her in anything so tight, or with makeup on, didn't mean . . . He shook his head. "You've changed," he said sadly.

She rolled her eyes. "Listen, Mr. Peterson, would you excuse me a minute? I need to talk about bulls with this horse's ass here."

The banker chuckled and told the two of them not to talk business too long. This was supposed to be a party, after all.

Sammie took hold of his arm and pulled. "Come on, party boy," she said. "Into the library."

He decided he'd go with her, and let her lead him off down the hall. Once they were alone he could straighten her out about what to wear, and what not to wear, in public. And she had mentioned something about a bull . . . "Say," he said, brightening as he opened the door to the library. "Are you thinking about selling me Big Ben after all?"

"Maybe." She followed him in.

He looked around, his eyes lingering when they encountered the desk against the far wall. His father's desk. "I hate this room."

"Sorry. I should have thought. This was your dad's spot, wasn't it?"

He nodded. Pete Evans had been a good father at

one time, but when a man spends years pouring alcohol down his throat he changes, and not for the better. "Never mind," he said brusquely. "I guess I should get used to this being my room. I'll need to keep my computer and my records someplace."

"I guess so." She chewed her lip for a second. "Tucker. What I wanted to talk to you about . . ."

"The bull?"

She nodded and took a deep breath, which pressed her chest against that shiny red cloth—and his attention went south.

"Tucker . . ."

"Hmm?" That top of hers was much too red. And too tight. And there wasn't nearly enough of it, which was why he was so aware of a couple of things he'd never really noticed about his buddy before. Two round, firm, absolutely delicious-looking things. With nipples.

He swallowed.

"Breeding is important, isn't it?" the owner of those nipples was saying. "I mean, you don't want to mingle just any bloodlines with your stock."

"You know, you really shouldn't wear that."

"What?"

"That." He nodded at her chest. A little glint of gold from an incongruously dainty locket around her throat almost distracted his attention for a moment. "I can see . . . well, hell, Sam, you must know what I can see, and I've got to say, you shouldn't be showing it—them—off this way. People will get the wrong idea."

She inhaled again. "I don't—"

"Now cut that out!" He glared at her. "If you can't quit breathing like that all the time—"

"Tucker, are you feeling all right?"

"I'm fine! I'm just fine, in spite of that teeny little scrap of cloth you've almost got on. But I have to say,

I'm mighty disappointed in you, tarting yourself up that way."

Her hands went to her hips and her eyes narrowed. "Tucker Evans, did you just call me a *tart*?"

"Well, if you dress like one and smear makeup all over your face, you can't be real surprised if people comment on it."

She made a loud, angry sound and stepped closer, tilting her chin up. "Oh, so now you don't like makeup and tight clothes on women! Have you mentioned that to Lynda? She'll be awfully upset, since everything she owns is at least one size too small—except those boobs of hers!"

"Now you just leave Lynda out of this!"

"Gladly! I'll leave her out *entirely*—but first I'd better warn you not to stay in here talking to me too long, or she'll latch on to someone else the way she did Monty Blake Wednesday when the two of you were in town. I heard all about that from his sister Anne. Poor Monty didn't know which way to look, he was so embarrassed about the way your lady friend was hanging all over him."

"You don't know what you're talking about!" he yelled. "My God, you're a menace, all right, talking about stuff when you don't have a clue. Not a clue! It's not as if you had any idea what things are like between a man and a woman!"

She went suddenly pale. And quiet. And the silence held and dragged on for one moment too long before she said, "No, I guess I don't. And it's none of my business, anyway. I'm sorry I said that."

He sighed and ran a hand over the top of his head, messing up his hair and feeling about snake-high. He hadn't meant to step on a sore spot. How was he to know little Sammie would be sensitive about something she'd never shown the least interest in? But he hated that he'd hurt her feelings. "My fault. I ought to know I can't shoot my mouth off without you coming back at me, right?" He tried a grin. "Now, what was it you wanted to talk about?"

She swallowed. "Breeding."

He perked up. "You mean you are thinking about selling your bull?"

"Maybe. Under the right . . . conditions."

"What are your conditions?" He couldn't think of what she might want. Some calves? Or the right to buy the bull back?

"Um," she said. And she turned away and started fidgeting with the books on the shelf behind her. "I want you to—that is, I, uh, wanyatgmprgn."

"Huh? Say that again?"

Her shoulders stiffened. Her head went up. She spoke clearly, though still with her back to him, and very fast, so that the words ran together. "I-want-you-to-get-me-pregnant."

Four

Tucker was calm. Very calm. "There is something wrong with my ears. Or the air in here is messed up. Or my brain is. Because you couldn't have said what I thought you said." A hint of desperation seeped past the calm. "Could you?"

"Well, I did," she said, still addressing the books. "But you don't have to do it *yourself,* if you don't want to. I mean, I wouldn't ask you to cheat on your bimb—on Lynda. But it's easy enough to do the thing nowadays without *that,* isn't it? I mean, when was the last time you let a bull impregnate one of your cows in person instead of using artificial insemination?"

"You want me," he said, speaking very slowly, "to trade my sperm *for your bull*?" His voice started to rise toward the end of the sentence, like the first strong gusts of wind announcing the arrival of the hurricane.

"Of course not." She did turn part way around now, and sneaked a glance at him. "Not *trade.* Good grief, Tucker, that bull is worth thousands! But if we can come to terms about *that,* then I'll sell you Big Ben."

The storm broke.

He told her what he thought about her offer, her intelligence, and her morals. How dare she try to use him in her latest campaign to infuriate her stepfather?

Because that's what this was about, wasn't it? He could think of a dozen things she'd done as a teenager to get Art's attention, but nothing came close to this!

He might have gotten a little carried away, because she was looking pale as death when he stopped to draw breath.

She didn't say a word. Just headed for the door.

"Where do you think you're going?" He grabbed her arm. "I'm not finished! By God, you can't go prancing around in that little scrap of nothing, saying you want to bear men's children and wanting to *buy* my semen like I was your damned bull, only you don't think I'm *worth* as much as your damned bull—"

"Let go of me."

He should have let go. He knew that, but his mouth ran on as if it had a life of its own, and another part of his body rose to the challenge she'd set it because the blasted thing *did* have a life of its own. "Be damned if I'll let you leave before I'm finished talking to you!" He gave her a little shake. He wanted to kiss her, dammit, and put his hand down that scrap of red covering her breasts and—"I'm not a bull at stud, and I'm not going to go around servicing—"

She turned and made one quick, sure movement with her knee. Right at his groin.

Stars exploded. His eyes fell out of his head and rolled around on the carpet. He bent over, clutching himself, while someone made the most godawful moaning sounds. He wanted to tell them to shut up, but he couldn't remember how to talk or breathe, or how he might go about finding his eyeballs when he couldn't see past the waves of pain crashing over him.

He asked for help. "Wha-wha-wha—"

"My name," she said in a tight little voice, "is Sherry." And after that baffling pronouncement, she turned and walked out.

* * *

Everything went wrong for Tucker the next day.

First his banker called. The money that was supposed to have been wired into his checking account from his mutual fund account, where he had stashed most of his prize money, had gone to someone in Arizona instead. Everyone was real sorry about the mistake and swore they'd have it straightened out right away, or at least by tomorrow, and in the meantime, his banker could *almost* guarantee that no checks would get sent back.

The pipe leading to the water tank in the west pasture sprang a leak, so he sent his one-and-only hand to fix it. Then the weatherman announced that a freak late-winter storm was headed their way, and that would play holy hell with his schedule because he'd barely started the new roof on the hay barn.

And Lynda was acting funny. She was bored, she said, and wanted him to take her into town, and she didn't mean that itty-bitty one nearby. Couldn't they head into El Paso for the day or something? She didn't seem to understand that he had to finish the roof before the storm arrived.

Maybe . . . he hated to admit it, but maybe his temporary disability due to Sam's knee had him seeing Lynda differently. More clearly. Until today, he'd thought those little-girl ways of hers when she wanted something were as cute as the cajoling of a kitten when it purred and rubbed up against you. From the day they'd met two months ago she'd made him feel special, looking at him with admiring eyes and touching him all the time, like she couldn't get enough of him.

But today she sounded more whiny than cute, and he couldn't help wondering if she admired anyone who let her have her way.

And he couldn't quit thinking about Sammie. It hurt,

which made no sense. He had plenty of reasons to be mad, and he was—but not mad enough to keep the hurt from coming through, and he could not figure out where the pain was coming from.

It wasn't until one o'clock that things got really bad—and better, too, in a confusing sort of a way. That's when J.J. rode over.

Tucker was nailing shingles as fast as he could when J.J. rode up. He didn't mind taking a break, so he walked over to the edge of the roof to meet the old man who had been more of a father to Sammie than her stepfather had.

But J.J. didn't look too happy with him when he reined his horse to a stop. He glared up at Tucker. "I don't know what you said to that girl, but you're gonna have to fix things, you hear me?"

"I am not about to cater to the whims of—" He broke off before he said something J.J. would see to it that he regretted. "Look, I've got two hundred cows coming in next week, and that storm's apt to hit before I'm finished here. I've got plumbing problems, too, and my banker says—"

J.J. suggested a creative and unlikely use the banker might have for the pipe, then said, "Sammie took off this morning after havin' words with Art. Whether she quit or he fired her, I can't say, but I gather she don't work there no more." He shook his head gloomily. "Guess I'll be giving notice myself, once she gets herself a place. Which she won't do, if she gets herself starved or froze first."

"What on earth are you talking about?"

"She's gone to the mountains. She was packing up her kit and muttering to herself when I saw her this morning. Wouldn't slow down or listen to a word I said, she was that worked up. She'd be all right up there for a couple days, even though she didn't pack any extra food, except for—''

''The storm.'' Fear chilled him. ''That stupid, crazy little—she'll turn around, though. Sammie's no fool. She knows to keep an eye on the weather, and once she sees that front piling up in the north, she'll head back.''

''I dunno.'' J.J. shook his head doubtfully. ''Maybe she won't notice until it's too late. She was awful upset.''

Because of him. The hurt that had plagued Tucker all day got stronger and sharper, lodging itself somewhere in his chest, but he couldn't turn his mind to that puzzle, not yet.

He thought furiously. The rocky hills that separated the two ranches bunched themselves up higher to the south, blending into the Davis Mountains. The three of them—him, Dan, and Dan's little sister—used to take their packs and head up into those mountains several times a year. He knew which spots she favored. ''Does she still head for Gopher Peak when she's upset?''

''Yep.'' The old man spat a brownish stream out of the corner of his mouth. ''I figure she'll make for the old line cabin on the edge of Art's land when she sees what's happening with the weather.''

Tucker nodded. That made sense. No matter how upset she was, Sammie would head for shelter once the weather got obvious about its intentions. ''I'll ride out right away. Probably I'll meet her heading down, but if I don't—well, I'll bring her back down if I have to tie her to Beast's saddle to do it.''

''What about your fiancée?''

''She'll understand.''

Lynda didn't understand. Tucker didn't listen to her wheedling, so she tried screeching, but he didn't have time to listen to that, either. It was three hours on horseback to that cabin, and it would be three hours getting back, too, and he had to make the most of what daylight he had left before the storm hit.

But Lynda seemed to think her need for attention was more important than Sam's safety. She complained that he was abandoning her to go "chasing off after that stupid little girl, who probably planned all this anyway." She thought he should have let J.J., who was seventy years old, go after Sam instead. Tucker listened to her opinion of his selfishness while he saddled Snickers, the quarter horse he'd raised from a foal.

By the time he had the girth tight on the saddle, he'd pretty much lost patience. By the time he rode out of the yard, he'd pretty much lost interest. Which was just as well, since she was in her room, packing to go home to her momma.

When a storm rolls in over the Davis Mountains, it gets dark quick and early. Sammie listened to the hammering of wind and rain on the walls and roof of the cabin as she felt around in the cabinet for the oil lamp. It was already so dark she couldn't see clearly. On the other side of the south wall, Beast shifted noisily.

She should have gotten the lamp lit earlier, but she'd been too busy lying on the cot and feeling miserable.

The cabin was really two rooms, both pretty basic. The smaller room had a wooden floor, a wood-burning stove, and a cot with a foam mattress for the humans who sheltered here from time to time. The larger side had two stalls, an earth floor, stacks of wood for the stove, and hay for the humans' four-legged partners.

Sammie didn't mind the commotion the storm was making. The howl of the wind suited her mood just fine right now. But when an even louder hammering rattled the front door, she jumped and dropped the match she'd just lit. Fortunately, it went out before it hit the floor.

She scowled at the door. The last thing she wanted was company. Lord, hadn't she ridden for three hours in order to be sure of not seeing another human face for a few days? Or maybe forever. Maybe she just wouldn't come back down again. She'd lost her job, so there was no pressing reason to ever have any contact with the rest of humanity again.

The knocking stopped—but only because her unwanted visitor started jerking on the door as if he planned to take it right off its hinges.

He might, too. It wasn't real sturdy. She sighed, set the globe back on the unlit lamp, and reached for her rifle. She supposed that if some fool camper had gotten himself lost she'd have to let him share a roof until the storm blew itself out. She kept her rifle in her left hand, just in case, when she opened the door.

Then she slammed it shut again. Or tried to.

"Dammit, Sammie, open that door!"

She got her back to the door, braced her legs and pushed, but he was bigger and stronger, and her feet began to slowly slide across the floor as the door opened bit by bit.

His shout blew in with the wind and rain. "Snickers is hurt!"

She moved away so quickly that the door slammed back against the wall. Tucker staggered in, wearing a dripping yellow slicker and a grim expression.

"Light the lamp, would you? The matches are on the table," she said, hurrying to open the cabinet by the sink. Reaching inside, she tried to find what she needed by feel. It was almost fully dark inside the cabin now, and the storm seemed to be building, hurling itself down on them in a frenzy of wind and rain. "You put Snickers in the other side?" That must have been what she heard earlier, she realized—not Beast moving around, but Tucker putting his horse up.

"Yeah. I looked for some salve, but didn't see any."

"She's cut, then. Will we need to sew it?"

"No. It's a puncture wound. Left front foreleg."

Puncture wounds were bad news, especially in the legs. Sammie frowned, worried. She heard the rasp of a match being struck, and a second later light bloomed behind her and she could see well enough to get the rest of her supplies. She stuffed everything in a plastic grocery sack and turned around. "So what happened?"

He'd closed the front door and moved to the only other door, which led to the other room of the cabin. He reached for the latch. "We were crossing the Agua Roja," he said, naming a tiny, seasonal creek that ran along a gulch halfway between here and home. "We've had a wet winter, and the creek was up."

"I noticed. The water came well over Beast's fetlocks when we crossed. The current wasn't all that strong, though."

"It's higher now, and stronger." He opened the door.

The smell of horses and hay greeted her, warm and comforting. She pulled a flashlight out of the sack and followed him in. "Did a branch catch her?"

He shook his head, disgusted. "A busted beer bottle, or a piece of one. It went in just above the fetlock."

They passed into the other side of the cabin, where the air smelled of hay and horses. Tucker set the lamp on a shelf near Snickers's stall. The mare greeted him with the funny little whicker that Tucker had always insisted was an equine laugh, and the reason for her name. Beast shifted in his stall, ears twitching.

Sammie set her sack of supplies on the hard dirt floor. "Hold her head, will you?" She knelt.

"I can take care of her," Tucker said.

She met his eyes. Maybe it was the dim, warm light of the oil lamp that made him look vulnerable. Or maybe it was the fact that he'd raised this horse, trained her, and ridden her to a championship. He loved her. Maybe he wouldn't ever say so, but Sammie knew it was true. "She'll stay calm if you're at her head, Tucker, and the quieter she is, the better for her. You know that. If I need help, I'll let you know."

He nodded, his face stiff.

For one dreadful moment, she thought she was going to cry. She didn't even know why, except that there was so blasted much emotion brewing inside her, with nowhere for it to go. She bit the inside of her lip to stifle the flood, and turned her attention to the horse.

The wound looked small, but it was deep and would be hard to clean adequately. They'd need to keep it open on the surface so no lingering infection got trapped inside, letting it heal from the inside out, and they'd have to keep Snickers quiet for a few days while it healed.

She worked in silence, letting Tucker's soothing voice be the only one the mare heard. He found a shedding blade, and used it to sleek the water from the mare's coat. By the time she was sure the cut was clean and was applying the pungent-smelling salve, he was currying Snickers with a brush. The horse obviously loved the attention.

What female wouldn't? she asked herself glumly. "Tucker," she started, but her throat closed up around the question she needed to ask.

"Hmm?" He continued crooning nonsense words to his horse while he brushed her with slow, smooth strokes.

She needed to know why he was here. Had he come all this way to apologize for the terrible things he'd said? Her heart began to pound. If he had, would she accept? Should she?

Damn right she would, she decided as she began winding a light gauze dressing around Snickers's foreleg. If she didn't, he'd hang around and pester her until she did. Tucker was nothing if not stubborn. And she wanted him gone.

She tied off the gauze. "Why aren't you down at your ranch, getting things fixed up for your bride-to-be?"

"Lynda's gone."

Her hands froze for a minute. She swallowed and reached for the elastic bandage that would keep the dressing in place, and tried to tamp down her joy. "Well. That's a shame."

"Don't add hypocrisy to your other sins," he said dryly. "You didn't like her, and I guess—well, she was a mistake. I thought . . ." He shook his head. "Never mind what I thought."

She finished winding the bandage. "So," she said as casually as she was able, "what are you doing up here, then?"

"J.J. told me you'd taken off," he said.

"He did?" She frowned. "Why?"

"You've noticed, maybe, that there's a storm? You know, the one that's throwing tree limbs around out there?"

"So? No offense, but you're the one who got caught in it, not me." She stood and dusted straw and dirt from her jeans. "Not that it was your fault or anything. You had to walk a long ways after Snickers got hurt, so it's not surprising the storm caught up with you." As a matter of fact, he'd had to walk almost as far to reach her up here as he would have if he'd turned around and gone back at that point.

She frowned, thinking that over.

His jaw tightened until something should have cracked. "I came," he said with awful patience, "to get you back down the mountain before you ran out of food. J.J. told me you'd taken off without packing anything."

"Well, of course I didn't pack much. The hands keep the cabin stocked. I've got standing orders for that—or did," she said, grimacing, "when I still had a job. Not much point in packing in more food myself when there's two weeks' worth of canned goods on the shelves. Except for some eggs and bread. I did bring those in."

His voice was level. "You're telling me that you don't need any supplies."

"No." When he cursed, low and heartfelt, her heart sank. "You, uh, came because J.J. made you think I didn't have any food?"

He nodded grimly.

"Oh." At least, she thought mournfully, Tucker hadn't wanted her to starve to death. The thought wasn't much comfort, since she knew he would have done the same for a stranger. She turned and started putting what was left of her medical supplies on the shelf next to the oil lamp.

He came over to her. "Sammie, I've been thinking about what happened last night."

Uh-oh. "Maybe you shouldn't. Think about it, I mean. Maybe we should both just forget about it. That might work, don't you think?" If they acted as if it had never happened, maybe they could still be friends. If they couldn't even be friends anymore . . . her heart hitched itself up into her throat, and she started for the other room.

"We have to talk about it." He was following.

"No, we don't." She moved faster. "Not tonight, anyway. Tomorrow, maybe."

"Sammie." His hand landed on her shoulder, stopping her, and he *was* close. Very close. She could feel the heat from his body. A dizzy mixture of lust and nerves tightened her muscles until she thought she might snap, just like barbed wire pulled too taut.

"I did some thinking on the way up here. I was wrong, wasn't I? About why you asked me . . . what you asked me."

They stood next to the doorway to the other side. The lantern on the shelf by Snickers's stall cast weird, flickering shadows, while Sammie's heart danced madly in her chest. It took all the courage she had to nod slightly.

"I should have known better than to say what I did. I mean, you've pulled some crazy stunts in the past, but a baby—you wouldn't have a baby for such a stupid reason. Only, if that wasn't why you did it . . ." He cleared his throat. "I wondered if maybe you had decided to, uh, practice on me."

"Practice?" Her voice cracked.

"Yeah. You probably thought it would be okay to try a little flirting, because you know you're safe with me. When I, uh, reacted kind of funny, you couldn't resist teasing me and got a little carried away."

She wanted to agree. They could both pretend that was the truth. Maybe deep down he knew better, but he wanted to believe this version of events, didn't he?

Anger flickered up from beneath the pile of other feelings. "Oh, so any time a woman asks you to get her pregnant, you assume she's flirting, do you?"

"Uh—well—"

She turned and faced him. His face was in shadow, so she couldn't read his expression at all. "You want to know why I said that, Tucker? It's simple enough. I want to have a baby."

The silence stretched and stretched between them.

At last he asked, his voice quiet and strange, "My baby, Sammie?"

Her heart jammed in her throat and thudded there, an insistent prisoner. She swallowed. "Tucker, do you know what my name is?"

Tucker was distracted. The rich syrup of arousal flowed in his veins, pooling hotly in his groin and stealing the blood from his brain. Dammit, no wonder he couldn't concentrate! He had no blood in his brain. His condition was absurd, because she looked just as she'd always looked—like Sammie, his friend, with her plain, long-sleeved shirt and thick, messy hair that he'd love to tangle his hands up in and—

He said the one thing his oxygen-starved brain could come up with. "Huh?"

"You don't get it, do you? My name is Sherry Anne Mathews. I don't think anyone even remembers that anymore. Do you know how long it's been since anyone called me Sherry Anne?"

He was confused. "But you liked it when Dan started calling you Sam, after your initials. Danny and Sammie—it was kind of cute. You *told* me to call you Sammie."

She rolled her eyes. "I was eight years old! My God, Tucker, do you even know how old I am now? I'm not 'little Sammie' anymore!"

"You're . . ." Math was a strain in his current state, but he managed. He was four years and two months older than Sammie, which made her . . . "twenty-three."

"That's right. I'm all grown up, Tucker, and I . . . I don't want to be just your good buddy anymore."

The hurt he'd felt ever since last night came splashing back over him. "But we've always been friends. Good friends, Sammie," he said, willing her to understand. "Friends are the ones you can really count on.

Don't you see? Sex is great, sure—but it's not exactly rare. Friendship is. Real friendship—that's a rare and powerful thing."

"Okay." She nodded. "Okay, that's all true, but have you ever thought maybe you could have friendship and—and all the rest, too? Maybe two people, the right two people, can do that."

"No." He shook his head, very definite. "No, Sammie. It doesn't work that way."

"Then I guess you're not going to kiss me," she said wistfully.

He realized, with a jolt, that he was standing so close he was practically on top of her. When had he moved? He'd even lowered his head slightly. Her face was tilted up to his, a pale oval in the dimness. Two small flames, reflections from the oil lamp, danced across the liquid surfaces of her eyes. Her lips were parted.

It would take no effort at all to bend down the last few inches and taste those pretty lips.

He wanted to. Wanted it so badly his hands shook. He stepped back, scared to death of himself, or of her, or of something he had no name for.

She sighed. "I hope you brought a sleeping bag with you. I'm taking the cot, and the floor is pretty hard. Good night." And she turned and walked into the darkness in the other room, leaving him hard and aching and confused.

And alone.

FIVE

Thirty minutes later, Sammie lay on her back between the thicknesses of her goosedown sleeping bag and stared at the darkness pressing down on her eyes like tears. The mattress beneath her back was thin and hard, but not as hard as the floor where Tucker lay, as far away from her as he could get and still be within the cabin. He had three blankets for his bed—two he'd brought with him, and one someone had left up here.

He was so close. And so horribly far away. Was there any way for them to go back to being friends, or had she ruined that for them? He seemed so certain that sex and friendship couldn't mix, and now . . . now, even though they'd never kissed, sex was part of their relationship. She'd seen that look in his eyes, and knew what it meant.

Could they go back?

Of course, his certainty about not mixing sex and friendship probably came from the fact that he wasn't in love with her, like she was with him. She sighed and rolled over on her side.

She had thought he was going to kiss her, though. When he'd stood so close to her, his body almost touching hers, she'd been all but certain he would kiss her. Even in the poor light, she'd known the look on his face for what it was.

Desire. For *her*.

Did she really want to go back?

If you were trying to cross a flooded river, she told herself, did you get to the middle, then turn around and go back? Of course not. Even if the water was higher, faster, and more dangerous than you'd expected, you didn't change direction in midstream. After a certain point, it was no safer to go back than it was to go on.

And she did have a powerful yearning to reach that other side.

No, having come this far, all she could do was hang on, pay attention to the current, and pray that her love was surefooted enough to carry her safely the rest of the way.

And come up with a way to seduce Tucker.

The floor *was* hard. And cold. And Tucker might have been only four years older than Sammie, but he'd spent enough of his twenty-seven years getting bucked off animals that outweighed him by half a ton or so that some of his body parts tended to stiffen up when he slept on the cold, hard floor.

Another body part often stiffened up in the mornings, too, but he was thankful to say that it had never been injured in his bronc-riding days. He lay in his corner of the floor the next morning with his eyes closed, smelling the heavenly scent of coffee brewing, and thought about ice water. Cold showers. And pointy knees right in the . . .

" 'Morning," said a cheerful voice. "I'm fixing your eggs sunny side up, 'cause that's the only way I know how to cook them. Ready in two shakes."

It had been years since he'd been camping with Sammie and her brother. He'd forgotten how blasted happy she was in the morning. He grunted, rolled into a sitting position, and scrubbed his face with both hands, leaving the blanket covering his lap. "I smell coffee."

"It's ready."

Every time she spoke, the part of him that he wanted to settle down tried to sit up and wave at her. He scowled and stood up, keeping his back to her. "I'll be back in a minute."

The bathroom facilities, such as they were, were outside. He grabbed his jacket, shrugging it on as he opened the front door—and froze. "Good God. It *snowed*." Snow was such a rarity in these parts, even in the mountains, that the possibility hadn't occurred to him.

"More like sleet, I think. It's slick in spots. I had hoped to head down the mountain today and bring the vet or at least bring some antibiotics back up for Snickers, but—"

He turned to scowl at her. "You're not going anywhere in this!"

"I know that," she said impatiently. "Shut the door, will you? You're letting all the warm air out."

He shut the door behind him and went to take care of necessities. In the process, the cold air sent the blood scooting back up into the rest of his body, where it belonged. Moving around eased the other sort of stiffness, too, the kind he got from sleeping on the floor. He was a good deal more comfortable by the time he went to check on Snickers.

He didn't remove the dressing. He'd do that when Sammie was there to help, since he'd probably have to reopen the wound to keep it healing from the inside out. But he stroked her, gave her a small measure of grain, and ran his hand along her leg, checking for heat or swelling.

When he went back into the people side of the cabin, he was feeling a good deal more cheerful.

Sammie wasn't feeling cheerful, exactly, but the exhilaration of setting a goal and breasting the current helped quiet the tangle of nerves that made it hard to sit still. "Your breakfast is keeping warm," she told him, nodding at the metal plate she'd set on the edge of the stove. She chased the last bite of her own eggs with her fork and a piece of bread. "How is Snickers?"

"No swelling, and the area is barely warm to the touch." He poured a cup of coffee and brought the pot to the table. "Need a refill?"

She breathed a sigh of relief. "Sure." She held her cup out.

He filled it, then paused. "Sammie—what happened with you and Art, anyway? J.J. said you'd quit, or gotten fired."

She shrugged. "You know how Art is. Gets mad anytime someone doesn't dance to his tune. I probably should have gone out on my own before this."

"You love the ranch."

"But it's not mine. And it never will be." She pushed her plate away. "The argument started with me asking for time off, but everything kind of blew up after that. He went on and on about how he'd done me a favor all these years by letting me work for him, how it was for my mother's sake and I should be grateful and all that rot. Didn't seem like I had much choice."

"You quit?"

She nodded.

"He's wrong, you know. You're a damned fine foreman. He's just too pigheaded to admit that a female could be better at managing the ranch than his son."

"Dan could do it if he wanted to," she said quickly. Dan was Art's son by his first wife, which made him Sammie's step-brother. She'd never thought of him that way, though. Dan had always acted like her big brother, and to Sammie, that's what he was.

"But he doesn't want to. That's the point Art keeps missing—Dan is never coming back to take over the ranch the way Art wants him to. He loves the ranch but he doesn't love ranching, and he seems to have found what he was looking for in the service." He dropped a hand on her shoulder and squeezed briefly, then went to get his plate. "Hang in there. Something will turn up. Or maybe that pigheaded stepfather of yours will be forced to admit he needs you running things."

"Sure," she said, cupping her coffee mug in both hands and trying to take a little comfort from the warmth. Never had her future looked more uncertain.

And she still had to figure out a way to seduce Tucker.

She brooded about that while he ate. It seemed a hopeless task, when she knew so little about acting female. Shoot, Tucker knew a lot more about that sort of thing than she did, just from watching all the females that had tried to trip him and beat him to the ground over the years.

After a few bites he put down his fork. "Quit chewing on your lip and tell me what's wrong."

"Nothing. Did your eggs get cold?" It was damned annoying. If their situation were reversed, Tucker wouldn't be having this trouble. He could have seduced her in a wink.

"They're okay." He eyed her warily a moment, then returned his attention to his breakfast.

Inspiration hit Sammie with all the subtlety of a freight train. Her mouth fell open as she absorbed the impact of an idea brilliant in its simplicity. If she didn't know how to conduct a seduction, and Tucker did—

why, then all she had to do was get him to do the seducing.

A few minutes' thought convinced her she could do this. She gave herself one last sip of coffee to fortify herself as she prepared to move forward, into the current. Then she set down her cup. "I'm sorry, Tucker."

"For what?" he asked, surprised. "I told you. The eggs are fine."

She looked at his head. Nice hair, but the skull was thick as stone, all right. Granite. "I'm not talking about breakfast. I'm talking about sex."

His fork clattered to the floor.

"I'm sorry I ever brought the question of sex up between us," she explained, leaning forward. "It seemed like a good idea at the time, but it confused everything. Why, look how confused you are right now, and I didn't suggest sex this time. I just mentioned it." She lowered her voice confidingly. "The thing is, I need some help."

He leaned back, alarmed. "I don't think I—"

"And look what happened when I tried to figure things out on my own! I wore the wrong clothes, said the wrong things—thank goodness you explained things to me last night, about not mixing sex and friendship." She smiled at him sweetly. "You were right. I should have come to you right from the start."

"I didn't tell you to come to me for, uh—"

"Oh, I don't mean come to you for *sex*! I'm talking about all the stuff that leads up to sex but isn't actually, you know, *doing* it. All that man-woman stuff you admitted I don't know anything about. Like flirting. You know all about that, don't you? And, like you said, I'd be safe with you."

"I didn't say it was a *good* idea. As a matter of fact, I think it's a terrible idea. Probably one of the worst ideas I've ever heard."

"Don't be so hard on yourself." She reached out and patted his hand. "It'll give us both something to do while we're stuck up here."

He looked ready to bolt.

"You don't mind, do you? All you have to do is answer a few questions. Like—what was wrong with what I wore to the party? J.J. said I looked real good."

"J.J. said that?" He was dumfounded.

She nodded and picked up her mug, pausing to take a sip. This was like fishing, she decided. You just kept throwing out your bait until you got the fish more curious than it was cautious. "He's been helping me figure things out. You know, how to dress, fix my hair, that sort of thing."

"No." He shook his head. "You didn't do that."

"What?"

"You didn't ask an old man who wears the same clothes until they fall off to help you with clothes and makeup."

"Now, don't exaggerate. J.J. changes his clothes. Not quite as often as he might, maybe—especially the jeans—but anyway, I didn't ask him. He volunteered."

He shook his head. "I don't get it, Sammie. You were never interested in girl stuff before. In high school, when most of the girls were hanging out together, giggling and talking about hairstyles and lipstick, you just wanted to hang out with the guys and talk about horses."

But in high school, the only way she'd been able to spend time with her big brother, when Dan was home from college—and with her brother's pal, Tucker—had been if she were "one of the guys." Besides, she *liked* talking horses. She shrugged. "I guess I'm a late bloomer. Does it matter? Listen, just tell me what was wrong with that bustier thing I wore to the party. J.J.

said it was just what I needed to get a man to notice me.''

''Yeah, but you aren't supposed to let men notice that much of you!'' He ran a hand over the top of his head, mussing that pretty brown hair of his, and scowled at her.

She wanted to smooth it for him, then run her fingers through it and tangle it up again. She tried to look innocent.

''Okay,'' he said at last. ''Okay, I guess I'd better help you. No telling what kind of trouble you'll get yourself into if I don't, because it's obvious you haven't got a clue.''

''Thanks, Tucker.'' She reached across the table and squeezed his hand. ''You won't regret this.''

Tucker had never regretted anything more. Not even the time when, as a cocky twenty-year-old, he'd gotten blind drunk on tequila and passed out in the back of a friend's pickup. He'd woken up in Albuquerque, New Mexico, the next day. That wouldn't have been so bad, except that his gear, his horse, and the rodeo where he'd paid his entry fee had still been in Lubbock, Texas.

At twenty, though, a man still has so much to learn about stupidity it may take him years to check out enough different versions of it to learn how to avoid looking an idiot in the eye when he's shaving. At twenty, Tucker had thought that watching his father slowly ruin himself with drink had somehow inoculated him against making the same mistake. It had been a shock to learn that the world didn't work that way.

But he had learned that lesson, so there had been some *point* to his suffering that time. Not now. He was convinced that what he was enduring now had no redeeming qualities whatsoever. How in the world had he let Sammie persuade him to teach her to dance? The lesson he'd given her in flirting had been bad enough. Compounding that by actually touching her was a whole new level of stupidity.

"No, dammit, Sammie, not like that," he said, his voice hoarse as he held her at arm's length for one desperate moment. "You've got to quit trying to lead."

"Sorry. But I'm not used to letting someone else set the pace and the direction. When I'm riding—"

"You're not riding me," he said, and shut his mouth, horrified at the wonderful images his statement conjured.

"No," she said innocently, "we're dancing. Or trying to. And I do appreciate you teaching me, but Tucker, wouldn't it be easier if we were a little closer together? I don't think I've ever seen people dance with this much space between them. I'm sure I could tell which direction you wanted me to go a lot better if we were closer. I mean, if I could feel which way your body was moving—"

"No," he said quickly. "You have to learn to do it the right way, first. Come on, now, pay attention. *One*-two-three . . ."

She started singing again, to give them some kind of music to dance to.

Somehow, Sammie had gotten the wrong singing voice. She should have sounded loud and brash, maybe slightly off-key. Instead . . .

" 'Stand by your man,' " she sang in a breathy little voice that made him think of tangled sheets and the musky perfume of arousal.

Somewhere, Tucker thought, *there's a big-busted brunette with a bee-sting mouth who loves to wear little lacy things, do her nails, and go shopping, and she's wondering who got her voice.*

Why was it he'd never noticed before what an absurdly sexy voice she had? They'd sung together over campfires any number of times in the past without him thinking of tangled sheets, or feminine fingers teasing the skin on his back. The bare skin of his totally bare back. And the woman with him between those sheets was bare, too. Entirely, delightfully bare, and he could easily imagine what her breasts looked like, because he'd seen quite a bit of them last— "Better," he said quickly. "You're doing much better. In fact, I think you've learned as much as you need to know for now."

She stopped singing. "No I haven't."

Oh, yes she had. He was pretty sure that his buddy Sammie, who had such pretty breasts, had never done half the things he was thinking of teaching her. "I need to check on Snickers."

"You checked on her thirty minutes ago. I'm barely catching on here, Tucker."

"I'd say you're catching on at the speed of light," he said grimly, and made himself let go of her. Only she still stood there, her hand at his waist, looking as pleased as if he'd just complimented her roping. "You're supposed to let go now, Sammie."

"Oh." Looking not a whit discomposed, she did finally stop touching him and step back—one whole inch. "I've been thinking."

"Have you, now?" Funny how he'd never noticed how creamy her skin was beneath those freckles. At the party, when he'd seen so much of her that wasn't usually exposed, he'd realized she had a true redhead's complexion, pale and fine as poured cream. He'd realized that she didn't have any freckles on her breasts.

At least, not the parts of them he'd seen so far.

She nodded. "I know you said that sex and friendship don't mix."

"Mmm-hmm." Did she have any freckles he hadn't

seen? Any shy, pale little freckles hiding in the soft undercurve of her breasts?

"Why not?"

Her mouth was freckle-colored, too. A warm rusty-rose color that made him want to . . . "Huh? What did you say?"

Patiently she repeated, "Why don't sex and friendship mix?"

He opened his mouth. And closed it again when he hunted around in his brain and found it empty. Dammit, she'd drained all his blood from his brain again. "They just don't."

"That's not much of an answer."

"I need some coffee," he said firmly, and turned away.

"I'll put some on if you'll fix lunch."

Since fixing lunch would involve opening a couple of cans and dumping their contents in a pan, Tucker didn't hesitate to agree.

She carried the little tin coffeepot to the sink, where she pumped water. Tucker went to the door, opened it, and stood looking out. It was nearly noon, and the patches of snow that the sun had shone on were mostly gone.

"What's the weather look like?" she asked.

"The sky is clear, but there's still icy spots in the shade."

"I guess I won't be heading back down the mountain yet, then," she said, sounding entirely too cheerful. "Not unless Snickers gets worse."

He grunted. Dammit, he'd hoped to break up their enforced intimacy in this little cabin by sending her after medicine for his horse. But not with icy patches still lingering. *Tomorrow,* he told himself, closing the door. Surely it would have melted by then. He only had to hold out one more day.

She was spooning coffee grounds into the basket. "Make yourself useful and build up the fire in the stove."

"Sure." Anything that put some distance between him and temptation sounded like a good idea. He headed for the stable.

The light in the other room of the cabin was dim, since the only window was shuttered for warmth. Still, he could see well enough to walk past Beast's stall to the woodpile, where he began collecting an armload.

He didn't see the snake, though. Not till it bit him.

SIX

Sammie had the coffeepot in her hand, but most of her mind was on the question of whether she was making progress with Tucker or just scaring him to death, when she heard him cry out.

She dropped the pot and took off running.

He stood by the woodpile, gripping his wrist tightly with one hand. Several pieces of wood lay tumbled at his feet.

"What? What is it?"

His face was pallid in the dim light. "Snake. No, dammit, stay back! It's in the woodpile." She moved forward instinctively, but he forestalled her by coming to her.

"Did you see it?" she asked. Blood welled slowly in two fang marks on the back of his hand. The fingers of his other hand were white where he gripped his wrist.

He shook his head. "I barely caught a glimpse when it flashed back beneath the logs, not enough to identify it. I didn't hear any rattles."

"Most snakes aren't poisonous."

"I know."

"No trouble breathing? Your hand—is it burning, like acid?"

"No." Their eyes met. His were clear, dark—and shaken.

She knew why. Tucker was afraid of snakes. Deeply, mortally afraid. When he was three, he'd been outside with his mother when she was bitten by a coral snake. She'd died pretty quickly. He didn't remember that day, he'd told her once, but he got shaky and sick if he so much as saw a snake.

"What color was it?" she asked.

"Dark. Maybe gray or black. Not banded."

She breathed a sigh of relief. Not a coral snake, then, and probably not a rattler. "Chances are it wasn't poisonous, then, but come inside and let's do what we can."

He followed her, stumbling slightly on the doorstep. She looked over her shoulder, anxious. It wasn't like Tucker to be clumsy. Was he reacting to having his deepest fear come true? Or had the snake injected some neurotoxin that was already weakening him?

"I'm okay," he said, disgusted. "Just shaking like an eighty-year-old virgin on her wedding night."

"Sit," she said, smiling in spite of herself, and pulled out the first-aid box.

"I don't need to sit. I need a drink."

"I've got some ginger ale."

He gave her a dirty look, but he did sit—on the cot, which was closest. "Damned snake shouldn't have been out in this weather. It's too cold."

"I don't think snakes listen to the weather channel. The storm probably caught it out for a little spring stroll away from its burrow, and it headed for the nearest warm place." She brought the box over and sat beside him. "Give me your hand—and quit holding your wrist so tight. You're cutting off the circulation."

"That's the idea," he said dryly, still gripping his wrist.

She looked at him. He sounded calm, but he was pale and, though it was cool in the cabin, there were beads of sweat on his upper lip. "Are you having any symptoms?"

"Other than the fear that I'll humiliate myself by fainting or throwing up?" He shook his head. "Not really."

"Well, I've seen you do that before." She saturated a cotton ball in peroxide. "Not faint, but—remember the Settlers' Days parade a few years back? You'd been on the rodeo circuit a couple of years by then, but you came back for a visit and—"

"And saw a snake, and threw up all over the place. Hey," he said when she pressed down on the wound. "Watch it, would you? I sure took some teasing over that."

"Yeah, you did," she said, swiping the cotton ball over the two neat puncture wounds on the back of his hand. The skin was slightly red around each entry hole, but didn't seem unusually sore. No swelling. She poked at the bite again, more gently, and he didn't flinch. "But you took care of the snake first." She looked up. "That was when . . ."

"When what?"

When I knew for sure I was in love with you. A forever kind of love, not just a schoolgirl's crush. "That rattler was on the float Cub Scout Troop 19 had made, curled up in the hay right between Mario Mendoza and little Wayne Redringer. You were riding Snickers alongside the float when the snake woke up, alarmed by all the commotion, and started shaking its rattles. You didn't hesitate. You leaned over, grabbed it, and pulled it straight toward you, away from the kids. You didn't throw up till it was all over."

She drew a shaky breath, remembering. "It was the bravest thing I've ever seen in my life."

"You're forgetting something, aren't you? After I grabbed the snake I dropped it and let my horse kill the thing." He shook his head ruefully. "Snickers was the real hero that day."

He didn't understand, did he? She could see that, but she didn't know how to explain to him that he *was* a hero. His fear of snakes was lodged in him belly-deep where it couldn't be reached by reason. But that fear didn't make him weak. When those kids had been at risk, he'd acted—quickly, unthinkingly. In spite of his fear, he'd done what he had to do.

So she acted, too. Quickly. Unthinkingly.

Because she wasn't thinking of herself, it wasn't hard to lay her hand on his cheek. And it was easy, maybe the easiest thing she'd ever done, to lean forward and skim her lips across his. And, when his lips parted on a surprised breath, it was the most natural thing in the world to touch the tip of her tongue to his bottom lip, and test that intriguing opening.

What happened next was neither easy nor difficult. Simply inevitable. If you touch a lit match to dried tinder, you have to expect flames. So Sammie shouldn't have been surprised.

But she was, oh, she was.

When her tongue touched his, little licks of heat curled up in her veins, all her veins, everywhere, all at once. It was like being tickled by flames from the inside out. She was astonished. Her fingers curled on his cheek just like those flames were curling inside her. He made a low, growly noise. His hands came up to her face—both hands, the hurt one and the whole one—and he tilted her head just the way he wanted it. And he took over.

For once in her life, Sammie didn't mind being told what to do. She was delighted with his wordless instructions when he showed her how their mouths could lick and linger while her breasts were crushed up against the hard wall of his chest. She liked his notion about fisting one of his hands up in her hair so much that she threaded both her hands into his hair, too.

Tucker had a great many suggestions to make, and each one pleased her more than the last. He wanted her on her back, and he put her there. Within seconds, she understood that this was a much better position, because now he could put his body on top of hers. The weight of him pressed along the lower half of her was such a delicious thrill that she quite forgot her name. When his fingers told her firmly that he didn't like her flannel shirt anymore, popping two of the buttons off during the explanation, she had to agree, especially when his hand captured her breast.

And when he showed her, with his mouth, another reason that he'd wanted her breast bare, she agreed so enthusiastically that her wanton legs curled up on either side of him as insistently as those flames were curling inside her—higher, hotter flames, flames that seared instead of tickling.

He made other demands now. While he sucked at her breast one hand went between her legs and cupped her there, the heel of his palm rotating against her with an exquisitely knowing pressure that made her suddenly frantic.

"Tucker." Her hands pulled at him, then tried to tug his shirt off, but she'd forgotten about buttons. "Tucker, I need you to—I need—"

"I know, Sammie. I know." His voice was harsh. His mouth came back to hers while his hands continued to inform her in mysteries that had her gasping for air. When he pulled his wonderful mouth away, she muttered a protest and tried to bring it back, tugging on his hair.

But he resisted, looking down at her.

One long strand of hair hung down across his forehead. His face was all tight and hard and hungry, with needs in his eyes as wild as her own. His hand still pressed between her legs, and she thought that if she didn't have him soon, she would die.

"Sammie," he said, his voice ragged, "I have to know. Have you ever done this? Been with a man?"

She thought about lying. She was afraid he might stop. But she couldn't lie, not when he held her like this and looked at her with all those needs churning in his own eyes. She shook her head shyly.

He groaned and closed his eyes. "I didn't bring anything, Sammie. I don't have any way of protecting you."

Protecting . . . ? "Oh." She licked her lips, trying to find words to tell him she didn't need to be protected *that* way. Hadn't she already told him she wanted to have his baby? "That's okay."

"No," he said. "It's not." All at once he pulled away from her. He sat up and leaned his head forward in his hands.

Sammie lay there, aching and confused, her breasts still tingling and the heat still ricocheting around in her body. He wasn't touching her anymore. He wasn't looking at her. Should she have lied?

After a moment he straightened. "This isn't right, Sammie."

She wanted to cry. "Why not?"

"I'm your friend. I'm supposed to be, anyway. Friends don't . . ." He stood. "Anyway, pregnancy isn't the only reason a man uses a condom."

Bereft, she clutched at the sides of her shirt, pulling them together to cover herself as she sat up. "You don't have to worry about catching anything from me, but if you aren't sure . . ."

"Hell, no." Tucker had never been so confused in

his life. Too many needs were tearing at him. He couldn't be still. "I mean, yes, I'm sure I don't have anything. That's not the point." There was nowhere to go, of course. But he could pace, so he did.

"Well, what *is* the point, then?"

"It's wrong, that's all."

"That doesn't explain anything! Or excuse anything. You were just as caught up in what was happening between us as I was." She paused. "Weren't you?"

The sudden doubt in her voice made him turn and look back. She knelt on the cot clutching her shirt to her chest, her face pale beneath the freckles, her expression achingly uncertain. Her hair was all over the place, the top button of her jeans was undone, and he wanted badly to go to her and pull the zipper down, too. And the jeans.

"Oh, I was," he said softly. "You know I was."

"Then *why* . . . ?" she cried. "Even if you didn't want to risk me getting pregnant, there are *other* ways to do things that would avoid that."

In spite of himself, he smiled. "And what would you know about those ways?"

"I read," she said with dignity.

His smile slipped. "I don't know if I could use any of those ways, though, Sammie. I want to be inside you too much."

Her eyes went wide, then angry. "Well, dammit, then! What are you doing over there?"

He felt raw and helpless to explain what he only half understood himself. "Friends . . ." He lifted a hand, let it fall. "They don't let you down. That's what it comes down to. With a lover—well, if both people just want a few smiles, a good time, it can work out okay sometimes. But if one person really cares—or if both do—they get each other all tangled up." He gave her a quick glance. "I do care, Sammie."

"Well." She swallowed. "That's good, though."

He shook his head. "When people care, they start expecting too much. Needing too much. Hell, haven't you seen that? Haven't you seen how often the people who are supposed to love each other the most are the ones who let each other down the worst?"

"But I wouldn't let you down." Her hands twisted together in the folds of her unbuttoned shirt.

"Maybe I'd let you down." He tried not to look at the way the cloth shifted over her breasts as her nervous hands clenched and unclenched in her shirt. "You don't think so now, but if I did what we both want me to do, we wouldn't be friends anymore, not for long. We'd start expecting the wrong things from each other."

She shook her head. "You're wrong."

"I've seen it happen too often." With his friends. With his family. None of the women his father had hooked up with after his mother's death had lasted long. None of them had cared enough to hang around when things got rough, but his father had had friends—a couple of them, anyway—who had stuck by him to the end. "Friendship lasts because friends don't expect more from each other than the other one can give."

"I wouldn't expect anything from you if we made love," she assured him. "I promise."

"You can't keep a promise like that." The cloth moved again as her hands twisted, revealing the curve of one breast. His mouth went dry and his feet took him one quick, involuntary step closer. "Quit that!"

"What?" She frowned. Her hands twisted again, and the rosy aureola of one nipple peeked out from the edge of her shirt.

It was the same color as her freckles. And her mouth. Warm rusty rose.

"That thing you're doing," he said, gesturing

wildly. "With your shirt and your nipple. Don't *do* that."

She looked down, turned a hot, bright crimson that clashed violently with her freckles, and jerked the shirt closed. Then she bit her lip . . . tilted her chin up . . . and opened her shirt again. Wide.

"Why?" she said, her head high. "I got the impression you liked looking at them. Among other things."

It wasn't the wave of lust sweeping over him that moved him forward, though that was sweet and hot and compelling. It wasn't the enticing picture she made, kneeling there with her shoulders squared, her chest out and her breasts bare, that drew him irresistibly to her. No, it was the look on her face as she stared up at him, an expression half afraid, half stubborn, and wholly challenging. That, and the memory of all the other times when he'd seen a similar expression on her face.

He knew Sammie. Once she made up her mind to do something, she was going to do it or die trying. And apparently she'd made up her mind to have him. "You are one stubborn woman, you know that?"

She smiled. "About time you noticed I'm a woman."

Her nipples were hard, and one of them—the left one—was still slightly damp from his mouth. "I'd have a hard time denying that at the moment," he said dryly, and he put one knee on the cot beside her. "You're determined to complicate things, aren't you?" He cupped both her breasts, rubbing his thumbs over their hardened tips.

She inhaled sharply. "Seems pretty simple to me."

He shook his head. Sex was simple, but there was nothing simple about what was happening between them, or what was about to happen.

He leaned forward and took her nipple in his mouth.

Sammie was a virgin. He reminded himself of that as he suckled and touched and explored, trying to clamp down on the need cramping in his gut. He told himself to go slow as he tasted and sampled and pulled at her clothes because he had to have her naked.

She was no help. Oh, no, she was all haste and impatience, as eager to get her clothes off as he was to have them gone, offering herself with a reckless generosity that stunned and excited him. How could he go slow? He did manage to get his own clothes off—she seemed to like that idea, too—but she was determined to be difficult. She wanted to do to him everything he did to her, and he couldn't take much of that.

All at once he rolled her onto her back, pushed her legs apart and paused, his chest heaving as he fought the urge to plow into her like a bull. Then, holding his breath, he eased slowly into her.

She was a virgin, but she'd been riding horses since she was five and she was hot, very hot, by the time he entered her. There was no membrane barring his way, and not much discomfort, either, judging by the way her hands urged him on, though she was so tight it was pure, agonizing delight to penetrate her. Then he was firmly, fully seated inside her, sweat running down the sides of his face from passion and the terrible strain of not taking her fast and hard and quick.

Her eyes opened wide. So did her mouth, in a round O of surprise. She gave a little wiggle, testing the fit and the feel of him, and he nearly had a heart attack. Then she smiled up at him, looking as pleased as if she'd invented sex. "Tucker, I *like* this."

He laughed—and started to move.

SEVEN

"Tucker?"

"Hmmm?" He was playing with the chain she wore around her neck, letting the little locket slide back and forth. The cot beneath them was hard and so narrow that, even snuggled up as close as they could get, his butt still hung off one edge and her knees stuck out on the other side. The air was too chilly for bare skin, since he'd never gotten more wood on the fire.

He'd never felt better in his life.

Mind-blowing sex will do that for a man. Of course, he told himself, it was probably just the novelty that had made their lovemaking seem like the best he'd ever had. He never went into a woman bare. Never. But he'd not only made love with Sammie without a condom, he'd climaxed inside her.

He suspected he was going to be worried about that, later.

"What about Lynda?"

"What?" He shoved up on one elbow, dropping the little locket. "What kind of stupid question is that at a time like this?"

"I want to know," she persisted. "If you don't think you should have sex with people you care about, where does Lynda fit in?"

''Nowhere.'' He bent to kiss her shoulder. ''She doesn't fit anywhere anymore, you understand?'' When his mouth reached the sensitive spot where her neck joined her shoulder, she shivered. Encouraged, he slid his hand around and cupped her breast. For a minute, while he kissed and caressed her, he thought he'd succeeded in making her forget her question.

''Tucker?''

''Hmm?'' He flicked his thumb over her nipple.

''Did you love her?'' She shifted in his arms to look up at him.

It took him a minute to speak the words he owed her, because that pain was back, the one he hadn't been able to figure out yesterday. He knew what it was now. ''Love is a cheat. It claims all sorts of things, but it doesn't work. People say they love you, then they let you down. No,'' he said, hurting because he was hurting Sammie. ''I didn't love her. I won't ever let myself be caught in that trap.''

She didn't say anything. But she blinked, quick and fierce, to banish the dampness he saw in her eyes just before she pulled his mouth to hers, so he knew she'd understood.

That night, when they started to make love, the cot broke. They laughed and unzipped Sammie's sleeping bag and used it for their mattress. Over the next two days and three nights they made love in all sorts of ways. Some of the time they even tried those ''other ways'' Sammie had spoken of, the ones where there was no risk of her getting pregnant.

But not every time.

When they weren't making love, they took turns caring for Snickers or exercising Beast. They did the few small chores necessary to keep themselves fed and tidied up after. And they talked. They talked about horses and cattle and the rodeo circuit. She told him all the best gossip about their neighbors and her brother, and he told her his plans for his ranch. But she didn't say anything about her plans for her future, and he didn't ask.

On the morning of the fourth day Tucker was in the stable half of the cabin, running his hand over his mare's fetlock. The big outside door stood open, letting in the sunshine. The air was cool, but not cold. The snow had been gone for two days.

Sammie stood in the doorway and watched him, so happy and sad all at the same time it made her chest ache.

Tucker could have been gone, too. If he'd really wanted to leave, he could have borrowed Beast and gotten back to his life as soon as the snow melted, leaving Sammie here to take care of Snickers. He had a ranch waiting for him, after all, while she had nothing . . . nothing but a few scattered dreams she didn't dare mention, because she'd promised him not to expect anything of him.

She hadn't known quite how much that would hurt.

She watched him run his hand over his mare's fetlock. They'd made love often enough that she was a bit sore from the unaccustomed activity, but looking at him made her ache anyway. She knew him differently now. When he ran his hand along Snickers's leg, she knew how that hand felt on her own leg. When he turned his head slightly and his hair shifted away from his neck, she thought of the texture of his skin just there, and how it felt different to her tongue than to her fingers.

"How's she doing?" she asked.

"No heat, no swelling, and almost no tenderness." He didn't look up. "Come have a look."

If Snickers's leg had healed, he had no reason to

stay any longer. And she had no idea what would happen between them once they went back down the mountain. "Sure," she managed to say, and came over and knelt beside him.

She ran her hands over the mare's leg, looking carefully at the wound, but there wasn't much doubt in her mind. "You don't even need to bandage it." She had to clear her throat before going on. "So. Are you going to ride her out of here today?"

"I wouldn't mind an excuse to stay a little longer, but I guess the vacation is over. I don't—Hey!" he said, taking her chin and trying to turn her face toward him. "What's wrong?"

"Nothing." She stood and dusted her jeans off.

He rose to his feet, studying her, then shook his head. "I'll be damned. You thought that once we were back home, that was it, didn't you? You thought I'd head back down the mountain and wouldn't want to be with you anymore."

"You haven't said any different. You haven't told me what you want."

His eyes were hard and intent when he looked at her. "You ought to know me better than that. There's a chance you're pregnant. Did you really think I'd turn my back on you if you were?"

"No, but . . . it's probably not the right time of month for that to happen," she said, wishing miserably that it had been.

"You know better than to count on that, and so do I. But you're right. I should have said something sooner." He took a deep breath. "All right, Sammie. If you're pregnant, we'll get married."

Her hands clenched into fists at her sides. "And if I'm not?"

He was silent a moment too long. "Then we take it

one day at a time, see how things work out between us.''

Well, that was clear enough, wasn't it? ''Tell you what,'' she said, turning and moving quickly over to the wall that held the tack. ''Let's just say that we won't get married, period.'' She reached for Beast's bridle.

''What do you think you're doing?''

''I'm getting the hell out of here.''

He grabbed her shoulders and pulled her around to face him. ''Look, you may not like my answers, but you asked for them. For some reason you decided it was time to get married. You picked me for the honor, and that's very flattering, but if you think I don't know why you wanted to get pregnant, you're fooling yourself.''

''Damn you, Tucker Evans!'' She had her hands too full of tack to hit him, and her eyes too full of tears to see straight. ''You think I was trying to get pregnant so I could trick you into marrying me? Is that what you think of me?''

''What else am I supposed to think? Good Lord, the first thing you did after you heard I was engaged was offer to have my baby! Then when we got stuck up here together—well, I'm not saying that it was all your idea to go to bed together, but—''

She screeched and jerked her knee up.

This time he was ready for her, though. He let go and danced back out of the way. ''Dammit, Sammie, would you calm down and talk about this? Why else would you act the way you have?''

''Because I love you, you damned idiot! I'm crazy in love with you and I need a little more than 'one day at a time' from you!''

His face went blank. He backed up a step—a quick, involuntary movement that ripped her heart in two. She blinked fast, trying to clear her eyes of the tears that insisted on coming. "Don't look at me like that. You must have known. How could you not have known?"

He didn't say anything. That was the worst thing, the way he just stared at her, as if she'd suddenly grown another head. She wanted to hit him, to hurt him. Or maybe she wanted to cry, but hitting him seemed like a better idea. "Dammit, Tucker. Say something."

When he spoke, his voice was tight, as if he had to force the words out. "It was a mistake. We should never have become lovers."

The funny thing was, she didn't even hurt. The world tilted and went flat, but she didn't hurt. She just stood there and breathed and watched all the color drain out of the world, along with her dreams. "I'll be heading back down the mountain now," she said, and walked over to where Beast waited, his ears flicking curiously. Her arms felt oddly heavy when she lifted the bridle to slip the bit into Beast's mouth.

"Sammie," he said. "I'm sorry."

"Go away, Tucker."

"I'm not letting you ride off when you're all upset."

"I'm not upset." She was numb. At some point that numbness was going to wear off. She had no intention of being anywhere around Tucker when it did.

Beast took the bit with no coaxing. He was probably sick of this place, too. Behind her, Tucker cursed, low-voiced and at length as she opened Beast's stall and led him out.

"You can't just ride off like this," he said. "What about your gear?"

"I'm not leaving anything that matters." Not anymore. She grabbed the saddle pad and threw it up on Beast's broad back.

Tucker didn't speak.

In spite of herself, she glanced over at him. His face was pale and set; his eyes—oh, his eyes looked about as bad she expected to feel, once she started feeling again. But he didn't stop her. It would have been so easy for him to do that. All he had to do was ask her to stay and work things out. All he had to do was give her reason to hope.

But he just watched in silence as she saddled Beast. He didn't say anything when she swung up into the saddle. She looked at him standing there in the doorway. Daylight streamed in around him, all hard and bright, so that his face was a dark blur to her. She licked her lips and waited, praying one last prayer. But he didn't speak.

She pressed with her knees. Obediently Beast moved forward. Her hand went to her throat and her fingers closed around the locket she'd worn every day for the past seven years. Just as she was passing Tucker she pulled once, hard, breaking the chain.

She threw the little gold heart in the dust at his feet, and rode away.

Eight

Tucker knew he was messing up. He knew it, yet he couldn't open his mouth, couldn't lift a hand to stop her. He stood there and watched Sammie riding away and he didn't say a word.

He was furious. Wasn't he? After practically wrestling him into bed, she was leaving him. Just because he couldn't say the kind of words she'd wanted to hear, couldn't give her pretty promises, she was riding that ugly black horse of hers right out of his life. Hadn't he known this was how it would be? Hadn't he told her that friendship and sex don't mix, and sooner or later they'd hurt each other by expecting the wrong things?

It had happened sooner than he'd thought, though. How could Sammie do this?

She had said she *loved* him.

The upheaval she'd created with those quick, angry words hadn't settled yet. Earthquakes and volcanoes were rumbling inside him. He didn't dare move or speak. If he did, something would erupt, and he had no idea what. So he stood completely still and watched her and Beast going around the rocky outcropping dotted with stunted oaks at the edge of the clearing.

In another moment they'd be out of sight.

He wanted to run after her, to yell at her to come

back. He didn't. He wanted to turn his back, to go into the cabin and start forgetting all the ways he'd messed up by making his friend into his lover. He couldn't.

You must have known, she'd said. *How could you not have known?*

Had he known what she felt? Maybe. Yeah, maybe deep inside he had known. He'd seen something in her eyes when they made love, something that made her glow. He'd liked that glow. He'd felt more whole, more complete, the past three days than ever before in his life. Dammit, she'd made him need her. How dared she do such a thing?

Because she loved him.

Tucker didn't have any trouble remembering the last time someone had told him that. His father had said it often enough, pretty much every time Tucker came back to the ranch. He'd get all sloppy with drink and say it right out: "I love you, son." Sometimes he'd cried when he said it. Sometimes he'd started talking about Tucker's mother, and how much he'd loved her, too. And always, always, he'd gone right on drinking. He'd loved Tucker the whole time he was drinking himself to death.

I'm crazy in love with you.

Tucker's fists clenched. What did those words mean? They were tricks, that was all, tricks that made you hope. He knew that.

He turned abruptly. Stupid to just stand here and stare at the place where Sammie and Beast had disappeared. They weren't coming back. Didn't he know that by now? The more you needed someone, the more sure they were to let you down. He went into the dimness of the stable and looked around, but there was nothing that needed doing, no chores, nothing to distract his mind.

It was time he left, too. He crossed to the other side

of the cabin, the people side. And stopped.

There, on the table, sat two coffee mugs. His still had half a cup left in it. Hers was empty. The plates from their breakfast were in the sink. It had been his turn to cook and hers to clean up, but she'd left. She'd left, but she was still there. Not in person. Inside him. She'd crawled inside and she wouldn't get out. Dammit, how did he get her out?

Tucker managed to hold himself together while he washed the dishes, dried them and put them away. He emptied the ashes from the stove and collected the trash he'd have to pack back down the mountain, then he gritted his teeth and went on to the harder chores. He folded the blankets from their makeshift bed and put them away. He looked at her clothes and her sleeping bag and left them where they were.

Someone else could come get her damned things.

Maybe there was a tremor or two, deep inside, when he closed the door and went to saddle Snickers, but he ignored that. It wasn't until he was leading the mare out of the stable that reality rose up and smacked him in the face.

He was looking down, feeling sorry for himself, when he saw her locket lying in the dirt.

His feet stopped moving. He let Snickers's reins trail on the ground and bent to pick up that little gleam of gold. And he remembered.

He'd gotten in the habit of giving Sammie a birthday present when she was still a little sprout, mostly because she seemed to get such a kick out of it. Usually he gave her something useful—a new snaffle bit, maybe, or a saddle blanket. But a couple of weeks before her sixteenth birthday he'd seen the little locket in a jewelry store in Laramie. For some reason—a whim, the purse he'd just won, fate—he'd bought it, and had them engrave her initials in a pretty, flowery script.

He hadn't made it back to Texas for another three weeks, so it was eight days after her birthday by the time he gave it to her, and he was feeling foolish about his gift. He'd wondered if she would look at the dainty heart and laugh, or maybe just stick it at the back of her drawer and never wear it. But he'd given it to her anyway.

He still remembered the way she'd smiled at the locket when she first saw it—a soft, dreamy smile that had made him ache deep inside.

All these years, she'd held on to his gift.

He stared at the little gold heart, running his thumb over the fancy engraving on the front. He'd seen that same soft sort of smile on her face a lot lately, like when he'd kissed her the first time, and when they woke up in the morning together. She had lots of different smiles, Sammie did. Tucker thought about how bright her eyes were when she laughed, and the way they turned dark with passion, or got all narrow and mean when she was mad. He stood there and, a little at a time, he saw *Sammie* instead of looking at his fears.

Oh, God. His hand closed in a tight fist around the little heart. He'd been such a fool.

Riding off into the sunset wasn't easy nowadays. With the best will in the world, Sammie didn't see how she was going to accomplish it before, say, April. Of next year.

To start off with, as soon as she got back to the house her stepfather had pulled the most low-down, sneaky stunt she'd ever seen him stage. He'd apologized. He wanted her to stay and manage the ranch. She was a good manager, he admitted, and he shouldn't have said different. If she couldn't see fit to stay on, she could damn well give him time to get someone else in.

So she agreed to stay a while, which meant she wasn't going to be able to just throw her things in a suitcase and take off. Of course, that might have been a bit difficult anyway. Big Ben wouldn't fit in a suitcase, and she couldn't exactly drop an eight-thousand-dollar Brahman bull at the vet's to board until she found a place of her own.

That night, Tucker called. Twice. She refused to speak to him. Sooner or later she'd have to, but not yet. Not yet.

The next day there were problems with the herd in the west field, with one of the hands, and with the feed order they'd just received, so at least she was too busy to brood. Tucker kept calling, but she spent the day moving cattle, so it wasn't hard to avoid his calls.

Avoiding him when he came over the next night was trickier, but when she saw headlights coming down the long drive to the ranch house, she slipped out the back, slipped a bridle on Beast, and went for a moonlight ride. She knew herself for a fool and a coward, but she just couldn't face him and see him looking worried or awkward, maybe embarrassed. He would want to know if she was pregnant. He'd want to know if he would have to marry her, for the sake of the baby.

So she rode off into the darkness. Out there, alone with the wind and the stars, she could admit that she'd done everything wrong. She'd pressed Tucker when she should have given him time, expected too much when he'd told her not to expect . . . anything. Not one damned thing.

And that's what she'd gotten. Nothing. She'd even lost her little locket, and that was what finally broke through the brittle shell around her grief—the stupid way she'd thrown away the little heart that she'd kept for so many years. She sat on a boulder a mile from the house, curled her arms around her raised knees, and cried and cried.

He quit calling after that. Which was okay with her, she assured herself during the day while doing her best to work herself into exhaustion. If, at night, she tossed and turned and ached for him, no matter how tired she was—well, things always seemed worse at night. She'd get through this. Somehow.

Six days after she came down from the mountain, two days after Tucker stopped calling, she got her period. And cried some more.

Then her brother came home.

Physically and emotionally, she and Dan were opposites. Dan was lanky, Latin-dark, and something of a loner. He was slow to anger, and even slower to trust. When he did give his trust, he gave it without reservations.

He got mad pretty much the same way.

A week after she came back from the mountains, a neighbor's truck pulled up in the yard when she was walking from the hay barn to the house. She paused. When she saw her tall, rangy brother climb out of that truck, she ran over, grabbed him, and hugged him hard.

"What are you doing here? I thought you weren't getting leave for another two months!"

"Emergency leave." He took her arm and started for the house.

"Emergency?" Delight changed quickly to alarm. "What kind of emergency?" Alarm mingled with the teeniest bit of irritation over the way he was towing her. Dan did have some high-handed ways. "Dan, what's wrong?"

"Nothing, with me." He propelled her up the steps and in through the front door.

Alarm was giving way to annoyance by the time he

closed the double doors to the living room behind them. "Good grief, what's up?"

"You tell me," he said grimly. "I got a call from Tucker—"

"You *what*!"

"—saying he'd gotten my little sister pregnant, but you refused to marry him."

Unlike Dan, Sammie was not slow to anger. It took all of one second for her temper to explode. She started moving at the same time she started cussing, and moved faster with every step until she was nearly running by the time she hit the hall.

"Come back here." Dan followed her into the hall, grabbing for her arm—and missing, which was remarkably clumsy for a Special Forces officer. "We have to talk about this."

"Later. Right now, I'm going to kill him." She skidded to a stop beside the entry table, where a cut-glass bowl held several sets of car keys.

"That's my job."

"No, you're his friend. Better if I do it." And she ran out the door.

The road leading to the Evans place was dirt—well-graded and firmly packed, but dirt. Her truck threw up a plume of dust behind it as she braked to a stop in front of the house. The dust drifted slowly to the earth . . . and to the wet white paint on the porch where Tucker knelt, paintbrush in hand.

By the time she slammed out of the truck, he stood on the single step that led to the porch. His face looked strained and tired, but there was an odd, hopeful light in his eyes. "Nice of you to stop by. I take it this means Dan is home?"

"How dare you call my brother?" She stopped in front of the steps. "You had no right!"

He shrugged. The ghost of his usual grin crossed his face. ''It worked.''

''Because you lied!''

''Was it a lie?'' He came off the step to stand in front of her. He grabbed her arms and looked at her intently. ''Was it, Sammie?''

All at once her anger drained away, leaving her no defenses at all. ''You're off the hook, Tucker. There isn't going to be a baby.''

''I'm sorry,'' he said softly.

His sympathy pretty much finished her off. ''Well, now that you know, I'll be going.'' She tried to pull away.

''Oh, no, you don't. I know you don't much like me right now—''

''Let go of me, Tucker.'' She had to get him to turn her loose before her blasted eyes started leaking again.

''You've made it pretty clear how you feel about me the past few days. I'm not saying I blame you, but I was getting desperate. If you hadn't come today, I don't know what I would have done. I—dammit, Sammie, hold still! I'm trying to say something important here!''

When she renewed her efforts to get loose, he tightened his grip on her arms. He braced himself against her efforts, took a deep breath, and said, very quickly with his words all rushed together, ''Will-you-marry-me?''

Stunned, she quit struggling to get loose. Only he was still pulling on her.

He looked as surprised as she was when he toppled over backward—taking her with him. He sat down hard on the freshly painted porch. She ended up mostly in his lap, with one of her feet trailing in the clean white paint. They stared at each other, their eyes only inches apart.

After a second her mouth twitched. "You're sitting in wet paint, Tucker."

"Yeah." He let go of her arms so he could get his arms around her. "So what's your answer?"

"There—there's supposed to be a little more to the question than that."

His mouth turned up at one corner, and the light was coming back into his eyes. "I didn't dare turn you loose long enough to do the thing properly, but if you're ready to settle down now . . . ?"

She bit her lip and nodded.

He put both hands at her waist—lifted her—and set her next to him. In the wet paint.

She looked down, incredulous. The paint was very wet. "Tucker!"

"Just a minute." He lifted up slightly and dug in his pocket. "Sit still now, and hold out your hand . . . Sherry Anne."

Her eyes big, she held out an unsteady hand. "What did you call me?"

"Here." He took her hand and turned it palm up, and then he dribbled a chain into it. A chain, and a locket.

Her little gold heart. She looked at him, puzzled.

"Read it."

She held it up. Her initials looked just as they always had, so she turned it over and saw that he'd had more engraving done, adding tiny little letters she had to squint to make out—tiny little letters that read, "I love you."

"The first time I gave that to you," he said, "I was late, eight days past your birthday, but you didn't hold it against me. I'm late this time, too. I didn't know what I felt. I was confused and I hurt you, and—just, please, tell me I'm not too late."

She looked down at the little heart in her hand.

"You aren't worried I'll let you down, or expect the wrong things, or any of that?"

He reached over and brushed the hair back from her face, smiling so tenderly her heart gave a jump, then started dancing. "I was an idiot, okay? I didn't stop to think. If there is one person in this whole world I know I can count on, one person I know is on my side, it's you."

Happiness was breaking out all over her in goose bumps. "And you don't feel trapped?"

"Sammie," he said, exasperated, "are you paying attention? I love you. I asked you to marry me after I knew you weren't pregnant."

"In that case," she said, her voice husky with emotion, "the answer is—no, you're not too late. And yes." She threw her arms around him and toppled him onto his back, giggling madly as she landed on top of him.

He lay there grinning up at her like an idiot. "This is some very wet paint I'm lying in."

"Yep." He had white streaks in his pretty hair. The palm of her right hand was white now, too, and so was her bottom, and she couldn't stop smiling. He felt good beneath her. Real good. She gave a little wiggle.

"Did you mean yes, you'll marry me?"

The river she'd had to cross had turned out to be a lot wider and deeper and scarier than she'd known it would be, but here she was on the other side. On Tucker's side. For good. "Damn right," she said, and bent and kissed him.

Survey

TELL US WHAT YOU THINK AND YOU COULD WIN

A YEAR OF ROMANCE!

(That's 12 books!)

Fill out the survey below, send it back to us, and you'll be eligible to win a year's worth of romance novels. That's one book a month for a year—from St. Martin's Paperbacks.

Name ______________________________
Street Address ______________________________
City, State, Zip Code ______________________________
Email address ______________________________

1. How many romance books have you bought in the last year?
   (Check one.)
   __0-3
   __4-7
   __8-12
   __13-20
   __20 or more

2. Where do you MOST often buy books? *(limit to two choices)*
   __Independent bookstore
   __Chain stores *(Please specify)*
      __Barnes and Noble
      __B. Dalton
      __Books-a-Million
      __Borders
      __Crown
      __Lauriat's
      __Media Play
      __Waldenbooks
   __Supermarket
   __Department store *(Please specify)*
      __Caldor
      __Target
      __Kmart
      __Walmart
   __Pharmacy/Drug store
   __Warehouse Club
   __Airport

3. Which of the following promotions would MOST influence your decision to purchase a ROMANCE paperback? *(Check one.)*
   __Discount coupon

__Free preview of the first chapter
__Second book at half price
__Contribution to charity
__Sweepstakes or contest

4. Which promotions would LEAST influence your decision to purchase a ROMANCE book? (Check one.)
    __Discount coupon
    __Free preview of the first chapter
    __Second book at half price
    __Contribution to charity
    __Sweepstakes or contest

5. When a new ROMANCE paperback is released, what is MOST influential in your finding out about the book and in helping you to decide to buy the book? (Check one.)
    __TV advertisement
    __Radio advertisement
    __Print advertising in newspaper or magazine
    __Book review in newspaper or magazine
    __Author interview in newspaper or magazine
    __Author interview on radio
    __Author appearance on TV
    __Personal appearance by author at bookstore
    __In-store publicity (poster, flyer, floor display, etc.)
    __Online promotion (author feature, banner advertising, giveaway)
    __Word of Mouth
    __Other (please specify)______________________________

6. Have you ever purchased a book online?
    __Yes
    __No

7. Have you visited our website?
    __Yes
    __No

8. Would you visit our website in the future to find out about new releases or author interviews?
    __Yes
    __No

9. What publication do you read most?
    __Newspapers *(check one)*
        __*USA Today*
        __*New York Times*
        __Your local newspaper
    __Magazines *(check one)*

__*People*
__*Entertainment Weekly*
__Women's magazine *(Please specify:______________)*
__*Romantic Times*
__Romance newsletters

10. What type of TV program do you watch most? *(Check one.)*
__Morning News Programs (ie. "Today Show")
(Please specify:______________)
__Afternoon Talk Shows (ie. "Oprah")
(Please specify: ______________)
__All news (such as CNN)
__Soap operas *(Please specify: ______________)*
__Lifetime cable station
__E! cable station
__Evening magazine programs (ie. "Entertainment Tonight")
(Please specify: ______________)
__Your local news

11. What radio stations do you listen to most? *(Check one.)*
__Talk Radio
__Easy Listening/Classical
__Top 40
__Country
__Rock
__Lite rock/Adult contemporary
__CBS radio network
__National Public Radio
__WESTWOOD ONE radio network

12. What time of day do you listen to the radio MOST?
__6am-10am
__10am-noon
__Noon-4pm
__4pm-7pm
__7pm-10pm
__10pm-midnight
__Midnight-6am

13. Would you like to receive email announcing new releases and special promotions?
__Yes
__No

14. Would you like to receive postcards announcing new releases and special promotions?
__Yes
__No

15. Who is your favorite romance author? ______________

WIN A YEAR OF ROMANCE FROM SMP

(That's 12 Books!)

No Purchase Necessary

OFFICIAL RULES

1. To Enter: Complete the Official Entry Form and Survey and mail it to: Win a Year of Romance from SMP Sweepstakes, c/o St. Martin's Paperbacks, 175 Fifth Avenue, Suite 1615, New York, NY 10010-7848, Attention JP. For a copy of the Official Entry Form and Survey, send a self-addressed, stamped envelope to: Entry Form/Survey, c/o St. Martin's Paperbacks at the address stated above. Entries with the completed surveys must be received by February 1, 2000 (February 22, 2000 for entry forms requested by mail). Limit one entry per person. No mechanically reproduced or illegible entries accepted. Not responsible for lost, misdirected, mutilated or late entries.

2. Random Drawing. Winner will be determined in a random drawing to be held on or about March 1, 2000 from all eligible entries received. Odds of winning depend on the number of eligible entries received. Potential winner will be notified by mail on or about March 22, 2000 and will be asked to execute and return an Affidavit of Eligibility/Release/Prize Acceptance Form within fourteen (14) days of attempted notification. Non-compliance within this time may result in disqualification and the selection of an alternate winner. Return of any prize/prize notification as undeliverable will result in disqualification and an alternate winner will be selected.

3. Prize and approximate Retail Value: Winner will receive a copy of a different romance novel each month from April 2000 through March 2001. Approximate retail value $84.00 (U.S. dollars).

4. Eligibility. Open to U.S. and Canadian residents (excluding residents of the province of Quebec) who are 18 at the time of entry. Employees of St. Martin's and its parent, affiliates and subsidiaries, its and their directors, officers and agents, and their immediate families or those living in the same household, are ineligible to enter. Potential Canadian winners will be required to correctly answer a time-limited arithmetic skill question by mail. Void in Puerto Rico and wherever else prohibited by law.

5. General Conditions: Winner is responsible for all federal, state and local taxes. No substitution or cash redemption of prize permitted by winner. Prize is not transferable. Acceptance of prize constitutes permission to use the winner's name, photograph and likeness for purposes of advertising and promotion without additional compensation or permission, unless prohibited by law.

6. All entries become the property of sponsor, and will not be returned. By participating in this sweepstakes, entrants agree to be bound by these official rules and the decision of the judges, which are final in all respects.

7. For the name of the winner, available after March 22, 2000, send by May 1, 2000 a stamped, self-addressed envelope to Winner's List, Win a Year of Romance from SMP Sweepstakes, St. Martin's Paperbacks, 175 Fifth Avenue, Suite 1615, New York, NY 10010-7848, Attention JP.

WAGONS WEST THRILLED MILLIONS OF READERS WITH ITS STUNNING DEPICTION OF THE AMERICAN WEST—AND THE MEN AND WOMEN WHO TAMED IT. NOW, AUTHOR DANA FULLER ROSS TURNS BACK THE CLOCK TO PORTRAY THE FOREBEARS OF LEGENDARY WAGON MASTER WHIP HOLT. . . . TRAVEL WITH THESE BRAVE PIONEERS AS THEY EXPLORE, CONQUER—AND LEAVE THEIR INDELIBLE STAMP ON THE WILD FRONTIER THEY CALL HOME.

EXPEDITION!

SHARE THE BOLD ADVENTURES AND BREATHTAKING EXCITEMENT OF THE EARLY HOLTS AS THEY CARVE OUT THEIR DESTINY IN THIS MAGNIFICENT LAND.

CLAY HOLT—

A superior marksman, he throws his flintlock into the battle to save a group of white strangers from hostile Blackfoot . . . only to end up as their guide on a journey straight to hell.

JEFFERSON HOLT—

A seasoned frontiersman and trapper, this second son travels east in search of his cherished wife . . . only to encounter danger on a wagon train bound for the Blue Ridge Mountains—and blackest treachery at the hands of a man he calls friend.

SHINING MOON—

Once free as the wild bird, she now roams the great frontier with her husband, Clay Holt. Brave, fiercely loyal, and adept with tomahawk and rifle, she risks her life on a perilous journey that will end in chilling violence and brutal capture.

MELISSA MERRIVALE HOLT—

This gentle beauty longs to be reunited with Jeff Holt—and share her precious secret. But for all she knows, Jeff is dead, while entrepreneur Dermot Hawley is very much alive, and waiting in the wings.

CHARLES MERRIVALE—

A successful North Carolina businessman seeking to expand into the shipping business, he schemes to remarry his daughter off to a ruthless tycoon—a man who will stop at nothing to see that Melissa renounces her marriage . . . only to become his wife.

DONALD FRANKLIN—

Distinguished Harvard professor, botanist, and friend of Thomas Jefferson, he heads an expedition along the route forged by Lewis and Clark. But it may be his last journey when his party is captured by hostile Indians and turned over to a murderous Brit.

LUCY FRANKLIN—

Franklin's lovely young daughter, she didn't know what she was getting into when she agreed to accompany her father into the wilderness. Now she's in love with Clay Holt, and she lives for the day when he will leave his Sioux wife . . . for her white woman's bed.

RUPERT VON METZ—

A handsome Prussian, he came to America to create a pictorial record of the life and landscape of the West. But his artist's arrogance will set him on a collision course with Clay Holt that will end in one man's death.

SIMON BROWN—

Traveling under an alias, this son of nobility has flown his rakish past to become a fur trapper for the London and Northwestern Enterprise. Now he has a chance to become a very rich, very powerful man . . . if he can break the American hold on the Rockies forever.

NED HOLT—

Jeff and Clay's hotheaded young cousin, his heart is filled with wanderlust. Vowing to escape his family's livery stables, he signs on as a sailor on a Carolina-bound ship—and meets his match in an unusual woman named India St. Clair.

INDIA ST. CLAIR—

A London slum orphan, she ran away to sea disguised as a cabin boy. A pickpocket and a rogue, she can swear, fight, and duel with the best of them . . . including brawny, handsome Ned Holt.

WAGONS WEST
FRONTIER TRILOGY
VOLUME 2

EXPEDITION!

Dana Fuller Ross

Producers of **The Holts, The Patriots, The First Americans,** and **The White Indian.**

Book Creations Inc., Canaan, NY • Lyle Kenyon Engel, Founder

BANTAM BOOKS
NEW YORK • TORONTO • LONDON • SYDNEY • AUCKLAND

EXPEDITION!
A Bantam Domain Book / published by arrangement with Book Creations Inc.

Bantam edition / February 1993

Produced by Book Creations Inc.
Lyle Kenyon Engel, Founder

DOMAIN and the portrayal of a boxed "d" are trademarks of Bantam Books, a division of Bantam Doubleday Dell Publishing Group, Inc.

ISBN 0-553-29403-2

Published simultaneously in the United States and Canada

Bantam Books are published by Bantam Books, a division of Bantam Doubleday Dell Publishing Group, Inc. Its trademark, consisting of the words "Bantam Books" and the portrayal of a rooster, is Registered in U.S. Patent and Trademark Office and in other countries. Marca Registrada. Bantam Books, 666 Fifth Avenue, New York, New York 10103.

PRINTED IN THE UNITED STATES OF AMERICA

OPM 0 9 8 7 6 5 4 3 2 1

Bantam Books by Dana Fuller Ross
Ask your bookseller for the books you have missed

Wagons West
INDEPENDENCE!—Volume I
NEBRASKA!—Volume II
WYOMING!—Volume III
OREGON!—Volume IV
TEXAS!—Volume V
CALIFORNIA!—Volume VI
COLORADO!—Volume VII
NEVADA!—Volume VIII
WASHINGTON!—Volume IX
MONTANA!—Volume X
DAKOTA!—Volume XI
UTAH!—Volume XII
IDAHO!—Volume XIII
MISSOURI!—Volume XIV
MISSISSIPPI!—Volume XV
LOUISIANA!—Volume XVI
TENNESSEE!—Volume XVII
ILLINOIS!—Volume XVIII
WISCONSIN!—Volume XIX
KENTUCKY!—Volume XX
ARIZONA!—Volume XXI
NEW MEXICO!—Volume XXII
OKLAHOMA!—Volume XXIII
CELEBRATION!—Volume XXIV

The Holts: An American Dynasty
OREGON LEGACY—Volume One
OKLAHOMA PRIDE—Volume Two
CAROLINA COURAGE—Volume Three
CALIFORNIA GLORY—Volume Four
HAWAII HERITAGE—Volume Five
SIERRA TRIUMPH—Volume Six
YUKON JUSTICE—Volume Seven

*Wagon's West * The Frontier Trilogy*
WESTWARD!—Volume One
EXPEDITION!—Volume Two

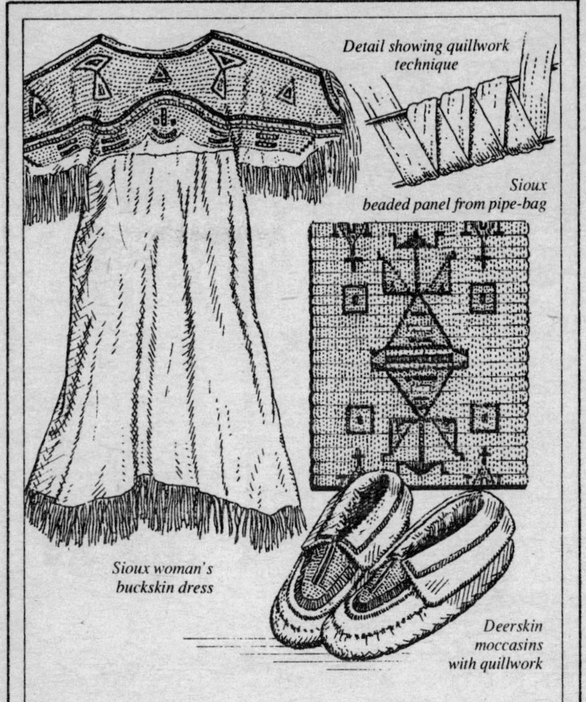

Before glass beads were brought to the New World by European traders in the fifteenth century, the decorative material used most often by native Americans was the porcupine quill. Considered a sacred craft, the art of quillwork was passed down from generation to generation. According to tribal lore, those who practiced the skill went blind or became ill, perhaps because of a disagreeable substance in the quills, which were softened in the quillworker's mouth before being sewn onto soft hide or clothing. Though beads of bone, shells, seeds, stones, and other natural materials were used for centuries, the more uniform glass bead became the choice material for ornamentation after it was brought to the continent by Europeans. The ornate quillwork patterns were readily adapted to beadwork, and the intricate, distinctive designs often served as identification for the tribes.

R. TOELKE '92

Man's beaver hat

Gentleman with
fur-trimmed cloak

As word of the frontier's bounty of beaver spread throughout the United States and Europe in the late 1700s, the demand for pelts skyrocketed and fur-trimmed clothing became *de rigueur* among the fashion conscious. By the turn of the century, every gentleman on the East Coast wore a beaver top hat, which could cost as much as fifty dollars. The hats were waterproof, retained their shape regardless of the weather, and could be brushed to a sheen. Women's clothing soon reflected the rage for fur, utilizing the skins of beaver, fox, marten, and otter to trim hats, collars, coats, and shawls. Benefiting from the increased demand for beaver pelts were companies such as John Jacob Astor's American Fur Company and the Rocky Mountain Fur Company, which purchased skins from the mountain men who had flocked to the lands of the Louisiana Purchase and changed forever the face of the American West.

 R-TOELKE '92

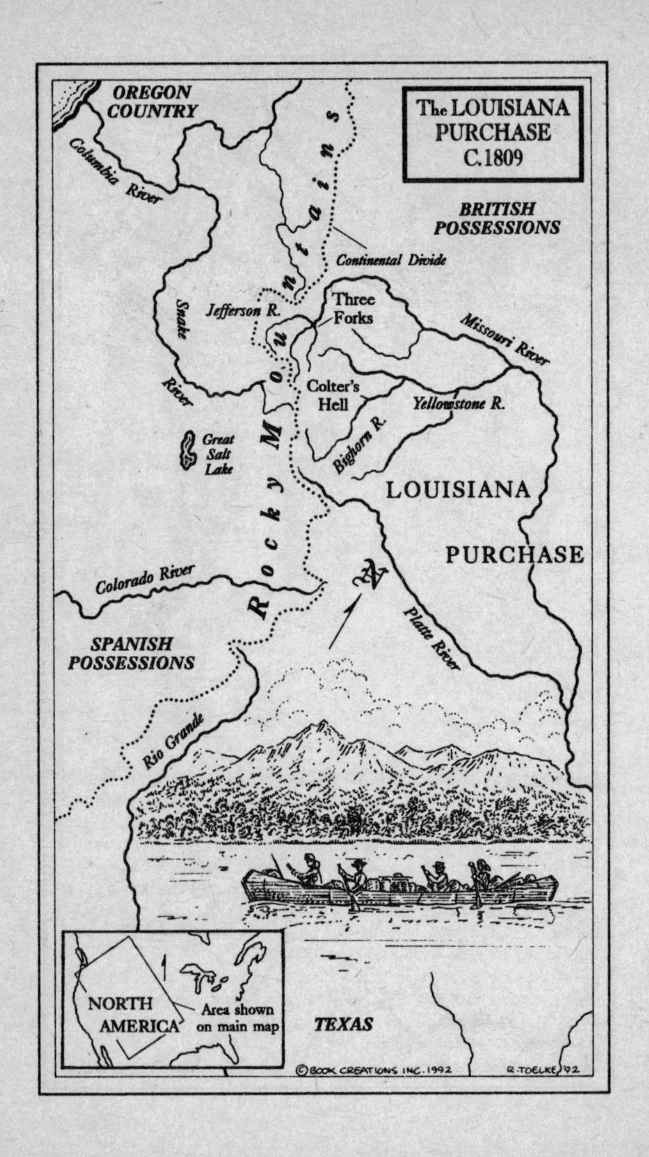

The LOUISIANA PURCHASE C.1809
OREGON COUNTRY
Columbia River
BRITISH POSSESSIONS
Continental Divide
Rocky Mountains
Jefferson R.
Three Forks
Missouri River
Snake River
Colter's Hell
Yellowstone R.
Bighorn R.
Great Salt Lake
LOUISIANA PURCHASE
Colorado River
Platte River
SPANISH POSSESSIONS
Rio Grande
NORTH AMERICA
Area shown on main map
TEXAS
©BOOK CREATIONS INC. 1992
R.TOELKE '92

The EASTERN UNITED STATES C.1809
LOWER CANADA
MAINE (Mass.)
VT
NH
CANADA (Great Britain)
Adirondack Mts.
Utica
Hudson R.
Boston
MA
RI
CT
UPPER CANADA
Syracuse
NEW YORK
New York City
MICHIGAN TERRITORY
Detroit
Allegheny R.
PENNSYLVANIA
Philadelphia
NJ
Pittsburgh
Monongahela R.
MD
DE
OHIO
Wheeling
Marietta
Washington
Ohio R.
INDIANA TERR.
VIRGINIA
KENTUCKY
PIEDMONT
NORTH CAROLINA
Blue Ridge Mts.
Cape Fear R.
Knoxville
Smoky Mts.
Wilmington
TENNESSEE
SOUTH CAROLINA
Charleston
ATLANTIC OCEAN
MISSISSIPPI TERRITORY
GEORGIA
SPANISH FLORIDA
©BOOKCREATIONS INC. 1992
R. TOELKE '92

PART I

This town is finely situated on both banks of the Muskingum, at the confluence of that river with the Ohio. It is principally built on the left bank, where there are ninety-seven houses, including a court-house, a market-house, an academy, and a post-office. There are about thirty houses on the opposite bank, the former scite [sic] *of Fort Harmar, which was a United States' garrison during the Indian wars, but of which no vestige now remains. Some of the houses are of brick, some of stone, but they are chiefly of wood, many of them large, and having a certain air of taste. There are two rope walks, and there were on the stocks two ships, two brigs, and a schooner. A bank is established here, which began to issue notes on the 20th inst. Its capital is one hundred thousand dollars, in one thousand shares: Mr. Rufus Putnam is the president.*

The land on which Marietta is built, was purchased during the Indian war, from the United States, by some New England land speculators, who named themselves the Ohio Company. They chose the land facing the Ohio, with a depth from the river of only from twenty to thirty miles to the northward, thinking the proximity of the river would add to its value, but since the state of Ohio has began [sic] *to be generally settled, the rich levels in the interior have been preferred, but not before the company had made large sales, particularly to settlers from New England, notwithstanding the greatest part of the tract was broken and hilly, and the hills mostly poor, compared with those farther to the westward, on both sides of the river.*

—FORTESCUE CUMING
"Sketches of a Tour to the Western Country"
The tour having been made in 1807–1809,
publication from a Pittsburgh press, 1810

CHAPTER ONE

God had made prettier country than the Ohio River valley, Jefferson Holt thought as he guided his horse down a road that ran alongside a stream. He had seen quite a bit of it, particularly those majestic peaks that formed the spine of the continent. Some called them the Rockies; to the Indians who lived there, as well as to men like Jeff Holt, they were the Shining Mountains.

But the rolling hills of Ohio, lush and green with the arrival of spring of 1809, were beautiful, too. To Jeff they represented home.

That was a beautiful word, Jeff thought. *Home . . .*

He was in his prime, twenty-four years old, with the strength and vitality that sprang from a frontier heritage and a vigorous outdoor life. He rode straight in the saddle, his keen brown eyes scanning the terrain ahead and to either side of him. A black felt hat was cuffed back on his head, revealing a shock of curly, sandy-blond hair. He wore a homespun shirt, laced at the throat with a rawhide thong, and fringed buckskin trousers tucked into high black boots. He carried a flintlock pistol under his broad black belt, which also supported a sheathed hunting knife. Balanced on the pommel of his saddle was a long-barreled .54 caliber flintlock rifle with brass straps, buttplate, and patchbox on the polished wooden stock, a product of the Harper's Ferry armory in Virginia. Slung over his shoulder were a powder horn and shot pouch.

Once Jeff had been a farmer. Now, however, he had the look of exactly what he was: a frontiersman. He had spent the past two years trapping beaver in the great western mountains with his older brother, Clay. The previous fall Jeff had voyaged down the Missouri River to St. Louis, along with a boatload of pelts belonging to the man who employed the Holt brothers, the shrewd fur trader Manuel Lisa. After waiting out the harsh winter in St. Louis, Jeff had struck out for Marietta, Ohio, which had, some twenty years earlier, been the first white settlement in what was then known as the Northwest Territory. The Holt family homestead was near Marietta.

Jeff frowned as bitter memories flooded his mind. He and Clay had left Marietta under a cloud, after an outbreak of violence that had resulted in several deaths, including those of their parents, Bartholomew and Norah Holt. Jeff intended to pay a visit to the family farm while he was there, but that was not the real reason he had come back.

He was there for Melissa.

Melissa . . . his wife, his love, the beautiful young woman he had been forced to leave behind when he and Clay headed west. Not a single day had passed during those two years when Jeff had not missed her terribly. Now that he was nearing Marietta, he felt his excitement build. Soon he would be holding Melissa in his arms again. After all this time, it was hard to wait.

He turned the horse away from the main road toward a path that ultimately led to the Holt farm. His primary destination, however, was another farm on the same path. It belonged to his father-in-law, Melissa's father, Charles Merrivale.

Would Melissa be surprised to see him? He had written her from St. Louis, but mail service was undependable, especially west of the Appalachians. It was entirely possible the letter had been lost or delayed so that Jeff would arrive before his message did. He almost hoped that would be the case; he would enjoy seeing the look on Melissa's face when he rode up, called her name, then swept her into his arms when she came running to him.

As that pleasant fantasy played itself out in his mind, he urged the horse on to a faster pace.

Soon the Merrivale farmhouse came into view. One of the most impressive structures in the area, it was built of planed and finished logs, which gave it a more sophisticated appearance than the crude cabins that were so common. The roof was covered with wooden shingles, and the windows had panes of glass in them, glass that Charles Merrivale had paid dearly to have transported from the East. Only the best for his family, he had been heard to say many times, only the best.

That had not included Jefferson Holt as a husband for Merrivale's daughter, his only child. But ultimately he had not been the one to make that decision. Jeff and Melissa were in love, and they had been married with her father's grudging acceptance, if not his blessing.

His heart pounding rapidly, Jeff reined the horse to a stop in front of the house. He could see no movement from inside or from the barn out back, and except for a few cows, the fields were deserted.

Everyone must be inside, he figured. It was about midday; Melissa and her parents were probably sitting down to dinner.

He was swinging down from his saddle when from out of the corner of his eye he saw the black snout of a musket emerge from a hole cut into the wall near the door for defense. Shocked by the sight, he froze.

The musket blasted. Instincts honed by his life in the mountains took over, and Jeff grabbed his rifle and flung himself off the horse as the musket ball sliced through the air where he had been an instant before. He landed hard, then rolled over, and the impact sent his own rifle slipping from his fingers. He rolled again and came up into a crouch, reaching for the pistol tucked under his belt. A second shot from the cabin whipped past Jeff's ear, making him dive forward. He sprawled on the ground, sheltered by a watering trough with thick wooden sides.

"Hold your fire!" he shouted without lifting his head. "It's me, Jeff!" Maybe Charles Merrivale had not recognized him, had perhaps taken him for a thief. Jeff knew his appearance had changed in the two years he had been gone. He was leaner, tougher, harder-looking now.

Or maybe Merrivale had recognized him after all. The man had never liked him. But would he try to kill him?

"It's Jeff, blast it!" he called again. "Jeff Holt!"

An unfamiliar voice shouted, "I don't know no Jeff Holt! Come on out of there with your hands up, stranger, and maybe I won't kill you!"

Who the devil . . . Jeff did not know whether to believe the man or not. If he stood, he might end up with a musket ball through him.

On the other hand, he could not lie there in the dirt all day. He had ridden hundreds of miles to see his wife, perhaps even to take Melissa back west with him, and he was damned if he was going to let some lunatic with a gun keep him away from her.

"All right," he replied, raising his voice but keeping his head low. "I'll stand up, but go easy on that trigger, mister. I don't mean anybody any harm."

"We'll see about that. Get up slow and easy, and you'd best not be holding a gun when you do."

Jeff slipped his pistol under his belt, took as deep a breath as he could lying on the ground, and pushed himself up onto his knees. Carefully he got to his feet.

After he had raised his hands, palms open to show he was unarmed, the door of the cabin opened, and a man stepped out, a musket clutched tightly in his hands. He trained the weapon on Jeff, who could see that it was cocked.

"Who the hell are you?" the man demanded suspiciously. He was tall, rawboned, and balding. "I don't like folks sneaking around my place. Now speak up, or I won't fire another warning shot."

Neither of the first two shots had been meant as warnings, Jeff thought grimly. They had come altogether too close to his head. But Jeff was not going to argue with him, not under the circumstances.

"I told you, my name is Jefferson Holt. I'm looking for the Merrivales. Are they here?"

"This is my place," the man snapped. "It don't belong to nobody named Merrivale."

Now that he'd had a chance to get a better look at the house, Jeff noticed some changes in it. The window glass of which Charles Merrivale had been so proud was dirty, with at least several months' worth of grime accumulated on it. Some of the wooden shingles on the roof had come off and not been replaced, and one of the puncheons that formed the porch stuck up at an angle. Jeff glanced at the barn and saw that it was in disrepair, too. Charles Merrivale never would have allowed such deterioration to go unchecked.

That realization sent Jeff's heart plummeting.

Charles and Hermione—and Melissa, too—were gone. He would have seen that right away had he not been so excited and full of anticipation when he'd ridden up to the house. And he had been too busy dodging musket balls since then to see what was now so obvious.

"Listen," he said urgently to the man holding the musket. "I'm not looking for trouble. Some people named Merrivale used to live here. Please, do you know anything about them? If you do, just tell me and I'll leave peacefully."

"You'll leave peacefully if'n I don't tell you nothing."

"Wait, Walter!" came a voice from inside the house. A woman leaned out the doorway. "Don't hurt the boy. He doesn't mean any harm."

"Get back in the house, Katey!" the man ordered without turning around. "I told you to stay in there with the young'uns, where it's safe."

"It's safe enough here," the woman said, stepping into view on the porch. "Mr. Holt's not going to hurt anyone."

"No, ma'am. I'm surely not."

The woman had the plain, hard-used features of most frontier wives, but as long as she was telling her husband not to shoot him, Jeff thought she was beautiful. Several children clustered around her, hiding behind her skirts.

"Look, I bought this place fair and square," Walter said, still pointing the musket at Jeff's chest. "We been here now for more than a year. I done paid my taxes. This farm is mine!"

"Nobody said it isn't." Jeff tried to remain calm and hoped Walter would do the same. "I'm not interested in your farm. My family has a place of its own, on up the road about a mile. The Holt homestead? Maybe you've heard of it."

The woman called Katey said, "I've heard of the Holts. Thought they'd all moved away, though."

"We have, ma'am," Jeff told her. "But I've come back for a visit, to make sure the place is all right and see that the taxes are paid on it. And to see my wife. I thought I'd find her here."

Walter shook his head. "Told you we don't know nothing about the Merrivales. Now I'll thank you to git."

"I swear, Walter, I've never known you to be so unsociable!" Katey exclaimed. "Now put that gun down. We might as well be civil to this young man. He looks as though he's ridden a long way."

"From the Rocky Mountains, ma'am," Jeff warmly informed her. "And I'd surely admire to put my arms down without having to worry about your husband blasting me with that blunderbuss."

"Aw, hell." Walter lowered the musket. "I reckon you ain't no thief after all. But don't try nothing, or I will shoot you, sure as anything."

Grateful, Jeff lowered his arms. "Thanks, but you don't have to worry, Mr. . . . "

"Seeger," Walter replied, still surly and suspicious. "Walter Seeger. This's my wife, Katey, and our young'uns."

Jeff tugged his hat off and nodded to the woman. "Pleased to meet you, Mrs. Seeger. I'm sorry if I've upset your family by showing up like this today. Like I said, I just want to find my wife."

It was taking quite an effort of will for Jeff to keep his voice calm and his words polite. Panic was scrabbling around in his mind like a crazed animal. *Where could Melissa and her parents have gotten to?*

"Why don't you come inside, Mr. Holt?" Katey Seeger asked. "We were just about to sit down at the table, and you're welcome to join us."

From the look on Walter's face, Jeff could tell that he was not happy about the invitation his wife had just issued, but he was bound by the code of hospitality that frontier folks lived by: No stranger was turned away from the table as long as he was peaceable.

Jeff tied his horse to a post beside the watering trough, then turned toward the house. Walter kept his musket tucked under his arm as he followed Jeff, Katey, and the Seeger children into the cabin. As he entered and looked around, Jeff saw that the expensive furnishings he remembered from his visits to the Merrivales were gone, replaced by rough-hewn tables and chairs that had probably been built by Walter. The floor was bare; no sign remained of the woven rugs in which Hermione Merrivale had taken such pride.

There were four Seeger children, three girls and a boy, all under the age of ten. They watched him shyly as he sat down at the table with their father.

The farmer placed the musket on the bench beside him, looked at Jeff shrewdly, and asked, "You say you used to live around here?"

"That's right. My father was Bartholomew Holt. My mother's name was Norah," Jeff replied. "My family's lived in these parts since after the Revolution, when the government paid off some of the soldiers with land in the Ohio Valley."

"I wasn't in the war," Walter said. "Not old enough. Would've fought the damned British if I could have, though."

"That was before my time, I'm afraid," Jeff said. "I heard my father talk about it some. He had a great admiration for Mr. Thomas Jefferson. That's how I came to have the name."

"Jefferson—" Walter made a face. "Nothing but a dandified whoremonger, if you ask me."

"Walter!" Katey exclaimed. "Think of the children and watch what you say!"

Grumpily Walter said, "Sure, sure. I just don't

have no use for any of them politicians, Jefferson included."

Jeff made no comment. He had never met Thomas Jefferson and knew little of the man's personal life, but he held some admiration for the former president anyway. It was Thomas Jefferson who had sent Captain Meriwether Lewis and Captain William Clark on their already legendary journey of exploration to the Pacific several years earlier. Jeff's own brother Clay had been part of the Corps of Discovery led by Lewis and Clark, and that experience had led Clay to return to the Rocky Mountains as a fur trapper, taking Jeff along with him.

Katey stirred the pot of stew simmering over low flames in the fireplace.

"Holt," she mused. "Seems like I do remember hearing talk in Marietta about a family named Holt. There was some sort of trouble a few years back, wasn't there?"

"Yes, ma'am," Jeff said, his features grim. "There sure was. My ma and pa were killed when their cabin was burned down."

"Oh, my!" Katey raised a hand to her mouth. "I'm sorry, Mr. Holt. I didn't mean to bring up any bad memories."

"That's all right," Jeff told her kindly. "It's all a long time in the past now. What I'm really worried about is finding the Merrivales."

Walter rubbed his stubbled jaw and said slowly, "I been thinking about that. I reckon I did hear something about them, after all. Took me a few minutes to recollect."

Jeff leaned forward, trying not to let his eagerness get out of hand. "What have you heard?"

"Just talk in Steakley's store, you understand. Seems they pulled up stakes and headed back East. Merrivale must've been a fool if he was willing to give up a piece of prime land like this," Walter added. "Either that, or he purely hated living out here."

"Some of both, I imagine," Jeff said. "Mr. Merrivale never was very comfortable as a farmer. He was a businessman from the East somewhere."

"Then I reckon that's what he went back to."

That made sense, Jeff thought. It had been a mistake for a man like Charles Merrivale to try to live the life of a gentleman farmer on the frontier. Jeff would not be surprised in the slightest if Merrivale had decided to return to his former home and go back into business. Hermione would have accompanied him, of course, and Jeff was sure, knowing Charles Merrivale as he did, that the man would have insisted Melissa go, too, even though she was married. Merrivale was used to running roughshod over the members of his family, and Melissa had a tendency to give in to her father's demands. Jeff had to admit that about his wife, no matter how much he loved her.

"You didn't hear anything specific about where they might have gone?" he asked.

"Nope. Or if I did, I've forgot it by this time. Been quite a while since I heard anything about the Merrivales, you understand."

Katey carried a wooden bowl full of the steaming, aromatic stew to where Jeff sat and placed it in front of him.

"We could try to find out, if you'd like," she offered.

"No, ma'am, but thank you, anyway. You've done enough, just showing me your hospitality like this." *And keeping your husband from shooting me,* Jeff added to himself. "I reckon Mr. Steakley at the store still remembers me. He'll know where the Merrivales went, if anybody around here does."

"You're right," Walter said. "Ol' Steakley usually winds up knowing just about everything there is to know about folks in these parts."

Katey gave Jeff a hunk of bread torn from a loaf that was warming on the hearth, then filled a mug with fresh milk from a pitcher before serving the meal to the rest of her family. The food was good, although at that time of year the stew was heavy on venison and light on vegetables. Jeff had little appetite, however, and ate without really tasting the food. He was too busy thinking about the unexpected development that fate had thrown his way.

For months now—years really, ever since he had left Ohio for the first time—he had been anticipating his reunion with Melissa. He had played out the scene countless times in his mind. But never in the wildest stretch of his imagination had he thought that she would not be there. Originally, she was supposed to go to Pittsburgh with Edward, Susan, and Jonathan Holt, his younger siblings. When he was in St. Louis, waiting with Clay for the fur-trapping expedition to head up the Missouri, Jeff had received a letter from Melissa explaining how she had decided to stay in Ohio with her parents. Jeff had accepted that, although he would have preferred her sticking to their original plan. But to get back to Ohio and then find her gone . . .

"Mr. Holt?"

Katey Seeger's voice interrupted Jeff's brooding thoughts. He looked up.

"Something wrong with the stew?"

He realized he had stopped eating and was just sitting there with a spoon in one hand and the hunk of bread in the other.

Smiling, he said, "It's all delicious. I was just thinking."

"About them Merrivales, I reckon," Walter said. He spooned stew into his mouth, chewed, and swallowed. "I wish we could be of more help, but there's just no telling where they went. Ain't you got no idea?"

Jeff had already begun casting his mind back over every conversation he could recall with all three Merrivales, not just Melissa. Had any of them ever told him exactly where they had lived before coming to Ohio? Jeff had never spoken much with Charles Merrivale, due to the tension between them, and although Hermione had been friendly enough to him, she had a tendency to ramble rather aimlessly when she was talking. His conversations with Melissa had usually centered around the present or the future, rather than the past. Besides, any time they had been alone, there had not been a great deal of talking going on.

"Back East" was the most precise answer Jeff could come up with to the question now plaguing him. And it was not much of an answer.

During the rest of the meal, he forced himself to be polite and pleasant to the Seegers, although impatience was building inside him again. They were curious about the Rocky Mountains, and he answered their questions about his life as a fur trapper. Since the Seeger youngsters were also listening avidly, he deliberately glossed over some of the more bloody and dangerous events—like Indian attacks, knife fights with other trappers, and a murderous Frenchman named Duquesne who had nearly plunged the whole frontier into chaos.

"You say your brother is married to a Sioux woman?" Katey asked eagerly, her eyes shining. People on the frontier were always hungry for a story, even one that had no real connection to them.

"Yes, ma'am. Her name's Shining Moon. She's mighty pretty, and I don't reckon we'd have made it out there without her and her brother, a young man called Proud Wolf. They are from the Hunkpapa tribe, part of the Teton Sioux. They've been helping us out right along."

"That's remarkable," Katey breathed.

"You trust them Injuns?" Walter asked with a scowl.

"Some of them I'd trust with my life," Jeff declared. "I've done just that, in fact. Shining Moon's people, the Hunkpapa, have always gotten along real well with the whites. The Blackfoot, now, they're a different story, and so are the Arikara and the Crow. We steer clear of them whenever we can."

Walter shook his head. "With all the stories I've heard about them savages, I wouldn't trust a one of them, not even them Sioux. That brother of your'n'll wake up one mornin' with his throat cut by that squaw."

Jeff said nothing. Shining Moon was about the prettiest, bravest, most gentle woman he had ever met—except for Melissa, of course—and he was sure Clay had nothing to worry about except being deserving of such a mate. But sitting there and arguing with Walter Seeger would not serve any purpose.

When he had finished the food, Jeff thanked Katey again and then reached for his hat. "I'll ride on into the settlement," he said. "I appreciate the help. And thanks for not shooting me, Walter. I know it wasn't for lack of trying."

Walter grunted. He looked a bit sheepish. "Sorry, Holt. A man's got to protect his family out here, though. Can't be too careful."

"That's right." Jeff said good-bye to the children, tipped his hat one more time to Katey, then went outside and mounted up. The Seeger family watched him from the porch as he rode away.

Nice folks, Jeff thought, although Walter was a mite on the unfriendly side.

Jeff kicked his horse into a fast trot toward the river road. When he reached it, he swung toward Marietta. Seeing his family's homestead would have to wait until he found out Melissa's whereabouts.

The settlement was laid out on the northwest

shore of the Ohio River, opposite the site of Fort Harmar, which had been established by General Rufus Putnam following the end of the American Revolution. At first, Marietta had been known as Campus Martius. Over the years it had grown into an attractive community, with several wharves built into the river and warehouses nearby. There were businesses, churches, and even a school. It represented civilization, picked up bodily and carried into what had been wilderness only a few years earlier.

The center of town, at least from the standpoint of community activities, was Steakley's Trading Post, a large, stout structure of logs with a porch that ran around three sides. It did a brisk business. If one was looking for someone in the Marietta area, Steakley's was the place to wait. Almost everyone went there sooner or later.

The establishment was busy as usual that afternoon, Jeff saw from the number of horses, wagons, and buggies tied up at the long hitching rail in front of the building. He found a place for his horse, flipped the reins around the rail, then climbed the three steps onto the porch. As he headed toward the main doors, one of them opened, and a man stepped out with a bag of sugar balanced on his shoulder.

"Jeff Holt!" the man exclaimed in surprise.

"Hello, Mr. Steakley," Jeff replied. "I'll wager you never expected to see me again."

"Hell, no, boy." The storekeeper grinned. He was a balding middle-aged man with stooped shoulders. "We heard that you'd likely gone west to the mountains, but most folks around here figured you'd get your hair lifted by some of those red heathens. What in blazes are you doing back in Marietta?"

"I came to pay the taxes on the farm, to make sure it stays in the family." Jeff paused, then went on, "And to get Melissa. But I'm told she and her parents don't live here anymore."

Rathburn Steakley pursed his lips. "Let me put this sugar on Hank Bradford's wagon, and then I'll tell you what I know. But I warn you, it's not much."

"Anything will help."

Several customers passed Jeff on the porch while Steakley loaded the bag of sugar onto one of the wagons in front of the store. Some of them looked at Jeff curiously, as if they almost recognized him but not quite, while others paid little or no attention to him. In the two years Jeff had been gone, Marietta had grown, and a lot of the people were strangers to him.

Steakley approached him and put a hand on his arm. "Come on inside. We'll go into the office to talk."

Jeff let Steakley lead him through the long room crowded with counters, shelves, and customers. Two young men wearing the white aprons of clerks were behind the main counter in the back of the store. Steakley's business had also expanded, Jeff noticed. He could remember when the man had run the trading post by himself.

Steakley opened a door behind the rear counter and led Jeff into a small office dominated by a desk covered with papers. There were two chairs, and as Steakley waved Jeff into one of them, he sank into the other with a sigh.

"It's not like the old days," the storekeeper said. "Bills of lading, ledger books, account books. . . . I recollect when folks would pick up what they needed and pay me with a nice fat pig or a couple of good roasting pullets. I never wrote down a thing in those days. Now it seems as if all I do is write things down." He shook his head and then looked at Jeff. "What have you been doing with yourself for the last two years, son?"

"Like you said, I've been out West. With Clay."

Steakley plucked at his bottom lip with his blunt fingers.

"Maybe you'd better not tell me anything about

that brother of yours," he said after a moment. "Jasper Sutcliffe'd still like to talk to him about Pete Garwood getting killed."

Jeff was not surprised to hear that Marietta's constable had not lost interest in the Holt-Garwood feud. Those tragic times had taken not only the lives of Bartholomew and Norah Holt, but also those of Luther and Pete Garwood. The whole countryside had been talking about it, and Sutcliffe probably would have charged Clay with Pete Garwood's murder if he could have caught up with Clay—even though Pete had met his death in a fair fight.

"I didn't come back to hash all of that out," Jeff told Steakley now. "What I really want is Melissa."

The man's hound-doglike features lengthened even more.

"She's gone, Jeff," he said quietly. "Her and her folks, too."

"I know. I stopped by their place and talked to the Seegers. They didn't know anything about where Melissa and her parents might have gone."

"They wouldn't; I don't reckon anybody does. Ol' Merrivale just up and hired him some wagons and drivers one day, loaded up all that fancy stuff from his house, and left, heading upriver."

"He didn't say where they were going?"

Steakley leaned back in his chair, clasped his hands together over his paunch, and frowned in concentration.

"Let me think," he said. "I don't remember anything right off, but you never know."

"Melissa didn't say anything to you before they left?" Jeff asked, anguish creeping into his voice. He could imagine Melissa giving in to her father's bullying and leaving Marietta, but he could not believe she had failed to leave a letter or some sort of message for him. "Did she give you anything to hold for me?"

Steakley shook his head decisively. "Now that

part, I'm sure of. I didn't speak to her or even see her before she and her folks left. Merrivale came in for a few provisions, I seem to recall, and he said . . . I think he said something about heading for New York!" Steakley's voice rose as the memory came back to him. "That's it. I'm sure that's what he said."

Jeff sat back and blinked, stunned. *New York?* It was a long way to New York, and it was a hell of a big place. How was he supposed to find her with nothing more to go on?

The storekeeper must have read the signs of confusion and frustration on Jeff's face because he said, "I know this has really hit you hard, Jeff. If you want my advice, you'll go back to the mountains and forget about Melissa Merrivale. Her pa's probably got her married off to somebody else by now."

"No!" Jeff was out of his chair before he realized it, and he found himself standing over Steakley, his left hand grasping the front of the man's apron, his right clenched into a fist and cocked for a blow. Steakley gasped in fear as Jeff lifted him half out of the chair.

"Take it easy!" Steakley pleaded. "Take it easy, goddamn it!"

Drawing a deep, ragged breath, Jeff released the storekeeper's apron and let him sag back into the chair.

"Sorry," Jeff said without looking at the man. "Didn't mean to jump you that way. But her name's Melissa Holt now, and she's not married to anybody else. She can't be."

"Sure, sure, I know that," Steakley said quickly, pale with fear of the reaction he had unwittingly provoked. "Don't know what I was thinking, Jeff. I'm the one who's sorry."

Jeff closed his eyes and massaged his temples. "I never figured . . . never even dreamed—"

"I know, son. The news has to come as a mighty bad shock. If there's anything I can do to help—"

"No, thanks." Jeff opened his eyes and squared his shoulders. "I'll ride over to the farm and stay there for a while, give myself some time to figure this out. Suppose I'll need some supplies."

"Whatever you want, it's yours. Be glad to put it on account for you."

"I've got cash money, but thanks, anyway."

"Jeff, the cabin wasn't ever rebuilt after—well, you know."

"After Zach and Pete Garwood burned it down and killed my parents, you mean?" Jeff smiled coldly. "Doesn't matter. I've spent a lot more nights outdoors in the past two years than I have under a roof. Besides, there's the cabin where Melissa and I lived."

"You're right." Steakley stood up and extended a hand to him. "Welcome back to Marietta, Jeff, and no hard feelings."

"Thanks." Jeff shook hands with him. "Reckon I'll pick up those supplies now."

His thoughts were a blur as he bought flour, sugar, salt, and bacon. One of Steakley's clerks put the things in a bag for him, and Jeff went out to his horse with the parcel slung over his shoulder. Sort of like the possibles bag he'd used back in the mountains, he thought.

And as he mounted up, still numb from the shocking news, he wished he was back in those mountains right now.

New York . . . God! How would he ever find Melissa?

"Arrogant young son of a bitch!" Steakley muttered under his breath as he watched Jeff Holt ride away. The Holts had always been a violent bunch, he thought, but Jeff's time in the mountains had turned him into little more than a savage himself.

Steakley turned and stalked back through the store to his office. He shut the door behind him, sat down, and leaned back in the chair. He could have told Jefferson Holt a thing or two if he had wanted to, yes, sir!

Like the fact that Melissa had indeed left a letter there for him, a letter that had no doubt told exactly where the Merrivales were going when they left Ohio. She would never go off without letting Jeff know where he could find her. The only problem was that Charles Merrivale had anticipated his daughter's actions, and he had visited the store after Melissa. He had been generous, too, paying Steakley well for that letter and a promise from the storekeeper to keep his mouth shut about where they were going.

Merrivale hated Jeff Holt, hated him with a passion, and so did Steakley. Maybe he *was* almost old enough to be Melissa's father, Steakley thought; that did not mean he would not have been a good husband to her. Every time he had started to hint around about that, however, Melissa had made it clear she did not have any romantic interest in him. She only had had eyes for Jeff Holt.

Well, that was over good and proper now. Melissa was thousands of miles away, and Holt would never find her. *Never.*

Steakley picked up one of his account books. He might not have Melissa, but he had a thriving business, and when the need got too great, he could always go see Josie Garwood. Josie was always glad to see him and his money. He had a pretty good life, Steakley decided.

But Jeff Holt, now . . . he had nothing.

Chapter Two

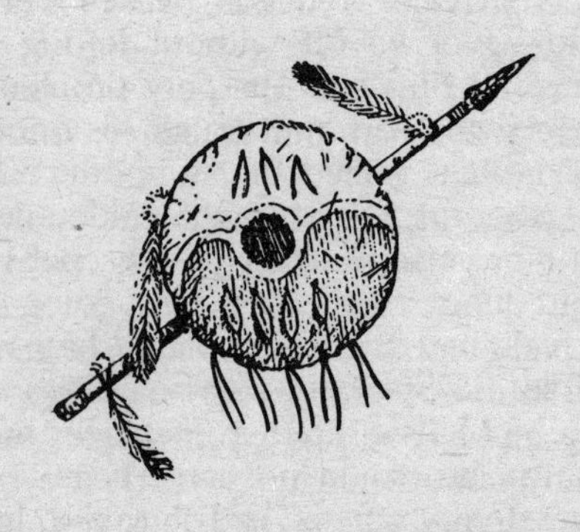

The Indians could not brook the intrusion of the whites on the hunting grounds and navigable waters which they had been in habits of considering as their own property from time immemorial.

—Fortescue Cuming
"Sketches of a Tour to the
Western Country"

The paddle in Clay Holt's hands bit smoothly into the waters of the Yellowstone River, sending the birchbark canoe gliding over the placid surface. The Yellowstone ran narrow and fast in places, but here it was wide and peaceful, sparkling with a blue and white shimmer in the midday sun.

Spring was Clay's favorite time of year in the mountains. The sun was warm during the day, and the nights were still cool enough for a man to sleep well, rolled up in a buffalo robe—especially when that robe was shared with a woman like Shining Moon.

Clay looked back at her, sitting in the rear of the canoe and lending her efforts with a paddle to his. Her dark eyes met his, and his expression softened. With his lean, hard features and the rumpled thatch of black hair under a coonskin cap, he could often appear rather grim, but Shining Moon nearly always was able to draw a smile out of him. A man could search the whole world over, he had thought more than once, and never find a better, more beautiful wife.

They made an impressive-looking couple as they paddled along the clear mountain stream that ran through a thickly wooded valley between rugged, snowcapped heights. Clay was dressed in a buckskin shirt and trousers, along with high-topped fringed moccasins and a coonskin cap, its ringed tail dangling on his right shoulder. He had tucked a brace of .54 caliber North and Cheney flintlock pistols under his belt, and he carried two knives, one in a fringed sheath on his belt, the other sheathed and strapped to the calf under his right moccasin. Resting against his left hip were his powder horn and shot pouch, hung from a strap that crossed his broad chest and right shoulder. His Harper's Ferry rifle, identical to the one he had given his brother Jeff, lay at his feet in the bottom of the canoe, where it would be easy to reach in case of trouble.

Shining Moon, a young Hunkpapa Sioux woman of twenty summers, also wore buckskins, but her dress was decorated with porcupine quills painted different colors and arranged in elaborate patterns on the garment. In addition, a band of brightly colored cloth was tied around her forehead to keep her long, raven-dark hair from falling in front of her eyes. She wore a hunting knife and, like her husband, had placed a rifle at her feet. She was not as expert a marksman as Clay Holt, but she could outshoot most male members of her tribe, who had only recently become proficient in the use of firearms. And none of the Hunkpapa, male or female, were as good at tracking and reading sign as Shining Moon. She had been invaluable on the journey, leading Clay and his companions unerringly to creeks and smaller rivers teeming with beaver.

As a result, Clay's canoe was heavily loaded with beaver pelts—plews, as the mountain men called them—as was the canoe being paddled by Proud Wolf, Shining Moon's brother, and Aaron Garwood, the fourth member of this partnership. Their canoe was directly behind the one occupied by Clay and Shining Moon.

Though it was still early in spring, Clay and the others had trapped enough beaver to require a visit to the fort established by Manuel Lisa at the junction of the Yellowstone and Big Horn rivers, where they could sell the pelts. The previous year, Clay and Jeff had worked for the Spaniard; this year, Clay had decided to go it alone except for his wife, her brother, and their friend Aaron. Instead of using equipment and provisions supplied by Lisa, they were responsible for outfitting themselves; but Lisa would provide a market for the furs, and Clay and his companions would keep the profits they realized, rather than work for wages. In the long run, Clay thought, they would make more money, though they would also have more at stake.

Clay wondered how Jeff was doing and if his brother had reached Ohio by now. Would he bring Melissa back to the frontier with him when he returned? Clay and Jeff had talked about that, but Clay had no idea what decision Melissa would come to. There were worse places to live than these mountains, Clay thought.

The past six months since he and Shining Moon

were married in a Teton Sioux ceremony had been like an extended honeymoon. Jeff might choose to remain in so-called civilization, but not Clay. This was his home now, and he would be happy to spend the rest of his life in the Shining Mountains.

It was about time to stop for the noon meal, so he gestured to Proud Wolf and Aaron to head for shore. Proud Wolf, sitting in the front of the second canoe, nodded his understanding.

Suddenly the sound of gunfire came floating to their ears, followed an instant later by bloodcurdling cries.

"What in blazes!" Clay twisted around to look at Shining Moon.

"I do not know," she said. "It comes from upstream."

Clay could tell from the anxious expressions on the faces of Proud Wolf and Aaron that they also heard the ominous noises. He pointed to the shore again, more urgency in his gesture.

The prow of Clay's canoe struck the grassy bank, and he jumped out, rifle in one hand, and after Shining Moon had stepped out, he reached back to haul the canoe onto dry land. A few feet away Proud Wolf and Aaron beached their canoe and joined Clay and Shining Moon.

The gunfire from upstream continued, sporadic blasts punctuated by shouts and cries. A battle was going on, no more than a few hundred yards away.

"What do you reckon that's about, Clay?" Aaron asked as he gripped his rifle. He was a slender young man with brown hair and a beard that did not totally disguise the surprisingly gentle cast of his features. He had been in the mountains less than a year and was not totally at home yet; given his nature, he might never be, in such rugged surroundings. His left arm was thinner and weaker than his right, the result of its having been broken in a fight with Clay back in

Ohio, when the Garwoods and the Holts were feuding. Those days were in the past now, and Aaron looked on Clay with a mixture of friendship and admiration.

Clay shook his head in reply to the young man's question. "Don't know, but I intend to find out before we go any farther. You and Shining Moon stay here, Aaron. Proud Wolf and I will go have a look."

Proud Wolf's chest swelled, and he smiled broadly. At sixteen the Hunkpapa Sioux was still young and his body was undersized, but he had a warrior's heart and spirit. He admired no one more than his brother-in-law, Clay Holt, and to accompany Clay on what might be a dangerous chore appealed to him.

"You should take me," Shining Moon said quietly. She had never been one meekly to accept a decision with which she disagreed, even if it came from her husband. "I can move as silently as the wind and without the exuberance of youth."

"You are only four summers older than me, sister," Proud Wolf reminded her.

"Four summers can sometimes be a great deal of time."

"Proud Wolf goes with me," Clay said. "He can keep quiet enough when he wants to, and I want you and Aaron covering our back trail, Shining Moon."

She nodded, realizing that Clay's decision had been based on logic rather than his feelings for her. He knew all too well that nothing got her dander up quicker than sensing that he was trying to be overprotective of her.

A fresh flurry of shooting exploded upriver. Somebody was burning a hell of a lot of powder, Clay thought as he and Proud Wolf made their way along the shore. Thick brush thronged the bank, growing in some places all the way to the river, and Clay was grateful for the cover it provided.

Behind them, Shining Moon and Aaron Garwood crouched at the edge of the growth, rifles held ready in case of trouble from an unexpected direction.

The river had been running straight, but as Clay and Proud Wolf made their way along it, they entered a stretch of twists and bends. With the thick growth on the banks, it was difficult to see past some of the turns, and Clay and Proud Wolf were almost on top of the battle before they got sight of the conflict. The gunshots were louder now, and as Clay parted the screen of brush to peer through it, he saw that some of the combatants were less than fifty yards away.

In the middle of the river was an island, little more than a sandbar, really, with a few trees and bushes growing on it. On that island, their backs to the shore where Clay and Proud Wolf crouched, were some two dozen white men, trying to fight off a band of hostile Blackfoot warriors on the far bank. Clay recognized the Blackfoot markings by the beadwork on their moccasins—a design ending in three prongs, which designated the three tribes that comprised the Blackfoot: the Siksika, the Blood, and the Piegan. The warriors were raking the island with arrows and musket fire, and as Clay and Proud Wolf watched, one of the white men crumpled, bending almost double over the arrow that had been driven through his midsection. Several more lay motionless on the sandy island.

"Damn!" Clay swore. "Those pilgrims are in a bad way."

"They have more guns, but the Blackfoot are many. They will attack the island, I think."

Clay agreed with Proud Wolf. The island was separated from the far shore only by a narrow strip of shallow water. The Blackfoot would wait, content to thin the ranks of the island's defenders before charging across those shallows to overrun the white men. Clay searched for any sign of canoes but did not see them. The white men must have been on foot; when they'd been jumped by the Blackfoot, they must have retreated onto the island, pinning themselves down.

"What will we do?" Proud Wolf asked quietly.

Clay looked over at him and saw that the young man was almost jumping out of his skin with eagerness to join the fight. The Sioux and the Blackfoot were ancient enemies, and Clay knew that Proud Wolf would like nothing better than to spill Blackfoot blood. Clay had no love for the Blackfoot, either. He had first clashed with them during the Lewis and Clark journey, and he knew them to be a treacherous, horse-stealing bunch.

But when you got right down to it, this was not his fight, and he hated to risk the lives of his wife, brother-in-law, and friend to help a group of men who had blundered into a bad situation. A man had to take care of his own troubles on the frontier, and if he could not, he went under. It was as simple as that.

At least that was what Clay tried to convince himself of for all of ten or fifteen seconds. Then he said, "I reckon we'll pitch in and do what we can to help. The way the river bends here, I think we can get our canoes up to this side of the island almost before the Blackfoot see us coming."

Silently, Clay and Proud Wolf retreated through the brush until they reached Shining Moon and Aaron Garwood. Clay explained tersely what they had witnessed.

Aaron said, "We're going to help those folks, aren't we?"

"I don't see as we've got much choice," Clay replied. "Don't reckon I could live with myself if we went off and left them there to die."

"Nor could I," Shining Moon said, "not at the hands of the Blackfoot." Her eyes were aflame with the same ancestral hatred of the Blackfoot that her brother possessed.

Quickly Clay outlined a simple plan. They would

approach the island from the deeper channel of the river and throw their four flintlocks into the battle on the side of the whites. There were too many people on the island for Clay and his companions to rescue; if only three or four had been in the party, the canoes would have had room enough to carry them away.

Shining Moon got into the canoe while Clay pushed it into deeper water. Likewise, Proud Wolf shoved off from the bank in the other canoe with Aaron. They made sure their rifles were primed and loaded, then took up the paddles and propelled the canoes toward the bend.

They could not waste any time, Clay knew. The arrows of the Blackfoot would probably not be able to reach them as long as they were in the stream, but musket fire was a different story altogether. They would have to cover over fifty yards of open water before they reached the shelter of the island itself. And since the river narrowed as it passed the sandbar, the current was liable to be stronger there, and paddling against it would slow them down. Still, they could do nothing else.

Hunched forward in the bow of the canoe, Clay dipped the paddle deep into the water, the corded muscles in his arms and shoulders working smoothly. Shining Moon was also strong, and together their efforts sent the canoe shooting through the current. Proud Wolf and Aaron followed behind them as best they could.

As they rounded the bend, the island came into view. A haze of black-powder smoke hung in the air over it and along the shore. Flintlocks still boomed, and arrows hummed in the air. Clay bent his back even more to the task of paddling, sparing only a brief glance toward the bank. Although he could see only a few Blackfoot warriors, he figured they outnumbered the defenders on the island two to one.

Four more rifles would not make a great difference, or at least one would not think so. But Clay had confidence in his own marksmanship, along with that of Shining Moon, Proud Wolf, and Aaron. If they could reach the island and make every shot count, the Blackfoot might decide the price they would have to pay to continue the attack was too high.

Ten yards slid under the canoes, then twenty, then thirty. They were more than halfway there, and so far the Blackfoot had paid no attention to them. That changed abruptly, however. Over the gunfire and the splashing of the paddles, Clay heard a sudden cry of alarm, echoed seconds later by other warriors. He saw a splash just ahead to the right and knew it was a musket ball hitting the water. As long as the aim of the Blackfoot stayed that far off, he was not worried.

More musket balls peppered the surface of the river near the canoes. Clay ignored them and kept paddling. A few seconds later, the sandbar loomed ahead to the right, between the canoes and the far shore where the Blackfoot hid in the trees. Clay dug down with the paddle and sent the canoe grating onto the sandy beach. He and Shining Moon leapt out with their rifles as Proud Wolf and Aaron safely arrived nearby.

Some of the island's defenders had seen them coming. Buckskin-clad bearded men jumped up and ran toward the newcomers. They would have been better off fighting the Blackfoot than greeting the reinforcements, Clay thought.

Then he realized that a greeting was the last thing these men had in mind. Without slowing down, one of them slammed into Clay, knocking him off-balance. Clay caught himself before he fell but had no chance to regain solid footing before another man slashed at him with a rifle butt. Clay blocked the blow, but this time he went down under the impact. A few feet away Shining Moon cried out in surprise and alarm as another man knocked her roughly aside and sprang into the canoe.

"Hey!" Aaron yelled as he and Proud Wolf were the victims of a similar assault. "What the hell are you doing?"

One of the bearded men paused long enough to throw him a hideous grin. "Getting out of here, sonny!"

Clay got to his knees and saw at least half a dozen men trying to pile into each of the canoes, fighting one another for space. They were making a desperate attempt to escape, abandoning the others to their fate. Clay's instincts cried out for him to put a shot in the middle of the ungrateful lot of them, but from the corner of his eye, he saw one of the Blackfoot emerge from the shelter of a deadfall on the shore—and train his musket on the fleeing men.

Throwing himself down on his belly, Clay brought his rifle to his shoulder, thumbed back the cock on the flintlock, and settled the sight on the chest of the Blackfoot warrior. He fired at the same instant as the Blackfoot. There was no way of knowing where the ball from the Indian's musket went, but Clay's shot caught the warrior in the chest and sent him sprawling backward.

Clay glanced over his shoulder and saw that both canoes were in the river now, riding low in the water with too many passengers. They were not even trying to paddle but were content to let the current carry them downstream.

A smaller band of Blackfoot detached themselves from the main party and raced along the shoreline, firing arrows and muskets toward the canoes. The men who were trying to escape soon discovered they had left the sparse shelter of the island for something even worse. A couple of them toppled from each canoe, arrows protruding from their bodies. Others sagged, wounded by musket fire, but managed to stay aboard.

The crude boats were awash within moments, however, perforated by balls from Blackfoot muskets. From the island, Clay saw the canoes sinking and uttered a heartfelt curse. He knew that when they went down, they would take all the supplies and a season's worth of pelts to the bottom of the river.

And he could do nothing about it, he realized. Supplies and pelts meant nothing if he and the others were killed. Clay helped Shining Moon to her feet, and together they ran toward a clump of small trees where several defenders were clustered. Aaron and Proud Wolf ran to a thicket nearby.

Clay and Shining Moon threw themselves to the ground beside the other defenders. Musket fire still rattled and popped around them. Clay's eyes widened in shock as he realized that one of the whites was a woman. A young woman, at that, with strawberry-blond hair underneath a hooded cloak. An older, round-faced man hovered beside her, one arm over her protectively. Neither of them seemed to be armed, but the men with them, all buckskin-clad frontiersmen, were firing toward the shore with pistols and rifles.

Debris was clumped at the base of the trees, and Clay guessed it had caught there during the spring floods, when the river had run higher. The driftwood and brush provided some shelter from the Blackfoot attack; it was unlikely to stop a musket ball, but it would prevent many arrows from getting through.

With fast, practiced ease, Clay reloaded, then rose up to get a bead on one of the Indians. The Blackfoot was showing only a few inches of shoulder behind a tree, but that was enough. Clay's rifle roared, and the warrior went staggering, his right arm dangling uselessly from a shattered shoulder.

"Good Lord!" cried the round-faced man sheltering the young woman. "That's quite some shooting!"

Clay put the rifle on the ground and jerked out his pistols. They did not have the range of the long gun, but in his hands they were accurate enough to down a couple more Blackfoot. Beside him, Shining Moon fired her rifle and sent another attacker spinning to the ground. From the nearby clump of brush, Proud Wolf and Aaron added their firepower to the efforts of the defenders, spacing their shots so that they would be firing while the others were reloading.

As he crouched down and reloaded the rifle and pistols, Clay glanced toward the river and saw that both canoes had sunk, leaving the would-be escapees floundering in the water. Some were floating facedown; others struggled back toward the island. The current was too strong for any of them to reach the far shore and escape that way.

Clay swallowed the revulsion he felt for those men. There would be time later to deal with them—if he came out of this mess alive.

His weapons reloaded, he fired again. This time one of the pistol shots missed, but the other one and the ball from the rifle hit their targets. Another Blackfoot died, and one more staggered away badly wounded. Clay had put five of the warriors out of the fight already; Shining Moon, Proud Wolf, and Aaron Garwood were taking an impressive toll with their fire, too.

"Pour it into them!" Clay shouted, his voice booming out over the island. "Keep firing!"

Leading by example as well as words, Clay rallied the defenders over the next few minutes, and although two more were killed by the attackers, the casualties suffered by the Blackfoot were much greater. Rifle fire raked the shoreline, the defenders shooting in volleys rather than offering the scattered, disorganized resistance they had before Clay's arrival.

He was not surprised when the attackers suddenly broke and ran.

A cheer went up from the men on the island as they saw the Indians retreating, but Clay stood up and shouted, "Give them a hot send-off, boys!" He had his pistols in his hands, and he fired both guns after the fleeing Blackfoot. The others followed his lead, sending more balls whining through the forest after the Indians.

One man let out an exuberant whoop, slapped Clay on the shoulder, and cried, "We showed 'em, didn't we? We really taught them redskinned bastards a lesson!"

Clay looked over at the man, saw that his buckskins were soaking wet, and savagely backhanded him. Only the fact that Clay had tucked away the pistol he had been holding in that hand saved the man from a cracked skull. As it was, he staggered back a few steps, tripped, and fell heavily to the ground.

"Touch me again and I'll kill you," Clay said coldly.

The man's face twisted with rage, and he scrambled to his feet, his hand reaching for the knife sheathed at his waist. He stopped short as he saw Shining Moon, Proud Wolf, and Aaron positioning themselves beside Clay.

"Here now, there's no need for fighting among ourselves!" exclaimed the heavyset, middle-aged man who had been hovering over the young woman. He pushed himself to his feet, helped the girl up, and said, "We've just saved ourselves from those savages. We should be celebrating."

Clay did not look at the man who had just spoken but nodded toward the buckskin-clad man on the ground. "No thanks to this son of a bitch and the others like him who tried to save their own skins. They stole my canoes and ran out on the rest of you."

"The hell we did!" flared the man in the wet

buckskins. "We were just—just tryin' to get around behind those redskins so that we could catch them in a cross fire." He folded his arms across his chest and glared at Clay. "That's what we were doing."

"Sure," Clay said, his voice filled with contempt. He turned to the older man, who seemed to be in charge of this group. "Name's Clay Holt. This is my wife, Shining Moon; her brother, Proud Wolf; and our friend Aaron Garwood."

"I'm exceedingly pleased to meet you, Mr. Holt. I am Professor Donald Elwood Franklin, and this is my daughter, Miss Lucy Franklin. We're from Cambridge, Massachusetts. Harvard, you know. I'm an instructor in botany there."

Clay greeted this announcement with some surprise. What the hell was a botany professor from Harvard doing in the middle of the wilderness, especially dragging his daughter along with him?

"Let's get off this island," he said. Explanations would have to wait.

Chapter Three

They made camp in a clearing not far from the island. The men who had been dumped in the river were miserable in their wet buckskins, and although Clay felt no sympathy for them, he built a fire so they could dry out. For the time being, he was stuck with this bunch; he might as well make the best of it, he decided.

Franklin was a talkative sort, and Clay could easily believe he was a professor. He seemed to be full of knowledge about anything and everything—except how to survive on the frontier. He wore a dusty dark suit, a silk cravat, a white shirt, and a beaver hat that Clay thought looked faintly ridiculous. His ruddy features were those of a fleshy, middle-aged cherub, and his cheerful expression caused his eyes to twinkle with amusement, even though as far as Clay could tell, he did not have much to be happy about in the present situation.

Lucy Franklin was not taking things so well. She was pale, and her green eyes remained wide and haunted with terror from the Indian attack. She said little and seemed content to huddle near the fire.

The professor brought out a pipe and a pouch of tobacco and was soon puffing away as he sat on a fallen log near his daughter.

"You saved our lives, sir," he said to Clay. "Those savages would have overwhelmed us if you hadn't come to our assistance."

"Just luck we came along when we did," Clay said, taking out his own pipe. "We were headed upriver with a load of pelts, bound for Lisa's fort." Clay was somber as he packed his pipe, then got a blazing twig from the fire and lit it. "Those plews are all on the bottom of the Yellowstone now, along with our supplies."

"I'm dreadfully sorry about that. Is there any hope of recovering your goods?"

"I reckon I can dive down and get some of the pelts, the ones I can find. Water won't hurt them. All of our supplies'll be ruined, though."

"We have plenty of provisions," Franklin declared. "We'll be glad to share them with you, of course. After all, you and your friends saved our lives."

As a matter of fact, several men had delved into the packs they carried with them and were cooking a stew made with dried beef, wild onions, and roots. One man already had pan bread ready to cook over the fire. The smell of the food reminded Clay it was past time to eat.

He looked at the professor and asked, "What in blazes are you folks doing out here, anyway? I didn't think there were any white men in these mountains except fur trappers."

"Well, as I told you, I'm an instructor in botany at Harvard. I'm also something of an amateur naturalist, like my friend Tom Jefferson." Franklin's words came faster as he warmed to his subject. "I'm on a botanical expedition, financed by President Jefferson and the American Philosophical Society of Philadelphia. Our purpose is to retrace the route of Lewis and Clark, collecting plant specimens, taking measurements, and the like. I don't know if you're aware of the scientific significance of the discoveries made by Captain Lewis and Captain Clark—"

"I was with them," Clay said. "I stuck more than one weed in a sack for Cap'n Lewis."

"Really?" Franklin's eyes widened. "You were a member of the Corps of Discovery, Mr. Holt?"

"Yes. All the way to the Pacific and back."

"Well, this is a most fortuitous meeting indeed!"

Clay was not sure he liked the sound of that, so he said nothing.

After a moment, Franklin went on, "You're aware, then, of all the information Lewis and Clark brought back with them, as well as the many specimens of their discoveries. However, you may not know that their findings were greeted with skepticism by some members of the scientific and philosophical community. Why, a few of my fellow naturalists have insisted that Lewis and Clark are madmen and simply imagined all the adventures they claim to have had."

"Kind of hard to do when they brought so much proof back with them, isn't it?" Clay said.

Franklin chuckled. "Never underestimate the stubbornness of the academic mind, my friend. At any rate, since President Jefferson sent the expedition to the Pacific for scientific as much as political purposes, I know that the doubt and resistance his ideas have met have been a great disappointment to him. I've come west to corroborate the discoveries of Lewis and Clark and try to convince the skeptics in the scientific establishment of their veracity."

"I reckon I follow most of what you just said," Clay mused. "But if these scientific rascals don't believe what Cap'n Lewis and Cap'n Clark had to say, what makes you think they'll believe you?"

"Preponderance of evidence, Mr. Holt, preponderance of evidence. Simply put, I'm going to beat them over the head with the proof until they finally open their eyes and look at it. Figuratively speaking, of course."

Clay could not help but like the professor, long-winded though he might be.

"Why'd you bring your daughter with you?" he asked. "The wilderness is no place for a young woman."

Franklin sounded genuinely surprised by the question as he replied, "Lucy goes everywhere with me. She's my assistant. She transcribes all my notes and helps me with my cataloguing and classifying."

"Reckon you've noticed by now this isn't Massachusetts, Professor," Clay said dryly. "There're all kinds of dangers out here you'll never run into back East. Indians, wild animals, bad weather—"

"Of course, of course," Franklin agreed. "I'm well aware of that, Mr. Holt. But I've read the journals of Captain Lewis and Captain Clark, and I'm also aware that they had a woman with them for most of the trip."

"An Indian woman," Clay pointed out. "A Shoshone named Sacajawea. Janey, we called her. She made the trip, all right, Professor, but it's not the same thing."

"You have your wife with you," Franklin said stubbornly, and Clay remembered what he had said about academic minds.

"Shining Moon is a Hunkpapa Sioux, born, bred, and raised in these mountains. This is her home. But I wouldn't drop her down in the middle of Cambridge, Massachusetts. She'd be plumb scared to death, I reckon." *I know I would be,* Clay added silently.

"Well, perhaps you're correct, Mr. Holt, but really, this discussion is pointless. Lucy is here, whether I should have allowed her to accompany me on this expedition or not."

"That's true," Clay agreed grimly. "And I guess that makes her your concern, Professor." Without waiting for Franklin to say anything else, he walked over to the fire and squatted on his haunches next to Shining Moon.

The man Clay had backhanded on the island was standing nearby, and after giving Clay a hard look for a moment, he said, "After we eat, we'll get organized and move on again. That all right with you, Professor?"

"Whatever you say, Mr. Lawton," Franklin replied. "After all, you are in charge."

Clay looked up sharply. "This gent's running the show?"

"Mr. Lawton is our chief guide, Mr. Holt. I hired him back in St. Louis, along with these other gentlemen."

Clay snorted in disgust, and that drew another glare from Lawton.

"No wonder you walked right into a Blackfoot ambush," Clay said.

Lawton stiffened. "Listen, Holt, I'm getting mighty tired of the way you're acting. I've heard talk about you, back in St. Louis and in some of the settlements along the Missouri. You're supposed to be some sort o' big skookum he-wolf. Well, you don't look like so all-fired much to me."

Slowly Clay stood up and faced Lawton across the fire. "I don't tell folks what to say about me or what to think about me," he said. "But I never tried to run out on folks I'd signed on to protect."

Lawton's hand went to the knife sheathed at his hip. Clay tensed and reached for his own blade. He felt an instinctive dislike for Lawton. *Might as well get this trouble over and done with now,* Clay thought.

Neither Shining Moon, Proud Wolf, nor Aaron Garwood said a word. They were well aware that Clay would not take it kindly if they intervened. Likewise, the others in the professor's party seemed willing to stand back and wait.

"Stop it!" Lucy Franklin cried. She had gotten to her feet without any of them noticing, and the hood of her cloak was thrown back so that her reddish-blond hair shone in the sunlight. She trembled as she went on, "We just escaped from those awful savages! We shouldn't be fighting among ourselves!"

"Lucy's right," Professor Franklin said, moving over so that he was between Clay and Lawton. "There's no need for this animosity, gentlemen."

A buckskin-clad man spoke up, his voice cool and arrogant. "I say let them settle it, Professor. A duel is the thing. That's what we would do back in Heidelberg."

Clay glanced at the man who had spoken. He was fairly young, probably in his mid-twenties, and for the first time Clay noticed that although he wore buckskins, he hardly looked natural in them. He had sleek dark hair and good looks that were almost too pretty for the surroundings. His hands were soft and uncallused, and he carried no weapons. A large leather case was propped against a rock next to him. Clay realized that he had been too busy earlier to notice the differences between this man and the others.

"I don't think we need a duel, Rupert," Franklin said sharply. "We're not back in Europe, you know. We don't settle things with sabers or dueling pistols at dawn."

The young man called Rupert shrugged. "Of

course, Professor. And I certainly would not wish to see anything occur that might upset Miss Lucy."

"Why don't you all just sit down and be quiet?" Lucy said shakily. "There's been enough fighting today."

His gaze still fixed on Lawton, Clay said, "Reckon the young lady's right. I'll stay out of your way, Lawton, and you stay out of mine."

"Sure," Lawton replied, his lip curling into a sneer. Clay knew by looking at him that the man considered this a victory; Lawton believed that Clay was backing down.

Let him think whatever the hell he wants to, Clay told himself. Anyway, this was none of his business. The professor was the one who had hired Lawton, so it was up to Franklin to deal with him.

The young man who looked out of place in buckskins approached Clay and gave a half-bow. "Rupert von Metz, at your service, Herr Holt. Professor Franklin neglected to introduce us earlier. I am honored to make the acquaintance of such a famous wilderness man as yourself."

So this Metz fellow has heard of me, too, just like Lawton, Clay thought. He'd had no idea folks were talking about him back in St. Louis. The trappers who had gone down the Missouri with him the previous autumn must have carried tales about his clash with Duquesne and the fight at the fort with Zach Garwood.

Even though von Metz had claimed to be glad to meet him, the young man's eyes were cold and calculating, Clay decided. He wondered what von Metz was doing on this expedition.

The explanation was not long in coming. Even though Clay had only grunted in acknowledgment of von Metz's self-introduction, the man went on as if Clay had asked for his life story.

"I'm an artist, you see," von Metz said. "I have

painted portraits of most of the noble lords and ladies in Europe, but my real ambition is to capture on canvas all the spectacle and majesty of the American West. To this end, one of my patrons, Comte Defresne, has generously sponsored my trip here and allowed me to join Professor Franklin's expedition." He smiled. "This land is much different from my native Prussia. There we have no red savages to menace us."

Aaron Garwood had sauntered over to listen to von Metz's discourse, and when the Prussian paused, Aaron spat on the ground and said, "Some of those red savages, as you call them, are the finest folks I've ever met." Aaron's eyes were narrowed with dislike as he spoke. "Proud Wolf over there is about the best friend I've got in the world."

"Of course," von Metz said, his handsome features stiff with resentment at Aaron's tone. "I meant no offense."

Clay did not believe that. Von Metz was like a bluejay; he did not care who his squawking disturbed.

"We'd better eat," Clay said curtly. "It's been a rough day."

He sat next to Shining Moon, who gave him a sympathetic glance. She understood his impatience with these pilgrims, he was sure. To Clay's way of thinking, a man had no business venturing into the mountains unless he could take care of himself, or at least pull his own weight in a group.

They ate in silence. Whenever Clay glanced at Lawton, the man was giving him a surly stare. With Lawton in charge, the professor and his companions were damned lucky to be alive, Clay thought. He had seen Lawton's kind before—a bully when the odds were on his side, a coward when he had to stand up alone. There was a good chance Lawton had run into trouble with the law back East somewhere, and heading west had seemed to him a good way to escape his problems.

Well, Clay mused, that description also fit himself in a few ways. He had come west in the first place to get away from Josie Garwood and her ridiculous claim that he had gotten her pregnant; he had returned to the mountains along with Jeff to put an end to the Holt-Garwood feud and all the blood-spilling that went along with it. And back in Marietta there was a constable who might still want to throw him in jail.

The feud had not ended when Clay and Jeff left Ohio. It had just traveled west with them, culminating in a final showdown between Clay and Zach Garwood, who had been accompanied by his brother Aaron. But now all that was over, the bad blood put to rest with Zach's death. Aaron had befriended the Holts, and Clay had left his past behind to make a life for himself in the mountains, a good life with Shining Moon and her people.

He wanted to get back to that as quickly as possible.

Professor Franklin was talking to Proud Wolf. The young Hunkpapa man was full of questions about Franklin's expedition, and the professor explained how the specimens he was collecting and the information he was gathering would be taken back East to further the knowledge available to the scientific community.

Frowning in confusion, Proud Wolf asked, "You mean there are people who spend all their time studying plants and animals and rocks?"

"Indeed there are, young man," Franklin replied. "They are called naturalists, and I'm proud to number myself among them. In fact, this journey has the support not only of former President Jefferson, but also of the American Philosophical Society of Philadelphia, the country's—perhaps the world's—leading organization of scientists. When I return, my fellow naturalists will pore over my findings until they've extracted every bit of pertinent information to be found."

"I understand your words—most of them—but not why you and the men like you do these things. A plant is here to eat, or to hide a warrior from his enemies, or to make his skin itch. An animal is here to eat and to give its skin to man for clothing. A rock is here to kill the animal—or a man's enemy. All of them—the plants, the animals, the rocks—have always been here, and they will always be here. What else is there to know about them?"

Franklin gave a booming laugh. "You do know how to reduce things to their most common element, don't you, Proud Wolf? That's the mark of a great mind, my boy. You should nurture it. But in the meantime, perhaps I can open your eyes to some things you haven't considered before now."

Clay had been only half listening to the conversation, but now he said, "There won't be time for that. We'll be moving on as soon as we can, and I reckon you will be, too, Professor."

"As a matter of fact, I've been wanting to talk to you about that, Mr. Holt."

Clay tensed. Ever since they had left the island and established this camp, he had had the feeling that something was on Franklin's mind, something that Clay did not particularly want to hear.

Franklin plunged on. "It seems to me that after the events of today, it would be perfectly logical for you to take over the leadership of our little expedition, Mr. Holt."

"Wait a minute!" Lawton protested, just as Clay had expected. "I'm the chief guide. That's what you hired me for back in St. Louis, Professor."

"And I'm a fur trapper." Clay hated to agree with Lawton but saw no alternative. "I've got business of my own to tend to, Professor."

"But you're a more seasoned frontiersman than

Mr. Lawton or any of his, ah, cronies," Franklin pointed out.

Lawton took offense again. "I've been in these mountains before!" he declared angrily.

"Yes, but for how long?" Franklin asked.

"Well . . . a few months."

The professor swung back to Clay. "And what about you, Mr. Holt? How much time have you spent in this wilderness?"

Clay shrugged. "Off and on—about three, four years, I reckon."

"So you see, it makes perfect sense for you to join us."

"Perfect sense to you, maybe," Clay said. "Not to me."

"Clay." Shining Moon spoke up, taking Clay by surprise. "These people may need our help. Besides, our supplies are gone. They sank into the river with the canoes."

Clay glared at Lawton. "It's because of him and his friends that we lost all our possibles."

Lawton returned the hostile stare but said nothing.

"Listen to your wife, Mr. Holt," Franklin advised. "We have more than enough supplies for everyone, you and your companions included. Besides, as I mentioned, I have the financial backing of both Thomas Jefferson and the American Philosophical Society. If you accept my offer, I can promise you enough compensation to recoup all of your losses and to outfit yourself for another trapping journey after our expedition has come to a conclusion."

Clay rubbed his stubbled jaw and grimaced in thought. This encounter had turned out exactly as he had been afraid it would. He did not want the responsibility of shepherding this bunch of inexperienced misfits through the Rockies. Chances were, they would all wind up dead, himself and Shining Moon included.

He looked over at Proud Wolf and Aaron. "What do you two think?" he asked. "You've got a stake in this, same as the rest of us."

"I think we should help these folks," Aaron said without hesitation. Clay saw his eyes dart toward Lucy Franklin, and he knew why Aaron had answered that way. The young man was attracted to her, and Clay could not blame him.

"I too think we should join this expedition," Proud Wolf said. "I would like to learn more of this . . . science and philosophy of which Professor Franklin speaks."

Franklin sensed that Clay was being won over. He concluded by saying, "Besides, Mr. Holt, if you refuse, we shall have no choice but to continue on with Mr. Lawton in charge."

Clay looked down at the ground for a long moment, and when he finally raised his eyes and looked at Franklin, he said, "You're a slick one, Professor. You reckon you've got it all figured so that I can't turn you down. And I don't suppose I will."

"Then you will take over?" Franklin sounded slightly surprised in spite of himself. "That's excellent, Mr. Holt, excellent!"

Clay stood up and looked over at Lawton. "But if I'm in charge, that means everybody's got to do as I say. That's the only way we've got a chance of getting you folks back to civilization alive."

"Of course, of course," Franklin agreed. "You'll be in complete command."

"Just want to make sure everybody understands that."

Lawton said, "We all know what you're getting at, Holt. I don't appreciate the way you been riding me, but I'll do what you say. Hell, I'm no fool. I reckon you do know this part of the country better'n I do."

"Damn right," Clay said. He turned to Franklin and extended his hand. "We'll do what we can for you and your people."

He just hoped he was not making the worst mistake of his life.

During his time in the Shining Mountains, Jefferson Holt had climbed ridges where no white man had stood before. He had looked out over valleys and mountains and known that he and his brother Clay were perhaps the only human beings, white or red, for fifty or a hundred miles around. Yet he had never felt as isolated as he did now, in the place where he had grown to manhood surrounded by family and friends.

His family was gone, scattered to the east and west. Those who had been his friends had either forgotten him or were uneasy in his presence. More than once in the first few days after his return to Marietta, he had noticed people looking at him as if they were watching a wild animal, fearful that it might spring at them without warning. Maybe Steakley had said something about the way Jeff had jumped him in the office of the trading post.

The worst thing, however, was that Melissa was not here.

There had been two cabins on the Holt family farm. One, the place where Bartholomew and Norah had died, was now a burned-out shell. Jeff could barely bring himself to ride past it. The other cabin, a smaller structure he had built with the help of his father and brothers, was the home to which he had taken Melissa on their wedding night. It held its own memories, most of them pleasant, but the good times were overshadowed by the tragedies that had separated the young couple. It was difficult for Jeff to go there, but he had no place else to stay.

The cabin had not suffered any more damage in his absence than had the Merrivales' place. Jeff chinked some places in the wall, working mud into the openings between logs, glad he had a chore to do that did not require much thinking. His brain was still numbed by the knowledge that Melissa was gone, and he wanted to keep it that way for a while. Maybe it would not hurt so much after time had passed.

It was a futile hope, Jeff knew, but it was all he had to cling to.

After a sleepless night, he rode into Marietta and paid a visit to the county offices, which were located in a building between a blacksmith shop and—of all things—a newspaper office. The newspaper had not existed when Jeff left Marietta two years earlier.

Taxes were due on the farm, as Jeff had known there would be. After he had paid the clerk, he said, "I don't like to see the farm sitting empty like that. The land's good; it needs to be worked."

"You thinking about letting somebody work it for shares, Mr. Holt?" the clerk asked.

"Yes, I believe I am," Jeff replied. "If you run into anybody who'd be interested, tell him to come see me. I reckon I'll be around for a week or so, anyway."

To tell the truth, Jeff had no idea what his future plans were, but he did not feel like explaining that to the county clerk.

The man pursed his lips and said, "That's not much time. But if I come up with anybody who wants to work like that, I'll send him right out to you, sir."

"Thanks." Jeff left the office, glanced up the street toward Steakley's, and considered paying another visit to the trading post. But there was no point in it, he realized. Steakley had already told him all there was to tell. Instead, he got on his horse and swung the animal's head toward the Congregational Church and the burial ground on the little hill behind it.

Jeff left his mount outside the wrought-iron fence around the cemetery and walked among the graves until he found the two he was looking for. His parents, Bartholomew and Norah, were laid to rest there, overlooking the broad sweep of the mighty Ohio River. It was an overcast day, with gray clouds thick in the sky and the air heavy with the threat of rain. Jeff thought that was just fine; the weather suited his mood.

He took off his hat and stood in front of the two gravestones.

"Hello, Ma. Hello, Pa. Reckon you probably thought I'd never be back this way." Jeff swallowed. He had figured he would feel foolish talking to dead folks, even if they were his parents, but somehow this seemed right, as if Bartholomew and Norah were with him somehow, listening to him.

"Clay's doing fine. He's married now, to an Indian woman named Shining Moon. I think you'd like her. She's a mighty fine lady. I haven't heard from Edward and Susan and Jonathan, but I'm sure they're all right. I know Uncle Henry and Aunt Dorothy are taking good care of them. I suppose the only one who's really made a mess of things is me.

"Melissa's gone. Her father took her and went east somewhere with her and her mother. New York, maybe, but I don't even know that much for sure. It'll be pure luck if I ever find her again, and I don't even know if I ought to try. If she loved me—if she *really* loved me—she wouldn't have let Merrivale drag her off like that!"

Jeff trembled as he spoke the angry words. He had not known he felt that way, but now he saw it was true. He was furious with Melissa. *She should have been here when I got back, dammit!*

Suddenly he felt ashamed. He had no right to

judge her like that. After all, he was the one who had left to go thousands of miles into the wilderness. True, he'd had a good reason for going, but still, Melissa had been left behind, a vital young woman suddenly without the man she loved. It had been hard for him, sure, hard as hell, but it must have been difficult for her, too.

Jeff took a deep breath, then said, "I wish you were here, Ma and Pa, to tell me what to do. I want to go after her, but what if I never find her?"

He left an even worse question unspoken, although it echoed in his mind: *What if I find her—and she doesn't want me anymore?*

His fingers clenched the hat in his hands, bending it out of shape.

"Jeff?" a voice asked behind him. "Jefferson Holt?"

He spun around quickly, his hand automatically going to the butt of the pistol in his belt. The black-suited man who stood inside the entrance of the cemetery took a rapid step backward, his round face paling in fear.

"Reverend Crosley!" Jeff exclaimed. He took his hand away from the gun as if the butt had turned white-hot. "I'm sorry, Reverend. You startled me. Old habits are hard to break, I guess. But I should have heard you coming."

Jeff knew he was talking too fast and too much, but he was embarrassed not only by his reaction but because Josiah Crosley had caught him talking to himself. At least, that was what it must have looked like. With the line of work Crosley was in, however, he ought to understand about such things, Jeff thought.

"I thought I saw someone come up here," the minister said, some of the color seeping back into his face. "I didn't know it was you, though, Jeff. I'd heard you were back in town. Have you returned to Marietta for good?"

Jeff shook his head without even thinking about the question. When he'd left the mountains, the possibility that he might not return had been an unspoken understanding between Clay and him; that, however, was when he thought he would find Melissa here. With her gone, Jeff was not sure where he was going, but he knew he was not going to stay in Marietta.

He glanced over his shoulder at the tombstones and neatly kept plots.

"You're taking good care of the place, Reverend. I thank you for that. I knew Ma and Pa would rest easy here—if they could anywhere."

Crosley moved closer to him. "You're more than welcome, Jeff. Your parents were fine folks. I guess nearly everybody in town liked them and were sorry when they, ah, passed away."

When they were murdered by the Garwoods was what the preacher meant, Jeff thought. And not everybody in Marietta had liked the Holts. Many had been convinced that Clay was indeed little Matthew Garwood's father and had blamed the Holts for the trouble with the Garwoods.

Jeff pushed those thoughts away. *No point in digging up the past now,* he reminded himself. What he had to worry about was the future.

"Reverend," he said, "did my wife say anything to you about where she was going when she left town with her parents?"

"No, Jeff. I'm sorry. None of the Merrivale family said anything to me. They left rather suddenly, you know."

"That's what I've been hearing."

"Melissa never wrote to you?" Crosley seemed to find that difficult to believe.

"Not once. I sure never thought things would turn out this way." Jeff squared his shoulders. He did not particularly like Reverend Crosley, and he did not want to pour out his troubles to the man. Anyway, since Crosley did not know where the Merrivales had gone, there was nothing he could do to help Jeff—except pray for him.

A fat drop of cold rain struck Jeff's cheek, followed by another and another. He clapped his hat on his head and brushed past Crosley, bumping the minister with his shoulder as he went by.

"I'll be going now," he said.

"Jeff, is there anything I can do?"

Jeff paused and looked back as the rain fell harder. "Say a prayer for me," he finally said. "I reckon it can't hurt."

Chapter Four

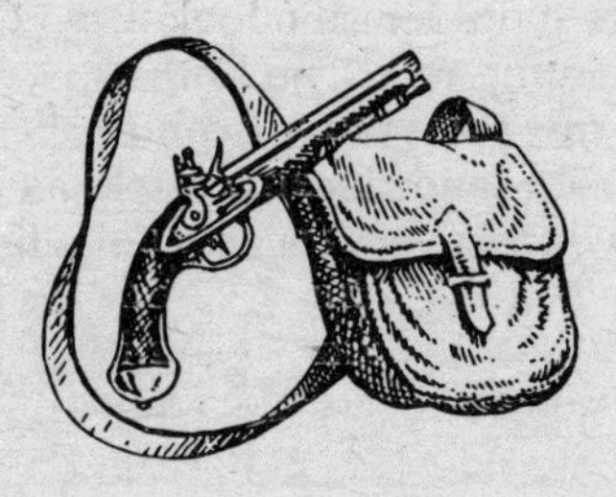

Charles Merrivale struggled with the cravat he was trying to tie around his neck. He cursed as he fumbled with the fine silk. His fingers, while not as blunt as a working man's, had not been made for such delicate work.

"Here, darling, let me do that for you."

Merrivale's wife, Hermione, came up from behind and reached around him. Standing on her toes and leaning to one side so that she could see their reflection in the mirror, she quickly arranged the cravat in a stylish knot.

Merrivale turned around, bent over, and brushed his lips across his wife's forehead.

"Thank you, Hermione," he said. "I was having a devil of a time with that thing."

"You were just nervous, dear. You always are when you have important business looming on the evening's horizon."

Merrivale frowned. Sometimes Hermione understood him all too well. It was a sign of weakness in a man, he thought, when his wife knew too much of what he was thinking.

Charles Merrivale was not a man who easily tolerated weakness, in himself or in others. He was tall and broad-shouldered and carried himself with an air of vitality that would have been more common in a much younger man. His thick hair was white, and his stern features gave him the look of an Old Testament prophet, which he resembled in more ways than one. Like those prophets of ancient times, he frequently laid down the law with unshakable conviction, especially where his family and his business were concerned.

So it had been when he resolved to leave Ohio and return to Wilmington, North Carolina, where he had run a profitable mercantile store for years before making one of the few incorrect decisions in his life—to move to Marietta, Ohio, and become a farmer. He had left no room for argument about his decision to return to North Carolina—although Melissa had given him one anyway—and while he had taken a loss on his property in Ohio when the man whom he thought was going to buy the place backed out at the last moment, forcing Merrivale to sell to someone else, he had not regretted his decision for an instant. Unable to repurchase the store he had left behind, he had simply established another one. Business was booming, and his enterprise was so successful that he had already expanded and built several warehouses near the docks. The growing shipping industry was just waiting for his entry into it, he had judged. Trading vessels regularly plied the coast up and down the Atlantic Seaboard, and Merrivale intended to carve out his own niche in this trade.

That was why the dinner that night was so important. He had invited a new business associate, a young man named Dermot Hawley, to join them.

Hawley owned a successful freight company, and he would be a natural ally for a merchant like Merrivale.

"What was that?" Merrivale asked suddenly, aware that his wife was speaking to him again. "I'm afraid I let my mind wander, dear."

"I just said I should go see how Melissa is doing," Hermione replied. "I'd so like for her to enjoy herself this evening. She spends altogether too much time brooding."

"Moping over that damned Holt." As usual, Merrivale could not even think about Jefferson Holt without his stomach clenching in anger and hatred. He thumped his chest lightly with his fist as the uncomfortable burning sensation grew stronger.

"Whatever," Hermione said. "I'd just like to see her happy again."

"She'll be happy when she meets Hawley. He's a very handsome young man."

Hermione gave her husband a look of concern, but Merrivale ignored it. He was counting on Hawley's being attracted to Melissa; that would go a long way toward sealing the arrangement Merrivale wanted to make with the young man. Besides, it would not hurt Melissa to think about a man to replace Jeff Holt as her husband. It would be easy enough, Merrivale knew, to have Melissa divorced from Holt; his lawyers had assured him that they could charge Holt with desertion and make the accusation stick. A divorce would cause a scandal, of course, but scandals had a way of blowing over, especially when the person involved came from a wealthy, influential family.

Merrivale glowered into the mirror. His grandson needed a father, blast it, and even if Jeff Holt was still alive somewhere out there in the wilderness, he would never be a suitable parent to a lad like young Michael Holt.

Shrugging into his dinner jacket, Merrivale

turned around. He was alone in the room. Hermione had left, and he had not even noticed.

Melissa Holt ran a bone-handled brush through her long, dark brown hair. In the glow of the lamp, her hair shone with brilliant auburn highlights, and she knew it was lovely. She kept it that way only out of habit these days, however. Since Jeff was not there to run his fingers through those silky strands, it really made little difference to Melissa how her hair looked.

In his bed in the corner of the room, nineteen-month-old Michael Holt gurgled in his sleep and rolled over. Melissa stood up from the bench in front of her dressing table and went over to check on the baby.

Of course, Michael was not really much of a baby anymore, Melissa thought, smiling as she looked down at his peacefully sleeping form. He had walked and talked at an early age, demonstrating a precociousness and daring that bordered on recklessness. Most of the time, in fact, Michael was a little terror, forever wandering away, drawn by his curiosity.

He had gray eyes and a thatch of sandy-blond hair, and every time Melissa looked at him, she saw Jeff in him with painful clarity. Michael was both blessing and curse, she thought, a part of Jeff she could cling to but at the same time a constant reminder of what she had lost.

But someday, *someday*, Jeff would come back, and then the three of them would be together.

"My goodness, Melissa, you're not even dressed yet!" Hermione exclaimed as she opened the door to her daughter's bedroom. "Mr. Hawley will be here soon, and we'll be going down to dinner."

At the mention of Dermot Hawley's name, Melissa drew the robe she wore tighter around her throat. She had never met the man, had never even seen him. For all she knew, he could be a perfect gentleman, the nicest man in all of North Carolina. Even so, she practically cringed at her mother's reminder. She knew what her father had in mind; Charles Merrivale's intentions were crystal clear.

"I'm not sure I'll be going down to dinner, Mother," Melissa began. "I'm not feeling very well—"

"No, Melissa," Hermione said sharply. "I'm afraid your father won't stand for that. He won't accept any excuses this time."

"He doesn't know how I feel!" Anger flared inside Melissa. "Surely he wouldn't be so cruel as to force an ill woman to sit through some dreadfully boring dinner—"

"Melissa." Hermione's voice was softer now as she stepped over to her daughter and laid a hand on her arm. "You're not really ill, and we both know it. You just don't want to meet this young man your father has invited."

Melissa pulled away from her mother. She loved her mother, she truly did, but at moments like this she felt almost as much rage toward her as she did toward her father. If her mother really cared about her, why had she never stood up to her husband and defended her daughter from his harsh, arbitrary decisions?

Hermione patted her carefully arranged red hair and straightened her gown. "Now finish dressing and come along downstairs, dear," she said absently. The brief argument was already over as far as she was concerned. "I'll send Sadie up to sit with Michael."

"All right," Melissa said, her voice so soft it was almost a whisper. She knew there was no point in being stubborn about this matter. When it came to stubbornness, Charles Merrivale could not be bested.

Hermione left the room, and Melissa turned to gaze into the cradle again.

"Why did you have to pick tonight to be so

good?" she asked the sleeping youngster. "Why aren't you crying and pitching a hissy fit the way you usually do? Then Father wouldn't make me do this."

Michael shifted slightly under his blankets but did not wake up.

Quickly Melissa put on a dark blue gown with white lace bordering the neckline, the wrists, and the hem. She passed the brush through her hair a few more times, then slid her feet into soft leather slippers. She wore no jewelry, no cosmetics. She was not going to fancy herself up for this man her father wanted to show her off to.

There was a quiet, diffident knock on the door, and Sadie, one of the housemaids, opened the door.

"Miz Hermione told me to come up here and sit with the baby," she said.

"That's right, Sadie," Melissa replied, summoning up a smile. It was not Sadie's fault that she was so unhappy, and Melissa did not intend to take out her anger on her. "Come in. And thank you."

Sadie slipped into the room. She was a slender girl of perhaps fourteen; it was difficult to put an accurate age on most slaves if they had been sold more than once, and Charles Merrivale was Sadie's fourth owner. Merrivale was not a strong proponent of slavery, but he felt a man in his position had to have servants. One of the first things he had done after returning to North Carolina and buying their house had been to purchase two maids, a cook, and a man to handle the gardening and the carriage. After a while, when Merrivale was confident they would continue working for him, he would free all four of them, or at least that was what he had promised Hermione and Melissa.

The constant evidence of slavery was one of the things that had shocked Melissa most when she returned to North Carolina. It had not been unheard of for a man to have slaves in Ohio, but it was rare. Out there on what had not too long ago been the frontier, a man might be poor—but he was still free.

"Michael seems to be sleeping soundly," Melissa said to Sadie. "But if he wakes up and gives you any trouble, you come downstairs and fetch me immediately, do you understand?"

"Yes'm," Sadie said. "But I don't figure Mr. Merrivale, he'll want his dinner disturbed. Don't you worry, ma'am. I'll take good care of this little one."

"Yes, I'm sure you will." Melissa understood all too well. An absolute emergency would have to occur before Sadie would be allowed to interrupt dinner. And Melissa could not wish such a thing on her own son, no matter how much she wanted to avoid the evening's ordeal.

"You best hurry, Miz Melissa," Sadie added. "Your daddy's guest is already here. Drove up in a fancy carriage, he did, just 'fore I was fixin' to come up here."

Melissa took a deep breath. So Dermot Hawley had already arrived. She could not postpone this meeting any longer. Grimacing, she left the bedroom and walked to the broad, curving staircase that led to the main floor of the house.

"And here's my elusive daughter now," Merrivale said in his booming voice when Melissa was halfway down the stairs.

She wanted to cringe. Her father's tone held a note of pride, but it was the sound of a man speaking of an inanimate object, a valued possession.

A pleasant expression pasted on her face, she continued to the bottom of the staircase. Her father, mother, and the young man who had to be Dermot Hawley stood in the doorway of the parlor where they could watch her. Merrivale and Hawley each held a glass of brandy.

Melissa could have used a drink herself about now, something to fortify her for this evening. Of course, it would hardly be ladylike or proper for her to take the glass from Hawley's hand and toss back the liquor it contained. Such a move would no doubt shock him beyond words.

She thought about it for all of five seconds, then regretfully discarded the idea.

"Mr. Hawley, may I present my daughter, Melissa," Merrivale said pompously. "My dear, this gentleman is Mr. Dermot Hawley."

Hawley took her hand, bent over it, and kissed it. "The pleasure is all mine," he murmured. "It's a great honor to meet you at last, Miss Merrivale. Your father has told me all about you."

"Then he should have told you that my name is Mrs. Holt, not Miss Merrivale," she said sharply, sliding her fingers out from Hawley's grasp.

"Melissa!" Hermione gasped. "Please, dear, don't be rude to our guest."

"That's right," Merrivale said ominously. "I've raised you to be more polite than that, young lady."

Before Melissa could say anything else, Dermot Hawley grinned and said, "That's quite all right. Actually, you're right, Mrs. Holt. I was aware that you're married. For a moment the fact just slipped my mind."

Melissa met his level gaze and nodded curtly. "Of course. I'm sure you meant no offense, Mr. Hawley."

"None at all, I can assure you." He kept smiling at her.

She had to admit, he was a strikingly handsome man, just as her father had said. In his early thirties, he had curly brown hair, a mustache of the same shade, and blue eyes that sparkled with intelligence and wit. He had a charming air about him. Melissa supposed he had most of the unmarried young women in town—and their mothers—swooning in the hope they might interest him in matrimony.

"Well, why don't we go in to dinner?" Merrivale asked gruffly. He ushered the others ahead of him into the dining room.

Hawley wore a brown suit, a ruffled white shirt, and a cravat of dark gold silk with an impressive-looking stickpin glittering atop it. The clothes were expensive, more testimony to the success of his business even though he was a relatively young man. His hand when he had grasped Melissa's was soft and smooth but strong, an indication that he had done physical labor in the past but not in recent years.

The long mahogany table in the dining room was lit by an array of candles in gilt holders at each end. The polished surface of the table shone brilliantly in the warm yellow light. It was set with fine china and crystal. Hawley commented on the beauty of the room, and when Melissa glanced at her father, she saw the same pride of possession on his face that he had worn when she came down the stairs.

Charles Merrivale was in his element; Melissa had to admit that. She wondered what had ever moved him to give up all this and move to Ohio to farm the land. Whatever it was, she was glad he had made that decision; otherwise, she never would have met Jefferson Holt.

Merrivale was seated at the head of the table, with Hermione at the opposite end, Melissa to his right, and Hawley to his left. The table was so long that Melissa thought her parents would have to raise their voices to be heard if they wanted to talk to each other. On the other hand, Dermot Hawley was relatively close to her, since he was sitting directly across from her.

The meal was every bit the ordeal that Melissa had expected it to be. Her father and Hawley talked business most of the time, and although she paid little attention, she gathered that the young man owned a freighting concern that was doing quite well. She understood why her father was trying to garner Hawley's favor. A partnership between the two men would profit both. Merrivale had the goods to sell—or he would as soon as he filled those warehouses he had built—and Hawley had the means to deliver those goods to people who would buy them. It made perfect sense for them to work together.

But she was damned if she was going to be an inducement for Hawley to strike a deal with her father!

Hermione was content to eat and be pleasantly silent, but from time to time, Hawley tried to draw Melissa into the conversation. For the most part, she responded to his questions in monosyllables, eliciting glares from her father.

At last, though, as he finished his dessert and reached for his brandy, Hawley said to her, "I understand that you have a child, Mrs. Holt."

"Yes, I do. A beautiful boy named Michael." Melissa could not help but smile fondly as she thought about her son. "I'm very proud of him. And I'm sure his father will be, too, when he arrives."

Hawley blinked in surprise. "I wasn't aware you were expecting your husband in the near future."

A dark glare had appeared on Merrivale's face. "She's not," he stated, "in the near future or anytime else. The boy's father went to the mountains and won't ever be back."

"That's not true!" Melissa cried, stunned by her father's blunt declaration. "I'm sure Jeff will come back, and when he does, he'll be just as proud of Michael and love him every bit as much as I do!"

Hawley leaned forward and asked, "You mean your husband doesn't even know he has a son?"

"That's hardly a proper question, Mr. Hawley," Hermione said coolly, "even if you are a guest."

Melissa could have hugged her mother for that show of support, but her father said harshly, "No,

Holt doesn't know anything about the child. He ran off before Melissa could tell him."

"That's not the way it was," Melissa protested. "You're making it all sound so awful—"

"It *was* awful," Merrivale cut in. "It was a dreadful mistake for you to ever marry that man. I knew from the start he'd come to a bad end. Why, he's been gone for over two years! I'm sure he's been killed and scalped by some of those wild red savages in the mountains."

"Charles!" Hermione cried.

Melissa paled. For the first time in her life, she was so angry with her father that she could have struck him. At the same time, a ball of sick fear had formed in the pit of her stomach. Her father had just put into words the horrible prospect that had haunted her for most of the past two years. All kinds of things could have happened to Jeff out there in the Rocky Mountains. Logically speaking, it was entirely possible he was dead.

But Melissa refused to believe it. She was sure she would know if Jeff were dead. She would know it in her heart.

"I'm not even going to dignify that absurd statement with a denial, Father," she said, forcing herself to sound much more calm than she felt. "You've always been wrong about Jeff, and you're wrong now."

Merrivale's face flushed brick-red with anger. "How dare you speak to your father that way?" he demanded. "Why, if you were still a child, I'd send you to your room—"

"But I'm not a child, am I?" Melissa interrupted. "I'm a grown woman with a child of my own and a husband who will be coming back for us. Mark my words, Father. You'll see."

"I'll see no such thing," Merrivale said coldly. "In fact, I've been considering instructing my attorneys to begin divorce proceedings so that this ridiculous union of yours will be dissolved!"

Melissa stared at him, as stunned as if he had just slapped her across the face.

At the other end of the table, Hermione said tentatively, "Charles, you can't mean—"

"I mean every word of it. I didn't intend to say anything about it just yet, but all this talk of Jeff Holt has convinced me that something has to be done. Otherwise, this foolish little girl is going to waste the rest of her life pining away for a phantom, a man she'll never see again."

Melissa was out of her chair before her father had finished speaking. Shaking with a rage she could barely control, she stalked across the dining room to the big french doors that led into the garden behind the house. She threw them open and stepped into the warm spring night. It was either get out of the house or start throwing things at her arrogant, pigheaded father, and she knew it.

Behind her, she faintly heard her mother saying in embarrassment, "Oh, Mr. Hawley, I'm so sorry about all this! I wanted you to have a nice dinner with us, not be subjected to such a—a scene!"

Melissa could not hear Hawley's reply, but she did not really care. It was none of his business. She had not wanted to meet him in the first place.

She was glad her father had not come after her and tried to force her back into the house. If he had, she was not sure what she would have done, but one thing was certain: It would not have been pleasant. The Merrivale family had already suffered enough embarrassment for one evening. The best thing that could happen now would be for Hawley to leave.

The sound of footsteps behind her made her turn around sharply to see who had followed her into the garden. A bright moon floated overhead, casting more than enough silvery illumination for her to recognize Hawley as he walked toward her. He was shorter than Merrivale, and he moved with a grace the older man had never possessed.

For a second Melissa thought about running deeper into the garden, where Hawley could not find her. But she stayed where she was. Her upbringing prevented her from being overly rude to anyone, even someone whose company had been forced on her. It was hardly this young man's fault that Charles Merrivale was such an awful, unfeeling parent.

Dermot Hawley came to a stop about five feet from her. She stood there, arms crossed over her chest, waiting.

After a moment he said, "I'm sorry, Mrs. Holt. I didn't mean to cause unhappiness between you and your father."

"It's not your fault, Mr. Hawley," Melissa said.

"Well, it was my question about your son that started things, even if it was indirectly. It wasn't my intention to bring up any unpleasant subjects. I didn't know what the—situation with your husband was."

Melissa relaxed slightly. Hawley sounded genuinely concerned and contrite, and she reminded herself that he was not the one who deserved her anger.

"That's all right, Mr. Hawley. I know you meant no harm. It's just that my father and I will never see eye to eye on the subject of my marriage, I fear."

Hawley chuckled. "I'll admit I haven't known your father for very long, but I have a feeling Charles Merrivale doesn't see eye to eye with people on a great many subjects, unless they agree with him, that is."

"You're right. He can be a maddeningly stubborn man."

"And what about his daughter?"

Melissa had to smile. "I suppose I can be a bit stubborn at times, too. But I come by it honestly, as you've seen."

"Indeed. Well, I just wanted to apologize for my part in this—"

"And as I've told you, it's not your fault. My father and my husband never got along well. But I'll never let my father bully me into a divorce! I won't hear of it!"

"Good for you," Hawley said firmly, which rather surprised Melissa. "You have to do whatever you think is best for you and your child." After a few seconds' hesitation, he added, "However, if your husband has been gone for over two years in the wilderness, perhaps—"

"No. I won't stand for any suggestion that Jeff may be dead. He's a good man, a strong man, a smart man. And he is with his brother, and Clay Holt knows those mountains as well or better than any other white man in this country. He was with Lewis and Clark, you know."

"No, I didn't." Hawley sounded impressed. "I'm sure Clay Holt must be quite a frontiersman. Were he and your husband going to trap beaver?"

"How did you know that?" Melissa asked.

Hawley shrugged his shoulders. "Most of the men who have gone into the Rockies are fur trappers. I hear there's a great deal of money to be made in that business, if one can endure all the hardships that come with it. Your husband may return from the mountains a rich man."

"I don't care about that. I just want him to come back."

"Of course. And I'm sure he will, if it's humanly possible. After all, what man wouldn't come back to a lovely woman like you?"

Melissa cast her eyes toward the ground, wishing that Hawley would not make such comments. He had somehow moved closer without her noticing it, so that now he stood only a couple of feet from her. She could smell his clean masculine scent, and it made her feel strangely disconcerted.

"Mr. Hawley—"

"Dermot."

"Mr. Hawley," Melissa insisted. "I'm not sure we should be out here like this. After all, I am a married woman."

"Which doesn't mean that you and I can't be friends. It's highly likely that your father and I will be doing a great deal of business together, Melissa, which means that you and I will be seeing more of each other."

"There—there shouldn't be any need for that. Father has an office in which to conduct business."

"Of course. But I've always believed in mixing business with pleasure whenever possible, and there's nothing more pleasurable than spending time in the company of a beautiful young woman."

"You dare too much, Mr. Hawley," she told him coldly.

He shook his head, and she could see him smirking in the moonlight. "Not at all. If I were going to dare too much, I'd be kissing you right now—Mrs. Holt." He drawled her name mockingly.

She wanted to slap him, but she sensed that would not bother him. In fact, he might regard it as the mark of a small victory. So she said, "I'm going in now. The night is getting rather chilly."

"Of course. I'll walk you."

"That's not necessary."

However, she could not stop him from striding along beside her as she retraced her path to the house. When they entered the dining room, they found Charles Merrivale still seated at the table, a goblet of brandy in his hand and the curved stem of his pipe clenched between his teeth. From the expression on his face, it was taking all his self-control to keep from biting right through that pipe stem.

"I see you found her, Dermot," he said to Hawley. "My thanks. My daughter is a rather delicate young woman and should not be out in the night air like that."

Hawley smiled. "We had quite an interesting conversation, didn't we, Mrs. Holt?"

"Yes," Melissa said. "Interesting." She looked at her father. "Where's Mother?"

"Your mother has retired for the evening. She was quite upset by your behavior, Melissa. You should apologize to her in the morning."

"I should apologize?" Melissa caught hold of her temper as it started to get away from her again. It would do no good to prolong this argument. Icily, she said, "I'm rather tired, too. Good night, Father." She turned to walk out of the room.

Merrivale stopped her with a sharp word. "Melissa!" When she paused and turned around, he went on, "Aren't you going to say good night to our guest?"

She looked at Hawley, whose expression was still enigmatic. "Good night, Mr. Hawley."

"Good night, Mrs. Holt," he replied. "I'm sure we'll be seeing each other again."

"I'm sure." With that, she got out of the dining room before anyone could stop her again.

Trembling with anger, she went up to her room, opening the door so sharply when she got there that she startled Sadie, who was dozing in a rocking chair near Michael's cradle.

The maid jumped up and blinked at Melissa. "The baby's been sleepin' just fine, Miz Melissa," Sadie said quickly. "Don't you worry, I been keepin' an eye on him—"

Sadie must have seen the fury on her face, Melissa realized, and mistakenly thought it was directed at her. "That's fine, Sadie," she said, softening her expression. "Thank you for watching him. You can go now."

"Good night, ma'am." Sadie scurried out of the room.

Melissa went over to the bed and looked down at the still-sleeping Michael. The sight of him drained the anger from her, and it was replaced with feelings of love and longing.

"Your father will come," she whispered to him. "Someday he'll come for us and take us away from here, and then we'll all be happy for the rest of our lives."

Chapter Five

Marietta is principally inhabited by New Englanders, which accounts for the neat and handsome style of building displayed in it.

—Fortescue Cuming
"Sketches of a Tour to the Western Country"

Of all the people in Marietta whom Jefferson Holt did not want to run into during his return visit, he wanted to see Josie Garwood the least. And yet as he stepped out onto the porch of the trading post, there she was, just starting up the steps. She held the hand of a little boy, four or five years old, who Jeff knew had to be her son, Matthew.

Jeff stopped in his tracks and for an instant thought about retreating into the store. He would have preferred to face a party of hostile Blackfoot than Josie Garwood.

But it was too late. She had seen him, and after a split-second's hesitation, she continued up the steps, bringing Matthew with her.

"Hello, Jeff," she said, pleasantly enough. "I heard you were back in town."

He nodded and lowered the bag of supplies in his hand to the porch. "Hello, Josie. How are you?"

"Keeping well enough, I suppose. You know how it is."

He did indeed. He knew about Josie Garwood, just as everyone else in the area did.

Josie was still a very attractive woman in an earthy way. Raven-black hair framed a face that was not beautiful but possessed a sensuousness that immediately drew the eye to it. Her figure had always been lush, and if her waist was a bit thicker now than when he had last seen her, her breasts were also fuller and more prominent. Her nipples prodded against the fabric of her dress. Jeff chided himself mentally for even noticing that fact, but it was hard not to notice Josie, and that was a fact, too.

The little boy at her side had the same coarsely handsome features and black hair as his mother. That was not surprising, and it was even less so considering that Matthew's father was none other than Zach Garwood, Josie's older brother. Josie had blamed Clay Holt for making her pregnant, an accusation that had caused the bad blood between the Garwoods and the Holts, but Jeff knew the truth. Zach himself had admitted it before Clay killed him in the savage knife fight at Manuel Lisa's fort the previous autumn.

But Josie was probably not aware that her secret had been revealed, and as far as Jeff was concerned, things could stay that way. Josie was already known far and wide as a trollop, and he had no wish to add to her shame.

Not that it was any shame to be viciously molested, as Josie had been by Zach. It was hardly her fault that her brother had forced her to give in to his perverted lust. But at the same time, Josie had lied about Clay, and that lie set in motion the chain of events that had ended with the deaths of Bartholomew and Norah Holt and Luther and Pete Garwood. If none of that had happened, Clay and Jeff would not have been forced to leave Ohio in hopes of avoiding any further bloodshed.

That was all over now, Jeff reminded himself. He smiled politely at the woman. "I'm glad to see you, Josie," he lied. "It's been a long time."

"It certainly has." She hesitated, then said, "Is Clay with you?"

"No, I'm afraid not. I don't know where he is." That was true; Clay had been planning to spend the spring trapping with Shining Moon, Proud Wolf, and Josie's youngest brother, Aaron, and they could be anywhere along the Big Horn or Yellowstone rivers by now.

"Oh," Josie said, her face and voice mirroring her disappointment. "I knew I hadn't heard anything about him coming back with you, but I was hoping. . . . " She let the words trail off and shrugged.

Josie had always been half in love with Clay, even when they were children, Jeff remembered. That was most likely why she had claimed he was the father when she learned she was pregnant. She had to have hoped that Clay would marry her. But Clay had not returned her feelings, and things had not worked out the way Josie had planned. Instead, Clay had headed west, joining up with the expedition led by Lewis and Clark. Josie had been left behind to denounce him bitterly.

"Have you seen him since you left?" she asked. "Everybody said the two of you had probably gone west together."

"I've seen Clay," Jeff admitted. He did not see any harm in easing her mind a little. "He was just fine the last time we got together." For a moment, he considered telling Josie that Clay was married now, but he stopped short of that. It would be better in the long run, he decided, to keep things as vague as possible.

Josie lifted her chin. "I'm glad to hear it. Clay and I, we had our differences, but I never wanted any harm to come to him. I never wanted any of that trouble—"

"I know, Josie." Jeff did not want her to hash over the past. "What's done is done. Let's leave it that way." A thought occurred to him, and he asked, "You knew Melissa, didn't you?"

"Melissa Merrivale?" Josie frowned. "Why are you asking *me* about her? You're the one who married her."

"That's right. But when I got back here, she was gone. Her father went back East and took Melissa and her mother with him. I was wondering. . . . Maybe you talked to Melissa before they left?" Jeff recalled that Melissa and Josie had not been what anyone would call friends, but he was unwilling to pass up any possible chance for information.

Josie sadly shook her head. "I'm sorry, Jeff. She didn't say anything to me. Do you mean to say you don't know where they are?"

Jeff sighed heavily, then said, "Mr. Steakley thinks they might have gone to New York, but he's not sure. Melissa didn't leave a letter for me or anything."

"That's awful!" Josie looked down at Matthew, who was impatiently tugging on her hand. "Just hold on," she said to the boy. "We'll go inside in a minute, as soon as I'm through talking to Mr. Holt."

"I want to go now," Matthew said, giving Jeff a surly look.

Jeff was sure the boy had been raised to hate the Holts.

"All right, all right!" Josie gave in, letting Matthew pull her toward the door of the trading post. Then she stopped abruptly and turned to Jeff, provoking a groan of frustration from Matthew.

"Zach and Aaron left here, too, Jeff. I guess you didn't know that."

Jeff had been hoping that she would not ask about her brothers. She would probably be happy to hear that Aaron was all right and had made peace with the Holts, to the point of joining them in their fur-trapping endeavor. But Jeff did not want to tell her that Zach was dead—and at Clay's hand.

"I had heard that they were gone," he said, still hoping to evade any direct questions about her brothers.

Thankfully, Josie did not ask any. Instead, she said, "Before they left, Zach talked about what a great place the West is going to be. There are all kinds of opportunities out there for somebody who's smart and willing to work, he said."

That sounded a little too perceptive and forward-looking to be a direct quote from Zach Garwood, Jeff thought, but he decided not to contest it. "That's right. I reckon it's going to be a fine place one of these days."

"I—I was thinking about going west myself. Making a new start. There's not much left for me here. Pa's dead, and I'm the only one left. I can't work the farm. All I can do is . . . well, you know what I mean."

Jeff could well understand why she would want to leave Marietta. Yet he worried that she might be intending to find Clay. The last thing Clay needed now, just as he was making a new life for himself with Shining Moon, was for Josie Garwood to show up, bringing Matthew along with her.

"What do you think?" she pressed him. "Do you think I should do it?"

"That's up to you, Josie. You're the only one who can make that decision. You should know, though, that the frontier is a hard place. St. Louis is the last real settlement. There's not much other than Indian villages and a few fur-traders' forts beyond it. It's not much of a place for a woman, especially one with a small child."

Josie's gaze darted back and forth along the street, and Jeff knew she was seeing the disapproving stares of the women, the knowing and lecherous glances of the men.

"Any place would be better than here," she declared fervently. She took a deep breath. "I'm glad I ran into you, Jeff. I think I've made up my mind."

Jeff bit back a groan. "It's up to you, Josie."

She patted his shoulder, then turned and continued into the trading post with Matthew. Jeff watched her go and wished he had not picked that afternoon to stop by Steakley's for a few more supplies.

He was going to be leaving soon. He still did not know where he was going, but the urge to be gone from Marietta was growing. As soon as he found someone to take care of the farm . . .

As if providence had just read his mind, the county clerk was walking along the street at that moment, and when he spotted Jeff on the porch, he called out, "Mr. Holt! I've been looking for you."

Another man was with the clerk. They were a mismatched pair, for the second man towered over the short, slender county official. Not only was this man taller, but he was wide enough to have made about three of the clerk, Jeff figured. He wore a thick, bushy black beard, and a battered felt hat was crammed down on his black hair. A coat that looked as though it had been made out of bear hide was stretched over his massive shoulders. Deep-set dark eyes squarely met Jeff's gaze.

"Mr. Holt, this gentleman is interested in talking to you about your farm," the clerk said.

The bearded man stomped up onto the porch of the trading post and extended a hamlike hand.

"Howdy, Holt," he said in a rumbling voice. "Glad to meet you. Name's Castor Gilworth."

Jeff shook hands with Gilworth, fully expecting the giant to crush his hand, but although there was immense power in the man's grip, he tempered it with restraint.

"Pleased to meet you, Mr. Gilworth," Jeff said. "Interested in some good farming land, are you?"

"Yup. Not to buy it, though. This feller"—Gilworth jerked a blunt thumb at the county clerk—"he says you got a place you need somebody to work for you. That sounds just like what me and my brother Pollux are lookin' for."

"You'd be willing to work the land on shares? I can tell you right now, I'm willing to be more than generous in the split. What I'm really after is somebody to take care of the place so that we can keep it in the Holt family."

"Sounds good to me," Castor Gilworth said. "You see, me and Pollux lost our place in Pennsylvania, and we got it in our heads that we want to head west one of these days. Ain't quite ready to do that just yet, though, so we need some work and a place to live. This farm of your'n sounds just right."

"Well, it sounds good to me, too."

Despite Gilworth's rough appearance, Jeff felt an instinctive liking for the big man. He had always been a pretty good judge of character, he thought, and his time on the frontier had honed that quality. Out there, a man had to know whom he could trust, and such decisions sometimes had to be made quickly.

"Draw up the papers any way you want," Castor

Gilworth said. "Reckon I trust you, so that's good enough for Pollux and me. We'll sign 'em." He grinned. "We can read and write, you know. Most folks figger we can't, but our ma taught us real good."

"I'm sure she did." For some reason Jeff's meeting with this massive man had lifted his spirits after that distressing conversation with Josie. "Where is this brother of yours, Mr. Gilworth?"

"He's still down to the county office. Ol' Pollux, he's a mite shy when he gets in a big town like this, so I figgered I'd come talk to you by myself first."

"Well, let's go get him," Jeff suggested. "We can work out all the details later, but right now I think you and me and old Pollux ought to have a drink."

Castor licked his lips. "I reckon we're going to get along just fine, all right, Holt. Come on."

He slung a huge arm around Jeff's shoulders as they started down the street.

"You'll like Pollux. Him and me are twins. Damn near as identical as two peas in a pod, 'cept he don't have no hair on top of his head. Bald as a stone. But he's a good feller, and we don't hold that agin him."

"Of course not," Jeff agreed.

"I hear tell you been to the Rockies. You got to tell us all about it. We're goin' to be out there one of these days, me and Pollux."

"I'm sure you will," Jeff said, realizing now that becoming friends with Castor and Pollux Gilworth would probably be somewhat akin to being swept up by a force of nature such as a flood or a cyclone. The chances of surviving would be pretty slim—but if you did, it would be one hell of a ride while it lasted.

The bend of the Yellowstone River where the Blackfoot attack had taken place was as good a place to camp as any, so Clay proposed that the expedition stay there for a few days, for a variety of reasons. He wanted to recover as many of the sunken pelts from the river as he could; that would mean diving to the bottom of the icy stream and taking considerable time to warm up between each dive. Also, he wanted to teach Professor Franklin, Lucy, and Rupert von Metz as much as he could about surviving in the wilderness. Finally, spending a little time there before continuing with the expedition would give Clay a chance to evaluate the skills—and the trustworthiness—of Harry Lawton and the men he had brought with him from St. Louis. From what Clay had seen of them so far, he was not impressed. However, he could deal with them being green as grass—as long as he could trust them.

Lawton raised more doubts in Clay's mind. As the party sat around the campfire that night after burying their dead, Clay announced his plan. Immediately, Lawton frowned and then spat expressively into the flames.

"Sounds to me like a damned foolish notion," he said.

Keeping a tight rein on his temper, Clay asked, "Why's that?"

"We already had to fight them Injuns once. Staying here's just begging 'em to come back."

Clay did not agree. "The Blackfoot's normal stomping grounds are a good ways north and east of here, though every now and then they come raiding down in these parts. That's what you ran into, a war party a long way from home. They've already been beaten once, so chances are that's where they're headed right now."

"You can't know that," Lawton said.

"No, I can't. But I know one thing: An Indian can be stubborn as a rock, but he's not stupid. Those Blackfoot may be nursing their wounded pride, but they won't regroup and come back this way until we've had time to be long gone."

"I think your idea is an excellent one, Mr. Holt,"

Professor Franklin said. "We need some time to lick our own wounds, so to speak, and you do have those furs to recover. I agree with you that we should camp here for a few days."

Lawton grunted. "Do what you want to do. I ain't in charge no more, am I?"

Clay wished the man was not so hostile, but under the circumstances, he would not have expected any other reaction. After all, Lawton's position as leader of the expedition had been yanked out from under him and handed over to somebody else, and a newcomer at that. No wonder he was angry.

But Clay had not asked for the job, either. Now that he had accepted Professor Franklin's offer, he intended to do the very best he could.

The Blackfoot raiding party that had clashed with the travelers earlier in the day was no longer a threat, in Clay's estimation, but that did not mean no other dangers lurked in these mountains. Consequently, Clay, Shining Moon, Proud Wolf, and Aaron Garwood took turns standing watch during the night. Clay would have let Shining Moon sleep, but he knew from experience that she would be angry if she was not included in any task that needed to be done.

For breakfast the next morning, Clay cooked hotcakes over the fire, and Proud Wolf picked berries from nearby bushes. Professor Franklin exclaimed over the tastiness of the berries and asked Proud Wolf how he had known they were safe to eat and not poisonous.

The young man just shrugged. "Any child of the Teton Sioux knows what to eat and what not to eat."

"You must give me a list," Franklin said enthusiastically, pulling out a sheaf of paper, a pen, and an inkwell from one of the supply bags. Breakfast was forgotten now that his scientific curiosity had been aroused.

When the meal was finished, Clay told Aaron to

keep an eye out for trouble, then walked over to the riverbank. Shining Moon went with him.

"You will look underwater now for the pelts?" she asked.

Clay nodded. He handed her his pistols and one of his knives, then tossed his coonskin cap on the ground and removed his shirt and moccasins. His skin prickled at the touch of the cool morning air. It might have been better to wait until later in the day when the sun was warmer, but he was anxious to recover as many furs as he could.

"Keep an eye on Lawton," he said in a low voice to Shining Moon. "I don't think he'll cause any trouble, but you never can tell."

"I will watch him," she promised solemnly.

Clay took a deep breath and waded into the chilly water, heading for the deeper part of the river. Some folks said it was better to go slow and get adjusted to icy temperatures, while others advocated plunging right in. As far as Clay was concerned, neither method had much to recommend it. There was just no good way to get into water this cold.

The frigidness hit him like a blow as he dove in, the stream closing over him as he stroked toward the bottom. At this point, the Yellowstone was not overly deep, perhaps ten or twelve feet, and it was clear enough for Clay to see the sunken canoes and their cargo. He swam quickly to them, trying to ignore the cold.

The pelts had been tied into bundles with rawhide thongs, which were then tied to the canoe. Quickly Clay cut the leather strips that lashed the furs to the sunken craft. He took hold of one bundle and tried to lift it, but a few of the water-soaked furs had caught on the canoe. Grimacing, he dislodged the bundle, then kicked off the rocky bottom of the river and knifed back to the surface of the stream.

He exploded from the surface, and droplets of

water sparkled brilliantly in the morning sunlight. His teeth chattering already, Clay swam to the bank and pulled himself out. Shining Moon was waiting for him with a blanket she had borrowed from the expedition's supplies. Clay shivered violently as she wrapped it around him.

"Come to the fire," she urged. "I asked Proud Wolf to build it up while you were in the river."

The campfire was indeed leaping higher now, and soon after he was seated beside it, the warmth from the flames seeped into his chilled body and put an end to his shivering.

"I can reach the pelts without any trouble," he said to Shining Moon, "but I'm going to have to take a rope down and tie it to the bundles. It'll probably take a couple of us to lift them out of the water. They're heavy from being soaked."

"Rest now," Shining Moon replied, "and let the cold leave you before you go in again."

Clay was not going to argue with that advice. He huddled beside the fire for a good half hour before he felt up to entering the river again.

The task went more quickly than he had expected. Using one of the expedition's ropes, he swam down to the sunken cargo, tied the rope to the rawhide thongs binding a bundle, and gave it a tug. That was the signal to Proud Wolf and two of Lawton's men who had been drafted to help. The three of them hauled the pelts out of the river while Clay swam to the surface.

Diving in and out of the icy water took its toll on Clay, and during the afternoon he needed more time to warm up between trips down to the canoes. By late in the day, with the help of the others, he had salvaged all the pelts he could. The binding around two bundles had come loose, and the furs had been washed away by the river's current.

Proud Wolf and Aaron Garwood had opened the

bundles and spread the furs out to dry. The sunshine would do a good job of that, but it would take several days before the plews were ready to bind up again. Clay did not mind the delay, since it would give him the time he needed to familiarize his charges with the wilderness.

Harry Lawton had spent most of the day sitting with some of his men, talking and laughing. Clay had paid little attention to them, since he was so busy with his own tasks. At one point Rupert von Metz joined Lawton and the others, took a small easel and canvas from his packs, and painted the lounging frontiersmen, who did not seem to mind the Prussian's attention.

A small hunting party had gone out during the afternoon and returned with a good-sized deer, so the group had venison stew that evening. By that time Clay, who was chilled to the bone and seemed unable to warm up no matter how much time he spent by the fire, was more than ready for hot food.

Lucy Franklin carried a steaming bowl of stew to Clay, who took it and said, "Thanks, Miss Franklin. You don't know what this means to a man as cold as I've been all day."

"I hope it helps, Mr. Holt. I made it myself, you know."

"No, I didn't know," Clay said. Lucy's demeanor led him to believe that she had recovered from the frightening experience of the day before. He spooned the stew into his mouth, then winced a little because it was so hot. But it tasted wonderful. He could almost feel the strength and warmth flowing back into him as he ate.

"It's good," he told Lucy. "Mighty good."

Her smile widened. "I'm glad you like it."

Clay glanced to the side. Shining Moon, Proud Wolf, and Aaron were waiting for their food, but Lucy was not in any hurry to take it to them. She seemed content just to stand there and watch him eat, Clay thought.

Feeling a little uncomfortable, he suggested, "How about some for my friends?"

"Of course. I'm sorry. I wasn't thinking." Lucy hurried back to the stew pot to dish up more of the savory concoction.

"Reckon I can fetch my own." Aaron stood, hitched up his buckskin trousers, and strode over to the fire. A few seconds later, Proud Wolf followed. They joined Lucy and took the bowls she handed them.

"Aaron and my brother have noticed that Miss Franklin is an attractive young woman," Shining Moon said quietly.

"Shoot, they probably figured that out right away," Clay said.

Shining Moon looked at him. "But Miss Franklin would prefer that *you* notice."

"What do you mean? You can't figure that gal is —is—" Clay frowned.

"Interested in you? That is exactly what I mean."

"But she just met me yesterday."

"When you helped save her from a band of 'bloodthirsty savages,' " Shining Moon said wryly. "You cannot blame her for feeling grateful. And when a young woman feels grateful to a handsome man, it can easily become something else."

"But, hell, I'm a married man!"

"That may not matter to her."

Clay suppressed a groan. "Lord, I hope you're wrong about this. I've got enough troubles right now without having to worry about some young girl making cow eyes at me."

Shining Moon lowered her own gaze and murmured, "Just so you do not return those looks."

"Not much chance of that!" Clay assured her.

He paid more attention now as Aaron and Proud

Wolf continued talking to Lucy Franklin. Maybe the two young men could distract Lucy from her budding interest in him. He fervently hoped so.

Warmed by the stew, Clay went over to speak with Professor Franklin for a few minutes, explaining that the expedition would stay for several days while the pelts dried on the riverbank.

"That's fine," Franklin said. "I've been picking the brain of that Sioux lad all day whenever he wasn't helping you, and I tell you, Mr. Holt, he's a veritable font of information. I've learned as much in one day about this land and its flora and fauna as I learned in all the weeks since we left St. Louis."

Clay could believe it. "Yep, Proud Wolf likes to talk, all right. Before we push on, though, I want to see how each of you handles a rifle. We need to go over your charts and maps, too, just to make sure they're accurate."

"Of course. And if anyone would know, it's you, Mr. Holt. After all, you've been over this ground before."

"Not all of it. This is a big country, Professor. There's plenty of it I haven't seen yet."

"Well, I'm sure you'll remedy that before you're through. You strike me as a man who needs to see all there is to be seen."

Clay shrugged. "Never really thought about it that way, Professor, but it could be you're right."

Exhausted by the day's grueling work, Clay went back to the other side of the fire, ready to lie down for the night. Using borrowed blankets, Shining Moon had made their bed just on the edge of the circle of light cast by the fire. She was nowhere in sight when Clay slid into the blankets, and he knew she must be off in the darkness tending to her personal needs before turning in. He planned to wait for her to join him before going to sleep, but weariness claimed him. His eyes closed as he drifted off.

He was not sure how much time had passed when he was roused from slumber by a soft, warm presence moving against him. Instinctively his arms went around the slender woman beside him. He recognized the scent of Shining Moon's hair as she pressed her face against his shoulder.

"You are awake, Clay Holt?" she whispered.

"I am now."

"And are you still cold?"

"A mite chilled," he admitted.

"You must be given warmth so that you will not become ill. And I know the best way to do that," she murmured. "It is an old Hunkpapa method."

"I'll bet." Clay chuckled. Then his mouth found hers, and his hand stroked her side, finding smooth, bare, silky skin that seemed to burn with its own special fire.

She was right, Clay thought. He was warmer already.

On the other side of the campfire, which had burned down to little more than coals, Lucy Franklin shifted uneasily in her blankets. She had seen Shining Moon slide in next to Clay Holt, and although they were being very quiet about it, she knew what they had to be doing.

Lucy's face flushed. There was nothing wrong with what they were doing, she told herself. After all, Clay and Shining Moon were married. Or at least they had been joined in some sort of Sioux ceremony, which was the same thing, as far as the two of them were concerned.

Lucy was not quite convinced of that, however. How could anyone be truly married without standing up in front of a preacher? When Lucy was quite young, her mother had died, and her father had never been comfortable with any sort of moral or religious instruction—despite the fact that Lucy probably knew more about botany than any other female on the continent—but even so she knew a real marriage had to be blessed in a church, not in the middle of some godforsaken wilderness.

At first, shaken and emotionally drained after the battle with the Blackfoot, she had not even realized that Clay and Shining Moon were a couple. It had seemed so much more likely that the Hunkpapa Sioux woman was paired with the other Indian, the young warrior called Proud Wolf. But Lucy understood now that Shining Moon and Proud Wolf were brother and sister. As for Aaron Garwood, he was just a friend and partner to the others.

Lucy was not blind. She knew from the way Proud Wolf and Aaron had hovered around her at supper that they were both quite taken with her. Aaron seemed to be a nice enough young man, but he was not nearly as impressive as Clay Holt. And Proud Wolf was an Indian, so Lucy knew there could be no relationship between them. But as for Clay . . . ah, Clay Holt was a different matter.

She had never seen a man who struck such a chord deep within her. He looked so stern, yet he was surprisingly gentle. And he knew everything there was to know about life on the frontier. He was the most compelling man Lucy had ever met.

Maybe she felt this way because she realized Clay was her best chance of surviving this horrible expedition. She wished she had never come along, but her father had never doubted that she would accompany him and assist him, as she had for the past several years, and Lucy had not wanted to disappoint him. So here she was, deep in the most hostile landscape she had ever encountered, probably surrounded by more savages, hundreds of miles from the nearest outpost of civilization. It was enough to make her weep with fear and desperation.

Except when she looked at Clay Holt.

Right now, that squaw might be enough for him, Lucy thought. But sooner or later, she vowed, Clay would realize that what he really needed was a white woman to love and care for. And that woman might as well be her.

She drifted into sleep with that thought in her mind and a faint smile on her lips.

Chapter Six

Holding his pounding head, Jefferson Holt staggered to the doorway of the cabin and threw open the door. A horrible noise outside filled the air; to Jeff's ears it sounded like a dozen waterfalls roaring at once. However, he saw it was just the Gilworth brothers, asleep in the back of their wagon and snoring so loudly the earth seemed to shake under Jeff's feet.

He was sick from drinking too much rum at Monsall's tavern the evening before, Jeff realized. He had bought a tankard for Castor and Pollux, and then each of them had insisted on buying one for him in return, and by that time Jeff had been fuzzy enough to start the whole thing around again. Where it had ended was impossible to say, since he remembered almost nothing after the sixth tankard.

Leaning on the doorjamb, he closed his eyes to shut out the brilliant morning sunlight and massaged his aching temples while wishing that the Gilworths would stop snoring. He must have managed to get on his horse and lead Castor and Pollux here in their wagon the night before. He had felt the same instinctive liking for Pollux Gilworth that he had for Castor, and settling the deal with them had been simple. They would work the farm and live in the cabin, taking care of the place and keeping all but ten percent of the profits. That ten percent would go into an account Jeff would open in Marietta's recently established bank, which was owned by old Rufus Putnam, the retired soldier who had led the first settlers down the Ohio River. In turn, Castor and Pollux had agreed to remain on the farm for at least two years, or until they heard otherwise from Jeff. They had shaken hands on the arrangement, and that was enough for Jeff.

Now all he had to do was decide what to do with his own life.

As Castor had said, Pollux was rather quiet, preferring to let his brother do most of the talking. But Pollux had said one thing the night before that came back now to Jeff. Talking about the reverses that had led the Gilworths to lose their farm in Pennsylvania, Pollux had said, "A man can't sit still when things're falling apart all around him. He's got to jump one way or t'other."

That was the choice facing Jeff now, he realized. Going west would take him to the frontier, back to the Rocky Mountains and his brother Clay. But Melissa had gone east. . . .

New York was a big place, sure, and he had no guarantee that was where the Merrivales had gone. But Jeff knew suddenly with crystal clarity that he was not ready to give up on being reunited with Melissa. She was his wife, and he loved her. They were meant to be together.

He straightened, his growing resolve helping him to forget about his headache and the uneasy feeling in his stomach. Now that he had made his decision, another idea occurred to him. The natural path to New York led up the Ohio River to Pittsburgh, where his two younger brothers and his sister were living with their aunt and uncle, Dorothy and Henry Holt. He could stop there and visit with Edward, Susan, and Jonathan on his way to New York. It would go a long way toward easing his mind to know that the youngsters were all right.

Jeff grinned. Despite the hangover, he felt better than he had at any time since returning to Marietta and discovering that Melissa was gone. He strode out to the Gilworth wagon, reached into the back of it, and shook Castor by the shoulder.

"Wake up!" he shouted cheerfully. "Rise and shine, Castor! Time to take a look around your new farm."

Castor stopped snoring. He rolled over and propped one eye open to regard Jeff balefully. He moaned. Beside him, Pollux stirred reluctantly as well.

"What the hell . . . " Castor muttered. He lifted a hand to his shaggy head. "Lord! Is that me yellin' like that?" He winced as he spoke.

"Come on," Jeff said, his enthusiasm clearing his head more with each passing moment. "We've got a lot to do before I leave."

"Leave?" Pollux echoed as he sat up and ran a hand over his bald head, which as Castor had said was as smooth as a polished stone. If anything, though, his beard was longer and bushier than Castor's. "So you made up your mind what you're going to do?"

Jeff nodded. "That's right. I'm going after my

wife. And I'm going to find her no matter how long it takes."

Castor clambered down from the wagon and slapped Jeff on the back, the force of the blow staggering the smaller man.

"That's the spirit!" he bellowed at Jeff, forgetting about his hangover. "I don't reckon you Holts ever give up, do you?"

"No, I guess not," Jeff said slowly.

He was beginning to realize that about himself and the rest of his family. They were Holts, and when they wanted something, or when there was a wrong to be righted, they went after it with every bit of their strength and determination.

And Lord help the man who got in their way.

Lucy Franklin was going to be a problem. Clay sensed that quite plainly over the next few days. It seemed as though every time he looked up, she was there in front of him, wanting to know if he needed anything or if she could do something to help him.

Maybe it was ungracious of him, he thought, but he wished to hell that the professor had left her back in Massachusetts.

Clay had a feeling Harry Lawton was going to give him trouble, too. So far the former chief guide had done nothing but mutter behind Clay's back, but whenever Clay caught the man looking at him, he saw hatred in Lawton's gaze.

The first thing Clay had done to prepare for the rest of the expedition was to make sure the supplies were in as good shape as Franklin claimed. He was glad to see they did indeed have plenty of everything —powder, shot, sugar, salt, flour, salt pork, jerky, and beans. That was enough for the trip to the Pacific, provided they were able to hunt game along the way. Franklin and his group were not planning to return overland. A ship chartered by the American Philosophical Society was scheduled to sail around the Cape of Good Hope and meet them at the mouth of the Columbia River. The ocean voyage itself was something of a scientific expedition, the professor had explained.

After checking the supplies, Clay and Franklin, with the help of Shining Moon and Proud Wolf, spent a day poring over the maps the group had brought along. Clay recognized some of them as copies of the charts made by Lewis and Clark during their journey. He recalled sitting by the campfire many a night while the two captains made laborious notes in their journals and struggled to get each detail correct on the maps they were making. Evidently much of the information gathered by the Corps of Discovery had been made available to scientific societies, such as the one in Philadelphia, although it had not yet been released to the general public. That time was coming, Franklin insisted, and perhaps not too far in the future.

"There's a great clamor among the population for more knowledge about the West," Franklin said to Clay as they looked over the maps. "They've heard a great deal about the expedition of Lewis and Clark, but much of what is being bandied about is just rumor and innuendo. Did you know, for example, that some people insist these mountains are inhabited by great woolly mammoths such as those that existed thousands and thousands of years ago?"

"Don't know about mammoths, whatever they are," Clay said, "but there's just about every other kind of critter out here."

"Some foolish individuals claim, however, that Lewis and Clark never reached the Pacific Ocean, that the entire journey was just a figment of the imagination of some scrivener hired by the government to dupe the public into accepting President Jefferson's purchase of the Louisiana Territory."

Clay shook his head. "Well, I know that's not true. I was there, from St. Louis all the way to Fort Clatsop at the mouth of the Columbia and back. If you ask me, nobody could make up something as far-fetched as what we did, no matter how much imagination they had."

"I agree wholeheartedly." Franklin traced a line on the map with the tip of a blunt finger. "Now, about this stream here and its location on the map . . ."

For the most part Clay found the professor's charts to be accurate, although he, as well as Shining Moon and Proud Wolf, did find a few mistakes to correct. By the time he and the others were finished studying the maps, Clay felt confident about using them.

The next morning—after Lucy had hovered over him so much during breakfast that he wanted to shoo her away like a troublesome insect—Clay announced, "Since we've got plenty of powder and shot, I want to see how everybody handles a rifle. You may all need to do some shooting before this trip is over."

"I handle a gun just fine," Lawton protested, "and so do the boys I hired."

"You won't mind showing me, then," Clay said.

"You're the boss, ain't you?" Lawton said bitterly.

Rupert von Metz folded his arms across his chest and stared at Clay. "Well, I for one refuse to be subjected to such a test."

"Why's that?" Clay forced himself to keep his tone civil and not show the impatience he felt.

"I am a Prussian," von Metz replied, as if the answer should have been obvious. "And despite the fact that I also have artistic abilities, I possess all of the natural Prussian aptitudes."

Clay waited a moment for a better explanation.

When it became apparent he was not going to get one, he asked, "And just what does that mean?"

Von Metz regarded Clay with disdain. "It means that as a Prussian, I am naturally better with a firearm than some unwashed backwoodsman."

"Really, Rupert—" Professor Franklin began.

But Clay held up a hand to stop the botanist. "That's all right, Professor. Reckon I know how Mr. von Metz feels. It's all right to be proud of the place you come from." Clay's mind was working rapidly as he spoke. Von Metz's arrogance was going to cause more and more trouble unless he was taken down a notch or two—now.

Clay continued, "Just because a fellow is from a certain place, though, doesn't mean he can do everything that other folks around there can."

Von Metz glowered at him. "You doubt my word?"

"Let's just say I need convincing." Clay's flintlock was cradled in the crook of his left arm, as it usually was when he was not busy doing something else. He shifted the Harper's Ferry rifle around so that it was held ready to use, then hefted the weapon and suggested, "Why don't we have a shooting match?"

"A competition? Between you and me?" Von Metz sounded surprised at first, but then his eyes began to shine with interest. The proposal seemed to appeal to his competitive nature. "Of course, Herr Holt. But why not expand the scope of this contest, say, to include cold steel as well?"

"What do you mean by that?" Clay felt a tickle of unease at the back of his neck. Von Metz was up to something.

"After our shooting match, as you call it, I propose that we also match our skill with sabers. I happen to have a pair of fencing sabers with me."

Somehow it did not surprise Clay that somebody like von Metz would haul a pair of fencing sabers hundreds of miles into the wilderness. You never knew when you might have to fight a duel, he thought, chuckling to himself.

He glanced at Shining Moon, Proud Wolf, and Aaron and saw the concern on their faces.

"Sure. Sounds like a good idea to me." Without warning, Clay tossed the rifle to von Metz, who reacted quickly and snatched it midair. "First let's see what you can do with this, though."

Von Metz lifted the rifle, checking its balance. He raised it to his shoulder and rested his cheek against the polished wooden stock, then squinted and sighted over the long barrel. Finally, he nodded.

"This weapon is crude, but it will do."

"It's loaded and primed," Clay told him. "All you have to do is cock it and fire."

"And what is my target?"

Clay looked around and spotted a small mark on a tree trunk about a hundred yards away. He pointed.

"See the blaze on that tree? A bear did that, rubbing up against the trunk until he knocked the bark off. See if you can put a ball into it."

Von Metz sniffed as if the challenge was too easy, but Clay thought he saw a glimmer of uncertainty in the young Prussian's eyes. Everyone in the group had gathered around by now and was watching with great interest as von Metz lifted the rifle to his shoulder again. He pointed it at the tree and settled his cheek against the stock.

"Better be careful," Clay warned him in a quiet voice. "You hold the gun like that when you fire and the kick's liable to bust your jaw."

"I know that," von Metz snapped. "I was simply trying to estimate the accuracy of these primitive sights."

Clay noticed that von Metz readjusted his grip on the rifle, however.

After a moment von Metz pulled the cock all the

way back, sighted again, and took a deep breath. Clay saw his finger whiten on the trigger as he squeezed off the shot. With a burst of smoke, noise, and flame, the rifle fired. Just as Clay had expected, the recoil of the heavy weapon knocked von Metz back a step.

A bit pale faced, he caught his balance and asked quickly, "What happened? Did I hit it?"

The distance was too far to be sure, so Aaron Garwood said, "I'll go check." One of Lawton's men hurried along with him as he trotted toward the tree.

When they reached it, both men examined the trunk intently. Then Lawton's man turned and held his hands about six inches apart. "That far under the blaze!" he called.

"Good shooting, Rupert!" Lawton exclaimed, and some of his companions echoed his congratulations.

Clay thought von Metz looked displeased, however, as he handed the rifle over.

"I should have done better," von Metz said. "If I had been more familiar with this weapon, I would have."

"I reckon so." Clay reloaded the rifle. "But that is good shooting, von Metz. That's no easy target I picked out. We'll see how I do."

He poured powder from his horn into the barrel, then dropped a ball on top of it and used the ramrod and wadding to seat the charge. After priming the lock and waving Aaron and the other man away from the tree, Clay lifted the rifle to his shoulder and cocked it. He sighted for only a couple of seconds before pressing the trigger.

The gun boomed again. As the smoke cleared, Aaron ran to the tree and let out a whoop of excitement. He placed his finger in the middle of the blaze and shouted, "Dead center!"

Clay's face was carefully expressionless as he asked von Metz, "Want to go again?"

The Prussian looked about ready to chew his way right through that tree trunk, Clay thought. Through clenched teeth he said, "You have already bested me. But there is still the test of steel."

"That's right. Let's get on with it." Clay handed the empty rifle to Proud Wolf.

Shining Moon put a hand on Clay's arm and asked, "Are you sure you want to do this?"

"Why not?" Clay grinned at von Metz. "This is just a little sport, isn't it, Rupert?"

"Of course," von Metz replied tightly.

Clay read another answer in the Prussian's eyes, however. Von Metz was serious about this, and Clay knew that if the man got a chance, he would run that saber right through Clay's vitals. He could always claim that the killing had been an accident. With Clay dead, Lawton would probably resume command, and Lawton and von Metz seemed to be friends. Besides, Clay had humiliated von Metz, at least in the eyes of the young artist; he would be eager to have his revenge.

Von Metz stalked to his tent and disappeared through the canvas flap to get the sabers. Meanwhile, Aaron dug both rifle balls out of the tree and rejoined the group, tossing the misshapen lumps of lead up and down in the palm of his hand.

"Good shooting, Clay," he said quietly to his friend. Echoing Shining Moon, he added, "Are you sure about this saber business?"

Clay smiled a little and looked at Proud Wolf. "Aren't *you* going to ask me the same question?"

Proud Wolf shook his head. "You will show that European fool how a true man of the mountains fights."

"Glad somebody's got some confidence in me," Clay said.

"I have confidence in you, my husband," Shining

Moon said. "But I do not want you spitted on a long knife like a rabbit ready for roasting."

Before Clay could reply, von Metz emerged from the tent carrying two long, slender, slightly curved sabers in brass scabbards. As von Metz brought the weapons over, Professor Franklin frowned.

"I'm not certain this is a good idea, Mr. Holt," he said.

Beside him, Lucy looked concerned as well.

"It'll be all right," Clay said quietly, hoping to reassure them. He was not as confident as he sounded, however. Von Metz moved with athletic grace, like a cat, and Clay knew that a single misstep could be fatal. Still, he had gotten himself into this, and now there was nothing he could do except go through with it. If he backed down, none of the group would follow him.

Von Metz held both sabers toward Clay and said, "You shall have the choice of weapons, even though by all rights it should be mine as the offended party."

"I thought we said this was sport, not a duel," Clay replied.

Von Metz's response was, "Pick your weapon, Herr Holt, and let us get on with this."

"Sure, if that's the way you want it." Clay wrapped his fingers around the bone handle of the hunting knife at his waist and slid the heavy blade from its sheath. "Don't need either one of those pig-stickers. I'll use this."

There were exclamations of surprise from those gathered around, including Clay's companions and the professor and his daughter.

Von Metz coolly asked, "Are you certain of this decision?"

"Yep."

Von Metz inclined his head. "Very well, then." He handed one of the sabers to a bystander, then slid the other from its scabbard, the blade emerging with a slight rattle of steel against brass. He tossed the scabbard aside.

Clay knew what the other man had to be thinking. The weapon Clay held had a long blade for a knife, but it was still only about a foot in length. The saber in von Metz's hand was close to two and a half feet long. In a fight like this, that extra eighteen inches represented a tremendous advantage in reach.

But Clay was certain that he would be lost if he used that flimsy little sword. A man was better off staying with what he knew. The bone handle of the hunting knife fit his palm as though it were part of him.

Von Metz put his feet together, lifted the saber in a salute, and said, "En garde!"

The onlookers moved back, forming a large circle with Clay and von Metz in its center. Nobody wanted to get in the way of a wildly swinging blade.

Clay said to von Metz, "Whenever you're ready."

The Prussian came at him then, sunlight flickering on the blade of the saber as it described a complicated arc through the air and flashed toward Clay's face. Clay took a quick step back, and the thrust missed. He brought his knife up, and steel rang against steel as it clashed against the saber, ruining any fancy move von Metz might have had planned for his backswing. The heavier hunting knife, with Clay's strength behind it, had no trouble turning aside the saber.

Von Metz stepped back and regarded Clay. "Very good," he said. "Very smooth, Herr Holt. You have fought with blades before."

"Once or twice," Clay said dryly.

Von Metz launched another attack, this time to the accompaniment of cheers from some of Lawton's men. Lawton had probably put them up to it, Clay thought fleetingly. Then he turned his full attention to von Metz. The Prussian's saber was leaping around like something alive, darting and jumping and slashing forward. But each time the blade approached Clay, the frontiersman's hunting knife parried the blow.

A light sweat broke out on von Metz's forehead as Clay used his knife to turn thrust after thrust aside. Clay seemed content to fight a defensive battle. That was sound strategy, given the longer blade his opponent possessed. He was going to have to bide his time, he thought, and wait for the right moment to strike.

That moment was not long in coming. Becoming angrier and more frustrated by the second, von Metz's movements grew wilder, more reckless. The saber swung wider as he slashed at Clay, who either ducked, dodged, or blocked each attack. Gradually, von Metz abandoned any pretense of fencing and merely hacked at his opponent. Clay retreated a little, drawing von Metz on. The Prussian cursed in his native language and lunged forward, swinging the saber wildly.

Clay knew the time had arrived. He darted aside, and as von Metz stumbled past him, Clay's knife slashed down and rang loudly against the saber. The lighter weapon snapped as Clay twisted his wrist in a time-honored maneuver to break an enemy's blade. Von Metz let out a howl of rage and tried to catch his balance.

He was too late. Clay's foot shot out and went between von Metz's calves. He hooked his toe behind the Prussian's left leg and jerked. Von Metz went over, landing hard on his back.

Before he could move, Clay dropped one knee lightly on von Metz's chest, then put the blade of the hunting knife against his throat. Von Metz froze motionless as the keen edge touched his skin. A surprised and horrified silence fell over the onlookers as they realized how close Clay was to cutting von Metz's throat.

But it was not really that close, Clay thought. If he had wanted von Metz dead, the Prussian would have a bloody gash from one side of his neck to the other right now. Shining Moon, Proud Wolf, and Aaron understood that and knew von Metz was in no real danger as long as he stayed still, but the others had no way of knowing the true situation.

Lucy gasped in horror, and Professor Franklin cried out, "For God's sake, Mr. Holt, don't kill him!"

In one lithe motion Clay got to his feet, taking the blade with him. He stood over von Metz. As he slid the knife back into its sheath, Clay said, "Never meant to kill him. If I did, he'd be dead already." He held out his hand to the prone von Metz. "You handle a blade pretty good, mister, and in case I didn't mention it before, that was fair shooting, too. I reckon you'll do to go over the mountains with."

At least that was true as far as von Metz's skill with weapons was concerned. His attitude, however, left one hell of a lot to be desired, Clay thought.

Von Metz sat up and pushed himself to his feet, ignoring Clay's outstretched hand. It seemed he was in no mood to be mollified by Clay's words of praise.

"You—you backwoodsman!" he said, his handsome face purple with rage. He turned on his heel and stalked off.

Clay shrugged. He had knocked some of the arrogance out of von Metz, but the young Prussian evidently still had a plentiful supply.

Turning to Harry Lawton and the other men, Clay said quietly, "You boys were going to show me how well you shoot."

"Yeah, we'll do that," Lawton said, giving Clay an ugly grin. "But you'd better watch out for that youngster, Holt. Next time, he's liable to shoot at you."

Clay doubted that. Rupert von Metz might be thoroughly unpleasant—and Clay knew the Prussian would not hesitate to kill him in fair combat—but he did not believe von Metz was the kind of man to shoot from ambush.

Lawton, now, was an entirely different story. As long as Lawton was around, Clay was going to do his damnedest to have eyes in the back of his head.

That night, as the campfire became embers and one by one the members of the expedition turned in, Rupert von Metz found himself sitting alone in front of his tent. No one had had much to say to him since the debacle that afternoon. He had already lost Lucy Franklin, of course, to Clay Holt. During the first weeks of the journey, Lucy had been taken with von Metz, who thoroughly enjoyed being charming whenever young women were involved. He had been hoping she would prove an entertaining diversion during this trip through the wilderness. Only the relatively close quarters and the fact that Lucy's father demanded a great deal of her time had prevented von Metz from instigating a dalliance already.

All that had changed with Holt's arrival on the scene, von Metz reflected. Now, not only did Lucy ignore him, but so did the other men in the group. Von Metz had no desire to become lifelong friends with any of these frontier ruffians, but their company was better than nothing.

In disgust, he stood up, brushed off the seat of his trousers, and turned to enter the tent.

"Wait up a minute, Rupert," someone said to him before he could push past the canvas flap.

Von Metz turned and saw a shape looming between him and the glow of the fire. He recognized his visitor as Harry Lawton, who had probably been the most cordial member of the expedition so far.

"What do you want, Harry?" the young Prussian asked.

"A bit of talk." Lawton chuckled. "Holt showed you up pretty good today, didn't he?"

Von Metz stiffened with anger. Lawton had no right to speak to him that way. "As I recall, you have had your own less than sterling moments against Herr Holt." Following Lawton's lead, von Metz kept his voice pitched low so that it could not be heard around the campfire or in any of the other tents.

"I reckon you could say that. I'm planning to do something about it, though."

"What?" von Metz asked scornfully. "So far you have done nothing but complain and utter vague threats."

"That's because I'm waiting for the right time," Lawton snapped. "You can take my word for it. Mr. High-and-Mighty Clay Holt is going to regret coming in here and bullying me out of a job."

"You will still be paid."

"That ain't the point!" Lawton insisted. "It's a matter of honor, too."

Von Metz tried not to laugh. It was ludicrous to hear a man like Lawton, little better than a filthy savage, talking about honor. Von Metz seriously doubted there was anyone on this misbegotten continent who fully understood the word.

"What is it you want with me, Harry? I'm rather tired."

"Sure, sure, I'll make it fast. I just wanted to know if you'd be interested in helping out when it comes time to settle the score with Holt."

Von Metz raised his eyebrows in surprise at the question. He had honestly thought Lawton lacked the courage to do anything about Holt except whine and complain.

"You have a plan?" he asked, curious.

Lawton shook his head. "Not yet. But I'm thinking on it. Can I count on you when the showdown comes?"

"Against Holt? You certainly can." There was a part of von Metz that believed Lawton would never get around to doing anything, but just in case he did, it would not hurt to form an alliance of sorts with the man. And if Lawton did not exact vengeance on Clay Holt, then von Metz would deal with the problem himself.

Lawton slapped him lightly on the arm, and Rupert tried not to show how distasteful he found the contact.

"Glad to hear it," Lawton said. "We'll show that—"

"You men better get some sleep," someone called from the other side of the camp. "We'll be pulling out in the morning."

Both Rupert and Lawton recognized the voice as Clay Holt's.

Lawton turned and gave Clay a wave of acknowledgment, then swung back to face von Metz and growled, "Ain't that just like the son of a bitch? He don't ever get through giving orders, not even when a man's fixing to turn in."

"So, we resume the journey tomorrow, eh?" von Metz mused. "Sometime during our trek, that opportunity of which you spoke will arise, Herr Lawton, and we must be ready to take advantage of it."

"Yep. And when we do, Clay Holt is a dead man."

Von Metz nodded slowly. He liked the sound of that; he most certainly did.

Castor and Pollux Gilworth went down to the landing to see Jeff off. It was a fine spring morning with a fresh breeze from the southwest. That breeze would fill the sail on the riverboat waiting at the slip and help carry the vessel upstream to Pittsburgh. Also aboard was a full crew to pole the boat along; against the current of the mighty Ohio, they needed all the help they could get.

Jeff had bought a new coat of brown wool, as well as some new shirts, from Steakley's Trading Post. He wore the same floppy-brimmed felt hat and carried the same weapons as when he had ridden back into Marietta. The Ohio could be a rough place to travel. Sometimes the boats were attacked by river pirates, and thieves and cutthroats might be traveling as passengers as well. But Jeff was not thinking about any of the hazards of riverboat travel that morning. He was filled with excitement and anticipation.

"Well, good luck to you," Castor said as he shook hands with Jeff. "Hope you find what you're lookin' for."

"Same here," Pollux echoed, also shaking hands with Jeff.

"I'm sure glad I ran into you boys," Jeff said. "You've taken a load off my mind, agreeing to work the farm. Once I've stopped off at Pittsburgh and made sure my brothers and sister are all right, I'll be able to turn all my attention to finding Melissa."

It would be good, too, just to see Edward, Susan, and Jonathan, not to mention his uncle and aunt. Jeff had not seen Henry and Dorothy Holt for more than ten years, when Bartholomew had taken the family to visit his brother Henry and Henry's family. That was the last contact Jeff had had with any of the Pittsburgh relatives.

His step was light as he crossed the gangplank to the deck of the riverboat, his powder horn, shot pouch, and possibles bag bouncing against his hip. He was traveling light, just the way he liked. He could move faster that way. In the mountains a man learned not to carry any more than he really needed.

Jeff turned at the low railing and lifted a hand in

farewell to Castor and Pollux. The burly, bearded Gilworth brothers returned the wave.

Jeff had been the last passenger to board. Not many people traveled upriver; most of the traffic still headed west. One of the crew members pulled in the gangplank, and within minutes other men had poled the boat away from the dock and turned it to catch the southwest wind.

Once again, Jefferson Holt was leaving his old home behind. And just as before, he had no idea what he would find when he got where he was going.

PART II

The Ohio into which we had now entered, takes its name from its signifying bloody in the Indian tongue, which is only a modern appellation bestowed on it about the beginning of the last century by the five nations, after a successful war, in which they succeeded in subjugating some other tribes on its banks. It was called by the French La belle Riviere, which was a very appropriate epithet, as perhaps throughout its long course it is not exceeded in beauty by any other river. It was always known before as a continuation of the Allegheny, though it more resembles the Monongahela, both in the muddiness of its waters, and its size: the latter being about five hundred yards wide, whereas the former is only about four hundred yards in breadth opposite Pittsburgh.

—FORTESCUE CUMING
"Sketches of a Tour to the Western Country"

Chapter Seven

"Could I interest you in a game of cards, Mr. Holt?"

Jeff was sitting on a stool atop the keelboat's cabin watching the steep, wooded hills slide by on either side of the Ohio River. The fellow passenger who had spoken to him was a man with red hair and a ginger beard. He was sporting a fancy waistcoat, a ruffled shirt, tight buff-colored breeches, and a beaver hat, canted on his head at a jaunty angle.

"No, thanks, Mr. Burke," Jeff said. "I think you'd find I'm not much of a card player."

The man called Burke smiled. "To a man in my line of work, Mr. Holt, that's not always a disadvantage. However, I won't press you." He ducked back into the cabin from which he had emerged a moment earlier.

Burke was one of only half a dozen other passengers on the boat. Jeff had met him the day the boat set out from Marietta, and Burke had not hesitated to declare right away that he was a gambler. He hailed from Pittsburgh, where he was returning after a trip downriver to pick up a recent purchase—one of the most impressive horses Jeff had ever seen.

"His name is Beau," Burke had explained to Jeff as he brushed the big, magnificent black animal. "He's been running races all over Ohio and Illinois for the past year, and he's never been beaten. I had to pay a pretty price for him, but he's going to win back that much and more once I get him to Pittsburgh."

Jeff recalled seeing horse races around Marietta in the past, but he had never heard of this Beau. From what Burke had said, however, the horse had not started winning races until well after Jeff had gone west with Clay.

The keelboat was a large one, nearly eighty feet long and eighteen feet wide. The walkway where the crew members poled the vessel took up only eighteen inches on each side, so there was plenty of room amidships for passenger cabins as well as a sizable cargo hold. The hold was only about half full, mostly with barrels of salt, so Beau was staying there, supported by a broad sling that passed under his belly and hung suspended from the ceiling.

The horse's new owner, Eugene Burke, divided his time between the cargo hold and the crude saloon that had been set up in one of the empty cabins. The bar consisted of several planks laid atop whiskey barrels. Barrels of salt had been rolled in from the hold to serve as tables, and the passengers and off-duty crewmen who frequented the place used kegs for seats.

A game of cards was usually going on, presided over by either Burke or one of the other passengers, a surly character named Wiggins, who also dressed well and had the look of a professional gambler. From what Jeff had seen, he concluded that Burke and Wiggins knew each other, but there was no friendship between them. In fact, they seemed to go out of their way to avoid each other.

Traveling against the current, the keelboat did not make particularly good time, and Jeff was keenly aware of each passing moment. He was eager to get to Pittsburgh, and even more eager to reach New York and begin his search for Melissa. Aided by the sail and a half dozen oarsmen in the boat's bow, the crew used their long poles to push the craft along, only a few yards offshore, where the water was shallower and the poles could reach the bottom. The captain—or patroon, as Jeff had heard the crew call him—stood aft on top of the cabin, controlling the long steering sweep and watching the river ahead so that he could call out instructions to his men.

Each night the riverboat was tied up to the shore, since traveling in the dark was too hazardous, but from dawn to dusk, the tall, gaunt, muscular crewmen in buckskin trousers and red flannel shirts followed a grueling routine. Standing at the bow, they planted their poles on the bottom of the river and walked toward the rear of the vessel, pushing it forward. Then they gripped the poles tightly and walked toward the bow and repeated the entire process. Their efforts moved the boat along at a slow but steady pace. In return, the boatmen received wages of approximately twenty-five dollars a month and meals consisting of hardtack, corn, and potatoes.

It made Jeff shudder just to think about it. He missed the mountains more than ever, the freedom, the clean air of the high country, the taste of water from an ice-cold mountain stream. These rivermen drank cups of muddy water dipped straight from the Ohio, usually followed by a cup of raw whiskey from the ever-present keg on deck.

Another day and the boat would reach Wheeling, the major settlement between Marietta and Pittsburgh. It also marked the approximate halfway point to Pittsburgh. Jeff was thinking about how surprised his relatives would be to see him when he heard a shout from the cabin beneath him.

"Don't be a fool, man! Put that gun down!"

Jeff tensed as he recognized Eugene Burke's voice. The saloon cabin was right under him, and it sounded as though Burke was in trouble. Jeff stepped to the edge of the roof, dropped lightly to the walkway, and ducked his head as he went down the three steps into the cabin.

The room was lit not only by the light coming through the open door but also by an oil lantern hanging from a hook on the ceiling over the makeshift bar. The boat's cook had been pressed into service as the bartender. Looking worried, he stood behind the bar. Five more men were gathered around one of the salt barrel tables, cards and money scattered on its lid. Burke stood on one side of the barrel, his hands held up in front of him, palms turned toward the three men opposite. The fifth man, whom Jeff recognized as the gambler called Wiggins, stood off to one side.

One of the three men who stood facing Burke had leveled a pistol at him. The flintlock was cocked and ready to fire.

"What the hell's going on here?" Jeff asked sharply, hoping he would not startle the man with the gun into pressing the trigger.

"Thank God you're here, Mr. Holt!" Eugene Burke exclaimed. "Perhaps you can talk some sense into these gentlemen. I seem to have offended them in some way—"

"Cheated us, you mean, you fancy-pants bastard," the man with the pistol growled. "We know all about you. Should've figured out before now why you always win more than you lose at these friendly little games." The man spat on the cabin floor in disgust.

To judge from their clothes, he and his two companions were tradesmen. They were better dressed than riverboat men but not as dandified as Burke and Wiggins. Jeff had exchanged few words with any of them during the voyage.

"What you're implying is just not true." Carefully Burke waved a hand toward Wiggins. "You've had your minds poisoned against me by the smooth words of my esteemed colleague here. I assure you, if I've won more than I've lost, it's only because of my greater experience at these games of chance."

"Experience at bottom-dealing, you mean," one of the other men said. "Go ahead and shoot him, Carl. It's what he deserves."

Burke looked wildly at Jeff again.

"Nobody's going to shoot anybody," Jeff said.

"Stay out of this, mister. It ain't none of your business. You ain't been playing cards with this fella, but we have. And we've all lost money."

"Then that's your own fault," Jeff said bluntly.

Wiggins spoke up for the first time since Jeff had entered the cabin. "Not entirely. Not when a man like Burke is sitting at the table."

Burke shot him a venomous glance. "You're just angry because I beat you to Beau!" he accused. "You wanted to buy him, too."

"I would have given that stupid farmer a better price for him than you did," Wiggins said coolly. "But if you think I'm holding a grudge against you, Burke, you're wrong. I simply told these men the truth about you because I thought they deserved to hear it."

Wiggins was lying, and Jeff knew it. He could see hatred glittering in Wiggins's eyes whenever the man looked at Burke. It was almost beyond comprehension to Jeff how a man could be so jealous over a racehorse that he would try to get another man killed. From what he had seen so far during the trip, Burke and Wiggins had a history of animosity toward each other; he supposed the horse was the last straw.

Jeff looked over at the bartender. "Better go tell the captain what's going on down here. I don't reckon he'll want anybody getting shot on his boat. Be hard to get bloodstains out of those planks."

Burke paled a little at that comment, and the bartender took a step toward the door.

"Hold it!" the man with the pistol barked. "We don't need the captain to settle this for us. We handle our own problems." He extended his arm a little farther. The muzzle of the pistol was only a foot from the forehead of the terrified Burke.

Jeff thought rapidly. His own pistol was tucked under his belt, and it was unlikely he could draw it and cock it in time to do Burke any good. The same was true of his knife. By the time he could slide the blade from its sheath, pull his arm back, and launch the knife in a throw, the man could easily put a pistol ball through Burke's brain. Jeff's rifle was in his cabin with his other gear; he had not expected to need it on what had started out as a peaceful day.

And that was my mistake, he realized, *thinking that a day would stay peaceful just because it started out that way.*

Jeff's gaze fell on a whip hanging on a peg beside the door. It was there, he knew, because sometimes when keelboats got stuck in shallow water or on sandbars, mules had to be used to pull the boat free. They would be brought to the riverbank, and ropes would be tied between them and the boat. In cases like that, the captain would use the whip to keep balky mules pulling on their ropes.

Right now, Jeff Holt put the whip to another use.

With his right hand he snatched the coil of braided leather from the peg. He had used a whip on mules and oxen back in his days of working the Holt family farm, but it had been awhile since then. Still, after one learned the necessary snap of the wrist, it was hard to forget. Letting instincts and old habits guide him, Jeff lashed out with blinding speed.

The whip uncoiled and then wrapped itself around the gunman's wrist with a sharp popping sound. Jeff jerked it back. The pistol boomed, but the ball thudded harmlessly into the cabin wall, missing Burke by several feet. There was another thud as the pistol fell to the floor, followed by a howl of pain as its owner clutched his wrist, which was circled by a bloody welt.

Everyone in the cabin was startled into a momentary state of inaction. Jeff took that opportunity to pull and cock his pistol. He aimed it in the general direction of the three men, but the muzzle menaced Wiggins a bit as well. With a slight shift of Jeff's aim, he would hit the gambler.

"Stand still, all of you," Jeff said. "Are you all right, Burke?"

Sweat beaded on Burke's forehead and trickled down his cheeks into his beard. He pulled a handkerchief from his pocket and mopped away some of the wetness.

"I'm fine," he said shakily. "Thanks to you, Mr. Holt."

The captain appeared in the doorway, drawn by the shot. Angrily he shouted, "What in blue blazes is going on down here? Who's shooting on my boat?"

"Just a misunderstanding, Captain," Jeff said without taking his eyes off the men he was covering with his pistol. To the redheaded gambler, he added, "It *was* a misunderstanding, wasn't it, Burke? I'd hate to think I risked my life for a fellow who cheats at cards."

Jeff's voice was cold and hard, and Burke seemed to realize he had better tell the truth. He swallowed and said, "You have my word, Mr. Holt. I didn't cheat these men. There was no need to."

"Are you willing to accept that?" Jeff asked the three men.

The one called Carl was still nursing his injured wrist. He glared at Jeff for a second, then jerked his head in an angry nod. "Don't reckon we've got much choice, do we?"

Jeff looked at Burke. "It'd be a gesture of goodwill if you were to offer them their money back, Burke."

"Give back money that was fairly won?" The gambler looked astounded.

"I know you have a hard time understanding that, but it might make the rest of the trip a bit easier."

Burke sighed heavily. "Very well. I suppose I should follow your suggestion, Mr. Holt. After all, you did save my life with that whip. Whatever gave you the idea of grabbing it like that?"

"Just luck, I reckon. Being in the right place at the right time, maybe."

Burke reached forward and picked up some of the money from the barrel, leaving most of it lying there. "That's my share of the pot. You gentlemen are . . . welcome to the rest." He winced as if the words pained him.

Carl and his companions scooped up the remaining money, and one of the other men said to Jeff, "You can put up that pistol now, mister. This is all over."

"How about you, Carl?" Jeff asked. "You're the one who got hurt. You holding any grudges?"

The man shook his head. "I guess not. I can be a little hotheaded sometimes, and I figure this was one of those times. I shouldn't have pulled a gun."

"I reckon you had some encouragement." Jeff looked over at Wiggins, who had watched the entire exchange stoically.

"I've heard enough of this to know what was going on," the riverboat captain said, "and it had better not happen again. I'm used to rough behavior from my crew, but they generally stop short of shooting at one another. I expect the same from my passengers. If there's any more trouble, I'll close this bar down, understand?"

The men all nodded, and Jeff finally lowered his pistol. As he tucked it away, Wiggins gave him a cold-eyed look, and Jeff sensed that the gambler's circle of enemies had expanded to include him. If Wiggins had succeeded in goading one of the other men into killing Burke, he might have been able to claim the racehorse for himself. Jeff Holt had ruined that scheme.

Burke stepped over to Jeff and said, "I can't thank you enough, Mr. Holt." With his handkerchief, he patted away the last of the perspiration from his forehead. "I shall never be able to repay you—"

"There's one thing you can do," Jeff cut in.

"Whatever you say."

"Stay out of trouble. I like you, Burke, but I've got other things on my mind right now besides pulling your bacon out of the fire."

With that, Jeff left the cabin to watch the landscape pass by and wait impatiently for the boat to get to Pittsburgh.

The crew and the other passengers on the keelboat were anxious to reach Wheeling for a variety of reasons. Instead of representing the halfway point to Pittsburgh, as it did to Jeff, Wheeling meant to the others a chance to go ashore to a settlement, to have a hot meal, to buy a drink in a real tavern, to sample the charms of the young women who worked in the waterfront dives.

Under other circumstances, a drink and a hot meal would have appealed to Jeff, although he could have withstood the temptation to hire a wench. He was not interested in the temporary pleasures of the flesh, not when his wife was out there somewhere waiting for him. He stayed on board the keelboat while the other passengers, the captain, and the crew went ashore.

During the night something disturbed Jeff's sleep, and he reached for his rifle as he rolled out of his narrow bunk. The boat was quiet now, but something had roused him, and Jeff trusted his instincts. Each of the cabins opened directly onto the walkway that ran all the way around the boat. Jeff swung the door back slowly to keep its hinges from squealing, then stepped out into the cool night air.

His thumb was looped on the cock of the flintlock, ready to press it back instantly into firing position. He stood stock-still, letting his eyes and ears do the work. From one of the other cabins, he heard the sound of snoring. Some of the other passengers or the crewmen must have returned to the boat after a night of carousing. Maybe that was what he had heard, Jeff thought—someone stumbling aboard, blind drunk.

Maybe . . . but maybe not. His instincts were warning him that something was wrong.

He turned quickly but quietly as the sound of a small splash reached his ears. It came from aft, and he stepped lightly toward the rear of the boat, listening for the noise to be repeated.

Moonlight washed over the scene. Nothing moved on the river. Other keelboats were tied up at the Wheeling docks, but they were silent and dark. Jeff reached the aft end of the vessel and stood next to the long sweep. Still nothing.

Several yards away a fish broke the water in a shallow leap, then splashed back under the surface. During the brief moment when it was out of the water, moonlight glittered on its scales.

Jeff grinned ruefully. The sound of the fish jumping was the same as the splash he had heard a few minutes earlier; he should have recognized it the first time. Nothing was happening on the keelboat. Everything was as quiet and peaceful as it should have been.

He tucked the rifle under his left arm and headed back to his cabin. His nerves were on edge from being anxious to get to Pittsburgh, he told himself. Nearly every waking moment he thought about Melissa, and at night his dreams were haunted by visions of her. No wonder he was jumpy.

He returned to his cabin, placed the rifle beside the bunk, and crawled under the blankets. Within moments he was sleeping.

The next day, as the boat resumed its voyage, Jeff noticed more traffic on the river. Keelboats and flatboats, barges and crude log rafts, the Ohio carried them all. Some, such as the boat on which he rode, were going upstream, but most were headed downstream.

Folks going west, Jeff thought as he watched the boats slide past. *Going after their dreams and hopes.* So was he, although his dream lay in a different direction.

Around midmorning the wooded, gently rolling hills they had been passing gave way to rugged, rocky bluffs, which rose over twenty feet on either bank. This formation ran as far as Jeff could see as he peered upstream, at least for two miles. As it happened, no other boats were traveling along this stretch of the Ohio at the moment. The breeze was fresh and strong, filling the sail, and with the efforts of the crewmen and their poles, the keelboat reached the fastest speed yet of the journey.

That did not last long, however. Jeff was sitting on the roof of the cabins near the bow, his usual spot, when he heard a commotion from the cargo hold aft. Eugene Burke emerged from his cabin, a frown on his bearded face as he listened to the same bumping and thumping Jeff heard.

"That's Beau!" Burke exclaimed. "If that son of a bitch Wiggins is trying to hurt him—"

The gambler left the rest unsaid and hurried to the door at the rear of the boat that led into the cargo hold. Jeff swung down and followed him.

The captain was already at the door of the hold, his attention drawn by the noises coming from inside.

He turned to Burke and said, "That's that horse of yours, Mr. Burke, acting like the very devil himself is after him. I knew I shouldn't have agreed to carry that animal. If he kicks a hole in our hull—"

As he spoke, the captain swung the door open, and what he saw inside shocked him into a momentary silence. Jeff and Burke crowded next to him, peered past him, and saw Beau jerking around frantically as swirling water rose around the horse's hocks.

Throwing his head back, the captain bellowed, "We're taking on water! Head for shore!"

Looking around, Jeff realized that there was no shoreline suitable for bringing the boat aground, only those steep bluffs. Warning bells went off in his head. This was more than a simple leak in the cargo hold, he sensed.

As the boat veered toward the shoreline, the captain splashed into the rising water in the hold, searching for the source of the leak. Burke went after him, reached for Beau's harness, and tried to calm the horse. Jeff stayed on deck, watching the shoreline.

Suddenly he spotted a narrow opening in the bluff about fifty yards ahead. At that point a small creek ran into the Ohio from the northwest, and as he watched, rowboats carrying men wearing buckskins and rough work clothes emerged from the opening and turned toward the foundering keelboat.

Following his instincts, Jeff lifted the flintlock rifle in his hands and reached for the cock.

"Pirates!" he shouted. "Pirates up ahead!"

He had heard plenty of stories about river pirates

and how they operated; now he knew that the splash he had heard the night before had been caused by someone sabotaging the keelboat. The pirate had bored a hole in the hull, plugged it loosely, and waited for it to work itself out. The scheme had worked perfectly, putting the boat in jeopardy here in this section of river between the bluffs, where the creek provided a good hiding place until the pirates were ready to make their move.

Of course, Jeff thought quickly, this was just speculation on his part. Maybe the approaching rowboats were not carrying pirates after all.

They answered that question by opening fire on the keelboat a second later. Rifle balls whined in the air above the boat and thudded into its sides. Jeff snapped his own rifle to his shoulder, settled the sight on the chest of a man in the lead rowboat, and pressed the trigger. The rifle boomed and bucked against his shoulder, smoke billowing from its muzzle. After the smoke had cleared, Jeff was able to see his target sag to the side, then topple into the water.

Lowering the rifle, Jeff drew and cocked his pistol. The range was still rather far, but he aimed and fired anyway and saw another pirate clutch a shattered upper arm.

The pirate rowboats were all to the port side of the keelboat, so Jeff decided to take the shortest route to the relative safety of the starboard side. He leapt onto the roof of the cabins and ran across it, then dropped to the walkway on the opposite side, where he crouched down to reload. The crew was gathering on that side of the boat as well, and the vessel began to list.

Jeff stood up, took aim with his rifle, and fired. This time he missed, the ball splashing into the water beside a rowboat. Grimacing, he snapped off a shot with the pistol. He could not tell if he hit anything.

The captain came bounding out of the hold and

pulled an old-fashioned blunderbuss pistol from under his long coat. Snarling an oath, he pointed it at the pirates and pulled the trigger. The weapon went off with a roar like a small cannon, and the heavy lead ball smashed into one of the rowboats with an explosion of splinters.

Burke emerged from the hold and joined in the battle, snapping off a shot with a small pocket pistol. The pirates were close enough now for the gambler's shot to have an impact. One of the men went over backward, clasping both hands to his face. Blood welled between his fingers.

More shots were fired by the keelboat's crew, most of whom carried pistols tucked under their belts, and as they fired a ragged volley, several raiders were hit. But the pirates had the rivermen outnumbered by more than two to one, and the rowboats were almost close enough now for the men in them to leap over to the keelboat. A moment later, while the crew members were still reloading, that was exactly what happened.

The pirates swarmed over the boat, and the fighting, now hand-to-hand, grew fierce. Jeff was in the thick of it. He reloaded his pistol and looked up in time to see a pirate leap across the cabin roof at him, an oar upraised to smash his skull. Jeff jerked the pistol up and fired without aiming, letting instinct guide his shot. The ball smashed into the pirate's midsection and knocked him backward, as if he had been punched by a giant fist.

Another raider took his place, however, hurling himself at Jeff, knife in hand. Jeff dropped his pistol and caught the man's wrist in time to turn the blade aside, but in the next instant the pirate crashed into him, and Jeff felt himself driven back toward the edge of the walkway. Suddenly nothing was under his feet but air, then a split-second later, the surface of the river itself. He and the pirate went under with a huge splash.

Twisting desperately, Jeff pulled himself out of the pirate's grip and searched with his fingers until he found the hilt of his hunting knife. He slid it out of its sheath. As the man grappled with him again, forcing his head underwater, Jeff struck out with the knife and sank the blade into his opponent's body.

The man gave a strangled yell of pain that was cut off by river water gurgling into his open mouth. His hands locked around Jeff's throat, holding him under the water. Jeff ripped the knife free and struck again and then again, plunging the blade well into the pirate's belly each time. The fingers fell away from Jeff's throat.

He kicked with his feet and stroked with his free hand, launching himself up and out of the water onto the shore. Inhaling a deep breath of air into his burning lungs, he shook his head to clear his eyes and looked up at the nearby keelboat. The fighting was still going on, but the crew was slowly getting the upper hand over the raiders. Men were battling all along the walkway, as well as in the water around the boat.

Eugene Burke was standing near the bow, and as Jeff watched, the gambler knocked one of the pirates into the river with a sharp right cross. Movement behind Burke caught Jeff's eye. It was the other gambler from Pittsburgh, Wiggins, creeping out of a cabin, gun in hand. Wiggins was finally getting into the fight, it appeared.

A second later Jeff realized he was wrong. Wiggins lifted the pistol and aimed it not at one of the pirates but instead at Burke's back. Instantly Jeff understood: Wiggins was going to use the confusion of the battle to get rid of his rival once and for all. Everyone would think Burke had either been killed by a pirate or hit by a stray shot.

From the shore, Jeff drew back his knife hand and shouted, "Wiggins!"

The man half turned toward him in surprise. Jeff's arm whipped forward, the knife flickering as it spun across the distance between them. With a solid thump, the blade caught Wiggins in the chest. He staggered back against the cabin wall. The gun in his hand dipped toward the walkway and went off as a death spasm caused his finger to jerk the trigger.

Burke whirled around at the sound of the shot so close behind him, turning in time to see Wiggins paw futilely with his other hand at the knife sticking out of his chest. Wiggins slid down into a sitting position, and his head fell limply onto his left shoulder as he died.

"Give me a hand!" Jeff called to Burke as he swam to the keelboat.

Burke knelt on the walkway next to Wiggins's body, grasped Jeff's upraised wrist, and helped him get out of the river. As water streamed from his clothes, Jeff bent over and pulled his knife from Wiggins's chest, causing the body to slump all the way over.

"It looks as if you've saved my life again, Mr. Holt," Burke said. "I'm quite grateful."

"Never mind that," Jeff said shortly. "Let's worry about the rest of those pirates."

They quickly realized, however, that the pirates were not going to cause any more trouble. The criminals who had survived were jumping back into their rowboats and pulling away from the keelboat as fast as they could. The price required to capture the boat was more than the pirates wanted to pay.

But the danger was not entirely over, for the keelboat was wallowing low in the water. With the pirate threat rapidly diminishing, the captain disappeared into the hold again, followed by several of his men.

The leak had to be found and stopped before the boat sank.

"I've got to get Beau out of there!" Burke said anxiously. "He can swim, but not if he's trapped in that hold!"

Jeff followed Burke down the steps into the big compartment. The horse was still thrashing around as much as it could in its restraints. Burke reached for the sling to unfasten it.

"No need for that, Mr. Burke," the captain called from the other side of the room. "We've got the leak plugged. If you want to help, grab a bucket and give us a hand bailing the water out of here."

For the next hour passengers and crew pitched in together to empty the boat of the water that had nearly sunk it. Soon the keelboat righted itself, and the hole bored by the pirates was temporarily plugged. As soon as the boat reached a spot where it could safely tie up, a more watertight patch would be put in place and covered with pitch.

"We'll be able to reach Pittsburgh; have no doubt of that," the captain assured Jeff and the other passengers. "This is only a minor setback."

A minor setback that could easily have proven fatal, Jeff thought. Luck had been with them, and although several of the crew were wounded, none had been killed or hurt so badly that they would not be able to pole the boat. Other than the pirates who had been killed in the fighting, the only one to die had been Wiggins.

Later in the day, when the keelboat was again heading upriver, Burke sought Jeff out and thanked him once more. "As I told you, you'll find I can be quite grateful, Mr. Holt," the gambler said. "I'd be glad to reward you—"

"No. I didn't do it for a reward," Jeff said curtly. He liked Burke, but he did not particularly care for the idea of having the man feel indebted to him. "I would've done the same thing for anybody about to be gunned down from behind like that. Didn't even really think about it much."

"Well, whatever you say. Just remember that I owe you a great favor. Perhaps when we reach Pittsburgh I can do something to repay you."

"We'll see," Jeff said.

He was not interested in being paid back, but the idea of reaching Pittsburgh greatly appealed to him. He was eager to see his relatives and then get on with his search for his wife. And if there was no more trouble along the way, that would suit him just fine. He had been apart from Melissa for much too long already.

Chapter Eight

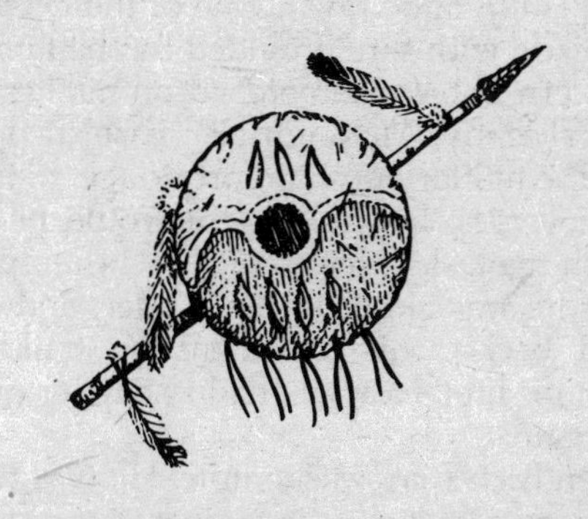

North of the border, on the edge of the Canadian Rockies, the finishing touches were being put on a sprawling fort surrounded by a high stockade fence made of unpeeled logs. Within the fort were several barracks, two storage buildings, a quartermaster's depot and store, a powder magazine, a smokehouse, a blacksmith's shop, and what would have been officers' quarters and the regimental offices —if this had been a military installation.

This was not an outpost of Her Majesty's Royal Army, however. It was privately owned and had been built by the fur-trading company known as the London and Northwestern Enterprise. The agent in charge of the company's Canadian operations had ordered the fort built, and he was the one who had named it Fort Dunadeen.

Fletcher McKendrick looked around at his handiwork and was well pleased.

He was a tall, rawboned, middle-aged Scotsman with curly, graying red hair and large, rough hands that still showed the marks of manual labor, even though McKendrick had spent most of the past few years behind a desk. Even in the wilderness he was well dressed, wearing tight brown breeches, a waistcoat, a silk shirt, and cravat. One of the D'Orsay beaver hats made with furs provided by the London and Northwestern Enterprise perched on his head.

Until recently, McKendrick's base of operations had been the military post at Fort Rouge, to the northeast. However, he had decided it would be easier to accomplish the task given to him by his employers in London if he was closer to the border, and the company had backed his judgment by building Fort Dunadeen for him. Now, he had to deliver on his end of the bargain.

McKendrick's job was simple: He was to expand the company's fur-trapping operation south into American territory by any means that he deemed necessary.

The London and Northwestern Enterprise was a latecomer to the fur industry in North America. The Hudson's Bay Company and the North West Company dominated the fur trade in the Canadian wilderness. Therefore, the owners of the London and Northwestern were more willing to cut a few corners in order to expand their business as quickly as possible. That suited McKendrick just fine; he was not a very patient man.

There were political considerations to his job, too, McKendrick knew. Borders in this part of the world were an uncertain thing, and the exact demarcation of the line between Canada and the United States had yet to be determined. When that time came, it would certainly strengthen England's claim to the territory it desired if the British leaders could point to a successful ongoing fur-trapping operation in the lower Rockies. Added to the greed of the London and Northwestern's owners had probably been some not-so-subtle urgings to expand, from ministers high up in the government.

Fort Dunadeen was only the first step. McKendrick had plans, indeed.

Several men were still working on the roof of one of the barracks buildings, but once that was completed, the fort would be finished. The stockade fence had been the first thing erected, to provide protection from the Indian bands that marauded in the area from time to time. When that had been finished, McKendrick had instructed most of the men to trap, leaving only a small contingent to continue the construction of the fort. The first buildings they had erected were the storehouses, to hold the furs brought in by the trappers. It was late spring, and the weather was more than pleasant enough for sleeping in the open in bedrolls until the barracks were completed.

McKendrick headed for his office. He liked to start the day with a stroll around the fort, but now he was ready to get to work.

His secretary, a man named Lloyd Hodgkins, was waiting for him. Hodgkins had recently been sent over from company headquarters in London, just as McKendrick had been a couple of years earlier. But unlike the burly Scotsman, Hodgkins had never done a day's physical labor in his life, and his slender frame, delicate hands, and pasty complexion were testimony to that. A pair of pince-nez perched on the narrow bridge of his nose as he regarded McKendrick sternly over the lenses. Hodgkins hated it on the frontier, as McKendrick well knew, but he was good at his job. He could keep up with the paperwork and had an eye for details that McKendrick sometimes overlooked.

"We now have enough furs in the storehouse to make up a load that can be taken east," Hodgkins said as McKendrick entered the office.

"Aye, and good morning to ye, too, Lloyd," McKendrick said dryly. Hodgkins had no time for small talk.

"And you're going to have to draft a letter to Lord Harbridge sometime soon detailing your plans for the upcoming expansion of the company's trapping territory."

McKendrick hung his hat on a peg near the door and stepped behind his desk.

"You're right, as usual," he said. "The lord and his partners will be getting impatient to hear what's going on out here."

McKendrick took out his pipe and tobacco pouch, then filled the pipe and packed it as he leaned back in his chair and frowned. Lord Harbridge was his superior in the London and Northwestern Enterprise, and he was not a man tolerant of failure. When McKendrick had reported the collapse of his first effort to extend the company's trapping south of Canada, he had received a scathing reply from Harbridge. The lord's attitude had softened a bit in recent letters, and he had provided the funds for McKendrick to have the fort built. But he would not be forgiving of another failure, and McKendrick was well aware of that fact.

As he raised his bushy red eyebrows, McKendrick asked, "What do ye think, Lloyd? You weren't here last year when we made our first try, but you've heard about it. What do ye think went wrong?"

Hodgkins sniffed. "Well, since you've asked me, sir, I believe you placed too much reliance in that man Duquesne. The French are so undependable, you know."

"Aye," McKendrick said slowly. "Mayhap you're right."

He had indeed placed a great deal of faith in the little mercenary who called himself Duquesne. The man had seemed to McKendrick to possess the guile and ruthlessness necessary to establish a foothold in the American Rockies. Duquesne had been well on the way to doing just that by stirring up trouble between the Indians and the American trappers when two men, brothers named Holt, had interfered. Duquesne had ended up dead. The only good thing to come of the whole affair had been that Duquesne's efforts could not be traced back to McKendrick. At least the Scotsman hoped that was the case.

"Duquesne made some mistakes," McKendrick continued, "but the real error was mine. I thought it best to operate behind the scenes and not come out into the open until all the Americans had been driven out. I can see now that's not going to happen so easily."

"What do you intend to do, then?" the secretary persisted.

McKendrick had been toying with an idea that would answer that very question. "We're going into that territory just as if we owned it and have nary a doubt of our right to be there," he declared. "The Americans can try to push us out if they want to, but they'll be risking an international incident if they do. Parliament has not recognized the boundaries of that land the Americans bought from Bonaparte, so they'll be quick to set up a howl if some of Her Majesty's subjects are harassed."

For a moment Hodgkins considered. Then he nodded and said, "A plan that is stunning in its simplicity, sir. But what if those barbarians don't care about causing an international incident?"

"We'll be there with enough force to keep them from running us off." McKendrick brought a knobby fist down on the desktop for emphasis. "I'll tell the men to lie low until they get a fort of their own built, and then the Americans can attack us—if they dare."

"You're going to build another fort?" Hodgkins sounded as if he regarded the suggestion with quite a bit of skepticism.

"Aye." Now that he had made up his mind, McKendrick was not the type to back away from the idea. "Not as fancy as this fort, mind ye. It will not cost much. But it'll be plenty strong to hold off those heathen Americans."

"I hope you're right, sir."

"I know I'm right," McKendrick said. "What I need now is somebody to take charge of the group that'll be going south."

"I'll make a list of the available men so that you can decide from among them."

McKendrick waved a hand in dismissal, and Hodgkins retreated into the smaller office set off to one side of McKendrick's chamber. After taking paper, pen, and inkwell from the desk, McKendrick began to compose the letter he would have Hodgkins copy to Lord Harbridge.

Never one who handled words easily, the Scotsman had to concentrate heavily on the task before him, and all of his attention was still fixed on the paper in front of him half an hour later. It was covered with blots, smudges, and crossed-out words, but Hodgkins would be able to make sense of it. That was his job.

Suddenly the outer door opened, and McKendrick glanced up in annoyance. He did not like to be disturbed when he was working on something like this. He glared at the two men who stood there, both of them wearing the buckskins and fur caps of trappers. They looked as nervous as cats.

"Well, what is it?" McKendrick demanded. "What in blazes do ye want?"

"Get in there, both of you," a man's voice said harshly.

The two trappers in the doorway stumbled into the office. Another man entered behind them, and McKendrick could see now that the third man had prodded them at gunpoint. He had a brace of flintlock pistols trained on their backs.

"What's the meaning of this?" McKendrick asked, blinking in surprise. "Hodgkins!"

The secretary hurried in from the other office but stopped short as he saw the two men standing in front of McKendrick's desk and the third man covering them with a pair of guns.

"What is this, sir?" he asked tentatively.

"I was hoping ye'd know." McKendrick got to his feet and peered past the two prisoners—because that was what they were, no doubt about that—at the third man. "You're Brown, aren't you?"

"That's right, sir," the man with the pistols said. "Simon Brown, at your service."

Simon Brown was a tall, strapping, handsome man with regular features, intelligent blue eyes, and thick brown hair. He wore a fringed buckskin jacket, whipcord trousers, and high black boots. McKendrick knew almost nothing about him except that he was one of the trappers, but he recalled now that Brown had impressed him before as being somewhat out of place in the wilderness. Looking at him now, McKendrick was struck by the thought that Brown would have looked more at home wearing an expensive suit and striding down a London street.

However, there was no mistaking the casual ease with which Brown held the two pistols. His attitude was that of a man accustomed to the threat of violence.

"What are ye doing here, Brown?" McKendrick asked. "And what have these two men done to warrant such treatment?"

"They've been stealing from the company, that's what they've done. I caught them hoarding pelts that should have gone into the storehouse."

McKendrick glowered at the two men, who refused to meet his gaze. In a voice that quivered with rage, the Scotsman asked, "Is this true?"

"N-no, sir, I swear it's not," one of the men said. "This is all just a misunderstanding. We'd never cheat the company, sir."

"I can show you the pelts, Mr. McKendrick," Brown said coolly. "Also the cave not far from here where these two have been storing them. I noticed them sneaking around there the last time I left the fort, so I thought I'd best see what they were doing."

Frantic, the other man said, "It's not true! Brown's out of his head—"

"Shut up." Brown prodded him in the back of the neck with a pistol muzzle. "I know what I saw."

"I believe ye, Brown," McKendrick snapped. "I thought it was taking longer than it should have to accumulate enough furs for our first shipment from this fort. Now I understand why." He looked over at Hodgkins. "Have these two locked up in the smokehouse, Lloyd. When the first shipment goes east, they'll go with it. I want them sent back to England to stand trial for their theft."

"Yes, sir," Hodgkins said.

Brown held up a hand. "Wait a moment. You're convinced of their guilt, Mr. McKendrick?"

"Indeed I am."

"Then there's no need to waste time and money putting them on trial, is there?"

With no more warning than that, Brown lifted the pistols in both hands and pulled the triggers.

The blast of the shots was deafening. The hapless thieves jerked forward, eyes bulging grotesquely, as the balls from Brown's pistols entered their heads from behind. Blood ran from their noses and ears as they pitched to the puncheon floor. The stench of death filled the room.

McKendrick stood behind the desk, rooted to the floor, his features frozen in a mask of shock. Hodgkins stared at the twitching corpses and let out a high-pitched wail before crumpling as if his bones had turned to water.

Finally McKendrick regained the use of his tongue. "My God, man!" he shouted. "What have ye done?"

"Simply carried out the will of the man who represents law and order in this part of the world, sir," Brown said as he reloaded the pistols. "I'm referring, of course, to you."

"But I didn't tell ye to kill them!"

"You said they were guilty. I thought this was the simplest, most direct way of dealing with the problem. I assure you, sir, once word of this gets around—and you know how the men talk amongst themselves—anyone who's been considering a spot of pilferage will think twice before they kipper off with any of the company's plews."

McKendrick passed a trembling hand over his face. His normally ruddy features were pale.

Slowly he said, "You're undoubtedly right about that, Brown. I trust you'll, ah, dispose of these two?"

"Of course, sir." Brown tucked away the guns.

Hodgkins let out a moan and pushed himself into a sitting position. His eyes were closed, and when he opened them and confronted the grisly sight before him, he swayed as if he might pass out again. But McKendrick's whiplash of a voice drove him to his feet before that could happen.

"Notify the company that these two men were killed in an unfortunate . . . accident, Hodgkins." McKendrick clasped his hands behind his back and rocked on his toes. Now that he had regained his composure, an idea occurred to him. "And, Hodgkins, never mind about that list of possible commanders for the expedition across the border. I think I've already found the right man for the job." He fixed his gaze on Brown. "Interested?"

"I'm not sure exactly what job you're talking about, Mr. McKendrick, but I'm always interested in anything that will help the company—and myself, of course."

McKendrick stepped around the desk, carefully avoiding the bodies and the puddles of blood that surrounded them. He extended a hand to Brown and said, "Get rid of these two, as I told ye, and then come back here. I think we have a great deal to talk about, ye and I."

"Yes, sir," Brown agreed.

And as he shook the young man's hand, McKendrick felt a surge of satisfaction. With Brown in charge of the group going south, the London and Northwestern could not fail to establish a foothold in the American Rockies—because Simon Brown would not hesitate to kill anyone who got in his way.

Clay Holt looked over the group gathered beside the Yellowstone River and tried not to dwell on the misgivings he felt. The majority of them were inexperienced or hostile toward him—or both. It would take more than a little luck for them to make it safely to the Pacific coast. And luck was sometimes in short supply out on the frontier.

"I believe we're ready to move out, Mr. Holt," Professor Franklin said with an eager expression.

"All right, Professor. We'll head northwest starting off. You've strayed a mite from your original path. If you'd kept going in the same direction, you'd have wound up down in Colter's Hell. Might've got through the mountains that way, but it would've been rugged."

"Whatever you say, Mr. Holt. You're in charge."

Clay felt the baleful gaze of Harry Lawton on him as Franklin made that statement. Lawton, after all, was the one who had gotten the party off the trail in the first place. It had to be galling to him to listen to this.

Not that Clay cared much about Lawton's feelings. As long as the man did as he was told, that was all that really mattered.

With Shining Moon at his side, Clay strode to the front of the group and angled away from the river. Professor Franklin and his daughter Lucy were behind him, followed by Rupert von Metz, Lawton, and the other men. Proud Wolf and Aaron Garwood brought up the rear. Clay wanted someone he could trust to keep an eye on their back trail.

Clay carried a bundle of beaver pelts on his back, as did Shining Moon and most of the others in the party. Despite the weight of the furs, Shining Moon would keep up with him all day and never lose a step. He knew that she prided herself on things like that.

They would be on foot for several days, perhaps a week or more, and the going would be tough. But once they reached the land of the Shoshone, they could trade furs for horses, and after that the trip would go more quickly. For the most part the Shoshone got along well with other tribes, even the Piegans and Bloods, and they had provided horses for Lewis and Clark's expedition several years earlier. He might even run into some who remembered him from that journey, Clay thought. He wondered how Sacajawea and her baby, little Pomp, were getting along.

The day was beautiful, with bright sky and towering clouds that seemed to mirror the snowcapped peaks below. The snow would remain on most of the peaks all summer long, despite the heat at the lower elevations. Today the spring air was crisp, not too warm, not too cool, and filled with the sweet scent of flowers blooming in the meadows that filled the valleys.

No wonder he loved this country and never wanted to live anywhere else, Clay thought as he walked along through it. It could be stark and hard at times, even brutal, but there was beauty here the likes of which could be found nowhere else on God's green earth.

The expedition pushed on all morning with few complaints, only those uttered in muffled voices by Lawton and his cronies. Clay had expected Professor Franklin and Lucy to tire quickly, but neither of them asked for extra rest stops, even when their pace slowed toward midday. Rupert von Metz also kept up, although his face grew taut with anger every time he glanced at Clay. Clay was aware of how von Metz felt, but he did not care as long as the Prussian caused no trouble.

They left the Yellowstone behind during the morning and stopped for the noon meal in a verdant park at the foot of a mountain. The men sank gratefully to the ground to sit cross-legged and gnaw on biscuits and hardtack.

Proud Wolf and Aaron moved up from the rear to join Clay and Shining Moon, and as they did, Clay asked them, "Any sign of people behind us?"

"I sure didn't see any. How about you, Proud Wolf?"

The young Hunkpapa agreed. "Those Blackfoot will not bother us again."

"Wasn't worried about the Blackfoot in particular," Clay mused. "But it's good to know they're not back there."

Professor Franklin and Lucy joined them, and as Franklin sat down, he gestured with a hand holding a biscuit. "These mountains around us, they're still part of the Rockies, correct?"

"The upper end of the range known as the Absarokas," Clay replied. "Another day or two and we'll be cutting west, through the valley of the three tongues of the Missouri. The going'll really get rough then, because we'll be heading up to the dividing ridge."

"The top of the Shining Mountains," Franklin said, awe in his voice. "I wasn't sure I'd ever get to see it for myself."

"We're not there yet," Clay pointed out dryly.

Franklin chuckled and said, "No, but you'll get us there, Mr. Holt. I have every confidence in you."

Clay was not sure he liked having somebody put that much trust in him, especially not a pilgrim like Franklin. However, he would do the best he could to keep his charges alive and get them where they were going.

Once they were past the dividing ridge it would still be a hell of a long way to the Pacific, Clay thought, but if they could get their hands on some horses, the route to the Columbia River would not be too hard to traverse. And when they reached the Columbia, they could build canoes to carry them the rest of the way. With luck they would reach the Pacific by early fall. If the boat from the American Philosophical Society was waiting, Clay and his companions could get this bunch off their hands and settle down to wait out the winter there on the Pacific coast. That would mean not returning to this part of the country until the next spring. He would lose a season's trapping, but Franklin had promised to make up for the loss. Besides, he could not leave these folks on their own out here in the wilderness; they would die for sure, and Clay did not want that on his conscience for the rest of his days.

Might as well make the best of it, he told himself. There were worse ways to spend a summer than trekking across this wild and glorious country.

* * *

Aaron Garwood pushed himself to his feet when the meal was over and Clay had called out the command to get under way again. The months he had spent with Clay, Shining Moon, and Proud Wolf had toughened him more than he would have thought possible. Even his left arm, weak from being broken by Clay during the bad times in Ohio, had grown stronger. When he had first come to the frontier with his brother Zach, Aaron had figured he would wind up frozen to death, drowned in some river, or stuck full of Indian arrows. He could still die in those ways, of course. But with what he had already learned from Clay and the things he would learn in the future, he figured he at least had a fighting chance for survival.

Nearby, Rupert von Metz was also getting to his feet, struggling with the cases that contained his canvases and paints.

"Would you like me to give you a hand with some of that?" Aaron said without giving it a thought.

Von Metz looked up at him and frowned. "No, I would not like for you to give me a hand, as you so quaintly phrase it. Do you think for an instant that I would entrust any of my work or materials to a man who is only half a step above the level of an aborigine?"

"Didn't mean to offend you," Aaron said shortly, reining in a surge of anger. "I just wanted to help."

"Well, I don't need your help."

"Fine." Aaron turned away, wondering if von Metz had been born with that burr under his longjohns.

Aaron drifted back to the rear of the column as it formed up again. Proud Wolf walked beside him.

"That man von Metz does not like you," Proud Wolf said quietly.

"I don't reckon he likes much of anybody except himself," Aaron said.

That was not strictly true, however, he saw a moment later. Although loaded down with the goods he was carrying, von Metz went over to Lucy Franklin and extended a hand to help her up. Aaron could not hear what she said to von Metz after he had assisted her to her feet, but she was smiling, and then she laughed at something he said in return. When the group set out, von Metz was walking beside Lucy and conversing with her.

Aaron's eyes narrowed. He did not trust von Metz, did not trust him at all, and he figured Lucy would be wise not to trust him either. Of course, it was not his place to say anything to her—

"Clay told us to keep an eye on the back trail, remember," Proud Wolf reminded Aaron, breaking into his thoughts.

"You're right. I reckon Miss Franklin can look after herself. After all, she is a grown woman."

And that, Aaron reasoned, was part of the trouble.

The afternoon passed without incident, although the party did not cover as much ground as it had during the morning. The professor and Lucy grew more exhausted, and Clay was smart enough to recognize that and adjust the group's pace accordingly. Aaron felt grateful for that; he did not want Lucy to suffer.

Von Metz walked alongside her most of the afternoon, allowing Aaron no opportunity to talk to her. But that evening, as they were making camp in a little bowl in the foothills of the Absarokas, Aaron saw his opportunity. Lucy had sat down on a large rock and slipped her shoes off, and she was rubbing her sore feet. He went over to her.

"Bear grease is good for that," he said.

Lucy looked up at him. "I beg your pardon?"

"Bear grease is good for foot miseries like that."

Flushing in embarrassment, Lucy quickly put her shoes on again. "My feet are fine, thank you, Mr. Garwood."

Aaron sensed that he had offended her, but he did not see how. Hurriedly, he added, "I was just trying to help—"

"Is this buffoon bothering you, Miss Franklin?"

Aaron's head jerked around when he heard Rupert von Metz's voice. The Prussian stood there, an expression of annoying smugness on his face.

Aaron knew he might be making a mistake, but he could not prevent himself from saying, "You just keep out of this, von Metz. It's none of your business."

"Perhaps it is," Lucy snapped. "Rupert is just trying to make sure I'm all right, and I appreciate that."

Von Metz smiled, then glanced coldly at Aaron. "I think what Miss Franklin is trying to say is that you should leave her alone, Garwood."

Aaron ignored the man's mocking tone and looked at Lucy. "Is that what you're saying, Miss Franklin?"

Lucy appeared more confused and upset with every second. She hesitated, then said, "I meant no offense, Mr. Garwood. You just took me by surprise, that's all."

"Then you don't want me to leave?" Aaron shot a triumphant look at von Metz, who glowered back at him.

"I don't know what I want."

Clay Holt stepped up behind her and said, "I think what Miss Franklin really needs is for you two young bucks to leave her alone. I reckon we've all got enough to think about without you two acting like a couple of bull moose."

"Damn it, Clay—" Aaron ended his objection

midsentence. Clay was right, of course; he nearly always was. There were more important things to worry about than scuffling with von Metz over a woman. There would be time enough for that once they had reached the safety of the Pacific coast.

Aaron sighed. "I'll gather some firewood."

"Good idea," Clay said dryly. "Why don't you help him, Mr. von Metz?"

Von Metz drew himself up and declared, "I do not turn my talented hands to such common tasks."

"Well, then, you might not turn them to eating, either," Clay said. "Everybody in this bunch pulls his weight from here on out, understand?"

For a long moment the tension in the air was thick as Clay and von Metz stared at each other. Lucy stood between them, turning from one man to the other.

Finally von Metz shrugged his narrow shoulders. "As you wish. I will be magnanimous enough to go along with your request, Holt, ridiculous though it may be."

"Don't care what you think of what I tell you, just as long as you do it," Clay shot back. He strode away, and Lucy watched him go.

Aaron took a deep breath and wished that he could handle himself as well as Clay did. He was not sure he would ever have that much confidence.

"I will gather firewood, but not with the likes of you," von Metz said icily to Aaron. "I will go that way. I would appreciate it if you would choose another direction."

"Fine by me," Aaron replied curtly. "I'm not that fond of your company, either." He turned on the heels of his buckskin mocassins and walked away.

"Wait, Mr. Garwood!" Lucy called after him.

Aaron stopped and looked over his shoulder. Von Metz had stalked off, too, but he also came to a halt and watched as Lucy walked over to Aaron.

"I'm sorry, Mr. Garwood," she said. "I didn't mean to cause trouble between you and Mr. von Metz."

"I don't reckon you caused the trouble," Aaron said, glancing at von Metz's taut expression.

"Well, I just wanted to say that I appreciate your concern."

And then she smiled at him.

Aaron felt as though his throat had constricted and he couldn't breathe. He could hear his heart pounding, and his face was getting warm. God, he had never known that the smile on a woman's face could be so potent!

Suddenly he was aware of the bustle of the camp going on around him. His friends Clay, Shining Moon, and Proud Wolf were only a few yards away, as was Lucy's father. None of them were paying much attention to the conversation now that Clay had broken up the potential trouble, but to Aaron it seemed as though all of them were staring at him.

He swallowed hard and said, "That's all right, Miss Franklin. Just don't you worry about it."

"Thank you, Mr. Garwood. I'll let you get on with your chores now. And I'll try that bear grease as you suggested."

Still smiling, she walked away.

Aaron forced his muscles to work. He strode out of the bowl where they were camped into the trees of the surrounding hills. He had no trouble finding branches on the ground there for firewood.

When he was about twenty yards from the edge of the bowl, von Metz stepped out from behind a nearby tree and said, "Garwood."

The two syllables were fraught with menace, and Aaron turned quickly toward the Prussian, halfway expecting to see a gun or a knife in the man's hand. He was ready to drop the armload of firewood and grab a weapon of his own if need be.

Von Metz, however, was unarmed, except for an armful of branches.

"Thought you were going the other direction," Aaron said.

"I circled around here so that I could talk to you in private," von Metz replied. "I abhor conducting personal business in full view of everyone else. It's quite undignified."

"What the hell is it you want?" Aaron asked bluntly.

"Just this: Stay away from Miss Franklin. She is a refined young lady who has no need of attention from a man like you."

Aaron's jaw tightened. "That's none of your damned business, is it?"

"You may dispense with the hostile attitude, my unwashed friend."

Somehow, von Metz made the word *friend* sound like a curse.

"I did not come here to fight you," he continued. "My wish is not to battle with you over Miss Franklin like two dogs squabbling over a bone. My sense of honor will not allow me to stoop to that level. However, I do wish to ask you a question. Just what do you believe someone like yourself could offer a woman such as Lucy?"

Aaron blinked. He had not thought about it that way. In fact, he had not really thought about the matter at all, other than to form a liking for Lucy and an intense dislike for this arrogant young Prussian. But he realized with a sinking feeling that von Metz was right. Lucy was accustomed to finer things than Aaron could ever hope to give her. And she was probably a lot smarter than he, too, considering that a professor had raised her. Aaron did not have a thing to offer her, at least nothing that really mattered.

"You made your point," he said quietly to von

Metz. "Now get the hell away from me and stay away."

"As you wish." Von Metz gave a mocking smile, then headed back toward camp, still carrying the firewood.

Aaron followed a moment later, his expression bleak. He had been fooling himself thinking that Lucy might be interested in him. That would not happen again.

They would probably be scalped by the Blackfoot anyway, he thought, so what the hell did it matter?

Chapter Nine

The situation of Pittsburgh is unrivalled with respect to water communication, with a great extent and variety of country; and would also be so in beauty was it not hemmed in too closely by high and steep hills.

—Fortescue Cuming
"Sketches of a Tour to the
Western Country"

Pittsburgh had grown since Jeff Holt had last visited the settlement. In fact, it could no longer be considered a settlement, he thought as he stood on the walkway of the keelboat and regarded it as they drew nearer. The place was now a city.

Situated in the triangle created by the Allegheny and Monongahela rivers as they came together to form the Ohio, Pittsburgh had originally been settled by the French from Canada and called Fort Duquesne. Eventually it had been taken over by the British and renamed Fort Pitt. The town of Pittsburgh had grown up around the fort. The British were long gone, of course, having been driven out during the Revolution, and now Pittsburgh was about as American a place as anybody could find.

The rivers and the city were enclosed by high, steep, wooded hills to the north, south, and east. The point of land on which Pittsburgh had been established was fairly level, as was the terrain to the southwest, where the Ohio flowed. As the keelboat passed Robinson's Point and Smoky Island, just south of the city, Jeff spotted several large buildings, which he decided must be factories of some sort, although he had no idea what was manufactured there. It appeared that Pittsburgh had become a center not only of trade but of industry.

Eugene Burke stepped up beside Jeff and laid a hand on his shoulder. "Well, what do you think, Mr. Holt?"

Jeff gave a whistle. "I never expected the place would have changed this much."

A faint tingle of unease went through him. Accustomed as he had become to the wide open spaces of the West, he had felt a little confined by Marietta, which was not much more than a village compared to Pittsburgh. How was he going to cope with all the buildings and the people? And if the thought of visiting Pittsburgh made him so uncomfortable, how the devil would he survive in New York?

Jeff swallowed hard and stared at the houses and stores rising on the point just ahead.

"Yes, Pittsburgh's come a long way from the frontier community it used to be," Burke said. "Why, when I first came out here, there were fewer than half a dozen taverns in the whole town. Now there are at least four times that many."

"Is that so," Jeff replied. He supposed people measured progress in different ways.

The keelboat veered into the Monongahela. Pittsburgh's wharves and shipyard were on the left bank, just past the main part of town. Jeff watched the streets and buildings slide by, then tried to count the vessels anchored ahead. He gave up when he reached two dozen—which, according to Eugene Burke, was approximately the number of taverns in Pittsburgh.

Henry and Dorothy Holt lived on Wood Street, about six blocks from the riverfront—at least that was what Jeff recalled from his previous visit to his uncle and aunt's house. He was certain he could find the place, but if he had any trouble, he knew someone would be able to direct him. Henry Holt was a cabinetmaker, one of the best carpenters west of the Appalachians, and surely well-known in the town.

As the crewmen tied the keelboat at a vacant dock, making fast a rope from the wharf to the cordelle in the center of the vessel's roof, Burke turned to Jeff and extended a hand.

"I hope you'll pay me a visit while you're here, Mr. Holt," Burke said. "You can find me at the Green Archer Tavern just about any evening. The least I can do is buy you a drink after you saved my life twice."

"I told you not to worry about that," Jeff said as he shook hands with the gambler. To take any sting out of the words, he added, "If I get a chance, I'll stop in and say hello."

"I hope so. Now, I'd best see about getting Beau unloaded."

Jeff could hear the racehorse moving restlessly below in the cargo hold. Beau was going to be glad to get his hooves back on dry land, Jeff thought.

One advantage of traveling light was being able to disembark easily. With his possibles bag, powder horn, and shot pouch slung over his shoulder and his Harper's Ferry rifle in his hand, Jeff was able to step across to the dock without waiting for a crewman to run a plank over the gap.

People, horses, wagons, and carts were everywhere, or so it seemed to Jeff. The air was full of shouts, laughs, and curses. Aptly named, Water Street ran the length of the town along the riverfront, and as Jeff took a deep breath to calm his jumping nerves, he plunged into what appeared to him to be utter chaos.

You could spend a year on the frontier and not see this many people, he thought as he wove his way through the crowds. To his left was the river, to his right a long line of warehouses and other businesses. Finally, after what seemed like a mile but was actually four blocks, he reached a broad avenue with a signpost declaring it to be Wood Street. Jeff had been hoping that Wood Street would not be as busy as the promenade along the river, but even more people were there.

He made his way past bakeries, tobacconists, saddlemakers, butcher shops, barbers, millineries, and general mercantile stores. His eyes were wide with amazement as he strode along. He had thought Steakley's Trading Post had carried a little bit of everything, but there were many more goods to be had here, a hundred times more.

And the taverns! Burke had been right about the taverns. Since getting off the boat, Jeff had not been able to walk a block without passing at least two of them. It seemed that people in this town worked a great deal and played just as hard.

But he noticed other signs of civilization, too. Up ahead on a corner were an Episcopal church and a Presbyterian meetinghouse. Beyond them, the street was lined with residences, and the heavy traffic thinned out somewhat.

He hailed a man in a wagon as he passed the

sanctuaries and said, "Excuse me, sir, but do you know if Henry Holt still lives near here?"

The man hauled his team to a halt and looked down at Jeff. "Henry Holt," he repeated slowly. "Any relation to Ned Holt?"

Jeff had a cousin named Ned, who had been about ten years old the last time Jeff visited. "That's right."

The wagon driver spat into the dust of the street. "I know where Ned Holt lives. Right up there. Third house on the left." He pointed to the house, and from the way his expression twisted, Jeff could tell that he was not fond of Ned.

That puzzled Jeff. He remembered Ned as an active, friendly boy. But he only said, "Thank you," then started down the street again.

The man in the wagon called after him, "If you've got a score to settle with Ned Holt, watch yourself. I hear he's a tricky one."

Jeff was bewildered. Why would the man assume he held a grudge against Ned? It sounded as if Ned was not thought highly of around here, which was surprising.

On the other hand, some folks in Marietta did not think much of the Holts, either. It was all a matter of how you looked at things.

The young blond man stretched lazily on the soft bed, enjoying the feel of the bed linens. The warm, silky smooth skin of the woman nestled against him felt even better.

It was the middle of the day, and sunlight was streaming in through the lace-curtained window of the bedroom. Somehow that made what had happened here earlier seem even more deliciously sinful. Affairs such as this were customarily carried out under the cover of darkness, when it was easier to slip in and out of a married woman's bedroom.

The young man propped himself up on an elbow and threw the sheet back. Preening under his gaze, the woman rolled onto her back and stretched her arms over her head, giving him a good look at her full, pillowy breasts, her generously rounded belly, and the lush curves of her hips and thighs. Her dark hair spread out on the pillow around her head.

"Do you like what you see, Ned?" she asked with a giggle that was only slightly unbecoming in a woman of thirty-some years. It was clear that the young man's attention made her feel like a girl again.

"You know I do, Phyllis," Ned Holt replied, leaning over to brush his lips against hers. He traced the kiss along the line of her jaw, then down to the soft hollow of her throat. Phyllis closed her eyes, tilted her head back, and shivered as his lips drew closer to the coral tip of one breast.

A door slammed downstairs.

Ned sat bolt upright, the passion that had gripped him an instant before fleeing as if it had wings. Phyllis gasped, brought her hands to her mouth, and uttered a mewling sound that was almost a moan of terror.

"Not your husband," Ned said hoarsely. "That couldn't be your husband."

"There's no one else it could be," she whispered. "But he wasn't supposed to be back until tomorrow!"

Heavy footsteps were coming up the stairs. The steps sounded purposeful, and Ned had no doubt where they were heading.

He saw no point in arguing about why Phyllis's husband had returned to Pittsburgh a day early; he had to get out of there—fast.

He was out of bed in a flash, no longer interested in Phyllis's brazenly displayed charms. Snatching up the breeches that he had hastily thrown aside earlier, he jammed his legs into them and pulled them up around his hips. He grabbed his shirt, which lay crumpled in a corner, tossed it over his shoulder, and picked up his boots as he hurried toward the window.

Next to it was a sturdy latticework trellis. Ned had checked on that out of habit the first time he had paid a visit to Phyllis Hastings. They had met in a Liberty Street tavern. She was quite beautiful—although he sensed her attractiveness would desert her before too many years passed—and so he had forgotten all about the pledge he had made to himself not to become involved with married women again.

That had been several weeks earlier, several quite enjoyable weeks. But now Ned listened to the footsteps coming down the hall and knew he had been a fool—again.

He slid the window open, threw a leg over the sill, and tossed his boots down into the alley behind the house. Then he tugged his shirt on over his head. Leaning to the side, he reached for the trellis.

Inside the bedroom, the door was thrown open, and a red-faced man stormed in to glare at Phyllis, who was still cowering nude and terrified on the bed.

"I knew it!" the man shouted. "I knew you were nothing but a no-good trollop—"

Ned did not wait to hear any more. Finding a handhold and foothold, he swung over onto the trellis. Phyllis's husband continued to rave at her, and Ned hoped that by reaching the ground in time, he might get away without having a shot taken at him.

It was awfully tiresome being shot at by angry husbands. That was one reason Ned had vowed to leave married women alone in the future.

"Fred! He's out here, Fred!"

The shout came from below Ned and startled him so badly that he almost lost his grip on the trellis. Grabbing the latticework more tightly, he pulled himself against the house and craned his head around to see who was down there yelling. He saw another pudgy, middle-aged man, probably one of Fred Hastings's friends or business associates.

Hastings's head emerged from the bedroom window. "Come back here!" he shouted at Ned. "Come back here, damn you, and face it like a man!"

Ned had no intention of doing that. He was only eight feet off the ground now. He jerked his head back and forth, looking from Hastings in the window to the man waiting in the alley, who called, "I'll get him, Fred! The bastard won't get past me!"

We'll see about that, Ned thought.

Suddenly Hastings stuck his hand out the window—and in it was a pistol. "Stop or I'll shoot!" he cried.

The whole situation was so ludicrous it would have been laughable, Ned realized, if he weren't the one with a pistol aimed at him. Stuck halfway up a wall outside a married woman's bedroom window . . . It was the kind of story that would have given him quite a chuckle had he heard someone else tell it.

But from the livid look on Hastings's face, the man was ready to shoot him.

With a yell, Ned pushed himself away from the wall and plummeted toward the man on the ground.

They crashed together with bone-jarring impact and fell to the dirt of the alley. Luckily, Ned landed on top, so that while he was shaken by the collision, the other man was stunned and had the wind knocked out of him. He lay there thrashing around and gasping like a fish out of water as Ned rolled quickly to one side and leapt to his feet.

His eyes searched wildly for his boots until he spotted them in the dust a few feet away. He lunged toward them and grabbed them up as Hastings shouted from the window, "Stop, damn you!"

Ned heard Phyllis cry, "Leave him alone, Fred!" He glanced up and saw her face over Hastings's shoulder as she struggled with him. Her arms were around his chest, trying to tug him back from the window. He shoved her away roughly.

While Hastings was distracted, Ned seized the opportunity to run. He dashed down the alley, away from the house. Behind him, a pistol cracked.

Grimacing, he hunched his shoulders as he ran, anticipating the horrible impact of a pistol ball striking his back. Nothing happened, though, and he kept running toward the narrow lane at the end of the alley. Hastings's shot had missed, and by the time the man could reload his pistol, Ned knew he would be out of range.

He had always been a fast runner, even as a boy. He put that skill to good use now.

Never again, he told himself as he sprinted toward safety. Never again would he dally with a married woman, no matter how lush or willing she was. Forbidden charms were often the sweetest, but they were not worth the danger involved.

Maybe this time he would keep that promise.

Behind him Fred Hastings leaned out the window and bellowed, "I know you! And you'd better stay away from my wife, by God, or next time I'll kill you, Ned Holt!"

Henry Holt's house was a whitewashed frame structure with two stories. He had built it himself with the help of his four sons, the youngest of whom was Ned. As a youngster Jeff had thought it large and roomy, and looking at it now, he was still impressed. His uncle had done well for himself.

Flagstones formed a walk leading across the neat front yard to a small porch. Jeff stepped up to the door and used the brass lion's-head knocker to rap sharply. After a moment he heard quick footsteps on the other side of the panel, and then it swung back to reveal a pretty young blond girl about ten years old.

Her eyes widened as she looked up at the visitor, and after a second she squealed, "Jeff? It *is* you!"

He had to look twice to be sure of the girl's identity, so much had she changed since the last time he had seen her. But then he grinned and said to his sister, "It's me, Susie."

Susan Holt threw herself into Jeff's arms and hugged him tightly around his waist.

"Edward! Jonathan!" she cried. "Come quick! Jeff's here!"

Rapid footsteps sounded in the hall just inside the door, and two young boys bounded out of the house. Both of them grabbed Jeff, staggering him. His little brothers had grown, too.

Dark-haired Edward, who would be thirteen years old now, was only about a foot shorter than Jeff. Jonathan, sandy-haired and stockier than any of his brothers, was eight. He hung on Jeff's left arm and whooped exuberantly.

His expression having lit up, Edward now tried to look more solemn as he stood back and held out a hand to Jeff.

"It's good to see you again," Edward said, holding back his joy in favor of the maturity he had always sought. But when Jeff grasped his hand, Edward gave up and pumped it for all he was worth before throwing an arm around Jeff's shoulders again.

"What's all this uproar?" a deep male voice asked. A slender man with iron gray hair appeared in the doorway and looked out at the happy group gathered on the step.

"Hello, Uncle Henry," Jeff said.

Henry could be a dour man at times, but a smile creased his leathery face as he recognized his nephew. He shook hands with Jeff, his grip as strong as ever from his carpentry work.

"Jefferson Holt! What in blazes are you doing

here in Pittsburgh? We all thought you were out west somewhere, trapping beaver and fighting Indians."

"I was until a while back," Jeff replied. "But now I'm heading east, and I couldn't come this way without stopping to see the youngsters, and you and Aunt Dorothy."

"Well, I should say not!" Dorothy Holt stepped out of the house to stand beside her husband. A diminutive woman, still attractive despite the silver streaks in her dark hair, she stepped forward and hugged Jeff tightly. "We're so glad to see you, Jeff! I couldn't believe my ears at first when I heard Susan saying that you were here."

"I'm here, all right, big as life and twice as ugly."

"You're not ugly!" Susan protested. "You're just . . . rugged-looking."

Jeff laughed. He supposed that was the polite way to describe him. He had a week's worth of beard on his face, and it had been longer than that since he'd had a bath—not counting the dunking in the Ohio during the battle with the river pirates. But the members of his family were certainly a sight for sore eyes, and he supposed they were looking at him the same way.

"Well, there's no need for all of us to stand around outside like this," Henry said. "Come in, Jeff, come in. Welcome to our home."

Henry took Jeff's hat and rifle, then led the group into a spacious parlor furnished comfortably without being ostentatious.

"I'll fix us some tea," Dorothy said. "Jeff, you just sit right down and make yourself at home."

Jeff settled himself on a sofa as Dorothy bustled off to the kitchen. Susan and Jonathan sat with him, while Edward took a wing chair at the end of the sofa. Taking out a pipe and tobacco pouch, Henry sat down in an armchair nearby.

"How long are you going to be with us, Jeff?" Henry asked as he filled his pipe with tobacco.

"Not very long, I'm afraid." Jeff hesitated, unsure of how much to say about the quest that had brought him there. Then he decided to plunge ahead and tell them the whole story. They were family, after all.

"I'm just passing through, heading for New York."

"New York?" Henry repeated in surprise, and the youngsters reacted the same way.

"You mean you haven't come to take us back to Ohio?" Susan asked.

"Why in the world are you going to New York, Jeff?" Edward said.

Jonathan just looked disappointed.

"I'm looking for Melissa," Jeff said heavily. "She's not living in Marietta anymore."

Henry put the pipe in his mouth, struck a match, and puffed. Then he said, "In that letter she sent upriver with the children, she didn't say anything about not staying in Marietta. In fact, I got the feeling that was what she was planning."

"That's what I thought, too." Jeff paused, then said, "Maybe I'd better back up a mite. I don't reckon I've ever thanked you for taking in these youngsters, Uncle Henry. I don't know what I would have done if it hadn't been for you and Aunt Dorothy."

With a wave of his hand, Henry said, "Don't you worry about that. We couldn't have been happier when they showed up and said they needed a place to stay. All of our own young'uns have married and moved away, you know. Except for Ned."

In his uncle's voice was a peculiar heaviness when he mentioned Ned, Jeff thought, and again he wondered why people acted strange when the subject of his cousin came up. But now was not the time to pry into that.

"Well, you really eased my worry," Jeff said,

"and Clay's, too. Melissa was supposed to come with the children, but she must have changed her mind at the last minute."

"You mean her father talked her out of it," Edward said. From the expression on his face, anyone could see that he did not care much for Charles Merrivale. "We were looking forward to her coming with us."

"I wish she had, Edward, I wish she had. Then I would have known where to find her. She and her folks were gone when I got back to Marietta, and the most I could find out about where they went was from Mr. Steakley. He seemed to remember something about them heading for New York."

Henry grunted. "Doesn't sound very certain to me."

"No, sir, it's not. But it's the only lead I've got."

"Well, I can understand why you're going there," Henry said. "It must've been quite a blow when you got to Marietta and found your wife gone."

"I felt as though I'd been punched in the stomach," Jeff said.

Henry puffed on his pipe one last time, set it in the ashtray on the table next to his chair, then clapped his hands on his knees. "Well, no point in dwelling on that now. Tell us what you've been doing with yourself these past couple of years."

"Yes," Jonathan echoed excitedly. "Tell us about fighting the Indians!"

"Actually, I haven't fought that many Indians, Jonathan. Most of the ones I've met have become good friends. In fact, you've got a sister-in-law who's a Hunkpapa Sioux woman named Shining Moon."

"No!" Susan exclaimed. "Clay married an Indian woman?"

"And she's as fine a lady as you'll find anywhere," Jeff said. "She's got a younger brother named Proud Wolf, and I reckon he's just about the best friend I've got out there in the West. Proud Wolf and Shining Moon saved our skins a time or two. And I mean *our* skins, not the beaver pelts."

Before Jeff could say anything else, the front door of the house opened again, and a man entered the foyer, slamming the door behind him and stopping short when he reached the parlor entrance and saw Jeff sitting there. He was tall, broad-shouldered, and brawny, with blond hair. He stared at Jeff in surprise.

"Hello, Ned," Henry said in a flat tone. "Come in. Your cousin Jeff was just telling us about his life in the West."

"Jeff?" Ned Holt acted as if he could not believe his eyes or his ears. "Is that really you, Jeff?"

Jeff stood up and held out a hand to his cousin. Just like Pittsburgh, Ned had grown considerably since Jeff had seen him last. Ned was four or five inches taller and about forty pounds heavier than his older cousin.

"It's me, all right," Jeff said. "How are you, Ned?"

A couple of long strides brought Ned face to face with Jeff. He ignored the outstretched hand and with an exuberant whoop swept Jeff into a bone-crushing bear hug. "Son of a bitch! How the hell are you, cousin?"

"Ned!" Henry said sharply. "Put the lad down, son. And watch your language! There are still children in this house, you know."

Ned set the startled visitor back on the floor and said sheepishly, "Sorry, Jeff. Hope I didn't squeeze the daylights out of you."

Jeff was trying to draw some air back into his lungs. "No, that's . . . that's all right, Ned. I reckon you're just glad to see me."

"Damn right!" Ned winced and went on, "Sorry again. Guess I'm just a little carried away."

Jeff could smell whiskey on Ned's breath, and he

realized that his cousin was a little drunk, even though it was the middle of the day. That came as a surprise. Henry and Dorothy were Congregationalists, like most of the Holts, and they had never approved much of drinking.

"Sit down and go on," Ned said eagerly. "I want to hear all about the West." He pulled up a straight-backed chair, reversed it, and straddled it as Jeff took his place on the sofa again.

A moment later Dorothy entered, cast a stern glance at Ned, and said tightly, "I thought I heard you come in, son. Have some tea with us. It'll do you good."

"No, thanks, Ma," Ned said. "I just want to hear all about Cousin Jeff's adventures out west."

"I'm not sure I'd call them adventures," Jeff said wryly. "Misadventures, maybe."

For the next half hour, he talked about some of what he and Clay had seen and done in the West, leaving out most of the violence and bloodshed and glossing over the rest. He explained about Shining Moon and Clay, and that he and Clay had been accepted into the Hunkpapa tribe almost as brothers. To his surprise Ned was even more full of questions than the children, and as Jeff looked at his cousin, he saw something shining there that did not come from liquor.

What he saw, Jeff realized, was wanderlust, the same thing that had gotten hold of Clay at an early age and sent him west at the first good opportunity. Jeff himself had experienced that feeling at times, although his odyssey to the mountains had come about by necessity rather than any great desire to roam. But he could understand how Clay had felt, and he saw the same thing now in Ned.

"I'm going out there one of these days," Ned said when Jeff paused in his storytelling. "I've got to see that country before it gets all civilized."

"I reckon it'll be awhile before that happens. It's a big land, and it's going to take a lot of people to fill it up. I don't know if that's even possible."

"Are you going back?" Ned asked.

Jeff answered without hesitation. "Someday. But I don't know when."

"Well, when you do, maybe I can go with you."

"If I were you, son," Henry said, "I'd worry more about exploring some unknown territory right here in Pittsburgh. Say, the inside of that factory where you're supposed to be working."

Ned shrugged off his father's sarcasm. "That's just a job, Pa. It doesn't mean anything. It's not like what Jeff and Clay have experienced out on the frontier. That's a whole different way of life."

"Not really," Jeff said, not wanting Ned to romanticize things too much. "A man has a job to do out there, too, and most of the time it's pretty hard work. But he does what he has to if he wants to survive."

"Yes, but he's free. There's no freedom in working for wages."

Henry scowled. "I don't believe I'll ever understand you, Ned. Why, if I felt like you do, this family wouldn't have any—"

"Jeff, you'll be staying a few days with us, won't you?" Dorothy asked, her question cutting across her husband's rapidly rising voice. It was clear she did not want the discussion to escalate into an argument. She gave Henry a stern look, and he settled back in his chair.

"I can stay for a few days. I'm anxious to get on to New York and start looking for Melissa, though."

"Why, I can imagine! It must have been horrible to go home expecting to find your wife and then her not be there."

"It's about as bad a feeling as I've ever run across."

Dorothy stood up. "We still have a spare room, even with the children here. Edward, why don't you show your brother where it is?"

"Sure," Edward said, bounding up from his chair. "Come on, Jeff."

As Jeff got to his feet, Ned popped up, too, and slapped Jeff's back.

"It's going to be great having you here, cousin," he said. "I know the best places in town to have a good time, and I'll show them all to you!"

"Well, I don't—"

"You'll do no such thing," Henry cut in. "It's bad enough you seem to have dedicated your life to carousing, boy. You're not going to drag your cousin into it as well!"

Ned shrugged. "We'll see. Come on, Jeff."

As Jeff followed Ned and Edward through the house, Susan and Jonathan trailed along behind, unwilling to let their big brother out of sight just yet. Despite the circumstances, Jeff had to admit that he was happy to see the three of them again. Knowing they were all healthy and in good spirits would make it easier to continue his search for Melissa.

Ned and Edward escorted him to a cheerful, airy room on the second floor of the house. A four-poster bed with an embroidered spread stood in the center of the room. Jeff rested a hand on the bed and pushed up and down.

"A bed to sleep on," he murmured. "The past couple of years I've gotten used to a rope bunk or a blanket roll on the ground."

"Sounds like a hard life," Edward said.

"It can be," Jeff admitted. "But it's got its advantages. When a man gets accustomed to the open sky over his head, it's hard to leave it behind."

"Damn, but that sounds good! You've got to tell me more about it, Jeff." Ned lowered his voice a little. "I, ah, might have to leave town before too much longer, and I've been thinking about heading west myself. Edward, not a word of this to my ma and pa."

Edward nodded. "Sure, Ned. I understand."

His brother might understand, but Jeff did not. "What's wrong, Ned? Are you in some sort of trouble?"

"Nothing you need to worry about, cousin." Ned grinned broadly and slapped Jeff on the back again. "You've come a long ways. You'd better get some rest. Before you move on, you're liable to need all the strength you've got!"

Jeff did not like the sound of that at all. But Ned was probably exaggerating, he reasoned.

From what Jeff had seen so far, Pittsburgh looked like a busy, industrious, but peaceful town. But appearances, as he knew all too well, could be deceiving.

Jeff talked more in the days that followed than he had in the past year. At least that was how it seemed to him. A man got used to silence on the frontier, to speaking only when necessary and keeping his words and thoughts to himself. But under the nearly constant questioning of his siblings, not to mention his cousin Ned, Jeff spun yarn after yarn. He answered their queries tolerantly and cheerfully, glad to be with them and remembering how he himself had reacted when Clay first returned to Ohio after his journey with Lewis and Clark. Jeff had been the one full of questions then.

He got some respite while the children were at school and Ned was at work. He spent that time helping his uncle in the cabinet shop behind the house. Unlike the others, Henry was as taciturn as a frontiersman himself, and he kept his attention focused on the work at hand.

Jeff enjoyed the sawing and hammering, the smell of cut wood, the faint hot tang of a saw blade warm from use. He had never minded hard work, and he found it kept his mind off his reason for being in Pittsburgh.

Always lurking at the edge of his thoughts, however, was Melissa. He had been willing to postpone his search for a few days to visit his family, but his patience was not as great as he had hoped it would be. By the time he had been in Pittsburgh a day and a half, he was itching to get started on his quest again, but he swallowed that impatience and forced himself to concentrate instead on his brothers and sister, his aunt and uncle, and his cousin. He enjoyed the time he spent with them, almost in spite of himself, although he resisted Ned's invitations to accompany him for a night on the town.

By his third night in Pittsburgh, though, he knew he would have to be moving on soon. He had enough money left to buy a good horse, so he decided that at supper that evening he would ask Henry to recommend a stable where he might find such a mount.

Shortly before the evening meal, Dorothy entered the parlor, looked around, and said, "Ned's not here yet. Where do you think he could be?"

Henry was sitting in his favorite armchair, puffing on his pipe and reading the current issue of Mr. John Scull's *Pittsburgh Gazette,* which boasted on its masthead that it had been established in 1784 as the first newspaper west of the Allegheny Mountains.

He rattled the newspaper and snorted. "Knowing that boy, he could be in any of a dozen or more taprooms."

"He always comes home for supper," Dorothy said. "You know that, Henry. I'm worried about him."

Jeff looked up and said, "Ned seems to be the type who can take care of himself, Aunt Dorothy." He was seated on the sofa, examining some of the schoolwork Susan and Jonathan had been proudly showing him.

"Oh, I know that, but I still worry. It's a mother's job, I suppose."

Jeff put down the paper Susan had given him. "I'd be glad to go look for him and make sure he's all right."

"Would you, Jeff? Supper won't be ready for a while. I'll tell you where to find the nail factory. You'll probably meet him on the way there."

Henry lowered his newspaper and sat forward in the chair. "You don't have to put yourself out, Jeff. I'm sure Ned's all right."

"I don't mind," Jeff said as he stood up. "I've been wanting to see a bit more of the city before I move on, and this will give me a chance."

"Can we come with you?" Susan asked.

Jeff glanced out the window and saw the shadows of evening. "No. It's getting dark, so I think it would be better if you two stayed here, Susan."

Both youngsters looked disappointed. Jeff was glad Edward was up in his room working on his studies; otherwise, he would have been asking to come along, too.

As Dorothy told him how to find the nail factory, located on Grant Street several blocks away, Jeff went into the foyer and put on his jacket and hat. His rifle was leaning in a corner, and his pistol was lying on a small table, but as he reached for them, he hesitated. He was going on a simple errand, and he should have no need for the firearms. If he did run into trouble, he always had his hunting knife. But it was unlikely he would encounter any problems in as civilized a place as Pittsburgh.

He strode out into the evening, enjoying the warmth that lingered in the air. Fewer people were on the streets now, since most were sitting down to their evening meal.

Jeff walked briskly toward Grant Street, which ran along the eastern edge of town. The closer he got to that district, the more taverns he saw. Given Ned's fondness for liquor, Jeff agreed with Henry that Ned had most likely stopped at one of them for a drink before going home. He decided to look into the ones he passed.

He had checked two taverns and seen no sign of Ned when a shout from up the street caught his attention. In the thickening dusk, he saw a figure dart out of another drinking establishment and run in his direction. The man was moving so quickly that his feet went out from under him, and he went sprawling on the cobblestones, rolled over, and sprang back to his feet. As he did, other men boiled out of the tavern.

"There he is!" one of them cried. "Get the bastard!"

Jeff froze as the fleeing man ran toward him. There was something all too familiar about him. . . .

"Come back here, Holt!" shouted one of the pursuers. "Stop, damn you!"

It was Ned, all right. His aunt had been correct, Jeff thought. Her youngest son was definitely in some sort of trouble.

"Ned!" Jeff called. "Over here, Ned!"

Ned was already racing in Jeff's general direction, but he veered directly toward him in response to the shout. As his cousin pounded up to him breathlessly, Jeff caught his arm and jerked him to a halt.

"What is this, Ned?" Jeff demanded.

Panting, Ned threw a frantic glance at the four men chasing him. They were not far away, but they were slowing down slightly since they had caught sight of Ned being confronted by someone else.

"Come on, Jeff!" Ned said desperately. "We've got to get out of here!"

"I'm not going anywhere until I find out what this is all about." Jeff owed a great deal to his aunt and uncle for taking in the children, and he was not about to turn his back on his cousin while Ned was in trouble—but he was not going to step into a fight without learning what it was about, either.

Ned hesitated, his wide-eyed gaze leaping wildly from Jeff to the other men and back again.

"They say I owe them money," he finally admitted, "but it's all a big mistake!"

The four men were close enough to hear what Ned was saying. They slowed to a halt ten feet away, and one of them laughed harshly.

"A mistake?" he growled. "You made it, Holt. Now pay up, or we'll take the debt out of your hide!"

"You've been gambling, haven't you, Ned?" Jeff asked.

Again Ned hesitated, but then he jerked his head in a nod.

Jeff asked the other men, "How much does he owe you?"

"It ain't us he owes," the spokesman replied. "It's our boss. But the debt's a hundred dollars."

Jeff gave a low whistle of amazement. One hundred dollars was a hell of a lot of money. He looked at Ned, who gave him a sheepish grin and shrugged.

"All right," Jeff sighed. "I'll pay you. But I'll have to go back to the place I'm staying."

"That won't do," the spokesman for the group said. "We got to have the money now. Either that, or Holt gets a beatin'. And he'll still owe the money after that." The man squinted at Jeff in the gloom. "Why're you trying to help this bastard, anyway?"

"He's my cousin."

"So you're a Holt, too, eh?"

"That's right," Jeff said sharply. He did not like the scornful tone in the man's voice.

"Well, get the hell out of here. You ain't got no part in this, even if you are related. Go ahead, turn tail and run like your cousin here."

Jeff looked at Ned, who was nervous and agitated and was clearly restraining himself from fleeing. The block they were standing on was practically deserted, and the other pedestrians in sight seemed to be avoiding the confrontation. In this part of town, it was doubtful that anyone would even summon a constable in the event of trouble.

Jeff took a deep breath. "I don't like the way you talk, mister. I said I'd pay you if you'll let me go get the money. You'll have to be satisfied with that."

The four men exchanged glances.

"Nope." The spokesman shook his head. "You're outnumbered two to one, mister. You got no right dictating terms."

"Then you'll have to settle for nothing," Jeff said coldly.

"Jeff . . . " Ned's voice was tight with anxiety. "I don't think this is such a good idea."

A faint smirk played over Jeff's mouth. None of the men were carrying guns as far as he could tell.

"You can run from this pack of dogs if you'd like, Ned. I'd rather not."

The leader of the toughs said, "You're a stupid bastard just like your cousin, mister. But don't say we didn't warn you."

With a shouted curse he leapt forward and swung a fist at Jeff's head. The other three hired ruffians were right behind him.

Jeff ducked the wild, roundhouse punch and stepped closer to the man, hooking a hard blow to his belly. A quick shove sent him staggering back into one of his companions.

In the meantime, one of the other two had slammed a punch into Ned's jaw, staggering the younger Holt. Ned caught his balance, blocked the next punch, and crashed his own fist into his opponent's face. The man's nose flattened under the impact, and he let out a howl of pain.

Jeff went on the offensive, tackling the fourth man and bearing him backward. The man's heel caught on a loose cobblestone, and he fell heavily, taking Jeff with him. Jeff landed on top of him and heard a satisfying *crack* as the man's head hit the street.

In the next instant a booted foot smashed into Jeff's side. The kick lifted him off his fallen adversary and sent him rolling along the grimy street. The man who had kicked him pounced after him and drew back his foot for another blow, but as his foot lashed out, Jeff twisted his head out of the way and grabbed the man's leg. A quick yank sent him tumbling.

Ned traded punches with the man Jeff had tangled with to start the fight. Now that the fracas was under way, he was holding nothing back. He slugged his opponent, took a punch, and slugged again, then reached out suddenly to grab the man's shoulders and jerk him forward. Taken by surprise, the man had no chance to resist. Ned lowered his head and butted the man in the face as hard as he could.

A few feet away Jeff threw himself on the man he had just spilled and hit him twice, a left and a right that drove the man's head first one way, then the other. The man went limp, stunned by the combination of blows.

Jeff rose to his feet and turned to face the next opponent, but he saw that he and Ned were the only ones left standing. Three of the men were either out cold or too stunned to keep fighting, while the fourth huddled on his knees and held both hands over his shattered nose. Blood made dark trails on the backs of his hands in the twilight.

Breathless, Ned said, "Well, I reckon we taught them a lesson. Come on, cousin. Let's go home."

"Hold on, Ned," Jeff said sharply. "Do you have any money?"

Ned blinked in surprise. "Some."

"A hundred dollars?"

"Not hardly."

"Give me what you've got." Jeff held out his hand.

"Wait a minute! What's the idea, Jeff?"

"A man ought to at least try to pay his debts," Jeff said stubbornly. "Give me the money."

Grumbling, Ned reached into his pocket and pulled out a handful of coins and a couple of folded bills. He handed them to Jeff, who walked over to the leader of the ruffians. The man was half conscious now, moaning and moving around a little. Jeff dropped the money on his chest.

"That's a start," he said, not knowing or really caring if the man heard what he was saying. "I'll see that your boss gets the rest of what he's owed." Jeff prodded the man in the side with the toe of his boot. "But stay away from my cousin. Holts don't take kindly to being pushed."

He turned and walked away, then looked over his shoulder and snapped, "Come on, Ned."

Ned hurried after him. "That was one hell of a fight, Jeff. You can really handle yourself. You must've been in a lot of brawls out there on the frontier."

"Not many," Jeff replied tightly.

He did not mention the urge he had felt during the fight to pull his knife and sink it into his opponent's belly. To Ned this had been nothing more than a rough game, but to Jeff, after spending two years in the wilderness, a fight was usually a matter of life and death. You killed your enemy before he could kill you.

He took a deep breath and pushed those thoughts away. He was back in civilization now, and things were different. But he was still the same man, and he knew now what he had suspected all along: No matter where he went, he would always carry some of the frontier with him.

Chapter Ten

As the expedition headed west through the valley where the three branches of the Missouri River ran, Clay was glad to see that Aaron Garwood and Rupert von Metz were keeping their distance from each other. Von Metz was a natural-born troublemaker, Clay had decided after their clash of a few days before, and the last thing he wanted was to have the two young men at each other's throats over Lucy Franklin.

Lucy seemed to be fond of both of them, although Clay had caught her casting longing glances in his direction several times. He ignored the looks—and hoped that Shining Moon would continue to do so, too.

The land of the valley was a flat, grassy plain, with the Absarokas falling away in the distance behind the travelers and the main body of the Rockies rising far ahead of them. Called the Shining Mountains by the Indians, the Rockies looked almost close enough to touch, but Clay knew he and his companions would have to travel for days before they reached the foothills.

As they hiked across the valley, Professor Franklin moved up alongside Clay and Shining Moon and asked, "Did you come through here with Captain Lewis and Captain Clark, Mr. Holt?"

Clay gestured to the north. "We were up that way about eighty miles or so on the westbound leg of the trip. On the way back, Captain Clark traveled through this area, but I wasn't with him. He and Lewis had split up into separate groups so they could cover more ground. I went with Lewis. And I've done most of my trapping south and east of here, around the Yellowstone and Big Horn rivers, so this is all virgin territory to me. I've heard plenty about it, though, from John Colter."

"John Colter," the professor repeated. "Oh, yes, I've heard of him. Supposed to be quite an adventurer. People have begun calling him a 'mountain man.' "

"Good name for him. He's seen more of these mountains than any other man alive, white or red, I reckon."

"I remember you made some mention several days ago of something called Colter's Hell. What's that?"

Clay chuckled as he replied, "John was out on one of his tramps through the mountains a couple of winters ago when he came upon a valley where hot mud bubbled up from the ground, boiling-hot water shot a hundred feet in the air, and demons rumbled around in the earth right under his feet—or so he said. The smell of brimstone was so strong it liked to have overpowered him. At least that's the way he tells it. Folks got to saying that he'd found the back door to hell, so it wasn't long before they started calling that area Colter's Hell."

"Incredible! Was there any truth to the story?"

"Most people didn't think so at first," Clay said. "But I've talked to enough Indians who have seen the same things that I sort of believe it now, even though I've never been there myself."

"This fellow Colter must be an amazing man."

"Tell the professor about the race," Shining Moon suggested.

"What race?" Franklin asked.

"Between Colter and about five hundred Blackfoot warriors," Clay said. "The stakes were his life. I know this one's true because I was at Fort Lisa when he came stumbling in after it was all over, naked and skinny as a rail with his feet cut almost to ribbons."

Franklin listened with rapt attention.

"Seems Colter was over on the other side of the Jefferson Fork." Clay pointed ahead of them. "That's on the far side of the valley. The Jefferson's the farthest west of the three tongues of the Missouri. Anyway, last fall he and another trapper name of Potts were up there on the canyon rim, about where it starts sloping down to the river. They got jumped by the biggest bunch of Blackfoot either one of them had ever seen. Potts tried to get away, but the braves filled him full of arrows. John had the sense to stay put. He figured he was dead either way, but he didn't see any point in rushing things.

"So the Blackfoot took his clothes and tortured him a mite—nothing too serious, you understand—then decided to have some real fun with him. They gave him a little start and told him to run for his life. Of course, they figured they'd catch up to him right away and kill him."

"How horrible!" Franklin muttered.

"Colter didn't care much for the idea, either," Clay said. "He'd told them he wasn't much of a runner, but that was an out and out lie. John Colter's about as fast on his feet as anybody you'll ever see. So he took off, running barefoot over those rocks, and when the Blackfoot came after him, they found they couldn't catch him after all. One by one, they fell back, their tongues dragging like a dog that's been running all day.

"All but one of them. He was the only one who could keep up with Colter. Now, John was heading for the Jefferson as fast he could, but he couldn't shake that one warrior. So when he got close to the river, he did the last thing that Blackfoot ever expected him to do: He turned right around and came straight at him.

"The Blackfoot was so startled that he tripped as he tried to throw his lance. He fell, and the lance went into the ground in front of John. That was all the chance John needed. He grabbed up that lance and stuck it right through the Blackfoot."

Clay glanced around and saw that Lucy Franklin and Rupert von Metz had moved up within earshot, too. He felt a little uncomfortable about relating the ghastly details while Lucy was listening, but he also knew from the expressions that she and the professor and von Metz wore that they would not be satisfied without hearing the ending.

"That Blackfoot was dead, but John knew the others would be coming along before too much longer. So he jumped into the river and found himself a place to hide, under a pile of driftwood that had floated along until it got snagged. Even in the fall, the Jefferson was mighty cold from snow melt, but Colter stayed there in that hiding place while the rest of the Blackfoot came looking for him. There was enough room under the driftwood for him to get air. Luck was with him; none of the Indians looked under that mess of wood. They went off searching for him, and he waited until it got dark. Then he slipped out from under the driftwood and swam downstream.

"Colter stayed in the river for about five miles,

then got out and rested some. There didn't seem to be any Blackfoot around, so his luck was still with him. He knew where he was well enough and figured the best thing to do was to strike out across country toward Fort Lisa. It was only about two hundred miles, and he'd walked it before."

"Two hundred miles! But he had no weapons, no food!" Professor Franklin observed.

"And he was buck naked, to boot," Clay agreed. "But he figured being hungry and footsore would be better than what the Blackfoot would do to him if they caught him. There were plenty of creeks along the way where he could get water, and for food, berries and bark were better than nothing. He started out that same night."

Clay concluded by saying, "Took him eleven days to cover that two hundred miles, but he made it. Like I said, I was there when he came in. I never saw anybody so worn out. But less than a week later, he'd outfitted himself and taken off again for the high country."

Into the awed silence that followed, Rupert von Metz said scornfully, "What a preposterous story! No one could possibly do such a thing."

"My husband does not lie," Shining Moon said coldly. "I, too, was there at the fort when John Colter arrived from his ordeal."

Von Metz scowled but was silent, as though unwilling to cast doubt on the word of a woman, even an Indian woman.

Quietly Clay said, "You'll find that lots of things happen out here on the frontier that might seem unbelievable to folks who have never been west. A man can do damn near anything, even outrun five hundred Indians or walk two hundred miles in his bare feet, if he wants to live bad enough."

"I'd like to meet this man Colter and talk to him," Franklin said. "I'm especially interested in that area you say he discovered called Colter's Hell. It sounds like something a scientist should investigate."

"Well, if we happen to run into him, I'd be glad to introduce the two of you, Professor," Clay said. "Or maybe sometime in the future, you and I could go take a look at the place ourselves."

"I'd like that, Mr. Holt." Franklin smiled. "I'd like that very much."

So would he, Clay realized. There were plenty of sights out here he had not yet seen, mountains he had not yet climbed, high grassy meadows he had not yet trod. The frontier was a beautiful place, and the best thing about it was that there were always new things to see and experience. This rugged wilderness was full of surprises.

Before he was through, Clay Holt vowed to himself, he would see all of it, from one end to the other.

They made camp that night beside the first fork of the Missouri. They had been able to trace its course for several hours before actually reaching it because the trees along its banks were visible as a low green line for many miles across the plain. The cottonwoods and willows grew to a respectable size here, and they would provide shelter and firewood so that the travelers would not have to burn dried buffalo chips.

Proud Wolf was given the job of gathering wood, and while a part of him wanted to protest that such a chore was woman's work, he did not argue with Clay. The time Proud Wolf had spent with his brother-in-law had taught him that everyone had to share in such tasks.

He picked up his rifle and ranged along the riverbank, heading upstream as he collected branches and twigs suitable for kindling. He had been in this broad valley once before, several years earlier, when the elders brought him and other young men there to teach them the buffalo hunt. The elders had demonstrated how to stalk the great shaggy beasts, using hides for concealment until they were close enough to bring down the massive creatures with lances and arrows. It had been a thrilling time for Proud Wolf, although he had never killed any of the buffalo himself. In fact, he had tripped and fallen on the hide he had been using as a disguise, and his feet had become so tangled in it that he could not get up. The debacle had almost caused a stampede, but Proud Wolf nevertheless remembered the experience with fondness, as it was the first time he had hunted with the warriors of his tribe.

Someday they will fully accept me as one of them, he thought as he filled his arms with firewood. *I will perform great deeds, and the women will sing songs of my bravery. . . .*

"Help! Dear Lord, someone help me!"

Proud Wolf's head snapped up. The cry was coming from somewhere behind him. He had traveled farther than he had intended, he realized, so caught up had he been in his recollections. The camp was probably a mile downstream.

The shouts continued, perhaps only a couple of hundred yards away, much closer to him than the camp was. Then he realized that he was hearing Professor Franklin's voice—and the man sounded terrified.

Proud Wolf dropped the firewood, grasped his rifle, spun around, and ran back the way he had come. As he ran he checked the weapon, making sure it was ready to fire as soon as he full cocked it.

He raced around a bend in the river, ducked past some cottonwoods, and came to a stumbling halt. The professor was fifteen feet up a willow, clinging to the trunk. Proud Wolf was a little shocked at the professor's climbing ability, given his bulky shape, but terror could give a man wings, and few things were more terrifying than a grizzly bear . . . like the one reared up on its hind feet at the base of the willow, swiping at Professor Franklin with a big paw.

The bear was a good-sized one, about seven feet tall and weighing at least six hundred pounds, Proud Wolf judged. He had seen larger bears before, but this one was undoubtedly big enough to pose considerable danger. Those paws with their long, curved, razor-sharp claws could open up a man from groin to gizzard. The beasts lost their temper easily, and Proud Wolf wondered what Professor Franklin had done to anger this one.

"Hang on, Professor!" he shouted. "Climb higher if you can, but do not slip!"

Proud Wolf was not sure if Franklin heard him over his own shouts and the bear's growling and snuffling. The grizzly's head swung around, and Proud Wolf knew it had noticed his presence. Silvertips like this one did not have good eyesight, but their hearing and sense of smell were keen.

The young Sioux lifted his rifle and cocked it, then hesitated. Killing a grown bear with one shot was a difficult feat, and once he fired, he would need at least half a minute to reload. In that amount of time the grizzly could easily reach him. Already riled, the beast would be angered that much more by being shot.

Proud Wolf had heard of men killing grizzlies with their knives, but he knew that was out of the question. He would be no match for the massive bear; the creature would tear him apart in seconds. But he had to do something. . . .

Then he heard a sudden rattling in the brush along the bank not far from him. Acting on a hunch, he darted toward the noise and pushed back the undergrowth: There he saw a single bear cub. The grizzly that had Professor Franklin treed let out a bellow of rage and lumbered toward Proud Wolf.

"Watch out, lad!" Franklin cried.

His pulse pounding in his head, Proud Wolf leaned over and scooped up the cub. It was still small enough for him to lift, but he had trouble hanging on to it as it struggled in his grip. He ran to the edge of the river, hesitated, and looked over his shoulder. The bear had covered more than half the distance between them and was closing rapidly.

Proud Wolf tossed the cub into the water.

The cub was crying as it landed with a splash, and the pitiful sound almost made Proud Wolf regret what he was doing. *Almost.* But he had to distract the mother bear some way, and the quickest method was to put the cub in danger.

Not that the cub was threatened too badly. The river's current was not swift, and Proud Wolf knew that bears could swim, even young ones such as this. But the cub's mother would probably dive into the water after it, anyway, so that she could grip the scruff of its neck with her teeth and haul it out of the river.

Proud Wolf was betting his life on that. He darted to the side, dropped the flintlock, and leapt toward a low-hanging branch as the bear thundered past him. Swinging his feet up, he hooked his knees over the branch and pulled himself up frantically, just in case the bear paused to swipe at him. However, the grizzly paid no attention to him, plunging into the river instead with a huge splash, sending a spray of water high into the air. It swam toward the cub.

Proud Wolf dropped from the tree and called, "Get down, Professor! Get down and run!"

Awkwardly, Franklin clambered down the willow, losing his grip near the bottom and falling the last few feet. He landed heavily and toppled onto the ground, and by the time Proud Wolf had picked up the rifle and raced over to him, he was sitting up and holding his left leg.

"I think I've twisted my ankle." Franklin looked

up at Proud Wolf, his normally ruddy features pale and drawn with fright and pain. "You run back to camp while that beast is occupied."

"No," Proud Wolf said curtly. "I will help you." He tucked the rifle under his left arm, then bent and slid his right arm around Franklin.

"But I can't run!" the professor objected. "That bear—"

"The bear is worried about her cub. If we can get out of here, she will forget about us." With a grunt of effort, Proud Wolf tried to lift Franklin.

The professor helped, levering himself to his feet with his other arm and his good leg while Proud Wolf supported the injured one. Proud Wolf looked over his shoulder again and saw that luck was with them. The grizzly was emerging from the stream with her cub—but on the opposite bank.

"Come on," Proud Wolf said, his voice showing the strain of hoisting even part of Franklin's considerable bulk. "We must hurry."

He thought about firing his rifle in the air in hopes of summoning help from the camp, then decided against it. Clay and the others might think he was just taking a shot at a deer to cook for their supper. Besides, he did not want to waste the time that would be needed to reload. It was more important to put distance between them and the grizzly.

Limping heavily, Professor Franklin made his way along the river with Proud Wolf's help. Every couple of minutes, the young Hunkpapa looked over his shoulder to make sure the bear was not in pursuit, but the brute seemed to have forgotten about them, just as he had hoped. The last glimpse he caught of the grizzly was of it disappearing into the brush on the far side of the river.

"We can slow down now," Proud Wolf told Franklin. "The bear will not bother us. They are quick to anger but equally quick to forget."

"Thank God for that! I certainly never intended to upset the beast. In fact, I didn't know she was anywhere near until I stumbled over that cub while I was studying the vegetation along the stream." Wincing in pain, Franklin went on, "All I could think to do was run and climb a tree. It wasn't until I was already halfway up that willow that I remembered bears can climb, too."

"The bear would have, when she got tired of swiping at you with her paw." Dryly he added, "You should not leave the camp alone, Professor."

"I know. But everyone else was busy, and I thought this would be a good opportunity to take a look at the foliage while there was still some light."

An idea occurred to Proud Wolf. "Next time you want to study something, will you take me with you?"

"So that you can protect me?"

"So that I can learn from you," Proud Wolf said sincerely. "This—this *science* of yours interests me. I wish to know more of it."

Professor Franklin smiled down at him. "You want to be my student, eh? That sounds like a fine idea, Proud Wolf. And at the same time you can keep me from getting into such trouble as I did today. It's a deal, my boy."

Proud Wolf beamed. He had already learned that the world contained many things about which he knew nothing. The arrival of the white men in the mountains had told him that; now, with the help of Professor Franklin, he would learn more about what lay beyond the territory roamed by the Hunkpapa.

He had already decided that one day he would travel to far lands and see the wonders they held. Great warriors were also great explorers, and he would be the greatest warrior of all.

* * *

"Oh, my God!" Lucy Franklin cried.

At the young woman's exclamation, Clay looked up sharply from his task. He had been forming a circle of rocks in which to build a campfire once Proud Wolf got back with the firewood, but that could wait. From the sound of Lucy's voice, there was trouble.

Proud Wolf and Professor Franklin were entering the camp. Franklin was limping heavily as though injured and was leaning on the young Hunkpapa man. Lucy ran forward to meet them. Clay followed at a slower pace.

"Father, what happened?" Lucy asked as she clutched the professor's arm. "Are you hurt?"

"Just a twisted ankle, that's all," Franklin told her. "But it would have been much worse had it not been for this lad. He saved my life."

Clay joined them and asked Proud Wolf, "Saved the professor's life from what?"

"Just a grizzly bear," Proud Wolf said in mock nonchalance.

"Old Ephraim?" Clay used the trappers' favorite term for the bears. "Don't see too many of them out on the plains like this."

"She was staying close to the river," Proud Wolf explained, "and she had a cub with her—as the professor found out."

"Oh, so that's what got her dander up. How'd you get her away from the professor?"

"I threw the cub in the river, then got out of the way."

Lucy stared at Proud Wolf. "You threw an innocent little bear cub in the river?" She sounded outraged by the admission.

"I had to get the bear's attention away from your father, Miss Franklin. She had him trapped in a willow tree."

"And soon she would have had me for dinner,"

Franklin put in. "Don't berate the boy, Lucy. His quick thinking saved my life."

"I'm sorry," Lucy said to Proud Wolf. "I didn't mean to snap at you. This—this wild country out here is sometimes beyond my comprehension."

Shining Moon, Aaron Garwood, Rupert von Metz, and Harry Lawton had gathered in time to hear what Proud Wolf and Franklin were saying, and following Lucy's comment, von Metz snorted and said, "It would take a lunatic to understand this land, my dear, since it seems to be wholly populated with them already."

Clay ignored von Metz and said to Franklin, "What were you doing when you got into trouble, Professor?"

"I'm afraid I wandered off quite carelessly while I was studying the trees along the river. I assure you, it won't happen again, Mr. Holt."

Lawton spoke up. "Next time you want to go off adventuring, Professor, let me know and I'll go with you."

The offer was one way for Lawton to get back in Franklin's good graces, Clay thought.

The professor winced with pain. "Thank you for your consideration, Mr. Lawton, but that won't be necessary. Young Proud Wolf here has agreed to accompany me each time I leave the camp."

"Sure, if that's what you want," Lawton said in a surly voice, then walked away.

Clay watched him for a second, then turned back to Franklin. "We've stood around here talking long enough. You'd better get off that bad leg, Professor. How'd you hurt it, anyway?"

"Falling out of the tree where that bear had chased me." Franklin limped to the center of the camp with Proud Wolf supporting him on one side and Lucy on the other. He sank down on the ground and stretched the injured leg in front of him. "I'm afraid I twisted my ankle rather badly."

"Well, this isn't a bad place to camp," Clay said as he hunkered on his heels next to the professor. "We've got more than enough supplies, so we'll stay here for a day or two or even longer, until you feel up to walking again. No point in pushing things and hurting that leg worse than it already is."

"Thank you, Mr. Holt," Franklin said fervently. "I'm sorry to be causing so much trouble—"

"Don't worry about it," Clay said. "This is your expedition, Professor, not mine."

"Perhaps, but we've put ourselves in your hands. I appreciate your understanding."

Clay clapped Franklin on the shoulder and then stood up. "We still need some firewood," he said, looking at Proud Wolf.

"I will return for it," Proud Wolf said.

Clay picked up his long rifle and cradled it in the crook of his left arm. "I'll go with you, just in case you run into Old Ephraim again."

Franklin lifted his head to look up at Clay. "Excuse me, Mr. Holt, but this is the second time I've heard you refer to the grizzly bear by that name. Can you tell me why?"

Clay had never really considered the question before. After he had thought about it for a moment, he said, "You saw that bear, with all the silver fur among the brown, like a grizzled old man. Didn't it look like somebody who'd be called Old Ephraim?"

"You know, now that I think about it in that light, you're correct. The name does seem suitable."

Clay strode off upriver, Proud Wolf beside him.

While the two of them gathered firewood, Shining Moon carefully removed Professor Franklin's boot and bound the injured ankle with wide strips of rawhide, tying them tightly so that the swelling would go down. Lucy watched as Shining Moon worked over her father's leg, as if suspicious that the Hunkpapa woman might try some heathen healing ritual. What Shining Moon was doing, though, was nothing more than good common sense. When she was finished binding the ankle, she propped Franklin's foot up on a round stone.

"Keep it higher than the rest of your leg, and that will help prevent more swelling," Shining Moon told the professor. "Tomorrow, I will make a poultice of roots and herbs and river mud to take some of the pain from your leg."

"Thank you, my dear," Franklin said gratefully.

"Are you sure that's such a good idea, Father?" Lucy said. "I mean, you won't know what's in this concoction Shining Moon prepares."

"I will be glad to tell you the things I will use, Professor."

"And I'd be very interested to know, Shining Moon," he said, "although I certainly trust you. But the medicinal and healing arts of your people are another area I'd like to investigate during this trip. I'm sure we'll have a profitable discussion."

Shining Moon traded smiles with the professor, and Lucy looked vaguely frustrated before she went back to unpacking the provisions.

That evening, as the entire group sat around the campfire, Professor Franklin related the story of his misadventure with the grizzly bear one more time. Proud Wolf looked rather embarrassed by the praise that Franklin heaped on him, but Clay thought the young man was enjoying being the center of attention.

After everyone had turned in for the night, except for the lookouts, Clay rolled up in his blankets with Shining Moon. There was nothing better than lying here, he thought, looking up at the brilliant stars in the huge vault of night sky, his woman's head resting on his shoulder.

She whispered, "Proud Wolf did a brave thing today."

"He did a smart thing today. Using that cub to distract the mama was quick thinking. But you're right about his being brave. It could've got him killed."

"I do not think Lucy Franklin realizes that. She does not like Proud Wolf or me."

"Oh, I reckon she just doesn't know what to make of you. Likely she never saw any Indians close up until she came out here. But I figure she wishes she were back in Massachusetts about now, right enough."

"Perhaps—if she could take you with her," Shining Moon said.

Clay looked at her in the starlight and saw that she was grinning. She was teasing him, but he did not mind. He leaned closer, intending to kiss her soundly.

A wink of light, seen for an instant from the corner of his eye . . .

He lifted himself on an elbow, peering toward the dark bulk of the distant mountains. Beside him, Shining Moon caught her breath in surprise at his reaction. She had been expecting a kiss, not this sudden tension on his part.

"What is it?" she whispered.

"Thought I saw something." His gaze was still fixed on the peaks. "A light, over yonder in the mountains."

Shining Moon twisted around to peer behind her at the Rockies. "They are too far away. You could not have seen anything."

"The light of a fire can carry a long way on a clear night." Clay lay down again. "But it's gone now, whatever it was."

"Perhaps it *was* a fire. It could belong to other trappers or to some of my people."

"Or to a band of Blackfoot or Arikaras."

She lifted a hand and rested her fingertips on his cheek. "Whatever you saw, it is far, far away and cannot touch us tonight. But you and I are together, as we should be."

"Can't argue with that." His head dipped toward hers, and his mouth found her warm, waiting lips.

But even as he kissed her, his mind was in the distant mountains, and he knew that whatever it was that had stirred his warning instincts was still there.

Waiting.

Chapter Eleven

From the number of religious houses and sects, it may be presumed that the sabbath is decently observed in Pittsburgh, and that really appears to be the case in a remarkable degree, considering it is so much of a manufacturing town, so recently become such, and inhabited by such a variety of people.

Amusements are also a good deal attended to, particularly concerts and balls in the winters, and there are annual horse races at a course about three miles from town, near the Allegheny beyond Hill's tavern.

On the whole let a person be of what disposition he will, Pittsburgh will afford him scope for the exercise of it.

—Fortescue Cuming
"Sketches of a Tour to the Western Country"

Jeff knew he could not stay in Pittsburgh any longer; his impatience to resume his search for Melissa was too great. The day after he had intervened in the trouble between Ned and the four toughs, he paid a visit to a nearby stable and bought a sturdy-looking bay mare.

"She'll make a good saddler for you, young fella," the liveryman said as he patted the mare's flank. "She's got a good gait, a pleasant nature, and plenty of sand."

"I'm sure I'll be well-satisfied," Jeff replied. "I'll need a saddle, blanket, and harness, too."

"Got quite a ride in front of you, eh?"

"All the way to New York City," Jeff said.

The livery owner, a short, slender, middle-aged man, squinted up at Jeff. "New York, did you say? You look to me more like the type to head west. What's in New York that'd take you back there?"

"A dream," Jeff heard himself saying.

That was true, he thought as the stableman went to get a saddle and the other gear he would need for the journey. As a young man—only a few short years ago, though the time seemed longer—he had dreamed of having a home and family: a good farm, a beautiful wife, a cabin full of rambunctious Holt kids. Melissa had been the centerpiece of that dream.

When Melissa and he were married, he had taken the first step toward fulfilling that dream. But their wedding had been marred by violence and death, and their happiness together had been short-lived. Fate, it seemed, had cruelly conspired to steal his dream away from him.

Jeff's jaw tightened. He was being maudlin, and he knew it. He and Melissa had had more than their share of bad luck, but there was no use in crying over it. The best thing to do was to forge ahead and try to put the situation right.

"Here you go," the liveryman said as he brought out a saddle, harness, and colorful blanket. "That'll take care of you. Whole thing'll run you, say—forty dollars?"

"Done," Jeff agreed. He took a pair of double eagles from his pocket and handed them over, then saddled the mare.

"Jeff!" a voice called from the street outside the livery barn. "There you are!"

Jeff saw Ned lunge through the entrance where the barn's double doors were swung back.

"Pa told me where he thought you'd headed. I need to talk to you, Jeff."

"I'm a little busy."

"This won't take long."

Jeff sighed. "All right. Wait until I get this horse saddled."

The liveryman looked Ned up and down and said to Jeff, "Friend of yours?"

"My cousin, Ned Holt."

"Oh." The man's voice was flat, hard. "I've heard the name."

Jeff looked at Ned. "Does everybody in this town know you?"

Ned just shrugged. "Word gets around."

"That it does," the liveryman said coldly. He walked off into his office.

Ned ignored the man's reaction and said to Jeff, "Let's go get a drink."

"Sort of early in the afternoon, isn't it?"

"Never too early for good whiskey. And I know a place that has the best in town."

Somehow that claim came as no surprise to Jeff. He cinched the saddle in place, then rigged the harness and bridle over the mare's nose. He took up the reins and led the horse out of the barn. Ned walked alongside him.

"The tavern's not far away. Come on."

Jeff let his cousin lead the way. Although he did not want a drink, playing along with Ned would be the quickest way to find out what he wanted to talk about. Jeff had a feeling he was not going to like what he heard.

Ned's destination was on Liberty Street, one of the two thoroughfares that paralleled the Allegheny River on the northwest side of town. As he and Jeff approached a sturdy-looking building, Ned indicated a signboard hanging from a pole outside the door. The sign showed the silhouette of a bowman with arrow nocked and bowstring pulled taut. The figure was painted a bright emerald green, and under it, in the same shade, were the words Green Archer Tavern.

Something about the name struck Jeff as familiar, but it took him a moment to recall that Eugene Burke, the gambler from the riverboat, had told Jeff that he could be found there. Surely there was only one Green Archer Tavern in Pittsburgh.

"I've heard of this place," Jeff said as he looked up at the sign.

"I haven't been here for a while, but the last time I paid it a visit, it had the finest liquor and the friendliest serving girls in the whole city," Ned said. "And that's all a man really needs to be happy, I always say."

Jeff could believe that, as well. Ned lived for the moment and had no concept of happiness that had to be worked for.

At the edge of the cobblestone street in front of the tavern was a hitch rail, and Jeff looped the mare's reins over it and fastened them with a jerk. "This won't take long," he murmured to the animal as he patted her.

"Here we are," Ned said, opening the door and ushering Jeff into the building. When Ned closed the door, the rectangle of afternoon sunlight that had fallen through the opening was cut off, and the interior of the tavern returned to its usual shadowy state.

Even in the early afternoon the shutters over the windows were closed. Lanterns burned at either end of the bar. The floor was sprinkled with sawdust. Thick beams stained a dark brown from clouds of pipe smoke supported the ceiling. Scattered around the room were heavy tables flanked by benches, and on the far side was a huge fireplace topped by a stone mantel. The fireplace was filled with cold ashes now.

A large circular table surrounded by chairs was tucked into a corner near the fireplace, and several men sat around it playing cards. Jeff glanced at the men, thinking that Burke might be one of them, but he did not see any familiar faces.

Women in low-cut dresses carried buckets of beer and glasses of whiskey on trays to the various tables, about half of which were occupied. A pair of bartenders in waistcoats toiled behind the long bar. The Green Archer was no common dive, Jeff decided as he looked around, but neither was it a high-class establishment. From the looks of things, it catered to men who took their drinking and gambling seriously.

The buzz of conversation in the room diminished slightly when Jeff and Ned entered, but it resumed so quickly that Jeff was unsure he had even heard correctly. Chances were, some of the men in the place had recognized Ned, who seemed to be known all over Pittsburgh, especially in places like this.

Ned steered Jeff toward an empty table and signaled to one of the bartenders by holding up two fingers.

"I don't want whiskey," Jeff said quickly. "Beer will be fine."

"Make it beer instead," Ned called out to the bartender, who nodded.

Jeff and Ned sat opposite each other, and a few moments later a serving girl brought them a bucket of beer and two mugs. Ned flipped her a coin and slapped her on the rump, drawing an outraged gasp and then a giggle from her.

"What did I tell you, cousin?" As she walked away, Ned watched her swaying hips. "Lovely, isn't she?"

Jeff had not paid much attention to the young woman, and if he had, he knew he would not find her nearly as attractive as Melissa. He grunted noncommittally.

"Why did you bring me here, Ned?"

Before answering, Ned dipped both mugs into the bucket, set one in front of Jeff, then took a deep swallow from the other. He wiped foam from his upper lip with the back of his free hand and leaned forward.

"I want to ask you a question, Jeff. It's about your trip to New York."

Jeff waited, and when Ned did not go on, he said, "Well? What about it?"

"Can I go with you?"

The words came from Ned in a rush, as if he'd had to summon up courage to voice it and did not want to wait until his determination bled away. For a change, the cocksure grin that bordered on arrogance was not on his face. Instead, he looked nervous and unsure of himself.

Jeff did not answer right away. He had been halfway expecting the question, but he was not sure what to say. To give himself time, he leaned back on the bench and drank from his mug. The beer was cool and, as Ned had promised, good.

"Why do you want to go to New York?" he finally asked.

"You saw the reason last night—or at least part of it."

"Those men who were after you?"

Ned lowered his eyes. "They're not the only

ones," he said quietly. "There are others I owe money to, and—well, there are some men who seem to be holding grudges against me."

"Now, why would they do that?" Jeff asked coolly. "It wouldn't have anything to do with their wives, would it?"

Ned managed to look proud and a bit ashamed at the same time, no easy task.

"Some women do seem to find my charms very appealing. I keep telling myself I should confine my attentions to the unmarried ones, but—"

"But it's hard for you to keep that vow, isn't it?"

Ned said nothing.

Jeff did not know whether to laugh at his cousin or chide him for his behavior. Ned was a wastrel, no doubt about that; his life was consumed by gambling, women, and liquor. *But he's so damned sincere about it,* Jeff thought.

"I take it you're really in danger," he said.

"As long as I stay in Pittsburgh, I am. But I could make a fresh start in New York—"

"A fresh start on more trouble, you mean."

"No. All that's behind me now, Cousin. No more women and no more gambling. I swear to that."

Jeff did not believe him for a second. Ned might think he meant that pledge, but Jeff knew it would prove impossible to keep. Still, Ned might be good company on the journey.

"What about Uncle Henry and Aunt Dorothy?" he asked. "How would they feel about your leaving?"

"They might be upset at first, but I'm sure they'd rather I go than stay here and get beaten up in some alley—or shot."

Ned had a point. For his own good he needed to get out of Pittsburgh. Jeff would be doing him a favor by helping him accomplish that, and surely his aunt and uncle would see it the same way, once they thought the situation over. It was a shame Ned had gotten himself into such trouble, but leaving town was probably the best solution.

He and Clay had left Marietta to prevent further bloodshed, Jeff recalled. Ned's problem really was not much different, except that it was of his own making, instead of being caused by some twist of fate.

Jeff was about to tell Ned he could come along to New York when the door of the Green Archer opened and a man entered, paused just inside the door, and peered around as if letting his eyes adjust to the dimness. Then he riveted his attention on the table at which Jeff and Ned were sitting. Quickly he yanked a pistol from his belt, cocked it, and leveled it at them, shouting, "I told you I'd find you, Holt!"

"Damn!" Ned grated. "Hastings!"

"That's right," the man said as he advanced toward the table, covering Jeff and Ned with the pistol. Behind him the other patrons of the tavern scurried for cover. "Fred Hastings. You've good cause to remember me, Holt, but I'll wager you remember my wife Phyllis even better. I thought you'd have the sense to stay away from her after I chased you out of her bed once! Instead, I find out you've still been sneaking around to see her!"

"Blast it, Ned!" Jeff exclaimed. "Have you completely lost your mind?"

"You don't know Phyllis, Jeff. That's really all I can say." He lifted his hands, palms outward, toward the man with the gun. "But I can promise you, Hastings, I won't bother her again. In fact, I'm leaving town. I'll be far away from Pittsburgh."

"You're not leaving," Hastings said grimly.

"Yes, I really am. I'm going to—"

"You're not going anywhere! You're going to be buried here in Pittsburgh, where I can visit your grave and have a good laugh every day, you goddamned—"

Hastings had moved up alongside Ned and Jeff's

table. Jeff saw the man's finger tighten on the trigger of the pistol, so he did the only thing he could: He upset the table, shoving it right into Ned and Hastings.

Hastings's flintlock pistol went off with a roar as he fell. Jeff could not tell if the shot hit Ned or not, and he did not take the time to find out. Instead, he jumped up from the bench and vaulted over the table. Hastings was struggling to get out from under it as Jeff landed on him. The man threw up an arm to block Jeff's blow, but he was too late. Jeff's fist caught him in the jaw, driving the back of his head against the sawdust-covered floor. Hastings went limp, his eyes open but glazed.

Jeff whipped around and knelt beside Ned, who was sprawled loosely on the floor. "Ned!" he said urgently. "Are you all right?"

Ned pushed himself into a sitting position and shook his head. "Banged my skull on something when I fell. But I'm not hurt. Hastings's shot missed, thanks to you."

Grasping Ned's upper arm, Jeff said, "Don't thank me. Let's just get the hell out of here."

As they stood up and turned toward the door, it was slammed open, and more men pushed into the tavern.

"There he is!" one of them exclaimed, pointing at Ned. "Where's Hastings?"

"Look there!" another cried, pointing to Hastings, still lying on the floor. "They've killed him!"

"Wait a minute—" Jeff began.

With clenched fists, the men moved forward.

"Fred wanted to do this by himself," one of them said grimly, "but now that you've killed him, Holt, we'll take care of you and your friend."

The odds were bad, but at least the men had not drawn more guns, Jeff thought. It looked as if once again, for the second time in less than twenty-four hours, he and Ned were going to have to fight their way out of trouble.

"Hold it!"

The voice crackled through the air from behind the bar. Jeff glanced in that direction and saw the familiar dapper figure of Eugene Burke. The gambler held a pistol, as did each of the two bartenders, and all three weapons were trained on the group advancing toward Jeff and Ned. The men stopped in their tracks.

Jeff noticed an open door behind the bar and figured that Burke had come through it, probably from a back room. The pistol shot must have drawn his attention.

"There's not going to be any more fighting in my place," the gambler said firmly. "Wrecked furniture costs money to replace, not to mention broken bottles of whiskey. Now, you men turn around and get out of here, and take your sleepy friend with you."

"But they've murdered Fred Hastings!" one of the men protested.

"No, they haven't, you damned fool," Burke said scornfully. "Look at him. He's coming around."

Indeed, Hastings was shaking his head and moaning. Jeff and Ned stepped away from him, and a couple of his friends hurried forward to help him to his feet. Hastings did not seem to know where he was or what was going on, but he was coherent enough to glare at Ned and start cursing.

"Get him out—now!" Burke said.

Hastings did not resist as his friends led him out of the tavern, but several of them cast baleful glances over their shoulders at Ned. Judging from their expressions, Jeff concluded that the matter was not yet settled.

After Hastings and the other men had left, Burke replaced his pistol under his coat, and the bartenders put their weapons under the bar. Burke went around the bar and walked toward Ned and Jeff, and for the first time he acted as if he recognized Jeff.

"I suppose that takes care of half my debt to you, Mr. Holt."

"As far as I'm concerned, the score is even." Jeff extended his hand toward Burke. "I have to admit, I was damned glad to see you. I remembered the name of this place and looked for you when we came in, but I didn't know you owned it."

"Yes, the Green Archer is one of my pride and joys, Beau being the other. He's running for the first time this Saturday. Why don't you come with me to the racecourse?"

"I'd like to," Jeff said, "but we won't be here by then. I'm heading on to New York, and Ned here is going with me. This is my cousin, by the way. Ned Holt. Ned, Mr. Eugene Burke."

"Oh, I know the notorious Ned Holt," Burke said dryly as they shook hands. "When we were coming up the Ohio on that keelboat, I didn't connect his name and yours, I'm afraid."

"I don't owe you any money, do I, Mr. Burke?" Ned asked nervously.

"No, my boy, you don't. You've always taken care of your losses to my satisfaction. Were those gentlemen after you because of a debt—or a woman?"

Ned looked sheepish. "A woman, I'm afraid."

"A man should never have more than two vices," Burke said. "That's all anyone can manage. You're just trying to do too much, Ned. That's your problem."

Jeff said, "We appreciate the help, Mr. Burke, but we'd better be going now. Ned probably has some getting ready to do if we're going to leave Pittsburgh tomorrow."

"I think that's a good idea," Burke agreed. "Sure I can't interest you in another drink to replace that spilled beer? On the house, of course."

"No, thanks," Jeff answered quickly, before Ned could accept the offer. "We've got to get going. Thanks again for the help."

"You're more than welcome. I'm glad you got to see my place—although it wasn't under the best of circumstances."

Jeff took hold of Ned's arm and steered him firmly out of the tavern. They paused just outside to look around in case Hastings and his friends were waiting for them, but they saw no sign of the men. Jeff untied his horse and led it down the street. Ned strode alongside.

"Do things like this happen to you every day, Ned?" Jeff asked.

"Well, not every day. But often enough that I think it's a good idea I'm leaving town."

"I hope your parents understand. But I'm glad you asked me if you could come along."

"Are you sure? I was afraid you'd say no."

"I thought about it," Jeff admitted. "But I don't think I could leave you behind now. I don't want you on my conscience, Ned Holt."

Henry and Dorothy Holt were understandably upset when their youngest son announced his intention of leaving town.

"Was this your idea?" Henry asked Jeff when he learned of Ned's plan.

"Don't blame Jeff, Pa. I was the one who asked him if I could go along. I just think it would be a good idea if I got out of Pittsburgh for a while. You know, until things cool off a bit."

"You mean until people forget about your gambling debts and your philandering?" Henry snapped.

"There's no need for talk like that, Henry," Dorothy said quietly. "We both know Ned has done some things he shouldn't have, but there's no point in dwelling on that now."

"I'm glad you understand, Ma. I'm only doing what I think is best for the whole family."

"And there are the other young men to consider, too," Dorothy went on. "It pains me to say it, Ned, but you haven't been setting a very good example for Edward and Jonathan."

"I know. And I'm sorry about that, too."

Henry looked at Jeff again and said, "Are you sure you want this rascal going along with you?"

"I don't mind. I think he'll be safer traveling to New York than he would be if he stayed here, at least for a while."

"How long will the two of you be gone?" Dorothy asked.

"I can't say. It depends on how long it takes me to find Melissa." *And I'll look until I do find her,* Jeff added silently.

"Good luck to you," Henry said as he shook hands with Jeff. "When will you be leaving?"

"First thing in the morning. I've tarried here long enough, not that I haven't enjoyed my stay. But it's time to be moving on."

"I understand." Henry paused, then added, "The young ones, though, they're going to be disappointed."

Jeff had already thought of that. He was not looking forward to their reaction, but the time had come to tell Edward, Susan, and Jonathan of his decision.

The first thing Edward said when Jeff had explained that he was leaving the next morning was, "Take me with you, Jeff. I'm old enough."

"No," Jeff said firmly. "You're still in school, Edward. All of you are. And you're helping Uncle Henry in his business. You're needed here."

"You mean you don't need me?" Edward asked in a voice tinged with bitterness.

"I never said that. But I'm going to be traveling quickly. That's why I decided to go cross-country on horseback, rather than continuing on up the Allegheny by keelboat. It's going to be a hard trip."

"I'm up to it," Edward said.

"You probably are. But that wouldn't stop me from worrying about you, and that would slow us down. My mind will rest a lot easier knowing that the three of you are in good hands here in Pittsburgh."

"I still don't think it's fair."

"It wasn't fair for my wife to disappear, either," Jeff told him, the words a little sharper than he intended. "Life takes all sorts of turns that aren't fair. All we can do is deal with them the best we can."

Edward nodded gloomily. "I guess you're right. But I don't have to like it."

"I don't like it, either," Susan said. She hugged Jeff tightly. "I was just getting used to you being here, Jeff, and now you're going off for who knows how long. Will we ever see you again?"

"Of course you will," Jeff promised. He returned Susan's hug, then slid an arm around the shoulders of Jonathan, who was struggling manfully not to sniffle. "I'll be back. One of these days, all the Holts will be together again. You have my word on that."

That promise mollified the youngsters a bit, and the family was able to enjoy a last quiet evening together. Ned stayed in, rather than going out one last time. It made no sense, he said, to risk getting killed on the very eve of putting all his troubles behind him.

Jeff made no comment, but he knew all too well that some of Ned's troubles might well follow him to New York. As long as Ned had such a healthy appetite for cards and women and whiskey, there was always going to be trouble in the vicinity.

Before dawn the next morning, Jeff was up, dressed, and going down the hall to Ned's room to shake him awake. Ned groaned and tried to bury his head beneath the pillow, but Jeff grasped his ankle and pulled him out of the bed, dumping him unceremoniously on the floor.

"Time to get stirring," Jeff told him. "I want to put a lot of miles behind us today."

"You're a cruel man, Jefferson Holt. It must be the middle of the night!"

"It'll be daylight by the time we leave. There'll be plenty of light to see the road. Come on."

Still grumbling and muttering, Ned got dressed, then followed Jeff downstairs. Dorothy was already in the kitchen cooking cornbread and ham and eggs for their breakfast.

"I'll send what's left of the cornbread and ham with you to eat on the road," she told them. "That way you'll have a little home cooking to start the journey."

"Thanks, Aunt Dorothy." Jeff sat down at the kitchen table in front of a steaming mug of tea.

"Henry's tending to your horses," Dorothy went on. "He knew you'd want to get a good early start."

She did not look at her son as she served breakfast to the two young men. When all the food was on the table, she said, "I'll go pack your things, Ned," and hurried out of the room before he could respond.

"Your mother's going to miss you," Jeff said into the silence that followed Dorothy's departure.

"I reckon so," Ned said gloomily. "I guess I've been quite a disappointment to her. All my brothers turned out so good, and me . . . Well, you've seen how I turned out."

"You're young yet," Jeff told him. "Things can change."

"Not easily. I figure some people were just born to trouble, and I'm one of them. But I'm going to try hard to make a fresh start in New York."

Jeff admired his cousin's determination while privately doubting Ned's ability to avoid the same sort of problems that had plagued him in Pittsburgh. Maybe Ned would surprise him, he thought.

Henry Holt came in from the small barn behind the house and said, "Your horses are saddled and ready to go, boys. Got your gear together?"

"Ma's tending to mine," Ned replied.

"Won't take me long to pick mine up," Jeff said. "I travel light."

"Comes from living in the mountains, I reckon," Henry mused as he slumped into a chair at the table. "I'd like to see those mountains one of these days."

"You, Pa? I figured you were the kind who'd be happy staying right here in town the rest of your life."

"There are things you don't know about your old man, son," Henry told him. "Bartholomew and I had a few rip-roaring times of our own, back in the days when everything west of the Alleghenies was dangerous ground. There comes a point in a man's life when he has to put all that behind him—but that doesn't mean he forgets what it feels like to be young and wild and anxious to see what's on the other side of the next hill."

Ned stared at his father as if he was amazed to hear such sentiments coming from Henry Holt's mouth. "You should have told me about all this sooner, Pa. I'd have liked to hear about it."

"You had enough of the wanderlust in you already," Henry said. "You didn't need me filling your head with stories and stoking that fire. Besides, your mother would've taken a broom to me if she'd heard me telling you about those days."

"What days?" Dorothy wanted to know as she came back into the kitchen carrying a pack for Ned.

"Never mind, dear," Henry said smoothly as he rose to his feet. He brushed a kiss across his wife's cheek. "The lads are ready to go. You'd best wake the young ones so they can say good-bye."

This was the part Jeff was dreading. He steeled

himself for the tearful farewells, and that was exactly what he got from Susan and Jonathan as the youngsters entered the kitchen still in their nightshirts and hugged him tightly. Edward's eyes were damp, but he managed to keep the tears from spilling as he shook hands with his brother.

"Next time you set off on some adventure, I'm going with you," he declared.

"I'd like that," Jeff said. Then he threw his arms around Edward for a last hug, not caring if he embarrassed his brother.

Meanwhile, Ned was saying his farewells to his parents. Dorothy was the only one crying, and she sobbed unashamedly as she hugged Ned and then Jeff, too. Jeff shook hands with his uncle while Ned said good-bye to his young cousins.

Then it was time to go.

They strode out into the gray dawn, two tall, brawny young men, carrying rifles and pistols and looking almost as grim as if they had been going off to war.

He was going to miss Pittsburgh, Jeff thought as he swung up into the saddle on the bay mare's back. He was going to miss his brothers and sister and his aunt and uncle. The visit had been a good one.

But it had only been a stopover on a much larger journey, and Jeff had known that from the first. It was time now to turn his eyes back to the goal that had led him away from Ohio in the first place.

It was time to go find Melissa.

"Well, that wasn't quite as bad as I expected," Ned said half an hour later as they rode their horses at a fast walk down the eastbound road from Pittsburgh.

Neither of them had spoken since the emotional parting at the Holt house. Now, Ned's flippant tone did little to disguise the fact that he had been shaken by the farewell, too, Jeff thought.

To change the subject, Jeff said, "Looks like it's going to be a warm day. The sun's only been up a little while, but it's already heating up."

"That's all right with me. I've had enough of the cold, gray winter. Give me some warm sunshine any day—and a pretty girl to share it with me."

Jeff heard the sudden thunder of hooves behind them and jerked his head around. Several riders came racing out of a lane Jeff and Ned had passed a moment earlier. They spurred their horses toward the two Holt cousins, the early morning sun glinting on pistol barrels.

"Hastings and his friends!" Ned said. "Damn it, I didn't think they'd come after us like this!"

"Ride!" Jeff called to him. "If we've got luck on our side, we'll outdistance them!"

As Jeff heeled the bay into a gallop, he slid his pistol out from behind his belt. He had no desire to kill any of their pursuers, but a well-placed shot might discourage them.

Twisting in the saddle as he and Ned pounded along the road, Jeff cocked the pistol and lifted it, then squeezed off a shot. He saw dust spout up in the road in front of the men chasing them. Several of the riders in the lead faltered as they flinched involuntarily from the shot, and that slowed down the others as well.

"Come on!" Jeff shouted to Ned, hunching forward over the neck of the mare and urging it on to greater speed. "We can make it!"

Ned's mount, a big buckskin gelding, ran neck and neck with the mare. Slowly the two of them pulled away from the pursuers.

Shots boomed behind them, and Jeff heard the faint whine of pistol balls passing near his head. He leaned forward even more, to make himself a smaller target. Beside him, Ned turned enough to throw a shot of his own over his shoulder, and then as Ned swiveled back to the front, Jeff saw that he was grinning.

This was all just an adventure to Ned, Jeff realized. And then to his shock he found that he was smiling, too.

He took off his hat, slapped it down on the rump of the mare, and cried out, "Faster, girl, faster!"

The mare surged ahead. Then Ned's mount drew even with the bay mare again, and side by side they plunged down the road, gradually drawing farther and farther away from their pursuers.

The chase was exciting, all right, Jeff admitted to himself. But he hoped fervently that the entire journey to New York was not going to be like this.

Part III

It may not be improper to mention, that the backwoodsmen, as the first emigrants from the eastward of the Allegheny mountains are called, are very similar in their habits and manners to the aborigines, only perhaps more prodigal and more careless of life. They depend more on hunting than on agriculture, and of course are exposed to all the varieties of climate in the open air. Their cabins are not better than Indian wigwams. They have frequent meetings for the purposes of gambling, fighting and drinking. They make bets to the amount of all they possess. They fight for the most trifling provocations, or even sometimes without any, but merely to try each others prowess, which they are fond of vaunting of. Their hands, teeth, knees, head and feet are their weapons, not only boxing with their fists, (at which they are not to be compared for dexterity, to the lower classes in the seaports of either the United States, or the British islands in Europe) but also tearing, kicking, scratching, biting, gouging each others eyes out by a dexterous use of a thumb and finger, and doing their utmost to kill each other, even when rolling over one another on the ground; which they are permitted to do by the byestanders, without any interference whatever, until one of the parties gives out, on which they are immediately separated, and if the conqueror seems inclined to follow up his victory without granting quarter, he is generally attacked by a fresh man, and a pitched battle between a single pair often ends in a battle royal, where all present are engaged.

—Fortescue Cuming
"Sketches of a Tour to the Western Country"

Chapter Twelve

Although Clay Holt kept his eyes open as the party he led crossed the valley of the three forks of the Missouri, he did not see any more unusual lights in the foothills of the Rockies' main range. As they drew nearer, what some members of the group had taken to be gray, overcast skies above the foothills were revealed to be the mountains themselves, towering seemingly to heaven.

As they paused one noon for a meal of jerky and hardtack, Professor Franklin peered in awe at the peaks that seemed to loom over them, although they were still miles away.

"My God," Franklin said. "They're so . . . majestic. But how in heaven's name will we ever get over them?"

Clay, squatting on his heels nearby, was smoking his pipe.

"It won't be easy, Professor," he said, "but there are ways. Trails and passes known to the Indians—"

"And to men such as yourself," the professor put in.

Clay shrugged. "I know some of them. But I'm mighty glad Shining Moon and Proud Wolf are with us. Any of the trails they haven't been over themselves, they've heard about from other members of their tribe."

Kneeling beside Clay, Shining Moon said to Franklin, "Teton Sioux do not like the high mountains, even though it is told by the old ones how our people came from them a long time ago. The hills and the plains are better. In my lifetime our people have moved slowly eastward and southward, coming down from the mountains in the land called Canada. We were driven to this land by the Blackfoot, the Crow, the Gros Ventre, and the Assinniboin. There is no shame in this, because always we have found better land awaiting us. And one day the Hunkpapa and the other bands of Teton Sioux will turn, and our enemies will regret ever rousing us from our sleep."

Soon the group packed up and resumed the journey, crossing the final and most westerly fork of the Missouri that afternoon. The land gradually sloped upward now, and they entered an area of sparse vegetation. This was the rugged, rocky terrain, dotted with cactus, over which John Colter had run his already legendary race with the Blackfoot. It was hard to imagine any man running naked and barefoot over such ground, let alone being able to outdistance attackers. But as Clay had said, people were able to accomplish amazing things when their lives were at stake.

Late in the afternoon, as they were looking for a

place to make camp for the night, Clay's gaze swept across the foothills before them, and he stiffened.

"Professor," he said, turning to Franklin, "you've got a spyglass in that gear of yours, don't you?"

"A telescope? Yes, indeed I do, Mr. Holt. Do you have need of it?"

"Break it out. I want to take a closer look at something."

"What is it?" Shining Moon asked.

"Not sure yet," Clay replied, his attention focused on the hills. "Thought I saw something moving around up there."

What he had seen could have been a family of bears, Clay thought, but the movement that had caught his eye had seemed human. He took the telescope that Franklin handed to him, then opened the instrument to its greatest length and lifted it to his eye. As he peered through the lens, the foothills seemed to leap closer to him. He moved the instrument slowly, scanning from side to side. After a moment he froze and held it steady.

"I thought so," he breathed as he watched a party of half a dozen or so white men outfitted in buckskins move along a ridge. He handed the telescope to Shining Moon and said, "Take a look. Right there above that white outcrop of rock." He pointed at the landmark.

"What is it, Mr. Holt?" Lucy Franklin asked.

"Looks like some other trappers."

Shining Moon handled the spyglass rather awkwardly, but finally she was able to hold it steady and locate the ridge where Clay had spotted the men.

"I see them," she said. "They are white men, that is certain. They have no pelts with them, though."

"Probably out on a scout," Clay said. "They must have a camp somewhere up there. Better let them know we're here." He turned to look at the group and ordered, "Three of you men fire your rifles into the air, one at a time."

Harry Lawton scowled. "Why would we want to do that? Waste of good powder and lead, if you ask me."

Clay suppressed the urge to tell Lawton that no one had asked him.

"Those fellows are right in the direction we're going. Chances are we'll be spending a night or two in the vicinity of their camp. I want them to know we're out here and heading toward them so that they'll be on the lookout for us. Life out here in the mountains is a pretty harsh, lonely existence most of the time, Lawton. Folks like to get together whenever they have the chance, swap some tobacco and a few yarns. You'd know that if you'd spent much time out here."

Lawton flushed angrily at Clay's last comment, but he said nothing. He nodded curtly to his men, and three of them raised their flintlock rifles. One by one they fired into the arch of sky, and the echoes of the blasts rolled across the hills.

Clay took the spyglass back from Shining Moon and again turned it toward the party of white men. He had located them and steadied the glass when the sounds of the shots must have reached them, for he saw them stop suddenly and lift their heads to listen, then look around. Even through the spyglass, he could discern little about their immediate reaction. But he did see that they turned abruptly and hurried in the direction they had come from, soon disappearing from view over the ridge.

"That's funny," Clay muttered as he lowered the telescope. "They took off like a grizzly was after them."

Lawton spat on a nearby clump of cactus. "Reckon they wasn't as anxious to make friends as you thought, Holt."

"Reckon not," Clay agreed, still puzzled by the men's reaction. But it was really none of his business, he supposed. Out here people did not force their company on others.

He waved his hand forward. "Let's move on. We've still got ground to cover before nightfall."

Simon Brown brought the ax above his head, then sent it slashing down against the log in front of him. The sharp edge of the axhead bit into the wood with a solid thunk. Brown grunted as he levered the ax free and lifted it for another strike.

He was shaping the log to join the others he had cut for the gate in the half-finished stockade fence that would soon enclose this outpost in the wilderness. The fort would be the London and Northwestern's first permanent foray into what was widely regarded as American territory.

But not much longer, Brown thought. Before he and his men were done, this entire area would be under British control—specifically, the control of the company and Fletcher McKendrick.

And McKendrick would be very grateful to one Simon Brown for all his help, grateful enough to pay Brown whatever he wanted. When he returned to England, it would be as a wealthy man, and he would spit in the faces of his father and older brother.

Damn the whole system of primogeniture anyway, Brown thought as he sunk the ax into the log once again.

The idea that Gerald was entitled to inherit his father's title and wealth simply because of an accident of birth was ridiculous as far as Simon Brown was concerned. If anyone deserved to become Lord Tarrant, it was he, not that simpering fool Gerald.

It was a shame that the doctor attending his mother at the birth had not been a bit more incompetent. Then he might have mixed up the order in which the twin boys had been born, might have said that Simon had come into this world first at five minutes before midnight on December thirty-first in the Year of Our Lord 1781, instead of five minutes after midnight on the first day of 1782. Twin boys, born in different years. How absurd . . . how unfair.

But Gerald was the eldest, and the law was unequivocal. Someday, everything would go to him, and Simon would be left with nothing. Gerald had made that perfectly clear before Simon left England. Of course, the way Simon had tormented his older but smaller, more fragile brother since they were children might have had something to do with Gerald's lack of generosity, Brown thought now with a cold, wry smile.

The ax bit once more into the log. Gerald had deserved it, Brown told himself. He was weak, so he had deserved the practical jokes, the beatings, the public humiliations, the nights when he had mewled in pain as Simon grunted above him and taught him all the ways a weak boy was meant to be used.

Brown warmed a bit as the memories came back to him. Those had been good days, and their parents—their damned, stupid parents—had never had any idea of what was really going on.

In the end, the system, and Gerald, had won, of course. But only for the time being. One day Simon Brown would return to England to reclaim his true identity. Gerald could have the birthright. Simon would be richer by far, and anyone who said money could not purchase contentment and prestige was a fool indeed.

Brown sleeved away the sweat from his forehead as he worked at shaping the log. The sun was sinking toward the mountain peaks, and night would be falling soon. He rested the ax over his shoulder.

"That's enough, lads," he called to the men

working on the fence and the buildings of the fort. "Pack it in for the night."

No one argued with the order to quit for the day. Of course, no one argued with Brown anyway, no matter what his orders were. Word had gotten around quickly about his killing the two thieves in McKendrick's office, and no one wanted to cross him. The men probably regarded him as either a lunatic or the cruelest bloke on the face of the earth—or both. That was fine with Brown.

To keep them off balance, he had set a fairly easy pace so far, both on their trip down from Canada and in the construction of the fort. Keep them guessing, that was his plan; make them wonder when he might explode into violence again. They stayed on their toes that way and did good work.

The fort was located in a small valley in the foothills. This was good beaver country, with many small streams running southeast from the mountains to join the Jefferson River. Brown had men out scouting those creeks at the moment, and as soon as the work on the fort itself was completed, they would begin trapping in earnest. Later, if anyone challenged their right to be there, they would have the fort itself to show as evidence that they had been trapping in the area for quite some time and therefore should have the right to continue.

Brown strode toward the long, low barracks building, the first structure the men had completed. It allowed them to sleep inside while they continued to work on the rest of the outpost, and it provided protection in case of Indian attack. The walls were made of thick logs, well-chinked with mud. In a number of places, loopholes had been cut so that rifles could be fired from inside in case of trouble. There were no windows and only one door. With enough food and water, a small force inside could hold off an army.

Brown had not yet reached the building when he

heard someone hailing him. He stopped, turned around, and was surprised and not a little annoyed to see a half-dozen men—the men he had sent out earlier to scout—hurrying toward him. As he walked forward to meet them, Brown saw that several of them looked worried.

"I didn't expect you boys back this soon," he said. "I expected you to camp out tonight and look for more beaver tomorrow."

"Sorry, Mr. Brown," the leader of the scouting party said. He was a slender, sallow man named Dobbs. "We saw something and figured we'd best get on back here and tell you about it. Might be important."

"Well, don't keep it to yourself," Brown said with impatience.

"Yes, sir. There're folks coming this way. White men."

"What?" Brown blinked in surprise. "How many? Two? Three?"

"More like a dozen and a half," Dobbs said.

A puzzled frown appeared on Brown's face. "Where?"

Dobbs waved toward the valley where the three tongues of the Missouri ran.

"Down on the plain," he said, "just this side of that nearest branch of the big river, the one called the Jefferson by the Americans. They spotted us first and fired their rifles."

"They shot at you?" Brown asked in amazement.

Quickly Dobbs said, "Oh, no. They were too far off to be shooting at us. I'd say they were signaling, sir. Trying to get our attention."

"What did you do?"

"We got out of sight as quickly as we could, just like you told us to if we ran into anyone, white or Indian. I'd say that if you want to keep our presence in these mountains a secret, sir, it's too late now."

Brown took a deep breath and tried to calm his raging pulse. Fury welled inside him, a blinding red haze of anger that threatened to overwhelm him. He wanted to lash out at Dobbs, to raise the ax and drive it deep into the man's neck. He could almost feel the satisfying crunch of steel against the man's spine, could almost see Dobbs's head topple off his shoulders to roll away, still in its coonskin cap. That would be an amusing sight indeed, Brown thought.

Gradually he brought his rage under control and said quietly, "How good a look did they get at you?"

"Fairly good, I'd say. I thought I saw the sunlight reflecting off the lens of a spyglass."

"But there was still quite a distance between your party and them, correct?"

"Yes. A couple of miles or more."

"So what they really saw was just a small group of white men moving through the foothills. They don't know whether you were American or English, so they'll assume you were just a party of American trappers."

"I suppose that's the most likely conclusion they could draw," Dobbs said.

"No harm done then." Brown looked around and saw that most of the men from the fort had gathered to listen to the discussion. He lifted his voice and went on, "But all of you men know our orders. We're not to reveal our presence here until the fort is complete and our trapping operation is established. You understand how important this is."

Some of the men muttered their agreement.

"We won't let this incident worry us," Brown continued. "But in the future, should any of you accidentally encounter Americans—and if they're close enough to see that there's something unusual going on—you're to deal with the situation immediately. Don't hesitate. Just kill them."

"Kill them?" one of the men exclaimed. "I say, is that really necessary?"

Brown fixed the man with a cold stare. "It is. And if you don't have the stomach for it, just take them prisoner and bring them here to the fort. I'll take care of the matter personally."

Judging from the uneasy looks on their faces, none of them doubted that for an instant.

Brown shouldered the ax again. Dobbs was a lucky sod, he thought. The man had no idea how close he had come to having his head lopped off. Brown was going to have to give that method of killing some consideration. If there were prisoners to be disposed of, it would be quite effective to use one of the broad-bladed axes and cut their heads off in front of the whole group. That would show his men that he meant business—and it would be quite entertaining at the same time.

Brown turned back toward the barracks. The day's work had given him an appetite that even Dobbs's bad news could not dispel, and he was looking forward to supper.

The botanical expedition camped that evening at the base of the foothills, and Professor Franklin took advantage of the opportunity to gather samples of the prickly pear, which grew in profusion in the area. Proud Wolf accompanied him, holding the box in which the professor placed his specimens. Franklin kept up a running lecture on what he was doing, explaining how scientific analysis would differ from casual observation.

In their quest the two had moved a short way up the gentle slope. Franklin bent over a plant with a large, pale blossom and studied it at length.

"What might this be, what might this be?" he muttered to himself.

"Bitterroot," Proud Wolf said. He bent beside

Franklin and reached out to grasp the plant at its base. As he pulled it out of the ground, a small, immature root shaped something like a carrot was revealed.

"Too early to eat this one," Proud Wolf went on, "but later in the year, when they are grown, these roots are peeled and eaten by my people. They are very good."

"I'm, ah, certain they are," Franklin said, regarding the scrawny root somewhat dubiously. "We'll take it with us. Lucy, come over here and make a note of this."

Lucy took her father's journal from one of the packs and carried it to the professor and Proud Wolf, along with pen and ink. She sat on a large rock and, as Franklin described the plant, wrote rapidly in the journal, making a sketch of the bitterroot as well.

Nearby, Rupert von Metz was doing some sketching of his own, using a large pad and a piece of lead from his gear. He roughed in the shape of the mountains that towered above them, then added pockets of light and darkness.

Seeing that the work of setting up camp was proceeding smoothly, Clay strolled over to the young Prussian and looked over his shoulder at the sketch.

"That's mighty good," Clay said after a moment. "Looks just like those mountains."

"It's supposed to," von Metz replied curtly. "Why else would I be doing it?"

"Just trying to give you a compliment, son."

"Oh. My work, which has won the praise of nobility and scholars across Europe, is now facing the critical judgment of an American backwoodsman whose only other exposure to art is the pitiful daubings of savages on rocks and tipis."

Clay's jaw tightened as he struggled to get a grip on his temper. "You're a mighty hard fellow to like, von Metz."

"I have never asked you to like me, Herr Holt.

Attaining your friendship is not one of my goals in life."

"I reckon surviving this trip is, though. You'd best think about that." Clay turned and walked away.

The exchange had been loud enough for most of the others to hear, and it contributed to a subtle air of tension that settled over the camp along with dusk's shadows. Clay chided himself for almost getting angry with von Metz. By this time he knew perfectly well that the Prussian artist was not going to accept his leadership with anything but ill will. Von Metz's arrogance, and his memory of being humbled by Clay in the competition with gun and blade, would not allow anything else.

But blast it, Clay thought as he sat by the campfire with Shining Moon, Proud Wolf, and Aaron, *the boy has talent.* He could draw pictures that did more than just look like their subjects. It was as though von Metz saw not only the outside of things but the inside, too, and a sense of that came through in his work.

Too bad he was such an unpleasant bastard.

That night, as Clay lay rolled in his blankets with Shining Moon, he heard the distant rumble of thunder and noticed a faint flicker of lightning near the mountains. Sometimes there were thunderstorms in the high country, brief but violent, full of pounding rain and crackling lightning. With any luck this one would blow over quickly and miss them. He knew the coming days would be difficult enough as they climbed toward the highest peaks of the Rockies; they did not need extra problems.

Contrary to his hopes, the rain came before morning. At first the drops, although large, were few and far between. Then they increased, and the wind picked up, bringing with it a raw chill as the group got ready to break camp after a cold breakfast. With the rain it was impossible to keep a fire going. As soon as they found a sheltered place, Clay thought, he would call a halt and have a fire built so that they could wait out the storm in relative comfort.

"Let's get moving," Clay called when the group was ready to go. "The sooner we find a good place, the sooner we can get out of this weather."

Everyone in the party looked miserable. Water trickled from the wide brim of Professor Franklin's hat down his back. Lucy had donned an oilcloth slicker, but it kept her only somewhat drier than the others. Rupert von Metz kept up a constant muttering in his native tongue, and Clay suspected he was cursing not only the weather but also everyone involved in this ill-fated expedition, especially him. As for Lawton and the other men, they had gone about the morning's tasks without complaint, but Clay caught more than one of them glaring at him through the drizzle. Even the normally exuberant Proud Wolf was more subdued than usual as he took his place at the rear of the party with Aaron Garwood.

Shining Moon, a blanket thrown over her head and shoulders, moved alongside Clay and said, "This rain is not good. It began in the mountains last night."

"I know," Clay said. "I heard it. But we'll stay out of any gullies that might flood. We'll be all right. You know of any caves around here?"

"Never have I heard any of my people speak of caves in these hills, but that does not mean there are none to be found."

"We're bound to find someplace to get out of the wind and rain. Keep your eyes open."

Clay knew Shining Moon's eyes were even keener than his, and he was glad she possessed such sight. It was hard to see anything through the rain and fog forming in the valleys between the hills. The sun was completely hidden by thick banks of gray and black clouds. The warm spring they had been enjoying seemed to have deserted them.

Throughout the morning the rain continued,

sometimes hard in a brief downpour, but mostly in a steady drizzle. The muddy ground made footing difficult and slowed their pace considerably, but Clay did not push the group to hurry. They were cold, wet, and uncomfortable, and he knew he might be faced with a full-fledged mutiny if he rode them too hard.

The beaver pelts got soaked again, and as they did, their weight increased until Clay considered abandoning them. But he hated the idea of giving them up; he and his companions had worked hard for the plews, and there was a chance the expedition might run into other trappers who would be willing to take the furs and split the profits. It would have to be someone Clay knew and trusted, however, before he would be willing to let him hold the money until he and the others got back from the Pacific coast, a year or more in the future.

Still he found no suitable shelter. The group had passed a few overhangs that looked promising, but the wind was swirling, and the formations would not have provided enough cover for a campfire. They had to have a fire, Clay had decided, not only for warmth and comfort but also to ease their minds. The professor, Lucy, and von Metz had to be frightened as well as uncomfortable, and a crackling fire to huddle next to always made one feel more secure and less inclined to panic. The Indians who had made their home in these mountains since time immemorial knew the truth of that: Give a person a nice snug cave and a circle of flame, and the world did not look nearly as bad as it might otherwise.

Suddenly the wind and rain lashed at them even harder than before. Clay bent forward against its force and heard a whimpering cry behind him. He looked over his shoulder to see Professor Franklin comforting Lucy, who was stumbling along beside him. Franklin had one arm around his daughter's waist and with his other hand held his hat on his head. In the dim, gray light their faces looked pale and haggard. Von Metz was behind them, equally unsteady on his feet.

Clay felt his wife's hand on his arm. "Clay, we must find some shelter soon. These people cannot go on."

"I know. Let's move over by that stand of pine and let them rest for a few minutes. I want to talk to Proud Wolf, too. Nobody's going to be coming up on our back trail in this kind of weather, so I think I'll send him ahead to scout."

Shining Moon agreed with his idea. As she walked along, her moccasins slipped in the mud, and Clay put his hand under her elbow to steady her.

They veered toward the trees, a sparse clump of pine that would offer some shelter from the rain but not much. The narrow trunks would not cut the wind at all. Normally, Clay would have avoided trees during a storm to lessen the chance of being struck by lightning, but other than the faint flickering in the sky and the distant rumbling the night before, no lightning had accompanied this storm. It was just wind and rain—but that was enough.

As the group huddled under the trees, Clay motioned Proud Wolf over to him and asked, "You feel up to going on ahead and taking a look around, maybe finding us a spot where we can get out of this mess?"

"I will go," Proud Wolf said. He loped away with a seemingly tireless gait and within moments had disappeared into the thick curtain of rain.

Clay lowered his bundle of pelts to the ground and told the other men carrying furs to do the same. Those with the lighter packs of supplies kept them on their backs. Clay leaned against the trunk of a pine and closed his eyes. His body had been hardened by the rugged existence he had led for the past five years, but he was no more immune to weariness than anyone else. He was tired, tired of slogging through the mud, tired of stumbling into trouble every time he turned around, tired of people depending on him. . . .

Shining Moon snuggled against him and rested her head on his shoulder. Her presence instantly drove away the gloomy thoughts. Life had its problems, but it also had its rewards, and the feel of his woman in his arms was one of the best rewards of all. Clay put an arm around her shoulders and drew her more tightly to him.

An ominous rumbling sound came from somewhere above them.

Rupert von Metz lifted his head sharply and asked, "What is that?"

"It sounds like—like . . . " Frowning, Professor Franklin groped for an explanation.

Clay knew what it was. "An avalanche," he said grimly, stepping away from Shining Moon and into the rain to peer up at the foothills and mountains. The rain pelted his face and made him feel almost as if he were underwater, in danger of drowning. He controlled his faint sense of panic and searched for the source of the steadily increasing roar.

Shining Moon gripped his arm tightly and said, "The mountains are falling."

Clay shook his head. "Just a few tons of rock and mud. The mud gave way under all this rain."

"We must get out of here," von Metz said wildly. "There is an avalanche coming, and you stand here calmly discussing it! We must run!" His voice trembled; he was on the verge of losing control.

"Can you see where it's going, von Metz?" Clay asked sharply. When the Prussian made no reply, Clay raised his voice to be heard above the thunderous rumble. "I can't, either. We might run right into its path if we leave here. At least these trees offer us some protection."

"Proud Wolf!" Shining Moon suddenly exclaimed. "He is out there somewhere!"

Clay caught her arm to prevent her from running out of the clump of trees. "There's nothing we can do to help Proud Wolf now. He's mighty fast on his feet, Shining Moon. If anybody can dodge an avalanche, it's him."

The noise was incredibly loud by now, and Clay had to shout to make himself heard. He had seen giant waterfalls, had heard thunder so deafening that it shook the very earth—but this sound was worse.

"Get behind the trees!" he bellowed, motioning for the others to move. If the pines were directly in the path of the avalanche, they would be swept away like everything else. However, if the main body of the slide passed on one side or the other, so that the trees were on the fringes of the disaster, they might provide enough protection for the explorers to survive. It was their only chance.

Suddenly, just when it would have seemed impossible, the noise grew even louder, like giant fists slamming against the ears of the terrified group huddled among the trees. Clay wrapped his arms around Shining Moon and leaned his shoulder hard against the trunk of a pine, bracing himself as best he could.

Then, looming up from the rain and fog like a monstrous beast, a gray wall of mud and rock appeared, dotted with trees it had uprooted higher in the foothills. The avalanche surged toward them like a wave. Several of the men screamed in sheer terror, broke away from the trees, and ran down the slope.

"Come back, you damned fools!" Clay called after them, but even though he was shouting at the top of his lungs, his words were lost, swallowed up by the roar of the slide.

Eyes wide, heart pounding, Clay watched as the bulging forefront of the avalanche swelled closer and closer—and then passed to the right. Rocks and clumps of mud pounded the grove of trees. Everyone was screaming now, Clay supposed—he knew he was —but nothing could be heard except the tumult of the avalanche. He pressed Shining Moon harder against the tree, shielding her with his body. He shuddered as rocks thudded against him, most of them small but packing significant impact. The tree shivered as it took the brunt of the blows. Mud swept around Clay's feet and tried to tug him away from Shining Moon, but he held on for all he was worth. The others were doing the same, using the trees for protection from the rocks and as anchors to keep from being swept away.

Clay twisted his head and saw the men who had made the fatal mistake of trying to outrun the avalanche. The leading edge of the slide was just now catching up to them, and as he watched, they disappeared into the boiling gray madness. He thought he heard their death shrieks, but he knew that had to be his imagination.

The mud was up to his knees now, pulling at him like giant hands. This time he really did hear a scream and jerked around to see Lucy Franklin being torn from her father's grip by the swirling mud. She started to fall, her face frozen in terror.

But before she could disappear under the surface of the mud, Aaron Garwood was there beside her, grabbing one of her flailing arms to hold her up. At the same time, Professor Franklin caught the back of Aaron's coat. The tough buckskin held without tearing, and together Franklin and Aaron were able to pull Lucy back to safety.

Then the air seemed clearer, the rumble of the avalanche having subsided slightly. Clay let himself hope that the worst of it was over. He leaned to the side to peer past the tree trunk, hoping he could see the end of the slide.

What he saw was a huge boulder weighing at

least several tons bounding down the hillside toward them like a pebble kicked by a little boy.

And it was coming straight at the tree where he and Shining Moon were crouched.

For a split second the thought flashed through Clay's mind that it would be ludicrous for him to be killed by something as unpredictable as an avalanche after all the other dangers he had survived. Then he was reacting instead of thinking. He flung Shining Moon to the side, the corded muscles of his arms and shoulders bunching under the buckskin shirt as he threw her to relative safety. He saw the flow of mud pull at her, spin her around; then her hands caught the rough bark of another tree trunk, and she held fast to it. Clay launched himself after her as the boulder slammed into the tree where he had been huddled an instant earlier. The pine was uprooted, plucked from the ground like the bitterroot plant the professor had found earlier. It spun crazily through the air.

Clay felt something hit the back of his shoulders just below his neck. He stumbled, the impact throwing him forward. Stunned by the blow, his balance deserting him, he fell. Cold gray mud slapped him in the face—

Then it closed in around him, drawing him deeper and deeper. He let himself go, surrendering to the inexorable pull as the grayness around him turned to black.

Chapter Thirteen

He is truly a philosopher, contrasting his former with his present situation, with much good humour and pleasantry.

—Fortescue Cuming
"Sketches of a Tour to the
Western Country"

Cantering his horse along the New Jersey palisades, Jeff Holt drew rein and looked across the Hudson River at New York City. He had thought Pittsburgh was impressive, but the Pennsylvania city paled when compared to the sprawling settlement spread out before him. The entire lower end of the island of Manhattan was crowded with buildings and people, and houses were scattered over the rest of it. A ferry loaded with travelers, horses, mules, wagons, and carriages traveled on the Hudson River, heading for the distant city.

Beside Jeff, Ned Holt let out a low whistle of

amazement. "Did you ever see anything like it, cousin?"

"No," Jeff admitted. "I never have."

During the past two months the young men had followed the Allegheny River out of Pennsylvania into New York, then headed east through the Finger Lakes region. It was beautiful country, full of wooded hills and valleys and deep, sparkling lakes. The roads were generally good, and there were quite a few farms in the area. An air of tranquillity hung over the entire region, and it was difficult to believe that less than fifty years before, smoke from the burning cabins of settlers had filled the sky as the Mohawk Indians fought a bloody, futile war to stem the tide of white expansion.

Jeff and Ned had taken their time on their journey. In each settlement they had come to, Jeff had questioned everyone he could find, hoping that someone had heard of the Merrivale family or knew of Melissa's whereabouts. He placed advertisements in newspapers, offering rewards to anyone who could furnish the information he needed. He had also checked the records of property transactions at each county courthouse, hoping to find some mention of Charles Merrivale's having bought land.

They angled northeast through Syracuse and Utica, continuing their search as they worked their way farther north into the Adirondacks. Everywhere it was the same story: People were hospitable and wanted to help, but no one Jeff encountered knew anything about Melissa or had even heard of the Merrivales. Finally he and Ned had turned south again and headed down the Hudson River valley, where again Jeff was struck by the beauty of the land.

Ned had enjoyed the journey, taking in the sights with wide, eager eyes. Once they had left Pittsburgh —and escaped from Ned's vengeful enemies—the young man had relaxed. He helped Jeff in his quest as much as possible; whenever they entered a community, they split up to cover more ground, and if Ned had any doubts about the potential for the success of their mission, he kept them to himself.

Jeff was grateful for that; he was plagued with enough doubts of his own. The task he had set for himself was impossible, he realized more with each passing day. The only way he would ever find Melissa was by sheer luck. He had to accept the possibility that he might never see her again.

But he was not yet ready to give up. Across the river was the most populous city not only in the state but also in the nation. More than sixty thousand people made their home in New York—and Jeff would talk to each and every one of them if he had to.

"We have relatives over there, you know," Ned said as they looked across the river at the city.

"No, I didn't," Jeff replied, surprised.

"We used to get letters from a cousin Irene. She was Pa's cousin, I think, which would make her your father's cousin, too."

"We were out of touch with everyone in the family except your folks in Pittsburgh," Jeff said. "I never heard anything about a cousin Irene."

"Ma and Pa haven't received a letter from her in several years, as well as I can remember. But she ought to be alive still. We could look her up."

"I suppose. New York's a big place, and it wouldn't hurt to have someone we know help us find our way around. Do you have any idea how we could locate her?"

Ned's forehead furrowed in concentration as he tried to cull details from his memory.

"Let me see. . . . She was married to a man named Marshall or Marsh or something like that—March, that was it! Her name was Irene March. Seems to me her husband was a shipwright."

"If we ask around at the docks, we can probably

find him. If the family is still here." Jeff heeled his horse into motion. "Come on. Let's see about getting a ride on that ferry."

They rode along the heights until they found a path that led down to the shore. The ferry was already making the return trip, and by the time they reached the landing, it had tied up at the small loading pier. More passengers were boarding.

Jeff paid for both of them, handing a silver dollar to the man collecting the fares. He and Ned led their horses on board the big bargelike ferry and found a place to stand near the railing around the edge.

Jeff felt a tingle of nervousness. It was partially because so many people surrounded him, and he was not used to being crowded. But his anxiety was even greater because New York City represented perhaps his last chance to find Melissa, and he knew it.

When the boat was full, it left the landing and made its way across the river, its steam engine thumping and roaring. The crossing took less time than Jeff had expected.

The boat docked at another pier on the western shore of the island. The main waterfront area was to the south, along the lower tip of the city. Jeff and Ned could see the tall masts of the many ships anchored there, showing plainly over the roofs of the buildings along Water Street and Wall Street. That was probably where they would find this man March whom Ned had mentioned.

Before they began checking into that, however, Jeff wanted to do something else. As they led their horses off the ferry, he spotted a sign that read *New York Weekly Journal* on a nearby building. He pointed it out to Ned.

"Let's stop there first. I want to place an advertisement."

"Might as well," Ned replied. "Can't hurt, can it?"

Jeff did not answer. They both knew all too well what a long shot it would be if someone saw the notice about Melissa and her family and could actually provide information about them. But Jeff was not ready to give up—not yet.

They entered the building and found a small reception area separated from the main part of the room by a waist-high railing. On the other side of the railing, the chamber was filled with bulky machinery, rolls of paper, and jars of ink. Jeff knew that the machine, which looked vaguely intimidating to him, had to be a printing press, but he had no idea how it worked.

Also beyond the railing was a man sitting on a chair tipped back so that his feet could rest on the scarred surface of an old desk. He had a magazine propped open on his legs and was scowling as he stared at its pages. Jeff read the name on the magazine, *Salmagundi*, and that made as little sense to him as the intricate arrangement of gears, levers, and plates that formed the printing press.

The man looked up, saw Jeff and Ned standing on the other side of the railing, and closed the magazine, then tossed it onto the desk.

"Scandalous." He grunted. "I don't know why people read such drivel." He lowered his feet to the floor, then put his hands on his knees, pushed himself upright, and said, "Can I help you gentlemen?"

"I want to put a notice in your paper," Jeff said. "When will the next edition come out?"

"Three days from now. We're a weekly, you know. Is that soon enough for you?"

"I suppose it'll have to be. I want the notice to request that anyone having knowledge of a young lady named Mrs. Melissa Holt or her parents, Mr. and Mrs. Charles Merrivale, should please contact me as soon as possible, in care of this newspaper. My name is Jefferson Holt."

The newspaper man raised his eyebrows. "You're the husband of the lady in question, I take it?"

"That's right."

"Ran away from you, did she?" The question was accompanied by a cynical expression.

Jeff wanted to lunge across the railing and knock the expression off the man's face, but he controlled the impulse.

"That's not important to you. What matters is that I intend to pay you whatever your going rate is for the space required to print that announcement."

"Of course." The mention of payment sobered the man. "I'll write up the notice and have it in the next edition. Let me figure out how much it will cost."

Ned patted the stock of the long rifle cradled in his arms. "Make sure you figure correctly, friend."

The newspaper man swallowed, blinked, and named a price that sounded fair to Jeff considering that the *New York Weekly Journal* was probably the largest paper in which he had yet placed a notice. He held a pair of coins over the railing, and the man stepped forward quickly to take them.

Now that the arrangement was completed, the man relaxed a bit and said, "If you want to reach a different group of readers, you might consider placing a notice in that magazine I was looking at. It doesn't have nearly as large a circulation as the newspaper, of course, but I suppose it's read by quite a few people."

"I thought you said it was scandalous," Jeff said.

"Oh, it is. But I know the man who puts it out. In fact, I do his printing for him." The newspaper man waved toward the building's grimy front window. "I see him coming right now. That's what led me to suggest you might want to place a notice in it."

Intrigued, Jeff turned and looked out the window to see a well-dressed man walking down the sidewalk toward the newspaper office. He wore a beaver hat, a silk shirt with an elegant cravat, a tailcoat, and high black boots over tight, fawn-colored breeches. His handsome features and air of elegance gave him the look of a fop, but there was genuine warmth on his face as he entered the office.

"Good morning, Collins," he said to the publisher, then turned to look at Jeff and Ned. "What have we here? Some gentlemen newly arrived from the wild frontier, by the looks of them."

Jeff was not sure whether to bristle at the man's tone or not. He nodded curtly to the newcomer.

"Washington Irving." The man smiled at Jeff and Ned as he held out his hand. "I'm glad to meet you."

Jeff shook hands with him and said, "I'm Jeff Holt, and this is my cousin Ned Holt."

"Glad to meet you, Mr. Holt, and you, too, Mr. Holt," Washington Irving said. "What brings you to the land of Knickerbocker?"

Warming to the man, Jeff said, "I'm looking for my wife, Mr. Irving. I just arranged to have a notice placed in Mr. Collins's newspaper asking for information about her. He suggested that I might advertise in your magazine, as well."

"We'd be glad to have your business, of course," Irving replied in a concerned tone. "And I'm sorry to hear that you've been separated from your wife, Mr. Holt. Was the separation . . . involuntary?"

"If you mean did she run away from me, the answer is no," Jeff said emphatically. "Melissa's father is the kind of man who likes to get his own way. When he and Melissa's mother left Ohio, he talked Melissa into going east with them, even though she and I were already married."

"Where were you at the time, Mr. Holt? I realize this is not really any of my business, but—"

"That's all right. I don't mind telling you. I was trapping furs in the Rockies with my brother."

"Really!" Irving exclaimed. "How fascinating. I must speak to you at length about this, Mr. Holt. For now, however, if you'll tell me how you want your notice to read, I'll see about getting it in the next issue of *Salmagundi.*"

Jeff repeated the same information he had given Collins, then said, "If you could word the notice so that anyone responding to it can get in touch with the *Salmagundi,* I'll check with you from time to time to see if anyone has answered."

"That'll be fine with me," Washington Irving agreed.

"Now, we've got to get down to the docks and look up another cousin of ours. He's supposed to be a shipwright, or at least he has something to do with boats."

"What's his name?" Irving asked. "Perhaps Collins or I know him."

Jeff looked at Ned, who said, "I'm pretty sure his last name is March."

"Not Lemuel March?" Washington Irving's eyebrows lifted in surprise.

"That's it, all right!" Ned said. "I remember now, Lemuel was his first name."

Collins and Washington Irving exchanged a look, and it was obvious to Jeff that both recognized the name.

Collins said, "You go down to the Tontine Coffee House, at the corner of Wall Street and Water Street. You'll either find March or someone who can tell you where he is."

"Thanks." Jeff shifted his rifle. "Let's go, Ned."

When they were on the street again, Ned said, "Did you see that look they gave us when we mentioned March?"

"Yes, I did. Reckon they've heard of him, all right. I wonder what it's about."

"We'll find out in that coffeehouse they mentioned, I suppose." Ned looked at the hustle and bustle all around them as they walked along the street toward the waterfront, and his gaze was eager and excited. Jeff wished he could share his cousin's anticipation.

The Tontine Coffee House was located at the angle where Wall and Water streets came together a block from the harbor. It was an impressive three-story building of brick and stone and mortar, with a flag flying from a pole on its roof and a railed wooden porch along the front of the building. The first floor was decorated with brick columns and arched windows, while the upper stories were less fancy. A dozen or more well-dressed men stood on the porch, sipping coffee from cups and talking animatedly. From the look of them, they were men of commerce—merchants, brokers, bankers, and traders—and successful ones at that.

The hum of conversation lessened as Jeff and Ned approached the steps leading to the porch and climbed them. Jeff in his buckskin and homespun and Ned in his rough store-bought clothing were out of place here, and naturally they attracted some attention. The weapons they carried made them stand out even more. None of the coffeehouse's patrons seemed to be armed. They were the kind to settle disputes with words and lawyers and money, not fists or knives or guns.

Jeff kept his face and voice civil as he said into the lull, "I'm looking for a man named Lemuel March."

That made them stare even more, and Jeff felt his jaw tighten in anger. Just because he was not from their city, they were regarding him as though he were some sort of lunatic.

He forced himself to go on politely, "I believe this man March has something to do with boats."

That drew a laugh, and a tall, slender man strode forward from the rear of the group. He had gray hair and a weathered face, and although he carried himself with the grace of a younger man, he had to be in his middle to late forties. He stepped in front of Jeff and Ned.

"So this fellow has something to do with boats, eh?" the man said. "Why are you looking for Lemuel March?"

Jeff returned the level stare. Although the man was dressed as expensively and elegantly as the others, something about him was different, a sense of personal strength that the rest of them did not possess.

"Not that it's any of your business," Jeff said coolly, "but Lemuel March is married to my father's cousin."

"My God, you're a Holt!" the man exclaimed. He looked at Ned and added, "And so are you. I should have known."

Jeff's eyes narrowed in surprise. "That's right. I'm Jefferson Holt from Ohio and more recently the Rocky Mountains. This is Ned Holt from Pittsburgh. And if you don't mind my asking, sir—who the hell are you?"

A grin spread across the man's face as he stuck out his right hand.

"I'm Lemuel March, of course. And I do have something to do with boats, as you put it." He jerked the thumb of his left hand over his shoulder, toward the waterfront. "I own about six of them back yonder."

Now it was Jeff and Ned who looked surprised. Jeff recovered first and shook hands with Lemuel March.

"It's good to meet you, sir. We meant no offense—"

March waved off the apology. "None taken, I promise you. It's been awhile since my wife has been in touch with either of your families. Come along and let me get you some coffee. You'll have to tell me all about your reasons for coming to New York."

Now that Jeff and Ned had been welcomed by March, the other men on the porch of the coffeehouse went back to their conversations. Grateful that he and Ned were no longer being gawked at, Jeff accepted a cup of the strong black coffee from a waiter summoned by March. Then Jeff explained the errand that had brought them to New York City. March listened intently as Jeff told him about the disappearance of Melissa and her parents from Ohio.

"You don't know for certain that they came here to New York, do you?" March asked when Jeff had concluded the tale.

"No, sir, I don't. And I've found no sign of them so far. But I can't give up."

"No, no, of course not," March agreed. "I have business connections not only here in the city but throughout the state. I'll be glad to pass the word that you're looking for your wife and try to help you locate her. If this man Merrivale has gone into business anywhere in the Northeast, we should be able to find him."

A surge of gratitude went through Jeff. For too long, Ned had been his only ally in his search. Now, with an influential man like Lemuel March on his side, perhaps he really did have a chance of locating Melissa.

"I'm sorry I had the mistaken impression that you were a shipwright," Jeff told the older man.

"I'm to blame for that," Ned said. "All I remembered for sure from Cousin Irene's letters was that you had something to do with boats, Mr. March. I never figured you owned them."

"That's all right, Ned," March said. "And both of you call me Lemuel. I don't stand on ceremony where family is concerned. Irene's going to be very happy to see the both of you. She loves to have visitors."

"Wait a minute," Jeff said. "We don't want to inconvenience you—"

"Nonsense. We have plenty of room, so both of you will stay with us while you're here in New York. Agreed?"

Jeff and Ned looked at each other, and Jeff said, "We'd be happy to. We've seen enough rented rooms in taverns and roadhouses over the past couple of months, haven't we, Ned?"

"Amen to that," Ned said fervently. "And slept out under the stars enough, too, although that never seemed to bother you much, Jeff."

"I got used to it in the mountains."

Lemuel said, "I want to hear all about that. You must have had quite an amazing experience out there. But I can wait until we're home so that you won't have to repeat everything for Irene and the girls. I'm sure they'll be interested, too."

"The girls?" Ned said.

"Our daughters," Lemuel explained. "Irene and I have three of them, you know." He clapped one hand on Jeff's shoulder and the other on Ned's. "I hope you lads enjoy being surrounded by beautiful females, because the March household is full of them!"

The March house was a two-story frame structure, its walls whitewashed and set off by trim painted a pleasant shade of green. It was about half a mile north of the Tontine Coffee House, facing a dirt street called Broadway that ran almost the length of Manhattan Island. Along the street were flagstone sidewalks, and the houses that lined it were set behind narrow yards that barely had room for a tree or two. The March house had a small brick entrance porch, little more than a pair of steps, built onto the front of it. The windows were narrow, and the shutters were thrown open on this warm day. Lemuel had insisted on driving Jeff and Ned in his carriage, which he handled himself. Their mounts were tied behind the vehicle.

Lemuel brought the team of matched black horses to a stop in front of the house and lithely stepped down. He had a hint of a rolling gait in his walk as he led Jeff and Ned up to the house, and that was enough to tell Jeff that at one time Lemuel had been a sailor. Lemuel ushered them inside, then removed the beaver hat he had reclaimed from inside the coffeehouse before leaving. He tossed it on a small table in the foyer.

"Irene! Girls!" he called out. "Come down here. We have company!"

A moment later an attractive blond woman appeared at the top of the stairs.

"Is that you, Lemuel?" she asked. "What are you shouting about?" Then, catching sight of the two visitors, she smoothed her dress and petticoats and started down the stairs. As she drew nearer, Jeff could see a few strands of silver among the blond hair, but her lovely features were unlined, and she looked youthful.

When she reached the bottom of the stairs, she smiled at Jeff and Ned and said, "Good afternoon, gentlemen." If she was surprised by her husband's bringing home two strangers, she did not show it.

"Do you know who these two lads are, Irene?"

As she glanced at Lemuel, Jeff detected a faint flicker of annoyance in her eyes, but the smile on her face did not budge.

"You know I don't, dear," she said. "Why don't you introduce them to me?"

"Of course. This is one of your cousins, Jefferson Holt, and another cousin, Ned Holt."

Irene March's green eyes opened wider when she heard the names.

"Ned?" she repeated. "You're Henry and Dorothy's youngest boy?"

"That's right, ma'am," Ned said.

Without hesitation Irene threw her arms around Ned and hugged him.

"Heavens, I haven't seen you in years!" she exclaimed. "And you've grown so much! Why, the last time I saw you . . . well, you don't even remember it, you were so small."

"I'm afraid I don't," Ned admitted.

Irene turned to Jeff. "And you're Jefferson? I'm afraid I don't remember you. You're not one of Ned's older brothers, are you?"

"No, ma'am. My parents were Bartholomew and Norah Holt."

Irene's mouth opened slightly as she stared at Jeff.

"Bartholomew and Norah," she said, her voice little more than a whisper. "I haven't seen Bartholomew since I was a little girl, but I knew he had married and had children. How is your father?"

"He's been dead for a couple of years," Jeff told her. "My mother, too."

"Oh, I'm so sorry! I had no idea—"

"It's all right," Jeff assured her. "I know you didn't. Our families have been out of touch for a long time."

"It's hard to keep track of everyone," Lemuel put in. "The country's so large, and the mail service isn't what it should be. But the two of you are here now, and that's what matters."

From the top of the stairs, a clear young voice asked, "What's going on down there? What's all the commotion?"

Jeff looked up as three young women started down the stairs with a clatter of heels. They came in descending order, from oldest to youngest, excited and eager to see who the visitors were.

The first one was a brunette, eighteen or nineteen years old, with a slender figure and brown eyes that studied Jeff and Ned with frank curiosity. Behind her was a blond like Irene, perhaps seventeen, whose already lush beauty foretold that she was going to be spectacularly lovely in a few years. Bringing up the rear, but not particularly liking it, to judge from the expression on her lightly freckled face, was a girl of fifteen or sixteen with green eyes and strawberry blond hair, which she pushed back out of her elfin face as she reached the bottom of the stairs. She gaped up at Jeff and Ned, unconcerned that she was staring.

"Girls," Lemuel March said, "these are your cousins, Jeff and Ned Holt."

Irene said, "Allow me to present my daughters. This is Rachel." She touched the brunette's shoulder. "And Jeanne." That was the lovely young blond. "And Barbara." Irene slid her arm around the shoulders of the coltish fifteen-year-old.

Rachel March stepped forward, held out her hand to Jeff, and in a husky voice said, "Hello."

"It's an honor to meet you, Miss March." Jeff took her hand awkwardly, unaccustomed to shaking with women.

"No need to be so formal, Cousin Jeff," Jeanne said brightly, bumping her older sister aside. "We're related, after all." She threw her arms around him and hugged him.

Jeff blinked in surprise as he found his arms full of soft, warm young woman. He managed to slip out of the embrace and hoped he did not offend Jeanne by doing so. She did not seem to mind because she immediately turned to Ned and repeated the greeting. Ned did not release her so quickly, Jeff noticed. Cousin or no cousin, Ned was in no hurry to let go of a pretty girl.

Barbara offered a shy nod and a timid greeting, to which he said, "Hello, Barbara. It's very nice to meet you."

"I told you I had a houseful of pretty women,"

Lemuel said proudly. "Well, come on in and sit down, you two. I'll have one of the servants take the carriage and your horses to the stable out back."

Lemuel disappeared toward the rear of the house while Irene led Jeff and Ned into a luxuriously appointed parlor. The two young men settled down on a long sofa with elaborately carved legs.

"That's a Duncan Phyfe, you know," Jeanne said.

"Uh, no," Jeff said. "Don't reckon I know this Phyfe fella."

"No, I mean he made the sofa," Jeanne said with a laugh. "He's becoming quite famous."

"Oh." Jeff shifted uncomfortably on the sofa. It might be pretty, but it wasn't much for sitting on. He would have preferred a log bench.

Irene sat in an armchair and gestured for her daughters to take seats on the floor at her feet. The girls lowered themselves gracefully to the large hooked rug on which the armchair sat.

"What brings the two of you to New York? Have you come for a visit?" Irene asked.

"No, ma'am. We're looking for someone. My wife."

Jeff thought Jeanne looked a little disappointed at the revelation that he was married.

Rachel leaned forward a bit and asked, "What about you, Ned?"

"Oh, I don't have a wife," he replied, grinning. "What I mean to say is that I'm helping Jeff. We hooked up in Pittsburgh."

Lemuel entered the room then and went to stand behind his wife's chair, his hands resting on her shoulders.

"Tell them the story, Jeff. I'm sure Irene and the girls will agree that we should help you all we can."

For the next fifteen minutes, Jeff gave Irene March and her daughters one version of the story involving himself and Melissa, Melissa's parents, and his brother Clay and the feud with the Garwoods, omitting the more lurid details so that he would not shock the young women. They all appeared to sympathize, especially when Jeff reached the part of the story concerning his return to Marietta only to find that Melissa was gone.

"That's dreadful, Jeff," Irene murmured when he was finished. "Lemuel is right. If there's anything we can do to help you in your search, we'll be glad to do it."

"They're going to be staying here with us while they're in New York," Lemuel said. "We've already agreed on that, haven't we, lads?"

"If that's all right with Mrs. March, sir," Jeff said.

"Of course it is," Irene said without hesitation. "We have more than enough room. If you want to bring in your things, I'll have the girls show you where to put them."

Jeff looked down at the possibles bag slung over his shoulder and then at the pack Ned had placed at his feet.

"I reckon we're carrying all our gear," he said. "We've been moving around pretty often, so we don't have much with us."

"That's fine," Lemuel said. "Rachel, take the boys upstairs and show them to the guest room."

"Yes, Father," Rachel replied as she got to her feet.

Jeanne and Barbara stood up, too, and Jeanne said quickly, "I could show them."

"No, dear, I think Rachel should take care of that," Irene said firmly, ignoring the look of disappointment on her middle daughter's face. "You and Barbara can go out to the kitchen and get started on dinner."

"But, Mother—" Jeanne began, stopping when she saw her father's face.

Jeff and Ned both looked down at the floor to

hide their amused expressions as they stood and followed Rachel from the parlor. She took them up the stairs and led them along a corridor to a large bedchamber at the back of the house. A window overlooked the rear yard and the small stable where the carriage and its team were kept. A four-poster, a wardrobe, a dressing table, and two chairs completed the room's furnishings, which Jeff thought looked quite comfortable. He and Ned had been lucky to find such a place to stay.

If only that same luck would rub off on his search for Melissa. . . .

"If you need anything, let one of us know," Rachel said. She pushed back her long brown hair and looked at them solemnly, which seemed to be her normal expression. "I hope you find your wife, Jeff."

"So do I," he said. "Thank you, Rachel. We appreciate everything."

"Dinner will be in about an hour." With that, Rachel left the room and shut the door behind her.

Ned let out a long, low whistle. "Lord, did you ever see such a lovely crop of young ladies!"

"They're your cousins, Ned," Jeff pointed out.

"Distant cousins," Ned countered. "I think I'm going to like it here."

Jeff closed his eyes for a moment and shuddered, remembering Pittsburgh. Ned's liking it here was exactly what he was afraid of.

Chapter Fourteen

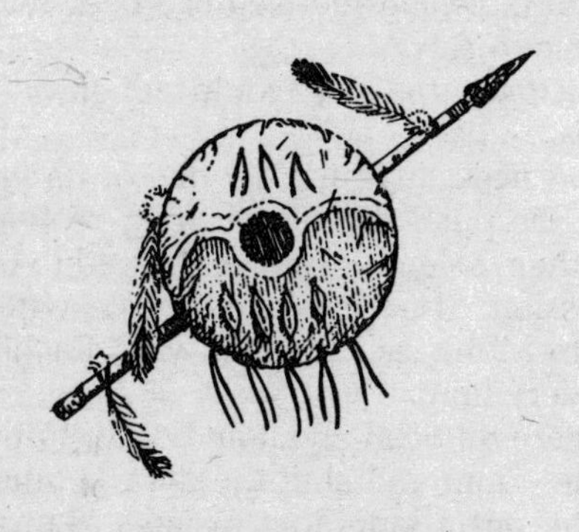

"Clay!" Shining Moon screamed as she saw her husband struck down from behind by a branch as the tree was uprooted and smashed aside by the plummeting boulder. Clay went down hard, landing face first in the torrent of mud and debris sweeping down the hillside.

Shining Moon did not hesitate. She abandoned her position of relative safety and lunged after Clay, reaching for the buckskin shirt he wore. Stumbling and staggering as the mud pulled at her, she managed to grab him and hang on tightly.

"Help me!" she cried as she tried to lift him. "Someone help me!"

She looked around frantically. Professor Franklin and Lucy were huddled behind another tree, one of the professor's arms wrapped around the trunk and the other around his daughter, both of them too terrified to move.

Not too far from her, Rupert von Metz and Harry Lawton were using trees for shelter and support, as were the rest of the men in the party. But neither the Prussian nor Lawton made a move to help Shining Moon. That did not surprise her. They were probably hoping the blow from the tree branch had killed Clay, Shining Moon thought bitterly, and anger surged up in her at the idea. The anger gave her strength, and she tugged harder at Clay's muddy shirt.

She was relieved when Aaron Garwood managed to reach her side. He bent over to get hold of Clay's left arm, and then he lifted while Shining Moon pulled up on his right side. Finally they pulled Clay out of the mud, which grudgingly released him with a great sucking sound.

Shining Moon bit back a sob as she saw how mud coated Clay's face and clogged his mouth and nose. Even if being hit by the branch had not killed him, he might have suffocated while his head was in the mud. Desperately she wiped away the thick, sticky gray mass. The rain, still pounding down, helped loosen the mud and wash some of it away.

The rumble of the avalanche was fading, and the flow of mud had receded a bit. The worst of the danger was over, at least for the moment. Under the circumstances another mudslide was all too possible. The travelers still needed to find shelter. In the back of her mind, Shining Moon knew that, but she could not give it much thought, not with her husband lying limp and motionless in her arms as she knelt there on the muddy slope.

She forced Clay's mouth open wider and dug out another great clot of mud with her fingers. Suddenly a spasm racked his body, a deep gasping cough that shook him and Shining Moon both. Relief welled up inside her. He was alive!

"Help me lift him," she said to Aaron. "We must leave this place."

"Wait just a damned minute," Harry Lawton protested as Shining Moon and Aaron struggled to get Clay on his feet. "As long as Holt's out of his head, I'm in charge again."

Shining Moon paid no attention to the man until he slogged across the dozen or so feet between them and grasped her arm. That made her grip on Clay slip, and he sagged to the ground again. The weakness in Aaron's arm made it impossible for him to support Clay by himself.

"Let go of me!" Shining Moon cried, jerking her arm away from Lawton. "How dare you—"

"Shut up, squaw," Lawton said harshly. "You ain't running this show, and neither's Holt anymore. He's unconscious and may never wake up, so I'm taking over again."

"You're crazy!" Aaron exclaimed. "Clay just got knocked out. He'll come to any minute."

"Look at his head," Lawton snarled. "I've seen men die from clouts like that."

It was true. A large lump on the back of Clay's head was visible now that the rain had washed away most of the mud and plastered his wet hair to his skull. There was a gash on the lump that had bled quite a bit.

Shining Moon felt a coldness in her belly that had nothing to do with the chill wind and rain. Lawton was right; sometimes when a man was hit hard enough in the head, he never woke up. The thought that Clay might be dying caused panic to well up in her, but with a determined effort she controlled that hopeless feeling. She was a Teton Sioux woman, a daughter of the Hunkpapa, and she was strong. Her people had known much hardship, but always they had persevered. She could do no less now.

Tossing her sodden hair back from her face, she

met Lawton's hostile gaze squarely. "My husband will not die, and until he is awake again, I will lead us."

"You?" Lawton laughed scornfully. "A squaw giving orders to white men? I don't think so." He turned to Professor Franklin. "What about it, Professor? Who's running things now?"

Franklin blinked, opened his mouth, and closed it again, as though too shaken by what had happened to offer an opinion. The same could not be said of Rupert von Metz, however.

"I think Mr. Lawton should be in charge again," the young artist said. "He knows more about what he is doing than anyone else."

"That is not true," Shining Moon objected. "I have lived in these mountains all my life."

"But you are a woman," von Metz replied with an infuriatingly smug expression. "I would not think it was necessary to point out something so obvious."

"You're wrong about Shining Moon," Aaron said as he knelt beside Clay, holding the unconcious man's head out of the mud. "She knows what she's doing."

"My boys ain't taking orders from a woman. Ain't that right?"

A rumble of tentative agreement came from the other men, most of whom had moved away from the trees now that the avalanche seemed to be over. The flow of mud had almost stopped. The rain had not let up, however, and it was sluicing down as hard as ever.

"This is a foolish argument," Shining Moon said. "We must have shelter. My brother will return soon and lead us to a place where we can get out of the rain and build a fire."

Lawton laughed, a harsh and unpleasant sound. "That brother of yours ain't coming back. The slide got him."

Shining Moon had feared that, but she did not let it show as she said, "Proud Wolf will be back."

"You can think what you want. I'm tired of arguing with you, lady. We're getting the hell out of here." Lawton jerked his head in a curt gesture, ordering his men to follow him.

"No!" Shining Moon cried, knowing that they would stand a better chance of survival if they stayed together. "You must not leave us!"

"Don't try to stop us," Lawton warned. He looked over at Franklin and Lucy. "What's it going to be, folks? You going with us or staying here with this squaw?"

Even though Lawton had not asked him, Rupert von Metz said without hesitation, "I will go with you, Herr Lawton."

The professor still appeared confused and frightened. Lucy huddled against him, not even looking around at the others. Franklin stammered, "I-I just don't know what we should do."

"Then to hell with you," Lawton said savagely. "I'm tired of waiting around here for you to make up your mind. Mr. von Metz, boys, let's go." He hefted his rifle and started along the hillside.

Rupert von Metz followed him, carrying the cases of art supplies he had somehow managed to hang on to during the mudslide. Although the other men muttered among themselves and shifted their feet nervously, none of them followed Lawton and von Metz.

A few moments passed before Lawton glanced over his shoulder and saw that von Metz was the only one behind him. Stopping short, he swung around.

"What the hell's wrong?" he demanded.

After a pause one of the men replied, "We ain't so sure about this, Harry. I mean, the squaw does know these mountains better'n we do."

"But she's a woman!" Lawton protested in disbelief. "Holt's woman!"

"Yeah, but what about that Injun gal who went along with Lewis and Clark?" another man asked. "She showed 'em where to go, and the way I heard it, they might not've made it back if it hadn't been for her."

"My husband knew the woman called Sacajawea," Shining Moon said. "She was Shoshone, and she was a true guide for the white explorers. I, too, will do my best to lead you to safety if you follow me." Even as she spoke the brave words, she wished Clay would wake up. She glanced at him, saw the slack, unconscious features, and wondered if she would be able to stay strong if he did not regain consciousness soon.

"Goddamn it!" Lawton exploded. He pointed along the hillside with his rifle. "I'm going this way. You can squat here with this redskinned bitch if you want to."

Shining Moon caught her breath. If Clay ever found out that Lawton had spoken of her that way, he would kill the man. *If Clay ever wakes up . . .* In the meantime, she had something else to worry about.

"I would not go that way," she said.

Lawton paused and sneered at her over his shoulder. "Oh? And why not?"

"There could be another avalanche. We are safer staying here and going straight up into the mountains. The rocks that will fall easily have already come down."

"That makes sense," Aaron said.

Lawton snorted contemptuously. "You saying there can't be another avalanche come through here?"

"One could, from higher up in the mountains," Shining Moon admitted. "But the chances are much smaller. The rain is still heavy. Rocks may fall in other places."

"Yeah, well, I'll take my chances. And so will the rest of you boys if you've got any sense." Lawton turned away again. "Come on, von Metz."

This time it was the Prussian who hesitated. "I am no longer so sure of this, Herr Lawton. What the woman says is logical."

Lawton swore. He had seen Clay Holt's injury as a chance to regain the control he had lost days earlier, but now it was all slipping away again. Shining Moon watched him closely, knowing that with Clay unconscious Lawton might decide to seize power by force.

The tension in the air grew as Lawton glared at each of them in turn.

"Shining Moon!"

The unexpected cry made everyone jerk around. Proud Wolf came loping along the hillside, his buckskins covered with mud, his long black hair matted with the sticky gray stuff. When he got close enough to see Clay lying motionless on the ground, Proud Wolf's face twisted with concern, and he ran faster. He approached the others and dropped to his knees beside Clay.

"Is he—"

"He lives," Shining Moon told her brother. "He was hit on the head by a falling branch, but he will be all right." If she said that often enough, she thought, perhaps it would be true. "I knew you would return to us, my brother. Your feet are fleeter than any avalanche."

"Just barely," Proud Wolf said. "I found a cave and was able to hide inside it in time. The slide passed over it. For a while I was afraid the entrance would be completely blocked, but when the rocks and mud were past, there was still a way in and out. We should go there now."

One of the men asked, "How far off is this cave, boy?"

"Half a mile, perhaps." Proud Wolf pointed

north along the slope of the foothills, in the opposite direction from where Lawton had been going.

"I say we head up there," another man declared. "Sounds like a good place to get out of this weather."

"The cave is dry," Proud Wolf added. "And we may be able to find enough dry branches inside it to make a fire."

"A fire sounds damn good to me," a third man rumbled.

Lawton hawked up phlegm and spat disgustedly on the muddy ground. "You're going to let a squaw and an Injun kid tell you what to do? Hell, I thought I knew you boys better than that. The whole damn lot of you make me sick." He strode over, picked up a pack of supplies, and turned to walk off again.

"Wait," Shining Moon said sharply.

Lawton stopped and looked around with a scowl. "What is it now?"

Shining Moon pointed to the pack in his hand. "You cannot take those supplies. The rest of us may need them. We lost several packs in the avalanche."

For a few seconds Lawton just stared at her in surprise. Then he shifted his body so that the barrel of his rifle was pointed in the general direction of the others.

"I'm not staying with a bunch of crazy people," he declared, "and I'm not going off without provisions. You want these supplies, you can damn well come and take 'em."

That same dangerous tension filled the air again as Lawton faced the rest of the group. Shining Moon's pulse pounded as she tried to figure out what to do. With all the rain coming down, there was a very good chance that Lawton's rifle would not even fire if they jumped him. But she knew he had a pistol under his coat, and the powder in it might be dry enough to ignite. Not to mention the long-bladed knife sheathed at his waist and the 'hawk tucked under his belt. They could overpower him and take the supplies away from him, she had no doubt of that, but how many of them would be hurt in the process? Someone might even be killed.

Clay would have known what to do, Shining Moon thought. So would Bear Tooth, the chief of the village where she had grown to womanhood. And Jeff Holt, who was now far, far away, also could have handled this situation. Perhaps Lawton was right: Perhaps she was just a squaw and had no business trying to lead a group of men.

"Give us the supplies," she heard herself saying, "or I will kill you, Lawton."

The direct challenge was too much for Lawton to bear. He swung the barrel of the rifle toward Shining Moon.

"You red whore!" he rasped. "Nobody talks to me like that!"

In turning toward Shining Moon, however, he took his eyes off Proud Wolf, who sprang forward with the speed of his namesake. The young Sioux's fingers closed around the barrel of Lawton's rifle and forced it up. Lawton grunted in surprise and staggered back a step. Proud Wolf hung on stubbornly to the gun.

Lawton slipped in the mud, caught his balance, and drove a kick at Proud Wolf. Proud Wolf fell, but as he went down he jerked hard on the barrel of the rifle, pulling it away from Lawton for an instant before he drove the butt of it back into the older man's stomach. Keeping his hold on the weapon, Proud Wolf dragged the muzzle down into the mud.

Before Lawton could do anything else, Shining Moon was on him, a fierce expression on her face as she whipped out her own knife and placed the edge of the blade against his throat. The move was too fast for him to counter, and he found himself staring into her eyes from a distance of only a few inches as the keen edge of the knife hovered against his skin.

"Let go of the rifle and the supplies and step back," she hissed.

Lawton's gaze darted over toward his men, and Shining Moon could read the plea for help in them. But she could not take her attention off Lawton to see if that plea was being answered. She stood there next to him, taut as a bowstring, ready to drive the knife into his throat.

"Forget it, Lawton." Aaron Garwood's voice came from behind Shining Moon. "Those fellas have too much sense to help you. They know you're likely to get them killed if they follow you, and they're probably as tired of hearing you run off at the mouth as the rest of us are."

Lawton was trembling with rage, but Shining Moon could see the bitter realization dawning in his eyes. He was on his own. With another shudder, he dropped the pack of supplies and the rifle and stepped back. Proud Wolf pulled the rifle over to him by the barrel. The confrontation was over.

"All right," Lawton grated. "If that's the way you want it, it's fine by me. Go with this stupid squaw and wind up dead for all I care. But you can't send me off into the wilderness with no provisions."

Professor Franklin spoke up. "He's right, Shining Moon. It wouldn't be humane to make him leave with no food."

"I would not do that," Shining Moon replied, breathing a little easier now. She sheathed her knife and said, "I did not want him to take the entire pack of supplies, but I am willing to let him have some of them." A faint smile appeared on her face. "Although if he is so much at home in the mountains, he should be able to fend for himself."

Glaring at her, Lawton began, "If you wasn't a woman—"

"If I were not a woman, you would not have tried to impose your will on me," Shining Moon broke in hotly. She controlled her anger by telling herself that a Hunkpapa always remained dignified, then went on, "I will not force you to leave the group. That is your own choice. You can stay with us, or you can go. If you go, you can take rations for four days."

"Four days?" Lawton repeated. "Where the hell can I get to in four days?"

"There is plenty of game in these mountains. Make the supplies last. A man who can make snares and traps can live here for a long time without any supplies bought from a store. My people have done it for hundreds of years."

"I ain't no stinking heathen."

Proud Wolf said coldly, "And the entire Sioux nation is glad of this."

"Are you going or staying?" Shining Moon asked.

"I'm going! I wouldn't stay here with you people if you was to ask me!" Lawton picked up the supply pack, took out some jerky and hardtack, a small pouch of salt and another of sugar, and a spare powder horn. He stored the supplies in his possibles bag, then tossed down the pack and asked, "That suit you, squaw?"

Shining Moon nodded gravely and gestured for Proud Wolf to return Lawton's rifle to him.

"Now go," she said.

Lawton turned and trudged away in the rain. Shining Moon watched his retreating figure for a moment, then turned back to where Aaron knelt on the ground beside Clay.

"Is he coming around?" she asked.

Aaron shook his head gravely. "Not yet."

Shining Moon bent to help Aaron lift Clay again. "Take us to the cave," she said to Proud Wolf.

Before they could get Clay on his feet, however,

two of the other men had stepped forward, and one of them said, "Let us take him, ma'am. We'd be pleased to."

Shining Moon looked up at them and saw the respect in their eyes, respect for the way she had stood up to Lawton. She saw admiration mirrored on the faces of the other men in the group.

"Thank you," she said sincerely, moving aside to let one of the men take her place. The other one got on Clay's other side, freeing Aaron to go over to Lucy Franklin and make sure she was all right. Shining Moon saw the look von Metz gave Aaron and knew the Prussian wished he had thought of that first.

The two men got Clay upright, wrapped their arms around his waist, and slung his arms over their shoulders. They were able to half carry, half drag him that way.

"Your man ain't steered us wrong yet," one of them said to Shining Moon. "Reckon the best thing we can do is let you take his place until he's up to running things again."

"I will do my best," Shining Moon said. She picked up the pack from which Lawton had taken his supplies and slung it on her back. To her brother she said, "Show us this cave you found."

Proud Wolf set off along the slope, quartering steadily up it toward the higher mountains. The others followed him, passing over the huge scar in the earth left by the avalanche. The rocks and mud had swept the hillside clean, leaving a swath of destruction more than a quarter of a mile wide. In a way that made the going easier, since all the obstacles had been wiped away, but the footing was still slippery and treacherous because of the mud and rain.

Eventually they reached a steeper slope, where outcroppings of rock were arranged almost like steps leading up to a narrow, dark opening in the hillside. Shining Moon recognized it as the mouth of a cave, partially blocked by rocks and debris left behind by the avalanche. She and Proud Wolf led the group toward it. As they went up, she glanced over her shoulder and saw that Aaron was still beside Lucy Franklin, helping her father assist her in the climb. Von Metz and the others, including the two who were supporting Clay's limp body, trailed along behind. It was difficult getting Clay up the slope, and several others pitched in to help.

When Shining Moon and Proud Wolf reached the cave entrance, she said to him, "You say you waited in here during the avalanche?"

"I did."

"There were no other occupants?"

"If you mean our friends Bear or Skunk or Badger, I saw and heard nothing of them," Proud Wolf replied, smiling. "I will go in first to make sure they are still not here."

Shining Moon started to object and say that she would go into the cave first, but then she saw the determination on her brother's face and knew from experience that it would do no good to argue with him. When Proud Wolf wanted to do something, only the Great Spirit, the Wakan Tanka, could stop the young man.

Shining Moon contented herself by saying, "Be careful."

Proud Wolf ducked his head and disappeared into the cave. Shining Moon leaned closer to the opening so that she could hear his footsteps as he proceeded slowly and cautiously into the darkness.

After a few moments, he called back to her, "The cave is not large. No one is here but us."

Shining Moon breathed a sigh of relief and stepped through the entrance, motioning for the others to follow. For the first time all day, rain was not pelting against her head, and the absence of it felt rather strange.

She straightened, raised a hand over her head, and her fingers barely brushed the rocky surface of the ceiling. *Good, plenty of head room*, she thought. But they would still need to be careful until they got a fire going and could see. She sank to her knees and felt around her, finding a large open space.

"Bring Clay over here," she said to the men carrying him. "Come slowly, and follow my voice."

She kept talking to guide the men, and a moment later one of them bumped into her with his feet.

"Sorry, ma'am," he said quickly.

"There is no need to apologize. Lay my husband down."

She reached up and helped them guide Clay's body to the floor of the cave. After tucking the depleted supply pack under his head for a pillow, Shining Moon let her fingertips stray over his face and brush his eyes. How she wished those eyes would open, how she longed to hear his lips once again whisper her name. . . .

But details needed to be attended to, and she was in charge now.

"Proud Wolf," she said.

"I am here, my sister."

"Search for dry branches or leaves, anything that we might use to make a fire."

"That is what I have been doing," Proud Wolf replied. "I will soon have enough."

"That is good," she said. "You have flint and tinder?"

"Wrapped up tightly and dry," came the answer.

Confident that Proud Wolf had everything under control, Shining Moon settled back on her heels beside Clay. Gradually, her eyes adjusted to the darkness. Enough grayish light filtered in from the narrow entrance of the cave for her to make out Clay's body, as well as the shapes of the other members of the party as they huddled around the chamber. Everyone was inside now, and Shining Moon could hear the chattering of teeth. They were soaked, and crouching in a hole in the ground did not provide much warmth. The sooner Proud Wolf got that fire going, the better.

He did so a few minutes later. First came only a spark as he struck his flint. Then a tiny flame grew in the tinder he had heaped in the center of a small pile of branches and leaves. The fire grew, caught hold, and spread. More red and yellow flames danced, casting their glow in an ever-growing circle on the floor of the cave.

Soon the fire was burning brightly. As he sat beside Lucy and Professor Franklin, Aaron pointed up at the smoke, which rose toward the ceiling and disappeared.

"Got a natural flue somewhere up yonder," he said. "It's sucking the smoke right out of here."

"That is good luck," Proud Wolf said as he hunkered by the fire, warming himself. "The passage must be small and crooked, for no rain is coming through it."

Shining Moon had noticed the same thing. It was doubtful that Proud Wolf could have found a better place for them to wait out the storm. The cave was big enough for all of them to get inside, yet its confines were close enough for the fire's warmth to spread quickly through the rock-walled room. They were lucky, Shining Moon thought. The avalanche easily could have killed them all, instead of just the few who had panicked and run. As it was, the only serious injury among them was Clay's.

She lowered her head and closed her eyes. Clay *had* to be all right. She could think of nothing else. If they had been in the village of her people, she could have brought a holy man to Clay's side to sing over him. Here there were no holy men. She was the one responsible, and she had done what she could for

Clay's body: She had led them out of danger, gotten him out of the rain and mud, and had made him comfortable on the floor of the cave by pillowing his head and spreading a blanket over him. Now she had to heal his spirit. Surely the Wakan Tanka would know that she meant no offense by singing the words of the healing song.

Eyes closed, Shining Moon began to sway slowly back and forth. In a clear voice that trembled with love and hope, she sang:

> "Oyate wan waste ca
> Wanna piyawakage-lo!
> Wankanta Tunkasila heya ca
> Wanna piyawakage-lo!"

No ceremony accompanied the song, as would usually have been the case; only the voice of Shining Moon. Then, as she repeated the words, Proud Wolf joined her. Tentatively, Aaron sang as well, struggling with the words. Even though they did not fully understand what was going on, the others must have sensed the gravity of the situation, for they tugged their hats off and sat quietly, solemn expressions on their haggard faces.

Professor Franklin and Lucy watched in awe, their own discomfort forgotten for the moment as they were swept up by the emotions in the cave. Only Rupert von Metz seemed unmoved as he sat with his head and shoulders slumped forward and his knees drawn up.

How long she sang, Shining Moon had no idea. She felt herself being transported away from that place, felt warm sunshine and the gentle kiss of a breeze on her face. The fragrance of flowers and pine trees filled her senses, and when she looked around, she found herself standing in a beautiful meadow, high on the side of a mountain. The sky was a gorgeous blue above her head, and she was looking up at it when she heard her name called. She turned and saw Clay, standing above her on the mountainside, having paused there in his climb. He called her name again, and Shining Moon beckoned to him.

"Come down, Clay! Come down from the mountain."

He hesitated, then started to move, and suddenly he was at the edge of the meadow, running toward her. She stepped forward to meet him, lifting her arms, opening them to draw him into her embrace—

Shining Moon slumped forward, her eyes jolted open by the shock, and she saw that she was not in a beautiful mountain meadow at all but rather inside a damp, cold, smoky cave in the side of a hill. Clay was still stretched out before her, motionless, eyes closed, features pale and drawn. Shining Moon's lips moved, and the final words of the healing song faded. She knew that she had failed, that her vision had been only that, a dream with no substance. She closed her eyes again and tried to choke back the sob that welled up in her throat.

"Sh-Shining . . . Moon . . . "

Her head jerked up at the sound of the weak, hoarse whisper, and as she looked at her husband's face, she saw something even more beautiful than the vision that had filled her mind moments earlier: She saw Clay Holt open his eyes, look at her, and smile.

Chapter Fifteen

Just as Jeff had surmised from his first visit, the Tontine Coffee House was at the center of commerce in New York City. Its proximity to the harbor and the offices of most of the city's shipowners made the establishment a busy place from dawn until after dusk. The day after Jeff arrived with Ned, Lemuel March took both young men to his office and from there to the coffeehouse.

"This is the best place to inquire about Mervale," Lemuel told Jeff as they entered the impressive building. "If it's all right with you, I won't mention your personal reasons for wishing to locate him. We'll make it sound strictly like a business matter. The men who congregate here understand those motives better than any others."

Jeff agreed. Whatever Lemuel thought was best was fine with him.

Most of the men at the coffeehouse had been there the day before and remembered Jeff and Ned. They were still staring today, some more blatantly than others, but evidently Lemuel March's presence was enough to make them accept the two visitors from the West. Clearly, Lemuel was highly respected in these circles.

He introduced Jeff and Ned to several men, all of whom had ships at the nearby docks.

"My friends here are trying to locate a man named Merrivale," Lemuel explained. "Charles Merrivale. Have any of you heard of him?"

"What line of business is he in?" someone asked.

"I'm not sure," Jeff said. "If I had to guess, I'd say he probably owns a mercantile store. But he could also be involved in shipping."

"Why are you looking for him?" someone else asked.

"It's a business matter," Jeff replied, taking his cue from what Lemuel had said earlier. "I have, ah, a proposition to make to him."

And a simple proposition it is, Jeff added silently. *Tell me where my wife is—or else!*

But all he received from Lemuel's friends were shakes of the head and a few expressions of regret.

"Sorry we can't help you, lad," one them said. "If we knew this fellow Merrivale, we'd tell you, I can promise you that."

"Could he have set up a business here in New York without you gentlemen knowing about it?"

Lemuel answered, "Not likely. It's our business to know all the store owners in the area. They buy the goods we bring in from England and France, you know. Except for the ones we ship on to other areas."

Ned had been paying little attention to the conversation. He seemed engrossed in the paintings that adorned the walls of the coffeehouse, paintings that featured all sorts of ships, from frigates to brigantines, plying the oceans of the world. His eyes widened as he studied the graceful vessels, their sails billowing with wind. He could almost see them moving across the waves, as if they had come to life before his eyes. Ned had been listening to what was going on with one ear, however, and he heard Lemuel's comment about shipping trade goods to other areas.

"You mean your ships go somewhere else besides New York?" Ned asked, turning to Lemuel.

"Certainly. The main trade routes run between either here or Boston and England, but the March Shipping Company also sends vessels up and down the Atlantic coast, from New Hampshire all the way down to Florida."

Ned glanced at the paintings again. "Lemuel, do you think we could go down to the harbor and take a closer look at your boats?"

"I don't see why not. Are we through here, Jeff?"

"I suppose so. I knew better than to get my hopes up, but I thought one of your friends might have heard of Merrivale."

"Don't be discouraged, lad," another trader said. "We'll all keep our ears open, and if we hear anything about this Merrivale, we'll get in touch with Lemuel."

"I'd appreciate that," Jeff said sincerely. Then he followed Ned and Lemuel as they left the coffeehouse and turned toward the docks.

Most of the ships in the harbor were the roomy, three-masted cargo vessels known as British East Indiamen, developed for the lucrative trade between England and the East Indies some twenty years earlier. Despite their age, they were sturdy craft with a great deal of life in them, according to Lemuel March.

"We can make the crossing to England in three to four weeks," he said as he pointed out the ships that belonged to him. "Coming back takes about two weeks longer, you understand. Have to sail against the trade winds rather than with them."

"What about the ships that sail up and down the coast?" Ned asked.

"Well, speed is less of a factor there, of course. And the ships make more stops along the way. But the distances involved are shorter, too. One of my ships can make the run from here down to, say, Wilmington, North Carolina, in about two weeks."

"Interesting," Ned muttered as he studied the ships lying at anchor.

"Since when did you become so fascinated with ships?" Jeff asked his cousin.

Ned shrugged his shoulders. "I didn't know I was until I started looking at these. But there's something about them, the way they look and the idea of skimming along over the surface of the sea. It just seems so—so free."

Lemuel clapped Ned on the shoulder and laughed. "You've got it, lad. You've summed it up in that one word. The sea has a powerful lure, just like a beautiful woman. And like a woman, if you're not careful, she'll be the death of you."

"Ned knows all about that," Jeff said dryly.

Lemuel laughed again. "There's nothing like dawn on the ocean with a strong wind at your back. It's a beautiful, powerful feeling, my boy. You should experience it sometime."

"Maybe I will," Ned said, still entranced. "Could I go on board one of them and have a look around?"

"I'll do better than that," Lemuel said. "I'll take you on all of mine that are here."

"Thanks, Lemuel. I really appreciate this." Ned's words were heartfelt.

Lemuel glanced over at Jeff. "What about you, lad? Do you want the grand tour, as well?"

"I don't think so. Since the courthouse isn't far, I believe I'll go there and check the tax and property records. Merrivale could have shown up here without drawing much attention to himself, but if he bought land or set up a business, there's bound to be a record of it."

"Yes, that's a good idea. Well, come along, Ned."

Jeff watched them go up the gangplank that led to one of the ships. Lemuel strolled across with the sure-footed ease of the sailor he had been in years past; Ned, looking a bit uncomfortable, clutched the ropes for support as he made his way on board.

Ned's interest in the ships came as something of a surprise to Jeff. With a shake of his head, he left the docks and walked toward the courthouse a few blocks away.

Back at the docks, on board the *Manchester,* Lemuel pointed out various sails to Ned, then took him into the cargo hold.

"This particular vessel will carry grain to England," Lemuel explained. "We'll start loading any day now. Once she's reached port on the other side of the Atlantic, she'll take on another cargo to bring back."

"What would that be?" Ned asked.

"That's hard to say. Might be manufactured goods, farm implements, or fabric or tea from the Indies. I have agents in London who are always on the lookout for suitable cargos." He cocked a bushy eyebrow. "This shipping is a bit of a hit or miss business. There's money to be made, but you need good luck as well as hard work."

Ned's forehead creased in thought. An idea had occurred to him, and like most of his ideas, it seemed quite appealing at first glance. He was determined to think it through, however, instead of plunging right in.

He pondered for a good ten seconds more before he said, "Sir, do you think I could have a job on one of your ships?"

Lemuel blinked in surprise. "Do you really want to go to sea, Ned?"

"When I stepped onto this vessel, I felt something I had never experienced before. It was the lure of the sea that you mentioned, the freedom to run before the wind and answer to no one but the gods of fate."

Lemuel laughed dryly. "That's quite poetic, lad, but there's not much truth in what you just said. It's true the sea has its appeal, but it can also be a harsh mistress. And as for answering to no one . . . well, you should know that the master of a ship rules his vessel like a king while it's at sea. He can have you striped with a whip or thrown into irons if you cross him. Discipline is stern. It has to be, if everyone is to survive the dangers of a crossing."

Ned looked rather crestfallen. "If you don't think I can handle it, just say so, sir."

A flicker of annoyance passed over Lemuel's weathered features as he said, "I meant no offense, Ned. It's just that you're all caught up in the romance of sailing, and you have no idea what it's really like. If you'd had experience aboard vessels like these, it might be different."

"There's only one way to get experience. Someone has to give you a chance." Ned looked shrewdly at the older man. "How did you become a sailor? Did you run away and ship out as a cabin boy?"

"I did not," Lemuel replied. "I was a cabin boy, yes, but I never ran away. My father was first mate on a ship of the line during the war. When it was over, I sailed with him, a lad of fifteen."

"I'm six years older than that now."

"And every bit as stubborn, I see." Lemuel paused for a moment, then said, "Tell you what, Ned. I'll think about it. If you're sure you want to ship out when Jeff is ready to leave New York, I'll find a place for you. It won't be on one of these big merchantmen on the English route, mind you. I want you to sail on one of my smaller ships on the coastal run. That way you can find out if you really have a taste for it. If you do, there'll be a berth waiting for you on a bigger vessel later." Lemuel held out his hand. "How about it?"

Ned hesitated only an instant before firmly gripping Lemuel's hand. "Fair enough."

"I warn you, though, you'll be sailing as a common seaman. There'll be no special favors for you because you're a relative. You'll follow orders and do your share of the work, or the captain will boot you off at the nearest port."

"That's exactly the way I want it," Ned declared.

"Good. Come along, then. I'll show you the other ships in the harbor."

They left the *Manchester* and proceeded along the docks, boarding several other vessels owned by the March Shipping Company. Ned's fascination grew with each visit. He was sure that when the time came, he would still be anxious to go to sea. Of course, that would mean parting company with his cousin Jeff, and Ned would regret that. He had to follow where his heart led, however, and right now it was telling him that his home was destined to be on the briny deep.

Of course, he had also toyed with the idea of going west with Jeff to the Rocky Mountains. He could see now what an immature notion that had been. He had made the right decision; he was sure of it.

As they left the last of the March ships and paused in front of a small office building, Lemuel said, "I've some business with the harbormaster, Ned. Why don't you wait here and watch that ship being loaded? It belongs to one of my competitors, but I imagine you can learn a few things by observing how the cargo's taken aboard. I'll be finished shortly, and then we can go back to the Tontine for lunch."

"All right, sir. That sounds fine to me."

While Lemuel went into the harbormaster's office, Ned turned toward the piers again and tilted his hat back on his head. Several wagons were pulled up on the dock next to the ship Lemuel had indicated, and a dozen or more men had formed a line to unload the crates from the wagons and pass them aboard the ship. From there, more men took the crates and carried them down into the vessel's cargo hold. As Ned watched, more wagons arrived, these loaded with large burlap bags, probably grain, he decided. Most of the workers were stripped to the waist, and a sheen of sweat glistened on their bare torsos.

Ned wandered closer for a better look at the loading operation. He was wondering how the crates were stacked inside the hold when a voice shouted hoarsely, "Watch where ye're goin', ye damned fool!"

Ned looked up and abruptly jumped aside as a crate crashed to the timbers of the dock only a foot or so from where he had been standing. He had inadvertently wandered into the way of a man unloading a wagon, causing him to drop a crate. The red-bearded worker, who was every bit as tall and burly as Ned, glowered at him.

"Sorry," Ned muttered. "Didn't mean to get in the way."

"Oh, ye didn't, did ye?" the man went on angrily. "Ye big landlocked oxen got no business bein' near a ship. Ye're a danger to yerself and to honest sailors who might stumble over ye."

"Wait just a minute," Ned said, feeling his own anger rise. "You've no call to talk to me that way. I'm going to be a sailor myself."

Redbeard stared at him for a few seconds, then threw back his head and bellowed a contemptuous laugh. "Ye? A sailor? Go back to yer farm, sonny boy. A sailor ye'll never be."

One of the other bare-chested workers tugged at Redbeard's arm and said, "Come on, we got crates to unload."

Redbeard shook off his hand and growled, "In a minute. I got to settle this with yon farmer." He fixed a cold stare on Ned. "And who would ye be shippin' out with, boy?"

"I'm going to have a berth on one of Lemuel March's ships."

"Oh, then that explains it," the man said in a contemptuous tone. " 'Tis well known that March will let anybody sail on his ships—even clumsy brutes such as yourself! That's why his vessels are the laughingstocks of the seven seas!"

Ned had been in enough tavern brawls to know that the bruiser was trying to goad him into a fight. Logically, he knew that if he threw a punch at the man, the man's companions would join in the melee. He would be badly outnumbered and would probably be in for the beating of his life.

That was what his brain told him. But his heart told him that he could not allow the insults to himself—and to his friend and host, Lemuel March—to pass unchallenged.

"You're a damned liar," he said.

Redbeard's eyes lit up. "Oh, 'tis a liar I am, is it? I can't let ye get away with sayin' things like that about me, boy."

"Then do something about it."

"I will," the man said. "I'll do—this!"

With no more warning than that, his hamlike right hand snatched up one of the curved, wooden-handled hooks that some of the men used to help them manipulate the heavy crates. With unexpected speed, he swung the point of the hook right at Ned's head.

Fortunately Ned had the presence of mind to duck, and the hook whistled over him, the point missing him by a matter of inches. He had not wanted this fight, but he was damned if he was going to run from it. Besides, running would not do any good. Redbeard and his companions would quickly overtake him. All he could do was try to end the battle as soon as possible.

While Redbeard was still off balance from the missed swing with the hook, Ned whipped a punch into the man's belly. His fist might as well have pounded into a block of wood, however.

Redbeard backhanded the hook at Ned, and this time Ned dived all the way to the dock to avoid being ripped open. Vaguely, he heard shouts and knew that the other crewmen from the ship were hurrying to witness the fight. If he was lucky, they would stand back awhile to see how Redbeard fared against him instead of pitching in right away.

Ned rolled across the heavy timbers and drove his shoulders into Redbeard's legs. He hung on tightly, heaved upward, and was rewarded by a resounding crash as the man tumbled to the dock. Ned scrambled to his feet and lashed out with a kick, his booted foot catching Redbeard on the wrist, sending the hook spinning. But the move left Ned open for his opponent to return the favor, and while he was balanced on one foot, Redbeard kicked the other out from under him.

Ned fell, but hands caught him before he could hit the dock, strong hands that jerked him upright and thrust him forward. The fight was entertaining and certainly better than working; Redbeard's friends wanted to keep it going as long as possible.

Hoots and catcalls came from the ring that had formed around the two adversaries, but Ned knew better than to be distracted by them. He had to keep his eyes on Redbeard, who was back on his feet and swinging a fist like a mallet at Ned's face.

Parrying the blow at the last moment, Ned tried to sneak one of his own through Redbeard's guard, but the burly sailor knocked it aside easily. Ned was overmatched, and he knew it. In the past he had fought when pride or circumstance drove him to it, but more often he had forestalled battles with his quick wit—or quick feet. Now he was trapped, forced to slug it out with a man who was stronger and more vicious than he.

Stepping back quickly, Ned knew that his opponent would follow, and Redbeard did not disappoint him. As the sailor charged toward him, Ned tried a move that he hoped would take the man by surprise. He ducked his head, dove forward, and rolled completely over. His feet came up together, and as he straightened his legs, using every bit of power at his command, he drove his heels right into Redbeard's groin.

The man's scream must have made the masts tremble on ships at the other end of the harbor. Redbeard folded up over Ned's legs and then slumped to the side, whimpering and writhing. Ned scuttled backward, propelling himself with hands and feet, then stood. The ring of Redbeard's friends was closing in around him, and the other men were muttering in anger and scowling darkly at him. They considered the blow Ned had just struck to be a low one, and they were going to avenge it.

Ned clenched his fists. He would not go down easily, he vowed.

"What the devil is going on here?"

The stern voice roared, and the crowd around Ned fell away almost miraculously. Two men strode through the opening. One was Lemuel March, the other a short, broad-shouldered, bullet-headed individual with graying dark hair clipped almost to his skull. He wore an expensive suit, and the shoulders of it bulged with muscle underneath the fabric. Ned knew that Lemuel had been intending to see the harbormaster, and he wondered if this man was he.

The man's next words confirmed the guess.

"I'll not have this sort of brawling on my docks! Since your own captains haven't seen fit to order you back to work, I'll take it upon myself to do so. Move!"

The other sailors hurried to follow the order, leaving Ned standing there alone to face Lemuel and the harbormaster. A few feet away, Redbeard was curled up, still mewling in agony.

The harbormaster cast a contemptuous glance in his direction. "Carney always was a troublemaker, as I've warned his captain more than once. I daresay he started this disturbance, but I want to hear your story anyway, sir." His cold eyes swung back toward Ned.

His pulse still pounding from the exertion of the fight, Ned drew a deep breath to calm himself and then said, "It was partially my fault. I got in his way while he was unloading a wagon. But then he insulted me and insulted my friend Mr. March, and when I called him a liar, he swung one of those hooks at me."

Lemuel was trying to look stern and disapproving, but a hint of amusement lurked around his mouth and eyes. "So you were defending my honor, eh?"

"That and trying to keep from getting killed."

"I don't like fighting," the harbormaster snapped. "Never have. But I have to admit I don't mind seeing somebody stand up to Carney for a change. He's accustomed to running roughshod over whoever strikes his fancy. I'll speak to his captain, but I doubt it'll do much good. Carney may be a bully, but he's also a damned fine sailor. As for you, sir"—he looked at Ned again—"stay the hell off my docks."

Ned blinked in surprise. "But I thought you agreed the fight wasn't my fault."

"I don't care about that. What's important is that Carney will have a grudge against you from now on, and if he doesn't try to settle it, someone else will, in an attempt to curry favor with him. You'll attract trouble down here, mister, and I don't want that."

Grudgingly, Ned said, "I suppose I see your point. And I'll stay away—until it's time for me to ship out."

"You're a sailor?" This time it was the harbor-master's turn to look surprised.

"I'm going to be," Ned declared. "Isn't that right, sir?"

"I, ah, promised the lad a place on one of my ships on the coastal run," Lemuel said.

"Well, that's your business, March," the harbor-master said gruffly. "Just keep your men civilized while they're in port, that's all I ask." With that, he walked toward his office, displaying the same rolling gait as Lemuel.

"Let's get out of here," Lemuel said in a low voice to Ned. He looked at Carney's companions, who had been watching the exchange with surly expressions.

"Get your friend up and take him below," Lemuel told them. He grasped Ned's arm and led him away from the ship.

When they had gone several yards in silence, Ned said, "Honestly, sir, I didn't set out to cause any trouble—"

"I know that, lad. No need to apologize. Sailors have to fight sometimes. It comes as natural to them as breathing."

Ned looked over at him. "Does that mean . . . you think I've got the makings of a sailor?"

Lemuel slapped Ned on the shoulder and said, "We'll see, son. We'll see. Now let's get something to eat. I imagine you've worked up quite an appetite."

The courthouse, which also served as New York's city hall, was an impressive building of three stories, constructed of white marble with a brownstone balustrade running around the top of it. Though not particularly attractive, it was one of the largest buildings in the city. Construction on it had begun in 1803, according to Lemuel, and was still not complete.

Jeff would not have cared if it had been a log hovel, if only it contained the information he was looking for. His search of the county records, however, reached the same dead end it had in all his other stops across the state. If Charles Merrivale and his family were in New York, they had not bought land or paid taxes.

His quest was over, Jeff thought bitterly as he went back to Lemuel March's house. He would never find Melissa.

Ned was full of talk that night, telling Jeff all about the fight on the docks and Lemuel's offer to let him sail on one of the trading ships that traveled up and down the Atlantic coast.

"I suppose that means we'll be splitting up," Ned said after supper in the room they shared. "That's the only thing I don't like about this, Jeff. I thought for a while I'd go back west with you. I know you never offered to take me, but—"

"You'd have been welcome, Ned. I'm sure Clay would have enjoyed getting to know you. But you've got to do what you think is best."

"What about you? Are you going back?"

Jeff peered out the open window at the night. A breeze was blowing in, carrying with it the salty scent of the ocean. That might hold the promise of magic and adventure for Ned, but to Jeff it just smelled fishy. He preferred the crisp, clean air of the mountains and plains.

"I don't know yet," he said honestly after a moment's thought. "I'm convinced now that I'm not going to find Melissa here in New York, but"—he groped for words—"I hate the idea of going back without her."

Ned rested a hand on Jeff's shoulder in sympathy. "I'm sorry, Jeff, I really am. I was hoping we'd find her, too."

"Well, there's still the advertisement in the newspaper, and the notice in Mr. Irving's magazine. Perhaps someone who knows something about Melissa or her family will see one of them."

"Sure," Ned replied, making his voice sound heartier than he felt. "There's always a chance, isn't there?"

"Yes," Jeff said quietly. "There's always a chance."

Dermot Hawley looked up, his expression automatically brightening as Melissa Merrivale entered the room. Melissa Merrivale Holt, he corrected himself, as she never failed to remind him. She was quite stubborn about that.

Just as she was infuriatingly stubborn about everything else, Hawley thought, his pleasant appearance betraying nothing of his thoughts.

"Mother says to tell you gentlemen that dinner will be served in five minutes," Melissa said to her father. "So you're to conclude your business in that time and not bring it to the table with you."

Merrivale just grunted, but Hawley said, "Of course. We wouldn't want to darken your mother's table with gloomy business talk, now would we?" His charming smile and twinkling eyes took any sting out of the words.

Melissa returned the smile. "Certainly not," she said as she withdrew from the study where the men had been talking.

That smile was a small victory, Hawley thought. But soon she would be smiling at him a great deal. Smiling and gasping in ecstasy and clutching at him and crying out his name as he made love to her, ravishing that beautiful body—

Hawley blinked and forced those enticing thoughts out of his mind. If he allowed his imagination to run wild like that for very long, he ran the risk of losing control and moving too fast.

And that might ruin everything, not only the plans he had for Melissa but for her father as well.

Charles Merrivale puffed on his cigar, then said around it, "That's an intriguing plan of yours, Dermot, taking a wagon train full of supplies overland to those new settlers in Tennessee. When do you intend to do it?"

"Everything is still in the preliminary stage right now, Charles," Hawley replied. He lifted his glass of brandy, sipped from it, and continued, "That's why I'm talking to you now. I wanted to give you the opportunity to be a part of the enterprise right from the start. It will take time to put together a large enough cargo of supplies to make the trip profitable, and I'm visiting several merchants in the area to see if they want to participate."

"Count me in," Merrivale said emphatically and without hesitation. "I can provide, oh, perhaps two wagonloads of goods."

"Excellent! I knew I could count on you, Charles. This arrangement is going to make money for all of us."

"Do you have anyone else lined up to provide supplies?"

"I'm working on that. I've spoken to an agent for a shipping line that brings goods across from England. He's expecting a ship here early next month, and I'm certain I can obtain some of that cargo." Hawley put his hand on Merrivale's shoulder. "You let me worry about these details, Charles. You just think about how you're going to spend all the money you make from this venture."

"I don't intend to spend it," Merrivale said,

somewhat stiffly. "I'm going to set it aside for my grandson. Michael will never want for a thing, not if I have anything to say about it."

"That's quite noble, Charles. I'm sure the lad will appreciate it when he's older."

Actually, Michael Holt would never see any of that money, Hawley thought. Once he had married Melissa, it would be only natural for him to assume control of her assets. One way or another, anything Merrivale made out of this enterprise was going to end up in Dermot Hawley's pockets.

Of course, Merrivale was not vital to the success of the plan, but his participation would make things easier. Despite his brusque, sometimes unpleasant personality, Merrivale had a reputation as an honest merchant, and so did the shipping agent Hawley had spoken to. By involving them in the scheme, it would give the whole thing a look of respectability. No one would dream that most of the goods Hawley intended to freight over the mountains into Tennessee were stolen.

Merrivale was talking again, and his words broke into Hawley's musings. "I'm sorry, Charles, what did you say?"

"I was proposing a toast," Merrivale said, lifting his glass of brandy. "Here's to our success, Dermot."

Hawley clinked his glass against Merrivale's. "To success," he said.

And if anyone got in the way? Well, he knew how to deal with such problems.

Merrivale downed the rest of his brandy and, placing the empty glass on a sideboard, said, "We'd better go in to dinner. We don't want to keep the ladies waiting."

"No, indeed," Hawley agreed. "That wouldn't do at all."

He would wait, though. He would wait for Melissa, at least a little while longer. The day was coming, the day that she would be his, totally and completely, to do with as he wished.

Dermot Hawley was still smiling as he and Charles Merrivale left the room.

Chapter Sixteen

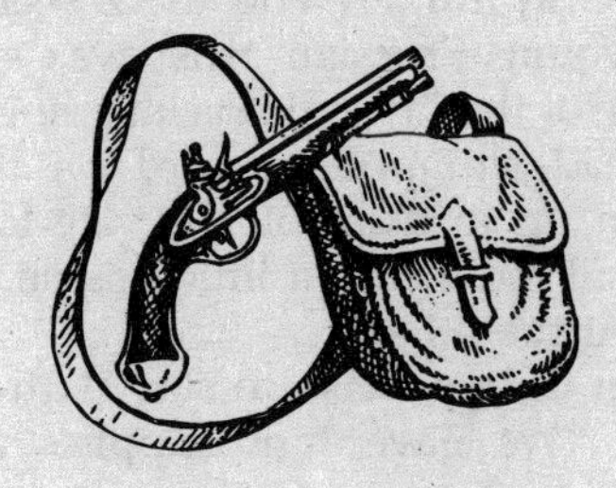

So he was alive after all. That had come as a great surprise to Clay Holt. As he leaned back against the rock wall of the cave and warmed his hands on a cup of hot stew from the pot suspended over the small fire, he looked at his wife and felt a grin spread over his face. He could not help it. He had been smiling a great deal, in spite of the ache in his head, ever since he had awakened earlier to find her gazing down at him in wonder.

On the back of his head was a good-sized knot with a gash on it that had bled profusely. The lump was painful to the touch, and other aches and pains spread throughout his body, but all in all he was fine —and grateful to be alive.

Outside, the rain continued to drum down. There had been no more mudslides, and the air in the cave had warmed somewhat, although it was still dank.

Shining Moon saw Clay watching her and asked, "Why do you smile so?"

"Just looking at the prettiest woman I've ever seen," Clay told her.

"That blow on your skull has addled your senses."

"Nope. I'm seeing things clearer than I ever have." After a moment he asked, "What happened to Lawton? Did the slide get him?"

He saw the quick looks the members of the party exchanged. Only Rupert von Metz seemed uninterested. The young Prussian artist was sitting on the opposite side of the cave, his back jammed against the wall, his head slumped forward on his chest, his knees drawn up in front of him. He looked utterly exhausted and more than a little hostile whenever he glanced up at the others.

"Lawton did not wish to stay with us," Shining Moon said. "We gave him supplies and let him leave."

"That's all there was to it?"

"All that matters," she said flatly.

Clay decided not to press the issue. Something had happened—most likely between Lawton and Shining Moon—but he could tell from her expression and tone of voice that she did not want to discuss it. He knew that later he would get all the details from Proud Wolf, complete with colorful embellishments. The boy certainly liked to spin a yarn.

Clay ate more of the stew, then said, "Well, we've got a snug place to wait out the storm, anyway. But there's another problem. Aaron, open those packs of supplies and dig out as many blankets as you can find."

Aaron looked puzzled. "Blankets?"

"That's right. We've got to get out of these wet clothes before all of us catch a chill. It's warmed up in here a mite, but the clothes aren't going to dry very well as long as they're on us."

Professor Franklin was frowning, and Clay knew

what prompted his concern. The presence of Lucy, not to mention Shining Moon, was going to cause a problem. But Clay had already thought of that, and he had seen a way to deal with it.

Aaron pulled a blanket from one of the packs, and Clay said, "Take that first one over there and tie a corner of it around that little knob of rock that sticks out. Then give the other corner to Proud Wolf."

Aaron nodded, seeing what Clay had in mind. Proud Wolf was sitting cross-legged beside the fire, but he stood up as his friend followed Clay's orders. When one corner of the blanket was tied around the rock as Clay had indicated, Proud Wolf took the opposite corner and held it up, pulling the blanket taut and forming a makeshift screen.

"You two ladies can shuck your clothes back there," Clay told Shining Moon and Lucy.

Shining Moon stepped behind the blanket, and Lucy followed reluctantly, her face burning with embarrassment. Proud Wolf could be trusted not to dishonor his sister by looking upon her nakedness, and if the young Hunkpapa man was tempted to sneak a look at Lucy, Shining Moon's wrath would discourage him.

"Pass out the rest of the blankets," Clay said to Aaron.

The other men awkwardly stripped off their wet buckskins and homespun. Three of the unloaded long rifles were leaned together in a tipi shape near the fire so that the wet clothes could be hung on them, a few garments at a time.

Aaron tossed two blankets behind the makeshift screen for Shining Moon and Lucy, then handed out the remaining ones for the men to wrap up in. There was no problem until Aaron tried to give one of the blankets to Rupert von Metz.

"Take that vermin-infested thing away from me," von Metz snapped. "If you think I am going to strip myself of my clothes and my last shred of dignity in order to garb myself like some sort of prehistoric aborigine, you are greatly mistaken."

"I think you've forgotten where you are, mister," Clay told him sharply. "If you catch a chill from wearing those wet clothes, it's liable to be the death of you. There's no doctor within a couple of hundred miles, and if you start running a fever, there won't be much any of us can do for you."

"Prussians are a hardy people," von Metz said haughtily. "We are accustomed to the cold and damp."

"All right, but I don't intend to sit around here nursing you if you get sick, von Metz. You may have to fend for yourself."

Von Metz glowered at him. "You would not abandon me!"

Clay thought the man sounded a bit less sure of himself than he had a moment earlier.

"Believe whatever you like. Have you ever seen a man burning up from the inside with the fever? It's not a pretty sight."

The Prussian took a deep breath, then snarled, "Give me that!" and snatched the blanket from Aaron's hand. His face set in angry lines, von Metz removed his wet clothing and hurriedly wrapped the wool blanket around his pale, slender form. Then he slumped back against the wall to glare around the cave as if daring any of the others to say anything.

Clay was satisfied. He would not have abandoned von Metz if the man had gotten sick, but he saw no point in letting the problem develop in the first place.

He finished the stew and set his cup aside, then pushed himself to his feet and traded his own clothes for one of the scratchy blankets. He was still lightheaded from the mishap earlier, so he moved carefully as he went over to Proud Wolf and said, "I'll hold that up now. You get those soaked buckskins off."

Proud Wolf turned over the chore to Clay while he changed, and Clay said, "You ladies about done back there?"

"We are ready whenever you are finished," Shining Moon replied.

Clay looked around, saw that all the men were covered with the blankets, including Professor Franklin, who looked rather ludicrous with his round, pudgy face sticking up above the blanket in which he was swathed. He lowered the screen as Shining Moon and Lucy resumed their places near the fire. Their hair, which had been soaked by the storm, was drying now, and it gave them a soft, fluffy look . . . sort of like a mountain goat after a rain. Clay figured they might not fully appreciate that comparison, though, so he kept it to himself.

Everyone settled back down around the fire, and after a moment Professor Franklin asked, "Well? What do we do now?"

Clay listened to the rain falling outside and gave the only answer he could.

"We wait."

The rain continued all day and well into the night, but sometime before dawn it finally stopped. When Clay stepped out of the cave the next morning, the sun was shining brightly, and a warm breeze moved over the face of the hillside. It felt good.

He had slept surprisingly well with Shining Moon snuggled against him. His slumber had been deep and dreamless, and when he awoke, he felt refreshed and even more clear-headed than the day before. He had been lucky to escape from the avalanche without any worse injuries than he had, lucky indeed, and he knew it.

The long rain followed by the strong southern

breeze had cleaned the air, and Clay inhaled deeply as he stared out across the valley of the Missouri's three forks. He could see for thirty or forty miles, all the way to the distant horizon where the Absarokas rose. He lifted his head to scan the mountains looming above him.

A thin plume of smoke twisted into the air, off to the northwest. Clay stiffened as he spotted it. Somebody was up there, a few miles away over the rugged landscape, and he did not think it was Indians. The smoke from an Indian fire was never so easily seen.

Lawton? Clay considered that possibility, but according to Proud Wolf, Lawton had started off in a different direction. Besides, Clay did not think Lawton could have covered that much ground in such a short period of time, considering the storm in which he would have had to travel.

That left the men he had seen through the spyglass, the unsociable group that had left hurriedly when they realized they had been spotted. The thought that they, or some similar bunch, were up there made Clay vaguely uneasy.

Three of the men Lawton had brought out from St. Louis emerged from the cave behind Clay. All of them were carrying their rifles.

"Mornin'," one of them said. "Thought we'd go out and see about pottin' a deer or a bear or an antelope, get us fresh meat."

Clay shook his head and pointed at the rifles. "Not with those. I don't want any shooting for a while unless it's absolutely necessary."

The men frowned at him, and one asked, "Why not? 'Fraid we'll draw Injuns?"

"If there are any Indians around, they won't need gunshots to know we're here," Clay said. "No, I don't want to start any more avalanches. It's still mighty muddy, and some of those rocks up there could slip and fall without much prodding."

"You're saying the sound of a shot could start another rockslide?" The member of the trio who spoke sounded skeptical, and the other two looked as if they shared that sentiment.

"That's right. There are places in the mountains where you don't dare fire a shot even when it hasn't been raining a lot. I've heard about more than one man who went out to shoot a deer and wound up with half a mountain falling on him."

"Well, what are we going to do for fresh meat, then?"

As if in answer to the question, Proud Wolf emerged from the cave carrying the bow he normally wore strapped to his back. A hide quiver full of arrows was slung over his shoulder.

"I will hunt now," he said to Clay.

"Figured you might be wanting to," Clay said. "I was going to suggest it if you didn't. Be careful, though. Don't try to take down Old Ephraim with an arrow."

Proud Wolf gave Clay a look of amusement. "My people have hunted grizzlies before."

"Well, we can't carry a bunch of bear meat. A deer'll do just fine."

Proud Wolf loped off along the hillside, avoiding the worst patches of mud, and soon disappeared in the heavy timber that covered most of the foothills.

Shining Moon stepped out into the sunshine. She was wearing her buckskin dress and leggings, both of which were decorated with feathers and dyed porcupine quills. Most of the mud that had coated the clothes the day before had dried and flaked off. She ran her fingers through her long raven hair, and as Clay watched her, he thought she had never looked more beautiful.

"Good morning," she said. "You did not wake me."

"Didn't have the heart to disturb you," Clay explained. "You'd been through a lot, and I figured you needed your rest."

"Are you all right this morning?"

Clay reached up to the knot on the back of his head. "It still feels like a mule kicked me, but I'll be fine."

Shining Moon nodded, and as the three men who had been planning to hunt returned to the cave, she went over to Clay and slipped her arms around him.

"It is a beautiful morning," she whispered.

Clay lowered his face to hers and kissed her. It was so good to taste the sweetness of her lips, to feel the warm strength of her body pressed against him. . . .

A tingle of unease went through him.

Shining Moon must have sensed it because she took her mouth away from his and asked, "What is it?"

"Don't know," Clay answered honestly, frowning. He lifted his eyes and scanned the mountaintops again, but no longer could he see smoke. Whoever had been responsible for the fire was gone.

But still he had the uncomfortable feeling of being watched. And he did not like it, not one damned bit.

Harry Lawton's fingers tightened on the flintlock rifle in his hands. He wished he could lift it to his shoulder and put a ball through Clay Holt's head. He ached with the desire to kill Holt and that Indian wife of his.

But he was not ready yet. The time would come, but this was not it.

Lawton sank lower behind the boulder that concealed him. He was close enough to see Holt and Shining Moon but far enough away to keep from being spotted, if he was careful. He intended to be mighty careful until he had taken his revenge on the people who had wronged him.

Shivering and miserable in his wet clothes, Lawton closed his eyes and leaned his head against the rock. He wished he could get warm. He was chilled to the bone, and no amount of bright sunshine seemed able to penetrate the frigid cloak that had drawn around him.

He had not gone far the previous day after leaving the group, just far enough to be out of sight. He had firmly believed that some of his men would see the error of their ways and come after him when he stalked off, might even beg him to come back and take over command again—the command that was rightfully his. But that had not happened. The sorry bastards had chosen to cast their lot with Holt and that Indian wife of his. Well, that was fine, just fine with Harry Lawton. They would *all* be sorry.

When it had become obvious that nobody was coming after him, Lawton stopped and turned around, then trailed the group to the hillside cave. As darkness fell, he had been able to see the warm red glow of the fire within the cave, and it had looked mighty appealing to him. But his pride would not let him go back. Besides, he knew that Shining Moon might have shot him if he had poked his nose in the cave. So he had huddled underneath a tree all night as the rain kept coming down. The tree did not offer much shelter, but it was better than nothing, Lawton supposed. Still, he was soaked to the skin, and with the soaking had come the cold.

Lawton's teeth chattered. Damn, he ought to have warmed up by now, he thought, especially the way the sun was shining. It was a beautiful day.

But it would be an even better day, he thought, when Clay Holt and Shining Moon were both dead. Then those other ungrateful sons of bitches would be glad to have him take over again. He had to handle this just right, though. He had to bide his time and wait until Holt was off away from the others. Better yet, Holt and the woman both.

A lot of fatal mishaps occurred in these mountains, and if an "accident" claimed their lives, the others would be quick to accept him again as their leader. The professor could not take over; he was an easterner and an inexperienced fool. Aaron Garwood was too green, and nobody was going to take orders from an Indian kid like Proud Wolf.

The thought of Rupert von Metz made Lawton shiver with rage. The Prussian had agreed to help him get even with Holt, but he had remained with him and the others, a traitor of the worst kind. Once he was in control again, Lawton would set the arrogant foreigner straight.

All he had to do was get rid of Holt and his squaw, and everything would be all right, Lawton told himself with great satisfaction. He could wait, too.

He just wished he could warm up.

Proud Wolf returned less than an hour after he had left the cave, the carcass of a young doe draped over his shoulders. He had brought it down with a single arrow, he explained, making the episode sound like an epic battle.

Clay and Aaron went to work skinning and gutting the deer, then carving off several steaks for the group's breakfast. They spent the rest of the morning smoking the remainder of the meat so they could take it with them.

The sun and the breeze dried the ground quickly, and by midday the mud had solidified. Clay and two of the other men scouted in a half-mile circle around the cave and found nothing threatening. The only interesting thing they found, in fact, was Clay's coonskin cap, hung on the branch of a bush that had been in the path of the avalanche. The cap had dried enough to wear it, and Clay settled it gingerly on his head, trying not to put pressure on the lump on his skull.

When he and his companions got back to the cave, Clay announced, "I don't see any reason why we can't move out and head on up into the mountains."

"You are sure you feel like traveling?" Shining Moon asked.

"I'm sure," Clay said. "You know me; I always feel better when I'm on the move."

She said with a trace of humor, "I have noticed this about you, Clay Holt."

Everyone was in good spirits as they gathered their gear in preparation for leaving. Even Rupert von Metz seemed to have recovered from his sour mood of the day before. During the morning he had set up his folding easel and taken a small canvas from his pack of artist's supplies. He had worked for hours depicting the impressive span of landscape around them. From what Clay had seen, von Metz had done a good job of capturing the view across the valley toward the Absarokas.

The remaining men Lawton had hired for the expedition in St. Louis had completely switched their allegiance to Clay, and they complied cheerfully with his orders as the group got moving again, heading higher into the mountains toward the dividing ridge. Clay suspected some of their newfound cooperation was due to Shining Moon. They had to respect her for the way she had handled herself during the aftermath of the avalanche, including the confrontation with Lawton. Some of that respect was rubbing off on him, as well.

They made good progress that afternoon and for the next three days. The fair weather held as the party climbed higher, leaving the foothills behind and entering the more rugged terrain of the mountains. They worked their way back and forth, following the valleys between the towering peaks and gradually treading higher and higher toward the passes that would take them to the other side of the Rockies.

Clay had no major aftereffects from the blow on the head. The swollen lump gradually went down, leaving a purplish-yellow bruise that was tender to the touch. His mind remained clear, however.

As they traveled Clay kept a lookout for more smoke, but none was to be seen. If that mysterious group of men was still up there, they were either on the move or had extinguished their campfire, he thought. From time to time he felt that same instinctive crawling of his nerves that told him someone was watching. Whoever they were, they were good at what they were doing, damned good, Clay judged. And that kept him on edge.

If anything, the harrowing experiences the group had been through had brought them closer together. The men joked among themselves and did everything Clay asked them to do. Professor Franklin went back to his collecting and cataloging of specimens, assisted by Lucy and Proud Wolf, who listened intently as the professor gave a running lecture on botany and natural history. Aaron Garwood spent a lot of time with the professor, too, but Clay suspected Aaron's real motive was to be around Lucy rather than to learn more about scientific subjects. Rupert von Metz was the only one who kept to himself, and even he was not as hostile as he had been.

The storm had been the last gasp of winter. The days were mild now, and the new growth of spring was everywhere. The arching dome of sky above the mountains was dotted from time to time with fluffy clouds, but there was no more threat of rain. It was sights like this, Clay thought more than once as he paused to take in the magnificent vista surrounding them, that made the hardships of living in the mountains worthwhile.

On the fourth night after leaving the cave, the group camped in a meadow high on the side of a mountain. The plateau was covered with grass and trees, and a spring bubbled out of the rock base of the steep slope bordering it. The water was cold, clean, and sweet. If he had not promised to take the expedition on to the Pacific so that they could meet the boat waiting there for them in the fall, Clay would not have minded making this place his base camp for a summer of trapping. It was as close to perfect as a man could find. But he was responsible for Professor Franklin and the others, and he was going to get them through or die trying.

That thought crossed his mind while they were setting up camp. He had come close to dying more than once already, but that was the way of the mountains. They gave a man beauty and bounty, but sometimes they demanded a high price. Clay Holt had always been willing to pay that price if need be, and he was not about to change now.

But he wished he could shake that uncomfortable feeling that was gnawing at him. . . .

Harry Lawton shivered as he stared down at the glowing campfire below. Heat as strong as that which came from those flames raged through him, and it was hard to believe that only a few days ago, he had been worried because he could not get warm.

Well, he was warm now. He was a long way past warm.

Deep in the recesses of Lawton's brain, a part of him was still thinking clearly enough to realize that he was burning up with fever, no doubt a result of huddling under that tree in the rain all night after he had been forced to leave the expedition.

That was the way he remembered the confrontation now. They had *forced* him to leave, kicked him out as if he were no better than some mongrel dog. But they would pay for the way they had treated him; all of them would pay. *Especially Holt and his red-skinned wife.*

For almost four days now, Lawton had trailed them, guided by instinct and whatever providence controls the fate of madmen. And he was undeniably mad, racked by fever and twisted by hate and resentment until his need for revenge was the only thing that kept him going. At first he had waited patiently for the perfect opportunity to kill Holt and Shining Moon, but he no longer cared about that. All he wanted was a chance, any kind of chance, to kill them all. He sensed that it would come soon.

When they camped in the meadow that evening, Lawton had skirted wide of the spot, staying out of sight as he moved beyond the campsite to the mountain above them. After darkness had fallen, concealing him, he climbed up to his rocky bower, where he would wait for morning. He was confident he could hold off an army up here if he had to. But he would not have to. The bastards would never know what hit them when he started cutting them down. Maybe he would save the two women for last, so he could have a little fun with them before he killed them.

Those insane thoughts were spiraling through his head as he fell asleep, exhausted by effort and illness. How long he slept, he had no idea, but suddenly something roused him, and he sat bolt upright from where he had slumped against the rocks. He saw the rosy glow in the eastern sky and knew that dawn was not far off. Already the predawn light was spreading over the face of the mountain.

Lawton lifted himself up so that he could peer over the rocks in front of him to the right and look down into the camp. But the sight that met his bleary eyes made him stiffen in surprise: Clay Holt was climbing up the steep slope, angling toward him.

Shining Moon awoke suddenly. Her arm went out, her fingers searching for Clay, who should have been lying beside her. Instead, her touch found only emptiness.

During the night she had been restless, unable to sleep. Something about this place bothered her, despite its beauty. Whatever it was had been enough to disturb her so that she did not fall asleep until long after midnight.

Exhaustion gripped her as she tried to pull herself awake now. Her eyes opened, and she saw the pinkish glow of approaching daybreak. She pushed herself into a sitting position, rubbed her eyes, and looked around for Clay but did not see him. No one else was moving around the camp either.

Clay must have gotten up early and relieved whoever was on guard duty, Shining Moon reasoned. She could not remember who that was. Her gaze went to the outer edge of the plateau, then moved over to the slope that formed the other side. There, movement caught her eye.

Two realizations burst upon her at once. Clay was climbing the slope above the meadow; Shining Moon could see that. The other was the reason this place had looked so familiar to her.

It was the meadow from her vision, the place where she had called Clay back from the mountain of death, summoning him back to life. That was how she had interpreted the vision later, and she knew it to be the truth.

Now, a hundred yards away, Clay was climbing that mountain again.

She threw her blankets aside. As she stood up, she cried as loudly as she could, "Clay! Clay, come back!"

She saw him stop and turn, saw another figure

suddenly lurch out from behind a clump of rocks about a dozen feet above Clay. Shining Moon recognized Harry Lawton. He was lifting a rifle, and she heard him howl out a curse as he pointed it at Clay. Then flame and noise belched from the muzzle of the rifle, and Clay fell.

Shining Moon screamed.

Too many things were happening at once. First Shining Moon shouting at him, then the scrape of a booted foot on stone and the insane cry of Harry Lawton from above him. Clay did not waste time trying to figure out how Lawton had come to be there. What the man wanted was all too plain.

He wanted Clay Holt dead.

Clay twisted aside, dropping to the rocky ground as Lawton fired. The rifle ball slammed through the air next to his ear—where his head had been an instant before. As he landed, his rifle slipped from his grip and went clattering down the mountainside.

Lawton tossed his empty rifle aside and reached for the pistol tucked under his belt. His eyes, deep-set in his haggard, bearded face, were shining with madness and, Clay thought, maybe something else. He thought Lawton looked sick, but that did not make him any less of a threat. Rolling over once, Clay jerked out his North and Cheney .56 caliber pistol as the muzzle of Lawton's pistol tracked toward him.

The two men fired nearly at once, and even over the twin blasts of black powder, Clay heard another noise—a deep, growing rumble from somewhere above Lawton. Hard on the heels of that sound came a whine as the ball from Lawton's pistol ricocheted off a rock six inches to Clay's left. A split-second later Clay's shot shattered the grip of Lawton's pistol, blowing it to splinters while neatly taking off the two middle fingers of Lawton's hand. He howled in pain and staggered back a step, shaking his wounded hand

and sending a spray of crimson into the air as blood welled from the stumps.

The roaring was louder now, and Clay knew that somewhere up there above them, a rock had fallen, prodded from its precarious perch by the vibration from Lawton's first shot. That rock had kept tumbling and bouncing downhill, taking another with it, and another and another . . .

"Get down, you damned fool!" Clay shouted at Lawton. "Rockslide!"

Lawton ignored the warning. Catching his balance, he used his good hand to jerk his heavy hunting knife from its sheath. He lifted the blade and staggered toward Clay, the knife poised for a killing stroke.

Down in the meadow a rifle cracked. The ball drove into Lawton's chest, pushing him back a step and standing him up straight. At that moment the avalanche caught him. A heavy rock, bounding through the air, slammed into the back of his head. Blood gushed from Lawton's eyes, nose, and mouth as the impact pulped his skull.

Clay barely had time to see that gruesome sight before he was rolling frantically toward a rock ledge overhang to his right. It would offer him some protection from the avalanche, provided the force of the slide did not dislodge it, too. If the overhang fell, Clay would be crushed like an insect. But he was already being pelted by the rocks that swept past Lawton, bearing the dead man with them, and the rock ledge was his only chance.

The roaring filled Clay's ears, and dust clogged his mouth and nose, choking him. He squeezed his eyes shut against the grit, but he could not keep from breathing it. Huddled there beneath the ledge, his arms crossed over his head for extra protection, Clay waited out the avalanche.

Although it seemed to take hours for the slide to

pass him, Clay knew it was only a matter of minutes. Compared to the avalanche and mudslide that had struck the expedition several days earlier, this one was not very large. It was massive enough to have deposited a good-sized heap of rocks and rubble at the base of the slope, however, and protruding from that heap were the feet and legs of Harry Lawton. The avalanche would have killed Lawton even if the shot had not come from the camp.

At the thought of the camp, Clay looked toward the meadow, blinking dust from his watering eyes and wiping them clear. With relief he saw Shining Moon, standing with a rifle in her hands, and he knew she had fired the shot that Lawton had taken in the chest. Clay stood up and waved at her, and she dropped the rifle and ran toward the slope. She scrambled up to meet him as he slowly descended, careful not to start another slide. She passed Lawton's impromptu burial mound without even a glance at it and flew into Clay's arms, holding him tightly around the waist.

"You are not hurt?" Shining Moon asked as she pressed her cheek against his broad chest. "You are all right?"

"Reckon I'll be fine. Thanks to you."

"No! It was my fault. I knew this was an evil place. I should have warned you there was danger here—"

"Wait a minute. Slow down, slow down." Clay put his hands on Shining Moon's shoulders and peered into her eyes. "I don't know what you're talking about."

"You do not understand! I saw this place in a vision, when I thought you were going to die. This mountain means death, and I called you back from it." Anger flashed in her dark eyes as she looked up at him. "Why were you not in camp? Why were you coming up here?"

"I just thought it would be a good place to take a look around. I-I don't really know any reason other than that."

"Death was calling you," Shining Moon said ominously. "Death was angry that you cheated it before."

Clay did not know whether to take her claims seriously or not. But Shining Moon believed in what she was saying, so he was not going to scoff at them. *And maybe she's right,* he thought. Maybe Death—in the person of Harry Lawton—*had* been calling him.

He looked down at the camp and saw that everyone was awake now, jolted out of sleep by the gunfire and the rumble of the avalanche. Their anxious faces were turned up toward the mountainside.

Clay slipped an arm around Shining Moon's shoulders and said, "Come on. They're waiting for us."

And as he led his wife down toward the camp, past the heap of stone where Lawton had been entombed, Clay noticed that the sun had come up, glowing bright and warm above the horizon.

Chapter Seventeen

There were no replies to the advertisements Jeff had placed in the *Journal* and the magazine called *Salmagundi*. Washington Irving was sympathetic when Jeff paid a call to the magazine's offices, which also happened to be Irving's living quarters.

"It's a shame you haven't been able to locate your wife, Mr. Holt," the well-dressed young man said as he leaned back in his chair behind a desk crowded with sheets of paper covered with handwriting. "Your tale is the stuff of great tragedy, worthy of the Bard or the ancient Greeks. Not that I want to trivialize your reality by comparing it to the fancies of literature. I mean no offense."

"None taken," Jeff assured him. He turned one of the sheets of paper on the desk around and looked at it. "What's this, if you don't mind my asking?"

"Oh, it's just one of a series of articles I've been

working on for the magazine. The history of New York, you know, as purportedly written by one Diedrich Knickerbocker. The readers seem to enjoy them, even if some of the more old-fashioned among them are a bit shocked from time to time. I've been thinking about collecting the pieces into a book."

"Well, good luck with it," Jeff said. He turned toward the door of the office. "And thanks for trying to help."

"Wait a moment!" Washington Irving said. "What will you do now?"

"I haven't made up my mind," Jeff replied.

It was a question that had been preying on him, however, and he considered it again as he made his way back to the March house. He could not continue to impose on the hospitality of Lemuel and Irene, although they did not seem to mind having Ned and him as guests—and Rachel, Jeanne, and Barbara were certainly enjoying the company of their cousins. But staying in New York would be a waste of time, Jeff sensed. It was time to get on with his life.

The real question was—which way was he going?

Ned gave him the answer to that, at least in the short run. When Jeff went in, Ned was waiting for him.

Ned took hold of his arm and said, "After supper, cousin, the two of us are going out to see what sort of entertainment this town's got to offer."

"I don't think so, Ned—"

"Now, I'm not going to listen to any arguments. I've watched you moping around here for weeks, and I'm tired of it. You need a drink in a place where people are enjoying themselves. And so do I if I'm going to be shipping out in less than a week."

"Lemuel has a berth for you on one of his ships?"

"The *Fair Wind*. Good name, isn't it? She's leaving New York for the Carolinas in three days." Ned smiled. "I'm finally going to be a sailor, after all this time."

Jeff refrained from pointing out that Ned had decided to become a sailor less than a month earlier.

"What about it?" Ned said. "After supper we go find us a good tavern, right?"

Impulsively Jeff agreed. "All right. I suppose a drink or two wouldn't hurt."

Ned rubbed his hands together in anticipation. "I hope we can find an establishment with pretty serving wenches. It's been a long time—" He stopped short as he remembered that he was talking to a married man who had been away from his wife for a much longer time than Ned had gone without the favors of a serving girl.

Jeff read those thoughts on his cousin's face and said, "It's all right, Ned. I wish you good luck, even though I'll not indulge myself in those particular entertainments."

Ned's look of concern vanished, and he slapped Jeff on the back. "This town won't soon forget that the Holts were here!"

That evening at supper, Lemuel and Ned talked about shipping, but Jeff was unusually silent.

"Well," Lemuel said after the meal had ended and the three men had withdrawn to the parlor, "what do you two lads have planned for this evening?"

Ned shot a startled glance toward Jeff, then looked back at Lemuel and asked, "What makes you think we, ah, have anything planned?"

"Nothing except that reaction of yours," Lemuel said. "It was just an innocuous question. But now I want to know—what *are* you up to, Ned?"

"We thought we'd go out and find a respectable tavern and have a short drink." Ned looked down.

"I see." Lemuel sounded unconvinced. "You didn't intend to pay a visit to some filthy dive, get stinking drunk, and paw the serving wenches all evening?"

"Of course not!" Ned's response was properly outraged.

"Good." Lemuel stood up, went over to the sideboard where his pipe and tobacco pouch were waiting for him, and picked up the pipe. He pointed its long curved stem at Ned. "Because I'm counting on you being a member of the *Fair Wind*'s crew when she weighs anchor in a few days. If you get yourself killed or hurt in some sort of brawl, or thrown into jail, I'll have to find a replacement for you at the last minute, and I don't like to do that. Do you understand me, Ned?"

"Yes, sir," Ned replied humbly.

"As for you, Jeff, I expect you to have a suitable influence on young Ned here."

"I'm not sure how much influence I can bring to bear," Jeff commented, "but I'll try, Lemuel."

"All right." Lemuel packed tobacco into the wide bowl of the pipe. "Whatever you do, stay away from Red Mike's down on Water Street. A more noisome place you'll never find. There's always some sort of sordid ruckus going on there."

"Red Mike's," Ned repeated. "We'll remember, sir."

"See that you do." Lemuel shooed them out of the room. "Go on, now."

The two young men got their hats and jackets from the rack just inside the front door and stepped outside, leaving their rifles in the house. It was doubtful they would need the long-barreled weapons that night. Both had pistols tucked into their belts, however, and Jeff carried his hunting knife as well.

As they strode down the street, Jeff asked, "Just where did you intend to begin the evening? I'm sure you have someplace in mind."

"Certainly I do." Ned grinned broadly in the twilight. "I thought we'd pay a visit to Red Mike's."

Jeff blinked in surprise. "But you heard what Lemuel said about that place."

"Indeed I did. Can you think of a better reason for going there?"

Jeff had no answer for that. He sighed, shook his head, and followed Ned.

From the outside, Red Mike's was just as squalid as Lemuel had made it out to be. It was located in a small stone building that did not open onto Water Street itself, as Lemuel had indicated, but rather onto a narrow alley running between that waterfront avenue and the next street over. A passerby had told them how to find the place, and the man had also said, "But only a fool'd go there. 'Tis sometimes worth a man's life to venture into such places."

Ned had not been impressed by the warning.

A red lantern hung over the doorway, which was probably what gave the place its name. The stench of human waste and rotting food from the alley made Jeff pause at the entrance to the passage.

"Are you sure you want to go in there?" he asked Ned.

"Of course. Why not?"

The answer seemed obvious to Jeff, but Ned was not in a mood to listen to reason.

"I don't much like the looks of this, Ned."

"It's just a tavern," Ned scoffed. "I've been in dozens worse than this. Come on."

Having been in worse places than Red Mike's seemed to Jeff a dubious reason to boast. He trailed after Ned, who walked boldly down the alley. The passageway was quite dark, the red-painted lantern giving off little light, and Jeff's boots slipped on the paving stones. He hoped he was not stepping in something too disgusting.

When they were halfway down the alley, the

door of the tavern swung open, and a slender figure stepped out, silhouetted for a second by the garish light within. The sound of coarse laughter floated out with the figure, and if anything, the smell in the alley grew worse. The man shut the tavern door behind him and walked toward Jeff and Ned.

Jeff could barely make him out against the faint glow of the red lantern. He touched Ned on the arm and said, "Better step aside." The figure was striding toward them with his head down. Jeff and Ned moved over to let him pass.

The stranger stalked by them without a word. The brief glimpse Jeff had was of a man in dark clothes, wearing a floppy-brimmed hat and a cloak with the collar turned up so as to conceal most of his face. Ned turned to watch him pass, then cocked an eyebrow.

"Strange gent, eh?" he commented.

The door of Red Mike's suddenly slammed open again, and this time three men hurried out, carrying themselves with a tense, angry air as they looked up and down the alley.

One pointed toward Jeff and Ned and exclaimed, "There he goes!"

"Get him! Stop that son of a bitch!" another man howled.

Then all three pounded down the narrow alley, straight toward Jeff and Ned.

"Watch out, cousin!" Ned yelled, grabbing Jeff's arm to jerk him out of the way. The men charged past, brandishing knives and pistols.

Relieved that the trio was not after him and Ned, Jeff turned to watch the pursuit. The man in the cloak had broken into a run, and despite the enveloping folds of the cloak, he moved with a lithe grace and speed. Barely slowing, he whipped around the corner onto Water Street.

"Come on!" Ned urged, tugging on Jeff's arm. "Let's go see what happens!"

Jeff had a pretty good idea of what was going to happen. After the three men caught up to their quarry, there would be a fight, and someone would be hurt, perhaps killed. The cause of the disagreement did not particularly matter: a perceived insult, an accusation of cheating at cards, the wrong look cast at the wrong woman—it could have been any of a hundred reasons.

While Jeff hesitated, Ned broke into a run and chased after the men who had just left Red Mike's. Sighing, Jeff went after him. Ned was just hotheaded enough to get involved with something that did not concern him in the slightest—and get hurt for his trouble.

When Jeff reached the end of the alley and emerged onto Water Street about ten feet behind Ned, he spotted the running figures at the end of the block. No one else was about at the moment, and it was easy to pick them out in the light of a streetlamp. The men were closing in on the figure in the cloak. Jeff drew up alongside Ned, and both of them trotted after the others.

One foot of the fleeing man must have struck a loose paving stone, for he fell, sprawling heavily in the street. With triumphant shouts his three pursuers closed in.

"We got him now!" one of the men yelled, pointing his pistol at the fallen figure.

Almost too quickly for the eye to follow, the man in the cloak rolled over and whipped out a pistol of his own. Coolly facing the muzzle of his adversary's gun, the man fired, his flintlock pistol booming as the orange flash of fire split the darkness. The other man had been too slow. He let out a shriek of pain, doubled over, and was carried past the man in the cloak by his own momentum. He stumbled a second later and went down.

The cloaked man dropped the empty pistol, rolled again, and came up onto his feet in one efficient motion. The other two were practically on top of him when he regained his feet, however, and each of them held a knife. The lamplight glinted off the blades as they were lifted to strike.

Before those blows could fall, the light glittered on yet another length of cold steel, this one long and slender and wielded by the man in the cloak. The sword flashed through the air, its razor-sharp point raking across the wrist of one of the men. He screamed and dropped his knife as blood spurted from the slashed veins, spattering the paving stones at his feet. Dropping to his knees, he grasped his injured wrist, cradling it against him.

The remaining member of the trio lashed out frantically with his knife. There was a tearing sound as the blade tangled for a second in the folds of the black cloak, then ripped free. It had obviously not found flesh, for the cloaked man smashed a fist into his opponent's face with more power than that slender figure should have possessed. The blow rocked the man back a step, and the sword gleamed in the light once more as its edge cut across the man's chest.

He stumbled away from the lethal blade, throwing his own knife down and holding up empty hands.

"Mercy, damn you!" he called. "Mercy!"

Mercy was not in great supply, however. The man in the cloak slashed the sword across the outstretched palms. The other man flinched away from the cutting edge with a cry, then turned and ran, following the example of his wounded companion, who had lurched back to his feet and was stumbling down another alley.

That left only the man who had been shot in the belly. The cloaked figure strode over to him, prodded him in the side with a toe, then nodded in satisfaction. The man was dead.

"You bloody sot!" the victor said in a voice startling in its clarity. "It's a shame you'll never know you've been bested by a woman."

Ned let out a low whistle of awe. Jeff was too shocked to respond.

The figure in the cloak whipped around and noticed Jeff and Ned for the first time. Her hat had come off in the fall, revealing close-cropped dark hair. She stiffened, then lifted the sword and pointed it at Jeff and Ned.

"Come ahead, if that's your wish," she challenged. "If it's trouble you're after, I can give you all you can handle."

Jeff found his voice first. "We want no trouble," he said. "We saw those men pursuing you and came along to see what was going to happen."

"Odds of three to one don't disturb you, eh?" The words were couched in scorn. The woman's voice had a British accent, and it was low and husky enough to pass for a man's.

Stung by her accusation, Ned said, "We would've pitched in to help you if you had seemed to need it. You handled those three with ease."

"It was a bit dicey for a moment or two," the woman said. She slid the sword into its sheath under the enveloping cloak and bent to pick up her hat and pistol.

Ned stepped forward impulsively and stuck out his hand. "I'm Ned Holt, and this is my cousin Jeff," he declared.

The woman hesitated and glanced over at the body of the dead man.

"This is hardly the time or place for introductions," she said. "Someone probably heard that shot and sent for the constable. I want to be well away from here before he puts in an appearance."

"All right," Ned said. "Come along with us."

"And why in blazes should I?"

"Because I'd like to know a woman who can fight like you can," Ned replied.

"How utterly charming. I'll wager you say that to all the ladies." With a jerk of her head she added, "Come along, if you've a mind to. I could use another drink. You lads might as well buy it."

"But not in Red Mike's," Jeff put in.

"No," the woman agreed dryly, "not in Red Mike's."

As they started along Water Street, heading in the direction of its intersection with Wall Street, Jeff cast a glance at the body lying on the paving stones. He had always been a law-abiding man—well, relatively so, at least—and it bothered him to leave the corpse. Also, even though the killing had been an undeniable case of self-defense, he was not sure he wanted to pass the evening in the company of this mysterious woman. But Ned seemed quite taken with her, and Jeff did not want to abandon his cousin.

"You haven't told us your name," Ned said.

"No, I haven't," the woman replied.

For a moment Jeff thought she was not going to say any more, but then she went on. "It's India. India St. Clair."

"That's an unusual name. A name for an unusual woman, I'd expect."

India St. Clair made no reply.

Jeff waited a moment, then asked, "Why were those men after you?"

"That's none of your business, now, is it?" India asked sharply.

"No, I suppose not. But surely you can understand why Ned and I are curious. It's not every day you see a fight between three men and a woman."

"Not with the woman emerging victorious, at any rate." India mulled it over for a few seconds. "I don't suppose it would do any harm to tell you. Those three didn't know I'm a woman. They saw me only as a potential victim. They were thieves."

"It looked more to me like they considered themselves the injured parties," Jeff commented.

"Well, you're wrong," India snapped. "Not that the attempt would have done them any good, even if they had overpowered me. I've no money. I'm flat broke, as you Americans say, and looking for a job."

"Flat broke?" Ned repeated. "That's absurd. A woman like yourself should always have money."

India paused and then said coolly, "Oh?"

"Of course. There are always means for a beautiful woman to earn a living."

Jeff knew what was coming and did nothing to prevent it. A lesson in manners would not hurt Ned.

India pivoted toward him, hooked her booted left foot behind his right knee, and drove her left elbow into his chest as hard as she could, while yanking his leg out from under him. Ned went down like a sack of grain and landed hard on the pavement. India was on him in a flash, slamming her knees into him and driving him down flat on his back. A small, wicked-looking dagger appeared in her right hand as if by magic, and she held the keen edge of the blade against his throat.

"I'll have none of that kind of talk," she informed him in a low, dangerous voice. "I'm a sailor and a fighter, not some tavern wench willing to let any man paw me for the price of a jug of ale!"

"All—all right!" Ned gasped, his eyes wide. He lay still, not daring to move with the dagger at his throat. His gaze cut over toward Jeff, who stood calmly with his arms crossed, a wry expression on his face. "You could give me a hand here, cousin!"

"It seems to me you're doing fine by yourself, Ned," Jeff said. "I'd rather you didn't cut his throat, though, Miss St. Clair. He *is* a relative of mine, after all."

"There's an old saying about how you can't choose your relatives," India said. Taking the blade away from Ned's neck, she stood up smoothly. "I'll not kill you, but mind your tongue in the future, Ned Holt."

"Oh, you can be sure I'll do that." Ned climbed to his feet and rubbed his backside, sore from the hard landing on the street. "I'm sorry, Miss St. Clair. I didn't mean to insult you. I spoke without thinking."

"A failing common to most men." She put the dagger away, the small blade disappearing somewhere under the cloak just as the sword and pistol had earlier.

Jeff laughed and gestured toward the Tontine Coffee House, less than a block away.

"Instead of finding another tavern somewhere, why don't we go to the Tontine? I'd rather have a mug of hot coffee than a drink, anyway."

"As long as you're buying, Mr. Holt, I don't care. As I told you, I've no money."

"I'm buying," Jeff said. "Come on, Ned."

Ned was feeling his throat to make sure he was not bleeding. As he fell in step alongside Jeff and India, he complained, "You could have killed me, you know."

"Only if I'd wanted to," she said.

The three of them were soon seated at a table inside the main room of the coffeehouse, which would not close for another hour or so. Few customers were in the place. The barman brought them mugs of coffee, and Ned's was laced with brandy at his insistence.

"I need fortification," he said. "It's been a trying evening. I don't often come that close to having my throat slit by a young woman."

"No, I'd wager you've been in more danger from

the husbands of young women," India said, drawing another chuckle from Jeff. She had not known Ned for long, but she already had him pegged.

After she had taken several sips of the bracing coffee, India said, "I'd rather not have it bandied about that I'm a woman, if you don't mind. I've gone to great pains to conceal that fact."

"Your hair, you mean," Ned said.

"And other things." She gave him a cool-eyed stare over the lip of her mug. "It helps being slender."

Ned slowly turned red as the meaning of her words sank in. Jeff would not have thought it was possible for Ned Holt to be embarrassed, but India had managed it.

"I think you must have an interesting story," Jeff said quietly. "If you'd like to talk about it, Ned and I would be glad to listen."

"Why should I talk to you two? I never saw either of you before tonight."

"That's as good a reason as any," Jeff said. "If you've been keeping it a secret that you're a woman, I imagine it's been pretty difficult not having anybody to talk to."

"Aye, that's the truth," India said, then hesitated, as if she realized she might be giving away too much of herself. Abruptly she shook her head, casting away that worry. "I suppose it wouldn't hurt to tell you. You strike me as honest blokes—even if Ned here is a bit too quick to assume he knows everything there is to know about the world."

Ned looked as if he could not decide whether or not to be offended by her comment, but he kept quiet.

"I was born in the slums of London," she began, "and a worse hellhole you're not likely to find. I never knew my father, and you can imagine what sort my mother was, a woman alone like that. She died when I was quite young, six years old, I think. It's difficult to be sure about things like that. Some sort of pox took her; it could have been one of a dozen different illnesses, considering the kind of life she led.

"Don't waste your sympathy on me, lads. I can see it on your faces. I made out just fine for a while. I was small and fleet of foot, the best thief and beggar Whitechapel ever saw. I would have been content to continue in that manner, but when I reached the age of about twelve, some of my mother's old 'friends' showed up and wanted to start the same sort of business with me that they had with her. I was having none of that."

"I should say not!" Ned muttered.

India took another sip from her mug. "So I cropped off my hair, and that let me pass as a boy, at least for a while. I was convinced that wouldn't work forever, though, so I left London. It seemed to be the only thing I could do."

"Where did you go?" Jeff asked.

"To sea, of course," India said.

"That's right, you told us you were a sailor," Ned said, "while you were holding that dagger to my throat. I'm going to be a sailor, too."

"Is that so? Well, I began as a cabin boy. The masquerade was easy enough. Thinking I was a lad, the sailors left me alone, except for a few who preferred young boys to women. And they quickly learned to steer clear of me once they saw how well I handled a knife."

Jeff could well believe that.

"And you're still sailing?" Ned asked. "Surely you can't still be working as a cabin boy."

"No, I'm a common seaman. And none of my shipmates have known that I was a girl. Some of the problems I was anticipating never, ah, developed as I thought they would."

Ned blushed again, and to cover his embarrassment, he asked quickly, "So you've been sailing the Atlantic trade routes?"

"For nearly eight years now."

That would put her age at around twenty, Jeff thought.

"I've lived and worked with some of the toughest seamen to stride a deck," she continued. "They taught me how to fight and drink and handle a sword and pistol. And they taught me as well how to do my share of the work. That's all I ask of life—a job and a fair chance to do it."

"What are you doing here in New York?" Jeff asked.

India sat back in her chair. "I grew tired of traveling back and forth between America and England. I'd rather make a life for myself here. But I can't do that until I can find a job and save some money."

"You're in need of work now?" Ned asked.

"That I am."

Ned leaned forward, his own cup of coffee forgotten in his excitement. "I'm shipping out in three days on a trading vessel called the *Fair Wind*. We're heading down the coast, bound for the Carolinas. If you'd like, I can speak to the owner about getting a berth for you. He's one of our relatives."

"Ned, I told you, I'm of a mind to give up the sea."

"But this is just a trading run up and down the coast. It's nothing like sailing to England and back."

"That's true enough, I suppose," India mused.

"If you were willing to make a few such voyages, your wages might give you enough of a stake to stay in America and do something else," Ned said.

The suggestion was logical enough, Jeff thought, but he had a hunch Ned was more interested in India for her beauty than he was for her abilities as a sailor.

After a few minutes India nodded. "I could give it a try, I suppose. But there's no guarantee this relative of yours would have a job for me."

"Oh, Lemuel will have a job for you," Ned assured her. "Either that, or he'll have to replace me. I won't sail without you, Miss St. Clair."

"I wouldn't back Lemuel into a corner if I were you, Ned," Jeff advised. "If you go giving him ultimatums, you're liable to lose your berth."

"Don't worry. I can handle Lemuel. Besides, I've lived this long without going to sea. If I had to wait a bit longer, I wouldn't be too bothered. But you'll see; it'll all work out."

Jeff wished he could muster up that much confidence about his own problems.

"You'll have to call me Max," India told Ned. "That's the name I've been using since I left London."

"Max St. Clair," Ned said. "I think I can manage that. I must say, though, India suits you better. It's a lovely name."

"Yes, well, I have no idea where my mother got it. She told me once that my father was an army officer who had been stationed there. At other times she told me I was the illegitimate grand-niece of the king or that my father was some sort of duke or earl. Which story she told depended on how much rum she'd had. All flights of fancy on her part, of course." India picked up her mug and drank from it. "You say this trading ship is going to the Carolinas?"

"Yes, but with several stops on the way—"

"Ned," Jeff interrupted, "do you think Lemuel would mind one more traveler on that ship? This one would be a passenger, though, not a sailor." For the first time in weeks, Jeff sounded lighthearted. "I'm afraid I don't know anything about the sea."

"You're going with us, too?" Ned looked genuinely surprised. He reached across the table to slap his cousin on the arm. "That's the best news yet! I really hated to think about us splitting up. We make a good team, you and I."

"I'm just considering it, mind you. But it's obvious I'm doing no good here in New York. And I'm not ready to head west again."

"I think it's a grand idea. We'll both get to see more of the country, and you know how the Holts are about new things."

"Well, I don't," India put in. "In fact, I don't have the foggiest notion what's going on here. But if you'll be sailing on the *Fair Wind*, Mr. Holt, I'll welcome your company. I've a hunch you may be able to help me keep this cousin of yours in line. That is, *if* I get the job, of course."

"I think you will," Jeff said. Now that he had gotten to know India a bit better, he liked her, although he still felt uncomfortable about the ease with which she had killed that man and the callousness that allowed her to leave his body in the street. But he was glad that he had decided to go along on Lemuel's trading vessel. Now that he had made his decision, he realized he had been dreading Ned's departure. If he were left alone in New York, he probably would have given up on his quest and returned to the mountains, never to see Melissa again.

"We need a real drink," Ned declared, signaling to the barman. "I want to celebrate the decisions we've all reached tonight. I think there's even more excitement to come."

"I'm not interested in excitement," India said. "Only in earning enough money to do as I wish for a change."

The barman brought over three jots of rum, and as Ned lifted his glass, he said, "Here's to adventure!"

Jeff and India looked at each other and shrugged. There was no dampening Ned's enthusiasm, and both of them sensed it was pointless to try.

"To adventure," Jeff agreed.

India echoed the sentiment, adding, "And may we have a fair wind indeed to Carolina."

The three glasses clinked together.

Part IV

Volumes might be written to prove the justice of the Indian cause; but in all national concerns, it has never been controverted by the history of mankind from the earliest ages of which we have any record, but that interest and power always went hand in hand to serve the mighty against the weak, and writers are never wanting to aid the cause of injustice, barbarity and oppression, with the sophistry of a distorted and unnatural philosophy; while the few who would be willing to espouse the rights of the feeble, have not enough of the spirit of chivalry, to expose themselves to an irreparable loss of time, and the general obloquy attending an unpopular theme; even in this so much boasted land of liberty and equality, where nothing is to be dreaded from the arbitrary acts of a king and council during a suspension of a habeas corpus law, or the mandate of an arbitrary hero in the full tide of victory.

Is not popular opinion frequently as tyrannical as star chambers, or lettres de cachet?

—Fortescue Cuming
"Sketches of a Tour to the Western Country"

Chapter Eighteen

There is something tremendously awful in the approach, and raging of a storm at sea, accompanied by dreadful peals of thunder, quickly following each other, and the quick flashes of lightning bursting in streams from the dark and heavy loaded clouds pouring down rain in torrents. This was the case now, and we prepared for it.

—Fortescue Cuming
"Sketches of a Tour to the
Western Country"

Dermot Hawley pushed through the crowd in the saloon, paying no attention to the resentful looks he garnered from some of the men he brushed past. This place, not far from the harbor in

Wilmington, North Carolina, was called Soapy Joe's, and its inelegant name fit it well. The patrons who drank there were working men: sailors, cargo handlers, freighters, and the like. Mixed in with them were a few individuals in buckskins, hunters back from the Blue Ridge Mountains. Most men in Soapy Joe's earned less money in a year than what Hawley's suit had cost.

Perhaps it had been foolish to come here, Hawley thought. He could have sent for the man he wanted to see and had him come to the office. But Dermot Hawley had never been one to let other men intimidate him, and he was not about to start now. If anyone in this dingy saloon wanted trouble, he would be glad to give it to him.

No one bothered him, however, as he made his way to the long bar and stepped up next to one of the buckskin-clad men leaning on the hardwood.

"Mr. Tharp?" Hawley said. "Amos Tharp?"

The man turned to look at Hawley. He was tall, rawboned, and broad-shouldered, and the buckskin shirt he wore was stretched tight over his muscles. Shaggy, reddish-brown hair hung almost to his shoulders below a wide-brimmed felt hat, and a mustache of the same shade drooped over his wide mouth. Brown eyes under bushy, rust-colored brows regarded Hawley with idle curiosity.

"I'm Amos Tharp," the man said after a moment of studying Hawley. "What do you want with me, mister?"

"A few minutes of conversation."

Tharp lifted his mug of ale from the bar and drained what was left in it. As he lowered it, he looked meaningfully at Hawley.

Hawley signaled the bartender to refill the mug, and when that had been done, he said to Tharp, "I'd prefer a bit more privacy for our talk."

"We can go over here." Tharp lifted his full mug

and gestured toward a table in the rear corner of the room. On either side of the table were a pair of high-backed benches, forming a booth of sorts. Tharp walked over to them and slid into one. Hawley followed and sat opposite him.

"I hope I can count on your discretion," Hawley began after he had introduced himself. "This is a business matter, and it's important that what is said here stays between us."

Tharp grunted. "Nobody ever accused me of flappin' my lips too much, mister. You got something to say, spit it out."

"All right." Hawley leaned forward slightly. "I'm told that you're a tough, dependable man, Mr. Tharp. I have need of just such an individual. I want to offer you a job."

"Figured as much. Doing what?"

"I'm putting together a wagon train of supplies to take over the Blue Ridge into Tennessee. I intend to sell them to the settlers there."

Tharp stared at Hawley for several seconds before saying, "Not a bad idea. I've been over there. Lot of those folks're pretty self-sufficient, but they miss goods from home. I reckon you'll find a market—if you can get your wagons through."

"That's where you come in, Mr. Tharp."

Slowly Tharp lifted the mug to his mouth and drank, then wiped his lips with the back of his other hand.

"You want me to take charge of that wagon train?"

"Exactly. I'm told you've been over the passes and into Tennessee many times. Is that correct?"

"I know the way," Tharp said. "It's pretty rugged in places, but wagons can get through all right. What you really got to worry about are Cherokees and bandits. They're thicker'n flies in those mountains."

"That's what I've heard. And that's why I need a strong man I can rely upon." Hawley lowered his voice a little and went on, "I'm interested in results, Tharp, not in how you achieve them. You'd have a free hand to hire some of the men you want to take with you. I'm not going along with the wagons. You'd be completely in charge."

Again there was a moment of silence as Tharp turned over Hawley's offer in his mind.

"What'd be stoppin' me from takin' the money I get for those supplies and headin' on west, or wherever else I might want to go?"

Without hesitation Hawley replied, "In addition to being told that you're tough and ruthless, I've also heard that you're an honest man. If you give me your word, I believe you'll bring the money back." Hawley leaned back. "Besides, if you don't, I'll hunt you down and kill you like a dog."

For the first time during this conversation, a hint of a smile played around Tharp's mouth. "I reckon you would, at that," he said. "What's this job pay?"

"Five hundred dollars," Hawley stated flatly.

Tharp cocked an eyebrow, but that was the only sign of surprise on his weatherbeaten face.

"That's a lot of money."

"It's well worth it to me to know that those wagons will get through safely."

Tharp took a deep breath and said, "All right. I'll take the job." He extended a callused hand across the table. Hawley took it and shook hands with him, sealing the arrangement.

Hawley told Tharp where the office of his freighting company was located, then said, "Come by there tomorrow afternoon, and I'll give you all the details. I don't yet know exactly when the wagons will be ready to roll, but it should be within the next couple of weeks."

"You say I can hire the drivers I want?"

"Within reason. I already have several lined up, but we'll need about a dozen more. They'll need to be men who can handle themselves in case of trouble."

Tharp nodded. "I understand. I'll start lookin' around, see who's available. By the time those wagons of yours are ready, I will be, too."

"Excellent."

Lifting his mug of ale, Tharp asked, "Stay and have a drink with me, Mr. Hawley?"

"I'd like to," Hawley lied as he stood up. He did not want to stay in Soapy Joe's any longer than he had to. The smell of stale, spilled beer and unwashed humanity was powerful inside the saloon. "I'm afraid I have to leave, however. I have another business meeting tonight. It's going to be a busy time between now and the wagons' departure. A great many details still remain to be arranged."

"I understand." Hawley raised the mug another few inches. "But in the meantime, I'll drink to the success of our little venture."

"I echo that sentiment," Hawley said. "Good night, Mr. Tharp."

Tharp was too busy swallowing ale to return the farewell, but he lifted a hand and waved to Hawley.

As he moved through the crowd again, Hawley noticed that the patrons did not regard him with as much disdain as when he had entered. His conversation with Tharp and his obvious agreement with the man had changed the opinion of the other customers. A man who met with Tharp's approval was probably not a worthless dandy, no matter how well he dressed. It was an interesting form of status discrimination, Hawley thought as he left the waterfront saloon.

His carriage was waiting for him at the curb, and the driver looked decidedly relieved as Hawley climbed into the vehicle. The man had probably been afraid Hawley would never get out of Soapy Joe's alive.

"We'll go to Mr. Merrivale's house now," Hawley told him.

"Very good, sir," the man said.

As soon as Hawley was settled inside the carriage, the driver picked up his reins and whipped the fine pair of horses into motion. The carriage rolled quickly away from the harbor.

Dermot Hawley leaned back against the rich brocade cover of the padded seat. The freighting business had been good to him. He had started with one wagon—stolen—several years earlier, and no drivers. Hawley himself had handled that chore. In a relatively short period, he had built the business into a thriving enterprise, sometimes honestly, sometimes cutting corners when that was necessary. On a few occasions the wagons of rival freight lines had mysteriously burned or crashed with the loss of their cargo. Hawley did whatever he had to in order to keep the business growing. The scheme he had concocted to dispose of stolen goods in Tennessee was a prime example. If it went off as planned, everyone would be happy—the men who were supplying most of the merchandise; Charles Merrivale, who would make a small, legitimate profit; and Hawley himself, who would make a large, dishonest profit.

He chuckled as he thought about the setup. Merrivale's involvement provided excellent camouflage, and Hawley would appear even more on the up-and-up once he married Melissa and was a part of Charles Merrivale's family. And there were added benefits to be had, too, such as Melissa's smooth white body in his bed.

Just thinking about that made Hawley tap on the roof of the carriage and call to the driver, "A little more speed, dammit! I'm in a hurry."

The ride got a bit rougher as the carriage clattered over the cobblestone streets at a higher speed. Hawley did not care, not as long as his thoughts were occupied with visions of Melissa.

Ten minutes later the carriage came to a stop in front of the whitewashed, two-story frame house that Merrivale had bought on his return to North Carolina. Hawley opened the door and alighted without waiting for the driver's assistance. He was eager to get inside and see Melissa.

"Go on around back," Hawley told the driver, who was only halfway off the seat. "I'm sure one of the servants will give you something to drink."

"Thank you, sir. I'll be ready to depart whenever you are."

Without acknowledging the man's comment, Hawley strode up the flagstone walk to the veranda that ran along the front and both sides of the large house. He went up the stone steps and crossed to the ornately carved front door. A lion's-head knocker was in the center of the panel, and he rapped it sharply.

One of the maids answered. Hawley had heard her referred to by name, but he did not recall it. Not that it mattered, anyway, he thought as he brushed past her and took off his beaver hat and the cloak draped around his shoulders.

"Tell Mr. Merrivale I'm here," he said coldly as he handed the hat and cloak to the young woman.

"Yes, sir," she said, never lifting her eyes to his. "I'll tell Mr. Merrivale. You can wait in the library if you want."

"Of course." Hawley adjusted the cuffs of his shirt as he walked from the foyer down the central corridor toward the library. He pulled the lace cuffs out just the proper distance from the sleeves of his coat.

By the time Charles Merrivale appeared in the library a few minutes later, Hawley had already poured himself a drink from one of the decanters on a sideboard, which he knew was always kept well-stocked.

"Good evening, Charles. I hope you don't mind my paying a visit this evening and helping myself to some of your fine whiskey." Hawley raised the glass of smoky amber liquid in a salute to his host.

"Of course not," Merrivale replied, although his ruddy face bore an expression of faint annoyance at Hawley's unexpected arrival. "I trust this is important."

"I think so," Hawley said smoothly after he had taken a sip of the whiskey. "I've just hired a man to be in charge of the wagon train. He comes highly recommended as a frontiersman and guide. I'm told he's fought Indians and hunted all over the Blue Ridge Mountains."

Merrivale's expression brightened. Finding the right man to lead the wagon train was one of the most important tasks involved in this undertaking, and Merrivale was as well aware of that as Hawley.

Merrivale crossed the room, took a glass from the sideboard, poured himself a drink, and asked, "What's his name?"

"Amos Tharp. I don't know if you've heard of him or not."

"Tharp, Tharp . . . " Merrivale mused. "No, I don't believe so. You say he was recommended to you?"

"By some other business associates." As a matter of fact, they were the same men who were providing Hawley with the stolen goods that would be transported on the wagons, but Hawley kept that information to himself.

"Well, if you trust him and think he's the man for the job, I'm sure he'll work out fine," Merrivale said. "Is there anything else we need to discuss?"

"Not relating to our business affairs. I was wondering, though—is Melissa here?"

"She has retired for the evening," Merrivale said, the look of vague annoyance returning to his face. "Caring for a young child can be quite tiring, even with servants to help."

"Yes, I imagine so." Hawley hesitated, concealing his disappointment that he would not be able to see Melissa. He had planned on carrying a fresh image of her beauty away with him when he left. But he could still take advantage of this turn of events.

"In that case, I'd like to talk to you about a personal matter, Charles. Have you said anything else to Melissa about that vanished husband of hers?"

Merrivale grimaced. "I've spoken to her until I'm blue in the face. She refuses to listen to reason. I've explained that with the help of my attorneys, she could easily divorce Holt in absentia or even have him declared legally dead, since he's been gone so long." Merrivale tossed off the rest of his drink. "Hell, for all any of us know, he really could be dead."

"One can only hope," Hawley said.

"I'm sorry, Dermot," Merrivale said sincerely. "I honestly thought Melissa would come around before now. I know how you feel about her, and I've considered ordering her to divorce Holt for her own good. She'd be much better off with you. But she's so damned stubborn. It would be just like her to pretend to go along with my wishes, then stand before a judge when the time came and claim that she was being pressured into it against her will. How would that look?"

"Not good," Hawley murmured, frowning. Merrivale was right; it would be much better if Melissa came around to their way of thinking of her own accord. Then she would not be able to back out once it came time for her to marry him. "We'll just have to be more patient, Charles. But I warn you, I'm not going to wait forever."

"I know, I know. I'll do what I can." Merrivale

glowered at the floor. "If her mother would just cooperate with me, blast it all. But Hermione's getting more and more intransigent with time. I suppose Melissa gets her pigheadedness from her. But it will all work out, Dermot. You have my word on that."

Hawley hoped Merrivale was right. He would hate to have to postpone his conquest of the fair Melissa for too much longer. Hawley was not a man accustomed to waiting for what he wanted.

He finished his drink and said, "I'll be going, then. I just wanted to stop by and tell you the good news about Tharp. We can proceed with all due speed now."

"My goods are ready. What about the ones coming in by ship?"

"According to what I hear at the harbor, the trading vessel should be here in less than a week. She will have stopped at several other ports on the way down the coast from New York, but I'm sure there will still be plenty of cargo in her hold."

"Do you know the name of this ship?"

"Yes, indeed." Hawley smiled. "And if I were a superstitious man, which I most assuredly am not, I'd think it was a good omen. The ship is called the *Fair Wind*."

Jeff Holt would not have believed a man could be as sick as he was during the first few days of the voyage and not die. Even though the ship rarely was out of sight of land and the captain spoke glowingly of what good weather they were having, the ever-present up and down motion of the vessel was enough to send Jeff dashing to the railing until it seemed nothing at all was left inside him, that he ought to collapse like an empty sack of skin. But somehow he did not. He survived—although he was no longer sure he wanted to.

Ned proved to be surprisingly adaptable. His features had carried a green hue the first day out from New York, but by the morning of the next day, he had his sea legs, as India put it. Of course, India—or Max, as she was known aboard ship—was not bothered at all with seasickness. She had been riding the plunging decks of ships for years now and was more at home there than anywhere.

It had not proven difficult to secure a berth for India on the *Fair Wind*. Ned had simply explained to Lemuel that he and Jeff had made the acquaintance of a young man named Max St. Clair, an experienced sailor who wanted to return to sea. Each time a ship was in port for any length of time, some turnover in the crew was to be expected, and as luck would have it, there was indeed a need for another crewman on the *Fair Wind*. India, accompanied by Jeff and Ned, had paid a visit to Captain Jebediah Vaughan, and India had told the captain the names of the vessels she had sailed on in the past. Vaughan, a stout, veteran sea dog with snow-white hair and beard, recognized the names of the ships and their captains.

"If you're a good enough seaman to sail with them, lad, you'll do to be a member of the *Fair Wind*'s crew," he had told India. If he had any inkling that there was a young woman's body under India's clothes, he gave no sign of it.

Lemuel had been equally delighted that Jeff intended to sail down to North Carolina as a passenger. "Good luck, my boy," he had said to Jeff when the entire March family congregated on the docks to see the ship off. "I pray that someday your search will finally be rewarded."

"So do I, Lemuel," Jeff said, shaking Lemuel's hand. "So do I."

Irene and the girls had hugged Jeff and Ned good-bye, and as usual Jeanne had been quite ardent in her farewell, especially with Ned. As the young woman hugged Ned, Jeff had glanced up at the deck of the ship and seen India there, watching the farewells, and he thought he detected disapproval on her face.

With Ned beside him at the railing, Jeff had waved to his relatives as the *Fair Wind* cast off and headed out into the harbor. Inside that somewhat protected haven, the waves had not been too bad, and Jeff hadn't minded the motion of the deck under his feet. The farther out to sea the vessel went, however, the worse he had felt, until finally his stomach clenched with nausea.

That had been the beginning. For almost three days, there had been no end in sight. By that time Jeff was pale and haggard, and he swore a solemn oath that once he reached North Carolina, he would never set foot on a ship again.

Until then, he would simply have to suffer if need be, although the sickness had improved greatly in the past day or so.

Elsewhere on board the *Fair Wind*, Ned Holt was learning what it was like to live the life of a common seaman. It was dirty, boring, exhausting work, he soon discovered. But he did not mind; he got to spend hours each day toiling alongside India, an opportunity that was worth all the effort.

She had not been lying about being an experienced sailor. Even though she had never been on the *Fair Wind* before, she had sailed on enough British East Indiamen that she seemed to know the vessel from stem to stern. Every time Captain Vaughan bawled out an order to trim the sails, India seemed to anticipate the command and hurried to obey it even as the captain's voice boomed out. Ned stayed close to her, and in a low voice she told him what to do.

The only problem with that, as far as Ned was concerned, was that her beauty was distracting. Everyone else on board might see a slender, athletic young man, but Ned knew she was a woman. In the loose white trousers and striped jersey she wore on board the ship, she was lovely, even when her face was coated with beads of sweat from wrestling with some balky rigging.

The ship was off the coast of Maryland when dark, billowing clouds took shape in the sky. Ned and India were sitting cross-legged on the deck, their backs against the wall of the forecastle while they mended one of the spare sails. Ned looked up at the darkening heavens to the northeast.

"What's that?" he asked.

"I'd say we're in for a bit of a blow," India replied. On board the ship, where it was necessary to maintain her masquerade as a young man, she kept her voice pitched low. She did not seem particularly disturbed by the approaching storm, barely glancing at the clouds before resuming her work.

Ned was worried, however. He looked toward the mainland, some two miles to the west.

"Shouldn't we be heading for shore?" he asked.

India shrugged. "That's up to Captain Vaughan. Sometimes it's easier to ride out these squalls if you steer clear of land. I think we should finish what we're doing and let the cap'n worry about it. There'll be plenty of time to finish up on this sail before the wind hits."

She sounded sure of herself, and Ned wanted to believe her. But the clouds were growing blacker now, and they looked to him almost as if they had teeth in them. For the first time since leaving New York, he wished he had not been so impulsive in coming along on this voyage.

Jeff emerged from the hatch where stairs led down to the cabins belowdecks. He spotted Ned and India and strode toward them, adopting the rolling walk that compensated in part for the motion of the ship.

"What's going on?" he asked. "Aren't the waves getting a little rougher?"

"There's a storm coming," Ned told him. "At least that's what Max says, and I believe him."

Looking up at the dark clouds, Jeff muttered, "So do I. Is there anything I can do to help?"

"No. You'd best go back belowdecks," India said. "You're a passenger on this ship, Jeff, not one of the crew. We'll handle things."

With a worried expression that matched Ned's, Jeff asked, "Are you sure?"

"I'm sure," India said.

"Well, all right. But if you have need of me, I'd be glad to lend a hand. I'm no sailor, but I can follow orders."

Captain Vaughan came up behind Jeff in time to hear his last comments. The captain slapped Jeff on the shoulder.

"We appreciate the offer," he said, "but Max is right, Mr. Holt. You go below and leave everything to us. We'll see you and the *Fair Wind* safely through this storm."

"Thank you, Captain," Jeff told him, then went over to the open hatch and ducked through it.

India folded the big square of sailcloth. She had finished patching it while Ned fretted over the approaching squall, and he felt a twinge of guilt as he realized he had left the rest of the work to her. He had not meant to become so distracted.

India rose lithely to her feet and thrust the folded sail into Ned's hands. "Take this below and put it back in the locker where we got it," she said.

"All right. Anything else I can do?"

"Get back above deck and keep your eyes open," Captain Vaughan said. "And do everything that Max tells you to do. He's been through blows like this before. Haven't you, lad?"

"Dozens of times," India agreed. "You're not going to sail for shore, then, Captain?"

"The coastline's too rugged along here. There's nary a good place to get out of a storm. The wind would just drive us ashore and wreck us. Best we try to skirt this squall and outrun the worst of it."

The wind hit then, a cold, swirling force. The sails were already full, but with the sudden change in wind direction, they fluttered.

Vaughan turned and bellowed toward the bridge, "Helmsman!"

The veteran sailor at the wheel was already spinning it, sending the vessel veering to starboard. The sails billowed again as they caught the wind. The ship would have to tack back and forth into the teeth of the gale to keep from being driven out of control. It was a tricky maneuver, but one an experienced captain such as Jebediah Vaughan would have carried out successfully scores of times.

Ned returned from stowing away the mended sail belowdecks, his face pale and drawn as he hurried to join India. On the way he passed Vaughan, who was striding toward the bridge.

"All hands to your stations! All hands to your stations!" the captain bellowed.

India was waiting for Ned. The wind tousled her short hair and pressed the blue-striped jersey and white trousers to her body. Ned could see the gentle curve of her bound breasts under the jersey.

"Stay close to me," she said to Ned, raising her voice to be heard over the wind, which was steadily increasing to a howl. "We have to watch these lines and make sure they stay taut!"

The two of them clambered atop the forecastle and made their way to the ropes that controlled one of the secondary sails. The *Fair Wind* was a three-master, and Ned and India were assigned to the foresail, along with several other seamen. As long as Captain

Vaughan and the helmsman kept the ship on the proper course, there should not be any problems, but with the changeable nature of winds in a squall, that was sometimes impossible to do.

The waves were higher now, and wind drove so much spray over the ship that Ned was soaked in a matter of moments. His stomach lurched each time the vessel plummeted into one of the troughs formed by the storm, and he wondered how Jeff was holding up below in his cabin.

Rain pelted down. Ned's feet, shod in rope-soled sandals he had bought in New York on India's advice, maintained a precarious grip on the deck as he made his way to his station alongside her. Feet spread wide apart to brace himself against the jolting ride, he stayed there for the next fifteen minutes, his hands on one of the ropes that controlled the foresail. He gripped the rope until his hands burned and his muscles felt aflame. He could barely see a foot in front of him, but still the storm raged.

Finally the force of the wind diminished somewhat. Though the squall had been fairly short in duration, to Ned it seemed much longer.

He leaned closer to India and called over the wind, "Was this a bad one?"

She shook her head, her hair plastered to her skull like a tight cap. "I've seen much worse, but this one may not be over yet."

Ned had hoped that within another five or ten minutes, the storm would be behind them, but that was not to be the case. After a lull of a couple of minutes, the wind strengthened again, and the popping of the sails as the wind caught them was like gunshots. Ned hung on tight to the rope in his hands as the ship again plunged wildly.

Suddenly he heard an even louder popping sound, but this one was much closer to India and him. He jerked his head around, and his eyes widened in shock as he saw the big boom of the mainsail whipping toward them, trailing a broken line behind it.

Ned dove to his right, acting immediately when he saw the threat. He wrapped his arms around India's shoulders, and as he crashed into her, the collision sent both of them sprawling to the wet planks of the deck. The heavy boom slashed through the air directly above them. Had it hit them, Ned realized, their backs would have been broken, at the very least.

Men were already leaping to grab the boom and wrest it under control. On the bridge Vaughan bellowed orders again. To Ned it was all chaos, punctuated by slamming gusts of wind and rain. But he did not care. He had saved India's life, and that was all that mattered.

"Get off of me, you great bloody oaf!" she shouted in his ear.

Surprised by her reaction, Ned realized he was lying on top of her, all the weight of his brawny form resting on her slender one. He rolled to the side and sat up, and India did, too, her chest heaving as she dragged air into her body. He had knocked the breath out of her when he landed on her.

"I'm sorry," he said, resting a hand on her shoulder.

"No need to apologize for saving my life. I'm the one who's sorry for shouting at you. I was having trouble breathing, you see."

Ned looked a bit sheepish at the thought going through his mind: If he was going to be lying on top of India, he would much prefer that it be under more pleasant circumstances.

He got to his feet and gave her a hand up. The wildly swinging boom was back under control now. It had torn a hole in the foresail, but that could be repaired. They were all lucky, Ned realized. Someone could have been killed, and the ship could have been crippled.

Minutes later the wind died down again, and this time the storm continued to slacken. Within a quarter of an hour, the clouds were scudding off toward the southwest, and slanting rays of afternoon sunlight were breaking through. The *Fair Wind* rode easily on a sea grown placid once more.

Jeff reappeared on deck, looking pale and drained. He found Ned and India and asked, "Is it over?"

"It's over," India assured him.

"Was it bad up here?"

"Bad enough," Ned answered.

"Your cousin saved my life." India looked over at Ned and went on, "And I don't believe I've thanked him properly yet."

Ned flushed. He wanted more than anything else to take India into his arms and express how glad he was she had not been injured, but of course he could not do that. Not with everyone except Jeff thinking that she was a young man.

"You can tell me some other time," he said gruffly.

"I'll do that," India said, her husky voice unusually soft. "I'll just do that, Ned Holt."

Chapter Nineteen

Three weeks had passed since Harry Lawton's death, and in that time the botanical expedition led by Clay Holt had climbed higher into the mountains. For the past week, however, they had been camped in a small valley just below the last approach to the pass that would take them to the dividing ridge of the Rockies. Professor Franklin had fallen in love with the spot as soon as he saw it and asked Clay if they could establish a temporary base camp there.

"Never have I seen such an amazing variety of vegetation and mineral formations," the professor had declared. "I must have some time in which to study them."

Clay had been happy to go along with Franklin's request. He had suffered no lasting effects from the injury he sustained in the avalanche, and his strength returned quickly. Nevertheless, he and the others had all traveled long and hard and could use the rest.

Spring was in full bloom now, and some days were so warm that they could have been mistaken for those of summer. The members of the expedition were happy to wait in this beautiful valley, surrounded by trees and wildflowers and the towering, majestic beauty of the mountains, while Professor Franklin dug up plants, chipped rocks, and puttered to his heart's content.

Even Rupert von Metz, while still not what anyone could call friendly, seemed satisfied by the decision to camp in the valley. He spent most of each day at his easel, painting the mountains around them. Part of the time, however, he worked on the maps he had been making all during the expedition. He unbent enough to allow Clay to take a look at the charts.

After studying them, Clay commented, "This is a fine job of map-making."

"What did you expect?" von Metz asked brusquely, and Clay did not push the issue any further.

After spending two days in the valley, Clay had come to a decision.

"If we're going to stay here awhile," he told the group, "we might as well fix some better places to sleep, instead of rolling up on the ground in our blankets every night. We'll build tipis, like Shining Moon's people. There're plenty of deer around here to provide buckskin."

So for the next few days, hunting parties went out and returned with deer. Clay, Shining Moon, and Proud Wolf were in charge of the skinning, and after the hides had been cured by the sun, Shining Moon taught Lucy how to sew them together, using thread fashioned from deer gut. The young woman from Massachusetts had been less than enthusiastic about the task, but she went along with what Shining Moon told her to do. In the meantime, the group ate well—venison steaks at some meals, a savory stew made from deer meat with wild onions and roots at others. The venison that was left over was smoked to preserve it so they could take it with them when they finally left the peaceful valley.

And it certainly was peaceful. Clay had been watching for smoke or other signs of habitation around them, but so far there had been none. In a way, that was bothersome.

Shining Moon felt the same way, and one day as they were scraping a hide before pegging it out to dry, she said, "We should have seen Shoshone by now."

"I agree," Clay said. "This is good hunting country for them. Something's got them spooked, I reckon, so they're staying away."

"Those men we saw from the valley of the Missouri? The ones whose smoke you saw?"

"Could be. The Shoshone have always gotten along well with white men, though. I wonder why they're avoiding this bunch."

Shining Moon put down the tool she was using. "I do not know. But dwelling in these mountains is something besides beauty."

Lifting his head to squint up at the peaks, Clay slowly stood up. "You're right. I feel it, too."

But other than keeping their eyes open and making sure guards were posted every night, they could do nothing about whatever was causing their unease —and wait for Professor Franklin to be ready to move on.

Aaron Garwood walked carefully through the woods, his long-barreled flintlock rifle held ready for use, his thumb curled around the cock. The deer droppings that had led him into this thick stand of trees were fresh, and he expected to spot the animal at any moment.

He had been foolish, he supposed, to wander off

from the others in his hunting party. But although he had gotten to know the other men and liked most of them, at times he felt the need to be alone, and today was one of those times.

It was hard to believe that Zach had been dead for less than a year. Sometimes it seemed to Aaron that his brother had been gone much, much longer. And in truth, Aaron mused now, the Zach he preferred to remember, the big brother who had protected and loved him, had been dead for a long time—if indeed that Zach had ever existed.

For years Zach Garwood had lived a lie. He had preached hatred for the Holt family, especially Clay, spewing his venom about Clay's having gotten poor Josie pregnant and run out on her—when all along it had been Zach himself who had committed the almost unthinkable sin of raping his own sister. But Luther, Pete, and he himself had listened to the lies and believed them, and they had hated the Holts with the same fanaticism that Zach possessed.

Now Luther and Pete were dead, along with Zach, and Aaron knew the truth behind it all. The way he had once felt about Clay was almost incomprehensible. He'd never had a better friend than Clay Holt, and although not a day went by that he did not feel the weakness in his left arm—the arm Clay had broken in a fight—Aaron never held that against him. Clay Holt might have broken his arm, but he had also repaired the damage done to Aaron's spirit by years of lies and hate.

Clay had not been able to do anything, however, about the melancholy that gripped Aaron from time to time. Aaron tried to keep the memories to himself, memories of watching his brothers die, of seeing his sister turn into a whore and his father grow old and bitter before his death. It was better for him to get out and do something when the recollections started to overwhelm him.

Like joining the hunting party today.

The valley where the base camp was located was two miles away. Aaron and the others had headed northeast along the range of mountains, making their way through other small valleys. They had splashed through several fast-flowing creeks that had looked like prime spots for beaver. Aaron did not have the expert eye that Clay did for such things, but he had learned from Clay and was developing his instincts. This would have been fine trapping country if they still had all their gear, Aaron thought.

He had split off from the rest of the men, telling them he would be back in a few minutes, when he had spotted the droppings. That few minutes had stretched into more than half an hour, and Aaron knew that if he did not spot the deer soon, he ought to return to the hunting party. But it was so quiet and peaceful and beautiful here that he just wanted to enjoy it.

It occurred to him that even if he found the deer, he might not shoot it. Some days were too pretty for killing.

The sound of voices drifted to his ears and made him stiffen. Had the other men circled around somehow and gotten ahead of him? That did not seem likely. Perhaps he was about to run into a band of Indians, Shoshone men out on a hunting party of their own. But as Aaron stopped in his tracks and listened intently, he decided the voices were those of white men, although he could not quite make out what they were saying.

Curiosity warred with his natural caution. Could they be the men Clay had seen a few weeks earlier, the ones who had avoided the expedition? Aaron pondered for a moment, then moved ahead quietly. Walking with the care that he had learned from Clay and Proud Wolf, he moved noiselessly through the woods toward the voices.

After a few minutes he reached the edge of the trees and found himself on a small ridge overlooking another creek. Men in buckskins and fur hats were checking beaver traps that had been submerged in the frigid, snow-fed waters of the stream.

Aaron knelt behind a screen of brush on the edge of the ridge and watched. There were nine men, and several of them carried bundles of pelts on their backs. Now that he was closer to them, he could make out some of what the men were saying. They were talking mostly about the traps. Then there were occasional bawdy comments and accompanying bursts of laughter. Aaron had heard plenty of men talking the same way during his time in the Rockies, especially around the fort built by Manuel Lisa, where he had first been reunited with Clay. But something about the conversation going on below him was different, and then he realized what it was: These men might be speaking English, but they were not Americans. Several had accents so thick he could barely understand what they were saying. A few others spoke in an altogether foreign tongue that Aaron thought might be French.

Canadians, he thought, a conglomeration of Britishers and Frenchmen. But what the devil were they doing down here? Unless he was badly mistaken, it was well over a hundred miles to the Canadian border, even as vaguely defined as that boundary was.

They must be the men Clay had spotted, Aaron thought. But they did not seem to be doing anything except trapping; they'd had no reason to duck out of sight that day Clay had seen them, not as far as Aaron could figure. Maybe he ought to go down there and ask them what the hell was going on.

Before he could make a move, the crackle of a foot stepping on a fallen branch sounded behind him. Aaron turned, instinctively lifting his rifle in case of trouble.

It was trouble, all right, but it came at him so quickly he did not have a chance to respond. He caught a glimpse of two buckskin-clad men lunging at him, both of them carrying rifles. One drove the brass buttplate of his weapon at Aaron's head in a vicious blow.

Aaron threw his left arm up, and the rifle butt thudded against it and sent agonizing pain shooting up his shoulder and neck. He bit back a yelp of agony.

"Hey! Wait—" he cried.

But the two men were not interested in anything he had to say. The second one clubbed him just as the first had. Aaron's left arm was numb. He twisted around to bring his rifle into play, but the second man's rifle butt slammed against his skull, the impact cushioned slightly by his coonskin cap. The blow glanced off to a certain extent because Aaron was trying to jerk his head out of its way. Still, the impact was enough to send him sprawling backward through the brush and over the rim of the wooded ridge.

Tumbling crazily down the slope toward the startled men along the creek below, Aaron tried but failed to hang on to his rifle. Rocks thudded painfully into his body, and gravel chewed at his skin during the fall. He dug in the heels of his moccasins in an effort to stop himself, but that just got him a twisted ankle. Finally, with a bone-jarring thump, he landed on the bank of the creek. Dirt and smaller rocks clattered around him as he lay there, some dislodged as he fell, others kicked loose by the two men who had attacked him as they slid down the slope behind him. The trappers hurried toward them, surprise on their bearded faces.

"Who the bloody hell is that?" one of them called harshly as he came up panting.

The two men who had jumped Aaron covered

him with their rifles as they reached the bottom of the ridge.

"Found him up there," one of them replied, jerking his head to indicate the top of the slope. "Spying on you, he was."

The numbness in Aaron's left arm and shoulder was giving way to a burning, throbbing pain. With his good arm he pushed himself into a sitting position. The men who were gathered around him stepped back, and more of them brought rifle muzzles to bear on him. They were treating him like a bigger threat than he was.

"I wasn't spying on anybody," he said thickly, then spat to get some of the grit out of his mouth. After wiping the back of his right hand across his lips, he went on, "I was just out hunting when I heard your voices. I don't know what the hell any of this is about."

"Oh, ye don't know what the hell this is about, eh? Ye don't expect us to believe that, do ye?" The questions came from a slender man with a scraggly black beard.

"It's the truth," Aaron said. "I didn't mean to cause trouble for anybody."

"The only one ye have caused trouble for is yourself, sonny," the man said. To the others, he snapped, "Get him on his feet, and somebody pick up his gun! We'll take him back to the fort."

Another man spoke up, this time with a French accent. "M'sieu Brown said we were to take care of such problems ourselves, *n'est-ce pas*?"

"I know what Brown said, but I'm not a cold-blooded killer. If he wants to dispose of this lad, he can blooming well do it himself!" The Englishman turned away. "Now come on. A couple of you take charge of this lot. The rest of us have beaver to get out of traps!"

Two of the men grasped Aaron's arms, hauling

him to his feet. Fresh pain shot through the left one as they lifted him, but he suppressed the urge to scream. A hand plucked the pistol from his belt while another took his knife.

"Ye are a well-armed blighter, I'll give ye that," one of his captors said.

"You can't do this," Aaron began. "You've got no right—"

"The nearest law's a hell of a long way away. We've got the guns, so we've got the right to do as we please. Now come along and don't give us any trouble. I doubt that our boss'd mind if ye were to get back to our fort a bit more battered up than ye are now."

Aaron swallowed his angry words. He was in trouble, bad trouble, no doubt about that. He had blundered into something not only strange but also dangerous. He was outnumbered and unarmed, and right now he could do nothing to get out of this mess. His only realistic course of action was to stay alive and find out as much as he could about what was going on.

Because sooner or later, he vowed, he was going to get away from these men, and when he did, he wanted to be able to tell Clay Holt what had happened. Knowledge was power, Aaron told himself.

Aaron's hands were not tied, but guards kept their rifles pointed in his general direction, discouraging him from trying anything. The group of trappers made their way along the creek, pulling up traps, removing the drowned beavers from them, and quickly and efficiently skinning the dead animals. These were experienced frontiersmen, Aaron thought. Getting away from them was not going to be easy.

As he listened to their conversation, he was able to pin down their nationalities. Eight of the eleven were English, while the other three were French-Canadians. They were none too careful in their talk, and it was clear to Aaron that they were part of a larger group that had established a fort nearby for the purpose of collecting as many beaver pelts as they could. Aaron wondered if they were Hudson's Bay men or if they worked for the North West Company or one of the smaller British fur-trapping and trading companies. One thing was certain: They had no business in American territory, harvesting the pelts of American beavers.

He was equally sure that they would not have been as free with what they were saying if they expected him to live. When they got back to the fort, wherever it was, this man Brown, whoever *he* was, would kill him. So Aaron knew he had to get away before they reached the fort if he wanted to live. It was as simple as that.

The rest of the hunting party that had accompanied Aaron from the expedition's base camp would know something was wrong when he did not rejoin them. Would they come looking for him? He was fairly certain they would, especially when Clay learned that he was missing. Clay was one of the best trackers west of the Mississippi, but even with his skill, it might take too long for him to find the trail of Aaron's captors. He had to do something himself, Aaron decided.

The trappers ate on the move, gnawing dried venison and hardtack as they continued toward the fort. Aaron was given food, which surprised him until he realized that these men were not much different from the ones he had been living and traveling with for the past year. They were harder and more ruthless, perhaps, than their American counterparts, and he was sure they would kill him if they had to, but they would not allow him to go hungry in the meantime. It was a curious code, but one he was coming to understand the longer he was on the frontier.

At midafternoon the bearded man who seemed

to be the leader of the group called a brief rest halt. The creek they had been following had merged with another, creating a larger, fast-flowing river. Spring's warmth had caused the snow on the higher elevations to melt at a faster rate, feeding the mountain tributaries. This one was about fifteen feet wide and five feet deep, and it made pleasant music as it bubbled and raced over the rocks in its bed.

The trappers drank deeply of the cold, clear water. Aaron joined them. He had given them no trouble since his capture, and he sensed that the men who had been told to watch him had relaxed their vigilance.

He looked downstream. About twenty yards away, the water dropped sharply into a falls that was thirty feet high, as best he could estimate. Aaron drank from the river, then stood up and stretched his back as if he was tired and stiff from his tumble down the ridge—which was true enough. At the same time, he took several steps and craned his neck to peer over the edge of the drop where the falls were located. He could see part of the lower section of the river. It was flowing even faster down there, almost fast enough to be called a rapids.

His plan formed instantly. It was more than daring, he realized. *Foolhardy* would be a better word to describe it. Yet he might not get a better chance to escape, and he knew he could not count on mercy from his captors.

He knelt beside the water again, leaned over as if to get another drink, and kicked out behind him with his feet, propelling himself suddenly into the river in a long, graceful dive.

Shimmering droplets sprayed high in the air as Aaron hit the surface with a splash. The frigid water closed over his head as his momentum took him under, cutting off the yell of alarm from one of the guards. Aaron's left arm still ached badly, but he forced himself to use it anyway, stroking hard with both arms and kicking. He had never been much of a swimmer, but he was swimming for his life now, and that made all the difference.

He stayed under, letting the current help him along, for almost a minute. Faintly, as if from a great distance, he heard the boom of guns going off and knew his captors were shooting at him. They would be able to see him through the water, but their view would be somewhat distorted. He beat back the panic that bloomed in his brain and swam as hard as he could toward the falls. Something tugged at his right sleeve, then again at the left leg of his trousers. *Rifle balls?*

Then, abruptly, he was tumbling half in and half out of the water; the river had dropped out from under him. He rode the falls down, slamming against outcroppings of rock along the way. The drop was not a straight one, but the slope was extremely steep. Aaron barely had time to hope that no jagged rocks awaited him at the bottom before he was plunging into a deep, icy pool.

He had no idea how far down he had sunk, but abruptly he was beating his way to the surface. The current tugged at him, tried to hold him down. Frantically, his desperation growing, he struggled against it, and after seconds that seemed like an eternity, his head broke the surface.

"There's the son of a bitch!"

The cry came from above, and a second later a rifle ball sizzled through the water beside him. Aaron flung water out of his eyes, opened his mouth, and inhaled as much air as he could. Then he dove again, this time into the downstream current, and he let it take him firmly in its grip.

Once the rapids had caught him, there was no getting free—not that he wanted to. With each passing second the racing water carried him farther from the men who wanted to kill him. However, it was also crashing him against the rocks and submerged tree trunks that turned this stretch of the stream into a white, frothing madness. Aaron was aware of the jarring impacts but discovered that he felt no pain, probably because he was numb from the bone-chilling cold of the snow-fed stream. For a few moments he tried to swim, then gave it up as an impossible task. The world had become a dizzying jumble of sky, trees, and water. Sometimes his head popped above the surface, only to be dragged back down a second later. Each time he came up, he gulped another breath and hoped he would not be knocked unconscious on a rock or impaled on a broken tree limb.

Eventually the river widened, and the insane pace of the water slowed. Battered and half-conscious, Aaron drifted along, letting the current carry him for more than a quarter of a mile before he summoned enough strength to kick his way feebly toward the shore. When he finally reached it, he pulled himself onto the grassy bank and collapsed, facedown, gasping for air and quivering.

If the Canadians caught up with him now, they would kill him and be done with it, he thought. He could not move a muscle, not even to save his life.

A few minutes later he was shaking with silent laughter at the audacity of what he had done. Only a madman would have attempted to escape the way he had; sometimes a touch of insanity was the only thing that would work.

Finally he was able to roll over and push himself into a sitting position. He looked back toward the falls, but they were out of sight. The rapids had taken him more than a mile downstream, he realized, and most of that distance was over rugged, rocky terrain that would slow down pursuit. If he could get to his feet and start moving again, he had a good chance of staying ahead of the men who would be after him.

Aaron looked around for a nearby tree with which he could pull himself up, but the closest one was twenty feet away. Slowly he climbed to his hands and knees, then rested for a moment before standing. He staggered, holding his arms out for balance. If he fell, he might not get up again.

He plodded from tree to tree, glancing toward the sky to determine which way was west, the direction he would have to take to find Clay and the others. Every few minutes he stopped and stood absolutely still, listening intently for the sounds of pursuit. Once he thought he heard voices, but they were far, far off to his right. He pushed on, and the next time he stopped, he heard nothing.

His whole body felt bruised from what he'd suffered during the wild ride through the rapids. His twisted ankle throbbed, and his left arm and shoulder ached. But his vision and thoughts were clear, and for that he was thankful.

Aaron walked the rest of the afternoon. The hot sun gave him strength and dried some of the moisture from his soaked buckskins. He was sure he looked like hell after everything he had gone through, but he felt surprisingly good. Escaping death would do that for a man, he supposed. Yet he was aware of a core of weakness deep inside him, and it grew a bit larger with each step he forced himself to take. He hoped he would find the camp soon. Once the sun dipped below the peaks to the west, the air would get chilly, and since his clothing was still damp, he could easily catch a fever.

As he studied the surrounding landscape in the fading light, Aaron thought some of the mountains looked familiar. He had covered another two or three miles since leaving the creek, and he figured he was somewhere close to the expedition's base camp.

If he'd had one of his guns, he could have fired it into the air and perhaps drawn the attention of his friends, especially if they were already looking for him. But his rifle and pistol were back with the Canadians; anyway, the powder in his horn was useless after that dunking in the creek. All he could do was keep trudging along into the gathering gloom.

He heard voices again, this time ahead of him. Aaron stumbled to a stop. Was it Clay and his friends —or the men who had captured him? Until he was certain, he would be risking his life to go blundering ahead and calling out to them, although that was his first impulse. He noticed a good-sized mound of rocks off to his left, which would afford some concealment and protection, so he started toward them as the voices grew louder.

Aaron clambered into the rocks and hunkered down among them, all the while scanning the line of trees from which the voices originated. He spotted movement, saw several men emerge from the shadows beneath the towering pines. He could tell they wore buckskins and carried rifles, but the light was too dim for him to distinguish any more than that. They might be his friends—or they might be the Canadians.

Then one of the figures that had been partially concealed by the others moved into full view, and Aaron felt a giddy surge of relief when he realized the person was wearing a dress and leggings. It had to be Shining Moon, he thought; there had been no women among his captors and no mention of any back at their mysterious fort. As the group of searchers came closer, Aaron could even make out Shining Moon's long, lustrous raven hair.

He pushed himself to his feet and stumbled out of the clump of rocks, waving his arms over his head and shouting hoarsely, "Clay! Shining Moon! Over here!"

They saw him and broke into a run. Aaron staggered to a halt, and at that moment the core of weakness inside him finally overwhelmed his senses. Everything spun dizzily around him, the earth changing places with the darkening, purple-streaked sky. He felt himself falling but was barely aware of hitting the ground.

Then Clay was beside him, lifting his head and saying urgently, "Aaron! Are you all right, Aaron? What the devil happened to you, son?"

Shining Moon and the others gathered around him, looking down anxiously at his torn buckskins and the ugly bruises that showed through the gaping holes.

Aaron clutched weakly at his friend's arm and fought off the blackness that was trying to engulf his brain.

"Clay," he managed to say. "There's something wrong. . . . I saw them . . . saw the men who . . ."

He slipped away then, carried along on a black tide every bit as inexorable as the rapids in that river.

Chapter Twenty

By the time the *Fair Wind* docked at the small harbor in Wilmington, North Carolina, Jeff had still not gotten completely over his seasickness. Ned was seldom bothered by the pitching of the vessel on the waves, however, and had acquired enough knowledge from India to be considered a capable sailor. As for India, Captain Vaughan was more than pleased with her performance during the voyage.

"You're one of the best sailors these old eyes have ever seen, lad," Vaughan told her as most of the crew prepared to go ashore for the night's stopover in Wilmington. "I hope you won't be running off and joining some other crew once we reach Charleston. I want you with me on the return trip. We'll be heavily loaded with tobacco, and I'll need all the good hands I can find."

"I'll have to think about it, Cap'n," she told him.

"But for what it's worth, I've enjoyed sailing on the *Fair Wind* so far. You work a man hard, but you treat him fairly."

"That's what I've always tried to do." Vaughan swung his gaze over to Ned, who stood nearby on the dock trying to catch his breath after unloading cargo. The crates had been put onto wagons and hauled off to nearby warehouses.

Vaughan asked, "What about you, Holt? You coming back with us to New York?"

"Well, I'd like to, Cap'n," Ned replied, sleeving sweat from his forehead. "But that depends to a certain extent on Max here. He taught me all I know about being a sailor, and I guess by now we're partners."

Jeff was listening to the exchange, and he saw the glance of surprise India shot Ned. She had clearly been expecting him to go his own way once the voyage was over. But she did not know Ned Holt as well as Jeff did; his cousin had set his sights on India and was not going to give up easily.

"All right," Vaughan said. "We'll be sailing tomorrow afternoon for Charleston. I don't care what you do tonight, but you'd better be here bright and early in the morning."

"We'll keep that in mind, Cap'n," India assured him.

She picked up her seabag and fell in step between Jeff and Ned as they walked away from the harbor.

When they were out of Vaughan's earshot, she said in a low voice, "You need to make up your own mind about what you do once we reach Charleston, Ned, instead of leaving it to me. I'll be no man's plaything, but neither will I be his keeper."

"Ah, hell, I'm sorry if I put you on the spot, India. I didn't mean to. It's just that I can't imagine signing on for another voyage without you along. We're friends, aren't we?"

"Aye, you've been a good mate," she admitted. "Both of you. And the wages we'll make from this voyage won't be enough to support me for very long. I suppose I'll ship out again, and I'd rather it be on the *Fair Wind* than any other vessel."

Ned clapped a hand on her shoulder and exclaimed, "That's great!"

India stiffened and said, "I put you on your backside and held a knife to your throat once before, Ned. Don't make me do it again."

Quickly Ned lifted his hand from her shoulder. "Sorry. I didn't mean anything by it."

"That's all right. It's just that I don't care for being touched."

Ned got a hangdog look on his face, and Jeff felt a little sorry for him as the three of them walked along. As friendly and helpful as India had been, she was still somewhat reserved, almost as if she had walled off a part of herself. Neither Jeff nor Ned could forget how she had handled herself in that fight back in New York or the way she had so coolly killed a man. India St. Clair's life had been fraught with a great many hardships, Jeff supposed, and the ordeals she had endured had certainly affected her.

Ned was nothing if not determined, however. "Why don't we go find a tavern?" he said. "I could use a drink."

"So could I," India agreed. "What about you, Jeff?"

"Might as well. There's a place up ahead." He gestured to a crudely painted sign over the door of a building that read Soapy Joe's.

India chuckled. "With a name like that, it must be a pub, all right. Come along, boys. First round is on me."

The tavern was a typical waterfront drinking establishment. Several of the sailors from the *Fair Wind* were already there, along with seamen from some of the other ships in the harbor. Quite a few dock workers were also in the place, along with two or three slatternly women serving drinks. Jeff even spotted a man wearing fringed buckskins and a floppy-brimmed frontier hat at a table in the rear.

Ned and India headed for the bar, and Jeff followed.

"Three rums," India told the gaunt man working behind the planks of the bar.

"And follow that with a bucket of ale, my good man," Ned added.

The bartender nodded dourly and poured the rum. Jeff wondered idly if he was Soapy Joe himself.

When he slid the smudged glass over to India, she picked it up and tossed off the drink without ceremony. Ned and Jeff followed her example. The rum burned mightily going down Jeff's throat, but the sensation eased as it hit his stomach and ignited a pleasantly warm glow there.

The bartender filled a bucket with ale from a huge keg, then handed it over to Ned along with three mugs. India took the mugs, then rattled a coin on the bar to pay for the rum.

Ned flipped one of his own coins to the man for the ale. "Come on," he said as he turned away from the bar. "Let's find a place to sit down."

They settled on benches beside one of the rough-hewn tables, Ned and India on one side, Jeff on the other. Ned took the mugs from India, dipped them into the ale, then passed them around. As Jeff sipped from his, he studied the surroundings. The walls, ceiling, and floor of the tavern were made of heavy beams, and oil lamps hung from the ceiling, casting a dim yellow light that made a haze of the smoke hanging in the air. The only decorations were several large stuffed fish mounted on one wall. No one came here because the place was elegant; Soapy Joe's patrons came to drink.

The cadaverous bartender was kept busy doling out rum, ale, and whiskey. The room was filled with the low rumble of conversation, punctuated by an occasional burst of laughter, but for the most part the customers took what they were doing seriously.

Ned took a healthy swallow from his mug and licked his lips. Looking across the table at Jeff, he asked, "What are you going to do when we get to Charleston, Cousin? I'm glad you came along with us, but I don't reckon you want to spend the rest of your days as a sailor."

Remembering all his visits to the railing of the ship, Jeff said, "No, I don't think so. In fact, I don't think I'm even going on to Charleston."

"What?" Ned exclaimed. "What are you going to do, then?"

Thoughts on that subject had been on Jeff's mind for several days now, and he said, "I've never been in this part of the country before, so I figured I'd look around for a while and see what it's like. Maybe I'll head on down to Georgia and Florida."

He left unsaid the thought that wherever he went, he would keep looking for Melissa. She was somewhere; she had to be. He would find her sooner or later.

"Are you ever going west again?" India asked. Then she added quickly, "I don't mean to pry."

"That's all right. I'm not sure what I'm going to do. I came east from the Rockies to find my wife, and I'm not going back without her."

Even as he spoke, Jeff realized that he was finally putting into words what he had felt all along without being fully aware of it. The thought crystallized into rock-hard determination. He missed Clay and Shining Moon and Proud Wolf, and he missed the mountains, but he was not going back without Melissa.

"I wish you luck, Jeff," Ned said sincerely. "I'm sure you'll find her one of these days."

"I am, too," India said. "And if there's anything I can do to help . . ."

"You've done enough by putting this big fella in his place a time or two," Jeff told her, gesturing toward Ned. "When I met him, he could have used being taken down a notch or two, and you've managed to do that."

"Hold on!" Ned said in mock anger. "I don't know where you get such ideas about me, cousin. I've always been the most modest, humble—"

A sudden commotion interrupted Ned's protest, and the three friends turned toward the back of the room to see what had happened. Several sailors had gathered around the table where the man in buckskins Jeff had noticed when they first came into the tavern was sitting. Another sailor was seated across from the frontiersman, and their elbows were on the table, their hands locked in an arm-wrestling stance. Shouts of encouragement went up from the sailors as they urged their friend to defeat the buckskin-clad man. From the sound of it, Jeff figured that several wagers must be riding on the contest.

The frontiersman was red-faced and straining as he pushed against his foe's arm, and the sailor seemed to be putting just as much into the effort, if not more. Their arms swayed back and forth as first one man gained the advantage, then the other.

"I want to watch this," Ned said, standing.

"Don't go mixing in, Ned. Sailors take their games seriously," India warned, still sitting.

"Well, I'm a sailor now, aren't I? Come on."

Jeff and India exchanged a look of concern and followed Ned nearer the table where the contest was going on.

The sailor was huffing and puffing as the back of his hand slowly dipped closer to the table. The buckskin-clad man was still red in the face, but he seemed in control, and it came as no surprise to Jeff when the sailor's strength finally gave out a moment later. The man's hand hit the table with a thud. He let out a groan of disappointment that was echoed by his friends.

The buckskin-clad man released the sailor's hand and pushed back his floppy-brimmed hat.

"That'll do it," he said. "I expect you boys'll be payin' up now."

"Wait just a damned minute," one of the sailors said angrily. "I think you cheated, mister. Nobody can take Peevey here in a fair match."

The frontiersman gave the sailor who had spoken an ice-cold look as he said, "Reckon somebody can, 'cause I just did it. And I don't much like being called a cheater. Now, are you going to pay up or not?"

"Ye got no right to be in here," a sailor said in a loud voice. "This is a tavern for seagoing men!"

"Aye," another said. "We don't want no backwoodsmen in here cheatin' us out of our hard-earned wages."

"Take it easy, boys," the buckskin-clad man advised, his voice clear and firm in the hush that had fallen over Soapy Joe's. "I know you're just on a tear and want a little fun, but you've come to the wrong man for it. You'd best pay up and be done with it."

"Listen to him talk," ranted the first sailor. "He wants our money, but he's too good to fight with the likes of us, he is!"

"Let's show him different," the second man growled. Clenching blocky fists, he tensed, ready to lunge forward and swing a punch at the head of the man in buckskins.

"I wouldn't," Jeff Holt said. As he spoke, he cocked the flintlock rifle cradled in his arms. The unmistakable sound caused a hush to fall over the room.

The sailors who had formed a menacing ring around the frontiersman stood stock still.

Ned had a look of anticipation on his face as he asked, "What are you thinking about doing, Cousin?"

"Those odds don't look fair to me," Jeff said. "Thought I'd lend a hand, maybe even things up a little."

Not only were the odds unfair, but Jeff felt an allegiance to the man in buckskins simply because he seemed to be the same type of man Jeff had known in the Rockies. The fellow looked as if he would be right at home in the Yellowstone and Big Horn country. Jeff could not stand by and watch a fellow mountain man being beaten by a bunch of sailors.

"I'm with you, Jeff," Ned said enthusiastically.

"And I as well," India added.

The buckskin-clad man looked at the source of his unexpected assistance, sizing up the three of them. Then he said to the sailors, "Well, boys? What's it goin' to be?"

The man who had been defeated in the arm-wrestling contest spat a curse, then said, "It's not worth getting busted up or shot and missing our ship when it sails. Here's your money, dammit!" He dropped a coin on the table, and his friends reluctantly followed suit. Then they stalked away, trying to salvage some of their dignity by glaring over their shoulders at Jeff and the others.

Jeff was amazed by his own behavior. Clay was the hot-headed brother; Jeff was always the one to use reason instead of resorting to violence. His time in the mountains had hardened him and made him more accustomed to taking fast action when need be, but it was still unusual for him to get involved in a brawl without a sound cause.

"Would've been a pretty good fight, I think," the man in buckskins said to Jeff. "If you gents would like to come with me, we'll find us a place to drink where we won't be bothered."

"All right," Jeff said. "How about you and Max, Ned?"

"Sure," Ned replied. He looked around at the patrons of Soapy Joe's, many of whom were still glowering at them. "The mood's getting uglier now that those gents have had time to think about it. If we stay here, we may have to fight our way out."

"I'll come along, too," India said quietly.

When they reached the street, the buckskin-clad man extended his hand to Jeff and said, "Amos Tharp."

Jeff took his hand. "Name's Jefferson Holt. This is my cousin Ned and our friend Max St. Clair."

"Pleased to meet all of you." Amos Tharp regarded Jeff shrewdly. "You've got the look of a frontiersman about you, friend. Been west?"

"All the way to the Rockies. I trapped beaver out there last year."

Tharp got a misty, faraway look in his eyes. "The Rockies. I've been wanting to see them ever since Lewis and Clark got back. You'll have to tell me all about them. Come along. I owe you gents a drink."

They found another tavern, this one farther from the waterfront and patronized by fewer sailors. Settling into a booth with another bucket of ale, they filled their mugs.

Tharp looked at Ned and India over his drink. "I'm a mite surprised that a couple of sailor boys sided with me like that."

"If my cousin's in the middle of something, then it's my fight, too," Ned said firmly.

"And I stand with my friends," India said.

"Well, here's to the three of you, then," Tharp said, lifting his glass. "You saved me from one hell of a beating, maybe worse. I'd have made those bastards pay for jumping me, but there were too many of them for me to stand up to them for long."

"Why were they ready to go after you like that?" Jeff asked. "Just because they lost some bets?"

Tharp shook his head. "Just looking for a fight, I figure, and they could tell by my clothes I wasn't one of them. If they hadn't come after me, they might've picked you, Holt. You're a frontiersman; anybody can tell that just by looking at you." Tharp downed a long swallow of ale, then studied Jeff. "Say, you wouldn't be looking for work, would you?"

"Work?" Jeff repeated. He had not really thought about what he would do next. He had left St. Louis with a sizable purse, but many months had passed since then, and his funds had shrunk considerably. Before long, he was indeed going to have to find a job, especially if he kept searching for Melissa.

After a moment he said, "I suppose I might be interested. Ned and Max are shipping out again tomorrow, but I've had my fill of the sea."

"Why don't you come with me, then?" Tharp asked. "I'm taking a wagon train full of supplies across the Blue Ridge Mountains into Tennessee. There's a good many settlers over that way now, and more going in all the time. Should be a profitable trip."

Tharp had not struck Jeff as the type to be a businessman. He asked, "Do you own these supplies?"

"Nope. I'm just in charge of the wagons and getting everything there safely. I've got enough drivers, but I've been hiring a few men to go along as guards and outriders. The Cherokees sometimes don't take kindly to folks crossing the mountains, and there're bandits up there, too, who'd as soon slit a man's throat as look at him. Might be a dangerous job, Holt. I got to admit that."

Jeff thought back to his days in the Rockies, to the battles against the Blackfoot and the renegades led by the man called Duquesne. He doubted that Tharp's wagon train would run into more trouble than that.

He knew he was acting on impulse, but the lure of being around men of his own kind and seeing some country besides coastal flatlands persuaded him. He stuck his hand across the table.

"You've got a deal, Amos. I'll be glad to go with you."

"Hope you won't regret it," Tharp said as he shook Jeff's hand. "Well, drink up, you three, and then I'll take Jeff to meet the boss. You'll like him." Tharp lifted his mug and said over the rim, "Fella name of Dermot Hawley."

With papers spread out on the desk in front of him, Hawley was not in the mood for visitors. But when his assistant stuck his head into the office and said that Amos Tharp was there, Hawley wearily agreed to see him.

The preparations for taking the wagon train across the mountains into Tennessee were almost complete. The *Fair Wind* had docked earlier that day, and Hawley had been there to purchase a good portion of the ship's cargo, making sure that plenty of people saw him. The goods had been taken from the ship to one of Charles Merrivale's warehouses for temporary storage until they could be loaded onto the wagons that would form the trade caravan. Hawley expected the wagons to pull out for Tennessee within a day or two, and the only thing Tharp had to do until then was hire a few guards. Hawley wondered if that was why Tharp had come to the office.

Hawley did not stand up as Tharp entered, followed by another man wearing a buckskin jacket and homespun shirt. The second man was younger than Tharp and not as tall, with sandy hair and clean-cut features. A long-barreled flintlock rifle was tucked under his left arm; hanging from his belt was a knife in a fringed sheath. He also carried a pistol. Hawley thought the man looked as if he knew how to use all the weapons.

"Howdy, Mr. Hawley," Tharp said, taking off his hat. "Got somebody I'd like for you to meet. I just hired him as one of the outriders for the wagon train."

Hawley stood up and held out a hand to the stranger. "Hello. Glad you're joining us. I'm Dermot Hawley, and I own this freighting company."

"Nice to meet you, Mr. Hawley," the stranger said, sounding more polite and a bit less rough-hewn than Tharp and most of the other frontiersmen involved in the scheme. "My name's Jefferson Holt."

Only Hawley's experience in hiding his true feelings allowed him to conceal the shock that went through him like a lightning bolt. The smile on his face never wavered as he said, "Holt, eh?"

"That's right."

Could there be more than one frontiersman with the name Jefferson Holt? Hawley wondered. He supposed it was possible, but as he looked into Holt's intelligent eyes, he knew without a doubt that this was the long-vanished Jeff Holt, Melissa's husband.

Swallowing to moisten his suddenly dry throat, Hawley asked, "What brings you to North Carolina, Mr. Holt?"

"Just drifting, I guess. I've been looking for . . . something for a while."

"Oh? And what might that be?"

"My wife," Jeff said bluntly.

Hawley saw Tharp glance at Jeff in surprise. From that reaction Hawley knew Holt had not told Tharp about Melissa. But did Tharp know anything about Merrivale's connection with the wagon train? Hawley tried desperately to remember, his agitation still well hidden behind his bland expression. He didn't remember ever mentioning Merrivale's name to Tharp, and he had certainly never talked to him about Melissa. Perhaps it would be safe to draw Holt out a little more, find out if he had any idea just how close to his goal he really was.

Hawley waved to the chairs in front of the desk, saying "Sit down, both of you. I like to get to know the men who are working for me."

Actually, Hawley had paid very little attention to the men Tharp hired, and he had never invited any of them to sit down and visit with him.

Hawley sank into his own upholstered chair and clasped his hands together on the desk. Looking at Jeff with a sympathetic expression, he asked, "You said you're looking for your wife?"

"That's right."

For the next few minutes, Hawley listened to a sketchy version of the story he had already heard from Charles Merrivale. Every time Holt mentioned the Merrivale name, Hawley waited anxiously to see if Tharp was going to say anything about having heard it mentioned around Wilmington. Tharp kept quiet, however, so evidently he was not familiar with Merrivale's mercantile business.

"I truly sympathize with you, Mr. Holt," Hawley murmured when Jeff had concluded his tale. "I hope you eventually find your wife."

"I'll never give up," Jeff said quietly.

"I'm sure you won't." Hawley straightened in his chair. "However, I'm glad you've decided to join our little venture for the time being." He turned to Tharp. "Amos, take Mr. Holt out to the camp and make him welcome."

"Camp?" Jeff repeated. "What camp?"

"The wagon train is forming just outside of town," Hawley explained. "We'll be leaving tomorrow, so you arrived in Wilmington just in time."

"I was planning to go by the courthouse and check the tax records for Merrivale's name. I know it would be a shot in the dark if I happened to find him that way, but . . ." Jeff shrugged.

His mind racing, Hawley pulled a gold watch from a pocket in his vest and flipped it open. "I'm afraid it's too late for you to find anyone at the courthouse. But I'll tell you what I'll do, Mr. Holt. I'd be glad to go there first thing in the morning to check those records for you. When I see the wagon train off, I can let you know if I found anything."

"Well, I guess that would be all right," Jeff said slowly. "Thanks, Mr. Hawley. It's mighty nice of you to help me like that."

"Glad to do it. I promise you, it's my pleasure." Hawley felt sweat form on his forehead and wished he could wipe it off, but that would draw attention to the tension he was fighting. Instead, he stood up and held out his hand to Jeff again.

"Good to have you with us, Mr. Holt."

"Same here," Jeff said, returning the handshake.

Tharp stood up, too, and said, "We'll be getting on out to the camp now. See you tomorrow, Mr. Hawley."

"Yes. Tomorrow."

Hawley stood there, hoping he did not look as stiff and tense as he felt, until the two frontiersmen had left the office. Then he sank back into his chair with a gusty sigh of relief.

That had been close, too damned close. If Holt had not run into Tharp and agreed to accompany the wagon train, he would no doubt have located the Merrivale family in Wilmington without much trouble. Now Hawley had the son of a bitch distracted and on his way out of town.

But that was not the end of the problem, Hawley knew. Sooner or later, Jeff would be back.

Hawley looked up sharply as the door opened again. Amos Tharp stepped in, pushing past Hawley's protesting assistant as he did so.

"Got to talk to your boss," Tharp grunted. "Now step aside, mister."

"What the hell is this, Tharp?" Hawley demanded as Tharp shut the door behind him. "I thought I told you—"

"I know what you told me," Tharp cut in. "I told Holt how to find the camp and sent him on his way, told him I'd catch up in a few minutes. But I wanted to talk to you first."

"You left Holt on his own?" Hawley's voice rose as he asked the question.

"Yeah, and that bothers the hell out o' you, don't it?" Tharp rubbed a thumbnail along his craggy jaw. "What's going on here, Hawley? Why'd you take such an interest in Holt? You never acted that way with none of the other men I hired."

Hawley sat there for a long moment, wondering whether or not to take Tharp into his confidence. Finally he asked, "Just how much does this man Holt mean to you?"

Tharp shrugged his brawny shoulders. "Only met him a little while ago. Seems like a nice enough fella. But it ain't like him and me are brothers, or anything like that."

"Good," Hawley said, reaching a decision. "Since you're here asking these questions, Tharp, I have a proposition for you."

"I'm listening."

"My reasons for being interested in Jefferson Holt are my own. But I want you to keep him out there at the camp until the wagon train leaves. Under no circumstances are you to allow him to come back into town. Do you understand?"

"Sure. There's bound to be more, though."

"There is." Hawley clasped his hands together again. "If he asks you anything else about anyone named Merrivale, you tell him you never heard of anybody by that name."

"Had a feeling you were going to say that."

"One more thing, and this is the most important of all." Hawley took a deep breath and plunged ahead with his idea. "I don't want Holt coming back from Tennessee."

"Don't see how I could stop him."

"Let me make myself absolutely clear. I don't want Holt to survive the trip."

Tharp's eyes narrowed. "You're talking about murder."

"I'm talking about five hundred dollars," Hawley snapped. "Over and above what I've already agreed to pay for your services."

"Five hundred dollars, eh? That's a hell of a lot of money." Abruptly a grin broke out on Tharp's rugged face. "But I reckon I'll try to see you get your money's worth, Mr. Hawley."

Relieved, Hawley returned the smile. "I knew we'd come to an understanding," he said.

"I want half of it now, though. I sort of like Jeff Holt. Might make it easier to keep in mind what I got to do if I've got some money to remind me."

"That can be arranged. Come back here tonight, and I'll have the cash then. You'll get the rest when you return from Tennessee—and Jeff Holt doesn't."

Tharp agreed and left the office.

Five hundred dollars, Hawley thought. As Tharp had said, a lot of money, but money well spent if it meant that Jeff Holt would never interfere with Hawley's plans for Melissa. No matter what incredible twist of fate had brought Holt here, so unwittingly close to the goal he had sought for months, it would not do him any good. Jefferson Holt was going to die, just as he should have died in the mountains a long time ago.

Chapter Twenty-one

Sitting in a tipi built by the members of the expedition, Clay Holt propped Aaron Garwood up and held a steaming cup of stew to the young man's lips.

"Try to get some of this down," Clay told him. "It'll help you get your strength."

Especially since Shining Moon added herbs to it to make it more potent than usual, Clay thought.

Aaron needed something strong. The boy's body was covered with bruises, including an ugly one on his upper left arm. His torso was wound tightly in makeshift bandages just in case he had any cracked ribs, and a piece of Lucy Franklin's petticoat was bound around his forehead to cover a deep gash there.

After Aaron regained consciousness, he had gasped out the story of his capture and subsequent escape from the Canadian trappers to Clay, Shining Moon, and Proud Wolf, who were with him in the tipi. The others were waiting anxiously outside to see if he would be all right.

As Aaron sipped at the broth from the stew, Clay looked up at Proud Wolf.

"Go out and tell the others he'll be fine," he said, "once he's rested up and gotten over those bruises."

As Proud Wolf stepped toward the tipi's entrance flap, he paused next to Aaron and rested a hand on his shoulder.

"I am glad you came back to us, my friend," Proud Wolf said. Then he went out.

Clay knelt in front of Aaron and asked, "You feel up to talking some more?"

"Sure. I'm feeling better now."

"These men who captured you," Shining Moon said, kneeling beside Clay, "you are sure they were British?"

"All except for a few Frenchies. I reckon all of them came down from Canada."

Clay agreed. "And they were taking you back to a fort they've built?"

"That's right. Their boss was there, a man they called Brown. He was the one who was going to kill me when we got there."

Shining Moon glanced at Clay. "Why would they want to kill Aaron? How could he be a threat to them?"

"He knew too much," Clay said grimly. "He could tell they weren't Americans, and they don't have any right to be trapping down here."

"For that they would kill someone?" Shining Moon sounded as if she found it impossible to believe.

Clay took his pipe and tobacco from his pocket and prepared to smoke. "Remember how Duquesne was trying to stir up the Sioux and the other Indians in these parts against the white trappers? We figured then that he might be working for some British outfit up in Canada that wants the furs in these mountains for themselves."

"But there are more beaver than anyone could ever trap," Shining Moon protested.

"To some folks, there's no such things as enough pelts or enough money. I've known men who'd cut your throat for two bits. There's a hell of a lot more than that involved in the fur trade. Not to mention the politics that get all mixed up in it."

"Politics," Aaron repeated as Clay took a burning twig from the fire, held it above the bowl of his pipe, and puffed it to life. "I don't understand."

"One of the reasons President Jefferson sent Lewis and Clark to the Pacific with the Corps of Discovery was to firm up the United States's claim to the Louisiana Territory he bought from that French fellow Bonaparte," Clay explained. "That's why we did so much mapping as we went along. It was sort of like surveying a new piece of property. Now, the agreement we made with Bonaparte sets out the boundaries of the territory, I reckon, but England doesn't have to recognize that agreement. They can sashay down here and claim a lot of the same land, and that claim'll be a lot stronger if they can point to a successful fur-trapping operation in these parts."

"So that's why they want to run everybody else out," Aaron mused.

"That'd be my guess." Clay had been thinking it through even as he explained it, and everything made sense to him.

"These men are dangerous," Shining Moon said. "That is why the Crow and the Shoshone have been avoiding them, as well as us."

"And the Britishers didn't want us getting close enough to see who they are," Clay said. "That's why they ducked away from us."

"What are we going to do now?" Aaron asked.

Clay rubbed his jaw as he thought that question over. As long as he was saddled with the responsibility for the safety of Professor Franklin, Lucy, Rupert von Metz, and the other men, he did not want any part of a clash between British and American fur interests. Every time he thought about how close to dying Aaron had come, anger sprang up in him, but the desire for revenge was overridden by caution.

"We've got our own business here," he said finally. "We'll stay out of their way and hope they stay out of ours. But I'll see if I can talk the professor into moving on right away, so we can put a little distance between us and them. You reckon you can travel in a day or two, Aaron?"

"Nothing wrong with me but some bumps and bruises," the young man replied. "I can travel tomorrow."

"Good." Clay clapped him on the shoulder, taking care to make sure it was the right one and not the left. "You get a good night's sleep. You ought to feel better in the morning."

"I am a mite tired." Aaron had finished the stew and looked stronger already. He set the empty cup aside and rolled up in the blankets that Shining Moon spread for him, and he was asleep almost before they left the tipi. As they stepped outside, Professor Franklin came up to them.

"Proud Wolf tells us the lad is going to be all right," he said.

"I think so," Clay said. "He'll need some rest, though."

"Of course." In the glow of the campfire, the concern in Franklin's face was evident. "The story about the British trappers he told you—is it true?"

"Seems to be. There's no reason for him to lie, and I trust Aaron not to have made any mistakes about what he saw and heard."

Franklin glanced over at his daughter, who was sitting near the fire with von Metz. Quietly he said, "Then we're in danger from them, too, aren't we?"

"We can't be sure of that. They probably don't know for certain that Aaron got back here and told us about them. I think if we stay away from them, we'll be safe enough. But I'd just as soon put this part of the country behind us as soon as we can."

Franklin sighed with disappointment. "I agree. I would have liked to stay here longer—there's so much to see and study—but we must do what's best for everyone. I don't want any more trouble with those men."

"We'll get everything together and move out tomorrow. That is, if Aaron is up to traveling."

"Of course. That gives me a little more time to collect samples."

"Don't wander off, Professor," Clay warned.

"Oh, I've no intention of doing that," Franklin assured him.

Despite what the professor said, Clay instructed Proud Wolf to keep an eye on the naturalist. The last thing they needed was for Franklin to go off and get into trouble.

Clay told the others that they would be leaving the next day, and no one gave him any argument. Aaron's ordeal had cast a somber pall over the expedition, which had recovered from the violence of Lawton's death and had been in good spirits again. Now, yet another threat had reared its ugly head.

Alone in their tipi, Shining Moon asked Clay, "Do you truly think we can avoid trouble with those men?"

"I don't know. But I'm sure going to try."

"You would like to go after them and pay them back for what happened to Aaron, wouldn't you?"

Clay slipped an arm around her shoulders and drew her close to him. "You know me too well," he said quietly. "But there're more important things now than settling a score. I've got to get this group out of here alive."

"You will," she whispered, lifting her mouth to his.

Now that the London and Northwestern fort was completed, Simon Brown was ready to send out more of his men to set traplines in the streams. The pelts would really start piling up in the storehouses, he reflected as he sipped from a bottle of the brandy he had in his pack. The other men did not know he had such fine liquor in his cabin; they might be envious if they did. But he had a right to enjoy fine things. After all, he was nobility—of a sort.

The man who should have been an earl, stuck in the middle of nowhere in a squalid little fort, he thought. It was enough to make him physically ill. Someday it would all be different.

He was about to drift off into the familiar fantasy of returning to England as a rich man and showing his high and mighty family just how little they really meant to him, when a shout from the sentry at the stockade gate drifted through the open door of the cabin. Brown had been half-reclining on his bunk, but he sat up straight at the call.

Someone was coming in.

He swung his feet off the bunk and went to the door, picking up one of his pistols and a blackhawk ax on the way. The keen-bladed, single-edged ax with its short, straight handle was as dangerous a weapon in his hands as a gun. He could throw it with great accuracy and power over a distance of twenty yards. He had heard that the Indians were good with their 'hawks, but he would match his trusty ax against such primitive weapons any day.

Striding toward the gate, Brown called up to the sentry in the guard tower, "Who's out there?"

"It's Robertson and his group, sir," the man replied.

"You're sure of that?"

"Aye, sir."

"Well, then, let them in," Brown said impatiently. The fort was dark except for a few candles burning in the windows of the barracks, but there was plenty of moonlight for the men at the gate to see his curt gesture as he ordered them to open up.

The rawhide thongs on the gate that served as latches were unfastened, and the small log used as a bar was lifted from its brackets. The heavy gate swung back on its hinges, and a group of almost a dozen men plodded on foot through the opening. They stopped in front of Brown as the gate was being closed behind them.

"I didn't expect you back for a few days yet, Robertson," Brown greeted the leader of the group in deceptively pleasant tones. "You must have had good luck."

"We brought in plenty of plews," Robertson replied. He was a slender man with an irregular patch of black beard on his lean cheeks. "But we ran into a spot of trouble."

"I don't like to hear that," Brown said, his voice still soft. "What happened?"

"An American ran into us. We had to catch him. We were going to bring him to ye—"

"An American?" Brown's voice, no longer soft, lashed at Robertson like a whip.

The bearded man shrugged. "He saw us before we saw him. Weren't nothing we could do but grab him."

"Perhaps not. I assume you killed him immediately."

"Well, some of the fellows brought that up. But I decided to bring him back here to ye."

"Bring him back?" Brown repeated venomously.

"I gave orders that if you encountered any Americans close up to kill them!"

Robertson nodded, looking as though he wished he were somewhere else. "Aye, ye did. But I thought ye might like to talk to this one, seeing as how he's from that scientific expedition we been dodging."

Brown's grip tightened on the handle of the ax. That group of Americans had been a thorn in his side for weeks now, ever since Dobbs had spotted them over in the valley. His men had remained on the lookout for them and tried to stay out of their sight at all times. No other trappers had been seen in the area, and Brown had congratulated himself on picking such a good site for the London and Northwestern's venture. Now, because of Robertson's carelessness, the Americans probably knew about the British presence in the Rockies.

Keeping a firm rein on his temper, Brown said, "So this man was one of that bunch, eh? We've been keeping an eye on them. They're not doing anything except digging up plants and rocks and measuring trees. I don't believe I need to interrogate the prisoner. Where is he, anyway?"

"That's the problem, Mr. Brown. The bastard's gone and got away, he has."

Rage burst inside Brown's skull. In a voice that trembled with emotion, he asked, "What did you tell this man before he got away?"

"That we were bringing him back here to the fort for ye to deal with."

"So," Brown said slowly, "he knows that you're British and that you have a fort in the area. And he got away and went back to the rest of his party."

Robertson quickly protested. "We don't know that, sir. We took quite a few shots at him, we did, and one of us might've hit him. Besides, he went over a waterfall and down some rapids, so he was pretty well banged up. I don't believe he could've got far through the woods. Probably lying somewhere, either dead or dying."

"But you don't know that," Brown said. "He could have gotten back to the others."

Finally, in a grudging voice, Robertson said, "I guess he could have. But it don't matter, does it? I mean, they were going to find out about us sooner or later anyway."

"Not yet," Brown snapped. "We haven't been here long enough to establish a strong claim. We can't afford to let the American government know what we're doing yet."

Robertson took a step closer to Brown and said, "If that bloke did get back to his mates, it's too late to do anything about it now, isn't it?"

"Perhaps not," Brown said softly.

And then he whipped the ax up in a motion too fast to follow in the moonlight and drove the blackhawk's blade into the front of Robertson's skull with a grisly *thunk*!

The blow split the man's head open nearly to the shoulders. A great quiver ran through his body, which stayed upright, and his rifle fell from nerveless fingers. Then, as Brown wrenched the ax free, Robertson's corpse crumpled like a rag doll.

The hideous violence had happened so shockingly fast that the other men present stood transfixed, as immobile as statues. Brown gave them a baleful stare.

"He shouldn't have disobeyed my order," he said calmly. "If he'd killed that American right away, we wouldn't have anything to worry about now." He flicked a hand contemptuously at Robertson's corpse. "Take him out and bury him. I don't want anyone bothering me for a while. I've got some thinking to do."

With that he strode back toward his cabin. He had already forgotten about Robertson; he had dealt with that problem, and it was behind him. His concern now was what to do about the American expedition.

He would feel a great deal better about the situation, he realized, if all of them were dead. And if they were, who would miss them? Who could ever lay the blame for their deaths at his feet? Those were intriguing questions indeed, Brown thought. All he had to figure out now was the best way to dispose of them. He had time to think about it, too. The Americans would not be able to move too fast, not fast enough to escape from him, anyway. After all, he made the rules here. This was his domain.

His lips curved in a smile at that thought. In England, if things had been different, he might have been an earl. Here in the Rocky Mountains he was king.

True to his word, Aaron Garwood was able to travel the next day, although he tired easily and Clay had to call frequent rest halts. But the expedition covered several miles that day, climbing still higher into the mountains. Two days later the party stood at the top of a high pass.

"This is it, Professor. The highest part of the Rockies." Clay held up his hand to bring them to a stop. "Thought you might like to take a look around."

"The top of the world." Franklin's voice was hushed with awe. "It's incredible."

Rupert von Metz sniffed in dismissal. "I see nothing so impressive, just more of these mountains, which have been looming over us forever."

Clay looked at von Metz and shook his head. True, this pass did not look any different from a dozen others they had seen, except that it was higher and the air, colder and thinner. Shining Moon had slipped on her capote, in fact, to ward off the chill. But it was what this place signified that made it important. It was the dividing line of the entire country. Every drop of rain that fell to the east wound up in the Atlantic Ocean, sooner or later, while all the water to the west ended up in the Pacific. That was oversimplifying it, but not by much.

Franklin turned to Clay and asked, "Can we stay here long enough for Herr von Metz to do a sketch?"

"I reckon that won't hurt anything," Clay said.

With a shrug of resignation, von Metz got his sketchbook and charcoal from his pack, and started to work while the others found rocky seats and settled down to rest.

"How are you doing, Aaron?" Clay asked as he sat down beside the young man on a large, flat rock near the wall of the pass.

"I'm all right," Aaron replied. "I feel better today."

Indeed, he looked better, Clay thought. Injuries seemed to heal more quickly in the high country, whether because of the air or the body's recognizing the need for quick recuperation in such harsh surroundings, Clay did not know. But he was glad that Aaron was stronger. It was hard to remember that he and this young man had once been mortal enemies. Aaron had turned into a staunch friend.

After von Metz had finished his sketch, the group moved down from the pass to find a suitable spot to camp for the night. Clay settled for a small, rock-littered bowl two miles downslope, where a tiny spring bubbled out of the stony ground. It would not be a comfortable place to sleep; they were above the tree line, and there were no pine needles or grassy swards to serve as a bed. Soon they would be back in that sort of country.

Two more days passed, and Clay was pleased with their progress. Crossing the dividing ridge had been more than a symbolic advantage; they were going downhill most of the time now, and that made travel easier on everyone. Clay was fairly sure they had left the bloodthirsty Britishers on the other side of the pass, and that eased his mind, too.

The next day they came to a stream that Clay identified as the Flathead River.

"We can follow this to the Columbia," he told the professor, "and that'll take us to the Pacific. There's still a lot of ground to cover, but if we build canoes, we can use the rivers. I'll get the men started right away."

"Excellent!" Franklin said. He opened his journal. "By my reckoning, the date is June seventeenth, eighteen hundred and nine. A momentous day, indeed."

Clay had no idea whether Franklin was right about the date or not, but June seventeenth sounded likely enough. It had been around the middle of April when he, Shining Moon, Proud Wolf, and Aaron had met up with the expedition, and a good two months had passed since then. *Two eventful months,* Clay thought. With all the trouble they'd experienced and the rugged terrain they had crossed, they had not really traversed much distance in that time. From here on out, once the canoes were finished, they would be able to go considerably faster.

While von Metz did another drawing and the professor, Lucy, and Proud Wolf collected and cataloged more plant specimens, Clay and the other men used their axes to fell birches along the riverbank. The small, supple branches would form the frames of the canoes, while the bark would serve as covering for the small boats. They would need six or seven canoes to carry all the members of the expedition plus the supplies, Clay estimated.

The woods rang with the sound of axes striking tree trunks, and to Clay it was a good sound. It meant they would soon be putting this part of the country, with all its dangers, behind them.

Not soon enough, however, as he discovered less than an hour later. He had stooped over to hack at the base of a tree, and as he straightened to stretch the cramping muscles in his back, something whipped by his ear with a fluttering sound. An arrow was embedded in the tree he had been chopping down, the shaft still quivering.

Then a man a few feet away dropped his ax and staggered forward, screaming. The bloody head of an arrow protruded a few inches from his chest, the feathered shaft sticking out from the middle of his back.

Cries came from the thick stand of trees as the dead man fell forward. More arrows cut through the air around Clay as he snatched up the long rifle lying at his feet. He went down on one knee, brought the primed and loaded weapon to his shoulder, and searched for a target. A flash of bright color caught his eye—streaks of red paint on a face contorted with hate. The Indian's arm was drawn back, ready to throw the 'hawk in his hand. Clay fired first, smoke and flame erupting from the muzzle of his rifle.

The Indian jerked backward, his face disappearing in a crimson smear even brighter than his war paint. Another warrior darted out from the trees and threw himself at Clay, 'hawk raised for a killing strike. Clay dropped the empty rifle and rolled to the side, and the attacker plunged past Clay and landed on the ground. Clay grabbed his knife from its sheath and lunged, driving the blade into the fallen man's back before he could regain his feet.

Clay ripped the knife free and rolled upright. The attackers were Blackfoot, probably from the southern band known as Piegan. It had been a raiding party of Piegan that had attacked the expedition all those months and miles ago, bringing Clay and his companions to their aid. This was a larger group, Clay saw to his dismay. The woods seemed to be full of them.

Guns boomed, arrows hissed through the air, and knives and 'hawks flashed in the sun. The cries of men in mortal agony furnished a grisly punctuation to the chaos.

Shining Moon! Where was she? The thought had barely flashed through Clay's mind before he grabbed his rifle and ran toward the river. But then a Blackfoot raider leapt at him. Clay drove the rifle's brass butt plate into the man's painted face, and the warrior fell away, blood spurting from his smashed nose. Clay sprinted on, hurtling over a body bristling with arrows. He did not pause to try to help the man; one of the arrows had caught the poor bastard in the throat, and he was far beyond what help Clay could give him.

Clay heard gunfire and saw powder smoke coming from a small cut in the riverbank, a gully that led down to the water itself. Part of the expedition must have taken cover there, he figured. He headed toward the smoke as fast as his long legs would carry him, the muscles of his back tensed in expectation of an arrow striking him. He jumped over the edge of the gully, landed hard, and tumbled down the short slope to roll to a stop at the feet of Shining Moon, who was aiming her rifle at the onrushing Blackfoot attackers.

Her rifle boomed, and as she knelt to reload, Clay scrambled back to his feet and peered over the lip of the cut. More men were fleeing from the nearby woods, Piegan warriors in hot pursuit. Clay pulled the pistols from his belt, primed and loaded them, then let loose with both shots. One ball smashed the breastbone of a charging Blackfoot, while the other left a bloody crease on a raider's head, sending him tumbling to the ground.

Clay turned to Shining Moon, and she thrust her reloaded rifle into his hands, taking the empty pistols from him. While she could handle a gun quite well, in a case like this she could do more good reloading for him. Clay looked at her just long enough to make sure she was not wounded, then turned his attention to the Blackfoot.

Smoothly he brought the rifle to his shoulder, settled the sights on the chest of another Piegan, and squeezed the trigger. The flintlock kicked hard against his shoulder as its charge of black powder exploded. Through the smoky haze, Clay saw his target jerk, the .56 caliber rifle ball knocking him backward.

Shining Moon had not quite reloaded both pistols, so Clay had a few seconds to glance around. Aaron and Proud Wolf were in the gully with Professor Franklin, Lucy, and Rupert von Metz. The young woman and the Prussian artist, both terrified, were crouched low, their hands over their ears. Franklin knelt beside Lucy, one hand on her shoulder, the other holding a small pistol. Five other men from the group had reached the comparative safety of the cut, and two others were almost there. The rest had fallen, either in the woods or trying to escape. Bodies were sprawled here and there, and a red rage burned inside Clay at the sight.

He took the reloaded pistols from Shining Moon and fired another volley, cutting down two more Blackfoot and giving the fleeing men time to reach the gully. They vaulted into it just as arrows slashed through the air where they had been an instant earlier. One of them was bleeding heavily from an arm wound, but the other seemed to be unhurt, just scared half out of his wits.

As any sane man would be, Clay thought. The Blackfoot outnumbered them more than two to one. Here in the gully, he and his companions might be able to fight off a direct assault, at least for a while, but they would be hopelessly pinned down in a cross fire if the Blackfoot got behind them and attacked from the river at the same time.

"We've got to get out of here," Clay said in a low

voice as their attackers loosed more arrows, then pulled back toward the trees.

"Looks like they're leaving," Aaron said.

"It might look that way, but they'll regroup and hit us again," he said grimly. "There's still a lot more of them than us. They're not giving up, not by a long shot."

"What—what do we do, Mr. Holt?" the professor said.

"Remember when they had you pinned down on that island in the Yellowstone? This is a lot like that. We're not on an island, but we're backed up against this river, so we might as well be. If they ford the stream and get behind us, they can pick us off however they damn well please. And there aren't enough of us to guard all directions at once."

"So what can we do?"

Clay turned his head and looked across the stream toward the far bank. There were trees and higher ground over there. It would be a lot easier to defend than this rock-strewn gully.

"We're going to get the hell out of here," Clay said.

He glanced at the trees again. The Blackfoot had disappeared, but he knew they were there, just waiting, letting their intended victims stew awhile in their own fear. In two minutes, or five, or ten, the warriors would burst out of concealment again and charge toward the river and the small group trapped there.

"Shining Moon," Clay snapped. "Take Proud Wolf and Aaron and get the professor, Lucy, and von Metz across the river. Fort up in those trees over there. The rest of us will cover you until you're across. Then you can lay some fire for us. Understand?"

The raven-haired woman nodded. She handed Clay his rifle, then picked up her own. Proud Wolf and Aaron had heard the orders, too, and were ready to go.

"I can't swim," Lucy said nervously. "And that river looks fast and deep."

"Hang on to me," Proud Wolf told her. "I will get you across."

"How about you, von Metz? Can you swim?" Aaron asked.

"Of course I can swim," the Prussian said. "But what about my paints and my canvases?"

"Leave them here," Clay said curtly. "Now get moving, all of you, before those Blackfoot start in again."

While Clay and the remaining men lined the edges of the cut, their rifles half cocked, Shining Moon, Proud Wolf, and Aaron herded their charges into the water. The Flathead was some forty feet wide at this point and like most mountain streams carried a swift current. It would have been better if the swimmers could have shed some of their clothing, but there was no time for that. Shining Moon swam next to Professor Franklin, ready to help him if need be. She carried her rifle and powder horn high above her head to keep them dry. Aaron and Proud Wolf did likewise. Proud Wolf had a more difficult time of it because Lucy Franklin clung to him, but like most of the young men in his tribe, he had learned to swim almost before he could walk, and he managed to get across with Lucy and dry powder and rifle.

Clay watched their progress while keeping an eye on the trees where the Blackfoot lurked. Just as the swimmers reached the far bank safely and pulled themselves out of the water, the war party attacked again. Several trade muskets boomed, but the old weapons were so inaccurate that Clay did not particularly worry about the fire from them. The Blackfoot were much more deadly with arrows and lances.

As the warriors came boiling out of the trees, Clay spoke calmly to his men. "Hold your fire just a little bit longer, boys. . . . Now!"

Rifle balls slashed through the charging men, knocking a couple of them off their feet. But others were still approaching. Clay hoped Shining Moon and her companions across the river were ready to rejoin the battle.

"Go!" he yelled, waving the other men toward the river. He hung back long enough to fire both pistols one last time, dropped them in the gully, then turned and plunged into the stream, careful to keep his rifle and powder horn above the water. He hoped he would have a chance to recover his pistols.

As he swam for his life, arrows splashed around him, but when shots rang out from the opposite bank, the Blackfoot fell back again. Shining Moon, Aaron, and Proud Wolf were laying down an effective covering fire, yet with the amount of time required to reload between shots, there was only so much they could do. Soon Blackfoot were darting forward again to throw lances after Clay and the other fugitives.

Abruptly the guns in the trees on the far bank fell silent. Fear, not for himself but for his wife, surged through Clay. Something must have happened to Shining Moon and the others, but he could do nothing except keep swimming.

The men with him reached the shore first and scrambled into the trees. Clay thought they would load and fire, but the eerie silence continued.

He was the last one to reach the other side of the river, and as he climbed out of the shallow water, a white man stepped from the trees on the bank and stood over him. Clay froze as the man, a total stranger, pointed a pistol at his head. Beyond him, at the edge of the trees, Clay saw other men herding his friends back into sight at gunpoint.

"Well, you've led my redskinned friends and I on a merry chase, my good man," the stranger said in a cheerful voice as he aimed the pistol at Clay. "But we've got you now."

Clay blinked water out of his eyes and glared up at the man. "You're working with those Blackfoot?"

"They're working for me," the man replied. "And you and all your companions are my prisoners. My name is Simon Brown." Though he smiled broadly, Brown's eyes remained as icy as the stream in which Clay still stood. "Welcome to my kingdom."

Chapter Twenty-two

For the first time since leaving Ohio on his quest to find Melissa, Jeff Holt's mind was at ease, or at least as much at ease as was possible these days. His wife was still missing, and her loss was like an empty spot in his soul, but the long days of riding and hard work had returned to him other things that had been missing: a sense of purpose over and above finding Melissa, a feeling of duty and responsibility to someone else, and a change from concentrating on his problems.

He was on the move again, and it felt damned good.

The wagon train had left Wilmington on an overcast summer day with clouds scudding in from the ocean. Ned and India had gone to the camp to see Jeff off, as had Dermot Hawley. Jeff had been glad to see Ned and India but disappointed in what Hawley had to tell him.

"I'm afraid I didn't have any luck at the courthouse, Holt," Hawley had said in a low voice after drawing Jeff aside. "There's no record of a Charles Merrivale buying or selling any property in the area, nor paying any taxes. In fact, there were no Merrivales listed at all. So it seems that your wife's family never visited this part of the country. I'm sorry to have to tell you this."

Dejectedly Jeff had said, "I appreciate your checking on that for me, Mr. Hawley. By the way, I posted a letter this morning to a fellow named Washington Irving, up in New York. He's the editor of a magazine up there, and I put a notice in it asking for information about Melissa or her family. I gave Mr. Irving the address of your office, just in case he ever gets a reply. I hope you won't mind holding them for me."

"Not at all," Hawley said heartily.

The man had been friendly and helpful, Jeff had to give him that. But for some reason, Jeff did not particularly like Dermot Hawley. He had not been able to put his finger on the reason, and he did not spend a great deal of time worrying about the matter.

He liked Ned and India, though, and he was going to miss them. Ned had shaken his hand, then grabbed him in a bear hug.

"I don't know how to thank you for everything you've done for me, Jeff," Ned said solemnly, or at least as solemnly as Ned Holt ever managed to get. "If it weren't for you, I'd be back in Pittsburgh, getting into trouble and worrying my folks to death."

"And now you're on the high seas getting into trouble," Jeff kidded gently.

"Maybe, but at least Ma and Pa don't know about it." He had lowered his voice conspiratorially. "Anyway, I reckon India'll keep me in line. She's something, isn't she?"

"You be careful," Jeff had advised his cousin.

"I'm afraid you're going to have your hands full with her."

Ned grinned. "I hope so."

After that, Jeff had shaken India's hand and told her to look after Ned for him.

"Oh, I shall keep an eye on young Mr. Ned Holt," she had said. "I can assure you of that." Then she'd thrown her arms around Jeff's neck for a brief hug.

A few minutes later, Amos Tharp had ridden to the head of the column of wagons and bellowed out the command to start the teams of oxen moving as he lifted his arm and swept it forward. They were on their way to Tennessee.

The caravan followed the Cape Fear River inland, making good time across the coastal plains. After a few days the terrain became more rolling, gradually climbing onto the Piedmont Plateau. The going was easy there, too, and enough settlers had followed this route into Tennessee to beat down a good path. The land became more wooded, and after several days on the plateau, Jeff had spotted mountains rising to the north and south.

"Those're the South Mountains and the Brushy Mountains," Tharp told Jeff as the two of them rode side by side at the head of the wagon train. "There's a valley between them where the Catawba River runs, and that'll take us on into the Blue Ridge. Once we get across there, we cut west between the Bald Mountains and the Smokies, and the trail's straight on into Tennessee. Pretty country up there."

"I'm looking forward to seeing it," Jeff said. "You don't think about how much you miss mountains until you get away from them for a while."

Tharp leaned over in the saddle and spat onto the ground. "I know what you mean. Ain't nothing uglier'n flatland. I'm not overly fond of flatlanders, either."

Jeff said nothing. It was true he missed the rough-and-tumble company of mountain men, but he had nothing against "flatlanders," as Tharp called them.

It was good to be back in a saddle again. Jeff rode alongside the wagons most of the time, on a mouse-colored gelding with a stripe of darker hair down the center of its back. The horse was part of Hawley's outfit, but Jeff would have the use of it as long as he was with the wagon train. From time to time, he relieved one of the drivers, and although it had been awhile since he had handled a team of oxen, the knack came back to him quickly. One of the most important qualities of a driver, Jeff soon remembered, was the ability to curse a blue streak, and that came back to him as well, although he shuddered to think what his mother would say if she were to hear him bellowing such profanities. Norah Holt had always been a God-fearing woman, and she had tried to instill that same feeling in her children.

Maybe it hadn't taken with him, Jeff thought as he cracked the whip and kept the oxen moving during his turn on a wagon. He hardly ever prayed, and he had not been inside a church in years—unless you counted those mornings when he awoke in the high country and saw eagles soaring majestically over snow-topped peaks and wooded valleys still partially obscured by morning mist. Places like that were the most magnificent cathedrals of all, Jeff had heard Clay say once, and while he was surprised to hear such a sentiment coming from his brother, Jeff understood completely.

He wanted Melissa to see those mountains, and one day, he vowed, she would.

As Amos Tharp had promised, the valley of the Catawba River provided a fairly easy route. Jeff and the other outriders ranged farther from the wagons most of the time now. Tharp had said that the Cherokee would not pose much of a threat until the caravan had crossed the Blue Ridge Mountains into Tennessee. Bandits and highwaymen could strike anywhere, however, so Jeff remained alert.

But trouble stayed away, and the miles rolled on. The only problem occurred when Jeff was relieving a wagon driver and was perched on the high seat, guiding the heavy vehicle along the trail, which was bordered to the right by a steep slope leading down to the river. Suddenly he heard a cracking sound, and the wagon lurched to the right. He felt it tipping over. He stayed on the seat as long as he dared, hoping the wagon would right itself, but after a couple of perilous seconds he gave up. Leaning forward, he yanked the pin that connected the wagon tongue with its double-tree, single-trees, and oxen to the body of the vehicle, then dove to the left as the wagon tumbled down the slope.

Jeff landed hard on his shoulder and rolled over, hearing the cries of alarm from the other drivers. He got to his feet and hurried over to the edge of the trail. The rolling wagon came to a stop short of the river, landing upright against a good-sized outcropping of rock. It had not fallen completely apart, but it was sagging at the seams.

Tharp galloped up, having been summoned from his position at the front of the train by the shouts from the other drivers.

"What the hell happened?" he called as Jeff gathered up the reins of the team. Once they had been cut loose from the wagon, the oxen had stayed stolidly in the trail.

"Front axle snapped near the right wheel," Jeff explained. "Threw the load to the side and unbalanced the wagon. If the trail hadn't been so narrow, all we would've needed to do was replace the broken axle."

"Never seen anything like it," the driver of the wagon immediately behind him said. "Holt had to've knowed that wagon was gonna tip over the edge, but he stayed on the seat long enough to unhook the tongue. Saved them oxen from a bad mess."

Tharp let out a low whistle of admiration. "Thanks, Jeff," he said sincerely. "We can repair that wagon, but we'd have been in bad shape if we'd lost the oxen. Not to mention that if you hadn't gotten off the seat in time, the wagon might've rolled right over you. If it'd taken the oxen down with it, they'd have landed on you, too."

"Reckon I'd be mashed pretty flat if that'd happened."

Tharp directed the salvage operation on the damaged wagon. After it had been unloaded of its cargo and carefully blocked up enough for the broken axle to be replaced, Jeff took a heavy rope down the slope and attached it to the ring on the front of the vehicle, where the tongue was normally fastened. Then he took the rope and dallied it around a tree on the other side of the trail. Tharp attached it to the harness of the team, then got them moving with a few shouts and some cuts from the braided rawhide quirt he carried. The oxen lurched into motion and pulled the wagon to the trail. Then several men got busy with hammers and nails, knocking the loosened boards back into place. The cargo was loaded again, and when the wagons were ready to roll, Tharp told Jeff to reclaim his spot as one of the outriders.

"I reckon you've spent enough time on a wagon today," he said. "I'd be pretty shook up, if I was you. You came damn close to getting killed."

"Not the first time," Jeff said casually.

Despite what he said, however, he still felt uneasy. A man never really got used to flirting with death.

The wagon train pressed on, and as if the incident of the broken axle had used up all their bad luck, everything went smoothly again for a time. Soon the Catawba River played out, forcing the caravan to swing south before picking up another river that would take it to the pass through the Blue Ridge.

One evening, after the wagon train had halted for the night in a grassy meadow, Jeff was walking behind a parked wagon, heading toward the rope corral where the saddle horses were kept to make sure his mount was settled down for the night. This particular wagon, unlike most of the others in the caravan, had no canvas top and was piled high with kegs of nails. As Jeff passed it he heard a sudden pop as one of the ropes securing the load gave way. The heavy kegs shifted, then began to roll—straight toward Jeff at the rear of the wagon.

For the second time on this journey, only Jeff's frontier-honed reflexes saved his life. Had he tried to step back, he would have been too slow, and the kegs would have crushed him. Instead, he dove without hesitation in the same direction he had been going, and although one of the kegs clipped him on the shoulder as it fell, he landed clear of the others, which crashed to the ground where he had been walking seconds earlier.

Amos Tharp ran up from the gathering shadows, followed soon by the other men.

"What's happened now, blast it?" Tharp bellowed. He looked at the pile of nail kegs that had fallen from the wagon and muttered, "Lord, I hope nobody's under them!"

"Nobody is," Jeff said, picking himself up from the ground on the far side of the wagon and brushing himself off. "Seems like things keep trying to fall on me, but I got out of the way in time again."

Tharp turned angrily to the men who had come up behind him. "Who in blazes secured the load on this wagon?" he demanded.

"Guess that'd be me," one of the freighters answered, his voice a little surly because he knew what was coming. "But I don't know how come this happened, Mr. Tharp. I swear them ropes was good and tight, and they hadn't been frayin' any."

"Well, one of them had to snap for those kegs to fall like that," Tharp growled. "Next time you tie down a load, Miller, you better make damn sure you do a good job of it. And keep an eye on the ropes in the future!"

"Sure, Mr. Tharp," the man muttered. "Sure."

Jeff went back to the campfire, his intention to check on the horses forgotten for the moment. As he poured himself a cup of coffee from the pot resting in the embers on the edge of the blaze, he looked over at Tharp, who had followed him.

"I'm not what you'd call a superstitious man," Jeff said, "but it's starting to look like I'm some sort of Jonah. Trouble seems to follow me around no matter where I go."

"I don't believe in no jinxes," Tharp said. "Accidents happen, Holt. Tonight's no different from the time that axle snapped and wrecked that wagon you were driving."

"Maybe you're right," Jeff said, but he did not sound convinced. Looking back on the last few years of his life, a lot of things that did not make sense—the feud with the Garwoods, the death of his parents, the disappearance of his wife—could be explained a little easier if there was indeed such a thing as a jinx.

And if that was the case, maybe it meant he would never find Melissa. . . .

Jeff tried not to think about that over the next few days as the wagon train climbed higher into the Blue Ridge Mountains. While the peaks were considerably lower and less rugged than the Rockies, the craggy, wooded elevations were still impressive. Jeff took advantage of the opportunity to ride out ahead of the wagons, and as the trail followed a winding path through the mountains, he was often out of sight of the others. At times like that, as he looked up at the deep blue summer sky and the mountaintops thrusting into it, he felt again as he sometimes had in the Rockies: as if he were the only man in a pristine wilderness, put there to appreciate its rugged, solitary beauty.

Of course, not all days were like that. Some started pretty but turned ugly before they were over.

One such day occurred a week after the nail kegs incident. The morning dawned clear and bright, but the sky had a brassy tinge to it that made Jeff uneasy, even though he was uncertain why he felt that way. He was not the only one affected, however. An air of tension hung over the camp, and men snapped at one another as they prepared for the day's journey. The oxen were balkier than usual, too.

"Don't much like the looks of the sky," Tharp muttered as he paused beside Jeff while riding toward his customary place at the head of the caravan. "Could be we'll be in for a storm later."

"Maybe," Jeff said. "The air's awful still."

"That's what I don't like about it," Tharp said darkly.

Jeff had seen some bad spring storms on the plains around the upper Missouri, as well as in the Ohio Valley, and he remembered the motionless, oppressive air that had been in evidence before such storms broke. Just about everything in North Carolina had seemed rather placid to him, however, including the climate.

"I guess we can stop if it gets bad," he said to Tharp.

"We may have to. For now, we'd best put some miles behind us." He stood in his stirrups, waved the wagons into motion, and shouted at the drivers. The call was repeated on down the train.

The weather did not change much during the morning. The air grew hotter and stayed as stale as it had been when the men rolled out of their blankets. Jeff ranged ahead of the wagons, following the road where it climbed steadily to a high pass. From there he looked to the west. On the far horizon was a dark blue line, and as he watched, he could almost see it move closer by the second. Soon it had resolved itself into a low, thick bank of clouds.

He turned his horse and rode back quickly to the wagons. A storm was coming, all right, and while he was no judge of such things, he figured it might be a bad one, just as Tharp had suspected.

Tharp spotted Jeff and must have recognized the urgency on his face. Reining in, Tharp waited until Jeff had ridden up to him.

"What's wrong?" he asked.

"There's a storm on the way, just like you figured. From up ahead there, I could see the clouds off to the west. I thought you might want to get the wagons off the road. Looks like it might become a cloudburst, and we'll need some shelter."

Tharp frowned. "You're right. Damn! This'll set us back some."

Scowling, he turned around in the saddle and motioned the wagons on at a greater pace. There was no shelter in the immediate vicinity; they would have to keep moving until they found a better place to wait out the storm.

Jeff rode alongside Tharp and watched the sky as the clouds loomed over the mountains ahead of them. A cool breeze suddenly was blowing, and after a long morning of breathing hot, torpid air, it was refreshing. As the wind increased, Jeff caught the tang of distant rain.

"Smells good, don't it?" asked Tharp. "Too bad we didn't really need it right now, or it might've been pleasant to hole up and watch it rain for a while."

"Those clouds look mighty dark."

"Sun shining on them makes them look that way."

It was not long before the clouds had swallowed up the sun, plunging the landscape into gloom. The wind, which had been cool and refreshing at first, quickly became dank and unpleasant.

The wagons finally arrived at an open stretch of road bordered by a thick stand of trees. As Tharp directed the drivers to pull the heavy vehicles off to the side, drops of rain began to fall, big drops that splattered onto the dusty surface of the road with thuds almost like those of fallen rocks.

Jeff expected the rain to become heavier. From the looks of the clouds, they were in for a real deluge. Instead, it remained intermittent. Maybe the worst of it was going to blow over and miss them, he thought, and the road would not become impassable after all. Lightning flickered in the sky and thunder rolled, making the horses and oxen nervous. Jeff stood beside his mount under one of the trees, stroking the animal's neck and talking softly to it.

Amos Tharp came over to join him a few minutes later. "Don't look like it's going to be as bad as we thought," Tharp said, confirming Jeff's impression. "Might be able to move on in a little while."

No sooner were the words out of Tharp's mouth than a low rumbling began, unlike anything Jeff had ever heard before. He was about to ask what it was when a frightened cry came from one of the other men.

"Tornado!"

Jeff felt his blood run cold. He had heard plenty about tornadoes back in Ohio, but he had never actually seen one. Now he did. An ominous black funnel dipped down out of the rapidly scudding clouds. It was hard to judge just how big the cylinder of whirling winds really was as long as it stayed aloft, but with a darting motion like a snake, its tail licked down to the ground and began laying a swath of destruction at least a hundred yards wide. The monster touched down at the base of a hill about a mile away from the spot where the wagons had taken cover and roared straight toward them.

The men gave frantic cries as they hurried around the grove of trees, but they could not outrun the tornado and had little chance of hiding from it.

"Get under the wagons! Hug the ground, boys!" Tharp called out.

He ran toward one of the wagons with Jeff close behind him. The tornado was covering ground with dizzying speed, and Jeff saw they were not going to reach the shelter of the wagon in time. Besides, crouching under a heavy wagon suddenly did not seem the wisest course of action.

"No, Amos!" he cried. He had spotted a slight depression in the ground, and without waiting to explain what he was doing, he launched himself into a dive, tackling Tharp around the waist. The big frontiersman fell with a surprised grunt. Jeff hung on tightly to him and rolled both of them into the little gully.

The roaring of the tornado grew even louder, a hellish sound that slammed against the ears. For an instant, Jeff felt himself lifted slightly, as if by a gigantic hand, and he knew that in that moment the tornado was passing directly over them. The wind tore at them, strong enough to pull them upward and suck out their souls. Then the unholy grip eased, letting Jeff and Tharp slump back to the wet ground.

Nearby was a crashing noise that seemed to go on forever, even though in reality it probably lasted only seconds. Then, with a startling suddenness, calm settled over the land again. Jeff lifted his head, blinked raindrops out of his eyes, and saw that with the capriciousness of nature, the tornado had abruptly disappeared. The threat was over.

Tharp pushed himself up onto his knees, looked around, and exclaimed, "Goddamn! Look at that wagon!"

Jeff saw the wreckage not far off and realized it was the same wagon under which Tharp had intended to take shelter. It was smashed to kindling, some of its cargo scattered around the grove, the rest of it plucked up and carried off by the tornado. The oxen that had been attached to the wagon were down, three of them dead, the remaining one badly injured. A couple of nearby trees were uprooted, as well.

But that seemed to be the extent of the damage. Evidently, the tornado had already been skipping, about to pull back up, when the edge of it struck the wagon.

Jeff got to his feet, brushed himself off as best he could, and offered a hand to Tharp.

"Looks like we were mighty lucky, especially me," Tharp said. He was looking at Jeff with a strange expression in his eyes. "If you hadn't tackled me, I'd have been under that wagon when it got hit. That tornado would've either crushed me or carried me off. Reckon you saved my life, Holt."

"I just did what seemed right at the time," Jeff said, checking his pistols for dirt. "I didn't stop to think about it or anything."

Tharp extended a hand to Jeff. "What you said earlier about being a Jonah . . . I reckon you proved today there wasn't anything to that."

"How do you figure?" Jeff asked, returning the handshake.

"Well, you were following me when you got the idea to dive in that ditch. You saved your own life as well as mine. Seems to me that if you think about it, you've been lucky all along. Most men would've got themselves killed in those accidents that happened to you. Somebody must be watching over you."

Jeff laughed. "I never believed in guardian angels."

"Neither did I." Tharp looked long and hard at the wreckage of the wagon where he had intended to seek shelter. He repeated quietly, "Neither did I."

Cracks appeared in the clouds overhead, letting stray shafts of sunlight come through. A few drops of rain still fell, and thunder continued to rumble in the distance as lightning flickered, but the storm was just about over.

"Let's get busy," Tharp said, clapping his hands together. "We got to gather up all the cargo we can find from that wrecked wagon and spread it out among the other wagons. Then we'll get back on the road. We've got some lost time to make up!"

Jeff followed him, ready to work. But as he did so, he was thinking. Maybe they were all luckier than he had thought—and maybe he was the luckiest of all.

Chapter Twenty-three

As soon as he looked into Simon Brown's cold eyes, Clay Holt knew instinctively that the man was the most evil person he had ever met. Duquesne had been ruthless and, yes, downright evil, but his depravity had been motivated by greed, at least at first. He had also been more than a little insane, Clay was convinced.

Simon Brown, however, was sane enough. It was just that he was possessed by a sheer love of killing.

Given that, they were lucky to be alive, Clay thought that night as the expedition and their captors camped near the river. Brown had ordered that everyone associated with the expedition be tied up, and he had spent the last few hours going through Professor Franklin's journals and specimens.

"Fascinating," Clay heard Brown mutter more than once.

Now Brown walked over to the professor and

said in his cultured British accent, "So you're a naturalist and a botanist, eh, Professor Franklin."

"That's right," Franklin replied, and Clay could tell he was making a great effort to keep his voice calm and steady. "Are you an educated man?"

"I spent four years at Oxford," Brown murmured.

"Then—then for God's sake, man, why are you doing this to us?" Franklin asked in astonishment.

"My reasons are my own." Brown reached over and stroked Lucy's hair. The young woman was sitting beside her father, and she flinched from Brown's touch. He did not seem bothered by her reaction.

"Be thankful I didn't have you killed out of hand," Brown said. "That's what the Blackfoot would like to do, you know. They hate all white men, but they hate Americans the most. That's why they were willing to help me track you down and capture you."

"But why?" Franklin asked again. "We weren't bothering you. We left you alone and continued our journey."

"You know of our existence," Brown replied. "You know about our fort. The company won't like that."

For the first time Clay spoke up. "The company?"

Brown cast a languid glance toward him. "The London and Northwestern Enterprise. I see no harm in telling you."

That simple statement sent a cold chill through Clay, and he could see that Shining Moon, Proud Wolf, and Aaron shared his feeling.

It had taken the expedition five days to reach the Flathead River after leaving the meadow where they had been camped when Aaron was captured by the British trappers. Now, as prisoners, they returned to that vicinity in only three days, because Brown set a brutal pace for them. Even Brown's men were exhausted by the journey, but no one complained. That told Clay a great deal about the fear with which they regarded Brown, and rightly so, he decided. Only the Blackfoot, accustomed to great hardships and grueling journeys, seemed unaffected by the trip.

Brown said little to the prisoners during the three days, preferring to wait until they had reached the London and Northwestern's fort before conducting any sort of interrogation. Clay saw the way Brown looked at Lucy from time to time, and he had to repress a shudder of revulsion and outrage. Brown had plans for her that extended beyond merely satisfying his curiosity.

Although Clay constantly kept alert for a chance to escape or turn the tables on Brown, no such opportunity presented itself. Several of the Blackfoot and three or four of the trappers, all holding loaded rifles, watched them at all times. Knowing Simon Brown as he already did, Clay figured it would mean the life of any guard who was careless. Terror had a way of sharpening a man's senses.

The group crossed the dividing ridge again, heading east this time, and late in the afternoon of the third day of their captivity, Brown called a halt atop a peak and waved expansively toward the sprawling log structure in the valley below them.

"Welcome to Fort Tarrant," he declared. "It'll be your new home—at least for a few days."

The prisoners were prodded down the slope, and the small force of men Brown had left at the fort opened the stockade gate. His step jaunty, Brown led them through the opening, the captives walking reluctantly behind him.

Clay looked at Aaron, who had suffered the most on the return trip. The young man's injuries had left him with less strength than the others, and now he was pale and exhausted. Even Rupert von Metz, who had been too petrified with fear to talk during the past three days, seemed in better shape than Aaron. Shining Moon and Proud Wolf had held up well during the journey, as had Clay himself, but Professor Franklin and Lucy looked almost as exhausted as Aaron.

The band of Blackfoot warriors balked at entering the fort, and Brown went back to talk with them in their own language. As the Indians turned and left, Brown returned to the others.

"The savages don't fully trust us, so they're going to camp nearby," he explained. "Their war chief says that we're to turn over at least half of the prisoners to them to be tortured and killed. Otherwise, they will be our enemies in the future."

The British trappers looked uneasy at that announcement, and after a moment one of them said, "You're goin' to give the bloody aborigines what they want, ain't you, Mr. Brown? I ain't fond of the idea of torture, but I don't want them savages goin' after *us* next time!"

A general muttering of agreement went through the group.

Brown said, "Don't worry. I'm sure our friends' bloodlust will be more than satisfied. In the meantime, let's make our guests comfortable in one of the storehouses."

Clay and his companions were taken to one of the windowless, sturdy log structures where the beaver pelts were stored. The one Brown chose was only half full, so there was room for all the prisoners, and once the small log that was used as a bar was dropped into place, it would be escape-proof.

The prisoners were silent as the door of the building was closed and the bar dropped into place outside it.

Then, into the blackness, Shining Moon said quietly, "Clay?"

"We wait," he declared. "We wait until the time's right. And then we'll make Simon Brown wish he'd left well enough alone."

An unknowable time after the door had been closed, Clay heard the bar being lifted from its brackets outside. Night had fallen, Clay was sure of that; the few chinks between the logs of the storehouse had allowed light to filter through, but he had seen nothing but blackness for what seemed like hours.

As the door was swung open, the flickering yellow light from a torch spilled into the building. Most of the prisoners flinched away from it, the darkness having made them sensitive to the torch's glare. The only ones who had quickly averted their eyes before the door opened were Clay, Shining Moon, Proud Wolf, and Aaron. Now, as they turned slowly to face the light, they could at least make out the shapes of the men who stood there, rifles in hand. Brown was the one who held the torch. He was behind the guards, but they stepped aside to let him pass. He stopped just inside the entrance to the storehouse.

"I do hope you're enjoying your stay here at Fort Tarrant," he said in mock politeness. "One's last night on earth should be a memorable one, much like one's last meal. And I've come to make you aware that this is, indeed, your last night."

Shining Moon's hand was on Clay's arm, and her fingers tightened at Brown's taunting words. Clay wanted to reassure her that everything would be all right, but he had no way of knowing if it would.

"Although I've decided to keep your papers and specimens to study, I've also decided I no longer have any need of you. In the morning, you'll be turned over to our Blackfoot friends, for them to do with as they will."

Clay had heard men say that their blood ran cold

when they were in bad trouble, but until now he had never experienced that particular sensation. He had faced death many times, but always on relatively equal footing, with a fighting chance for survival. To be given to the Blackfoot for a long, slow, agonizing death by tortures . . . It might be better to jump Brown now and be shot by the guards.

Only Clay's stubbornness kept him from doing just that. He was still alive, and as long as there was breath in his body, he was not going to give up. He would not give Simon Brown the satisfaction of seeing him panic.

"If you're not giving us to the Blackfoot until the morning," Clay said coolly, "why don't you get the hell out of here so that we can get some sleep?"

"You're a very annoying man," Brown said to Clay, examining him as he walked around him. "I'll leave you alone, but not before I give you one more bit of information to ponder. The young white woman will remain at the fort. I will enjoy her company. Also, a community of men such as this one can always use a woman to help with the cooking and cleaning, and when I tire of her . . . well, I'm sure the rest of the men can find other uses for her as well."

"You—you—" the professor sputtered. Even a man such as he, with an almost limitless vocabulary, was unable to find words to describe Brown's villainy. Aaron and Proud Wolf each grabbed an arm to hold him back.

"The Indian woman will also go to the Blackfoot," Brown added. "I'm certain they know how to deal with a woman of their enemies."

The verbal thrust went into Clay like a knife. The Blackfoot would turn Shining Moon into a slave and eventually kill her.

"Remember," Brown said as he backed out of the

building with the guards. "First thing tomorrow morning."

Then he was gone, and the door was shut, cutting off the torchlight and plunging the fetid interior of the storehouse once more into darkness. Clay felt Shining Moon close beside him, felt a tremble go through her.

"This must not happen," she whispered, her voice strained.

"It hasn't happened yet," Clay told her. But he was damned if he could see any way to stop it.

Not surprisingly, none of the prisoners locked in the storehouse slept much that night, despite the comfort provided by the piles of beaver pelts. Clay curled up with Shining Moon beside him and tried to calm his racing mind long enough to drift off, but with little success. He could tell from Shining Moon's restlessness that she was having as much trouble sleeping as he was. Finally, along toward morning, exhaustion claimed them, and they fell into a light sleep that was easily broken when the bar on the door was removed at dawn.

The reddish glare of the rising sun shafted into the building as the door opened. As he sat up, blinking against the light, Clay saw guards armed with rifles. Simon Brown was with them.

"Rise and shine, my friends. Time to go," Brown called in a maddeningly cheerful voice.

Again Clay thought about jumping Brown, but all that would get him would be a rifle ball in the head. Then Shining Moon would be left on her own. He would wait awhile longer, he decided, and hope for a chance to turn the tables on their captors.

None of the prisoners were eager to walk to their own deaths, naturally enough, and several trappers had to go into the storehouse to prod them out at riflepoint. The men kept as much distance as possible between themselves and the captives, however, so again Clay had no chance to make a move. He stumbled out into the dawn with Shining Moon beside him and the others behind.

Rupert von Metz was the last one out of the storehouse. He had to be dragged out by a couple of men who handed their rifles to their companions so that von Metz could not grab one of the weapons. As they hauled him bodily from the building, he began to scream.

Clay felt a wave of disgust. He could understand being afraid—he was about as scared as he'd ever been—but he could not imagine letting his fear get the best of him like that. He might die—hell, everybody died sooner or later, he thought—but when the time came, he would die with dignity, and if at all possible, he would die fighting. But he would not go to his death kicking and screaming.

Von Metz seemed to be strengthened by his own terror, however, and as he was pulled into the morning light, he suddenly tore away from his guards and ran toward Simon Brown.

Brown let out a startled curse, and a couple of the trappers swung their rifles toward von Metz. The young Prussian dropped to his knees and flung his arms around Brown's legs in supplication.

"Please don't let them kill me!" he pleaded. "You said you didn't have to give all of us to the Blackfoot, Herr Brown. Please, for God's sake, spare me!"

Brown looked down at the quivering man. "Why the hell should I?"

"I can help you!" von Metz cried. "I have been making maps ever since we left St. Louis! I can show you where the Americans are and how you can avoid them. I can help you find new places to trap beaver. I will do anything!"

Brown's forehead wrinkled in thought. "A map-maker, eh?" he mused. "And I suppose it's you who painted all those pictures we found back where we caught you."

"That's right! I am an artist, too! I have painted all the crowned heads of Europe. Surely you would like a portrait of yourself, Herr Brown!"

Clay had to give credit to von Metz. The Prussian knew how to reach Brown. He went straight for the Englishman's vanity, and the plea fell on receptive ears.

"All right," Brown said abruptly. "You can stay here at the fort—for now. But I'll want to see that portrait before I decide if you live or die, my friend. You'll understand if I don't trust you fully just yet. Get back in there."

Blubbering in relief, von Metz scrambled back through the door of the storehouse. He giggled as he flung himself down on a pile of pelts. One of Brown's men shut the door behind him.

"As long as you're sparing people," Clay said coolly to Brown, "what about my wife and the professor?"

"I'm afraid not," Brown said. "Although keeping the professor alive is tempting. It would be good to have another educated man to talk to out here in this godforsaken wilderness. But I'm afraid I could never trust him. Better to make a clean sweep of things now, eh? No offense, Professor."

Franklin regarded him through eyes narrowed with hate. "I'll see you in hell, you devil."

Brown threw back his head and laughed. "Quite possibly."

"What do you intend to do with Shining Moon?" Clay asked.

"Ah, yes. The squaw. I do believe that the Blackfoot will appreciate her much more than I. I do believe that young Lucy will keep me well enough occupied for a while." Brown reached out and grasped Lucy Franklin's arm, plucking her out of the group.

Lucy screamed, "No!" and in fear and desperation flailed at him.

Her father uttered a heartfelt oath, then leapt toward Brown and Lucy with surprising speed. But he was not fast enough for Brown, who nonchalantly whipped a pistol from his belt and clubbed the professor over the head. Franklin staggered and went down, stunned, as Lucy screamed again.

Every fiber of Clay's being wanted to lunge forward and launch an attack of his own, but he knew that if he did, Brown's men would shoot him down like a dog. He controlled himself with an effort of will, telling himself that he could do more good in the long run by waiting for a better time to strike.

"Get him on his feet," Brown told a couple of his men, indicating the half-conscious professor. He turned to Lucy and slapped her, a hard forehand and backhand that rocked her head from side to side. She subsided into stunned silence.

"That's better," Brown said.

Professor Franklin was lifted to his feet and shoved along with the others.

Brown gestured curtly to his men. "Now get them out of here. The Blackfoot will be waiting outside the stockade. I'm taking the fair Lucy back to my cabin. After she's tied up, I'll return to enjoy the festivities we've planned for today."

The gate was swung open, and as Brown had said, the Blackfoot were there to take charge of the prisoners. Clay scanned the paint-streaked faces of the warriors and saw grim anticipation of the joy they would take in torturing the helpless men to death. All three bands of the Blackfoot tribe—the Blood, the

Northern Blackfoot, and the Piegan—were brutal and bloodthirsty, but the Piegan were the worst of the lot.

And now Clay and his friends were in their hands.

Chapter Twenty-four

The weather had been clear since the storm. Jeff Holt looked up at the towering peak of Mount Mitchell from below, where the wagon train was traveling in a pass of the Blue Ridge Mountains. Again he was reminded of the Rockies. True, these mountains were more heavily wooded and lacked the stark majesty of the Rockies, but being here felt almost like being back home.

As that thought went through Jeff's head, he realized for the first time the Rockies were home to him now. No longer did he think of Ohio and the farm near Marietta as his home, although he would always have a soft spot in his heart for that place. Home now was far to the west, the wild, high country where he and his brother and men like them were carrying the banner of civilization—and at the same time, perhaps, mourning it a bit because the land they found would be irrevocably changed by their coming.

Jeff heeled his horse into a faster trot alongside the line of wagons. Right now, he had to concentrate on getting these wagons and their cargoes safely to Tennessee. After that . . .

Well, he had to admit, after that he was not quite sure what he would do.

Amos Tharp had changed since the tornado that had nearly taken his life. He had been friendly to Jeff all along, but now the feeling seemed more genuine. Most of the time the two men rode together, Tharp pointing out landmarks and spinning yarns about the adventures he'd had in this country when he had first come over the Blue Ridge. He had hunted, guided settlers, and fought Indians, and as Jeff listened to Tharp's stories, his liking for the man grew. They were a lot alike, and that feeling was confirmed by the look in Tharp's eyes whenever Jeff talked about the Rockies and his experiences out west. Jeff recognized a yearning in Tharp's expression: the wanderlust of the pioneer, the need to see what was on the other side of the next hill or mountain or river. Many times Jeff had seen the same look on Clay's face, and he had felt the same thing in his own heart.

As the wagons went through a pass Tharp called Newfound Gap between the Bald Mountains to the northeast and the Smokies to the southwest, Tharp declared, "Well, we're in Tennessee now. Ought to start seeing some farms before too much longer."

"Think we could stop at one of them, maybe trade a few goods for a home-cooked meal?" Jeff asked.

Tharp grinned. "Sounds like a good idea to me."

Two more days had passed before the trail took them near a homestead, however. Jeff had ridden about a quarter of a mile ahead of the train, and when he spotted a thin column of smoke climbing into the sky, he followed it to the chimney of a good-sized log cabin a short distance from the road. Behind the cabin were plowed fields, a barn for milk cows, and a pig-pen made of saplings. Two small children were playing in the dirt in front of the cabin while their mother sat beside the open door churning butter. Perched on a nearby stump was a young man in buckskins, using a rag and a long stick to clean the barrel of an old flintlock. He looked up with a friendly expression as Jeff rode into the small yard.

"Howdy," the farmer called in a deep voice. "Light and set awhile, stranger."

"Thanks." Jeff swung down from the saddle. "How're you folks doing?"

"Fine and dandy," the young man replied as he stood up. He was a tall, well-built man, and his jovial demeanor took any sting from his words as he asked, "Mind if I ask what you're doin' in this part of the country?"

"Outrider for a wagon train bringing in supplies from North Carolina," Jeff answered, pitching his voice loud enough so that the woman could also hear. The children had stopped playing and run to their mother, and now they shyly regarded Jeff from behind the chair on which she was sitting.

"Wagon train, eh?" the young farmer said. He turned to his wife. "Hear that, Polly?"

"I heard." The pretty young woman smiled at Jeff. "Would you and your friends like to stay to supper, Mr. . . . ?"

"Holt," Jeff supplied. "Jeff Holt."

The farmer stuck out his hand. "I'm Davy, and this is Polly. These are our young'uns. Pleased to meet you, Mr. Holt."

"Same here," Jeff said as he returned the firm handshake. "And we'd be honored to stay for supper, ma'am, but there're quite a few of us."

"Don't worry, Mr. Holt. We have plenty," Polly assured him. "Our garden produced well this year, and we always have more than enough meat on hand. I can't seem to keep Davy from going out hunting, even when we don't really need any more food."

Davy let loose with a rumbling laugh, then said, "I do like to hunt." He patted the gleaming stock of his rifle. "I wouldn't want ol' Betsy here to feel neglected."

"I swear, Davy, sometimes I think you're married to ol' Betsy instead of me."

"Glad I ain't," Davy said with a twinkle in his eye. "This here gun's never let me down, but it ain't much for keepin' a man warm at night."

"Davy!" Polly, with a look of mock sternness, stood up from her butter churn and turned to Jeff. "Go fetch your friends, Mr. Holt. We'll be glad to have you all stay for supper."

The young homesteaders welcomed the other members of the wagon train, and true to her word, Polly fed them all. After weeks of eating on the trail, the meal of roast venison, potatoes, greens, cornbread, and fresh apple pie was like a taste of heaven to Jeff. And seeing the obvious love between Davy and Polly was a poignant reminder of his own relationship with Melissa. They had dreamed of just such an existence as this—a comfortable cabin, a good farm, youngsters running around underfoot. . . .

Jeff ached inside as he thought about what he had missed so far in his young life. True, he had seen and done things that few men had ever experienced, but he had been denied the commonplace pleasures of everyday life.

Davy talked a blue streak, and when he was not spinning a tale of his own, he was asking questions. When he found out that Jeff had spent time trapping in the Rocky Mountains, the young farmer's eyes lit up.

"Lordy, I've always wanted to go west," he said fervently. "I reckon there's more sights to see out there than a man could fit into a whole lifetime."

"It's pretty country," Jeff said. "Good country. But don't let that wanderlust get too strong a hold on you, Davy. You've got good things to live for right here in Tennessee."

"Yep, I reckon you're right. Still, I'd sure like to see more of the country one of these days."

Amos Tharp joined them and said, "I surely do appreciate the hospitality, mister. You mind if we camp here overnight? I promise we'll keep our animals out of your garden and not bother you."

"You're welcome to stay, Mr. Tharp. Make yourself to home. We're glad for the company, ain't we, Polly?"

The young woman nodded as she carried another platter of potatoes to the table. She seemed genuinely pleased to have so many visitors.

Jeff sat up late that night, talking to Davy, who smoked his pipe and asked questions about the West. When Jeff finally turned in, he slept well, rolled in his blankets under one of the wagons, and the next morning, the smell of bacon and biscuits cooking woke him and made his mouth water in anticipation.

Polly fed her guests as cheerfully as she had the night before, and Jeff was not the only one feeling regretful when the wagons were ready to roll again. They would miss the good food and pleasant company.

As he sat on his horse near the head of the train, Jeff leaned over to shake hands with Davy, who was walking along the line of wagons saying farewell to the drivers and outriders.

"You boys take care of yourself," he told Jeff sincerely. "And if you ever come back through this neck of the woods, Jeff, you be sure and stop."

"I'll do that," Jeff promised. "So long, Davy."

"So long," the farmer said, and Jeff knew it would be a long time before he forgot Davy's sheer zest for life.

As Jeff joined Tharp at the head of the train and the wagons began to roll, Tharp said in a low voice, "That boy sure can talk, can't he? Ought to be a politician with that gift of gab he's got."

"Maybe he will be," Jeff said, turning in the saddle to look back at Davy and Polly Crockett and lift a hand in farewell to them.

"We're heading for a settlement called Knoxville," Tharp said to Jeff later that day. "It's getting to be a pretty good-sized place, and I figure we can sell the whole load of supplies there. It's about two or three days from here." He turned to Jeff. "Looks like your luck's turned around since that twister, just like I said. Haven't been any more accidents."

"Reckon that's true enough," Jeff said. "I just hope the luck holds for all of us. Davy told me that the Cherokees west of here have been raising a ruckus from time to time."

"Yep, that's right," Tharp said. "The Chickasaws have mostly made peace with the government, but the Cherokees are still holding out. We'll have to pass through their land before we get to Knoxville."

Jeff shot his companion a sharp glance. "You think they'll attack the wagons?"

"Could happen," Tharp said with a shrug. "We'd best keep our eyes open. Why don't you pass the word along to everybody else to do the same?"

Jeff wheeled his horse around to convey Tharp's warning to the other men. An air of tension settled over the train as everyone got ready for the possibility of an Indian attack. Jeff, returning to the head of the line of wagons, rode alongside Tharp, his rifle poised in his hands.

The trip through the wooded Tennessee hills proceeded peacefully, however, and when they camped that night in a swale between two hills, they saw no sign of hostile Cherokee. Maybe Tharp was right, Jeff thought. Maybe their luck had turned for the better and would stay that way for the rest of the journey.

The next morning dawned hot and clear, and again the sun had a brassy tint to it as it began its long climb through the sky. By the time Jeff had gotten up, seen to his horse, and eaten breakfast, his homespun shirt was wet with sweat. The weather was similar to the morning the tornado had struck, and Jeff felt edgy because of it. But a hot, dry breeze was blowing that he hoped would keep any such storms from developing.

He finished his coffee, scrubbed out his cup and plate with sand, and was headed back to the rope corral to saddle his horse when he heard a startled cry from a sentry Tharp had posted the night before. The yell was cut off abruptly.

A second later someone shouted, "Let 'em have it!"

Gunfire erupted all around the camp. Rifle balls plowed up dirt near Jeff's feet, and as he spun around in shock, he saw several wagon drivers knocked off their feet by the shots. He dove for the shelter of one of the nearby wagons, landed hard on the ground, and rolled under the vehicle as he gasped for the air that the impact had knocked out of him.

Jeff bellied over to the far side of the wagon and peered out past the spokes of the big rear wheel. He saw men rising from concealment on one of the hillsides overlooking the camp. Bandits! The grass was tall there, and the men must have crawled up close to the wagons during the night and then lain there quietly until given the word to attack. Now some of them were firing toward the wagons while others ran forward to carry the fighting closer.

Quickly Jeff loaded and primed his flintlock, then

settled the butt of the Harper's Ferry rifle against his shoulder. Lining the sights on the chest of a raider, he squeezed the trigger. The weapon blasted and bucked hard against his shoulder, and the bandit running toward the wagons was flipped backward by the heavy lead ball driving into his chest.

Jeff twisted around, pulled his powder horn and shot pouch around his body where he could reach them more easily, then took a patch from the patchbox on the stock of his rifle. As he started the reloading process, he heard balls thud into the wagon above him. From the sound of it, one hell of a lot of lead was flying through the air up there, and he was glad he was below the level of most of the shots. He wondered where Amos Tharp was. Tharp was the closest thing he had to a friend in this bunch.

From the sound of the shooting, Jeff realized that the bandits had surrounded the camp. He and the others were going to have a hard time fighting their way out.

When the rifle was reloaded, he picked out another target, this time one of the gunners crouched on the hillside, and let fly with another shot. The ball knocked the man on his backside in a bloody, inelegant sprawl.

The stench of burned powder was heavy in the air, stinging the nose and making the eyes water. The constant crashing of guns blended into a constant, ear-numbing roar. But even that noise was not enough to drown out the cries of wounded and dying men. Jeff blinked to clear his eyes and did not waste time wondering if they were watering because of the smoke—or because once again violence and death had dogged his trail.

Some of the bandits had reached the wagons and were engaged in hand-to-hand fighting. The men on the hillsides, unable to continue firing for fear of hitting their friends, abandoned their positions and charged down toward the wagons, yelling stridently as they came. Pistols barked and knives flashed in the early-morning sunlight. The timing of the attack had been good; while most of the men in the camp were awake, not all had been fully alert when the shooting started. The defenders were in danger of being overrun, even though from what Jeff had seen so far, the men with the wagon train outnumbered the bandits.

Heavy feet ran past the wagon where Jeff had taken cover. He laid the rifle aside, then waited for a chance to emerge from under the vehicle. When the opportunity came, he pulled his pistol, made sure it was ready to fire, then rolled out and jumped to his feet.

A bandit who was coming toward him stopped in shock at Jeff's sudden appearance. The man was ugly, with a large nose that had been broken more than once and a bushy black beard. He growled an oath and lifted a brass-barrel flintlock pistol in his hand.

Jeff reacted fast, firing almost from the hip, and the ball took the bandit high on the left side of the chest, spinning him around with its impact. As he staggered, he nearly dropped his unfired pistol, but Jeff sprang forward to snatch it from his fingers. As the man toppled to the ground, Jeff whirled in search of another target, the raider's pistol gripped in his left hand.

He saw a man about to plunge a long, heavy-bladed knife into the back of an unsuspecting wagon driver. Jeff snapped up the pistol he had taken and hoped it fired accurately as he squeezed the trigger. The pistol's recoil was stronger than what Jeff was used to. It must have had a heavier charge in it, Jeff thought. But the shot had been on target, and the ball propelled by the heavy load of black powder tore through the body of the man with the knife, killing him instantly.

Something smashed into Jeff's back, sending him stumbling forward and nearly knocking him down. He felt an arm loop around his neck and then jerk up hard under his chin, exposing his throat for a killing slash with a knife. He drove his elbow back as hard as he could into the midsection of the man grappling with him and lifted his shoulder to block the knife. The blow with his elbow had done the job, knocking him loose from the man's grip. Jeff pivoted smoothly, ducking even lower, and left his feet in a dive that sent his shoulder smashing into the bandit's belly. Both men slammed to the ground, but Jeff landed on top. He caught the wildly flailing wrist of the man's knife hand and wrenched it around with all his strength as he shoved down at the same time. The would-be robber's own blade buried itself in his chest.

Jeff rolled off the dead man, sprang to his feet, and bent over long enough to yank the knife from the man's body. He straightened just in time to meet the charge of another bandit, this one clubbing at Jeff's head with an empty pistol. Acting instinctively, Jeff flung his arm up to block the blow, and the blade of the knife in his hand sliced neatly across the bandit's wrist, grating on bone. Blood spurted from the severed veins and arteries, and the suddenly nerveless fingers released the pistol, which fell harmlessly at Jeff's feet. The bandit shrieked, clutched his wrist in an effort to stem the spouting blood, and stumbled away. Jeff let him go.

In the chaos that surrounded him, Jeff could not judge how the battle was going. Men ran and shouted through a haze of gunsmoke tinted red by the rising sun. He managed to reload both pistols during a lull in the frenzy, and that was all that saved his life when two raiders jumped him at the same time, one brandishing a knife and the other wielding a club. Jeff did not hesitate. He shot them down, one after the other.

"Tharp!" Jeff shouted over the din of battle. "Amos! Where are you?"

For a moment, no one answered. Then he heard someone call, "Holt! Over here!"

Jeff spun around in time to see Tharp lifting a pistol about twenty feet away. The muzzle of the gun looked like the mouth of a cannon; it was trained on Jeff.

Jeff's eyes widened in amazement. Bright orange flame bloomed from the barrel of the gun, and for one crazy instant, Jeff almost thought he could *see* the ball emerge from the barrel to speed toward him.

Then it whistled past his ear, and behind him someone grunted. Jeff jerked his head around and saw a man crumple to the ground, an ugly round hole in the center of his forehead where Tharp's shot had caught him. A bloodstained hatchet slipped from the man's fingers.

Jeff turned back to Tharp, remembering the way he had saved the man's life by knocking him off his feet during the tornado. He saw the broad grin on Tharp's rugged face and knew Tharp was thinking about the same thing.

Then one of the bandits loomed out of the smoke next to Tharp and sank the foot-long blade of a knife into his side. Tharp staggered, and the bandit ripped the knife free only to plunge it into him again.

"No!"

Jeff was not even aware of the ragged shout that came from his throat as he flung himself forward, covering the ground between him and Tharp in a flash—but not before the robber had stabbed Tharp a third time. The man tried to meet Jeff's rush, but he was too late. Jeff swung the empty pistol in his right hand in a roundhouse blow that crashed into the bandit's head. The man staggered and thrust weakly at Jeff with the knife. The blade ripped the sleeve of Jeff's shirt and drew a fiery line across the skin of his arm, but Jeff ignored the pain. He slammed the pistol into the man's head again, driving him to the ground. Even then, Jeff did not stop. He landed on top of the bandit and battered his skull until it was barely recognizable as something human. Only then did Jeff regain control of himself; he felt a sickening wrench deep in his belly as he saw what he had done.

He crawled away from the dead man, then pushed himself upright. Gradually he became aware that less fighting was going on around him. Lifting his head, he wiped the back of his hand across his eyes, leaving a streak in the powder-smoke grime that had settled on his skin. He saw that the wagon train's defenders were finally routing the rest of the bandits. Their superior numbers and the fighting ability of the men Tharp had recruited had finally won out.

But not in time to save Amos Tharp himself. Jeff went to his knees beside Tharp's sprawled, bloodstained form. Tharp's mutilated chest rose and fell in a ragged rhythm as he fought to breathe. Jeff got a hand under his head and lifted it, and Tharp's eyes opened.

"Looks like . . . my luck changed, too," Tharp gasped out.

"Hang on, Amos," Jeff told him. "The fight's over. We'll take care of you. You'll be all right."

"Hell! Don't . . . lie to me, Jeff." Tharp's hand came up and clutched feebly at Jeff's arm. "Just listen. . . . Got something mighty important to tell you."

"I'm listening, Amos," Jeff said grimly. It was about all he could do for his friend now, and both of them knew it.

"Glad I could . . . even the score."

"You saved my life," Jeff told him.

"Fair enough. I tried to . . . to end it a couple of times."

Jeff leaned closer to Tharp and frowned, not sure

he had heard the man right. "What are you talking about, Amos?"

"Those accidents back on the trail. . . . They weren't accidents. . . . Was trying to . . . to kill you."

The hubbub of the battle's aftermath faded away for Jeff. He was sure now that he had heard Tharp correctly, but he still could not understand what Tharp was trying to tell him.

"Why would you want to kill me?"

"Hawley paid me to . . . to make sure you didn't come back alive." A shudder ran through Tharp's body as he forced the words out.

"Hawley," Jeff repeated in amazement. He had never even met Dermot Hawley until he arrived in North Carolina. Why in the world would Hawley want him dead?

Tharp's fingers tightened on Jeff's arm again. "You got to . . . to promise me something," he rasped. "These wagons . . . you get 'em through, Jeff." His voice seemed to strengthen for a moment. "Get 'em to Knoxville and take care of things. Whatever money you get, take it back to Hawley . . . and his partner."

"Partner? What partner?" The revelations were coming almost too fast for Jeff to keep up with them.

Tharp chuckled. "Hawley figured I didn't know nothin' about it . . . but I kept my ears open, knew more than he thought I did. Don't know why he wanted you dead, Jeff. Just promise me . . . you'll take the money back."

"I will, Amos," Jeff vowed. "You can count on it."

"Good. When you get there, you can . . . ask him yourself." Tharp's voice faded away, and his eyes closed. Jeff could almost feel the life slipping from him.

Leaning closer again, Jeff said urgently, "Ask who, Amos? Hawley?"

Tharp's eyelids fluttered. In a hoarse voice little more than a whisper, he said, "Ask . . . Hawley's partner. Man named . . . Merrivale. . . . Could be he's the one . . . you been look—"

Stunned almost beyond belief by what he had just heard, Jeff stared down into Tharp's open, sightless eyes for a long moment before he realized the man was dead. Then, moving slowly and awkwardly as if all his senses had been numbed, he gently lowered Tharp's head to the grass and stood up. Looking down at the knees of his buckskin trousers, he saw crimson stains from the blood that had leaked from Tharp's body and pooled where Jeff had been kneeling.

Merrivale. Dermot Hawley had a partner named Merrivale, and Hawley wanted Jeff dead. There had to be a connection with Melissa.

"I'll get the wagons through, Amos," Jeff whispered, even though Tharp could no longer hear him. "And I'll go back to North Carolina, all right. Because if Charles Merrivale is Hawley's partner, I want to see the expression on his face when I hand him his blood money!"

Chapter Twenty-five

Screams filled the mountain air as the men who had joined the ill-fated botanical expedition in St. Louis were systematically tortured to death. Clay Holt's wrists were tied behind his back. He was bound shoulder to shoulder with Proud Wolf, both of them lashed to a stout tree trunk facing away from the gory arena where the torture was taking place. They could not see what was being done to the others. That was part of the fiendish Blackfoot plan: let them hear what was going on but not see it, so that their imaginations could furnish all the horrible details.

Clay knew all too well what was happening—and so far, he had not been able to do a damned thing to stop it.

Already three men had been dragged to their deaths, and their cries of agony had torn at Clay's soul. As he listened to the hideous sounds and smelled the stench of burning flesh and freshly spilled blood, he blamed himself for what was happening.

He had undertaken to get these people through the mountains and safely to the Pacific, and he had failed.

Of course, he had never dreamed they would encounter such a monster as Simon Brown.

Professor Franklin and Aaron Garwood were tied to the tree next to Clay and Proud Wolf, and beyond them were the other four men left from the original party put together by Harry Lawton. The Blackfoot were working their way down the line of trees, saving Clay and Proud Wolf for last; Clay because they knew that Brown wanted him to suffer the longest, and Proud Wolf because the youngster was a Sioux, a hated enemy of the Piegan.

Shining Moon was lying on the ground in front of the tree where Clay and her brother were bound. Her wrists and ankles were lashed together with rawhide. So far, she had not been hurt, only tied up and shoved onto the ground. From where she lay, she was able to see what was going on behind the other captives, but she had quickly averted her eyes when the torture started. Clay knew that his wife was the strongest, bravest woman he had ever met, but even Shining Moon had her limits.

Two Blackfoot men strode past Clay and into his line of sight. Clay saw something he had been afraid of: They were carrying earthen jugs, occasionally lifting them to their lips to take long swallows from them. The British trappers had provided the liquor, Clay guessed, and whatever it was, rum or whiskey, the stuff was doing its work. The Indians were well on their way to being drunk—and that meant they would become meaner and more inventive in their torture.

One of them bent and took hold of Shining Moon's arm, jerking her roughly to her feet. He cut her ankles loose from the rawhide binding.

"Come," he grunted.

The other was more fluent in English. "We are

tired of killing," he said to Shining Moon. "Now we take woman."

Shining Moon tried to pull away from them, and both Clay and Proud Wolf strained futilely at the ropes that held them.

"Leave her alone, you bastards!" Clay bellowed at the two Blackfoot men, knowing it would do no good but unable to contain his rage.

One of them released Shining Moon and stepped over to Clay. Casually, he backhanded the captive, driving his head against the tree.

"Shut up, or we make you watch," he growled. "Or maybe white man would like that?"

Shining Moon tore herself from the grip of the Blackfoot and flung herself toward Clay. With her wrists tied in front of her, she could not throw her arms around him, but she pressed tightly against him anyway, moaning and sobbing. She slid her arms past his side and behind his back, hunching against him as if she were trying to hide behind him. She looked up at him, and her desperate eyes met his for an instant.

Then one of her captors grabbed the shoulder of her buckskin dress and jerked her away from Clay. She cried out as the Blackfoot lifted a knife and cut away the dress. The other man held her as the first one slit the dress most of the way down the front and peeled it away from Shining Moon, leaving her nude except for her leggings and moccasins.

Clay watched, his face stony as they shoved her past him, out of sight. They were laughing, and he heard the slap of brutal fists on her flesh as they beat her to the ground. Then came the awful grunting as they took turns mounting her.

Clay's head dropped forward, and his chest heaved. He knew the significance of what he was hearing. He also knew that Shining Moon had perhaps given him what he needed to take revenge.

In that instant when their gazes had met, he had

seen that her eyes were clear and cold and calm, despite the hysterics she was demonstrating. Then she had shoved something into his hand, and his fingers had closed tightly on it. Now, as he tried not to think about what he was hearing, he explored what she had slipped to him.

It was one of the stones from her necklace, he realized, and even though he could not see it, he knew which one it was. She had taken it from the bottom of a clear stream, a beautiful piece of translucent crystal that had been slightly rounded by the action of the water. Now, though, it had a sharper edge on it, and Clay knew that for the past few hours, as men were being tortured behind them, she must have been surreptitiously rubbing the crystal against the stones under her, putting an edge on it.

An edge that could fray rope? Maybe, Clay decided, carefully testing its sharpness.

If the Blackfoot had used rawhide thongs to bind all the prisoners, there would have been no hope of cutting through them. But these bonds were rope, no doubt provided by Simon Brown as part of his payment to his Blackfoot henchmen.

Well, that bit of bribery might just backfire on Brown, Clay thought.

Still trying not to think about what was going on behind him, he maneuvered the stone, fraction of an inch by fraction of an inch, maddeningly slowly, until the edge rested against a rope around his other wrist. He and Proud Wolf were tied with the same ropes, and if he could loosen the right ones, they could slip out of the bonds.

With a deep breath and a prayer that none of the Blackfoot would notice what he was doing, Clay got to work.

The next few hours were the most agonizing of his life. His fingers, already partially numb from his wrists being tied so tightly, refused to work some of the time, and it took a supreme effort of will to keep rubbing the stone against the ropes. From time to time he shifted the stone in his hand and tried to explore the bonds to see how much damage he had done to them, but his blunt fingertips were too deadened to sense much.

The sounds of Shining Moon being beaten and raped accompanied his efforts. The first two Blackfoot had finished with her, but others had taken their place. Clay knew what kind of hellish ordeal his proud young wife was suffering, and while he would not allow himself to dwell on that knowledge, it nevertheless made the fires of hate burn more brightly, adding to his determination to free himself.

Proud Wolf knew what Clay was doing and occasionally gave him a glance of encouragement. Clay also saw the pain in Proud Wolf's eyes, caused by what was happening to his sister.

The other four men from the expedition had been untied from the trees and hauled off, kicking and screaming and flailing, but it had done them no good. Their screams and shrieks sliced through the air like knives, the sounds fading one by one into pitiful, bubbling whimpers before fading completely into silence —a silence even more awful than the screams.

By late afternoon the only prisoners left were Clay, Proud Wolf, Aaron Garwood, and Professor Franklin. The Blackfoot were no longer molesting Shining Moon, and Clay could hear the rasp of her breathing and knew she was still alive behind him, probably unconscious. Considering what had been done to her during this endless day of agony, perhaps that unconsciousness was merciful.

He strained against his bonds, and this time he felt a sudden give to them. One of the strands of rope had parted.

But it was not enough, he realized. His hands were looser now, and the ropes had more play, but he still could not get free. There was hope, though, and that propelled him to keep working. Soon his fingers began to tingle and burn as blood returned to them. The pain of restored circulation was greater than he would have imagined, but he gritted his teeth against it and forced himself to continue as the sun touched the mountaintops to the west.

He froze as the sound of footsteps told him the Blackfoot were approaching again. Their last victim had died several minutes earlier; they were probably ready for some new thrills. To Clay's surprise, about a dozen of them stumbled drunkenly past the prisoners and continued on toward the fort.

One of the warriors stepped in front of the tree where Clay and Proud Wolf were tied.

"My brothers go to get more white man's water from the British chief," he said. Three more Blackfoot came into view, and the spokesman waved a shaky hand toward them. "But the rest of us will stay here and take care of you." The man leaned over and spat into Clay's face. "Waaugh! Killer of Blackfoot! You will cry and beg for your life while we take your eyes and your skin and your tongue from your body."

One of the other men said worriedly, "The British chief told us to save this one for last."

The first Blackfoot shook his head. "We take him now. He has suffered long enough, endured the torments of hearing what we have done to his wife and friends. Let him die now—so that I can drink more of the white man's water and go to sleep."

"I say!" Professor Franklin exclaimed. "You filthy heathen savages! I've never seen a more cowardly lot of dogs!"

"Better shut up, Professor," Aaron advised him quickly.

It was too late. The four captors stumbled over to the tree where Franklin and Aaron were tied.

"What is this you say, fat white man?" the leader demanded.

"I said you're cowards, each and every one of you," the professor declared, sneering in contempt. "You attack helpless women, and you do the dirty work of an even more cowardly white man. And for what? A few jugs of liquor! You're disgusting."

The Blackfoot put his face up close to Franklin's and warned, "You shut up, or we take you next." Then he brought his knife up and placed the tip against the professor's cheek. As he drew the point down, a bright red line of blood appeared. "We cut you open like a fat buffalo cow."

"Go—go ahead," Franklin jeered through his pain. "I'm not afraid of you."

The man moved his knife to the other side of Franklin's face and slit that cheek as well. A shudder ran through Franklin's body, but he did not cry out. Clay never would have expected such a display of bravery from him.

"Maybe you are a man of courage. We will see." To his companions, the Blackfoot snapped, "Cut him loose!"

Professor Franklin looked over at Clay then and said calmly, "I imagine you've been praying, my friend. I implore you—keep doing what you've been doing."

Understanding blossomed in Clay's brain. The professor must have seen what he was doing with the stone, must have known that Clay was in the process of loosening his bonds. He had taunted the Blackfoot and goaded them into taking him for torture next so that Clay would have more time to free himself. *He is sacrificing himself for the rest of us*.

Clay wanted to say something to the professor, but no words came to his lips before the Blackfoot slashed Franklin's bonds and jerked him out of sight.

Beside Clay, Proud Wolf breathed some words in the Sioux tongue; Clay recognized them as a prayer.

Almost ten minutes passed before the professor surrendered to his first scream. Clay shut his ears to the sound and concentrated on severing the ropes. He was not going to give up. The ropes were fraying more. It was just a matter of time—time that Professor Franklin had bought with his life.

As the professor's cries finally became whimpers and moans, Clay bunched his shoulders and prepared for one more attempt to break the ropes. He strained with all his might, and Proud Wolf did the same, until suddenly, almost surprising them, the ropes parted.

Clay pressed back against the tree behind him so the Blackfoot would not notice. They were free!

"Wait!" Clay whispered urgently to Proud Wolf. "Just wait."

Proud Wolf understood. The time had to be right.

After Professor Franklin had finally fallen silent, the four Blackfoot returned to the tree. The leader pointed his bloodstained knife at Clay.

"Now you," he said. "No one will stop us this time."

"Just me," Clay said.

And then he moved.

He was glad he had worked some feeling back into his hands and arms, for it allowed him to move quickly. Like a striking snake, his left hand darted out and grabbed the leader's knife wrist while his right fist whipped through the air and crashed into the man's jaw. Taken totally by surprise, the Blackfoot was knocked backward into his companions by the blow. Clay followed like a deadly whirlwind, plucking the man's knife from his hand and flicking the blade across his throat. Blood spurted, and Clay felt its hot spatter on his face. His lips drew back in a savage snarl as he threw himself into the midst of the remaining captors.

Proud Wolf was right behind him, picking up one of the heavy branches that had fallen from the trees and swinging it through the air like a war club. The branch crushed the skull of one Blackfoot.

Clay plunged his knife into the belly of another, ripping the blade from one side to the other, spilling the screaming man's entrails on the ground. Clay shoved him aside and went for the fourth and final Blackfoot, who managed to dart aside, avoiding Clay's lunge. He was carrying a lance, and as Proud Wolf leapt at him, the man whipped the lance around and cracked the weapon's shaft against Proud Wolf's skull. Stunned, Proud Wolf stumbled and went down.

As Clay recovered his balance and turned to face the Blackfoot again, the man tossed aside his lance and pulled a pistol from the waist of his trousers.

"White man!" he howled at Clay, making the words sound like a curse. "I will kill you with your own weapon."

He pointed the gun at Clay and pulled the trigger. A grin split Clay's blood-streaked face as nothing happened.

"Should've cocked it first, you damned fool," he said.

Then he bolted forward, crashing into the man. The pistol sailed off into the gathering twilight.

Clay and the Blackfoot went down hard, rolling over and over as Clay tried to sink his knife into the man's body. A knee slammed into Clay's groin, causing a red haze of agony to wash through his brain. Vaguely, he heard Aaron shouting encouragement. If there had been time to cut Aaron loose, he could have dealt with this last man. As it was, Clay had to finish him off.

But that seemed doubtful. As they rolled on the ground, one of the Blackfoot's hands caught hold of Clay's hair, and he used the grip to smash Clay's head against the hard, rocky earth. Combined with the knee to the groin a moment earlier, this blow was enough to send Clay spinning into blackness. He hung desperately on to consciousness, fighting his way back toward the light, but he felt the Blackfoot slam his hand down against the ground and knock the knife loose from his fingers. Perched on Clay's chest, the Blackfoot snatched up the knife and raised it high over his head, poised to bring it down in a killing strike.

A gun boomed, and the Indian's head jerked back, a hole appearing between his eyes and a much larger opening erupting in the back of his head as the pistol ball blew away most of his brain and skull. Dead instantly, he rolled limply off Clay and fell to the side.

Shocked back to full consciousness by the shot, Clay turned onto his side, then pushed himself onto his hands and knees. He lifted his head, and by the light of the fire that had been built by the Blackfoot earlier, he saw Shining Moon's recumbent form. In her hand, smoke curling from its muzzle, was the pistol with which the last warrior had tried to kill Clay. Nude and battered, she had pushed herself off the ground enough to aim and fire the weapon just in time to save her husband's life.

"I knew to cock it," she said, smiling wearily at Clay.

The gun slipped from her fingers, and she slumped down again, either dead or out cold.

The sight of his wife renewed his strength, and Clay jumped up and ran to her side. As he knelt beside her and rolled her onto her back, he saw her bosom rising and falling. She was alive! He put his hand on her neck and felt a pulse, erratic but strong. Shining Moon was alive, and somehow Clay knew that she would be all right.

Proud Wolf, having regained his senses, hurried over to them. "My sister! Is she—"

"She's alive." Clay gestured toward the remaining prisoner. "Cut Aaron loose and gather up any guns you can find. The rest of those Blackfoot may come back here any minute."

If they did, Clay vowed, they would get a hell of a different reception from what they expected!

But no one seemed to have heard the shot. Either that, or the men at the fort were ignoring it on the assumption that a Blackfoot had used a pistol to finish off one of the prisoners.

Clay felt better after Proud Wolf, Aaron, and he had found enough rifles and pistols to arm themselves. As they divided the weapons, Clay avoided looking at the mutilated bodies of their companions, especially the professor. But then a moan came from the slumped, bloody form of the naturalist.

Proud Wolf jumped in surprise and exclaimed, "Clay!"

"I heard," Clay said. He hurried over to Franklin and knelt beside him. "Professor! Can you hear me?"

Franklin turned his head toward the sound of Clay's voice. His eyes were gone, and his face was a mask of blood. He lifted a hand, and Clay clasped it gently and said, "I'm right here, Professor."

"M-Mister . . . Holt," Franklin rasped.

The Indians had not cut out his tongue, as they had threatened. He had probably passed out from the pain before they got that far, Clay guessed.

"You just take it easy, Professor," Clay told him. "Everything's going to be all right now."

"L-Lucy."

"We'll take care of her. You have my word on that."

Franklin's hand tightened slightly on Clay's. "Take her home. . . . Promise me you will."

"I promise," Clay said quietly. It was a pledge he meant to keep.

"I knew you would free yourself . . . if you had the chance. Thank you . . . Mr. Holt."

"Thank you, Professor," Clay said, making an effort to control his voice. "We couldn't have done it without what you did. You gave us the time."

"Knew you were . . . Lucy's best chance. Never should have brought her."

"She'll be all right, Professor. She'll be all right." Clay hoped that was true, hoped that Lucy was not already dead.

"My journals—" Franklin arched slightly off the ground as a spasm seized his mutilated body. Then he eased back down, and his next words were spoken in a clear voice from which all the pain had vanished. "My, these mountains are a beautiful place, aren't they? So many plants, so many trees . . ."

After almost a full minute of silence, Clay knew that Franklin was dead. He pulled out a bandanna and covered the man's face. Then he stood up slowly and turned to Aaron and Proud Wolf.

"Tie the bodies of all four of those Blackfoot on the trees, so it'll look like we're still there."

"What are we going to do, Clay?" Aaron asked, his voice shaky.

"We've got to get into the fort. Lucy's still there, and so's von Metz." Clay's grip tightened on the rifle in his hands. "And Brown. He's got a little surprise coming to him."

It was less than an hour before dawn, and the grayness of approaching day tinged the sky to the east. Fort Tarrant slept under the fading stars. One man dozed fitfully in the guard tower beside the gate, fighting to stay awake. He knew that if he went to sleep at his post, Simon Brown would have his hide.

Inside the stockade the dozen or so Blackfoot—whose distrust of the white man had disappeared after a couple of jugs of rum—were curled up next to the barracks, sleeping off their binge.

The guard in the tower shook himself awake, stumbled to the edge of the small platform, and peered blearily into the night. He thought he had heard something; probably just a small animal, he told himself.

The arrow flew out of the darkness. The arrowhead pierced his throat, scraped past his upper spine, and emerged from the back of his neck. He dropped his rifle and for a moment pawed feebly at the shaft, then tumbled lifelessly over the railing to the ground outside the fort. The soft thump his body made as it hit the grassy earth was not loud enough to disturb anyone inside.

"Good shot," Clay said to Proud Wolf as they crouched, along with Aaron, at the edge of the woods near the fort. "He never had a chance to make a sound."

Continued silence was crucial if they hoped to get into the fort, rescue Lucy and von Metz, and have their vengeance on Simon Brown and the other trappers.

The night had been an eventful one. As Clay wrapped Shining Moon in robes from the Blackfoot camp, she had regained consciousness, and he gave her the remaining rum from one of the jugs the Indians had tossed aside as empty. The liquor had been enough to blunt her pain.

"I am all right," she had told Clay, her voice surprisingly firm. He explained what had happened—the professor's sacrifice, the battle with the remaining Blackfoot, the promise he had made to Franklin—and Shining Moon had said, "You must go to the fort and save Lucy. I will wait here."

"I can leave Proud Wolf or Aaron with you."

Shining Moon had shaken her head. "No. It may

take all three of you to rescue her—and von Metz, even though he is a craven dog."

Clay had to grin at that. "I reckon we feel the same way about him. But I'm not going to leave him there."

"No, you must help him, too, if you can. I ask only one thing of you, my husband: Leave a pistol with me so that I can fight my enemies this time if they come for me."

"Nobody's coming for you except me," Clay promised. But he had left the pistol and a powder horn and shot pouch there with her anyway.

He, Proud Wolf, and Aaron had scouted around the fort in a wide circle, looking for any sign of the Blackfoot who had left the camp earlier. They were nowhere to be found, so Clay had concluded that they were inside, probably passed out from drinking. He hoped so, anyway. That would mean their enemies were concentrated in one place. By this time the rum had probably put them into a deep sleep.

Now, with the guard dead, Clay and his two companions were ready to make their move. He thought of Jeff for the first time in a while. He wished his brother were here. With Jeff at his side, Clay thought, he would not hesitate to charge straight into the jaws of hell itself. But Proud Wolf and Aaron Garwood were valiant allies, too. The odds were against them, of course, but then Holts had a habit of overcoming odds.

"Let's go," Clay said in a whisper.

Little more than shadows in the gloom, they flitted forward. When they reached the wall, Clay and Aaron boosted Proud Wolf over it, since he was the lightest of the three. A few minutes later he tossed one end of a rope back over, having secured it on the other side, and Clay and Aaron used it to climb into the stockade. They had discussed having Proud Wolf open the gate but decided against it because of the noise involved and the possible difficulty.

As they dropped lightly to the ground inside the fort, Clay motioned for Proud Wolf and Aaron to come closer to him.

"I'm going to find Brown's cabin," he breathed, the words too faint to be heard more than a couple of feet away. "Proud Wolf, see about getting von Metz out of that storehouse. Aaron, take a look around and see if you can find their powder magazine."

Both young men faded off into the darkness while Clay catfooted toward the buildings to find Brown's cabin.

Aaron's pulse raced as he stole among the crude log buildings of the fort. He had survived more dangers in the past few months than he would have thought possible. He had stared death in the face, and so far, luck had been on his side. But anybody's luck was bound to run out eventually. Would this be the day for him?

He put that thought out of his mind. Clay had given him a job to do, and by God, he was going to do it. The British trappers had to have stored their supply of black powder somewhere inside the fort, and he was going to find it. He checked the other storehouses. Their doors were latched, but the bars were not in place except on the one where von Metz was being kept, and Proud Wolf was tending to the Prussian. Aaron looked in each of the other buildings he came to, carefully opening the doors to avoid making any noise. The sky was lightening enough now for him to see inside the buildings once his eyes had adjusted.

The powder was in the fourth one he checked, half a dozen large barrels of the stuff.

Proud Wolf slowly lifted the bar that closed the door of the storehouse where von Metz was being held. He hoped the Prussian would not be awakened and call out; that could alert the enemy.

He had already noticed the sleeping figures near the trappers' barracks. The Blackfoot were sleeping peacefully only a few feet from their grudging allies. Under other circumstances, the Blackfoot and trappers would be doing their best to kill each other. Politics, and liquor, did strange things to men, Proud Wolf reflected. He would just as soon have nothing to do with either.

Quietly he set the bar aside, then unfastened the rawhide thong that served as a latch. After swinging the door open, he stepped into the darkness of the storehouse. With the light filtering in from the fading stars and the approaching sunrise, Proud Wolf was able to see the sleeping form of Rupert von Metz. He was curled up on a pile of beaver plews and was snoring softly. Proud Wolf crept over to him, knelt beside the pelts, and closed his hand over von Metz's nose and mouth.

Shocked out of sleep by Proud Wolf's touch, von Metz jerked wildly until the Hunkpapa leaned close to his ear and hissed, "Be still! It is Proud Wolf. I have come to take you from here. If I take my hand away, will you be quiet?"

Von Metz's head went up and down in a nod, and Proud Wolf released him.

Von Metz whispered, "What . . . how did you—"

"Never mind about that now. Come." Proud Wolf rose and led him to the door. Von Metz was trembling and stumbling, and Proud Wolf hoped he would not make so much noise that their erstwhile captors would be roused.

Clay stepped up onto the porch of the cabin and walked across to the door with all the skill he had learned from his years on the frontier. His passage was as close to soundless as possible. Unlike the storehouses, the cabin had a window, and it was open. Clay bent slightly to the side to peer through it. He could barely make out a bunk and a chair. Lucy was still tied in the chair, he realized, and Brown was on the bunk, flung across it, wearing his clothes and boots. One of his hands hung over the bed, and near it was an overturned liquor bottle. Lucy's dress was torn off one shoulder. Perhaps Brown had become too besotted to harm her, Clay thought. It was the first glimmer of brightness he had seen for some time.

He walked to the door and silently let himself into the cabin.

Proud Wolf and von Metz emerged from the storehouse just as Aaron stepped out of the building that served as the fort's powder magazine, leaving the door open behind him. Proud Wolf lifted a hand to get his friend's attention, and at that moment Rupert von Metz did something totally unexpected.

He grabbed the rifle from Proud Wolf and shouted at the top of his lungs, "Help! Help me! Everyone wake up!"

Proud Wolf whirled around and lunged at von Metz, but the Prussian darted nimbly out of the way.

"Shut up, you fool!" Proud Wolf said, though he knew it was much too late for such a warning.

Von Metz cocked the flintlock as he lifted it. "I will show Herr Brown he was right to spare me!"

Proud Wolf twisted aside as the rifle blasted and the ball lashed past him. Aaron was running toward them now.

The Blackfoot warriors roused themselves groggily from their drunken slumber, but the British trappers were more alert. Several of them hurried out of the barracks, rifles in hand, awakened by the shouts and gunshot.

"Over there!" a trapper yelled as he spotted

Proud Wolf, Aaron, and von Metz in the shadowy light.

Proud Wolf saw muzzles swing toward them, and he called to Aaron, "Get down!"

Both men dropped to the ground. Von Metz, however, whirled around to face the trappers, the empty rifle still in his hands. His eyes widened in shock as he saw what was about to happen, and he just had time to cry, "No, wait!" before thunder and flame volleyed from the guns of the British trappers.

Three of the heavy lead balls caught him in the chest, lifting him off his feet and driving him backward in a loose-limbed sprawl. He landed on his back and was dead in a matter of seconds.

Von Metz had served as a valuable distraction. As the Prussian was dying, Proud Wolf and Aaron dove behind a stack of logs left over from the construction of the fort. The trappers had left them there to use as firewood during the next winter, but right now they functioned quite well as cover for Aaron and Proud Wolf. More rifle balls thudded into the logs.

Inside Brown's cabin, the Englishman rolled over and sat up sharply at the sound of the first shot. He looked at Lucy in the chair and murmured something to her, and when she did not respond, he backhanded her across the face. Even in this bad light, Clay could tell that her face was swollen and covered with bruises. He lifted his rifle, ready to bound across the room and smash Brown's skull with the butt.

Brown's hand came up holding a small pistol, which he had cocked and trained on Clay before the tall frontiersman could move.

"Hold it!" he snapped, and Clay froze, knowing that Brown would not hesitate to kill him. More shots rang out, and a smile stretched across Brown's face.

"So, you've come back to haunt me like a ghost. Well, we'll soon put a stop to that."

Outside, Proud Wolf and Aaron crouched behind the logs.

"Rush 'em!" they heard one of the trappers yell. "The little bastards can't reload fast enough to get all of us!"

Proud Wolf turned to Aaron and said, "It has been good to know you, my friend. Now we will sell our lives for as high a price as we can."

"I wouldn't count on that," Aaron said.

The trappers charged toward the makeshift barricade, shouting as they came. Their route took them beside the storehouse where the barrels of powder were kept, and as they passed the open doorway, Aaron popped up from behind the logs, the butt of his rifle socketed firmly against his shoulder and a prayer on his lips as he squeezed the trigger.

The flintlock cracked, and the ball sped past the running men, going through the open door and smacking into a powder barrel.

The whole world blew up. At least that was what it sounded like to Aaron as he dived behind the logs again, hoping they would shield him and Proud Wolf from the force of the explosion. In the brief instant before he had taken cover, he had seen flame and debris erupt from the exploding storehouse and engulf the trappers.

The blast shook the entire fort, including Simon Brown's cabin.

"What the hell—!" Brown yelled.

Clay lunged forward and to the side as Brown fired the pistol. The ball clipped Clay on the right shoulder, making his arm go numb. He dropped the rifle.

Brown jumped up from the bed and reached for the blackhawk ax lying on a nearby table.

Clay hit him just before his fingers closed around the ax handle. The collision drove both of them away from the table. Clay tried to reach the pistol in his belt with his left hand, but Brown grabbed his arm and wrenched it away from the gun. Grappling desperately with each other, the two men fell to the floor and rolled over and over.

That brought them bumping up against the legs of the table, overturning it. The ax fell, and Brown snatched it up and whipped it toward Clay's head. Clay jerked aside just in time, and the ax blade bit deep into the puncheons of the floor. Brown tried to pull it free, but while he was doing that, Clay smashed his left fist into the Englishman's face.

Brown shrugged off the blow and pulled the ax free, however, and Clay jumped frantically backward to avoid another swing of the razor-sharp blade. He was near the open door of the cabin as he scrambled to his feet. Brown flung himself forward, tackling Clay and knocking him out of the cabin.

Clay got hold of the ax handle with one hand as he and Brown tumbled across the porch and into the dirt in front of the cabin. The sun was peeking above the tops of the trees to the east, but Clay had no time to notice it. He was holding off the ax with all his strength. His right arm was still numb, and fighting one-handed put him at a definite disadvantage, especially since Brown seemed possessed by a demon that gave him the strength of ten men. Clay brought his leg up between them and tried a trick he had learned from the Sioux. He flipped Brown up and over his head. The Englishman sailed through the air and came down hard on his back. Both men had lost their grip on the ax, which skittered away in the dust.

Brown recovered first, and Clay was barely on his feet in time to meet his charge. Brown's fists battered Clay, forcing him back. Clay managed to block a few of the blows, but with only one good arm, he could not throw any punches of his own. He tripped on something and fell backward.

The ax! He reached for it, but Brown got there first, snatched up the blackhawk, and slashed at Clay's head. Clay rolled aside, but Brown came after him, flailing the deadly instrument. Clay kicked out with his foot and caught Brown in the knee, spilling him, and as Brown fell, Clay grabbed the ax, jerking it out of Brown's hands. He swung it wildly, and both men came to their feet for the final time.

With an impact that shivered throughout Clay's arm, the blackhawk's blade met the side of Simon Brown's neck. The keen steel sliced through flesh, sinew, and bone with a grating sound, then came free in a shower of blood. His chest heaving from exhaustion, Clay stood there, facing Brown. The head of the self-styled king of the Rockies had toppled from his shoulders—and hit the ground before his body crumpled.

Letting the ax slip from his fingers, Clay looked around. On one side of the fort was a crater, put there by the explosion. The barracks was on fire, and the other storehouses had been flattened by the blast. Dead men littered the open area inside the stockade. Any trappers or Blackfoot warriors who had survived the explosion had fled into the woods.

Proud Wolf and Aaron hurried toward Clay, both of them unhurt. Proud Wolf grasped his brother-in-law's arm.

"Clay?" he said anxiously.

"I'm all right. Where's von Metz?"

"Dead," Proud Wolf replied flatly. "He was the one who tried to warn the trappers."

Clay's grimy features were bleak.

"Lucy's in the cabin," he said. "Let's get her, and then let's get the hell out of here."

The three men went inside to where Lucy was tied to the chair. As Aaron freed her, Clay spotted a dispatch case lying next to the table. He picked it up and read Brown's name, and beneath it were the words *London and Northwestern Enterprise.* Clay opened the case quickly and pulled out a piece of foolscap, folded into thirds and originally sealed with wax imprinted with the letter *M.* The seal had been broken. Clay opened the documents. It was from a man named Fletcher McKendrick, the North American manager of the London and Northwestern Enterprise, and the only address given was Fort Dunadeen in Canada. The body of the letter informed Brown of the supplies that were being sent to him at the fort, a long, detailed list against which Brown could check the delivery "to ascertain the reliability and integrity of the men hired to transport the goods."

Clay was intrigued. His speculations about the British incursion into American territory had just been confirmed. But it was the last sentence of the letter that caused all the elements of the theory to fall into place: "I expect a shipment of furs to arrive within a month, since I do not anticipate that you will have failed to accomplish your mission, as the Frenchman Duquesne did."

"Fletcher McKendrick," Clay said. "I reckon I'll have to pay your Fort Dunadeen a visit. We've got some scores to settle."

"Where's my father?" Lucy said. She was wrapped in blankets.

"Let's go outside," Clay said. He knew this was not going to be easy.

Aaron supported Lucy after she had heard the news. A couple of pouches were slung over his shoulder, and Clay recognized them as the ones that held Professor Franklin's journals.

"She wouldn't leave without them," Aaron explained.

"That's fine," Clay said. His face was grim as he

remembered the professor's courageous death. "In fact, it's just right. Let's go."

Clay opened the gate, and then the four of them walked out of the stockade, leaving the blazing ruins of Fort Tarrant behind them. The black smoke climbed high into the clear morning sky.

CHAPTER TWENTY-SIX

Lucy Franklin was asleep, and Clay was grateful for that. She needed the rest after the ordeal she had been through. But Shining Moon had been passed out when Clay and the others returned for her, and now, hours later, she was still unconscious. Clay stared broodingly at her motionless form as he sat by the campfire Proud Wolf and Aaron had made.

With the British trappers and their Blackfoot henchmen dead, they did not have to worry much about being discovered by enemies, so Proud Wolf and Aaron had built the fire high, and the flames danced merrily, casting a large circle of flickering light around the clearing. The ruins of Simon Brown's fort were half a mile away. Once the fires started by the explosion had died out, Proud Wolf and Aaron had spent some time in the late afternoon poking through the rubble. The flames had not reached

Brown's cabin, and inside they found all the rock and plant samples Professor Franklin had gathered during the expedition. They had salvaged the specimens to go along with the professor's journals.

In the meantime, Clay had already begun keeping a vigil over his unconscious wife, a vigil he had continued into the night after gently carrying her limp form to this spot.

Proud Wolf and Aaron were sitting nearby, and not far away was the blanket-swathed shape of the sleeping Lucy Franklin. She had been battered by Simon Brown and then devastated by the news of her father's death, but overall, she seemed to be holding up well. Lucy was stronger than even she knew, Clay suspected.

"When will Shining Moon awaken?" Proud Wolf asked, sounding as though he was talking as much to himself as to anyone else.

"I don't know," Clay answered. "She's hurt bad."

"But she will be all right. She *must* be all right."

They had had this conversation before, earlier in the evening. Clay made no reply now. There was nothing left to say, nothing to do but wait.

"What are we going to do about Lucy?" Aaron asked, looking at the sleeping woman.

"I don't see that we have much choice," Clay said. "We promised her pa we'd take her back to civilization. That means St. Louis. From there, she can head back East. We've got the professor's journals and his specimens. Reckon Lucy'll know what to do with them."

"We cannot leave until Shining Moon is better," Proud Wolf pointed out.

Clay agreed. That went without saying. He would never leave his wife.

Aaron wearily got to his feet. "Think I'll try to get some sleep."

"That's a good idea," Clay said. "Proud Wolf, you might as well do the same."

Proud Wolf shook his head stubbornly. "As long as Shining Moon—"

"As long as Shining Moon's unconscious, there's nothing you can do for her," Clay cut in sharply. In gentler tones, he added, "Get some sleep, son. I'll stand the first watch."

And all the ones after that if I have to, he added silently.

Reluctantly Proud Wolf followed Aaron's example and rolled up in his blankets. Despite his vow that he was not tired, his breathing soon became heavy and regular, and Clay knew he was asleep. Aaron was resting easily, too, and silence settled over the camp, broken only by the crackling of the fire and an occasional rustling noise as a small animal moved in the nearby brush.

Clay felt a pang deep inside as he looked at Shining Moon's face, so still in the firelight. He knew she was breathing, was alive, but that was all he could tell about her. He did not know if she would ever recover.

But one thing he did know. When they returned after taking Lucy to St. Louis, the three of them were heading north, toward Canada.

Two names were burned into Clay Holt's brain: the London and Northwestern Enterprise, and Fletcher McKendrick. The company, and the man, that had been responsible for everything the renegade called Duquesne and then the monster known as Simon Brown had done.

It was time for a showdown, and Clay would not rest until McKendrick had paid for all the evil he had set in motion.

A sudden snap made Clay jolt in alarm. He blinked his eyes, realizing that he had made one of the worst greenhorn mistakes a man could make on the frontier. In his brooding he had looked too long at the fire, and the flames had hypnotized him, at the same time stealing his night vision. He could not see—

A shadowy form stepped into the ring of light. Clay spotted it and surged to his feet, clutching his rifle. He had cocked the weapon, and his finger was on the trigger, ready to fire, before his vision cleared enough for him to recognize that the shape belonged to an old Indian woman, her bent, twisted body wrapped in a tattered blanket.

Clay relaxed, but only a little. How in the hell had an old woman come to wander into their camp? Were there other Indians around?

Easing off on the flintlock's trigger, he said, "Greetings, grandmother. Why have you come here?" He was not sure if the old woman was Sioux or not, but that was the tongue he used.

The bent figure made no reply, although he sensed that she understood his words. Instead, she slowly lifted her arm and pointed with a gnarled finger. Clay realized with a shock that she was pointing at Shining Moon.

He frowned. "I don't understand. Are you a medicine woman? Have you come to help?"

The old woman just smiled, a hideous, toothless grin that stretched her weathered, lined face into something only vaguely human.

Clay's heart pounded, and a coldness settled deep in his belly. He lifted his rifle a little.

"I think you'd better get out of here," he said.

She kept pointing at Shining Moon, unafraid of his rifle. In the black pits of her eyes was a look that seemed to say she considered him no threat at all. She shuffled forward, and even though her gait was slow and halting, she moved as if supremely confident that he could not stop her.

Clay moved quickly, putting himself between Shining Moon and the old woman.

"You've come for her, haven't you?" he asked, knowing that his voice had risen and become ragged with tension and emotion. "Well, you can't have her, damn it! You hear me? You can't have her!"

The woman continued to move toward him.

Clay wondered fleetingly why Proud Wolf and Aaron and Lucy did not wake up and help him. They all seemed to be sleeping so soundly. He was alone, alone to face the strangest menace he had ever encountered.

But he would not give up. Not with something so precious to him at stake.

"Take me," he said suddenly, not sure where the words came from but knowing somehow that they were right. "If you've got to take somebody, then take me!"

The old woman pointed past him, pointed at Shining Moon.

"No," Clay whispered. "You can't have her. Not unless you take me, too."

The old woman stopped, and a heavy sigh shook her frail body. She pointed one more time at Shining Moon, but Clay stood firm.

Something glittered in the old woman's eyes, and Clay could hear her words in his mind as clearly as if she had spoken: *We will meet again someday, Clay Holt. We will meet again, you and I.*

"That's fine," Clay said out loud. "But not here and not now."

She inclined her head just a little, as if acknowledging his point. Then she turned, and in the same halting gait with which she had approached, she walked out of the camp and vanished into the surrounding woods.

It was strange, Clay thought as beads of sweat broke out on his face, but he could not hear the sound of her going.

"Clay?"

He heard the whispered name and whirled around, falling to his knees beside Shining Moon. Her eyes were open, and she looked up at him with an expression of wonderment.

"Shining Moon?" he said.

"Was there . . . someone else here just now? I was waking, and I thought I saw . . . something—"

"No," Clay said firmly. "There was no one here. Nobody but me and Proud Wolf and Aaron and Lucy." He leaned closer to her and brushed his lips across her forehead. "How do you feel?"

"Better. Rested. I think I will be all right."

"You will be. I know you will."

She held out her hands to him, and he lifted her into a sitting position and settled down beside her so that he could put his arms around her and hold her close. She leaned against his shoulder and made a sound of contentment.

"I love you, Clay Holt," she murmured. "I will always love you."

"And I love you. But that's enough talking. You still need some rest. Just take it easy, lean on me, and close your eyes."

"Yes. I will do that."

This time, as her eyes closed and her breathing became deeper, Clay knew she was only asleep. Shining Moon was going to need a lot of healing, but tonight she had taken the first step on that journey.

Strange things were said to happen in these mountains. Clay supposed staring into the fire could have disoriented him until his imagination had played a trick on him. But he was not going to worry about what he had seen, was not going to concern himself about whether it had been real or only a product of exhaustion and worry. He had the only reality he needed right here in his arms.

* * *

The roll of money in Jeff's pocket seemed to be on fire as he rode through the streets of Wilmington, North Carolina. He supposed he should have gone to Dermot Hawley's office first, but he did not trust himself to face the man, not yet. And he had to see if what he suspected was true. He had to find out if Hawley's partner was none other than Charles Merrivale.

The wagons had reached Knoxville without further trouble, and as Amos Tharp had predicted, it had not been difficult to sell the supplies once they got there. Jeff did not consider himself much of a businessman, but he thought he had gotten a fair price for the goods. He had even sold the wagons, which had not been part of the plan, but he was long past worrying about doing anything to upset Hawley. After all, the man had tried to have him killed.

Some of the drivers were going to stay on in Tennessee and settle there, while others were returning to North Carolina. Jeff had paid them off and left all of them behind, retracing the route across the mountains and the Piedmont in much shorter time than the westbound journey had taken. He had ridden long and hard to get back.

And now the real payoff was about to take place.

It had not been difficult to find someone who could tell him how to find the Merrivale Mercantile Company. If Hawley had not hustled him out of town practically as soon as he arrived on the *Fair Wind* weeks earlier, he would have no doubt stumbled onto Merrivale then. Hawley had done his best to prevent that, just as he had lied to Jeff about checking the records at the courthouse.

He still did not know the reason why, but he would soon, he vowed.

Spotting the sign he was looking for, he reined in and studied the big building in front of him. Merrivale's business took up damn near a whole city block, with the big double-doored main entrance on the corner. Jeff swung down from the saddle, looped the horse's reins over a long hitch rack, and stepped up onto the store's porch.

He opened the doors and stepped inside, then strode toward the rear of the building. That was where he would find Merrivale, he knew. He ignored the long aisles bordered with shelves stacked high with all sorts of goods, just as he ignored the clerks who asked him if he needed help. He pushed past them, his eyes fixed on a door behind the rear counter. Somehow, he knew that door led to an office.

"You can't go—" one of the white-aproned clerks started to say, edging over in front of Jeff, but he stopped short as he saw the expression on Jeff's face and the look in his eyes. Hastily, he backed out of Jeff's path.

Jeff put his hand on the knob, turned it, and thrust the door open. As he stepped into the room, he saw that it was indeed an office, with two large windows in the wall to the left. In the center of the airy, well-lit room was a big desk, and behind it a man with white hair and stern, craggy features looked up in annoyance from the ledger book open before him.

"What's all this?" he demanded. "Who—"

Then Charles Merrivale saw who had barged into his office without knocking, and his lined features turned almost as white as his hair.

Acting calmer than he felt, Jeff took the roll of bills from his pocket and tossed it onto the desk in front of Merrivale.

"There's the money from the wagon train," Jeff said. "You can split it up with your partner, Hawley."

Merrivale's mouth opened and closed two times, but nothing came out except a croaking sound. He swallowed hard.

"What are you doing here, Holt?" he said in a low voice.

Jeff kicked the office door closed with his heel.

"Surprised to see me, aren't you, Merrivale? You figured I was dead by now. That was some plan you and Hawley came up with, hiring Tharp to kill me like that. But it didn't work."

"Tharp?" Merrivale repeated. A look of genuine confusion appeared on his face. "I don't know what the hell you're talking about. But yes, I did think you were dead. I believed some red savage had probably killed you by now."

"You don't know anything about Hawley arranging to have me killed?" Jeff sounded skeptical.

Merrivale pushed himself to his feet. "That's insane," he said brusquely. Some of the color had come back into his face as he recovered from the shock of seeing his son-in-law again. "It's true I've had some business dealings with Dermot Hawley, but I don't know anything about hiring someone to kill you." He hesitated, then added, "Although perhaps it might not be a bad idea."

"You sorry old son of a bitch," Jeff grated. His fists clenched, and it took every ounce of his self-control to keep from leaping across the desk and battering that smug look off Merrivale's face.

"I don't know what you're doing here in North Carolina, Holt," Merrivale went on, "but you're neither needed or wanted here. Melissa has forgotten about you and made a new life for herself. If you have the least bit of common decency left in you, you'll leave town without bothering her and go back to whichever little squaw you've been living with for the past few years."

"You're lying," Jeff said stubbornly. "I've been true to Melissa. I promised her I'd come back, and now I have. Where is she, Merrivale?"

The older man drew himself up and glared across the desk.

"I won't tell you. And if you don't get out of here and leave Wilmington immediately, I'll have you arrested! I'm a man of some influence in this town, you know."

"I'll just bet you are," Jeff said softly. He reached across his body and let his fingers curl around the smooth wooden grip of the pistol at his waist. If he could not make Merrivale talk one way, there were always others. . . .

As Merrivale's eyes widened in fear, a voice came from the other side of the door. Jeff recognized it as belonging to the clerk who had tried to stop him.

"Wait!" the man was saying urgently. "You can't go in there, Miss Melissa! There's a crazy man in there with your father—"

Jeff whirled around and threw the door open.

"Melissa!" The cry was torn from the core of his soul.

She was there, only a few feet away from him, after all these years. And as she turned to face him, he saw that she was just as lovely as ever, though her face was ashen with shock at the moment. Then, as he stepped forward to meet her, she threw herself into his arms. All the old familiar sensations—her warmth, the scent of her hair, the taste of her mouth—came flooding back to him as he kissed her.

The long search was over, and none of it mattered, Jeff realized now. He and Melissa were together again.

"Mama?"

The little voice made Jeff stiffen. He took his lips away from Melissa's and looked down to see a child tugging at her skirts. The boy was a sturdy youngster, with blond hair and clear blue eyes, almost the color of the high country skies.

"Ours?" Jeff whispered.

Melissa nodded.

"My God," Charles Merrivale said. "My God."

Jeff glanced back at him long enough to see the look of defeat on his father-in-law's face. Then he forgot about Merrivale and turned his attention to the child, kneeling in front of the boy to smile tenderly at him.

"Jeff," Melissa said, "I want you to meet Michael."

Jefferson Holt looked into the eyes of his son and knew that nothing in his life would ever be the same again.

WAGONS WEST
FRONTIER TRILOGY
VOLUME 3

OUTPOST!

by

Dana Fuller Ross

Clay Holt confronts his nemesis, Fletcher McKendrick, when he travels north armed with the desire for vengeance and the knowledge of the man's diabolical deeds. His wife, Shining Moon, remains behind, struggling to rebuild her life after the brutal attack by those in McKendrick's employ.

Meanwhile, Jeff Holt has his own troubles in the form of his father-in-law, Charles Merrivale, who refuses to accept Jeff's marriage to Melissa, even though that young family, once torn apart, is now happily reunited.

And Josie Garwood, the woman who once accused Clay of fathering her child, appears in the wilderness village of New Hope, where Shining Moon lives. But the baby that Josie bore is now a boy, one who has been taught to despise Holts—and who poses a grave threat to anyone who stands in his way.

* * *

Read on for an exciting preview of *Outpost!*, the third book in the Frontier Trilogy, on sale in September 1993 wherever Bantam paperbacks are sold.

Do not grieve—misfortunes will happen to the wisest and best men. Death will come, and always comes out of season: it is the command of the Great Spirit, and all nations and people must obey.

—Sioux burial oration,
as quoted by John Bradbury
"Travels in the Interior of America
1809–1811"

The Absarokas shouldered up out of the plains, their steep sides covered with evergreens except where sheer rock thrust out or deep gullies were carved in the stone. Splashes of orange, brown, and russet stood out where the leaves of deciduous trees had turned with the advent of fall. The wildflowers, so common earlier in the year, were gone now.

As Clay Holt and Aaron Garwood paddled closer to the mountains, they saw moose, antelope, and deer grazing in the distance on both sides of the river. Prairie dogs and ground squirrels stuck their heads up, peered inquisitively at the intruders in their canoes, then disappeared into the tall grass.

With each stroke of the paddle Clay's joy at being home increased. Soon he and Aaron would spot the Hunkpapa Sioux village, where they would be welcomed with feasting and dancing. When that was over, Clay would join his wife, Shining Moon, in her tipi, and their reunion would be complete.

"Smoke over yonder," Aaron called.

Instantly Clay's instinct for survival was uppermost in his mind as he lifted his paddle from the water and let the gentle current carry his canoe to a halt alongside Aaron's. The younger man was pointing south toward a curving valley between two peaks.

Clay frowned as his blue eyes spotted the thin column of grayish-black smoke.

"Too much smoke for a campfire," he said grimly. "There's trouble over there."

"You reckon it could be coming from Bear Tooth's village?"

"I aim to find out," Clay declared. He stroked the paddle, sending the canoe ahead.

About a quarter mile farther, a small creek ran into the Yellowstone from the south. Clay piloted his canoe into the smaller stream, Aaron following closely behind. The creek was shallow, but since the canoes did not require much draft, they easily navigated it toward the valley where the smoke continued to climb.

It was all Aaron could do to keep up with Clay, whose paddle rose and fell with amazing speed and strength. But when Clay finally grounded his canoe on the bank of the creek, Aaron was behind him.

"We'll get there quicker going overland now," Clay said as he climbed out and pulled the canoe higher on the shore. "I remember this creek. It winds around as it gets closer to the mountains."

He took an extra powder horn and shot pouch from the canoe and draped them over his shoulder. Aaron followed suit. They were venturing into the unknown, and it always paid to have plenty of ammunition along whenever one did that. After checking his Harper's Ferry rifle to make sure it was loaded and primed, Clay set off at a ground-eating pace toward the origin of the smoke, which was growing thicker.

The Sioux could run all day over these plains and rolling hills, and Clay's stamina approached the same level, but he could see that Aaron was having trouble staying with him. He couldn't bring himself to hold back, however. The heavy smoke could mean that tipis were on fire—which suggested a raid by a war party from a rival tribe, most likely the Blackfoot, Crow, or Arikaras, who were also called the Ree. All of them were dangerous and antagonistic toward the Sioux, but of the three the Blackfoot were the most hostile.

As the two men topped a small rise above the mouth of the valley, Clay's worst fears were realized. He saw the half-circle of tipis, open to the east, with their entrances facing east as well so that the Hunkpapa could greet the sun each morning. The camp should have been a tranquil scene; the sun overhead was warm, and the sides of many tipis were rolled up to allow the crisp autumn breeze to pass through. But a half dozen of them were blazing, transforming the once-peaceful camp into a place of chaos, havoc, and death.

Clay recognized the markings on a few of the tipis untouched by flame. "It's Bear Tooth's village, all right," he called to Aaron, his voice choked with anger and fear for the safety of his wife and friends.

Aaron was panting from exertion. "Are . . . are those Blackfoot?"

Clay nodded grimly. "Piegans, I'd say. And they're getting more of a fight than they bargained for, I reckon."

Indeed, the Hunkpapa were battling back with the desperation of a people defending their home from savage invaders. Muskets boomed, arrows flashed in the sun, and blood flew from the heads of tomahawks swung through the air.

Clay and Aaron were too far away to discern the details of the fighting, but Clay pointed out one individual, a tall, brawny Blackfoot warrior wearing an elaborate headdress of eagle feathers and ermine fur.

The warrior, though not joining in the fighting, was waving his arms and exhorting his comrades on to greater atrocities.

"That's a leader in the Blackfoot Horn Society. He's got powerful medicine, supposed to be able to point at a man and strike him dead." Clay lifted his rifle to his shoulder and cocked it. "Let's see how he likes being pointed at."

"But Clay, it's at least three hundred yards down there," Aaron protested.

Clay's rifle boomed, and a second later, the Blackfoot warrior in the ermine headdress was thrown backward, arms flung out to the sides as the heavy lead ball struck him. The warriors near him howled with surprise and outrage.

"Reckon Horn Society medicine's not as strong as powder and shot and a Harper's Ferry rifle," Clay said with a tight smile as he quickly reloaded. "Come on!"

He charged down the hill toward the Sioux camp, stopping to fire the flintlock again. Aaron had waited to shoot until now, and both men's lead found their targets. Clay pounded forward again, covering the ground in leaping strides. In a matter of moments he would be in the thick of the hand-to-hand fighting, and he knew he had to focus his attention on what he was doing. Yet an inner voice frantically cried out for Shining Moon, fearful for her safety. The part of Clay Holt that still prayed sent a plea heavenward that she was not already a victim of the Blackfoot.

Proud Wolf sat outside the tipi he shared with two other young men, Walks Down the Wind and Cloud That Falls, carving shafts for arrows. The band's arrow-maker could not keep up with the need for arrows, and the men of the Hunkpapa Sioux village carved their own shafts for hunting, allowing the arrow-maker to fashion war arrows.

But on this day war came with no warning, announcing its bloody presence in the boom of muskets and the screams of the women.

Proud Wolf leapt up, dropping the shaft he had been carving, and reached for the rifle that lay near his feet. He brought it to his shoulder, setting the sights on a Blackfoot warrior about to smash the skull of a Sioux brave with a tomahawk. Before the 'hawk could fall, Proud Wolf pressed the trigger. Powder flashed in the pan, and the weapon kicked against his shoulder with a loud explosion, its ball knocking the Blackfoot backward, his collarbone shattered.

There was no time to reload. The Blackfoot were everywhere, swarming through the village, killing wantonly. Proud Wolf wondered how they had gotten so close to the Hunkpapa without being discovered, but he had no chance to ponder the question. A raider leapt toward him, and with one hand Proud Wolf swung the rifle to block a sweeping knife thrust. He plucked his own knife from its sheath and plunged it into the belly of the Blackfoot.

He had no idea where Shining Moon was, but he fought his way toward the center of the camp to Bear Tooth's tipi, where the Sioux defenders would rally. The back of the Blackfoot attack would be broken there, he knew, and he wanted to be a part of it.

He could hear a high, keening chant above the chaos of the battle, and he looked over to see a Blackfoot in an ermine and eagle headdress. Proud Wolf felt a chill as he recognized the trappings of the Horn Society. Its leaders had the most powerful medicine of any warrior society. For a moment Proud Wolf's spirit faltered. If they were opposed by the Horn Society, surely the Sioux would not defeat these invaders.

Then the Blackfoot in the ermine headdress was driven backward by something, blood suddenly appearing on his beaded buckskin shirt as he fell lifelessly to the ground. Some of the warriors with him shouted in rage and gestured toward the hill that overlooked the village.

Proud Wolf also looked that direction and saw two men in buckskins who carried long rifles. His heart bounded. The men were too far away for him to see clearly, but somehow he knew they were Clay Holt and Aaron Garwood.

And as some of the white men Proud Wolf had known might have phrased it, those damned Blackfoot didn't know how much trouble they were in now.

As he ran past a burning tipi, Proud Wolf saw a young Hunkpapa woman sprawled on the ground, trying to back away from the Blackfoot warrior who loomed over her, 'hawk raised for a killing strike. With a harsh cry, Proud Wolf flung himself at the larger, older man, grabbing his arm and diverting the blow as the 'hawk fell.

The impact as Proud Wolf crashed into the Blackfoot threw both of them off-balance. Falling, Proud Wolf tried to catch himself but was too late, and he slammed into the ground with enough force to knock the breath from his lungs. Gasping, he rolled over, and at that instant the Blackfoot's 'hawk smashed into the ground where Proud Wolf's head had been an instant earlier.

Proud Wolf looked up into the face of his enemy, an ugly face made uglier by the diagonal stripes of red paint running across features twisted by hatred. The Piegan lashed out again with the 'hawk, aiming for Proud Wolf's head, but the young Hunkpapa blocked the blow with his forearm, the 'hawk's wooden handle cracking against it with numbing impact. The knife he held in that hand slipped from his fingers, which suddenly refused to obey.

Desperately Proud Wolf swung his own 'hawk at the Blackfoot. The raider ducked, giving Proud Wolf the chance to roll to the side and put some distance between them. He sprang to his feet as the Blackfoot lunged at him again.

Proud Wolf used his quickness and smaller size to avoid the next two blows, then dove under a third swing, somersaulted, and came up next to the unprepared Blackfoot. A fast sideways swipe with the 'hawk opened the enemy's belly, but the man made no sound even as he grabbed at himself to keep his entrails from spilling out. Proud Wolf swung his 'hawk in a looping blow that drove the blade deep into the man's neck. With a gasp, the Blackfoot tumbled to the ground in a heap as Proud Wolf wrenched the 'hawk free.

"Proud Wolf!" a voice cried, and he turned to see that the young woman whose life he had just saved had scrambled to her feet. He recognized her now as Butterfly, a young woman from his village. Despite being a year younger than Proud Wolf—and a female —she was taller than he was, and her shoulders were as broad as his. Her body was lithe and strong in a buckskin dress, and lustrous black hair fell around her shoulders. She would have been quite attractive, Proud Wolf had thought many times, if she were not the most annoying female on the face of the earth.

He was taken aback when she threw herself at him, swung her arms around him, and pounded him heavily on the back as she embraced him. "You have saved me!" she said. "My vision was right! Oh, Proud Wolf—"

The last thing he wanted to hear during a battle with Blackfoot raiders was Butterfly's chatter about a vision. Over the years he had heard more than he ever wanted to hear about her visions, most of which had to do with the ridiculous notion that someday the two of them would be married. Proud Wolf pushed her away and prodded the fallen Blackfoot with his foot, just to make sure the invader was dead. His chest filled with pride as he saw the man's head loll loosely on his shoulders.

Something slammed into his back, and the impact drove him forward over the Blackfoot's body. As he fell facedown on the ground he heard an arrow whip through the air over his head. Someone let out a hoarse cry of anger, and only as he rolled over did he realize that the noise had come from Butterfly. She snatched the tomahawk that had been dropped by the dead Blackfoot and threw it unerringly, the 'hawk flickering through the air until the blade thudded into the forehead of the Blackfoot who had loosed the arrow at Proud Wolf. The man dropped to his knees, then fell forward in death.

Proud Wolf swallowed hard as Butterfly turned toward him with a solemn look. Like it or not, she had just returned the favor and saved his life; the arrow would have hit him had she not knocked him out of its path. And judging from the expression on Butterfly's face, she was just as aware of that as he was.

"It is meant to be," she said softly. "Fate cannot tear us apart."

Proud Wolf scowled, climbed quickly to his feet, and said, "Find a safe place with the other women." Then he picked up his knife to join the battle again. There were still attackers to be driven off.

Just as he turned away, he saw the injured expression flare in Butterfly's eyes, and guilt gnawed at him. The girl sometimes buzzed around him like a fly after rotten meat, but he had truly not meant to hurt her. Perhaps it was for the best; her visions could never come true.

Shining Moon huddled against the buffalo-hide wall of her tipi, hoping no Blackfoot would come in and discover her. She heard the raiders' cries as they spread their destruction through the camp, smelled the acrid smoke from the burning tipis that drifted into her haven. She was more frightened than she had ever been in her life, which had lasted twenty summers. She knew she might not see another.

Her gaze rested on the long rifle lying nearby with its powder horn and shot pouch. She could load it, prime it, and be ready to fire in less than a minute; her husband had taught her well in that regard. Clay Holt had taught her many things, in fact: how to smile, to kiss, to revel in the feelings he had aroused in her during their courtship and the early months of their marriage. She had given herself fully to those things, and she knew she had been a good wife to him.

But everything had changed, and no matter how much she wanted her life to be the same as it had been, she knew it never would be.

Before, she had been quick to fight when challenged. She had battled at her husband's side, had taken charge when he was injured. She had killed evil men to save herself and her friends.

Now she could only sit and shiver and pray to the Great Spirit to protect her, because in her mind she heard not only the cries of these Blackfoot warriors, but the cruel laughter of the others, the ones who had worked for the man called Simon Brown, the ones who had violated her, tortured her until she had prayed for death. Their laughter, their harsh grunting as they took her, her own screams as their knife blades bit into her flesh . . . those sounds echoed endlessly in her mind, and the proud spirit that had once been hers had been driven out by those hellish noises.

Shining Moon cried out in terror as the flap over the entrance of the tipi was thrust aside and a leering face, striped with white and vermilion paint, looked in at her. She screamed as the Piegan stormed in and reached for her. At her belt was a knife, but she did not pull it from its sheath to slash at the raider, as she once would have done. Instead she cowered, futilely pawing the air while her feet pushed against the ground and she tried to scuttle out of his reach. When his hand caught her arm, it closed so tightly on her flesh that she cried out again, this time in pain. The Blackfoot dragged her toward the entrance.

You must fight back, screamed a part of her brain, but to no avail. Fear and pain paralyzed her, and in her mind she was once more at Fort Tarrant, far to the northwest, where she had undergone the ordeal that had so scarred her. Not physical scars—those wounds had healed, and she was as lovely as she had ever been—but scars on her soul, scars that would never go away.

She would not have to live with them for long, she thought. This Piegan would no doubt kill her within minutes.

He dragged her through the opening into the autumn sunlight. Her eyes wide with terror, Shining Moon saw the bodies scattered around the camp, bodies of Sioux and Blackfoot alike. She stumbled over the limp, outstretched arm of a young Hunkpapa girl, no more than twelve, whose throat had been slit, and would have fallen if not for the grip her captor had on her arm. He pulled her along, and suddenly the most frightening realization of all burst through Shining Moon's thoughts: He did not intend to kill her; he was taking her prisoner.

She knew what that meant. When they reached a place of safety after fleeing from this attack, the Blackfoot warriors would rape her repeatedly until they tired of her. Then, if the whim struck them, they would kill her. Either that, or take her with them back to their village, where she would be a slave, tormented daily by the Blackfoot women.

Shining Moon stiffened. She could not endure that. Better to die here and now.

With a sharp cry, she threw herself at the warrior, trying to get her hands on the 'hawk he held. She kicked him, clawed at his face, tried desperately to twist out of his grip. Growling a curse, he swung around, released her arm, and backhanded her viciously, knocking her off her feet. His thoughts were clear to read on his face: If she was going to be this much trouble, he might as well go ahead and kill her now. He stood over her and raised his 'hawk, ready to strike.

Instead, his back arched abruptly as a gun blasted nearby. The Blackfoot swayed momentarily over Shining Moon, his mouth opening soundlessly, blood trickling over his lips. Then he collapsed beside her.

She looked up in amazement and saw Clay Holt standing ten feet away, a tendril of gray smoke drifting from the muzzle of one of the flintlock pistols he held in his hands.

"Shining Moon," he said, his voice hollow with emotion. Then he put away the guns and came to her side, kneeling to take her into his arms.

A Sioux woman did not cry, she reminded herself, ashamed of the tears that had already dried on her cheeks. But she shuddered violently as Clay held her and finally lifted her to her feet. His arms tightened around her, as strong as iron yet as gentle as the touch of the breeze on the petals of a wildflower.

She had been anticipating and dreading Clay's return, knowing that she was no longer the woman he had married, and now he was here. All he seemed to be feeling was joy at being reunited with her; he stroked her hair and murmured in her ear. But soon he would see the change in her, she feared, and then he would be repulsed by her, would no longer want to call her his wife.

That was in the future. For now, she did not want to think any longer. The only thing she wanted to do was stand there and be held by him.

Gradually, they became aware that the sounds of

battle had died away around them. Clay took a deep breath and surveyed the scene, his arm around Shining Moon's quivering shoulders. She was shaking like a deer, he thought, but then a Blackfoot attack was enough to make anybody a little jumpy.

The raiders had been driven out of the village but at a great cost. The fire had spread until half the tipis were destroyed. Bodies were sprawled everywhere, and while many of them belonged to the Blackfoot, too many were Sioux. Young and old, men and women and children alike, all had fallen victim to the bloodthirsty Piegans. Clay felt a certain satisfaction when he looked at the body of the Horn Society leader he had shot from atop the hill, but as satisfaction went, it was damned little. At least Shining Moon had survived the raid, and so had Proud Wolf. Clay saw him nearby, trying to ignore a young Hunkpapa woman who was talking to him. The young warrior wasn't succeeding very well, Clay thought.

Aaron walked up, his face grimy with powdersmoke, the sleeve of his jacket ripped and bloodstained where a Blackfoot 'hawk had left a shallow cut. "Well, we're home, I reckon," he said.

They were home, all right.